Winter
Fire

By
Susannah Leigh

A SIGNET BOOK
NEW AMERICAN LIBRARY
TIMES MIRROR

COPYRIGHT © 1978 BY SUSANNAH LEIGH

 SIGNET TRADEMARK REG. U.S. PAT. OFF. AND FOREIGN COUNTRIES
REGISTERED TRADEMARK—MARCA REGISTRADA
HECHO EN CHICAGO, U.S.A.

SIGNET, SIGNET CLASSICS, MENTOR, PLUME AND MERIDIAN BOOKS
are published by The New American Library, Inc.,
1301 Avenue of the Americas, New York, New York 10019

FIRST SIGNET PRINTING, APRIL, 1978

1 2 3 4 5 6 7 8 9

PRINTED IN THE UNITED STATES OF AMERICA

Part I

Love and Loss

1

WANTED: Serious, well-bred, intelligent woman between the ages of 25 and 35 sought for marriage by wealthy rancher. American or English background preferred. Widow acceptable. Address inquiries to Jason Hamilton, Triple Crown Ranch, Jasper Springs, Territory of Wyoming. Serious replies only.

Kate's lips turned up in amusement as she sat in the small writing salon of her aunt's Boston home, staring down with fun-filled eyes at the newspaper in her hands. How ridiculously quaint the advertisement was, she told herself gleefully—and how very American! Where else but in this brash new land could such a peculiar phenomenon as the mail-order bride have become an acceptable, almost ordinary fact of life?

American or English background preferred. Kate let herself laugh aloud as she reread the words. English, indeed! Whoever this bold, presumptuous rancher was, she was afraid he would have to settle for an American. He must have been very naive indeed if he thought any well-bred Englishwoman would tolerate being married off to a man she had never met—or even laid eyes on.

Serious replies only. Kate's eyes lingered on the tantalizing words that leaped out of the page like a red cape waved in front of an angry bull. What fun it would be to pen a coy response to this man's advertisement, she told herself mischievously—what fun to try to coax from him a letter that would provide hours of amusing diversion in the salons of her friends, the other young English ladies of quality visiting in Boston. The more she turned the temptation over in her mind, the more intriguing it became.

Not that she had any need of a mail-order husband, she reminded herself with a certain smug satisfaction. Even had she ever been willing to consider such a degrading thought, it would hardly have been necessary. Why, she had always had more beaux than any other girl she knew. Besides, now that she had met Philippe . . .

Philippe. She let the newspaper slide from her fingers, falling to her side on the divan as she half-closed her eyes, feeling her thoughts drift back to the man she had come to adore in the last few weeks. Philippe. Dark raven hair, ending in little curls at the nape of his neck. Black flashing eyes that always seemed half-filled with laughter, half with desire. White teeth glittering boldly against the darkness of his mustache. She let her eyes close completely, feeling an electric thrill of excitement run through her body, as it always did when she thought of him.

Yes, now that she had met Philippe, she had no need of either familiar beaux or mail-order strangers. When the time came to marry—and she was sure that time would be soon—it was Philippe and no other whose hand would be joined to hers, no matter how her father felt about it.

Kate could not quite control the soft smile that formed on her lips and lit up her eyes as she thought of the violent opposition she would face from her father the instant he found out about her love for Philippe. Far from being frightened by it, she was almost exhilarated, as if his anger would indeed offer nothing more than a taste of spice to her already forbidden affair.

Poor Papa, she thought with a light laugh. What chance did a stocky, barrel-chested, fiery-haired, and fiery-tempered Irishman have against the reckless, willful daughter whose temperament had grown so exactly like his?

Not that he hadn't tried to raise her differently, she had to admit. He had done everything in his power to mold her into the proper young Englishwoman her mother would have wanted; and if Aunt Caroline hadn't left to come to America, he might have succeeded, at least to a degree. Indeed, if he hadn't longed so desperately for Caroline's steadying influence on his daughter, Kate was sure he would never have allowed her to make the long trip to the New World alone. Even so, he had been nervous about it, partly—or so he claimed—because of the disastrous war between the North and South that had ended only a few short years before, but mostly, Kate was sure, because he was afraid to let his headstrong daughter escape from the rigid enforcement of his discipline.

And he had been right, Kate thought, letting herself chuckle at the idea. No sooner had she slipped out from under his strict thumb than she had gone and done the one thing he had feared the most. She had met—and fallen in love with—a totally unsuitable man.

The monotonous sound of raindrops battering against the windowpanes broke in on Kate's thoughts, and she glanced up impatiently, irritated at the heavy spring rains that crashed through the thick foliage of the stately oaks, soaking the rich green lawn beneath. Soon it would be time to meet Philippe, and she had looked forward to riding through the sun-drenched city streets on the pretty little filly her aunt had bought just for her. Now it looked as if she would have to find a carriage for hire instead.

Her eyes flitted toward the dainty hands of the porcelain clock on the mantelpiece, fully expecting them to tell her it was nearly time for the eagerly awaited rendezvous, but to her irritation, she saw that they had barely moved since the last time she had seen them. One hour. She still had one long, tedious hour to wait before it would be time to leave.

Glancing again at the window, she felt her impatience grow as she glowered out at the rain that held her half a prisoner in her aunt's sedate home. The silence that hung over the entire house seemed to her like a heavy pall, dampening her rebellious, fun-loving spirit even more effectively than the drab, gray atmosphere that lingered outside the windowpanes. How she missed the noisy, boisterous exuberance of her seven brothers, and even the incessant, frivolous prattle of her younger sister, Colleen. At least, when the house was filled with siblings, there was no time for boredom or for discontent.

Oh, if only it were time to meet Philippe, she thought with a new burst of impatience. How unfair it all seemed. Whenever she was with her lover, the hands of the clock seemed to race by, moving almost faster than the eye could see, yet now that she was away from him, the minutes seemed to crawl by interminably. Restlessly she pulled herself up from the divan, thinking to pass the rest of the hour quietly in the privacy of her own room, when suddenly her eye fell again on the advertisement in the newspaper.

Well, why not? she thought with a quick flash of mischief. After all, she had an hour to kill—and besides, what harm could it do? It was only a bit of frivolous diversion. Impulsively she picked up the ad, carrying it with her to the ornate gilt-and-marble writing table her aunt had shipped all the way from France.

She held the ad before her for a few minutes, pondering it

carefully, then reached for a piece of Aunt Caroline's writing paper, not the heavy monogrammed stationery she usually used, but rather the translucent white parchment that bespoke of quality without hinting at aristocracy. Dipping her pen neatly in the inkwell, she began to write, admiring the clean contrast of black lines against the snowy whiteness of the paper.

"My dear sir," she wrote swiftly and easily, leaning back when she had finished to peruse her handiwork. She liked the way it looked, the words standing out boldly in the center of the untouched expanse of paper, liked too the way it sounded, *my* dear sir, as if he were indeed her dear sir, belonging to her in some mysterious way by virtue of the silly, secret little joke she was about to share with him. She raised her pen to continue, then stopped, bewildered, her hand still poised in the air. It hadn't occurred to her that she would have difficulty writing to him, and she was surprised to find herself at an uncharacteristic loss for words. Why on earth should it be so hard to find the right words to say to a man she neither knew nor cared about?

What on earth could she say to him? "My dear sir, I am a well-bred but somewhat ill-mannered young lady of nineteen who is utterly, utterly bored because I must wait an hour to meet my lover, and I am not used to having to wait for what I want. Therefore, I am amusing myself by answering your quaint and rather diverting advertisement. Please *do* answer me. I assure you, your reply will provide hours of delightful entertainment for me and my friends."

No, that would hardly do. The man couldn't be expected to answer such an insulting letter, and besides, fond though Kate was of frivolity, she drew the line at malicious ridicule.

"My dear sir." She looked at the words again, sweeping cleanly across the paper, and tried to imagine what should follow them. "My dear sir, I have read your advertisement with great interest." There! That was perfect. It was a good opening, and it had the additional advantage of being true.

Little enough of what followed would be true, Kate knew. While she could boast honestly enough of being well-bred and intelligent, she hardly dared claim seriousness as one of her virtues, and as for the matter of age, well, that was bound to be a deliberate lie. "I am a well-bred lady of 25," she wrote, superstitiously crossing her fingers against the flagrant falsehood "and I am both intelligent and well-educated." She paused, looking back at what she had written, then impulsively crossed out the number 25. That was the minimum age specified in the ad, and as such, it was too blatant, too obvious. Tentatively she wrote in the number 26 and stared at it for a moment. Yes, that was good. It was a year farther from the truth, but it had a ring of honesty about it.

Kate leaned solemnly over the writing desk, scribbling in sentences, then crossing them out again with an intensity unwarranted by the triviality of the task she had set herself. By the time she had written and rewritten the letter several times, she finally reached the point where she was satisfied with the results of her labor. Pulling out a fresh piece of paper, she copied the sentences over neatly, then leaned back with a smile of satisfaction as she read it over to herself.

My dear sir,
I have read your advertisement with a great deal of interest. I am a young Englishwoman, 26 years of age, who has enjoyed both a good background and education. Although I am presently residing in Boston, I have seriously considered removing my residence to the West. Since it would be most improper and impractical for me to consider such a move without the devoted protection of a husband, I feel that the relationship you suggest in your advertisement might be mutually beneficial to both of us.
I am sure you realize, sir, that a woman of good breeding and reputation could not possibly consider such a proposition as yours without knowing the full background of the other party involved. Therefore, I am sure you will understand and forgive me for declining to send any further information about myself until I have heard more fully from you.
Looking forward to your earnest reply, I remain,
Yours sincerely,

Kate laughed with delight as she read the letter. It was perfect! How clever she had been to insist that he divulge information first. It saved her from writing all the tedious details that were so difficult to manufacture. Besides, wasn't that exactly the answer he would expect from a lady of good breeding and background?

She dipped her pen one last time in the ink, then reached forward to sign her full name at the bottom of the letter. Just at the last moment, as the tip of her pen touched the paper, she realized her mistake, and laughing at her own foolishness, she pulled her hand back. She had nearly ruined it all. Lady Catherine Devlin, indeed! Why, she might as well add a postscript: "P.S. My mother was a distant cousin of the queen."

The very signature alone would tell him that her letter could hardly be a serious one—and that his reply would be intended only for amusement and ridicule in the salons of the bored young ladies of Boston and London.

Still, Catherine Devlin alone had a strange sound about it. It was a name she never used without the title. She hesitated for a moment. She could hardly sign "Katie," as her father called her, nor would she select "Cathy," the pet name Philippe had chosen for her, rolling it softly on his tongue, the "h" almost forgotten, as though it were really "Cat'y." On impulse, she reached forward again and signed her name boldly, "Kate Devlin." She liked the way it looked on the paper, strong and informal, without the slightest hint of coyness. It sounded like the name of a woman who would have the boldness and confidence to answer such an advertisement.

Kate reread the letter one last time, whispering the words aloud to herself. Satisfied that she had written the perfect response—one that could not fail to provoke the interest of her unknown correspondent—she folded the letter neatly, and hastily stuffed it into an envelope, addressing it carefully to Mr. Jason Hamilton, Triple Crown Ranch, Jasper Springs, Wyoming.

When she finished, she turned again toward the fragile clock and learned to her amazement that she had not only passed the tedious hour but had actually overextended it. As she raced from the room, she realized with amusement that, instead of having to kill time as she had expected, she would be forced to hurry. It wouldn't do to be late—no, it wouldn't do at all. Philippe, so casual about his own appointments, was nonetheless remarkably intolerant of tardiness in others.

She fairly flew through the hall toward the wide, elegantly curved stairway that led to the second floor, pausing only long enough to drop her letter on a small table, where the maid would find it, giving it to the coachman to post.

2

THE RAIN THAT ONLY AN HOUR BEFORE HAD BEAT A FIERCE, incessant tattoo on the windowpanes had slackened to a fine drizzle, and Kate noted with pleasure that it showed signs of letting up altogether. She had always loved the crisp, clean feel of the air after a storm, even as a small child, and now it promised to make the short ride to Philippe's boardinghouse doubly enjoyable.

Hastily she reached for the green riding habit she had laid out on the bed earlier in the day, and as she lifted it up, her fingers luxuriated in the smooth, rich feel of the thick velvet fabric. Ordinarily she would have changed her mind at least half a dozen times, discarding the outfit she had chosen earlier and selecting another, only to discard that one, too, but today she was in too much of a hurry to play her usual games. She slipped into the outfit quickly and sat down at the dainty vanity table that Aunt Caroline had considered suitable for one of her age and station. Grasping the delicately crafted silver hairbrush, she began to put the finishing touches on her thick auburn curls before crowning them with what Papa always insisted on calling a "silly little bit of fluff and feather."

She paused for a moment to gaze at her reflection in the mirror, offering a tentative smile to the girl who looked out at her so solemnly. The girl in the mirror smiled back, and Kate was both captivated and bewildered by this image of herself. It was only recently that she had discovered she was pretty, and it seemed to her as if she had come into possession of a lovely, glorious secret. It was, in truth, a secret she could hardly claim with any exclusivity, for the rest of the world had seen the promise of beauty in her face years before, but it was new to Kate, and unexpected—and therefore all the more thrilling.

Even when her carrot-bright hair—the subject of innumerable taunts from other children over the years—had mellowed to a rich, deep auburn, Kate had no idea that its dramatic red highlights could be considered beautiful. Only when Philippe told her that her hair reminded him of the fiery excitement and passion of flames set against the dark, mysterious beauty of the night did she begin to sense the truth, and she could hardly wait to get home to her mirror to see if he was right.

Her eyes, too, that odd, dark color of green, had always seemed embarrassingly peculiar; yet, Philippe only laughed at her when she had confessed how much she hated them. "But, *chérie*, they are beautiful," he protested, taking no pains to hide the hints of mockery in his laughter. "They are like pools in thick, silent forests, all bright and sparkling and dancing in the sunlight, but deep and unfathomable by the light of the full moon." And again her mirror told her he was right.

Every girl should see herself reflected in the eyes of a man who loves her, Kate thought contentedly. Every girl should see that high cheekbones are not funny-looking or awkward, but serve instead as a lovely frame for huge dark eyes; that full lips are neither ugly nor fat, but rather sensual and warm, offering the promise of passion and love.

Kate caught herself daydreaming, the hairbrush suspended in midair, and she laughed aloud at the vanity that let her admire her own reflection so openly. Still, she couldn't make herself feel too guilty about it. It was so new to her, this idea of being pretty, that she couldn't believe it was wrong to delight in it, at least for a little while. She picked up the little velvet bonnet, decorated so becomingly with a white ostrich plume, and perched it neatly on the top of her head.

There, I'm ready, she thought triumphantly as she rose to glance at the full-length reflection of her figure in the mirror. She liked the way the expensive folds of velvet clung to her body, accenting the fullness of her breasts and the slender neatness of her waist. She liked the way the dark green fabric seemed to deepen the color of her eyes; liked, too, the bold contrast provided by the tiny bursts of white in the feather in her bonnet and the lace at her pale, slender throat. She was ready, and she looked charming—and Philippe would have to adore her. He would just *have* to.

She flitted through the door, humming a cheerful tune to herself with all the confidence and joy of youth. When she got to the stairs, she flew down them two at a time, delighted at the childlike, exuberant gesture that seemed so at odds with the womanly sensuality she had seen in her mirror only seconds before.

She was still humming when she reached the foot of the stairs and noticed, to her great satisfaction, that not even the tiniest drop of rain was visible against the windows that flanked the heavy front door. A perfect day for riding!

"Sure, now, you're not thinkin' of ridin' on a day like this!"

Kate had been so engrossed in her own thoughts that she failed to notice the drab little girl whose cap and apron seemed to overpower her fragile presence.

"Why, it's a day not fit for man or beast!"

Annoyed, Kate turned to face the girl directly. Aunt Caroline always seemed to have a steady stream of young Irish maids, arriving one after another in quick succession, and disappearing just as rapidly a few weeks or a few months later. Kate supposed this must be another of them, for she could not recall having seen the girl's face before, but she couldn't be sure. After a while, they all seemed to look and sound alike, blending into one vast montage of personality.

"The rain's stopped now," she told the girl firmly, wanting to halt her protests before they drew Aunt Caroline's attention. "It's a lovely day for a ride."

"Ah, now, it isn't," Maureen or Maggie or Molly or whatever her name was protested unfittingly. Obviously the girl must be new, Kate thought angrily. She hadn't yet learned to keep her place. "Sure'n it'll all come down again anytime now, what with those black clouds threatenin' out there."

Kate opened her mouth to snap out a fitting retort, then shut it again abruptly as the smooth swish of silk against the highly polished floors warned her that it was too late to try to quiet the little Irish maid. Aunt Caroline had already heard the fuss she created and had come to investigate. With sinking heart, Kate turned slowly to face the look of hurt concern she knew she would see in her aunt's eyes.

"I'm only going to run a few errands," she told her aunt quickly, feeling the color rise in her cheeks at the transparency of her lie.

The sharp look in Aunt Caroline's troubled blue eyes showed that she knew the truth, as Kate had known she would, but she was too much of a lady to call her niece a liar. She gazed at the girl in silence for a moment, her eyes veiled with unspoken anxiety. She knew better than to challenge Kate's stubbornness by forbidding her to go out, yet her sense of responsibility would not allow her to remain silent. In the end, she decided on a compromise.

"I wish you wouldn't go," she said simply, her mellow voice laden with genuine concern.

"I won't be gone long," Kate hastened to promise her, knowing that it was a promise she could easily keep. With the threatening weather, a long walk was out of the question, and she could hardly hope to linger long over tea at Philippe's rooming house under the watchful eye of his landlady. Kate reached out her hands beguilingly toward her aunt, offering her the same coaxing smile she had often used so effectively when she was a little girl.

This time the smile did not work, and her aunt remained unmoved. "I still wish you wouldn't go," she insisted; then, noting the resolved look on Kate's features, she quickly abandoned the attempt to dissuade her. "At least not on horseback," she pleaded, looking toward the window, where heavy black clouds could still be seen massing in the sky. "I don't like the looks of the weather."

"Don't worry," Kate promised her, glad to have found one small point on which she could compromise graciously. "I'll take the carriage." The look of relief that flooded her aunt's gentle features only served to make her feel more guilty. What a difficult position she had placed her aunt in, Kate thought regretfully. What a trial she must be to her!

She turned the thought over and over in her mind as she sat in the carriage, feeling herself jostled back and forth as the wheels rolled over the rough, cobbled Boston streets. She knew Aunt Caroline was too loyal to report her transgressions to her father, but she also knew her aunt loved her too much to want to see her enter into an alliance her father considered unsuitable. What a mess she had made of it all! She was alternately angry at herself for hurting her aunt and furious with her father for having placed her in a position where she had no choice. How absurd it was anyhow, how totally absurd! Surely she should have the right to choose the man with whom she would spend the rest of her life.

Kate pressed her face against the window, looking out idly at the nearly empty streets through which the carriage passed. As her nose touched the cold glass, a plump raindrop landed almost on the tip of it, splattering forcefully in all directions. It was followed by another and yet another, until the entire surface of the window was a solid sheet of water. Looking out at the heavy rain, Kate shivered involuntarily and reached for a heavy blanket, pulling it up warmly around her shoulders. She was glad now she hadn't been too stubborn to give in to her aunt.

She had meant to leave the carriage a block or two from Philippe's rooming house and go the rest of the way on foot, but as the heavy rain continued unabated, she leaned forward and gestured to the driver, beckoning him around the corner and down the street. Philippe would be angry if he knew, but she could solve that problem easily enough. She just wouldn't tell him. Let him assume she had taken a hired carriage. Besides, he was just being foolish. Even she knew that.

From the very beginning, Philippe had insisted on keeping his residence a secret from her family, even from the servants. He seemed in some strange way to be afraid of Papa, but of course, that was ridiculous. If Papa found out about their romance, he might well be expected to drag his daughter home with unceremonious haste, but he would do nothing to Philippe. He wouldn't bother. What would be the purpose? Besides, even if Philippe were right, they were in no danger from the coachman. He had been with Aunt Caroline for years. Surely he was too loyal, too honorable, to take a bribe from her father or his Boston cousins.

Kate beckoned the coachman into the little lane that led to Philippe's rooming house, and when he stopped opposite the small wood-frame dwelling, she opened the door of the coach tentatively. Feeling the raindrops splatter into the protected interior of the carriage, Kate glanced down hesitantly at the expensive velvet folds of her skirt, realizing only too well that her favorite riding costume would be ruined even by the short run to the house. Impulsively she grabbed the blanket, throwing it over her head as she hiked her skirt up above her knees and raced madly for the front door.

Without waiting for the maid to answer her knock, Kate burst through the door and laughingly dropped her skirt to the floor as she flung the blanket away from her, shaking the excess moisture onto the threadbare rug. She felt exhilarated by the challenge of the storm, and as she threw the blanket in the corner for the maid to recover, she looked defiantly toward the double doors, half-expecting them to be tightly closed against the outside world.

Instead, the doors had been flung wide open, as if to issue an invitation of welcome. To Kate, however, they looked anything but inviting. She realized with sinking heart that she had hoped, albeit unrealistically, that the landlady would be absent that afternoon, and she and Philippe would be able to close the doors, at least partially, availing themselves of whatever modicum of privacy the house could offer.

The look of disappointment was clear on her face, and

13

Philippe laughed as he saw her in the doorway and rose to greet her.

"The dragon walks, I fear." The note of affectionate teasing, so apparent in his voice, was reflected in the depths of his dark, flashing eyes. She forced herself to smile in spite of her disappointment as she swept across the room toward him, extending her hands in greeting. As always when he saw her, he was surprised by the radiance of her beauty. It was as if each time they met she had somehow managed to grow even more beautiful, or perhaps it was only that her loveliness was like an elusive will-o'-the-wisp that never quite seemed tangible when he was away from her. He reached out his hands to take hold of hers, drawing them gently toward him as he bent down and caressed her fingertips lightly with his lips.

He was aware of the heavy rustle of taffeta in the hallway beyond the open doors, and he held Kate's hands to his lips a moment longer than he had intended. That would scandalize the meddlesome old bat for sure, he thought angrily. He wondered if she wore taffeta petticoats on purpose, the better to make her unwelcome presence more obvious.

Kate heard the sound almost as soon as he did, and abruptly pulled her hands away, frowning with anger and disappointment.

"Why so sad, *ma petite?*" Philippe teased her, deliberately misinterpreting her expression. His lips were unsmiling, but his dark eyes laughed at her. "How is it that you look so unhappy when you see me, my little Cathy? Can it be you are disappointed in me?"

"Oh, no," she cried out hurriedly, not catching the note of teasing in his voice. "It's just that . . . well, I mean, I hoped . . ." She broke off awkwardly. How could she explain that she had hoped to be alone with him, at least for a moment, to enjoy the boldness of the very advances that decorum made her reject?

"I know, *chérie.*" He couldn't help laughing aloud at her obvious confusion. "You were hoping we could be alone so I could tell you freely how beautiful you look in that dress, though I expect you know it already. You've probably spent hours in front of the mirror admiring yourself."

She laughed prettily at his teasing, and he admired her coyness, the way she tilted her head to the side and glanced up at him out of half-closed eyes. He wondered if she could maintain her coolness if he carried the game one step further.

"How beautifully it fits you, *chérie,*" he continued, deliberately letting his eyes play insolently up and down the length of her body. "The soft velvet touches every inch of your body, as if it were your lover's hands. How I envy that fabric, caressing the smoothness of your skin just as I long to caress it." He was careful to keep his voice low, in case the rustle of taffeta in the hallway returned again.

The confused blush that met his words was enough to melt even the most careless of hearts, and Philippe was almost sorry he had teased her so mercilessly. Still, as he glanced at the youthful pink flush of her cheeks, he couldn't help delighting in her all the more. What an intriguing creature she was, this child-woman who stood so uncertainly on the threshold of maturity. There was still a hint of the awkward adolescent she had just left behind, but already she showed the promise of the sensual woman she was about to become.

"Really, sir, you are too impertinent," she told him firmly as she moved toward the settee beside the tea table. The words were a shade too hesitant, but they were nevertheless flippant enough to let him know she didn't intend to take his teasing without fighting back. "I shall have to bring a chaperon next time, if you are going to assault my ears with such unbecoming conversation." She had begun to sound more sure of herself, more in control, and he was delighted to see how quickly she had recovered her composure. What an exquisite woman she was going to become!

"Shall I pour you some tea, sir?" she asked lightly as she sat down, the rich green fabric of her skirt making the cheap red velvet settee look all the more vulgar and tawdry in comparison. She was still playing the part of the coy young lady of quality, and he enjoyed it immensely. "I think I must give you some extra sugar, to make you a little more sweet."

"If you please." He wondered where she had heard that line. Probably in the salon of one of her titled friends. It amused him greatly.

He watched her pour out the tea, expertly and gracefully, and he marveled again, as he frequently did, at the ease with which she moved from one role to another. One moment, she was the gracious English aristocrat, all elegantly prim and proper, and the next, she showed promise of all the charm and coyness of a highly paid courtesan. He wondered if those were only superficial layers, and if he scratched beneath the surface, just a little way, he might not find the passionate soul of a common harlot.

She must have known what he was thinking, for she looked up at him coyly and put a note of mock scolding into her voice. "Really, sir, you must not look at me that way. I get the feeling you are thinking thoughts that are not quite nice." She was still playing the proper young lady, taunting him to pay her the risqué compliments she was already planning to rebuff. He was tired of the game.

"I was thinking how much I want to tear that pretty dress off your body and touch your naked skin, running my hands over your breasts, your thighs—"

"Philippe!" There was no coyness in her voice now, only an urgent plea, and he broke off abruptly. She sat absolutely still, stiff-backed and rigid, barely even daring to draw a breath. Her face turned a vivid shade of crimson, and her eyes were nearly closed, the long lashes softly caressing her cheeks. He was angry with himself for hurting her. He hadn't intended to. The words had somehow just slipped out, almost without his being aware of them.

"I'm sorry, Cathy." There was no hint of teasing in his voice as he leaned forward and laid his hand gently on hers.

"I don't know what to do when you talk to me like that, Philippe," she told him simply. She looked up at him with troubled green eyes, and he felt himself begin to squirm under the intensity of her haze. He knew he had treated her unfairly. He had only tried to appeal to the harlot in her because at that moment he wanted very badly for her to behave like one.

"Forgive me, *ma petite*."

Philippe was suddenly aware of the faint rustle of taffeta again, and he pulled away from Kate abruptly. Picking up his teacup, he leaned back in his chair, trying to look casual and nonchalant.

"We can't go on like this, Philippe," Kate told him urgently, taking care nonetheless to keep her voice low enough to prevent the landlady from eavesdropping. "Don't you understand? I want you to say things like that to me. I want it very much, and yet I know I shouldn't. I just don't know what to do."

He was surprised that she was able to express her feelings so openly and unashamedly. Most of the women he knew could not. "It's a game, *mon coeur*," he told her lightly, angry with himself for not being able to match her honesty. "You must learn to play it well."

"No," she said abruptly, and he was surprised at her firmness. She was usually careful not to let her obstinacy show in front of him. "No, I can't play that game . . . and I don't want to. I want to get married. Now. Right away."

He stiffened instantly at her words, and she was aware that

she had pushed too hard. He set his cup firmly on the table and looked across at her, his usually sparking eyes cold and stern. "You know we can't do that, Cathy."

"Why not?" she persisted. "If we love each other—"

"You know very well why not," he interrupted angrily. Was that the sound of taffeta he heard in the hallway? Goddammit, would the bitch never leave them alone, not even for a few minutes? He lowered his voice cautiously. "Your father would never allow it."

Kate, too, was aware of the sound of rustling in the background, and she whispered her reply. "I know it won't be easy, darling," she conceded.

"I think, *ma petite*, that is an understatement."

Kate sighed as she realized how right he was. Her father would not accept Philippe easily. The fact that he was handsome and charming might make him welcome in the salons of the young ladies of society, but it would only serve to make Papa distrust him more. All he would notice or care about were the superficial aspects of Philippe's character. All he would see was that Philippe was poor, and a French Canadian to boot.

"It's so unfair," she protested angrily, forgetting to keep her voice low. And it *was* unfair. How could Papa despise Philippe for his poverty, when he himself had once been poor, accumulating his fortune only through his own ambition and ingenuity? And while a French Canadian was hardly popular among the Boston Irish, surely Papa must have met with even worse prejudice as an Irishman amidst the English aristocracy.

"On the contrary," Philippe disagreed. "I don't blame your father at all. If I had a beautiful daughter like you, I wouldn't want her to marry someone like me. A man with no prospects for the future, and a very dubious way of earning a living, at that."

Kate listened to his words, and she wished he hadn't said them. That was the one thing she didn't like to think about, the one objection her father could raise that she had no answer for. And yet, that was unfair too. All right, so Philippe was a gambler, so what? Didn't Papa realize how difficult it was for a poor man to make his way in this new country? What else was Philippe to do if he didn't want to remain poor forever?

"You see," Philippe said gently, watching the helpless look on her face. "It's going to take a long, long time to convince him."

"But I can't wait a long time," she protested petulantly. He noticed that her lower lip was trembling, and the moist pink tip of her tongue reached out to lick it slowly, as if that could stop its quivering. He watched with fascination, wondering if she knew what she was doing, if she knew what effect it had on him. Could she possibly know how desperately he wanted to touch those lips with his own, feeling that same moist tongue flickering against his mouth?

Dammit, he thought angrily, and he rose abruptly, turning his back on her. Why did she have to affect him that way, anyhow? All right, she was a beautiful woman—beautiful, sensual, and desirable—but he'd known a lot of beautiful women in his life, and there were a lot more to come. He hadn't married any of them, or even been tempted. Cathy was different, he knew that; but the difference lay not in her beauty or her charm, but rather in the fact that she had a wealthy, indulgent father. Without her father's fortune, all her beauty and sensuality would mean nothing in the end. Without that, she would only be a burden he would have to drag around with him for the rest of his life.

"We'll have to wait, Cathy," he said, rather more harshly than he had intended. "There's nothing else we can do."

"We can elope."

"My God, do you know what you're saying?" Seeing the startled look on her face, he realized he had shocked her with his language, and he took a moment to control himself before sitting opposite her again. "Cathy, that's impossible," he told her with a cold finality he would have avoided if possible. Long experience had taught him that coldness was not a good way to get whatever he wanted from a woman, but he had to stop her from thinking about elopement, at all costs.

"But don't you see, Philippe?" she argued. "When it's over and done with, what can Papa say? He'll have to forgive us."

"And if he doesn't?"

"Well, then, he just won't, that's all. He can't do anything about it."

"Can't he?" Philippe asked with calm sarcasm. "Of course he can, *ma petite*. He can cut you off without a cent."

Kate had never heard Philippe talk that bluntly about her father's money before, and she struggled to compose her features. "Is the money that important to you, Philippe?" she asked, trying to make her voice sound calm, as if she were merely asking a casual question.

"Of course it is," he told her simply. When he saw the look of pain that crossed her face, he realized he had played his cards too openly. He leaned forward, looking at her earnestly. "You're used to money, Cathy. You've had it all your life. You wouldn't be happy living the way I do."

"Of course I would, Philippe," she told him happily, relieved to find that he wanted the money only for her sake. "I like having the things money can buy, but I can do without them."

He smiled at her gently. "Really, *chérie?*" he asked softly. She was disconcerted to see that his smile bore a trace of mockery. "That dress you have on—tell me, how much did it cost?"

She blushed at his words, for the remark had hit home. The dress *was* an extravagance, a ridiculously expensive indulgence that she had teased and cajoled her father for days to get. She didn't try to answer Philippe, for she knew there was nothing she could say. There was no way to convince him she could do without the luxuries she had grown accustomed to, and in truth, she was not totally sure herself that he was wrong.

"I didn't mean to be cruel, *mon coeur,*" he told her gently, "but you must see what I am trying to say. You've never been poor. You don't know what it's like. Oh, it might be fun for a while, just like a new game. But after the first year or two—after the first child or two—life would become only a drudgery for you. Soon you would grow to hate me." He did not add: Soon we would grow to hate each other. But it was implicit in his tone.

For the first time, Kate began to realize the hopelessness of her love for Philippe. She was near tears, but she did not want him to see them. She could not trust herself to speak.

"Now you are too sad," he said, laughing gently at her. "You are too quick, too impetuous. You run from one end to the other so fast, I cannot even see you go. See, first you want to be married now—*right now!*— then you think we will never be married at all. We will belong to each other, my love, I promise you, but you will have to be patient. You will have to talk to your father, and coax and wheedle and beg. You will have to use all your beguiling feminine charms, until he does not know how to say no. You will know what to do."

She tried to smile at him, but she couldn't feel hopeful. She knew her father so much better than he did. He reached out a hand to touch her lightly on the arm, and the gentle gesture of comfort moved her greatly.

"I love you, Philippe," she whispered softly.

"And you, *ma chère, je t'aime.*" The words were too easy, too fluent to be convincing, and he struggled to make them sound more sincere. "I do love you, Cathy, really I do, but I love you too much to want to ruin your life for a few months of pleasure."

He saw tears well up in her eyes at his words, and to his surprise, he found himself growing nervous at her reaction. Surely she's not going to give up so easily, he thought, and he was annoyed with himself for caring. Usually he was so cool in these situations, so nonchalant and devil-may-care, always ready to risk everything on one bold roll of the dice. Why did it matter so much this time whether he won or lost? What was it he would miss the most if he lost her—her beauty . . . or her money?

She looked up at him tenderly, her dark lashes heavy with tears. "You're right, Philippe," she said softly. "We must wait. Of course we must." She laid her hand lightly on his arm. "I'm lucky to have found someone like you, someone who cares enough about me to be sensible and not take advantage of my love."

He smiled with relief at her words, delighted that it had been so simple after all—just as simple as it always was. He wondered why he had doubted himself, even for an instant.

"Come, *chérie,*" he said teasingly as he pulled his arm gently out from under her hand. "Take up your teacup like a good little girl and pretend to be a casual friend come to call. I don't want to give that old bat a chance to spread a lot of evil gossip about you."

She picked up her cup dutifully, but her hands trembled with emotion, and it clattered loudly against the fragile china saucer. He laughed softly at her, but there was no laughter in his eyes, only desire. She knew he longed to reach out and draw her into his arms. Setting the cup down carefully on the table, she sat silently, waiting for him to move toward her, her eyes filled with expectation.

He shook his head gently. "Time to go home, *chérie,*" he whispered softly, and he looked at her silently for a moment before rising slowly and taking a step toward the door. "Time to leave, *petite chère,* before I forget all my good resolutions and betray that trust I see glowing in your eyes."

She walked beside him reluctantly toward the door. She longed to reach out and touch him, but she knew that even if the landlady were not home she would never dare to be so bold. All she could do was walk close to him, letting her hip brush up against the outside of his thigh for a brief second.

He felt the sensual touch of her body against his, and the unexpected gesture inflamed him with desire. Damn the landlady anyhow, he thought angrily. What right did she have to snoop and pry? And what did he care what she thought or said anyhow? Impulsively he reached out and grabbed Kate around the waist, swinging her abruptly into the corner behind the door.

She was surprised by his move, but she was ready for him, and as he buried his lips in the softness of her neck, relishing the rich, heavy scent that emanated from her hair and skin, she drew her arms possessively around him, clutching him even closer to her body. When he drew his lips toward hers, leaving a trail of passionate kisses along her neck and cheek, he found that her lips were already parted, waiting for him. There was no trace of the coyness he had expected, and to his delight, her mouth was as hungry as his. He felt her press herself against him until he was aware of every supple curve of her body. All the self-control he had built up so carefully during their encounter vanished as rapidly as if it had never existed, and he would have pulled her roughly to the floor had she not surprised him by twisting agilely out of his grasp and flitting to the center of the room.

"But you told me to go home, Philippe," she protested coyly. Her eyelids were half-closed, her head tilted down, and she looked at him artfully in a manner he knew had to have been practiced many hours in front of the mirror.

Damn the girl, he thought angrily. She can't tease me like that and get away so easily. He would have reached out and pulled her back to him, but she realized his intention even before he did. Pirouetting quickly, she darted out the door, stopping on the threshold only long enough to blow him a kiss from full red lips before she disappeared into the light rain that still fell outside.

Damn her anyhow, he thought again, but he knew he wasn't really angry. She had only turned the tables on him, repaying him in kind for having teased her so mercilessly, and he was delighted to see how cleverly she had learned to play his own game. The corners of his eyes crinkled together in lines of laughter.

Let her tease now, he thought with satisfaction, but when we are married. . . . When she is mine . . .

He smiled to himself as he thought of the days that lay ahead. Let her try to tease me then, he thought.

3

THE PAPER CRACKLED IN PATRICK DEVLIN'S ROUGH FINGERS, and the sound of it filled him with irritation. He glanced down in disgust at the elegantly expensive parchment, which looked so out of place against the coarse redness of his large peasant hands. White parchment indeed, he thought angrily. What a ridiculous affectation of his cousin's—his wife's idea, no doubt. Patrick remembered Michael's wife as a slow, stupid woman, the kind who would have no trouble forgetting her humble origins the instant her farmer husband made a little money in the New World. He wondered if she really thought a few expensive accessories would fool anyone into thinking she was a lady. Anne had used the same kind of paper, he remembered, but for Anne it had been different. Anne was a lady, born to elegance and refinement. It annoyed him to see an Irish potato farmer's wife pretend to be her equal.

Anne. He remembered her, as he so infrequently did, feeling the familiar stab of pain he had tried to eliminate by eradicating her gentle memory from his heart. *Anne.* He caught a fleeting vision of her the way she looked the first time he saw her, soft and lovely, her fair hair blowing lightly in the wind. He had been happy with her, those few years they had together, and she had been good for him, tempering his rebelliousness with her own gentleness of spirit. Perhaps if Anne had lived . . .

But Anne didn't live, he thought bitterly. Anne died at the birth of her last child, the little golden-haired beauty who looked so much like her, and with her death, her children were robbed of the gentle but firm influence that would have strengthened their lives. Caroline tried to take her place, and she was enough like her sister to succeed for a while, but then she had married and followed her young husband to the New World. Even when he died there, fighting in a war he had no part in making, Caroline had remained, making the new land her home.

Now, after all these years, Patrick had decided to reintroduce his sister-in-law's steadying influence—and now it was too late! He looked down angrily at the letter that was now crumpled from being crushed between his strong fingers. He should never have let her go alone, he thought angrily, not this stubborn, headstrong girl who was so much like her father. He should have gone with her, or never let her go at all.

"Pardon me, sir."

He was surprised to hear Gilchrist's voice break into his thoughts. The man must have moved on cat's feet, Patrick thought, so silent was his entry into the spacious, comfortable library. He considered berating him for sneaking in so quietly, then thought better of it. There was no point taking his irritation out on the servants.

"What is it, Gilchrist?" he asked, making at least a minimum effort to cover his annoyance at the interruption.

"I thought I should remind you, sir, that Lord Burton-Styles is still waiting."

"Good God, let him wait," Patrick snapped, irritation finally getting the better of him. "I haven't time for the bastard now."

"Very good, sir," Gilchrist responded coolly as he moved from the room with the efficient dignity of a skilled British servant. Patrick was pleased to note the tiniest edge of surprise that sneaked through Gilchrist's well-trained voice. He knew Gilchrist wasn't shocked by his language—heaven knows, he had heard enough of that in the Devlin household—but even a well-oiled serving machine obviously couldn't remain icily aloof in the face of keeping such an important dignitary waiting.

Had he not been so worried about his daughter, Patrick would have smiled at the ludicrous situation. Lord Burton-Styles was not only old, fat, and ugly, he also had one of the most unpleasant personalities Patrick had ever encountered. But he was one of the wealthiest and most powerful men in England. He was used to being flattered and fawned over, and like nearly everyone else, Patrick had never disappointed him. The fact that he was now sitting alone in Patrick's salon, cooling his heels and undoubtedly cursing impatiently, would ordinarily have amused Patrick greatly. Today, he had other things on his mind.

He turned the paper over carefully in his hands, rereading the unwelcome words scrawled roughly on its elegant surface. He felt a flash of anger at his cousin for having intruded so violently on his peace of mind, though he was aware of the unfairness of his response. It wasn't his cousin's fault he had let his headstrong daughter go across the Atlantic by herself, and it wasn't his fault she had set her cap for the one man she knew she couldn't have. That was just like Katie—tell her no and heaven and earth couldn't combine to stop her from trying to do it. Why, if he had that little minx there right now . . .

He spent a pleasant five minutes thinking of all the strong, angry words he would shout at his daughter if she were standing in front of him at that moment, but he had enough perspective and enough of a sense of humor to know that things would not really go the way he imagined them. He would shout at her, all right, and he would say all the things he meant to, but she would shout right back at him, giving at least as good as she got. She would stand up to him face to face, the sunlight catching in her hair until it looked like dark flames, and her eyes would dance with the deep green fire of perfect emeralds. He would yell and scream, scold and shout, but deep in his heart he knew he would be taking a special, secret delight in her courage and her determination. She was too like him, too much a part of him, for him to be able to stand up against her successfully, and the worst of it was, the little vixen knew it. She would wait until the fighting began to die down, and then she would begin to wheedle and coax, wrapping him slowly and securely around her little finger until he knew he would probably give in to her.

Sighing, he looked back at his cousin's letter. Perhaps, after all, it wasn't so bad. Perhaps there was a way he could give his favorite child to this man without too many qualms. Michael had always been quick to overreact—and without too many brains, at that. Perhaps he was wrong this time.

Patrick read the words again slowly and carefully, trying to think with his mind instead of his heart this time. The man was penniless, Michael said, and a French Canadian, no less. Michael's awkward hand had written the words a little smaller than the others, as though a French Canadian was something so shameful that it needed to be whispered, even in writing. Patrick found himself chuckling a little at his cousin's snobbishness. Who were they—he and his cousin both—that they could afford to be such snobs?

Well, it wasn't good, Patrick thought to himself as he pondered the problem, but it wasn't so bad, either. He remembered a time, not that long ago, when young Paddy Devlin had been only a poor potato farmer come to seek his fortune in an alien land. There was a young girl then, too, a lovely young aristocrat, and she had been the only one to believe in

24

him. Her family had been none too pleased, either, but she had insisted on marrying him, and he hadn't given her a bad life, not a bad life at all. Perhaps this young man of Katie's would prove to be as good for her.

His eyes continued to scan the letter, relief showing candidly in them for a moment, until they paused on a single word, narrowing ominously as they stared at it. *Gambler*. There it was, the word he had skimmed over before, the one he had pushed to the back of his mind. *Gambler*. The one thing in the whole letter that made it impossible for him to accept his daughter's choice.

Though he had never seen him before, Patrick could picture Philippe in his mind—dark and handsome and charming. He had seen enough men like him to know how easily a young girl's head could be turned, especially one like Katie, who was only beginning to learn how beautiful she was. He would woo her and charm her, but in the end the looks and the charm would fade away, and there would be nothing left but the shallow uselessness of his character.

Katie was beautiful. Patrick knew that, but he knew, too, that it was not her beauty that would attract a handsome gambler. Philippe would be more interested in her father's money, and he would count on using it freely, both to uplift his life-style and to honor his gambling debts. What he wouldn't consider was the fact that, after providing a livelihood for seven sons, there would be little left of Patrick's fortune to support a wastrel son-in-law. When he discovered that, he would tire quickly enough of his wife, leaving her to return, bitter and abandoned, to the protection of her father or one of her brothers.

"No, goddammit," Patrick shouted aloud, not caring that no one was there to hear it. "I won't let it happen." Not to Katie, not to his beautiful, lively Katie. He'd see the man dead and in hell before he'd let him do anything to hurt Katie.

"Sir . . ."

Gilchrist's voice was hesitant. As before, he seemed to materialize from nowhere.

"Damn it all, what do you mean, sneaking up on a fellow like that?" Patrick's face was red with rage.

"I'm sorry, sir." To Patrick's surprise, Gilchrist seemed uncharacteristically awkward and unsure of himself. "But Lord Burton-Styles—"

"All right, all right," Patrick interrupted impatiently, though his anger was channeled at Burton-Styles, not at Gilchrist. He had known his lordship long enough to realize how thoughtlessly unkind he could be to servants, treating them almost as if they were animals. It was not an uncommon trait among the aristocracy, but Patrick was not far enough removed from his own humble origins to be able to consider himself a species apart from the serving class. "Show his lordship in."

Patrick settled himself impatiently in a heavy chair. He wasn't looking forward to Burton-Styles's visit, but he knew there was no way for him to avoid it. It crossed his mind to wonder, as he often did, what caused Burton-Styles to seek out his company. It could hardly be his wealth, for there were far wealthier men than he, nor his influence, for he was far from the most influential man in England. Until a couple of years ago, Burton-Styles hardly seemed to know Patrick existed. Now, all of a sudden, he seemed interested in cultivating his friendship.

Unlike Gilchrist's, Burton-Styles's footsteps echoed down the long hallway, and Patrick was aware of his approach long before his bulky form appeared in the doorway.

"Well, there you are." Burton-Styles's voice was filled with petulant annoyance. He was breathing heavily, as if the exertion of carrying his fat body down the long hallway had been almost too much for him. "What do you mean, keeping me waiting so long?"

Patrick stared at him in silence for a moment. It seemed to him that Burton-Styles was the epitome of everything he disliked in a man. Although his lordship was obviously well into his sixties, and had rolls of loose fat, he dressed and talked as if he were a fashionable young dandy. He had never been compatible with his wife, and even before her death several months before, he seemed to consider himself one of society's charming, eligible young bachelors. It was a measure of his power and influence that no one contradicted him.

"Do you good to wait for someone else for a change," Patrick snapped after a long pause. He was in no mood to humor anyone.

"Ah, such a temper," Burton-Styles replied calmly. He showed no sign of irritation as he settled his body into a large, well-made chair across from Patrick. It was one of the secrets of his success to know when to press a man and when to back off. This was obviously a time to back off. "What have you been doing with yourself lately, Paddy?" he asked calmly. "I haven't seen much of you for the past few weeks."

"Keeping busy," Patrick snapped. "Just everyday business

sort of things. I couldn't expect someone so grand as your lordship to know about things like that."

Burton-Styles laughed easily. "A rough day, Paddy?" The question was casual, but his tone had a disarming air of sincerity.

"No worse than most," Patrick parried.

Burton-Styles eyed the letter still clutched in Patrick's rough hands. "News from abroad? From the pretty little daughter, no doubt." His voice was casual, but his eyes gleamed unnaturally, and the slightest trace of a leer pulled up the corners of his lips. For the first time, it occurred to Patrick that the older man's gestures of friendship had coincided remarkably with the emergence of his elder daughter into young womanhood.

"Not from her," Patrick replied cautiously. He was suddenly reluctant to talk about Kate with the grinning figure seated opposite him, though he was aware of a need to get the problem off his chest. "Can't expect her to write—much too busy—not that it would make the least amount of difference if she did. Young people don't seem to write the truth to their fathers nowadays. Unfashionable, I suppose."

Burton-Styles picked up the note of worry in Patrick's voice. "A little problem with Catherine?" he hinted. "A display of temperament, I suppose." He chuckled a little at the thought. "That girl always had a strong will about her, much too strong for a woman. But Lord, she is beautiful." He took no pains to conceal the look of admiration that glowed on his ugly features.

Patrick watched him with repugnance. The idea of any man chuckling obscenely over a girl young enough to be his granddaughter was particularly disgusting to him—particularly when the girl was his own daughter. In a ridiculous way, he felt as if the man had profaned Kate with the lust in his eyes almost as much as if he had touched her with his gross hands.

"Wipe that filthy smirk off your face," he snapped angrily, not even noticing how blatantly he had insulted the man he had once held in such awe.

Burton-Styles only laughed. "As bad as all that?" he asked coolly. "A little indiscretion, perhaps—the girl's passionate, anyone with half an eye can see that. Or worse?" His eyes glittered with undisguised enjoyment. "A ruinous love affair?"

As Patrick eyed the older man in anger and revulsion, he suddenly realized that what he had mistaken for ghoulish amusement was in reality avid hope. Burton-Styles would like nothing better than to see Kate dragged home in disgrace, ruined forever, with no possibility of making a decent marriage. She would be an easy prey then for a man like him.

He didn't want to answer Burton-Styles. The man was the last person in the world he wanted to confide in, but he was the only person there, and Patrick needed desperately to talk to someone. Against his will, he found himself pouring out the whole story to Burton-Styles, even reading Michael's letter aloud to him. To his surprise, the older man seemed genuinely concerned.

"Good Lord, Patrick, you can't let that happen!" There was no trace of a leer on his face anymore. "That would be the worst thing that could happen to her. A love affair—all right, it might be ruinous—but someone with Catherine's beauty could turn it to her advantage. But to be chained to a husband like that . . . Good God, it would be a constant degradation."

"But what am I to do?" Patrick pleaded. "You know Katie. You know how stubborn she can be if I say no. . . ."

"Don't say anything," Burton-Styles counseled firmly. "Just write to your cousin and have him put her on the next boat home, with any kind of chaperon he can lay his hands on. Don't give her time to think. Just get her back here and keep her here. Put her in chains if you have to, but keep her here! You don't have to worry about him. He won't have the sense or guts to follow her."

Patrick eyed the older man with newfound respect. It was easy to see why Burton-Styles had grown so influential. Aside from his wealth and family connections, the man had an astute brain hidden under all those obscene layers of fat.

"You're right," he agreed, and for the first time since he had received Michael's letter, he began to feel cheerful. Burton-Styles's motives might be different from his—he was undoubtedly more interested in seeing Kate again than he was in her welfare—but his advice had been good.

"I'm bringing her home," he said happily. "On the first ship. I'm bringing my Katie home."

4

Kate saw the pile of trunks and boxes the instant she entered the front doorway of her aunt's house, but at first she was only bewildered by them. She felt a curious sense of detachment, as if it were not her belongings but someone else's that had been heaped so hastily in a corner of the large hallway. It took only an instant, however, for a cold chill of apprehension to creep through her body, and suddenly she realized what had happened. She was aware of it even before she recognized the strident sound of her cousin's voice as it spilled out the open doorway of the front salon.

The little Irish maid was unfortunate enough to stumble out into the hallway at just that moment, and Kate pounced on her angrily.

"What's going on here?" she demanded, even though she was sure she already knew the answer.

"Oh, Miss Catherine . . ." the maid stammered awkwardly, her mouth open in surprise and fright.

"They're sending me home?" Kate asked, half-hoping the frightened girl would deny it.

"Oh, mum, I don't know if I should be tellin' you," the girl replied helplessly.

"I want to know," Kate told her obstinately, her voice filled with angry determination. "Tell me just what they said."

"Well, I suppose it's all right." The girl was obviously intimidated by the force of Kate's anger. "There was a letter from your father, mum—to the gentleman in the parlor. He said your father wanted you home on the first boat, and without no warnin', either."

Without any warning! Kate felt the blood rush to her face. How could he play such a cruel trick on her? Not only was he calling her home, but he wanted to make sure she had no chance to see or talk to Philippe before she left. Furious, she whirled around, hurrying back toward the outer door. Only when she reached it did she turn around and face the bewildered maid.

"Don't you dare tell them I was here," she hissed in warning, then raced out the door and hurried on toward the street. Her last glimpse of the frightened maid, eyes wide in horror and lips quivering, told her the girl would not dare repeat the conversation. Still, she could not be absolutely certain, and she forced herself to hurry faster, racing along the uncobbled street so swiftly that she could feel the mud spattering against the red balmoral petticoat that peeked fashionably from beneath the hem of her walking dress.

When she reached the main street, she found a carriage for hire, and she sank gratefully into its cushions, trying desperately to control the breathing that came in heavy, painful gasps. Instead of helping her to relax, however, the journey only provided additional time for her to work herself into a frenzy, and by the time she reached Philippe's house, she was nearly frantic with anxiety.

She jumped out of the carriage so hurriedly that she nearly forgot to pay the driver, and darted up the walk toward the front door. She was so engrossed in the immediacy of her errand that she nearly failed to notice the flash of color at the stable door as Philippe rode his dark, spirited mare out into the bright sunlight. Only at the last moment did the frisky prancing catch her eye, and the instant she saw him, she turned quickly and began to run toward him.

"Philippe," she called out indiscreetly, not caring who heard her. If he got away from her now, it might be hours before he returned, and who knew what might happen before then? She waved frantically to make sure he saw her.

She needn't have bothered, for he had seen her even before she caught sight of him. He reined in his horse and waited patiently for her to approach, carefully restraining the impulse to turn and gallop away. He was not at all pleased with her unexpected visit. He had an appointment with a delightful Frenchwoman with whom he had developed a certain rapport—a woman who did not suffer from the conflicting emotions of a gentlewoman's duties and a harlot's joys—and he was eager to keep that appointment. He did not look forward to another afternoon of teasing and frustration with Kate.

"What are you doing here?" he asked as she reached his side. His features were set in a mask of cold displeasure.

She was frightened by the unexpected lack of welcome in his manner and his tone, but she was too out-of-breath to be able to defend herself. As he looked at her more closely, he saw the distraught expression on her face and was sorry he had treated her so unkindly. Hurriedly he dismounted and put an arm comfortingly around her waist, leading her into the dark, silent stable, where they would be safe from prying eyes.

"What is it, *chérie?*" he asked tenderly. "What's wrong?"

"It's Father," she told him as soon as she had caught her breath enough to speak. "He's sending me home."

Philippe felt his body stiffen with apprehension at the words. He had expected them, of course, but not so soon. He wondered if he had laid his groundwork well enough. Had he established a firm enough relationship with Kate to be sure she would suffer all the anguish that would be necessary to ensure their union?

"When?" he asked tensely. He wanted to know how much time he had left.

"Now." She looked up at him, her troubled green eyes brimming with tears. "They were waiting for me—my Irish cousins—when I got home this afternoon. They were supposed to take me away with them, without even giving me a chance to say good-bye to you."

"Well, then, *ma petite*, it isn't so bad," he said lightly. It *was* bad, but he didn't want her to sense how nervous he was. "We have outwitted them after all."

"Oh, Philippe," she cried out happily, and in a flurry of excitement she flung her arms around his neck. "I was hoping you would say that, but I was so afraid you wouldn't. I know how you feel about eloping."

"Eloping?" She felt his body go rigid under her touch. She knew she had said the wrong thing, and she pulled away from him uncertainly. As she looked up into his face, she saw that his eyes were cold and hard.

"But I thought . . ." she stammered awkwardly. "I mean, you said . . . well, when you said we outwitted them . . ."

"I didn't mean *that*, Cathy," he said quietly. As he looked at the anguished confusion written poignantly on her features, his anger melted away, and he slipped his arms tenderly around her. "I only meant that you found a way to see me anyhow."

The look of hurt frustration that greeted his words called out for sympathy, and he pulled her firmly toward him, holding her comfortingly in his arms. At first he meant only to assuage her disappointment, but soon he became aware of the soft, womanly warmth of the body he clasped so firmly against his.

She did not pull back, as she always had before, when she felt his strong hands begin to caress her. This was no time for false modesty, she told herself firmly, no time for the rigid rules of propriety. This was her man, and she loved him. She turned her face toward his and gazed at him solemnly, trying to memorize the features she knew she might never see again. She made no effort to conceal the tears that glittered like morning dew on her long, dark lashes.

"It will be a long time, Philippe," she whispered softly. "You won't forget me?" The questioning note in her voice held more than a touch of fear.

"It's you who will forget me, *chérie*," he said lightly. "All the men in London will be chasing you." He tried to say the words teasingly, as if he were making a foolish little joke he didn't expect anyone to believe, but he couldn't drive away the icy chill that insisted on penetrating his body. Perhaps, after all, he was only speaking the truth. She was young and passionate, full of a zest for life. How long could he expect her to stand patiently on the threshold of womanhood, feeling the first strong stirrings of desire, yet forcing herself to deny them? Soon other lips would awaken her passion, just as his lips had done, and she would forget her love for him.

She saw the look that came into his eyes, and though she didn't understand it, she was frightened by it. She suddenly felt cold, cold and very, very lonely, as if she were witnessing a preview of what her life would be like when Philippe was far away from her. She began to tremble uncontrollably, and only when he clasped her even more firmly in his arms did she begin to feel warm again.

"It's all right, *petite chère*," he whispered tenderly, stroking the soft little curls that fell delicately to the nape of her neck.

She was comforted by his caress, and even when he pulled the fashionably frivolous bonnet from her head and tossed it roughly to the floor, she did not protest. It seemed natural to feel his fingers in her hair, pulling at the pins that held it up until he released it to fall in a rich, silky cascade to her waist. Even as he buried his fingers in her thick tresses, luxuriating in their smooth softness, her hands reached out for him, clutching at him desperately, pressing the warmth of his body against hers. If only she could hold him tightly enough, perhaps he would never get away. Perhaps nothing would ever be able to part them.

He sensed the eager acquiescence of her body as she clung

to him, and he knew at that moment there was nothing she would deny him. It gave him a giddy sense of power to realize the completeness of his mastery over her, and he wondered, with an oddly detached sense of curiosity, what he was going to do about it. He was keenly aware that he stood at a crossroads of his life. He could go on playing the gentleman, courting Kate and her fortune, or he could give it all up, trading everything away for one glorious afternoon.

He buried his face in the fragrant curls that nestled abundantly on her neck and shoulders, listening eagerly for the soft sigh he knew must escape her lips. It suddenly occurred to him that he did not have to make a choice after all—he could have his cake and eat it too. Even if he possessed her that afternoon, she would never reject him as a suitor. Quite the contrary, the shared experience of awakened passion would only make her remember him all the more tenderly, yearning for him—and only for him—with an added urgency.

He moved his hand cautiously from her back, sliding it slowly around her body, carefully gauging her reaction. He didn't want to move too quickly. He didn't want to do anything to frighten her or make her pull away from him. He tried to be subtle as he reached his foot out and kicked the heavy door closed. Although it groaned in protest as it swung slowly shut, she didn't even seem to notice it.

She was aware only of the strong hand that moved slowly toward her breast, and she was unable to keep her body from quivering at the bold touch of his fingers. She knew she should pull away indignantly, loudly protesting the impudence of his advances, but the very impropriety of it only made her relish it all the more. She would have to stop him soon—she knew that—but she couldn't help giving herself a few minutes more to savor the wicked sinfulness of the forbidden fruit that was offered so temptingly to her.

As his hand finally came to rest softly on her breast, gently cupping and caressing it, her body began to respond to his touch with an urgency that both frightened and delighted her. She tried to force herself to pull his hand away, but even when he moved it slowly inside her blouse, gently caressing the bare skin that lay beneath, she could not bring herself to say no to him. Although the touch of his hand against her naked flesh burned with the intensity of a searing flame, the pain it brought with it held, not agony, but delight. Her body strained toward him, as if it had a will of its own, and she no longer attempted to resist the passion that seemed to carry

33

her along in the wake of its force. She pressed herself tightly against him until she could hardly breathe, and it seemed as if their two bodies must join and become one. She felt his fingers catch at the mass of hair that flowed freely down her back, and as he grasped it roughly, pulling her head back, her face turned up obediently toward his. The pain of his roughness only added to her exhilaration, and even before he bent his head over hers, her mouth was open, ready to receive him.

She had never known a kiss like that, rough and savage and brutal, yet all the while filled with a sweet passion that made her whole body ache with a desperate hunger. As if in a dream, she felt herself falling backward, floating on the arms of passion. It wasn't until the spikes of rough straw scratched through the sleek velvet of her dress that she realized she had been supported instead by Philippe's strong arms as he lowered her gently to the ground.

"Mon coeur, mon ange," he whispered tenderly, kissing her between each word. All the while, his hands searched her body, making her writhe with pleasure at his touch.

"Oh, my darling," she replied eagerly. "I love you. I love you so much." She kissed him hungrily, and her hands caressed his body with an eagerness that almost matched his. She felt no shyness with him, even when he began slowly to remove her clothes. Finally, as she lay naked in his arms, she pressed him tightly against her breast, her body still quivering with excitement at the passionate touch of his hands and lips.

Only when he pulled away from her, drawing himself up to his knees and struggling to undo the front of his pants with overeager fingers, did she begin to feel truly naked. Her body shivered in the unexpected chill of the air, and she began to feel embarrassed under the intensity of his gaze. Self-consciously she pulled her hands up, trying awkwardly to cover her nakedness.

"You have no reason to feel ashamed, *chérie*," he assured her, his voice harsh with desire. "You have a magnificent body."

His eyes swept over her figure with a naked lust that terrified her in its frankness. This was not what she had expected, not what she had wanted of her first encounter with love. Where was the romance, the tenderness, the gentle delicacy she had expected in a lover? He made her feel, not like the cherished object of his love, but like a common harlot, to be taken with uncomplicated, unsentimental lust. She cowered deeper into the straw, feeling both ashamed and stupid for having let him go so far with her.

"Philippe, please . . ." she pleaded. She knew he could not help seeing the terror in her eyes.

He stared at her tensely for a moment, then rose slowly, his pants still half-undone. She stared at the hard bulge in front of them, her eyes filled with fascination and embarrassment. She had never seen that part of a man before, although she had heard stories about it before, mostly from the serving women in the kitchen. It had never occurred to her it would look so big or so menacing.

"I'm sorry," she whispered softly. She didn't even try to hold back the tears that flowed down her cheeks.

"So you're just a tease, after all," he said harshly. He was angry with himself, and that made him all the more angry with her. What a fool he'd been! Now he would neither marry her nor possess her. "Don't lead a man on like that if you don't mean to go through with it. Next time, you might not be so lucky." He turned abruptly on his heels and started toward the door.

"Philippe!" She was on her feet almost before he began to move, and forgetting her nakedness, she hurried after him, catching him just before he reached the door. "Please, darling," she pleaded urgently, placing her hand tentatively on his arm. "I didn't mean to tease, truly I didn't. It's just that I was frightened."

She placed her hands lightly on his cheeks and gazed up at him imploringly from beneath lashes damp with tears. As he looked down at her, the anger on his face began to subside, and she was filled with the hope that his hands would soon caress her body again, this time lightly, gently, easing away her fears with the sensitive touch of his fingers. Instead, his face grew hard again, and as if to challenge her, he threw his arms around her roughly. As he pulled her brusquely toward him, she felt the harsh pressure of his mouth assaulting her unwilling lips. She wanted to recoil in horror from the unexpected violence of his lovemaking, but she was desperately afraid of losing him forever. Was it always this frightening, she wondered, this ugly—the act of love for a woman?

She knew her lips must feel like ice against his, and she was terrified that he would pull away from her in anger. She tried to make her actions more feminine, more inviting, but there was no way she could force herself to feel anything but revulsion at the insistent roughness of his strong male hands against her naked flesh. Finally she could bear it no longer, and she started to push him back, but even as she did so, she felt her body begin to glow again with the same fierce flames that had touched it before. Unreasonably, she tried to fight the very feeling she had cultivated, confused and angry at the conflicting emotions that pulled her back and forth against her will, but the emotion was too strong for her, and she found herself seeking the burning fire of his lips with agonizing passion.

This time it was she who drew him down to the straw, it was she who held his throbbing body close to hers, relishing the sweet, yearning pain that carried her along in its swift, surging current.

He was wise enough not to pull away from her again, but kissed and caressed her carefully as he awkwardly unfastened his trousers with one hand. He tried to keep her from noticing the gesture, but she was aware of it instantly, and she found to her surprise that she was filled with an overwhelming curiosity. She remembered how frightened she had been by this vivid proof of his masculinity only moments before, even when he had been clothed, yet she was unable to keep her eyes from glancing toward it now. The minute she saw its massive hardness, she recoiled from it in alarm.

"But, Philippe," she protested, "it's so big." She was horrified at the very idea of being assaulted by such a formidable weapon.

She was afraid he would be angry with her for pulling away again, but he only laughed. "To give you more pleasure, *mon coeur*," he promised. "You'll see."

She was keenly aware of the touch of his hand as it slid down the smooth, naked skin of her body, pausing only for a moment on the inside of her trembling thighs. Then slowly it continued upward, moving with an increasing insistence, until it finally came to rest on the center of the sweet pain that had engulfed her body. At last, she felt him prepare to penetrate her, and all thoughts of fear vanished from her heart. Her body rose up eagerly to meet his, and she knew with a sureness born of instinct that she was ready for him.

At the first strong thrust of his body, she felt a swift stab of pain, and she cried out in protest.

"But, Philippe, it hurts."

"Only for a little while," he promised, kissing her tenderly. "Trust me, *mon ange*. It is only for a little while."

She was confused at the unexpected pain, so unlike the sweet anguish that had seemed to fill her entire body, but she did not dare protest again. She lay obediently beneath him, biting her lips against the pain, until she discovered, to her delight, that he had been telling her the truth. Slowly, almost unnoticeably, the pain began to subside, and in its place was an overwhelming pleasure, far beyond any she had imagined or dreamed of. Instinctively, her body began to move in unison with his. All sensation of pain left her, and she could feel nothing but the swift, all-encompassing rapture that enveloped her, lifting her toward a peak she could neither understand nor envision.

Suddenly she felt the strong, rhythmic thrusts of his body cease, and a moment later the crushing force of his weight fell heavily on top of her. She was surprised to hear the sound of his breathing coming in short, painful gasps, as if only a few moments of strenuous exercise had been too much for his powerful physique.

"Don't stop, Philippe." She nudged him eagerly with her hands, trying to urge him to continue the movements that had driven her to such heights of ecstasy.

He pulled himself up on his elbows and looked at her strangely for a moment; then, as his face lit up with comprehension, he began to laugh softly at her. Laying his hand gently on her cheek, he leaned down and kissed her lightly.

She realized then that the moment of lovemaking was over, and her anguished body called out to her in frustrated anger. Why had he driven her to such heights, she wondered, only to leave her bewildered and unsatisfied?

The disappointment was written keenly on her features, and as Philippe glanced down at her, he knew he dared not leave her so unsatisfied. He had wanted her return to England to be dominated by the memory of a beautiful afternoon, not a frustrating, unfulfilling one. He knew what he had to do, but he knew, too, that he had chosen a clumsy place for it. He glanced nervously toward the door. If he was lucky, no one would stumble in before he had a chance to complete her initiation into the rites of love.

Kate saw him glance toward the door, and misinterpreting his intentions, she thought he wanted to end their encounter.

"Is that it, Philippe?" she asked, puzzled and hurt. "Is that all there is to it?"

He began to laugh again. "You have so much to learn, *chérie*," he told her tenderly, taking her in his arms and caressing her gently. She tried to ask more questions, but each time she opened her mouth, he sealed it effectively with his lips.

As he played with her body and encouraged her to play with his, she felt a renewal of the yearning that had filled her before, this time stronger than ever. She wanted to cry out in frustration at the pain that engulfed her body, yet offered no hope of appeasement. Even as she despaired of ever finding release, she glanced down and saw, with a surge of hope, that he had grown large and hard again. Instinct told her that she dared to hope.

She sought his mouth eagerly, greedily trying to suck the sweetness of his body into hers, and as she felt him enter her again, she moaned with pleasure. He began with more tenderness this time, more patience, and he moved her slowly along with him toward heights of passion that far exceeded any she had felt before.

As her excitement rose, her hips again began to move with his, at first tentatively, then with more confidence, more passion. This time there was no cessation of her pleasure. The tension in her body rose to a pitch that was almost unbearable, and she wanted to cry out that she couldn't bear it anymore. Still it rose, ever higher and higher, until she thought she must die from the agony. Finally, when it seemed as if she would burst from the delicious pain, she felt her whole body explode, like a series of tiny firecrackers. She was surprised to hear the sound of her own voice as she cried out, but it did not embarrass her, and soon the sound of her cry had mingled with the moan of pleasure that escaped from Philippe's lips.

Afterward, she clung to him eagerly, not even noticing that her breath, like his, was drawn in a series of harsh, panting gasps. All she wanted to do was lie next to him forever, clasping him tightly against her body for all time. She felt an agonizing rush of tenderness, at once so beautiful, yet so painful.

After a moment, she felt Philippe move impatiently in her arms. He began to glance more and more frequently toward the door.

"Please, darling," she whispered softly. "Stay in my arms. Don't run away from me."

Philippe turned his dark, penetrating eyes toward her face, taking note of the hopeful eagerness it so innocently displayed, and he knew he must not be too impatient with her. The moment of love that followed the act of lovemaking was important for a woman. No matter how awkward and uncomfortable he might feel lying on the straw in the stable and waiting for someone, friend or stranger, to intrude on their idyll, he must not pull away too quickly. He wanted her to remember that afternoon for a long time.

He cradled her tenderly in his arms for a few moments,

whispering sweet promises of love in her ear. When he finally decided it was time to leave, he eased her gently to her feet.

"We must go now, *chérie*."

"I don't want to go." She sounded confused and frightened, as if she had forgotten that the moment of parting was to come so soon.

"It's all right," he told her comfortingly. "We must part for a little while, *mon coeur,* but we will remember each other and we will meet again."

"I *will* remember, Philippe," she promised. "I could never forget."

He stood by the door, his back to her as she dressed. Try as she would to make her fingers hurry, they stubbornly contrived to move slower and slower, and she silently cursed the conventions that forced women to wear so many layers of clothes. It seemed forever, but finally she was ready, and she carefully hooked up her skirt on the four clips that descended from her belt, so that the red and black balmoral petticoat could peek demurely from beneath it.

She twisted her long hair on top of her head and knelt down to search hurriedly in the straw for the pins Philippe had tossed away so carelessly. She could find only a few of them, hardly enough to hold the heavy tresses securely on her head, and she was grateful for the windy day that would justify its disarray. As she finished, she called to Philippe, and he turned toward her, smiling approvingly at her loveliness.

His smile was the same, Kate thought, and yet it looked different. She knew he would never look the same to her again.

"I will always remember," she promised.

5

IN SPITE OF HERSELF, KATE FELT A WARM GLOW OF ANTICIpation spreading through her body. The pure apple green of her watered-silk ball gown was just pale enough to lend an air of fragility to her healthy figure, but still rich enough to bring out the deep emerald green of her eyes, and her mother's jewels gleamed at her ears and throat, the crisp flash of diamonds and the darker fire of rubies contrasting becomingly with the smooth whiteness of her skin. She had forgotten how much she enjoyed the elegance and traditions of England, and as her ears caught the first strains of music that floated up the marble staircase, she could not keep her toes from tapping with impatient eagerness on the floor beneath her feet.

"Katie, aren't you ready yet?" Her younger sister, Colleen, swirled into the room like a powder-blue hurricane, her long golden hair piled for the first time in adult splendor on top of her head. "They're starting to come. Can't you hear the sound of hooves in the courtyard? Do hurry. Oh, Katie, you look so pretty. Do I look all right? Don't go downstairs without me. Please don't forget me. Promise you won't forget."

She broke her nervous chatter for a second to catch her breath, and Kate took advantage of the brief second of silence to laugh with amusement. Colleen was just sixteen, and this was her first ball. Kate remembered with a sudden rush of nostalgia how exciting it was—and how terrifying—to go to your first dance and not know whether you were going to be the belle of the ball or some poor little wallflower sitting in the corner.

"Why, it's Lady Elinor, I do believe," she said with mock seriousness, taking advantage of a touch of humor to acknowledge Colleen's new adult status. "Lady Elinor Agnes Caroline Colleen Devlin."

"Oh, Katie, don't be so silly," Colleen protested, but Kate was pleased to see that the nervousness in her face had abated for the moment. "I'm still just 'little Colleen.' You wait and see. Watch Lady Harseford when she sees me. She'll chuck me under the chin in that abominable way she has, and she'll say, 'Well, if it isn't little Colleen. My, how we've grown!' You just wait and see."

"Not on your life," Kate protested, laughing. "She'll look at you with the same gape of amazement she always has when some girl puts her hair up for the first time, and she'll make a great show of saying, 'Why, this can't be *Elinor*. Quite the young lady now, aren't we, Elinor?' "

Colleen rewarded her with a giggle. "Do you really think I look all right?" she asked nervously.

Kate rose swiftly, and with the confidence of a girl whose dance card had been filled for the past three seasons, did not cast a single backward glance at her mirror. "You look lovely," she said generously, linking her arm through her sister's and leading her out into the wide hallway. As she watched the radiant smile that lit up Colleen's face, she smiled to herself. There was no chance the girl would be a wallflower that evening, but Kate knew better than to try to tell her now. Only time and the new awareness that would light up in the eyes of boys who had known her since early childhood would convince her of that.

She felt Colleen hesitate awkwardly as they reached the head of the heavy marble staircase, and she grasped her young sister's arm more tightly, remembering how sharp and treacherous each slab of Italian marble had felt beneath her feet the first time she descended those same stairs with her dress flaring around her toes and her head proudly held too high to look down and watch her footing. Under her guidance, Colleen floated down the stairway as gracefully and effortlessly as if she had made the same entrance a thousand times before, her eyes alight with excitement and hope.

We must look the same, Kate thought with a sudden burst of surprise. Colleen and I. And yet, how different the reason. The glow on her sister's face came from the sight of the bright lights and stylishly dressed young cavaliers at her first ball, while the excitement on her own face reflected the vision of the last great ball she would ever see in her father's home.

She looked down at the room below, barely noticing the faces that had turned upward to watch her entrance, and thought, with a surge of pride that surprised her, how very beautiful the massive old entry hall looked. She had always lived in the house that had been in her mother's family for generations, and until that night she had always taken it for granted. It had never occurred to her to notice how perfectly the satiny sheen of white marble brought out the subtle highlights in dark wood paneling that had stood for centuries, or how superbly the glow of dozens of tiny candle flames was absorbed in the heavy brocades and velvets that draped the room. Nor had it occurred to her to marvel at the medieval tapestries, priceless beyond description, that hung against the wall as casually as if they were quite ordinary possessions. There would be nothing like that in America, she knew. There, everything would be new and shiny, even a bit tawdry and crude in comparison to everything she had ever known. She slowed her step deliberately, letting her eyes sweep around the room in a childlike wonder at the beauty of it all, determined to impress it on her memory forever.

Patrick Devlin followed his guests' gaze and turned to watch with pride as his daughters descended the staircase. He did not fail to notice the look of eager anticipation in Colleen's eyes, or to be delighted by it, but it was his elder daughter's expression that pleased him most. Since the day Burton-Styles had suggested he call her back, he had been apprehensive about the plan, and even when he carefully organized all her favorite diversions—long rides across the meadows, picnics beside the river, formal teas and casual dinners with friends—he had been afraid he would fail. At each new entertainment, he carefully searched her face, and while he read quiet enjoyment there, he was disappointed to see that she did not throw herself into any of the activities with real enthusiasm. Not until that night had he seen her eyes light up with excitement and anticipation.

It worked! he thought, congratulating himself in a burst of triumph. My plan worked. For by now, it had become *his* plan, and all thoughts of the odious lord who originated it were erased from his mind.

His look of triumph was not lost on Kate, for his expression was as transparent as hers, and for a moment it spoiled her pleasure. She was silent as she reached the foot of the stairs and glided quietly across the floor to take her place in the reception line between Patrick and her older brother Edward and his wife. She had been only too aware of her father's carefully plotted attempts to draw her back into her old life, just as she was aware of the fact that he had been careful not to give her even a few minutes alone with him to plead her cause. To be reminded of it at that moment only made her realize all too poignantly how easily she had let the past few weeks drift by. She made a firm resolve not to let it go on any longer. She would force her father to talk to her soon—the very next day if she could.

She was startled to notice Colleen's eyes fixed on her face, staring at her with a puzzled expression. Determined not to spoil the fun, either for her sister or herself, she quickly drew an arm around the girl's waist and pulled her into the line, between herself and Edward. Let her share in the fun of receiving guests at her first ball for a few minutes, at least until the dancing began. Glancing around the hall, she caught sight of the various shades of red and golden that capped the heads of her other brothers, and smiled as she watched them circulate among the guests, greeting them warmly—especially the young and pretty ones—and steering them toward the grand hall, which had been cleared of all but long rows of chairs set against the wall.

Only her brother Eamon stood apart, his expression dark and guarded as usual beneath his deep auburn hair. Kate shuddered for a second as she watched the brooding intensity that lay on his brow, even on such a gay occasion, and she thought again, as she often had, how little she really knew this strange brother of hers. Although he was only the third eldest, his strength of will made him a natural leader, and whenever Patrick was absent, Kate had learned to expect the same strict discipline from him that she did from her father—but with a difference. Where Patrick's severity was tempered with humor, Eamon's was not. Nor could Kate, or any other woman for that matter, wheedle him or twist him around her little finger.

Her thoughts were interrupted by the sharp sting of fingernails in her bare arm, and glancing around quickly, she realized that Colleen had pinched her to gain her attention. The younger girl's eyes were filled with mirth, and Kate turned quickly to see what had amused her.

"Lady Horseface," she whispered as loud as she dared, and Kate grinned appreciatively at her impudence. Lady Harseford did indeed have the long, equine features of a draft horse.

True to form, Lady Harseford swept through the doorway and descended on Patrick and his family with a gushing enthusiasm that was no more palatable for its obvious sincerity. Kate waited, holding her breath eagerly, until she got to Colleen. Just as she had predicted, the woman took a giant step backward, as if she were stunned by what she saw.

"Don't tell me this is *Elinor*," she enthused vociferously. Her back was half-turned toward Kate, enabling her to risk an outrageous wink at her younger sister. "Why, my dear, I would never have known you. Don't we look grown up? Quite the little lady, aren't we, now?" Only the fact that she didn't chuck Colleen under the chin saved the girl from breaking out in a fit of schoolgirl giggles, and Kate grinned as she watched her sister's valiant struggle for self-control.

"Well, well, so the prodigal daughter's returned."

Kate heard the booming voice with a rush of loathing, and as she turned reluctantly, she realized that only Lady Harseford's timely entry could have diverted her from seeing the man.

"You look beautiful, my dear, if you'll permit an old man to say so—even more beautiful than when you went away. America must have agreed with you."

Kate gaped at Lord Burton-Styles with undisguised disgust, too dismayed at seeing him to be able to think of even the most perfunctory reply. She had always disliked the man, but

43

he seemed particularly repulsive that night, with the vivid purple satin of his waistcoat stretched ludicrously across the wide expanse of his body. Besides, she hated the way he looked at her, as if his eyes had the ability to remove her clothing layer by layer from her body.

"I brought Katie home so I could watch over her," Patrick replied abruptly, and Kate suddenly realized to her surprise that her father had not reprimanded her for failing to greet the important nobleman with suitable courtesy. "I didn't want a bunch of dirty old men leering at her."

Both Colleen and Lady Harseford turned around to gape at him in amazement, and even Kate was surprised at her father's words. Feisty as he was, she had never heard him talk back to the powerful lord before. Only Burton-Styles seemed completely undaunted.

"Quite right, quite right," he agreed amiably, calmly continuing to undress Kate with his eyes.

Kate tried with little success to ignore him, but she found his lecherous expression hopelessly distracting, and she wished he would move on into the grand hall, although she was painfully aware that he showed little inclination to do so. Not until she glanced toward the new arrivals and saw a familiar face, one she had not expected to see, did she begin to forget him.

"Why, Charles," she said, reaching her hands toward him with genuine delight. "What a pleasant surprise. We hadn't expected to see you here."

"I hope you don't mind, Patrick," Charles's companion added hastily. "I've brought along a houseguest. You remember Charles Stratton."

Patrick did remember Charles Stratton—and he did mind—but he couldn't risk a second rudeness so close on the heels of his sharp retort to Burton-Styles, so he bit his tongue and greeted young Stratton graciously. Kate watched him in amusement, even managing to feel a little sorry for him as she watched his carefully laid plans go so badly awry.

Charles, four years older than Kate, had been her first crush, and she had waited eagerly for him to notice she had grown up and begin to succumb to her appeal. That Patrick disapproved, because of his lack of wealth and social status, had only made him more attractive to his stubborn daughter, and Kate suspected it was partly to keep her away from Charles that her father agreed to send her to America. Poor Patrick! Once there, she had only gone out and found someone even more unsuitable than Charles.

"I just came down for the week," Charles told her. "It was a spur-of-the-moment decision. Otherwise, I would have told you I was coming, and waited for a legitimate invitation."

Something in his eyes made Kate wonder if he had made the trip especially because he heard she was home, and the thought made her sad. Only a few months ago, she would have been thrilled at the idea, but now it meant nothing to her. Now she could look at Charles and see, not a handsome, dashing suitor, but only a comfortable old friend.

She heard the unpleasant sound of Burton-Styles's moist, throaty chuckle, and as she glared in anger at the man, she realized he had been taking in the scene with a great deal of relish. The idea infuriated her, but she could think of no way to rebuke him that would not merely enhance the amusement he already felt. Why couldn't he just go away? she thought furiously. Angry as she was at her father for interfering in her life, she didn't like to see his discomfort become a source of malicious pleasure for that obese toad.

To her relief, she heard the musicians strike up a dance tune, and all thoughts of Burton-Styles vanished from her head as she felt her toes begin to keep time with the music. The light touch of a hand on her forearm reminded her that it was time for her first partner to claim her for the waltz she enjoyed so much, and she turned eagerly to follow him. Only at the last moment did she remember Colleen, and she tossed a quick glance over her shoulder to make sure that her sister was also going to dance the first dance. She needn't have worried, for Colleen was already being led off by a red-faced, stammering young man, obviously in awe of the elegant young lady who only a short time before had been nothing more than one of his playmates.

Kate loved to dance. She felt as if her feet barely touched the floor as she floated through the graceful steps of the waltzes and cotillions and the lively, exhilarating galops, moving easily from partner to partner, with barely a moment to catch her breath or even glance around to make sure Colleen, too, was enjoying every dance. For a time she was amused by the lighthearted banter she exchanged with her young gallants, remembering it as part of the excitement of a life that already seemed to belong to the past, but soon she began to weary of it and wished her partners would give at least a moment or two of silence to enjoy the sweeping music and almost hypnotic rhythm of the dance.

I wonder what's happening to me, she thought. Once she had loved the casual flirtation and teasing that seemed as much a part of a ball as the music, but suddenly it amused her no longer. What a difference it makes, she thought in amazement. What a difference to fall in love! Now even the idea of superficial flirtations did not appeal to her. Soon, she would be like all the other matrons who sat along the sides of the room, content to dance a dance or two every now and then with their own husbands.

The idea frightened her for a moment, and she glanced apprehensively toward the dark-robed matrons, sitting patiently against the wall, smiling as they watched their daughters enjoy the excitement of the dance. Breathing a sigh of relief, she remembered with gratitude that she was going far away to America. At least the Boston ladies, while they did not dance as often or flirt as outrageously as the young girls, did not feel they had to shroud themselves in somber grays and blacks the minute they exchanged their marriage vows.

She heard the music change, and dropping a brief, coy curtsey to her partner, she turned quickly to extend her arms to the man who had materialized by her side. Glancing up at him from beneath properly demure lashes, she was delighted to see that she was gazing into Charles's warm brown eyes.

"Oh, Charles," she breathed with a sigh of relief. "I am so glad to see you. I was getting tired of all that nonsense."

"Nonsense?" He looked both puzzled and amused at the same time.

"I mean all the silliness and the flirting. Everyone keeps saying the same things over and over again, and it gets so boring after a while. It really is a tiresome game."

"I always thought so," he agreed, laughing. "But you seemed to enjoy it."

She felt a light flush cross her features. "I suppose it must have looked that way," she conceded, feeling as if she had to defend herself. Then, realizing how silly she must sound, she too burst out laughing. "To be honest, I suppose I did enjoy it, but not anymore. Maybe I've grown up too much for that."

"You *have* changed," he agreed, and she thought she caught the sound of admiration in his voice. "I could see that the instant I walked through the door. You've changed a lot . . . and I like it." His eyes glowed with a look Kate had never seen in them before, and she felt a wave of confusion sweep over her as she responded to his flattery.

The intricate steps of the dance took them away from each other for a moment, and Kate was glad for the respite that gave her at least a few seconds to sort out her tangled feelings. How could her heart beat so wildly at hints of love from a man she no longer wanted? she wondered. Was she so fickle that, even with the depth of her love for Philippe, she had to dangle other men's hearts like ornaments on a necklace?

He seemed to sense her confusion. When he reached out his arms to enfold her again in the casual lovemaking of the dance, he offered neither bold looks nor bold compliments, but held the conversation to polite questions about her trip. She was grateful for his tact, and forgetting her discomfort, soon relaxed easily in his arms to enjoy the rest of the dance. By the time the music had ended and he prepared to turn her over to her next partner, she had nearly forgotten the incident, and it probably would not have come to mind again had she not glanced across the floor and caught sight of her father's angry eyes focused on her face.

Patrick's scowl was as dark and obvious as a spoiled, thwarted child's, and Kate almost had to laugh at him. Here he had pulled her back from America and an objectionable alliance, only to see her in the arms of a man who, save for the fact that he was an Englishman, was nearly as unsuitable. In a burst of mischief, not untouched by resentment, Kate looked back at Charles and flashed him a bright, happy smile, taking care not to miss Patrick's reaction out of the corner of her eye. The deepening of his scowl told her the gesture had not been in vain.

She had already begun the steps of the new dance when a sudden thought flashed through her mind, almost causing her to stumble over her own feet. What if her father thought she was going to marry Charles? What then? If he was truly convinced, once and for all, that she intended to marry below her station, might he not give in at last? And if she was going to marry someone he didn't approve of, would it really make any difference *who* that someone was? Wouldn't he just surrender then, letting her marry Philippe?

She saw instantly that the idea was a good one, and only one small misgiving crossed her mind. She was fond of Charles, and the idea of using him or hurting his feelings was repugnant to her, but it took her only a few seconds to talk herself into believing she could handle that problem when she met it. After all, Charles was young and popular. Besides, he barely knew her—he hadn't seen her at all for months. It was just a passing fancy for him, and he would get over it quickly enough.

Ignoring her partner, she turned her head, seeking out

Charles to see if he was still watching her. She was flattered to find that he was. Making sure her father's eyes were also on her, she sent Charles another bold, flirtatious smile. It gave her only a small twinge of conscience to see how his face lit up in response.

Preoccupied as she was with her new plan, even the dancing no longer excited her, and when the musicians stopped to allow a break for refreshments, the passage of time seemed almost interminable. One glance at the heavily laden dining table was enough to tell her that her father's French chef had overdone himself with elaborate aspics and pâtés, which the local matrons and portly gentlemen were piling unashamedly on their plates, but even had her stays not been laced so tightly that there wasn't a spare quarter of an inch, she would not have been hungry enough to eat more than a bite or two. Her eyes fell with amusement on Colleen, her plate heaped high with the cold meats and jellied fish she adored, surrounded by a bevy of young men, each competing eagerly for her favor. Now that she was sure she wasn't going to be a wallflower, the appetite that had deserted her at dinner had returned at least twofold.

Despite the attentions of no less than half a dozen devoted young swains who hovered over her, trying to tempt her with one dainty morsel after another from the heavily laden table, Kate could not manage to feel contented. Finally, when the prattle became too much for her, she excused herself on the pretext of overseeing the serving arrangements. It was an idle duty, for the housekeeper who had served the family since she was a small child always had everything perfectly organized, but at least it took her away from the social banter for a few minutes.

"You've escaped your young cavaliers?"

Kate whirled around at the sound of the words, then laughed with relief when she saw that it was Charles who had accosted her.

"I told you I was bored with all that."

"Then why don't we wait out the intermission in the garden?" He took her arm lightly, leading her toward the door that had been opened to let in the fresh summer breezes.

Kate hesitated. She could see the musicians readying themselves to begin playing again. Soon the dancing would start, and partners would be searching to claim her. Still, if she were missing for the first dance or two . . . well, surely that

48

would add kindling to the fires that must be raging inside her father at that very minute.

"Come on," Charles urged. "You'll be safe from all your young suitors there. All except me, that is." There was a twinkle in his eye as he said it, but she got the uncomfortable—though not totally unwelcome—feeling that he was half-serious.

She allowed herself to be maneuvered through the doorway and out into the cool summer evening. The garden was heavily perfumed with the sweet scent of roses, and the dim light and soft noises that drifted out through the doorway made the party seem very far away. Kate leaned against the heavy masonry wall and looked up at the thousands of bright stars punctuating the deep blue of the sky.

"How beautiful the garden is," she said softly.

"You always loved it," he reminded her. "Do you remember? You said it was your favorite place."

"I remember. I always loved the sight and smell of it—the earth and the grass and the beautiful fresh flowers."

"Except the roses," he teased.

"The roses?"

"You always used to be afraid of them." He reached over and neatly plucked a full red rose from a nearby bush. "You said they bit you."

She laughed as she recalled the long-forgotten bit of childish nonsense. "How on earth did you remember that? It was so long ago."

"I remember a lot of things about you," he said quietly. His eyes were serious, far more serious than she wanted them to be.

"That's silly," she retorted quickly, eager to cover her confusion. "You never even noticed me."

"I always noticed you. You were so much more vibrant and alive than the other children. Besides, even then it was obvious how beautiful you were going to be."

She felt herself blushing. The game had gone too far, and she wished he would stop staring at her and turn away. Instead, he reached out his hand, offering her the single rose he held.

"Well, I'm not afraid of them anymore," she told him, trying to change the subject, as she carefully took the flower from his hand. "I stay away from their sharp teeth." He did not draw back his hand, but let it rest lightly on hers. She wondered why she was so intensely aware of it.

"Isn't it lovely?" he asked, staring down at its velvety

smoothness. "In the evening light it looks almost like your hair, dark and rich, with the red only half showing through."

His voice was soft as a caress, and she turned away from him in embarrassment. "You shouldn't say such things to me, Charles," she told him, not quite as convincingly as she had intended.

"Why not?" Though his voice was light, it still had an underlying current of seriousness. "What's wrong with telling you you're beautiful? Don't the other young men tell you the same thing?" He reached his hand up, and placing it lightly on the side of her face, forced her to turn and look at him.

"Yes," she agreed hesitantly. "But they don't . . . Well, it's just something they say to all the girls. You sound like you really mean it."

His laughter was soft and light as he continued to look down into her eyes. "I do mean it. I think you're the most beautiful woman I've ever seen."

She felt her heart beating faster with excitement, and she knew she should turn away from him or reprimand him, but she couldn't force herself to do it. It was as if the sight of his dark eyes had mesmerized her.

Taking her silence for encouragement, he dared to continue. "Oh, Cathy, you look so lovely."

With the sound of the nickname she was used to hearing only from Philippe, Kate was jolted back to reality for a second. "Oh, Charles, you mustn't," she protested, but he pretended not to hear her.

"If you only knew how you looked with the moonlight shining like dark fire on your hair. And those mysterious green eyes—they're enough to drive any man wild."

He leaned his head toward her, his hand lightly caressing her face, and she realized in a moment of panic that he was going to touch his lips to hers. Still, she could not force herself to pull away. He did not hurry, but drew his mouth down slowly, until the gesture ended in a soft, lingering kiss. It was tantalizingly sweet and made Kate's body long for remembered pleasures, but for all its hints of passion, it was gentle and light enough to be, if a trifle daring, at least within the bounds of propriety. When Charles finally pulled his head away, it was only for a few inches, and he continued to stare into her eyes with a hunger that matched the aching in Kate's body.

He must have read the longing in her eyes, for he drew his mouth again to hers, at first lightly, as before, then with an urgency that reminded her of the passion that had haunted her dreams every night since that moment, so many weeks ago, when she had surrendered herself completely and whole-heartedly to Philippe. Without even being aware of it, her arms were suddenly around his neck, clutching at him as desperately as he clutched at her, and her body seemed transported across time and space to that deserted stable and the man she loved. Only thoughts of Philippe and the memory of dark hair and laughing eyes saved her from the passion threatening to engulf her, and in a burst of horror and self-disgust, she pushed Charles roughly away from her.

"Oh, my God," he stammered, stumbling awkwardly away from her. "What have I done?" His face was crimson with embarrassment and shame.

She stared at him in shock, appalled not by what he had done, but what she herself had come so close to doing. She was suddenly aware that Philippe had awakened in her a deep vein of passion that, once aroused, could never be stilled, and it terrified her. She knew she would never again be satisfied with a light, romantic kiss, and a cold wave of fear flooded over her as she realized how easy it would be to succumb, if not to Charles, then to the intense passion of some other man's touch, forgetting, in her need to share the strength and pleasure in a man's body, the depth of her love for Philippe. How long would it be, she wondered, before she talked herself into thinking she was in love with someone simply because she desired him? In a sudden rush of panic, she knew she had to get back to Philippe, and she had to do it soon. Nothing was too great a sacrifice if it accomplished that.

Charles, misunderstanding the anguished flush on her face, tried awkwardly to stammer his apologies. "I'm sorry, Catherine. I know that doesn't . . . Dear God, I wish I could explain. I don't know if you can ever forgive me."

She shook her head impatiently, angrier with herself than him. She meant the gesture as a negation of his words. It was meant to say: It's all right. It's as much my fault as yours. But he took it differently.

"Oh, Cathy, don't say that," he pleaded. "I know I'm a cad, but you have to forgive me. I didn't mean to do that. With God as my witness, I didn't mean to. It's just that you're so beautiful, and I wanted . . ." He broke off abruptly. "Dammit, I'm only making things worse." He stopped pacing and smiled ruefully at himself. "And swearing in front of you besides."

He walked toward her slowly, taking one of her hands in

his, then dropped it again in embarrassment. "Listen, Cathy. What I'm trying to say is that my intentions are honorable. Oh, I know I'm not good enough for you. I don't have the family or the money that you do, but I'm a hard worker, and my prospects are good. And I love you. That counts for a lot. You'll find out later how important love is. I don't expect you to answer now. I know I don't even have a right to ask you, but I want you to be my wife."

Kate could only gape at him in amazement. She had gone too far, much too far. She had not wanted a declaration of love, much less a marriage proposal. All she had been after was a mild flirtation, just enough to make her father nervous. *And yet* . . . She couldn't still the little voice in the back of her mind. And yet, if her father learned that Charles had proposed, and if he learned that she had not definitely refused him, what would he do then?

"You don't have to answer now," Charles reminded her gently. "Just tell me I may hope."

She stared at him helplessly. She didn't want to hurt him, but she wanted so desperately to return to her lover. She wanted Philippe and needed him. She had to go to him soon, and this seemed to be the only way.

"Charles . . ." she began awkwardly, wavering in an agony of indecision. When the time came to say the words, she still could not make up her mind. Encourage Charles, and hope to trick her father; or tell him the truth, and not hurt him. Finally, when she could bear the silence no longer, she heard herself say in a quiet little voice, "I don't know."

She meant it to say: I don't know what to do. But he did not understand. "That's enough," he assured her quickly. "It's enough to know you haven't completely rejected me."

She felt sick with guilt as he slipped his arm tenderly through hers and led her toward the open doorway. "We'd better get back in," he told her gently. "They'll come searching for you soon."

The gay strains of dance music did nothing to revive her spirits as they stepped into the brightly lit ballroom and watched the dancers whirling by in a bright montage of colors. She was painfully aware of the eyes fastened on her face, and she knew tongues would soon be clicking over the confusion that must be written on her face, as well as the stiff, embarrassed demeanor of her escort.

Only when she caught sight of Patrick's face did she begin to feel better, for across his features lay the blackest expression she had ever seen. She knew he had missed her absence and guessed the cause of it, just as she knew her reappearance with Charles had confirmed his worst suspicions.

It worked, she thought in triumph. Just the way I knew it would. Now, he'll have to let me marry Philippe.

6

To KATE, THE MUSIC SEEMED TO DRAG ON IN AN ALMOST MOnotonous repetition of rhythm and melody, and she found herself yearning with increased intensity for the moment the musicians would pack up their instruments and the servants would begin to clear away the chairs and return the room to its natural order. It was the first time she had failed to enjoy a ball, and the sensation was an unpleasant and bewildering one.

Wherever she turned, she could not seem to avoid the vision of Charles's eyes as they followed her around the room. She moved rapidly from partner to partner, whirling from one end of the hall to the other and back again, but no matter where she went or how swiftly she flitted away, his eyes did not leave her for a single instant. He did not try to dance with her again or engage her in conversation, but seemed content to watch her from afar, a soft smile on his lips, as if for him her popularity was a source of enjoyment and not of jealousy. It was that same proud, gentle smile that cut her more deeply than anything he had done or said before, for it reminded her more poignantly than words ever could how cruelly she was using him.

Finally, when she was sure she must scream aloud with impatience and frustration, she heard the musicians begin their final piece, a waltz for her instead of the traditional galop, because her father knew it was her favorite. As the last strains of music died away, she saw the guests begin to gather in little groups, laughing gaily and saying good-bye to friends they might not see until the next party. She was grateful for the hostess duties that kept her surrounded by departing guests in the entry hall, for they prevented her from having even a moment alone with Charles, who could find no reasonable excuse to linger after the others had gone home.

"I thank you for a remarkably pleasant evening," he told her quietly, holding her hand in his a brief moment at parting. "I hope I may look forward to seeing you again soon."

His voice was heavy with meaning, but she pretended not to notice as she lowered her eyes, blushing becomingly. Misinterpreting her reticence for shyness, he gave her hand one last comforting squeeze as he bowed politely and took his leave. Kate felt herself heave a deep sigh of relief as she watched his tall, slender back disappear through the doorway.

As the last of the guests began to drift away, Kate turned back toward the ballroom, which the servants had already begun to clear. She was eager to find her father. Never of a patient temperament, she was especially determined that night to have it out with him once and for all. She knew it would be impossible to settle things so quickly, but at least she could set the wheels in motion. She could tell him of Charles's proposal, and hint at the possibility of acceptance.

It would be like waving a red flag in front of an angry bull, she knew, but she was not the least bit intimidated by the idea. Her father would rant and rave like a madman on a rampage, but the vision of his fury filled her more with amusement than fright. She had no fear of her father, and she was more than confident in her own ability as a bullfighter.

Eagerly her eyes searched the grand hall for the sight of his stocky figure, but at first, as she saw nobody save the scurrying servants, she felt her heart sink in dismay. She had been so sure he would be there. What if he had anticipated her move and outsmarted her, leaving the party early to retire to the locked privacy of his room?

It was with a gasp of relief that she finally spotted him in a distant alcove, and she hurried across the hall, anxious to capture him before he had a chance to slip away. It was only when she was halfway there that she noticed that one of the guests had lingered behind, and she halted in dismay as she caught sight of a broad expanse of fawn-colored trousers capped by the gaudy shimmer of violet satin.

"Damn him anyhow," she said aloud, but she was careful to keep the words to a whisper, for she knew they were permissible only for her father and brothers. Why did Burton-Styles, of all people, have to remain behind after everyone else had left?

Kate hesitated in the center of the room, carefully eyeing

the pair in the alcove. After a minute or two she saw Burton-Styles glance her way, as if he had felt the force of her eyes fastened on his bulky figure. Hastily she turned away, busying herself with a series of unnecessary orders to the already efficient servants. The action did little to discourage his attention, however, and Kate found herself growing more and more uncomfortable as she felt the full force of his offensive gaze directed pointedly at her. Searching around avidly for a means of escape, she saw with relief that the door to the garden was still open. It took only a few moments of cautious waiting before she saw Burton-Styles turn briefly toward her father in a feigned display of polite interest, and she used the respite it gave her to slip outside.

The air was cold, far colder than it had been before, or perhaps it was just that the bright lights and music no longer floated out through the doorway to give the garden an illusion of warmth. Kate found herself hugging her bare arms with her hands, massaging them to make the blood run warm again. Either from instinct or from memory, she stepped over to the high masonry wall at the edge of the rose garden, where she had stood earlier that evening. To her surprise, she saw that the single rose Charles had given her still lay on the cold stone of the wall, and she lifted it up gently, careful to avoid the thorns that used to bite childish fingers so many years ago. Lost in thoughts and memories, she stared down at the deep red glow that shone with a soft luster in the clear moonlight.

"A gift from a suitor?" The voice was raspy and smooth all at the same time. To Kate it seemed like the sound a stone grinding mill would make if it had been greased until the oil poured down its sides.

"Lord Burton-Styles?" Kate's voice reflected her surprise. She had been so certain she had slipped out unseen. "What are you doing in the garden?"

"I am an admirer of beauty, my dear." His eyes were not looking at the roses, but were fastened instead, with no pretense of subtlety, on the white expanse of bosom that pressed up from the front of her low-cut gown. She knew from the leer in his eyes and in his voice that he had indeed observed her escape and followed her deliberately into the garden. Kate suddenly noticed that the sounds from the ballroom had stilled, as if the servants had finished their tasks and gone away, and she was painfully aware of how unprotected she was in the garden. She felt herself shiver again, but this time it was not from the cold.

"Why, you're trembling, Catherine." Behind the leer lurked the essentail politeness of the era, and even to Kate's wary ears the solicitude sounded almost genuine. "Shall I have one of the servants fetch your shawl?"

"No, thank you. I was just about to go inside anyhow." She took a step toward the door, then hesitated, waiting for him to move aside and let and let her pass. To her dismay, his massive form remained rooted in the same spot, completely blocking her escape.

"Would you please let me by, Lord Burton-Styles?" She was surprised to hear how calm her voice sounded. Her heart was beating so loud, she thought for sure he must be able to hear it.

"Surely you would not deprive me of the pleasure of your company, Catherine?"

Kate was frightened by the quiet determination she heard in his voice. Over the years, she had listened with scandalized curiosity to far too many tales of Burton-Styles's brutality, tales of abuses and liberties taken with the daughters of commoners and lesser nobles, and she realized with desperation what a compromising position she had placed herself in. Glancing up at the dark, hard eyes that showed through narrow slits in his puffy face, she decided that softness and pleading would have no effect on such a confirmed libertine. All she could hope to do was match his stubbornness and boldness with her own.

"I don't like it when you look at me in that impertinent manner, sir," she told him as coolly and firmly as she could manage. "A gentleman does not behave in that manner toward a lady. Please lower your eyes and let me pass."

She saw instantly that her ploy was not going to work, for his look remained rudely presumptuous. "I am not inclined to do that, my dear," he told her calmly, clutching her upper arm with surprising strength in his pudgy fingers.

"Take your hands off me!" Despite her resolve, anger and fear were replacing the coolness in her voice. To her alarm, the urgency in her tone only seemed to amuse him.

"Why should I?"

She knew she should answer him in the polite vernacular of the era, for it was only by playing the game well that she could protect herself. She knew she should say again, "A gentleman does not behave in that manner toward a lady," but rage and loathing fought for dominance in her emotions, and try as she would, she could not stifle them.

"Because you're fat and ugly and vile as a toad, and I despise you!"

She hissed out the words with a vehemence that amazed her, for she had never spoken so harshly to anyone in her life, but as she watched the cruel eyes glinting in his face, she could not find it in herself to be sorry for the bluntness of her words. She was no longer shivering with cold or even with fear. Instead, the trembling that overcame her body was a reflection of her horror and disgust.

She was surprised to see a quick, answering glimmer of rage flashing out from dark, beady eyes, but frightening as it was, she minded it less than the look of lascivious hunger that had preceded it. Then, to her amazement, the anger disappeared as quickly as it had come. The slender slits that let his eyes shine through closed until they were even narrower than before, and tiny, crinkly lines appeared in the puffy fat around them. It was only a second before his mouth opened wide, saliva glistening on gross lips, and he began to roar with laughter.

"Just as I always thought," he gloated between bursts of mirth. She was even more frightened by the exultant triumph ringing in his voice than she had been by his crude lechery. "You are no lady, my dear." Still clamping her flesh tightly in his heavy paw, he forced her a few steps backward, pressing her effectively against the wall.

"And you are no gentleman!" she gasped in shock, horrified at the brazen coarseness of his gesture.

"Why should I be a gentleman with you?" he retorted quickly. "You're as crude and vulgar as I am."

Suddenly she realized what had happened, and as she understood the source of the gloating pleasure in his voice, she felt a cold wave of fear spread over her body. What a fool she had been! She'd played right into his hands. Now she had nothing at all to protect her from him. Her family name and influence was nothing he would either fear or respect. The only thing that had held him away from her was the tenuous Victorian code of chivalry that said no gentleman, no matter how wealthy or important, could take advantage of a defenseless lady. But now she had proved she was at heart no real lady, and even that fragile barrier of protection was lost to her.

"What a delightful little morsel." He grinned, lowering his face until it was only inches from hers. "Don't look so frightened, my dear. With the vulgarity of your nature, I'm sure you'll enjoy this as much as I will."

Kate felt a sickening sense of nausea flood through her body as she watched his thick lips draw nearer and nearer to hers. Desperately she turned her head away, until her cheek was pressed against the cold wall, but it did no good, for he still managed to twist his mouth around until it pressed against hers.

Only the strong rigidity of the cold masonry wall held her erect as she fought the waves of nausea that swept over her, until, for a few merciful seconds, she slipped away from consciousness. When she became aware again of what was happening to her, she was brutally conscious of the bruising impact of his fingers gouging at her breasts, as if he was trying to dig his way into her body, but for a moment they caused no impact on her fear-numbed senses. It was as if her brain, in terror and revulsion, had shut off its power of reasoning to protect her from the knowledge of his bestiality. Only when she looked down and saw the massive streaks of red his rough fingers had left across the smooth whiteness of her breast did she at last fully comprehend the indignities he intended to practice on her body, and mustering up every ounce of her strength, she managed to wrench herself away from him.

The momentary limpness of her body had lulled Burton-Styles into a false sense of acquiescence, and he was not prepared for the sudden burst of resistance that pulled her from between the hard pressure of the wall and the soft flabbiness of his body. She was already several steps away before he was able to react to her sudden flight, but then he wasted no time. Despite his age and weight, he moved with surprising swiftness as he reached out and caught hold of her arm, whirling her around with vengeful force and flipping her brutally back against the wall. She felt her body strike the hard stone with a pressure that knocked all the air out of her lungs in a loud, agonizing gasp. The outward evidence of her pain only seemed to increase the vicious pleasure that lit up his eyes.

"Oh, please," she pleaded desperately as soon as she managed to regain her breath enough to force out a tortured whisper. She was no longer interested in a contest of will or strength with the brutal lord, and she was far too frightened to feel self-conscious about the tears that were streaming freely down her cheeks. "Please don't hurt me."

"Spare me your whining, my dear," he told her coldly. "You should have tried that before, when it might have done you some good."

She watched in horror as his fingers reached out again toward her breast, clutching the thin fabric of her dress and tearing it away from her body as easily as if it had been a delicate piece of gossamer. The sickening sound the soft green silk made as it tore apart and fell from her body seemed as if it were part of a hideous nightmare. In her terror, she began to shiver even more violently in the cold night air, but her suffering did not move him. Instead, he grabbed hold of the heavy corset that was now her body's only defense against his assault, and snatching it roughly in his hands, pulled at it with a strength that astonished her. She heard herself cry out in agony as the stays dug into her ribs and flesh, but finally, just as the pain became unbearable, the laces tore apart, and corset and chemise both fell to the ground, leaving her body exposed to the night air and the foul lewdity of his gaze.

"Hush, my dear," he scolded, amused. "You wouldn't want to call attention to your plight, would you?"

She understood with a frightening rush of awareness that he was laughing at her—not for crying out in pain, but for not calling for help sooner. Of course! That was what he was waiting for! He had expected her to scream. The fact that she made no sound had only encouraged him. She cursed her own folly for thinking she would be able to handle him by herself. Why had she been too stubborn to call for help? Now, she knew, it was too late. Now she would rather die than have anyone see her like that, with the marks of his fat hands on her body.

He gave a low, coarse chuckle as his fingers clamped down on her arms, holding her firmly, while he used his free hand to unfasten the front of his trousers. Kate's attention was caught by the gesture, and despite her horror, she could not keep her eyes from following his hand. As she caught sight of the hideous bulge that pushed at the rich fabric of his pants, she found herself shuddering with revulsion. The anticipation was so ugly that she knew there was no way she could ever suffer him to touch that part of his body to hers. With all her strength, she pressed her hands against his stomach, pushing him violently away from her. Raising her foot, she aimed it at his crotch with a force that was calculated to double the size of the swelling, but he was too quick for her. Fending off her foot, he grabbed her shoulder with one hand, forcing her back against the wall, while he used the other to slap her briskly across the face, first on one cheek, then the other. She sensed the bitter taste of blood in her mouth from the cut he had gouged in her cheek with the heavy ring he wore on his hand.

"That will teach you some manners," he snarled savagely as he watched her sob in fear and anger. "Now I'll show you what a real man can do!"

She felt the pressure of both his hands against her shoulders, forcing her downward, and desperately as she fought, she knew it would only be a matter of time before his superior strength won out. Finally her legs crumbled beneath her, and her body dropped painfully to the dirt and stones at her feet. In an agony of disgust, she looked up at the leer of pleasure that was stamped on his face as he tore open the front of his trousers and pulled out the red and ugly proof of his crude, drunken masculinity. The vividness of its surprisingly slender vulgarity, set against a mass of dark hair, horrified her in a way nothing had ever done before, and she knew that no matter what the cost, she must stop him from playing his filthy games with her. No shame was too great to bear if it would save her from the ugliness that confronted her. As she felt the crushing burden of his weight sink down to envelop her slim figure, she forced her mouth open. At first, her throat seemed too dry to make a sound, and even when it finally came, the scream that issued from her lips sounded remote and far away, as if the rasping cries came not from her, but from someone else.

Please, God, let someone hear, she thought in despair. Please don't let it be too late.

Even before she heard the sound of running footsteps, she felt the oppressive weight pull away from her body, and glancing up, she was amazed to see a look of stunned surprise on his face.

Why, he didn't expect me to scream, she thought, astonished at the idea. That slimy pig! He really thought I was going to let him do this to me.

He pulled himself up hurriedly from her prostrate figure, giving her a look of pained anger and reproach, as if the entire incident had been her fault instead of his. As he stepped away from her, the massive red threat that had pointed at her from the front of his trousers curled away until it was no bigger than a fat pink worm, but his pants still hung open, and he made no effort to redo them. His features quickly relaxed into the same arrogant, amused expression they habitually wore.

In another instant, the garden was filled with rushing figures and the harsh sound of angry voices. For a moment everything was too confusing to piece together, and as Kate pulled herself to her feet, she backed unsteadily toward the stone wall, gazing around her in bewilderment. It took her a few seconds to sort things out, and then, with a rush of relief, she picked out the figures of her brothers as they hurried to protect her. At first, their presence was a comforting one, and she almost forgot her embarrassment and fear, but soon the face of her brother Eamon began to stand out from everything else, and Kate gaped at him with a fascination born of terror.

This is the face of a man who can kill, she thought, stunned at the discovery. Even the horror of the past few minutes faded from her mind in the midst of the sudden cold fear she felt looking at her brother. Eamon had always been the strange one, different from the others, more intense, but never until that moment had Kate actually been afraid of him.

"No, Eamon. No!" she shouted urgently, desperately anxious to keep him from committing an act from which there could be no recall. It was only after she cried out that she realized her oldest brothers, Edward and John, had their strong arms around Eamon, stoutly holding him back. Glancing around in relief, she saw that Patrick, too, his face black and raging, was being held by two of his sons. Tension hung heavy in the air, and for a few seconds Kate barely dared to breathe. Only Burton-Styles seemed completely at ease.

"We seem to have had a slight misunderstanding," he said coolly, the traces of a deliberately insulting smirk playing around the corners of his mouth.

His words seemed to anger Eamon even more, and Kate could see the muscles in his arm straining through the thin silk of his shirt as he fought to free himself from the brothers who held him back.

"Don't, Eamon," she urged.

He turned his dark, angry eyes toward her. "Would you be telling me you liked it?" he asked hoarsely. "Was I wrong about what I saw? Were you encouraging those fat hands to crawl across your flesh?"

His words reminded her of her nakedness, and she clutched her hands across her breasts in embarrassment, as if they could somehow help to hide her shame. She was surprised to feel a light touch on her arm, and turning quickly, she saw her younger brother, David, more sensitive than the others, standing beside her. Sensing her discomfort, he had hurried to the stable and grabbed a blanket from one of the carriages. Now he held it open while she gratefully wrapped herself in its folds.

"No, Eamon," she said coolly, feeling a measure of pride and dignity restored by the protection of the blanket. "I didn't encourage him, but I don't want you doing anything rash. He didn't hurt me. You got here in time. Besides, if they let you go, I'm afraid you'd kill him. They'd hang you for that . . . and believe me, he's not worth hanging for."

"For once, the girl's talking sense," Patrick's voice cut in. As Kate turned to face him, she saw that, while her father's visage was still dark and angry, he had at least relaxed enough to encourage his sons to let go of his arms. "As for you"—Patrick turned his black scowl toward Burton-Styles— "I want you out of here."

Her brothers, with the exception of the two who were still holding fast to Eamon, stepped toward Burton-Styles as if to enforce their father's command, but the lord offered no resistance.

"Good evening, Paddy," he said calmly. "I hope I'll find you in better humor tomorrow. And to you, Catherine, I can only say it's been a pleasure." He lingered over the last word as if to emphasize it. Kate was amazed at how cool and arrogant he could be, even in the face of being thrown out of another man's house.

Even after he had passed through the doorway, Eamon still strained to get loose, and Patrick glared at him sternly. "Up to your room, lad," he said sharply. "And just to make sure you do what you're told, your brothers will go up with you and lock the door."

It was only a minute before Kate found herself alone with her father, and even the warmth of the blanket could not keep her from shivering as she looked into his eyes. It was a long time before he spoke, and when he did, his voice was curt and severe.

"Get to your room," he said coldly. She was stunned at his abruptness, and opened her mouth to protest, but he would not listen. "None of that now," he warned her harshly. "I'll have none of your excuses. Get to your room."

Angry and hurt, she pulled the blanket tightly around her and rushed from the garden, unshed tears stinging her eyelids. How could he be so thoughtless, she wondered so unsympathetic? Was this the same father who never failed to find time to laugh away all the hurts and sorrows? Why, he was treating her as if everything had been her fault, as if she were, in reality, the instigator instead of the victim.

She was all the way across the ballroom and halfway up the stairs before she realized why Patrick was so angry with her. He was worried about her, and he felt like he had been backed into a corner. Patrick always got angry when he was backed into a corner.

She paused at the top of the stairs to relish the discovery she had just made. Despite all the ugliness of the scene that had just occurred, Lord Burton-Styles had played right into her hands. With the interest he had displayed in her—and the lack of nicety he showed in pursuing it—it would hardly be safe for her to remain unwed for long, at least not if she stayed in England. He was too rich and powerful to be denied what he wanted—and it was obvious he wanted Kate.

Well, then, her father would have to see her married, and soon, too. And if she had to be married quickly, and perhaps to someone unsuitable, why shouldn't it be Philippe?

She hugged herself under the blanket and began to hum a cheerful little tune as she headed for her room.

7

"LORD BURTON-STYLES, SIR."

The ill-concealed disapproval that lay just beneath the surface of Gilchrist's voice warned Patrick that the servants had not missed the commotion the night before. Even Burton-Styles's wealth and title were not enough to save him from the contempt that so easily permeated the below-stairs world, where the manners and decorum of the era were even more rigidly defined than in their masters' quarters.

"Tell the bastard to go hang himself," Patrick snapped furiously, but both he and the stiffly proper servant knew the message would never be delivered, for the heavy, shuffling sound of Burton-Styles's footsteps already echoed in the long hallway just outside the study. As Patrick looked up in annoyance, Gilchrist dutifully slipped out through the open doorway.

"Now, now, Paddy," Burton-Styles wheezed as the sides of his enormous body rubbed against the narrow door frame.

His tone was surprisingly humble and conciliatory. "Don't start ranting and shouting. I've come to apologize."

"I'm not interested," Patrick told him shortly. "Take your fat body and get it out of here. I don't want you in my house."

"My, my, such a temper," Burton-Styles replied coolly, easing his body into the only chair in the room that would accommodate it. "Surely you can forgive a man a little amorous mischief when he's had too much to drink. I told you I came to say I'm sorry."

"Amorous mischief?" Patrick knew his sturdy Irish face was turning as red as his hair, but he didn't care. Pretending to a dignity and self-containment he didn't feel had never been part of his character, and now he was content to fume and rage like the hot-tempered peasant he was. "Foul-minded lechery is more like it. And as for being sorry, like hell you are! I'd be a fool to let you in my house as long as I've a young daughter around, and you know goddamn well that's the truth. Do you mean to tell me you wouldn't try the same thing again if I let you?"

"Of course I would." Burton-Styles seemed neither surprised nor angry at the question. "She's a beautiful wench, and I intend to have her."

The calmness of his declaration only seemed to add fuel to the fire that was raging inside Patrick, and he could barely sputter out his indignant reply.

"You mean to have her! Why, you filthy, lewd, black-hearted son of a bitch! How the hell do you dare say that to me?"

"Because for the first time in nearly fifty years, I intend to do the damn thing honorably."

Patrick's mouth had already opened to shout out an angry retort when the impact of Burton Styles's words stopped him abruptly. He didn't like the sound of them. For the first time, he noticed that the powerful lord was dressed with unaccustomed discreetness, the black wool of his jacket tightly buttoned despite the heat that was making sweat run down his chin onto his collar. He had never seen Burton-Styles dressed like that before, and his discomfort began to increase. Patrick never liked it when people behaved out of character. Dealing with the unexpected always unnerved him, putting him at a disadvantage.

"What do you mean?" he asked cautiously.

"Why, you old fool, I'm offering to make an honest woman of your daughter. As you know, my wife died several months ago, so I am now free to marry again. I'm asking for your daughter's hand."

"You want to marry Katie?" Patrick was so incredulous that he forgot to sound angry. "You filthy old lecher! Don't you think I'd burn in hell before I'd see my girl marry an old swine like you? Why, you're old enough to be her father. *Her* father, hell—you're old enough to be *my* father."

"Precisely," Burton-Styles agreed. "I *am* an old man, but you have to admit, I'm a very *rich* old man."

Despite himself, Patrick felt an unwilling wave of response. The man was a disgusting old pig, no doubt about it, but he *was* rich, richer than Patrick could ever dream of being. And there were no sons or daughters to make a claim on his fortune. If Katie were to marry him, she would be assured of enough money to provide the kind of security Patrick wanted her to have.

"That's obscene," he said stubbornly, but Burton-Styles noticed with gloating satisfaction that his protests were growing weaker. "Do you think I'd sell my daughter for money?"

"Hardly," the lord hastened to interject. "Quite the contrary. I am sure you have only her welfare at heart, but think of it this way, man. I'm over seventy now, and with the weight I carry around and the amount of liquor I consume, how much longer can I live? A few years—or if the girl's lucky, only a few months—of being a dutiful wife, and Catherine will become a very rich widow."

Patrick's eyes narrowed as he looked at the massive rolls of flesh that enveloped the man's body. It pained him even to imagine his daughter's body violated by that huge, obscene lump of flesh.

"Money isn't everything," he insisted, his lower lip protruding much the way his daughter's did when she found she couldn't get her way.

"Use your head," Burton-Styles insisted. "You have no choice." His voice was unexpectedly kind. He wanted Kate, and he was willing to use every advantage he had over her father to get her, but he couldn't help liking the feisty little Irishman. It didn't give him any particular pleasure to watch him squirm.

"What do you mean?" Patrick's voice was defensive and wary, but Burton-Styles got the feeling the hot-tempered redhead had already glimpsed the truths he intended to point out.

"Paddy, your daughter's a headstrong, hot-blooded wench. What are you going to do with her if she doesn't marry me?"

"Marry her off to someone a damn sight better than you, that's what."

"Who? Young Stratton?"

Patrick bristled. Burton-Styles had touched a sore spot, and he obviously knew it. "She's not interested in him. She was only dangling him in front of my nose so I'd let her marry the other one. I know all her little tricks by now."

"Of course. That was obvious. But she's just stubborn enough to go through with it. And then what? How long do you think it would last? She'd be bored with him in a month, and doubly resentful because she had to marry him instead of the man she really wanted. I'll make you a wager, Paddy. If she marries young Stratton, he'll be a cuckold within a year."

Patrick scowled at him in silence, but he did not attempt to deny the charge. He had no illusions about his vivacious, temperamental daughter. He was only too well aware of the sensuality that lay behind her full, passionate lips and the fiery light in the depths of her deep green eyes, and he knew there was far more of himself in his beautiful daughter than there was of the gentle, well-bred woman who bore her.

"Of course, you could always relent," Burton-Styles pressed. "You could let her marry the other one—the gambler."

"I'd see her dead first," Patrick barked out angrily, then shut his mouth with a loud snap as he realized what he had said.

"You see what I mean," Burton-Styles urged softly. "There really isn't any choice. The gambler or young Stratton . . . or me."

The silence that hung tensely in the air remained for a long time as the two men faced each other, each unwilling to break the heavy stillness. Finally, when Burton-Styles spoke, his voice was low and kind.

"There's no help for it, Paddy. The gambler's in the girl's blood. If it isn't him, it'll be the next man that comes along with romantic eyes and a flashing smile. If she marries young Stratton now, who will protect her when she starts breaking the rigid laws of society? But if she marries me . . . well, she'll have to be faithful while I live, I grant that. I'd never tolerate nonsense of that kind. But after I die . . . Think of it, Paddy. As Lady Burton-Styles, she can do anything she wants. She can marry her young gambler, or keep him on the side—or anyone else she wants. She'll be so wealthy and so powerful that nobody—*nobody*—will be able to ruin her."

Burton-Styles could see the despair that shone bright as tears in Patrick's eyes, and he was wise enough not to press the point. He knew he had already won. There was no other way Patrick could protect his daughter from her own tempestuous temperament. He would have to give Kate to him.

"Suppose I agreed," Patrick offered tentatively, his voice heavy with indecision and unhappiness. "What good would it do? You'd never get her to say yes."

"There are ways of persuading her," Burton-Styles replied calmly. "You know that as well as I do. If you agree, she won't have any choice."

Patrick was silent. He knew the words were true. Still, he hated to force his daughter into an unwilling marriage, one that would cause her great unhappiness, even if it was for her ultimate good. It was a long time before he could bring himself to speak.

"All right," he agreed wearily. "You can have her."

Kate watched the sunlight streaming in through the window, and her heart sang with excitement as she waited impatiently for the summons she knew must come. No matter how diligently her father had avoided her for the past few weeks, he would have to see her now. After the incident that occurred the night before, he had no choice. Soon he would send for her, and she was ready for him.

She had taken care to put on one of her most becoming dresses, a pale yellow organdy frock that brought out the rich red tones in her hair and gave her a deceptively fragile appearance. It had always been one of her father's favorites, and she knew he could not resist it. Soon she would float into his study, looking properly feminine and helpless, and when she glanced up at him from beneath long lashes, smiling a soft, demure smile, she was sure he could refuse her nothing.

When the gentle knock finally came at the door, it sounded to her ears as loud as a clap of thunder, and she half-jumped out of her chair, then fell back on the cushions, laughing at herself for the unconscious nervousness that had come so unexpectedly to the surface. Opening the door eagerly, she gazed out at Gilchrist's impassive features and listened to the polite monotone of his voice as he intoned the words she had been waiting to hear.

"Your father wishes to see you in the study, Lady Catherine."

Clutching up her skirt in nervous fingers to keep from tripping over it in her haste, Kate rushed past Gilchrist's somber figure and hurried down the hall toward the stairway. Common sense told her she should wait a few minutes, giving Patrick a little more time to stew before she began her assault, but she was too impetuous to force herself to hold back. Eagerness lent speed to her feet, and she fairly flew down the stairs and through the hallway, the leather of her dainty heels clicking a sharp tattoo on the polished wooden floor.

She had nearly reached the door of her father's study when the sound of voices warned her he was not alone. She stopped abruptly, her feet sliding awkwardly along the floor for a brief second before she could bring herself to a halt. She stood motionless in the hallway, listening to the slow, surprisingly soft sound of her father's voice as it spilled out through the open doorway. This was hardly what she'd expected. She thought she would see her father alone. What on earth had prompted him to call for her now?

As she heard the coarse, loud voice that answered her father's, she caught her breath with a sharp gasp of foreboding. Lord Burton-Styles! What was he doing in her father's study? That he had chosen to call was no surprise—hadn't he hinted as much the evening before?—but that Patrick agreed to see him was something else again. Kate was conscious of an icy chill clutching at her heart as she forced herself to step across the threshold.

"You wanted to see me, Father?"

"Ah, yes. Come in." Patrick's face was flushed with embarrassment, and he could not bring himself to look his daughter in the eye. "Say good morning to Lord Burton-Styles, Catherine." Kate felt her fear deepen. Never in her memory had her father called her anything but Katie.

"I'll do nothing of the kind," she replied coolly, raising her head proudly as she swung around to give the offensive nobleman a disdainful look. "I would not have thought, my lord, you'd have the effrontery to come here after the grossness of your actions yesterday."

"My God, what a beauty," Burton-Styles cried out, laughing in delight at her outburst. "What spirit! What fire! Look at her, Paddy. What a magnificent wife she's going to make!"

Kate felt the blood drain out of her face at his words, but she was determined to stand her ground, her head still held high, despite the confusion that poured through her brain. Wife? What did he mean by that? Surely she had misheard him.

Patrick's flush deepened. "Goddammit, can't you let me tell her in my own way?" he complained.

For an instant the room seemed to whirl around, and Kate

was afraid she was going to faint. "Tell me what?" she asked weakly. "Wife? Whose wife?"

"I should think that would be perfectly clear, my dear," Burton-Styles's hoarse, oily voice replied. "I have asked your father for your hand, and he has been gracious enough to give it to me."

"My father has given me to you?" Her voice was soft and stunned. At first she could not believe it, but as she turned slowly to face Patrick, she saw by his downcast, embarrassed expression that it was true. "Well, I don't care what my father said. You're a filthy, fat old toad, and I won't marry you!"

"Now, Katie, be reasonable," Patrick pleaded. Kate was alarmed to see that the embarrassment on his face had been replaced by a dark frown. "He's an old man. It'll be only a year or two, I promise you, and then you'll be a widow—and a rich one, at that."

"I don't care if it's only for a day. I won't have him, and that's that. I don't give a fig for money, and you know it."

"That's because you've never been without it," Patrick reminded her ominously. "I have, and I know what it's like." Why did he have to choose those words? Kate wondered—almost the same words Philippe had spoken to her only a few short weeks before. "You're a headstrong young woman, Katie. I don't know what to do with you, and that's a fact. Be a good lass, now, and marry the lord. He'll make you a tolerable husband for a while, no worse than some I know, and when you're a rich widow, you can do anything you want. Marry that damn fool gambler of yours if that's your fancy, or make a fool of a dozen young Strattons."

Too late Kate realized with a jolt of horror that she had stepped into a trap—and it was one of her own making. She had outwitted herself by flirting so outrageously with Charles the night before, not realizing she was setting into place the last piece for her own checkmate.

"I can't do it," she whispered softly. "I'm sorry, but I can't." She made no attempt to control the tears that flowed freely down her cheeks, knowing they were her last chance to melt Patrick's stubborn heart.

"Goddammit, none of that," Patrick shouted, turning away from her to make sure the tears did not weaken his resolve. "You'll marry him, and that's final."

"No," she replied. She was still crying, but there was a new firmness in her voice. "You can't make me do it. You can drag me to the altar, but you can't force me to say yes."

"You'll say yes, or you'll go to the convent."

"The convent?" Kate was too surprised for a moment to be frightened. She was aware of her father's Irish background, of course, but her Anglican mother had imposed her own religion on the family long before Kate was born, and thoughts of the convent had never occurred to her.

"The convent," he affirmed. "They have high walls and strict discipline, strict enough to keep you in. Let you dine on bread and water, missy, and dress in simple clothes, and we'll see how long you like it."

The picture was a dismal one, and for the first time Kate began to comprehend the extent of the danger she faced. Spending the rest of her life behind high gray walls terrified her, and for half a second she was tempted to relent, but a quick glance at Burton-Styles's corpulent body and carnal face quickly dissuaded her. There was no way she could ever tolerate those obscene rolls of flesh pouring over her white belly and soft young breasts.

"Then I choose the convent."

Mustering up as much dignity as she could, she stiffened her back and pushed her chin up as she turned and swept out of the room. From the hallway outside, she could not see the puzzled, concerned look on her father's face, but she was not to be spared the ugly sound of Burton-Styles's laughter ringing in her ears.

"Let her go, Paddy," the odious lord urged cheerfully. "A few weeks in the convent, and she'll be glad enough to come out at any price."

Kate felt her feet hesitate as she neared the end of the hallway. Now that she was out from under the watchful eyes of the two men, all semblance of confidence left her, and she felt herself begin to shake violently. She knew Burton-Styles had spoken only the truth. A few weeks imprisoned behind high walls, contemplating a life of emptiness, and she would be on her knees in no time. But how—*how*—could she ever bring herself to wed, much less bed, that hideous man?

The sound of his triumphant laughter followed her down the hall, and she was forced to listen helplessly to the snatches of conversation, sometimes more shouted than spoken that echoed through the empty hallway.

"Well worth waiting for, I assure you, my friend. What beauty she has, what fire—yet all the while still untouched, still radiant with the enchanting glow of innocence."

Innocence?

Kate's breath came in a sharp, painful gasp as she realized

the implication of that single word. And yet, how natural it seemed. How foolish she was not to have realized it before. Of course Burton-Styles thought he would be marrying—and taking to his bed—an innocent virgin bride.

But she wasn't innocent.

She shut her eyes, feeling a sick wave of horror flood over her as she recalled hot summer evenings, hidden beside the stove in the kitchen, listening with one or another of her siblings to the servants' gossip they were still too young to understand. How the old biddies had delighted in chuckling over the weddings, clacking their tongues against the roofs of their mouths, making a noise that sounded even to Kate's young ears vaguely obscene, as they relished the telling and retelling of the morning after, when bloodstained bedsheets had been draped from upper-story windows, proudly displayed for all the neighbors to see. What a stupid, barbaric custom it was, and yet, it was just that sort of peasant custom that would appeal to a man like Burton-Styles. How would he feel when he realized he had been thwarted in that pleasure? When he found that his bride's marriage blood had been spilled, not on the white silk of his sheets, but on the crude straw of a stable floor thousands of miles away?

He would not be kind about it, that was for sure. How he would resent the idea of being tricked into marrying a young girl who was far from innocent! No doubt he would find ways to make her life a living hell to pay for it.

Well, perhaps it was just as well, she thought. It was like burning her bridges behind her, cutting off all her escapes. Now there was no possibility she could relent, no possibility she could give in at the last minute to that repugnant marriage. Now she had no choice.

In her mind, she was already packing her bags as she hurried up the stairs, choosing what frocks to leave behind, what few to carry with her. Somehow—she didn't know how, but *somehow*—she had to get hold of some money and make her way to the coast, perhaps to Plymouth or Southhampton, where it would be easy to find a ship to the New World. Soon she would lie in her lover's arms again.

8

THE SCENE AT DOCKSIDE IN THE BOSTON HARBOR AS THE *Star of India* pulled in from England was both frightening and chaotic, and Kate clutched her heavy bag frantically to keep it from being torn away by the jostling of the crowd. She had never been part of a huge, milling mass of people before, and she was terrified by the mindless movement that pushed her first this way and then that, with no seeming pattern or reason behind it. Finally she caught sight of an empty area of the deck, near the railing on the far side, and grasping her suitcase tightly against her body, she pressed her way through the crowd. When at last she stood alone beside the railing, her weary arms gratefully let the bag drop to the surface of the deck, and she took a deep gulp of the cool morning air. The fresh, salty taste of the sea in her mouth and nostrils seemed almost a miracle after the fetid air she had been forced to breathe for weeks.

The long sea voyage had been agonizing and grotesque. To Kate, its ugliness seemed an accumulation of all her childhood nightmares. Jammed like animals into the crowded hold of the ship—the lucky ones crowded two or three to a narrow berth, the unlucky ones scrambling for a few inches of floor space to spread their blankets—the passengers endured the seemingly endless days with a fatalism that was terrifying in its totality. By the end of the voyage, the only reality that held meaning for any of them was the constant sound of sick and frightened whimpers and the all-pervading stench of vomit and urine.

But unbearable as the journey had been, it was over now, and as the fresh, clean scent of salt air cleansed her nostrils, Kate already felt the horror of it fading into distant recesses of her memory. Yes, the voyage was something easily forgotten. Harder to forget were the days that preceded it.

Kate still had to close her eyes against the faintness that swept over her when she recalled those days. She had been terrified enough when she learned her father's plans for her, but the terror grew even more intense as, bit by bit, she realized the desperateness of her situation. Everywhere she turned, she found no help, no friend or relative who dared defy either her father or the powerful Lord Burton-Styles, and in the end she had to swallow her pride and go to the one person whose aid she had no right to beg.

She still recalled with painful clarity the look of hurt in Charles's eyes when she confessed the truth to him. She had dreaded that look for days, knowing even before she saw it that it would tear her apart with guilt, but she forced herself to face it. Charles, she knew, was too much of a gentleman to refuse to help her, no matter how callously she had used him or how deeply she had hurt him.

In the end, he had given her the money she needed, money he could ill afford, and taken her to Southampton to wait for the next ship to Boston. He had known one of the mates on the ship, an old school chum he told her, and he bribed the man to get her a good cabin. Kate could only suppose the man pocketed the money with a sly grin, for despite Charles's efforts, she ended up in steerage with all the penniless immigrants arriving to try their fortunes in the New World.

"Well, that's all over now," she told herself firmly, not caring if anyone overheard her talking to herself. It *was* over, and there was no sense dwelling on the past. The past was dead, and she had to look to the future. Buttoning her coat against the chilly morning air, she forced her aching arm to pick up the heavy bag again as she moved with determined steps toward the gangplank, now almost clear of departing passengers.

A small group of ship's officers had gathered near the gangplank, and Kate noticed the captain among them. He looked up in surprise as he saw her heading toward them.

"Anything wrong, miss?" Kate noticed a trace of insolence in his voice.

"You'd think she doesn't want to get off," one of the ship's mates quipped. "Maybe she can't bear to leave us." Kate wondered if he was the same mate who had stolen Charles's bribe.

"I just don't want to be part of that mob scene," she retorted coolly.

"Can't say as I blame you there, miss," the captain responded quickly. His tone had grown more respectful, as if he recognized from Kate's careful enunciation that she was not one of the usual riffraff he was accustomed to transporting. "I think you'll be all right now. They seem to have cleared out."

He took Kate's arm and helped her onto the shaky gangplank. She was grateful for his assistance, for it took a second or two to get a good hold on the thick, oily rope that served as a railing. Watching her feet carefully to keep her heels from catching in the rough, uneven planks, Kate made her way slowly down the rickety wooden ramp. She was nearly halfway down before she realized she had forgotten the most important thing of all.

"Oh, Captain," she shouted, craning her neck around so she could see him.

"Yes, miss?"

"When is the next ship due in Boston? From England, I mean?"

"You must be expecting someone," he guessed. "Some relatives, I suppose." Kate nodded her head quickly, grateful that he had provided her with a ready-made excuse for her query. "Do you know what ship they'll be on?"

"They said they'd try to get the next one," she lied.

"That'll be the *Mary Ann*. But I'm afraid it'll not be here for another three weeks."

She thanked him, then turned her head away quickly from his sympathetic glance, afraid he would catch the look of triumph in her eyes. He must already be curious enough about her. Well-bred young ladies were not usually wont to travel unchaperoned in steerage. There was no point making him even more suspicious.

Three weeks! She could hardly believe her luck. Three long weeks before she needed to dread the arrival of a hot-tempered Irishman and his seven strong sons. More than enough time to make plans with Philippe, plans for the elopement he would have to agree to now.

The sound of excitement rang in her heart, blocking out the loud, raucous clamor of the docks, and she barely noticed the sweaty crowds that continued to jostle her as she went off in search of a carriage. After a number of fruitless efforts to make her way toward one of the few vacant coaches, she finally gave up, deciding she would have better luck on the streets that led to the harbor. Picking up her satchel with a renewed burst of energy, she made her way toward the edge of the crowd. She had nearly reached the street when she heard a familiar voice call her name.

"Why, Cousin Katie, what a surprise."

Whirling around in an agony of suspense and fright, Kate

was stunned to come face to face with the half-witted grin of young Christy O'Conner, Cousin Michael's boy. How could she have forgotten he worked on the docks? What a fool she was not to have wrapped herself up in a veil and mingled with the crowds until she could get out of the area safely.

"Why, Christy," she said, feigning a warmth she did not feel. "How are you?"

Ignoring the superficial politeness of her question, he gaped at her in amusement, a slow, moronic grin spreading across his features.

"We weren't expecting you back so soon, Cousin."

"No doubt," she replied crisply. "But as you can see, I'm here."

"We didn't think your pa'd let you out."

She bristled at the comment. Where did he think she'd been, in a cage? Though in truth, when she thought it over, he wasn't far from right. "Papa can never deny me anything, you know that." She was careful to smile her warmest, most flirtatious smile, as if to reinforce the truth of what she was saying.

"I reckon he couldn't," Christy agreed readily. "You was always a right pretty one, though I can't say as how you look so perky now. What's the matter, Cousin? You look as pale as them what's come out of steerage." The idea seemed to cause him a great deal of mirth, for a low, guttural chuckle began to gurgle in his throat.

You ghoul, Kate thought angrily, but she didn't dare speak the words aloud. "It was a rough voyage," she retorted curtly. Then, anxious to get away from him before even his slow brain could begin to suspect something, she added, "It's been nice seeing you, Christy, but I'm eager to get to my aunt's house. Be a good boy and fetch me a carriage."

He began to look around hesitantly, and for a moment Kate thought he was planning to obey her sharp command, but his next words quickly dispelled that hope. "Where's your chaperon?" he asked, puzzled.

Kate had been dreading the question she hoped he was not clever enough to think of, but she had already prepared her answer. "Still on board. She's in even worse shape than I am. She'll follow when she feels better—with my luggage." She hoped her words would stifle not only the question he had already asked but also the one she was afraid was on the tip of his tongue.

He seemed to accept her answer, but she knew only too well that his slow, dull features rarely showed any expression

75

other than childish amusement, so it was hard to tell what he was thinking. "I'll see you to your auntie's house," he told her.

"That's not necessary, Christy," she replied firmly. "I'm sure you have work to do. Just fetch me a carriage, and I'll be fine." She was desperately aware that she needed more time. The minute Christy got to his father with the news of her arrival, the game was up. Michael was far too shrewd to be taken in by the ruse for a minute. If she could just keep Christy on the docks until evening, she and Philippe would still have time to make their escape.

"No, indeed," he protested stoutly. "My pa'd whup me sure if I let you go alone. You just wait here while I tell 'em where I'm going." He hurried off to talk to another lad, whose hair was even redder than his own.

Kate considered bolting when she saw that Christy was nearly halfway across the yard, but she thought better of it. There was no vacant carriage in sight, and with her heavy bag, she would be lucky to get even half a block before he caught up with her. Besides, running away would only arouse his suspicions. She decided her only chance was to stand her ground and bluff him out.

It was only a few minutes before Christy got a carriage and Kate found herself seated beside him as they rode through the heavily cobbled streets. Despite the incessant, half-witted chatter that poured out of his mouth, Kate managed to ignore him, except for a perfunctory nod every now and then, and concentrate on the task that lay before her. Time was of the essence, she knew, and the timing was something she had to work out quickly How long would she have after Christy left her aunt's house—half an hour? forty-five minutes?—before he reached his father? She had to count on the shortest time. She didn't dare take any chances. Half an hour, then. Thirty minutes to greet her aunt, calm her fears, bid her good-bye, perhaps for the last time, and get out of the neighborhood before her cousins came to search for her. It was a close schedule, one that didn't allow for any mistakes, but she was sure she could make it.

And yet the moment she caught sight of her aunt, rushing anxiously down the steps of her home to greet her unexpected arrival, she knew it was going to be far more difficult than she had anticipated. One look at her aunt's pale, worried expression warned her that the flippant excuse she had tossed out so boldly to Christy would not fool her for a moment, but with her cousin standing at her side, staring at her with crude amusement on his face, she dared do nothing but repeat her lie.

"Papa has sent me back." She tried to force a light gaiety into her voice, but she only half succeeded. "You know how he can never hold out against my wheedling."

It took only one quick glance at her aunt's troubled eyes to realize she had not been taken in for an instant, but Kate knew she would never call her a liar in front of Christy. Time enough to find a better excuse for her aunt when Christy was gone, Kate told herself guiltily, remembering how much grief she had already caused her aunt—and knowing how much was yet in store for that gracious lady. She didn't know yet what she was going to tell her—how she was going to find the words to allay her fears—but she knew there was no sense worrying about it until Christy left. She could say nothing in front of him.

But the confrontation she feared never came, for Kate was not to leave the house that day. She hadn't seen the shadowy figure beside the wall when they rode in, but she couldn't miss him a few minutes later when Christy, refusing her aunt's polite offer of tea, went out to take his place beside him.

It was her Cousin Sheamus, Christy's brother.

Too late Kate realized what had happened. The message her cousin had given the redheaded boy was not a message for his employers on the dock as she had assumed, but one for his father and brothers at home. Now she could no longer hope to fly to Philippe's arms that day, but would be forced to stay in her aunt's home, keeping up the ridiculous farce she had already begun, pretending her father had succumbed to her coaxing and sent her back to Boston to enjoy herself.

The two young men lingered by the gate with no pretense at concealment. Kate realized that the silent declaration they were making was an obvious one. There they were, and there they would remain until her father either came or sent word. Whenever she tried to leave the house, one or both of them would go with her, making it impossible for her to see Philippe or even send him a secret message.

She felt a cold fear begin to clutch at her heart, a fear even worse than the one that had overwhelmed her when she faced her father and Lord Burton-Styles in his study that day that now seemed so long ago.

She had thought when she got off the ship that everything would be all right—but instead, it had only gotten worse. The walls around her aunt's house may not have been as high as the walls of a convent, but they were high enough to keep her in when the only means of exit, the gate at the front, was guarded by her cousins.

Three weeks! It had seemed like a long time before, but now it seemed terribly short. Three weeks before the *Mary Ann* docked in Boston with a message for her uncle, demanding her return home—a *message*, if she was lucky!

If she wasn't lucky, the *Mary Ann* would hold Paddy Devlin and his sons, angry and bound for vengeance.

9

HUGE WHITE ROLLS OF FOG CAME BILLOWING IN FROM THE sea, as they had nearly every day for a week, drowning the last rays of late-afternoon sun in their haze and changing the entire city into a twilight world. Kate sighed as she watched the thickening mist, knowing with the certainty of past disappointments that the winds would soon begin to disperse it, breaking it up into delicately swirling clouds of white that would float slowly inland, to evaporate in the warmth of the sun.

The first day the fog rolled in, Kate had watched it with a mixture of excitement and hope, waiting avidly for the atmosphere to grow dim enough to obscure the two patient figures who stood in solemn vigilance beside the gate. She had already been in Boston nearly a week, and the time that was so precious to her seemed to be slipping away like sand between her fingertips. Then, with the advent of that first fog, everything seemed suddenly to have changed.

With eager, trembling fingers, she had taken her dresses from the closet and jammed them into the carpetbag she had bribed one of the servants to buy for her. All that remained was to sneak down the steps without being seen and slip out the side door, easing her way toward the gate under cover of the shrubbery until she could find a convenient corner to hide the bag. Returning to the house the same way she had come, she forced herself to sit meekly in the parlor, pretending nothing was amiss, while she anxiously watched the window, waiting for the mist to grow heavy enough to cover her escape. She wore the same gray walking dress she had on the last time she saw Philippe, but she was careful not to pin up the skirt, letting it hang instead to her ankles, covering the pretty red petticoat, so no one would suspect she was planning to go out.

But the fog did not deepen that evening, and Kate watched in an agony of disappointment as the air grew clearer and hopes of escape became more and more remote. Though she slept in her clothes that night, getting up frequently to check the weather, the enveloping mist she had been hoping for never materialized, and in the early-morning hours, before the sun had a chance to rise, she crept downstairs to rescue her carpetbag from the shrubbery where she had secreted it. She did the same thing the next night, and the night after that, and every night for nearly a week. Carefully, in the late-afternoon hours, she would creep out to hide her bag beside the wall, and just as carefully in the hour before dawn, she had to sneak it back into the house and hang her dresses once again in the closet so the servants would not grow suspicious.

Now, watching the fog deepen once again, Kate was tempted for the first time to give up. It seemed so pointless to hide her bag in the garden and wait the long, futile hours for that one perfect moment when she could slip away unseen. Still, she had no other plan, and she knew, with time so short, that she couldn't afford to pass up even the slimmest chance of escape. With a sigh of weariness, she forced herself to step over to the closet and begin again the evening ritual she had started so hopefully the week before.

Despite her caution, every stair seemed to creak under her feet as she descended, and Kate cursed the secrecy that forced her to creep down stealthily each night, her heart in her throat for fear of being caught. She made it safely to the bottom, but no sooner had she set foot on the highly polished floor than she heard the sound of scurrying footsteps bustling toward her. She barely had time to step into the little writing salon before she saw one of the Irish maids rushing by, her heels clicking busily on the floor. Fortunately, the girl did not turn into the writing room, for there was no place for Kate to hide her bag, and in a few moments, everything was silent again. The only sound Kate could hear was the loud thumping of her own heart as it echoed ominously in her ears.

Peeking out from the doorway of the salon, Kate saw that the hall was indeed empty, and picking up her carpetbag, she made her way quickly toward the servants' quarters at the side of the house. Inching her way along the narrow corridor, Kate felt her cheeks begin to burn with anger and humiliation at the stealth she was forced to practice. How unfair it seemed! At nineteen, she ought to have been able to choose her own destiny, right or wrong, wise or unwise, without the father and the brothers and the cousins who were all determined to impose their will on her. And yet, it would be like that all her life, she knew. When she escaped the dominance of her family, it would only be through marriage, and that would be nothing more than a transferal of the title of ownership. Instead of belonging to her father, she would become the property of her husband.

For the first time, she began to catch a glimpse of the life her father was trying to offer her with Lord Burton-Styles, and her inherent honesty forced her to admit grudgingly that he was not totally wrong. As the widow of a wealthy and powerful man, she would at least have the independence she craved. She would be one of the few women in England—perhaps one of the few in the world—who would have the right to govern her own destiny. If the odious Burton-Styles hadn't gone along with it, she might have been tempted to consider the proposition, but even the vaguest memory of his bloated, leering face was enough to dispel the idea from her mind forever.

As she cautiously eased the side door open and poked her nose out into the cold autumn air, Kate was surprised to see that the thick haze had deepened considerably in the short time it took her to creep downstairs. The entire yard had a mystical, fantasy-world quality about it, and she had to strain her eyes even to see the trees that lay barely ten feet away from her. For the first time in days, she began to feel hopeful again. Perhaps, after all, tonight would be the night she finally managed to slip away.

Taking care to close the door tightly behind her, she stepped out into the heavy white mist. She moved boldly, feeling no fear of being caught, for even had the thick fog not enveloped her in its cloak of invisibility, the heavy shrubbery alone would have been sufficient to block the side yard from her cousins' watchful eyes. Only as she neared the gate did she begin to feel any sense of danger, and then she was careful to stay close to the wall, where the veil of greenery could still protect her. Inching her way slowly forward, she slid her hand along the wall until it dripped with cold moisture that the dark red bricks had picked up from the heavy condensation in the air. She silently cursed the long skirt that picked up tiny drops of water from the blades of grass, but she did not dare take the time to pin it up.

As she reached the last thick clump of bushes by the gate, she quickly found the little indentation she had carved out of the earth for her bag and shoved it easily inside, pulling the branches of greenery over it to conceal it completely. Her task done, she prepared to slip back inside the house, but a quick glance at the atmosphere around her made her hesitate. The fog seemed to have grown heavier, even in the brief time she had been outside, and it occurred to her, with a rapid acceleration of her pulse, that the time of her escape might be only minutes away.

On impulse, she pressed her way into the shrubbery, forcing open a narrow space between the stout green branches and the high brick wall. Saber-sharp edges of twigs gouged painfully into the skin of her bare hands and caught at her skirt, holding her prisoner until she could rip the fabric angrily from its clutches. How ill-equipped she was for such an adventure, she thought bitterly. Whoever had decreed that women must always wear full skirts and masses of voluminous petticoats, even in the most inappropriate of circumstances?

Finally, when she had inched her way nearly to the end of the wall, she paused to catch her breath. Under cover of the foliage, it was hard to gauge the intensity of the fog, but Kate was reasonably certain it had not grown any thinner. She felt confident enough to risk a peek outside to reconnoiter her situation. Cautiously she separated the leaves that lay in front of her, squinting eagerly into the pale white mist.

Instinct forced her to catch her breath, hardly daring even to exhale for fear of the soft noise she would make as she found herself staring into the cool gray eyes of her cousin Sheamus, not two feet away from her. At first, she thought for sure he must see her, but she quickly realized the eyes that gazed back at her were as unseeing as those of a blind man. The heavy mist that half-shrouded his tall, gaunt figure had served with equal effectiveness to conceal the subtle movement of the leaves as she peered out at him. It gave Kate an eerie feeling to see her cousin so close to her and yet know he was completely unaware of her presence.

The low, guttural sound of Sheamus clearing his throat carried across the cold air to her ears, and Kate was startled to hear how loud it sounded. With a shock of realization she remembered her own noisy progress through the shrubbery only seconds before as she trampled heavily on the moist earth and snapped twigs off with a loud cracking sound. How lucky she was that her cousins were not paying close attention! Otherwise, surely the heavy rustling sounds would have aroused their suspicion. She must be more careful.

The sound of plodding footsteps made her peer more intently into the fog, and she recognized the tall figure that approached as one of her other cousins, but in the indistinct haze she could not be sure which one it was. Only after he had nearly reached Sheamus' side did Kate realize it was Christy, the same youth who had spotted her on the docks nearly two weeks before. It seemed to her an omen—a good omen. How fitting it was that these two, who had begun the vigil her first afternoon in Boston, should be the sentries on her final evening.

"Brrr, I hate this!" Christy's voice sounded unpleasantly near. "I'll be glad when it's over."

He'd be glad when it was over! Despite her anxiety, Kate felt herself bristle with indignation. How dare he complain about the discomfort of his vigil! He and his brothers were there of their own free will, taking turns to stand guard over her like some criminal in prison. If he didn't like it, all he had to do was go home!

"It won't be long now," Sheamus assured him calmly.

Oh, yes, it will, Kate thought angrily, a little surprised at herself for gloating so vehemently at their discomfort. It would be a week before the *Mary Ann* pulled into the Boston harbor. Even if Kate escaped that very night, her cousins would have no way of knowing about it. They would have to keep up their stern, uncompromising vigil until Paddy and his seven sons arrived. She found herself hoping the fog would turn into an icy sleet that would give them all pneumonia.

"They should be here by now," Christy complained.

Kate felt her heart jump into her throat at the sound of his words. They couldn't be here yet! The *Mary Ann* wasn't due for a week. She was sure of it. Anxiously she fought back the panic that threatened to overwhelm her, taking a deep breath and forcing herself to think clearly. As soon as she did, she had to smile at her foolishness. She had been so wrapped up in her own thoughts that it never occurred to her everyone else wasn't thinking the same thing. The minute Christy had said "they," she had visions of a redheaded Irishman and his seven sons, yet Christy no doubt meant nothing more ominous than the two brothers who were due to relieve them. She let herself relax enough to breathe a sigh of relief, but her newfound sense of security was quickly shattered by her cousin's next words.

"Pa's been at the docks since early morning. The ship must have come in by now."

It was all Kate could do to keep from gasping aloud. Her first instinct had been right! Christy was expecting Patrick and her brothers. Yet, surely he must be mistaken. Patrick couldn't be arriving that day. The captain she'd spoken to assured her the *Mary Ann* wouldn't arrive until next week.

"They'll be here." Sheamus spoke with a confidence that only added to Kate's despair.

"Why are you so sure they'll be on that ship?"

"Use your head, lad." Sheamus spoke patiently, as he always did with his slower-witted brother. "The ship from England isn't due till next week. Sure'n you don't think Cousin Paddy'll wait that long, do ye? No, lad, the smart thing is to slip across the channel and take ship at Le Havre."

Kate gasped as she realized how logical it was. Le Havre! Of course they'd go to Le Havre!

Or would they?

Kate recalled with the urgency of a drowning man clutching at a life rope how deathly afraid Paddy was of the wild waves that often rocked small boats crossing the channel. He'd turned green as a patch of new spring grass the one time he'd attempted it, so they said, as much from fright as from seasickness, and he'd vowed never to go near that narrow, surprisingly treacherous body of water again. Surely, feeling as he did, he'd wait for the *Mary Ann*.

And yet, if he was angry enough . . . Kate felt the rapid beating of her heart quicken at the thought. If Patrick was angry enough, and he well might be, he could easily let his stubbornness override his fear. And even if he didn't, even if he chose the more comfortable crossing for himself, wouldn't he send his sons ahead as his emissaries?

Even without realizing it, Kate's hand had slipped stealthily through the shrubbery, and suddenly she was surprised by the feel of something hard in her hand. It was the handle of her carpetbag.

Even as her fingertips brushed against it, she knew what she had to do. She had to pull it toward her through the bushes until it lay by her side, and then she had to peek again through the branches, choosing a time to slip past the two guards at the gate. She could no longer afford to wait for the fog to thicken. Even without its cover, she had to try to slip out and make her escape.

It was hard work dragging the bag toward her through the tangle of branches, harder than she had imagined. No matter how careful she tried to be, twigs snapped ominously in her hand, and leaves rustled heavily, until they sounded as loud as waves crashing against the rocky shore. After each new sound, Kate held her breath in terror, wondering if they had heard, but she dared not part the outer branches to peek out, for fear they were staring curiously in her direction. Finally, after what seemed to her forever, she managed to inch the bag over to her. Although her hands were cut and bleeding, she felt a sense of exhilaration as she clutched it against her breast. Holding it tightly, she strained her ears for any sound that would tell her her presence had been noticed. Instead, she heard only silence—a heavy, ominous, unnatural silence. When it was broken, it was broken only by the eerie howling of the rising wind.

The sound of the wind struck terror into Kate's heart, for she knew it was capable of breaking up the fog and driving it in scattered clusters inland. Knowing she must move quickly, she forced herself to find the courage to peek again through the leaves, seeing to her relief that the fog had, if anything, grown denser. Tensely she curled her fingers around the suitcase handle and inched her way as close to the edge of the shrubbery as she dared.

Suddenly, as if in answer to her prayers, the wind curled itself around Christy's head, picking up the cap that was settled on top of his red curls as neatly as if it had fingers of its own to clutch with. Christy let out a yowl and started to chase it down the street. Sheamus called after him angrily, obviously annoyed at having to guard the wide gate by himself in the heavy fog, but if Christy heard him, he paid no heed. Kate could hear the heavy clumping of his boots as he rushed awkwardly down the cobbled street.

This was her chance, Kate realized, her mouth suddenly dry with fear. Sheamus' back was turned as he stared after Christy, and she would have at least a few seconds to slip past him. If only he didn't turn around too soon, she would be able to get away. If he did . . .

Kate forced herself not to think about what might happen. It was now or never. This was her only chance. Grasping the bag tightly in her hand, she forced herself to move out of cover of the bushes, dashing more by instinct than by sight down the slippery cobblestones.

Fear tempted her to look back over her shoulder to see if her flight had been discovered, but reason forced her to keep her eyes straight ahead. Turning around would accomplish nothing. If Sheamus had seen her, there was no way she could avoid capture. If he hadn't, even the pause of a single second might mean the ruin of all her plans. She had to keep running straight ahead, running as fast as she could.

Her feet slid on the treacherous stones, but she managed to keep from stumbling as she ran down the road. After the first few seconds, she was no longer sure where she was or even what direction she was going, but it didn't matter. All she wanted was to put distance between herself and her two cousins. Even after she began to feel safe, certain she had long since passed out of Sheamus' range of vision, she avoided the temptation to turn and look back. She didn't hear the sound of pursuit, but she didn't dare take any chances.

Suddenly, without any warning, she felt herself run abruptly into some hard object that impeded her way, and she gave out a cry of pain as she stumbled and half-fell to the ground. The instant she heard the sound of her own voice echoing ominously on the still air, she wished she could recall it. If Sheamus and Christy heard it, surely they would recognize her voice and come after her.

Kate's first instinct was to begin to run again, but she realized with a mounting sense of horror that she had completely lost all sense of direction. If she tried to run now, she was as likely to move toward the dreaded Sheamus and his brother as away from them. She knew she had to pause for a moment to get her bearings, groping through the fog for something—some familiar landmark—that would tell her where she was.

Fearfully she stretched out her hand, surprised to feel how much it was trembling, and reached for the object that had blocked her way. It took her a moment to find it, and when she did, its cold, slippery surface caused her to pull her hand back in fright. Forcing herself to reach for it again, she was surprised to feel a smooth, round pole beneath her fingers. As she leaned forward to catch a glimpse of it, she saw to her amazement that she was standing before the ornately decorated hitching post in front of the hotel.

But the hotel was way down the block, hundreds of yards from her aunt's house! Kate could hardly believe she had run so far. No wonder there had been no response to the sound of her voice when she cried out in fright. Sheamus and Christy were both much too far away to hear. A sudden surge of relief flooded over her, and she leaned wearily against the post, the strain of exertion weighing down her trembling limbs. She had made it! She was safe at last.

The first wave of exhilaration had barely passed through her body when troubled, disturbing thoughts began nagging at the back of her mind. At first, she could not figure out what was wrong. She was safe. She had escaped. Why did the anguished fear keep gnawing away at her without respite? Then suddenly, in a horrible flood of recognition, she remembered, and all sense of excitement was gone.

Cousin Michael was at the docks!

Kate felt as if her heart had stopped beating, and the muscles of her chest seemed to contract around it like icy fingers of fear. She tried to tell herself she was being foolish. She had no proof that her father and brothers were on that ship, or even if they were, that the ship would be able to dock in such a heavy fog. It was ridiculous working herself up into a state like that. If the worst had happened and they were already in Boston, they still had to find her. It would take hours, or even days, to discover where Philippe lived.

Then suddenly a stab of recognition shot through her body, feeling as sharp as a physical pain. The image flashed through her mind of a rainy afternoon, months before, when she had succumbed to temptation and ridden in the carriage all the way to Philippe's door. With a rising sense of urgency, she realized that time was even more important now than it had been before.

Instinct urged her to hold close to the buildings, groping her way along them as she crept down the street, but she realized now that that would be impossible. It would take her at least an hour, more likely two or three, to reach Philippe at that rate. She had to abandon safety and force herself out into the middle of the street, listening carefully for the sound of hooves to keep from being run over by one of the few carriages trying to press its way through the heavy haze. Somewhere in the wide avenue, she had to find a carriage for hire. It was the only way she could get there in time.

At first, she despaired of the task, for try as she would, she could not manage to keep in a straight line, but moved instead from one side of the street to the other in an odd zigzag pattern. At that rate, she thought bitterly, she wouldn't reach Philippe's house before sunrise. Finally, just when she felt she must cry from fear and exhaustion, she felt her outstretched hand come in contact with the rough, hard surface of a carriage wheel, and she knew luck was with her.

Hurrying forward to the coachman's seat, she called out

eagerly to the driver. Receiving no answer, she dropped her bag on the pavement and climbed up to the driver's seat, searching for him with her hands as well as her eyes. There was no one there.

Tears of anger and frustration welled up in her eyes. For a moment she was tempted to give up hope, but she quickly pulled herself together and forced her mind to work logically. Surely, she reasoned, no coachman would leave a valuable horse and carriage alone in the fog. He must have gone inside to escape the moisture and the cold.

Running to the side of the carriage, Kate cupped her hands over her eyes and attempted to peer into the dark interior. Even when she saw nothing, she refused to give up, tapping against the cold glass with the ring on her hand.

The face that materialized suddenly from the dark bowels of the carriage startled Kate, and she jumped back for a moment in fright. It seemed to her as odd and eerie a face as she had ever seen, with pale, puffy skin half-glowing in its whiteness in the midst of the gloom, and thin, scraggly locks of hair sticking up in all directions. Only a pair of browned, decaying teeth leered out from a broad grin that looked both comical and sinister at the same time. Half covered as it was by the fog, the face looked as if it were disembodied, floating loosely on the dense gray air, as if it were some netherworld ghost or goblin come to haunt her.

"Well, missy, what d'ye want?" The voice, both gruff and resonant, was as strange and frightening as the face, and Kate was tempted to run away.

"I need a carriage," she said firmly. She hoped the fog would keep him from seeing how much she was shaking.

The nearly toothless mouth gaped open even farther, and a dry, cackling sound greeted her ears. "Not tonight, missy. Be ye such a fool as to risk your neck in a fog like this?"

"I must have a carriage," she cried out desperately. "I'll pay you well, I promise you."

"You'll not get a carriage tonight. Not me nor any other will carry you through this. Why don't ye come inside and wait out of the damp?" His ugly face seemed to leer even more broadly, and to her horror, a heavy, lashless lid winked down boldly over one eye.

Kate pulled away from the carriage in disgust and hurried back toward the buildings at the road's edge, a flurry of anxious thoughts rushing through her mind. The man was hideous and obnoxious, but for all that, he had an air of honesty and common sense about him that left her no doubt he was right. There was no way she would find a carriage that night. No one would risk his life or that of his horse in such a heavy fog. No one, that is, except her cousin Michael.

Michael had always been a hotheaded fool. It would be his idea of fun to rush madly through the crippled streets, bouncing his carriage against fragile peddlers' stands and heavy stone walls alike. And Michael was waiting with his carriage at the docks!

Suddenly, time was no longer on her side. She was ahead of them, but they could move faster. How long would it take to get from the docks to her aunt's house? An hour, perhaps? And another hour to Philippe's. That might be all the time she had. Two hours. It barely seemed enough, but she knew she had to try. Picking up her bag with an arm that had already begun to ache from its weight, she began to grope her way along the fronts of the buildings, stumbling against posts and stoops and the few other people adventurous enough—or needy enough—to be out on a day like that.

The fear began to gnaw like a tumor in the pit of her stomach until it rose all the way up to her throat, where it lay like a monstrous obstruction, threatening to choke her in her own saliva. It couldn't be true, she kept telling herself. They couldn't have landed. The fog must have kept them out. But still the fear kept rising, until finally she could barely manage to breathe.

Her arms were desperately tired; and hot, sharp pains began to shoot through her shoulders, bringing tears to her eyes. She stopped again and again to change hands, but soon it did no good at all, and each arm that raised the suitcase was as tired as it had been minutes before when it laid down its burden. She was sorely tempted to leave the bag behind, to hide it in some obscure doorway, hoping she and Philippe would be able to find it later, but prudence and practicality forced her to keep hold of it. Everything she owned was in that bag, and all her money, too. She didn't want to go to Philippe a pauper.

Kate had no idea how long she continued to walk down the road, stumbling and picking herself up, then stumbling again. She only knew that it was a long time, much longer than she had hoped—and time was running out. Her skirt was coated with mud and her feet soaked clear through, but she did not care or even notice. Her body had become as mechanical as a robot, and she forced herself to move forward, one foot at a time, somehow managing to eke out just one more ounce of endurance, and then another, even when she thought she could no longer go on.

Stumbling against the rough edges of a stairway that protruded out from one of the buildings, Kate felt the impact of a loose wooden board as it flipped up and hit her sharply in the knee. Crying out in pain, she was surprised to hear a soft, mewing reply. Creeping closer to the house, she peered through the loose slats that enclosed the foundation and came face to face with the bright, inquisitive eyes of a gray tiger kitten.

"The cats!" she thought exultantly.

She had found the house with the cats! That meant she was already at the corner of the street that led to Philippe's rooming house. She had made it at last. Picking up her carpetbag, she shoved it hastily in beside the cats. There was no need to carry it any farther. It would be easy to find there, and she and Philippe could pick it up on their way.

Unencumbered by her burden, Kate made better time, half-walking, half-running down the familiar street. Now that she had almost reached her destination, she could laugh at the foolish fears that had been terrifying her. In a few minutes, she would be there. She would be with Philippe, and he would take care of her. She would never have to worry or be afraid of anything again.

By the time she reached his house, she had completely forgotten her weariness, and the exuberance that carried her up the steps and through the doorway was one that made her want to sing aloud with joy.

"Philippe!" she cried as she flung open the door and crossed the threshold. "Oh, my darling, I'm here."

The silence that greeted her outburst was as deep and terrifying as the stillness in the foggy world outside. Dim candles flickered in the room, but even their pale light seemed strong at first to Kate's eyes, and she could not make out the figures standing in the hallway and the salon. She only knew they were silent, far too silent.

It took her eyes a few seconds to become accustomed to the sudden light, but even before she recognized the shadowy figures. she knew what she would see. The taste of failure was bitter in her mouth and stung her eyelids.

She did not break their silence as she cast her eyes around the room, counting the seven tall figures in the pale, flickering light. At first, she felt an easing of the tension when she saw that Patrick had not come with his sons, but as soon as she caught sight of her brother Eamon's face at the far end of the small salon, she found herself wishing for her father's tempering influence. She had never seen as dark and evil a look as the one that lay heavily on his brow.

This is the face of a man who can kill.

How long ago had she first thought those words? Weeks ago, she remembered. The night of the gay and glittering ball. Even then, they had struck a momentary pang of terror into her heart. Was it a premonition, she wondered, a subtle forewarning of the terror she would feel that night?

It was a long time before she lowered her eyes from Eamon's dark face and saw the man who lay facedown on the carpet. The blood that had poured from a gaping wound in his side stained the bright red carpet an even darker red.

"Oh, my God," she cried. "Philippe!"

She was on her knees beside him in a single second, hoarsely calling out his name and listening in vain for a reply. As she struggled to pull him toward her, she noticed with a sickening rush of horror the sticky feel of congealed blood that lingered on her hands.

"Philippe!" she cried again, but she knew he would not answer. Even as she cradled his head in her arms, she knew there was no use calling out again. Even before she laid her fingers against his cheek, she knew his skin would have the icy feel of death.

Only then did she notice the small, almost bloodless hole in the side of his head, and it affected her even more deeply than the sight of the ugly, gaping wound in his side. She leaned her head close to his for a moment, letting her tears pour over his cheeks, as if their warmth could somehow take the death chill from his body.

He had died because of her, she reminded herself bitterly. Died because she had dared to love him and let him love her. Slowly, almost imperceptibly, she felt the grief in her heart begin to die away, only to be replaced by a deep, tearless hatred.

Her eyes were dry as she looked up again, though traces of tears still lingered on her cheeks. The past was over, she told herself sternly. She could do nothing to change that. All she could do now was maintain whatever dignity she could still find in front of his killers.

She rose slowly, her eyes fixed firmly on Eamon's face. The look in his eyes no longer terrified her, but filled her instead with an overpowering sense of anger. It was no longer the look of a man who *could* kill, she reminded herself. Now it was the look of a man who *had* killed.

"Murderer!" she hissed.

Eamon's face barely changed at the sound of her voice, but Kate detected a faint flicker of excitement glowing in the depths of his eyes. Suddenly, she realized with horror that Eamon was not only capable of murder—he enjoyed it! Sick with disgust, she turned away from him.

As she moved slowly back toward the hallway, where her other brothers stood, she found herself gazing at them not so much in anger as in disappointment and sadness. She saw her brother Edward standing on the stairway beside the youngest, David. Their eyes were carefully averted so they would not have to look into her face.

"Why, Edward?" she asked softly. "Why?"

But Edward kept his eyes cast down, and did not attempt to answer her question.

"And you, David?" Tears began to choke her voice. David was a year younger than she, and had always been her favorite. "Not you, too."

"We had to, Katie." His voice was firm, but he, too, could not bring himself to meet her eyes. "Don't you see, we couldn't let him ruin you? We had to do it."

"You had to!" Her voice was heavy with revulsion as she backed away from them, until the cold, hard metal of the doorknob jabbed her in the back. They *had* to kill her lover? Why? Because they didn't approve of her choice?

The idea of seven self-righteous brothers dictating her movements for the rest of her life, even if it meant killing someone to keep her in line, suddenly began to suffocate her until she could barely breathe. She knew she would rather die than spend the rest of her life under that hideous yoke. For a second, she was even sorry she had refused Lord Burton-Styles. With his money, at least she would have been free. She would have had enough to buy and sell every last one of them.

But she couldn't have married Burton-Styles, she reminded herself bitterly. She couldn't have married him then, and she couldn't marry him now. Not when she wasn't the innocent virgin bride he expected. Even that choice was gone. She slid her hands behind her back and was surprised to feel the touch of cold metal.

Of course! That was it! She couldn't have Burton-Styles's money, but she could still have her freedom. She curled her fingers around the knob. She would have to make a life for herself. It would not be the easy, luxurious life she was accustomed to, but at least it would be free. Slowly, carefully, so they would not detect the movement, she turned the knob in her hand.

It took only a fleeting second to thrust open the door, whirl around, and leap boldly down the steps. Before anyone even knew what had happened, Kate enveloped herself in the dense gray mist.

She heard the sounds of pursuit behind her, but they did not frighten her, for she knew they had no idea where she was. She set a straight course down the road, turning by instinct at the corner as confidently as if it had been a clear, sunlit afternoon. From a distance, she heard a voice call out, "Katie," and then another joined it, and yet another. What fools they were, she thought. Why did they waste their breath? Surely they knew she would never willingly go back to them.

When she reached the old house where she had left her bag, she paused for a moment, kneeling down in the mud at the side of the road, while the bright-eyed kitten stared out at her, obviously bewildered by this inexplicable human who stayed outside in the wind and cold fog instead of creeping beneath the house. Kate touched her hand to the soft fur and felt the kitten begin to purr in contentment. The life and warmth beneath her fingers reminded her with its cruel contrast of the cold touch of Philippe's flesh as he lay in a pool of his own blood on the parlor floor. Hot tears stung her eyelids and threatened to blaze a trail down her cheeks.

Abruptly she snatched up her satchel and forced herself to begin walking down the street. There was no time to sit there, no time to wallow in her own self-pity. She didn't know where she was going or what she was going to do, but somehow she had to force herself to keep moving. Somehow she had to force her feet to take her out of the area and keep on walking until she found some sort of shelter, some place where she could hide for a few days while she took stock of her life.

There was no point trying to think any further than that. The future was bleak for her, and empty, and it would be terrifying if she let her mind dwell on it. It was enough just to keep her feet moving, one after the other down the road.

The little gray kitten kept staring out at her with solemn, unblinking eyes until she finally disappeared into the deepening fog.

Part II

An End and a Beginning

10

THE WELL-WORN, MUD-SPATTERED SIGN OUTSIDE MRS. SMALLey's boardinghouse proclaimed home-cooked meals, but from the heavy smell of grease that permeated even the small, shabby second-floor bedroom, Kate judged that the food would offer little in the way of taste or nourishment. Not that it mattered. She had no appetite. She wondered if she ever would again.

She had been sitting in the same straight-backed chair beside the small, curtainless window since late morning, when she finally discovered the one landlady willing to take her in despite her disheveled appearance. From time to time she turned away from the dirt-encrusted window to stare dispassionately at the dark patches of brown that boldly streaked her skirt. At first, she could not bear the sight of them, but now she could gaze at them impersonally, no longer able to distinguish the marks of her lover's lifeblood from the telltale streaks of mud that had spattered up out of grimy city streets.

How strange it was to feel so detached, she thought. So calm in the face of grief. It was as if her heart had grown numb in the hours that passed since her lover's death, and she could no longer feel anything, not even sorrow or despair.

She knew she could not sit in the same straight chair forever, but she felt no inclination to leave it. Finally, reminding herself it would do no good to sit and brood, she forced herself to rise wearily and walk over to the bed. Picking up the carpetbag, which seemed to have grown even heavier in the hours since she had laid it down, she set it on the bed and began pulling out its contents, tossing her dresses in haphazard fashion across the dirty spread.

She barely noticed the white envelope that fluttered to the ground. Picking it up automatically, she glanced with little curiosity at the coarse paper and bold handwriting that scrawled her name across the front. "Jason Hamilton," she said to herself, reading with faint surprise the name of the sender in the corner. Jason Hamilton? Why did the name sound familiar?

And then suddenly she remembered. Jason Hamilton. Her wealthy Wyoming rancher. How long had it been since she had written that mischievous letter to him? How many months . . . how many lifetimes? The answer had come days ago, while she was still staying in her aunt's house, but she had been too wrapped up in her problems even to look at it. She had simply tossed it carelessly into her bag, where she had promptly forgotten about it.

She was tempted to cast it aside again, as casually as before, but then thought better of it. If she let her thoughts drift back to Philippe, she would only begin to brood again. Better to avail herself of whatever distraction she could find, even so shallow a one as the letter. She carried it back to the small window, holding it up to catch the meager gray light that filtered through its grimy panes. As she tore it open, she noticed that a small, flat object had been enclosed with it. Turning the object over, she saw to her surprise that it was a photograph.

It was an inartistic picture, appearing both dim and stilted; and to Kate, the man who sat rigidly posed in a stiff black suit that pulled tightly across overly broad shoulders had a strange and unfamiliar air about him. She could not tell his coloring from the poorly made print, but she judged him to be dark rather than fair. His face was of a squarish cast, with bones that were strong and well-chiseled, and there was an air of power about him, of strength and rude force, that bespoke of the rough, hardy pioneer stock of which the West was shaped.

Eager to study his face, Kate held the picture even closer to the window, tilting it to catch the faint rays of light. The subtle strands of sunlight that glimmered across its surface caught up highlights she had not guessed at before, and she found herself searching his face in earnest, looking for clues that would tell her what kind of man he was. It was his eyes that intrigued her most. They seemed to be dark, she decided, but she could not be sure, for they were deep-set and picked up heavy shadows that gave them a sad and haunted air. How stern they looked to her, stern and uncompromising, and yet, they also seemed fair—like the eyes of a wise judge, or one of the fiery young prophets she had read about in her mother's Bible. Here was a man who was strong and bold, she judged, but a man who could be stubborn too, and perhaps even, if the occasion demanded, cruel.

She suddenly felt curious about this man whose picture evoked in her such contrasting feelings, and hoping she could learn more about him from his letter, she unfolded it eagerly and began to read.

My dear miss or madam,

Forgive me for the ambiguity of my opening, but you did not tell me if you were unwed or widowed. I was pleased to receive your letter, and also, I may add, impressed by your candor. I am afraid, living in the West as I do, I have too much forgotten my manners. Of course I could not expect any well-bred young woman to supply me with the particulars of her life before I had disclosed anything about myself.

I was born thirty-five years ago in Virginia, into a family of much greater refinement than my ill-mannered advertisement would seem to indicate. As I am sure even an Englishwoman must be aware, the War Between the States has changed the course of every Southerner's life. I do not tell you this in bitterness or to brood about the unhappiness of the past, but only to explain why I forsook my native soil to settle far away.

I am more than moderately wealthy in my new life, and while I will not bore you with great details of it, I have considerable land holdings in the territory of Wyoming. I also have a large and well-built home, one in which I am sure my wife would be proud to receive guests.

No doubt you are wondering why I feel the necessity to advertise for a bride in an Eastern newspaper. Let me assure you, dear madam, that it is not because all the local ladies have refused me, but simply because there are no unmarried ladies here of a proper age and station. A Westerner, when he wants a bride, must usually find one from the East. I am enclosing a photograph of myself, which, while it is hardly a good likeness, will at least assure you that I have no more than one head, one nose, and one pair of eyes.

If you are as well-bred as your letter sounds, and of serious intentions, pray let me hear from you again. I am not looking for beauty or excitement, I promise you, but rather for a kind and devout heart, together with a gentle disposition. I am afraid I cannot promise you the same, for I would be lying were I to list gentleness among my virtues, but I can at least promise that whatever loyalty I receive will be returned to the giver at least twofold.

Hoping to have your reply soon, I remain,

Your faithful servant,
Jason Hamilton

She had been right about the man after all, Kate decided as she lowered the letter to her lap and picked up the photograph to stare at it again. She was right about what she saw in his eyes. He was strong and uncompromising, just as she had guessed, but he was honest too, and just—and not without a touch of humor. This must be what the West was like, a vast new land peopled with a new breed of men, men who were in touch with the earth and the elements, men who were not afraid to fight for the basic ideals "civilized" lands had all too long ago buried beneath the superficial layers of their manners and their codes. It would not be a bad life, living with this man, Kate thought as she gazed at the picture. Not a bad life at all.

It would not be a bad life.

As the words played around in her mind, Kate realized that even while she was reading the letter, she had been formulating a tentative plan, a plan that involved a new life in a new land. And why not? she asked herself boldly. Just because the correspondence had begun in jest didn't mean it had to end that way. Besides, what other choice did she have? A conventional marriage was out of the question, and there was no one she could turn to for help, no one who would dare defy her father and his murderous wrath. As for making her own way, what could she do? Without references, no employment would be open to her, not even as a maid or governess in someone else's home. The letter in her hand represented her only chance, but it was a chance she would have to grasp boldly and quickly.

Before she could change her mind, she rushed to the door, calling out to the landlady to borrow a scrap of paper, an envelope, and a pen. With these supplies grudgingly given, she pulled the rickety chair up to the side of the narrow bureau and sat down to write.

It would be simple enough to devise a story, she decided. He had given her the clue himself. She would say she was a young widow, a common enough circumstance in the years following the foolish war these stubborn Americans fought to tear apart their country. No more worrying about blood on wedding bedsheets for her! As for her situation . . . Well, what else could she claim to be but a maid or governess?— and she readily chose the latter, sure that Jason Hamilton would be tempted by one of those modest, self-effacing creatures, intelligent and well-educated, but docile and quiet nonetheless.

And the picture!

She jumped up in glee as she remembered it. Yes, there it was, safely tucked away in the bottom of her carpetbag. She had had it taken for Philippe, but it turned out dreadful, making her look drab and plain, and years older than she was. She had saved it only because she knew he would enjoy seeing it. What a good laugh they would have had over it!

Philippe! Dark and shining eyes flashing with mirth.

But she mustn't think of him, she reminded herself firmly. She dared not think of him. She would only cry if she did.

Turning the photo facedown on the dresser, she picked up the pen resolutely and began to write. To her surprise, the words flowed easily across the paper, as if she were writing a chatty, gossip-filled letter to a friend. How odd, she thought, that it should be so simple. The first letter—the one that hadn't mattered at all—was something she had labored over, yet this one flowed recklessly from her pen. It was no more than four or five minutes before she was finished and could lean back to peruse her handiwork.

Dear Mr. Hamilton,

Thank you for your very kind letter, and thank you in particular for understanding why I could not divulge more information previously. I must admit, when I first saw your advertisement, I felt rather as if someone were playing an enormous practical joke, but now that I have read your letter, I know you must be sincere.

As you seem to have guessed, I am a widow (as are far too many young women in these bitter days), but like you, I would prefer to bury the past and begin again. I, too, have a refined family background, but I now find myself orphaned and impoverished, forced to work as a governess in other people's households, with no hope of forming a home of my own.

Your letter seemed to me the answer to my prayers, but while I am eager to have you accept me as your wife, I can do no less than match your candor with my own. I can offer you a heart that is both kind and devout, and at least as much loyalty as any other woman you will find, but I doubt if I can promise always to be of a gentle disposition. Perhaps no one truthfully can, and I only hope that my gratitude (coupled perhaps with your patience) will teach me to be the kind of wife you seek.

I, too, am enclosing a photograph, though it is a dreadful one, and I fear it will do nothing to persuade you to choose me for your wife. I wish I could find the words to tell you, sir, what devotion I would give to you, or how hard I would work to please you, but I find I do not know what to say. I feel rather as though I were a bottle of cure-all tonic on a carnival wagon with a dreadful, bald-headed man shouting out all sorts of exaggerated claims about my virtues, and I am afraid I don't know quite how to handle the situation.

I remain in loyalty and devotion,

> Your faithful friend,
> Kate Devlin

It was a foolish letter, she told herself irritably. A letter with absolutely no information and more than its share of inanities. And why on earth had she put in that silliness about the medicine show? Now he would think she was nothing more than the giddy, empty-headed creature she really had been until a few weeks ago.

Well, that was just too bad, she scolded herself sternly. There was nothing she could do about it now. She had one piece of paper, and only one, and the letter would have to stand as it was. Folding it up decisively, she slipped it into the envelope, followed it with the photograph, and quickly sealed it.

Getting the letter to the post office was going to be another matter. Kate did not for a moment underestimate the problem. If her brothers were clever, it was one of the places they would be watching, knowing she would have to communicate for help. Well, never mind. She would cross that bridge when she came to it. Perhaps when she got close enough, she would be able to bribe one of the little street urchins to carry it for her. In the meantime, she had better take stock of her situation.

She spread her clothes out on the bed and surveyed them objectively. Except for a nightdress, an extra petticoat, and a heavy black shawl, she had only four garments. The lovely white lawn, low-cut and delicately sprigged with green, was perfect for an afternoon garden party, but hardly suitable for dinner at Mrs. Smalley's, and she rolled it up in a ball and stuffed it back into the bag. After a moment's thought, she did the same with the sleek green taffeta. Its fashionable bustled skirt and elegant deep green velvet trim would not be of service to her there. That left only a modest gray-green afternoon dress, badly rumpled from being packed in the bottom of the satchel, and the torn, soiled walking dress she had on.

The situation was not promising, but she refused to let it discourage her. Reminding herself that two dresses were, after all, better than nothing, she decided to set about getting them in order. Resolutely, she stepped over to the door and threw it open.

"Mrs. Smalley!" she called down the dingy staircase. Waiting in vain for a reply, she repeated the summons again, slightly louder than before.

"Yes?" Mrs. Smalley's head appeared reluctantly at the foot of the stairs, wearing its perpetual scowl. Mrs. Smalley always looked as if the half-dozen teeth left in her mouth were continually aching. "What d'ye want?" Her tone was far from cordial. She did not like being disturbed during her daily vigil of watching at the window to see what the neighbors were doing, and she felt no need to cover her aggravation with courtesy.

"Tell the maid to run the bath for me," Kate told her forcefully. She was determined to match the woman's surly disposition with firmness. "And then I have some dresses that need mending and pressing."

"The maid?" Mrs. Smalley's face showed mirth for the first time since Kate had encountered her. "Where d'ye think ye are? One o' them fancy hotels down to the smart side o' town? Bath's down the hall, and there's an iron in the kitchen—if ye know how to use it."

She shuffled away, chuckling maliciously to herself, while Kate was left to stand alone in the narrow hallway, choking down her anger and bewilderment. Know how to use it, indeed! Why, she had never even seen an iron, much less learned how to go about working it.

"Don't let her get to you, dearie," a kind voice called out. Turning around, Kate saw a figure silhouetted in the dim light that poured out of a doorway at the end of the hall. At first, she could only stand and gape at her. The woman was wearing a bright red dressing gown that was trimmed with more frills and feathers than Kate had ever seen in her life, and her hair, which was fixed in hundreds of frizzy little curls, was the most amazing shade of red. Traces of heavy makeup had settled into the deep creases of her skin, and there were dark bags under her eyes.

"Why, you poor little mite," the woman cried out as soon as she caught sight of the tears of fright and discouragement welling up in Kate's eyes. "You don't belong in a place like this, do you? Come to Stella, dearie. Come on here, that's a good girl."

Without even being aware of moving, Kate suddenly found herself in Stella's comforting arms, her head resting against a surprisingly motherly shoulder. Stella did not try to stop the girl's sobbing, but patted her head instead in a kindly manner.

"There, there, dearie," she said after a few minutes, when the torrent of tears finally began to diminish. "Come and tell Stella all about it." She led Kate gently into the room and urged her to sit down on the edge of a large rumpled bed. "Now, then, tell Stella what's the matter."

Kate longed to do as she was told, for she was desperately eager to spill out all the grief and agony she had suffered, but caution would not let her take the chance. After all, Stella was only a stranger. Besides, if she was poor enough to live in such a slovenly dwelling, mightn't Patrick's money be enough to tempt her to betray her new friend?

"I'm a governess," she said impulsively, picking up the lie she had written to Jason Hamilton. "I'm supposed to be going to a family out West." How easily the lies flowed, once they had been started! "They were supposed to send me tickets and money, but there must have been some mix-up. Now I have to wait."

"And you're half scared out of your wits, aren't you?" Stella said comfortingly. "Well, don't you worry, now. Stella will take care of you." She held Kate at arm's length for a moment, taking a good long look at her. "I guess you wasn't joshin' when you said you needed a good pressin'—and cleanin' too, I'll warrant."

Kate could only smile weakly.

"Well, now, you get that dress off. Do you have a nice warm robe? No? Well, here, take this." She tossed Kate a dressing gown that was the same shade of red she was wearing, but trimmed with even gaudier decorations. "You go and take yourself a nice hot bath. Then come on down to the kitchen for a spot of tea, and I'll show you how to get this clean and pressed."

"I don't know how to thank you—" Kate began.

"Don't you worry none about that," Stella interrupted, beaming. "What are we put here for, if it ain't to give each other whatever mite of help we can? And listen, dearie, take this." She pulled a small object out of the dresser drawer, where it was hidden beneath a pile of lingerie. "Nothing like a nice bar of perfumed soap to make a girl feel more like herself, don't you think?"

Despite the unhappiness Kate had suffered, she found herself smiling back at Stella's warm, homely grin. It wasn't that her plight was any better or any less terrifying. Indeed, it was every bit as bad as it had been only a few minutes before, when she had sobbed her heart out on the older woman's shoulders, but somehow, with a friend like Stella, nothing seemed quite as black and ugly anymore.

Stella may have had the strangest hair and the gaudiest clothes Kate had ever seen, but as time went by, she began to look more and more like an angel from heaven. It was Stella who carried Kate's letter to the post office, never once being tactless enough to ask why she was afraid to go herself, and Stella who made the same long walk every day to see if a reply had come, returning each time with a crisp shake of the head and a new joke to take Kate's mind off the long waiting. It was Stella, too, who carried her English pounds to the bank, coming back with American money. And Stella who sat beside her each night at the dinner table, fending off questions from the other ladies with frizzled red or saffron curls and the tight-lipped, elderly men who stared at her with suspicion in their eyes. And in the end, when her money ran out, it was even Stella who gave her the few dollars she needed to pay for her board.

"Don't you worry your head about it, dearie," she said when Kate protested. "Things'll work out soon enough, and then you'll be able to pay me back, you'll see."

At first, Kate found herself wondering where Stella's money came from. She seemed to have an income of her own, though it must be a small one if she lived in that hovel, for she never had to go out to work. She would lounge around the house all day, then deck herself out in her gayest finery each evening for whatever party or entertainment she was planning to attend. It seemed to Kate that she must not get back until the early hours of the morning, for no matter how often she sat up waiting for her friend to return, she never seemed to be able to catch her.

Then, finally, one night, her vigilance was rewarded, and she was delighted to hear Stella's rich, throaty laughter echoing in the hallway. Eager for a few minutes of cheerful conversation, she hurried over to the door and threw it open quickly, only to shut it again almost as abruptly when she saw that Stella was not alone. She caught only a glimpse of the man who was with her, but it was enough to tell her he was as repulsive a creature as she had ever seen. He was nearly as fat as Lord Burton-Styles, and every bit as lecherous too, she'd wager, for she hadn't missed the sight of his plump hand resting on Stella's ample posterior.

It didn't surprise Kate—or shock her—that Stella had a

lover, but it grieved her to see how ugly and unpleasant he was. She wanted better for her friend.

The next night, when she heard Stella on the stairs again, she couldn't resist opening the door a crack to peek out. To her surprise, she saw, not the fat man she had expected, but rather a gaunt, elderly man who crept up the stairs behind Stella, his fingers lewdly slithering up beneath the skirt of her bright red dress. Even that did not shock Kate. That Stella could have two lovers was not outlandish—since the afternoon Kate had willingly given away her own virtue, she was no longer quick to judge others—but that they should both be such disgusting specimens of humanity appalled her.

When she saw Stella come in with a third man, and then a fourth, the truth finally began to dawn on her; and at last, she was shocked. She had never before met one of those ignoble women who sold their bodies to the lust of coarse men, and indeed, she had never even seen one of them. She had been permitted glimpses of high-priced courtesans, of course, from behind the demure shield of her fan, but from the ladies who walked the streets or plied their trade in cheap barrooms, she had always been protected. For the next day or two, she found herself ashamed of her new friend, and she could not look her in the eye.

Stella seemed to understand, for she did not press herself on Kate, but gazed at her instead with a sad smile and mournful eyes whenever they passed in the hall. However she felt about Kate's rejection, she continued to make the long, futile trek to the post office every day.

And yet, who am I to scorn her? Kate asked herself one gray afternoon when Stella returned from the post office, empty-handed as usual. The thought struck her like a bolt of lightning out of a clear sky, and she felt herself blush in shame as she looked at the hurt in her friend's warm, kind eyes. Who was she indeed to look down on Stella? Hadn't she been tempted to sell herself to a man she loathed, for the power and freedom his money could buy her? She would have sweated beneath the gross lust of his foul body no less than Stella did with the strange men who passed through her life, a different one each night. And for Stella, there was not even the consolation of power and wealth, but only a grubby day-to-day subsistence in a shabby, wretched boardinghouse.

Impulsively, she reached out her arms and threw them around the older woman, as if to say: I'm sorry. I don't care what you are. You're my friend and I love you. Stella seemed to understand the silent gesture, for her face glowed with happiness, and Kate felt that at last she had repaid, in some small measure at least, Stella's many kindnesses to her.

Later that evening, she thought of it again as she sat alone in her room. How cruel she had been to judge Stella so harshly, and how unreasonable. What else could Stella do? She was a woman alone in the world, without a husband or father to protect her, and she had no other means of earning a living for herself. What else was left for a woman alone?

Kate felt herself shiver, though that evening was not a cold one. Suddenly, she was keenly aware that she, too, was a woman alone—alone and without resources. She had but four days left of the rent money she had borrowed from Stella. After that, what could she do? She had no way to earn a living, and her one last, slim hope—the letter she had written weeks ago—was now fading fast away.

She squared her shoulders and forced herself to face her dilemma realistically. There was, after all, only one choice open to her. She could swallow her pride—and her anguish—and go crawling back to her father, or she could borrow one of those feathery red dresses from Stella and ask her to teach her how to make a living. It was a grim choice, but an easy one nonetheless. She decided to borrow the dress from Stella.

The four days passed quickly, and still there was no word from Wyoming. Feeling her courage falter, Kate borrowed the money once again from Stella, but she promised herself it would be the last time. The prospect that faced her was an ugly one, but it was one she would have to confront sooner or later, and there was no point putting it off any longer.

As she sat in the shabby front parlor one morning, still trying to brace herself for the ordeal that lay ahead, she stared out of the window at the ominous gray clouds gathering in the sky above. Suddenly, she was surprised to catch a glimpse of fiery red at the end of the block as she saw Stella running full speed toward her. It was not until she was nearer that Kate noticed the broad grin on her face. Looking down, she saw a flash of white in her hand.

Kate met her at the door, her heart in her mouth for fear the answer would be a rejection, but the minute she saw the envelope at close hand, she knew it was all right. It was far too thick to contain only a short, polite note. Eagerly she tore it open, hardly noticing the tickets that fluttered to the floor, along with a plain, brown-wrapped packet. Tears of relief flooded her eyes as she sat down to read it.

I was most touched by your letter, and impressed not only with your honesty but also with that saving grace of humor you seem to have retained despite your troubles. Do not fear that your picture would dissuade me from you. When I told you I was not looking for beauty, I assure you I was speaking the truth. I prize a plain face and an honest heart over a pretty visage that masks a shallow soul.

I have enclosed with this letter train tickets to Cheyenne, Wyoming, where I will meet you. You will also find a modest sum of money to discharge any small debts you may have accumulated and to see to your needs throughout the journey.

At first she felt only relief. The money he had sent was sufficient to pay her debts, both to Stella and to Charles, and still leave enough for the journey, and the tickets would carry her far away, to a land where her father and brothers could never find her.

Only after a few minutes did she begin to realize the enormity of the step she was about to take, and she slipped back upstairs to take another look at the picture of the man to whom she had entrusted her future. Her hands were trembling as she pulled it carefully from the drawer where she had hidden it.

Stern, uncompromising eyes in a strong, severe face. An expression she could not fathom. And yet, this stranger was going to be her husband.

She felt a cold rush of fear that seemed to penetrate even her bones as she stared down at the likeness in her hand. It was not so much the strangeness of the life to which she had committed herself that frightened her, for she was young enough to take bold steps recklessly, but rather the death of all her youthful daydreams. Gone forever were visions of handsome, dashing cavaliers and gay, glittering balls. Gone all the last shattered hopes of love and romance. Instead, there would be only rough rancher's hands to touch the smoothness of her naked skin. In exchange for protection and security, she would allow the strong, lean body of a stranger to impose itself on hers.

She was glad she had decided not to condemn Stella too harshly.

"Whoever you are, Jason Hamilton," she whispered to the cold likeness in her hand, "I hope you are kind."

11

"BUFFALO!"

The cry that began with one voice was soon taken up by others, until it echoed up and down the corridors of the train. "Buffalo!" the men shouted, grabbing up their guns and casting aside their coats as they raced toward the front of the train. "Buffalo!" the women squealed excitedly, hitching up their skirts to race after the men. "A whole herd of them. Hurry up, before you miss them!"

"Do you see them, miss?"

Turning away from the window, Kate found herself looking into the shining eyes of a young boy, fourteen or fifteen years old. His hands were clutched eagerly around the barrel of an expensive new rifle.

Kate nodded her head, smiling. She had spoken to the boy before, and she liked him. This was his first trip West, and his vitality and enthusiasm had provided most of the few bright moments she had experienced on the long, dreary journey. Now, the light that glowed in his eyes was so compelling that she almost forgot her own excitement in her enjoyment of his.

"They're really something, aren't they?"

They really were astounding. There must have been hundreds of them—or perhaps thousands—a milling sea of dark brown fur extending miles into the distance, as far as the eye could see. This, at last, was the West, Kate thought, feeling a long-overdue thrill of anticipation run up her spine. This was what she had been waiting for.

So far, she had been disappointed. Throughout the long, tedious days of staring out of gray, mud-smeared windows, she had seen nothing of the excitement and vitality she sought. Instead, the neat white houses of the Eastern landscape, surrounded by tidy picket fences and well-kept gardens. gradually gave way to crude, unpainted buildings, weatherbeaten to a drab, uniform gray, and all too soon, the green, rolling hills of Missouri became the long, flat, monotonous Kansas prairie.

Even the people were not what she expected. True, the men who climbed aboard the train at each stop were not burdened with the exaggerated, overly proper manners of the East, but they had their own kind of superficiality about them, for all that. They gave the impression, not of quiet strength and self-assurance, as Kate had imagined, but rather of a raucous, boisterous arrogance that was as repulsive as it was ridiculous. As for the cowboys—well, the only cowboys Kate had seen were scrawny, filthy men with tired and lonesome faces. And the Indians—even the Indians weren't frightening. They were only pathetic little bands of scraggly captives, all decked out in dyed chicken feathers and herded into the depots to beg a few coins from the passing travelers.

Yes, the West had been a disappointment, a big disappointment. But now it was different! Here at last was something vast and strong and exciting. This was what she had been waiting to see. Eagerly Kate joined the throng of men and women pushing their way toward the front of the train, where the beasts were congregated.

As she hurried through the crowded aisles, she felt the train jolt to a sudden stop. Grasping the side of a nearby seat to keep from falling, she listened to the sound of a jubilant shout that rose from the front of the train.

"A buffalo hunt!" The boy turned around to shout over his shoulder. "They're stopping to let us hunt them!"

By the time Kate pressed her way into the forward car, she saw to her surprise that the windows had all been lowered, and many of the men were already positioned at one or another of them, their guns resting against the window sash. Gazing out in wide-eyed wonder, she found that she could see the beasts with perfect clarity, and for the first time she realized how huge and strong they were. Suddenly, she was grateful for that crowd of boisterous men, always so ready to hoist a gun at any impulse. They might not be pleasant, but at least they would provide her with protection.

And yet, there were so many of the beasts! Hundreds upon hundreds milling quietly around the train. If they were to become angry . . . if anything were to set them off . . . Kate shuddered at the thought. A hundred guns or a thousand would avail little against them. They would just come on, body after massive body, until they had trampled the train and all its occupants beneath their heavy hooves.

She backed away nervously toward the end of the car, pressing through the excited, chattering throng of people until she heard the first sharp crack of a gunshot in her ears. It was followed quickly by another, and yet another, until the entire car seemed to explode with the force of a gigantic roll of thunder. Kate strained her eyes to see if the beasts were preparing to attack, but thick billows of smoke poured out of the guns, stinging her eyes and clouding her vision.

Please, heaven, don't let them attack, she thought desperately, pressing a trembling hand against her heart, as if she could still its violent beating. She kept her eyes glued tensely to the windows, watching for one of the few brief seconds when a strong gust of wind would clear away the smoke for an instant. Each time it did, Kate saw to her relief that the gigantic brown forms were still standing patiently and stolidly in the same places, waiting for the heavy crack of a gun to bring them to earth with a massive crash that would make the ground tremble in its wake.

Slowly, she began to realize that the creatures were not going to stampede into the train. They were not even going to run away. To her amazement, they seemed insensitive to their danger as they gazed around in slow bewilderment at their fallen comrades. Sick with disgust, Kate stared at the eager eyes of the men at the windows. They were alight with the lust to kill.

Why, this isn't sport! she thought angrily. What kind of sportsman would enjoy killing a beast that neither fought nor ran? Turning away from them, she pressed her way back through the crowd toward the exit door.

A cold wind stung her cheeks as she stepped out onto the platform between the cars. Even there, men had stationed themselves to shoot. Some of the bolder ones had even leaped to the ground, obviously feeling very brave and adventurous as they faced the defenseless beasts on their own turf.

"Here, girlie," one of the men shouted, thrusting a gun toward her. "Want to have a try?"

Kate could only stare at him in horror. A dozen scathing remarks occurred to her, but even angry as she was, she knew better than to cross a kill-crazed maniac with a gun in his hands. She shook her head briskly and hurried to the next car.

"Delicate little lady, ain't she?" Kate heard the sound of rough male laughter echoing after her until the door slid shut behind her.

She had expected the car to be empty, but to her surprise, she caught sight of a lonely figure at the far end. As she approached, she recognized the same young boy who had rushed forward only moments before, eager to experience the thrill of the hunt. Now he was trembling with excitement, his gun on the seat beside him, and Kate had to choke down the revulsion that rose in her throat as she gazed at him. After all, he couldn't help it, she reminded herself. He was only a boy. With a rush of sadness, she realized how very like her own younger brother he was. Like David before he became a murderer.

"Did you get any?" She forced her voice to remain cool and kind.

"Aye," he admitted. She was surprised at the lack of expression in his voice. "Early on. I was one of the first. I wanted to get one before they started to run."

"But they didn't run," she reminded him gently.

"That's just it!" His eyes were filled with suffering as he looked up at her, and she realized she had been wrong. The boy was trembling, not from excitement, but from loathing. "It's nothing but senseless slaughter. They aren't even going to wait to pick up the hides or the meat. They're just going to kill as many as they can and let the carcasses rot in the sun."

"Senseless slaughter," she echoed softly, her voice hollow with despair. Unlike the boy, she realized the deeper implications of the words, and they made her sick with dread.

So this was the West—the land to which she had entrusted her future. This ugly, brutal, violent land was going to be her home, and these cruel, arrogant people her neighbors. One of them was even going to be her husband.

"Cheyenne!" The conductor's voice was loud and clear as he called out the name, but he still took a minute to stop by Kate's seat to make sure she had heard. "Cheyenne, miss. We'll be pullin' in in five minutes or so." He had three grown daughters of his own, and he found himself taking a fatherly interest in the safety of the pretty, solemn-faced girl who had come such a long way alone. "Someone goin' to be there to meet you?"

"Yes," she assured him, smiling in response to his obvious concern. She could see the relief flooding his round pink cheeks as he hurried on his way, calling out the name of the town again and again for the people in the other cars.

I wish it were all that simple, she thought. I wish I could reassure myself as easily as I reassured him.

She turned to look out the window again, willing the rapid *chug-a-chug-chug chug-a-chug-chug* of the wheels to slow down, to give her just a few minutes more before she had to face her future; but ignoring her fear, they hurried on as rapidly as before.

It's going to be all right, she tried to tell herself. Of course it would be all right. She was foolish to worry so much. Hadn't the ugly, flat prairies of Kansas dissolved subtly into the green grasses of Colorado and then into the even lusher plains of Wyoming? And hadn't the faint haze in the distance slowly materialized into tall, snowcapped mountains that broke with their majesty the ugly monotony of the flatlands? Surely, after all, this new country was going to be as beautiful as she had dreamed.

But what of the men who peopled this brash new land? Kate felt herself shiver as she thought of them. Every time the train stopped, a new group of men had boarded, each dirtier and coarser than the ones who passed before. Either too silent or too boisterous, they took their seats in the car, spitting brown tobacco juice from between stained teeth and leering boldly across the aisle at her. These were the men of the West; and soon, she would call one of them "husband."

She slid her fingers restlessly across the smooth taffeta of her skirt. Perhaps the plain gray walking dress would have been a wiser choice, she thought nervously. It made her look more like the simple, unaffected governess she was supposed to be. Still, she had worn the dress every day of the journey, and it was soiled and rumpled from traveling. Besides, the deep green taffeta, trimmed with even darker velvet, was undoubtedly becoming, and she was desperately eager to make a good impression on this strange new husband she had never met.

After a few minutes, the train began to slow down. Kate felt her heart leap into her throat as she realized the moment she had been dreading was at last drawing near. Only a few minutes ago, she had wished the wheels of the train would move more slowly. Now she longed for them to speed up, rushing through the town at breakneck speed and never turning back, but all too soon they hesitated, and the train jerked to a rough and awkward stop. Kate knew the time had come. Picking up her carpetbag in a cold and sweaty hand, she forced herself to move toward the doorway.

She made her way carefully down the steep metal steps, scanning the crowd anxiously with her eyes as she searched for dark hair and an ill-fitting black suit stretched across shoulders that were too broad for the body that bore them. When she did not see him at first, she felt a sensation much akin to relief, but after a few minutes of standing alone on the platform, the feeling began to give way to one of panic. What if he were not there after all? What if the whole thing was nothing more than a monstrous practical joke?

As the crowd began to thin out, Kate noticed a man standing alone at the far end of the platform, his tall lean body clothed in the casual style of the West. It was quickly apparent to her that this was not the man she had come to meet, for there was nothing plain or stodgy about him, but she could not keep her eyes from returning to him again and again with a fascination she knew was unseemly in a promised bride.

Despite the slender lines of his body, hard, tense muscles rippled plainly beneath the thin fabric of his shirt. He was surprisingly graceful for one so tall, and as he leaned against the side of the station with all the casual elegance of a London dandy, Kate slowly became aware of a tenseness and vibrancy about his body that made her think of a panther poised to strike. With a sudden quickening of her heartbeat, she realized that this stranger, whoever he might be, was the most exciting man she had ever seen in her life.

He raised his hand easily, slipping off his hat and lowering it to his side as he turned and met her eyes. His hair, thick and unfashionably long, was golden where the sunlight caught it, and his eyes were the most piercing blue she had ever seen. With a sudden stab of regret that pained as deeply as the cut of a sharp knife, she found herself wishing that this was the man she had come to meet . . . and wed.

In that brief instant, as their eyes met, Kate suddenly realized what a fool she had been. When Philippe died, she had given up all her dreams, all her deep longings for love. She had thought that life—for her—was over. And yet, in reality, it was just beginning. She was still young. She still had years of love ahead of her. Her grand passion for Philippe—that all-powerful love that would endure to the grave and beyond—why, that was nothing more than a schoolgirl infatuation. Nothing more than the tender stirrings of desire in the body of a maturing young woman. Never for an instant had she sensed in Philippe the depths of strength or animal magnetism that radiated from the body of this stranger who stood before her. She could almost feel it in the air, the electric charge that passed from his eyes to hers like static current that snapped through the air on a rainy evening. Here was a man the likes of which she had never seen before.

The stranger was staring back at her quite openly now, as brazenly and suggestively as the men on the train, but she could not bring herself to draw her eyes away. Slowly he lowered his eyelids, until his eyes seemed to be hooded, like the head of a cobra, and a slow, arrogant smile formed at the edges of his mouth.

Good heavens, she thought, alarmed. He looks like he's undressing me with his eyes!

The man was insolent, almost too insolent to bear, but he was exciting, too, and she stared back at him for a moment in fascination until she realized with a gasp of horror that her gaze was far too open, too direct. No wonder he felt free to take such bold advantages with his eyes. No doubt he thought she was encouraging him. Blushing heavily, she forced her eyes to settle demurely on the ground at her feet.

She did not know how long she remained like that, standing quietly at the edge of the platform with her eyes carefully averted, but after a while, the sounds began to die away, and she sensed she was alone in the station. Slowly, she looked up again. To her surprise, she saw that the stranger was still there, as if he, too, were waiting for someone who did not come. There was no longer insolence, or even boldness in his eyes, but only a puzzled expression as he carefully studied her face.

Then, suddenly, a preposterous idea struck her, and she gasped aloud in amazement. What if . . . ? But no, it couldn't be true. Still, there was something about the strong, square set of his jaw, or perhaps it was the high, sharply chiseled cheekbones. The eyes were deep-set, too, deep-set and filled with shadows, and hair that was golden could have been darkened by a poor photograph. Could it be . . . ?

His eyes flickered with recognition at the same moment as hers, and then she knew she had hit upon the truth. This man—this tall, exciting stranger—was Jason Hamilton, the man she had traveled across the continent to wed.

She was surprised not to feel even a small surge of joy at her discovery. Only a moment ago, she had longed to meet this man, yet now she felt nothing but a cold sense of fear as she gazed into his unfathomable blue eyes. Jason Hamilton was undeniably exciting and dynamic, and there was an animal magnetism about him that made the blood run hot through her veins, but she sensed he could be dangerous, too. Dangerous both in the strength he carried in his powerful body and in the power he would have over her. She was determined not to let him guess she was afraid of him. He must never know that; it would give him too much of an advantage. Forcing herself to look bolder than she felt, she lifted up her chin, squared her shoulders, and marched over to him, remembering only at the last moment to tilt her head coyly and smile her softest, most flirtatious smile.

"Mr. Hamilton?" She made her voice low and sweet, with what she hoped was the proper balance of coyness and demure naiveté.

"Mrs. Devlin?" His voice was heavy with scorn and disbelief. Even in her worst nightmares, Kate had not imagined so cold a reception, and she felt almost as if he had slapped her in the face.

Stunned, she could think of nothing to say, and the two of them stared at each other for several minutes in silence, Jason's piercing blue eyes searching Kate's face inquisitively, while Kate's green eyes stared up hesitantly from beneath dark lashes. It was Jason who finally spoke.

"You don't look like your picture." He threw the words out angrily, as if they were a challenge.

"Well, neither do you!" she snapped irritably. Jason Hamilton might be handsome, but he certainly was a boor! Here she had traveled thousands of miles to be his bride, and instead of finding kind words of welcome, he could only criticize her because she didn't resemble a perfectly ugly photo. "Anyhow, I told you it was a dreadful picture. Didn't you believe me?"

"You also told me you didn't have a gentle disposition," he reminded her, the traces of a mocking smile playing at the corners of his lips. "It seems you were honest about that, at least."

"I was honest about everything," she retorted indignantly, forgetting in her anger the complex of lies she had written in her letter.

His face grew hard and cold at her words. "You are not at all what you claimed, madam."

"What do you mean?" She felt traces of pink beginning to burn in her cheeks. He could only be remembering the immodesty in her eyes as she had stared at him on the platform before she knew he was the man she had come to meet.

"For one thing, you said you were twenty-six. I doubt you're a day over nineteen."

"Oh, that," she said, smiling with relief. So that was all he was worried about. "Of course I lied. I had to, or you'd never have sent for me. But I'm not nineteen. I'm twenty-two." There, that was a good compromise. Halfway between the truth and what he had wanted. Surely he'd be willing to settle for that.

"And you're no more a governess than I am. I may not know much about fashion, but I know that dress is far too elegant and expensive for a servant."

Why, oh, why, hadn't she worn the plain gray frock instead? she berated herself. Instinct had warned her, but she'd been too vain to listen. "That's not so—" she tried to protest, but he would not let her finish.

"I haven't the patience to listen to any more of your lies," he warned her, grasping her arm tightly and pulling her toward a rough wooden wagon waiting at the side of the station. "I'm afraid the transportation isn't what you're used to. If I'd known I was picking up such a fine lady, I'd have hired a carriage."

"Oh, you are maddening," she cried out, furious with him for the high-handed treatment he was giving her. "Do you have to be so sarcastic about everything? It isn't fair to blame me because I don't look the way you thought I would. You aren't exactly what I pictured either, you know."

"Are you disappointed?" Sarcasm and mockery fought for dominance in his voice, and Kate knew he was remembering the fascination in her eyes when she first looked on him. Would he never let her live that down?

"If you mean about your looks, no." She was determined not to blush. "But I'm not crazy about your personality."

"Well, that makes two of us," he told her, laughing bitterly. "Now, hop on up, and I'll take you to the hotel at Jasper Springs until I decide what to do with you."

Jason jumped lightly onto the high seat, but Kate remained on the ground, gaping up at him. "What do you mean, what to do with me?"

"You are not what I bargained for, madam. Surely you don't think I intend to marry you."

"But you brought me all the way out here!" Kate's cheeks glowed a hot, bright red, and her voice trembled with indignation. "Why, you son of a . . ." She caught her breath sharply to keep from finishing the phrase. Nineteen years in the same house with an Irish father and seven boisterous brothers had taught her to express herself when the need arose, but she had a feeling it wouldn't go far toward impressing this strange, cold man.

She was right. His only reaction was to throw back his head and roar with laughter. She hated it only slightly less than the cool mockery that had preceded it. Setting her lips in a thin, tight line, she vowed not to say anything else to him, no matter how long the journey was.

She looked up with dismay at the high seat beside him, wondering how she was going to climb up without help. Then, determined not to beg him for anything, she set her foot on the heavy metal rung of the wheel, trying to get enough leverage to propel herself upward. Instead, the slippery sole of her shoe slid along the rung, thrusting her forcibly back toward the earth. To her disgust, she was unable to regain her balance and landed in a heap in the dust at his feet. Still laughing, he jumped down to help her up.

"Don't you touch me," she screamed, pulling herself hastily to her feet. "I can get up by myself, even if I am a 'fine lady.'" She knew she was being childish, but she didn't care. She was determined to prove that she didn't need him. Her foot slipped again on the treacherous wheel, but the third time, she finally made it to the seat beside him. As she turned to glare at him in triumph, she saw that he was still laughing at her.

Why did he have to be so infuriating? she thought angrily. Why did he have to make fun of her? And why, above all, did he have to be so maddeningly attractive? If only he were plain and dour, the way he looked in his photograph, then she wouldn't have minded so much. She wished she could cry in fury and frustration, but she was determined not to give him the satisfaction of seeing her tears.

"What are you going to do with me?" she asked as he took up the reins and coaxed the horses into a brisk trot. She hadn't meant to talk to him, but she was frightened, and she couldn't bear the sound of silence, even for a minute.

"I don't know." She cast a glance at him out of the corner of her eye, hoping he was looking at her, but his eyes were fixed straight ahead.

"You can't just abandon me here."

"Oh, I'll get you back to Boston," he assured her irritably. "And I'll see that you get some money for your trouble, if that's what's worrying you."

She barely heard his last words, so appalled was she with the destiny he had chosen for her.

"Boston?" Boston, where her father and brothers would be searching for her. Boston, where her lover's body must now be lying in some unmarked pauper's grave. "I can't go back there."

"Are you running away from something, Kate?" He turned to look at her intently. For the first time, his voice held genuine concern, but Kate did not notice—nor did she notice that

116

for all his arrogance and show of disinterest, he had slipped and called her by her first name.

"Of course not," she lied. She didn't dare tell him the truth. He already despised her enough. "But I won't go back there."

"Oh, yes, you will," he replied ominously, all the hardness returning to his voice. "There's a train next week, and I'm going to put you on it."

"Go ahead," she retorted. "But you can't keep me from getting off at the next stop."

"Get off where you like—just stay away from Jasper Springs."

"If you want to keep me out of there so badly, you can stop the wagon and let me out right here!" Furiously, she reached behind her and tugged at the heavy carpetbag. She had followed this man's promises all the way across the country—and even made a fool of herself by letting him see how attractive she found him the first moment she saw him—and all she had gotten in return was hostility and coldness. She wasn't going to stay with him another minute, no matter how handsome and exciting he might be.

"Stay where you are," he ordered, shifting the reins to one hand as he reached out with the other and caught her arm in a viselike grip.

"Let go of me, you boor!"

"I may be a boor, but I'm not going to leave a woman alone in the middle of nowhere."

"Why not?" she shouted, raising her voice to keep him from noticing the tears that still threatened her eyes. "It seems to be the custom out here. The whole lot of you Westerners are nothing but a pack of barbarians."

She expected him to flash back an angry retort, but his voice was surprisingly calm. "I'd think you'd reserve judgment until you had a chance to meet a few Westerners."

"I saw enough on the train. Chewing tobacco and spitting it on the floor and upholstery. Leering at me as if I were some sort of cheap harlot. Tossing their guns around every chance they got. Why, they even stopped the train to shoot a lot of buffalo that were just milling around, not doing any harm. They didn't even want the meat. They just enjoyed the thrill of killing. What a lot of big, strong men they were! Shooting a bunch of defenseless animals that were just about as ferocious as a pack of old cows!"

"You didn't find that exciting?" He turned to look at her

with an expression she couldn't understand at first. Slowly it dawned on her that it was a look of surprise.

"This may not have occurred to you," she informed him indignantly, "but civilized people don't act like that."

He didn't seem to hear what she said. "Years ago, there used to be herds of buffalo living all over this land," he told her. "The Indians killed them, but only for the meat and hides. They left the ones they didn't need to grow and breed. Then along came the white man . . . and now there are only a few left."

"Well, it sounds like the Indians are more civilized than you are!" She knew it was a ridiculous thing to say about a bunch of savages, but she was so angry she could not help herself. To her surprise, he seemed to take her comment seriously.

"Do you think so?" he asked softly. There was a hard edge to his voice that warned her not to continue.

Why was she quarreling with him anyhow? she asked herself bitterly. Why were there only harsh and angry words between them, when instead she longed so desperately to impress him, to speak the words that would begin to build a new and growing bond between herself and this handsome stranger who was to have been her husband? How could everything have gone so horribly wrong? The neat little curls she had worked so hard to train around her finger, the pretty green dress with the fashionable bustle—why had these things only antagonized when they were meant to please? Oh, if only she'd just had the sense to keep her temper when he'd first spoken to her so coldly. Then perhaps she could have mended things.

Well, small matter now, she reminded herself. Now it was too late. Glancing at his profile in the bright midday sun, she saw that he was deep in thought, lost in a world that would never include her.

Why, she thought again, *why* did he have to be so attractive? How could fate have played such a cruel trick on her? Had she come halfway around the world to find a man she longed for with a deep and hungry yearning—beyond anything she had ever known before—only to discover he was the one man she could never have?

12

KATE RAN HER FINGERS OVER THE FRESHLY PRESSED FOLDS
of her gray-green muslin skirt, then turned slowly to check
her reflection in the small chipped mirror that hung above the
dresser. She was not going to make the same mistake again.
The grim expression on Jason's face when he had let her off
at the hotel only an hour before warned her there was little
chance he would change his mind about her, but she was determined to try, at least one last time. If nothing else, her
pride would not let her give up this handsome man without a
fight. When he came to her door, ready to escort her to dinner, she wanted him to see a different woman, one in a
primly modest dress, her hair pulled sedately back into a bun
at the nape of her neck. She wanted to be able to hold out
her hands to him, as if to say: If you had seen this woman at
the station this morning, would her welcome have been so
cold?

But when the knock came and she threw open the door,
she saw standing before her in the dim light of the hallway,
not the one man she had expected, but two. She could only
stare at the second man in dismay.

"Good evening, ma'am." The stranger intoned the words in
a soft, well-modulated voice as he hastily removed his hat
and held it casually in his hands. After a moment, Jason followed his example, and Kate saw with a pang that his hair
was even more golden in the faint light than it had been in
the bright rays of the sun. He stared down at her coolly,
mockery and amused surprise playing in his piercing blue
eyes, but he did not attempt to speak, either to greet her or to
explain the other man's presence. It was left to the stranger
to introduce himself.

"Marcus Arundell, ma'am, at your service . . . but we're
informal out here, and I hope you'll call me Marc."

Despite the dismay she had felt only seconds before when
she had first seen him, Kate couldn't help liking this polite,
soft-spoken stranger. "I'm pleased to meet you, Mr. . . ." She

caught herself quickly, and the traces of a smile began to form on her lips. "I mean, Marc."

He returned Kate's smile easily, and she found herself keenly aware of soft brown curls twisting gently onto his forehead, and dark, sympathetic eyes that called back memories of another man whose gaze was much the same. She found herself wondering with an odd sense of premonition whether this stranger would prove to be as good a friend as Charles. He seemed aware of the intensity of her gaze, for even as he smiled casually at her, his eyes were scanning her face with faintly concealed curiosity.

"You seem quite taken with Mrs. Devlin." Jason's deep, resonant voice had an icy sharpness as it cut through the air. "You can't take your eyes off her." Kate turned quickly to glance at him in surprise, unable to understand the harsh sarcasm in his tone. If she hadn't known better, she would have thought for sure he was jealous. Yet, how could a man be jealous of a woman he didn't even want?

Marc only laughed good-naturedly. "She is a beauty, Jason. I concede that." His eyes grew serious as he turned to look his companion directly in the eye. "But we've been friends a long time. There's no way I'd set my sights for a woman that belongs to you—even if I thought I stood a chance."

"Don't worry about it, Marc," Jason responded with an unexpected burst of joviality. Laughing, he clapped his hand heartily on his friend's shoulder. "Mrs. Devlin is not my woman—nor is she likely to be. Look at her all you want."

Kate was stung by the brutal force of Jason's outspoken rudeness, and even Marc seemed disconcerted as he turned to glance awkwardly at Kate, standing silently in the doorway, her face ashen with humiliation. When she looked up and saw the expression on his face, she suddenly found herself growing almost unbearably furious with Jason. What a crass, insensitive beast he was, to embarrass not only her but also the friend who was only trying to be kind.

"It seems Mr. Hamilton is completely without manners," she said tartly, forgetting in her rising fury that she had resolved to prove herself meek and ladylike. "Perhaps it should make me feel better to see that he's rude not only to me, but thoughtless to his friends as well."

Marc looked surprised for a moment, as if he had not expected to find such a bold display of temperament beneath her sleek, neat cap of auburn curls, but he soon recovered enough to chuckle softly.

"Good girl," he said warmly. To Kate's surprise, there was

no disapproval in his voice at her sudden outburst of temper. "Don't let him get away with that. But look here, I told you we were informal. Go ahead and call him Jason—even if he is rude to you."

Kate glanced quickly toward Jason, expecting to find taut lines of anger beginning to form on his face, but she saw instead, to her relief, that the corners of his mouth had turned up in amusement. They were obviously good friends, these two, she realized. They knew each other's moods and tempers well. No doubt Marc's warmth and easy humor acted as a gentling influence on Jason, and Kate found herself suddenly grateful for the presence that only moments before had seemed like an intrusion.

She was to have more than one occasion to renew her gratitude before the evening was over, for without Marc's laughter and good cheer, dinner would have been a dismal, shoddy affair. The instant she set foot in the drab, ugly hotel dining room, ringing with the loud cacophony of rough male voices, Kate knew she had stepped into a world in which she was doomed to feel alien and ill at ease. Without Marc, it would have been intolerable, for it was he and not Jason who sensed her discomfort and took her firmly by the arm, leading her through the crowded room to a table by the window.

It was, Kate decided, the grimmest and most depressing place she had ever seen. Completely unadorned, save for a few plain candles that provided illumination at the tables and in sconces set into the filthy, unpainted walls, the room was as coarse and raw as the frontier men who sat at its tables and spit dark brown tobacco juice on the rough wooden floor. Even the long window that ran the length of one wall provided neither character nor distinction, and the curtains that screened off its lower half had decayed and torn, until large gaping holes appeared in their surface, leaving ample space for passersby to peer through with all the subtlety of visitors to the monkey house at the zoo. Watching their inquisitive faces, Kate quickly realized that women—at least, women who didn't wear bright red dresses with feathers—were a great curiosity in this land of bearded, tobacco-stained men.

So this was the West, Kate thought bitterly as she glanced around the squalid dining room. This was the brave new land she had journeyed to with so much hope. Not even the hints of coarseness she had encountered on the train prepared her for anything so relentlessly ugly. Why, even Mrs. Smalley's boardinghouse was better than this pigpen! The tablecloths might have been gray and stained from careless laundering, but at least they were not streaked with vivid mementos of dinners long past; and the flatware, if a bit greasy at times, had never been encrusted with dried tidbits of food from other people's mouths.

Kate was constantly aware of Jason's intense eyes fixed on her throughout the meal. If only they hadn't been such a clear, deep blue, she told herself desperately, then perhaps she could have ignored them, at least for a few minutes. His eyes followed her hand each time she dipped the spoon valiantly into the thick layer of clear grease that coated the soup, determined not to complain, not to give him an excuse to call her a "fine lady" again. They followed her lips as she gnawed fiercely on the tough, overcooked beefsteak, trying to break each piece up so she wouldn't have to swallow it whole, half-choking on it as it caught for a moment in her throat. And yet, unyielding as his eyes were, they were nowhere near as intimidating as she had expected. There was something in them, some nuance or expression that she couldn't quite put her finger on. When she finally figured out what it was, it was all she could do to keep from gasping aloud in surprise.

There was no mockery in his eyes, no scorn—not even a hint of amusement! Instead, Kate caught sight of an expression that bespoke approval, and perhaps even grudging admiration, as if despite all his anger and antipathy, Jason had noticed how hard she was trying to please him and couldn't help appreciating it. Kate felt as if she had just been thrown a small crumb of comfort, the only one to be offered her since she had arrived in Jasper Springs.

Even with the little surge of triumph she allowed herself to feel at the subtle change in Jason's attitude—and with the flattering attentiveness that distinguished Marc's easy social discourse—dinner was an ordeal for Kate, and the strain she felt made it seem to drag on interminably. It was a relief when finally she could set down the thick, bitter coffee and push her chair back from the table. After the grimness of the dining room, even the shabby, threadbare lobby, for all its smoky, raucous crudity, seemed like a welcome oasis.

When Jason and Marc stopped to greet an acquaintance, Kate took advantage of the opportunity to slip away from them for a moment. She felt almost as if a burden had been lifted from her shoulders as she found herself alone at last, no longer needing to pretend at social chitchat or even to hide the deep hurt she felt at Jason's rejection. Crossing the room, she stopped beside a large painting that hung on the opposite wall, staring at it not because she liked it but because it made her feel a little less conspicuous in a room filled with men.

It was a depressing painting, she decided. All done up in brown and gray and muddy yellow, it depicted a bunch of filthy cowhands, half-obscured in a cloud of dust as they chased after a herd of cattle. To Kate, it seemed to typify the West as she had seen it—drab, and dirty, and ugly beyond description.

Slowly she became aware of eyes staring at her, their intensity making her squirm with nervousness. Glancing around cautiously, she was surprised to see Jason standing by himself across the room, his eyes fixed intently on her profile. For one swift instant, before he raised his guard again, Kate caught in his eyes an unexpected look, one she knew he never meant her to see. It was a look of deep hunger, as suggestive as the intensity of his gaze at the railroad station, but with none of the scornful mockery he affected when he knew she could see him. It was the look of a man who desires a woman.

Why, he wants me as much as I want him, she thought in amazement. Only he's too stubborn to admit it.

She had to smile softly as she realized how foolish she had been—how foolish they both had been. Why on earth was she so determined not to let him see the hurt and the tears, when those were the very things that might have won him over? And as for Jason, how could he let his anger push him into a corner until it was almost impossible to back down?

Pride, that's all it was, foolish, stubborn pride. Well, she was proud, she had to admit that, perhaps as proud as he, but at least she had the sense to know when to let go. At least, she was not afraid to make the first move.

"It's a lovely night, isn't it?" she said quietly, walking over to stand at his side. "Could we go for a walk?"

"The streets of Jasper Springs are hardly suitable for a woman at night," he replied curtly. His eyes were hard and expressionless, as if he had drawn a shade down over them.

Kate was stunned by the coldness of his response. How unfair he was! Here she was, willing to extend herself, willing to meet him more than halfway, but even that wasn't good enough for him. She felt her temper begin to flare up again.

"If you won't escort me, I'll go by myself!" she snapped angrily as she turned and headed toward the door. She didn't care if he followed her or not.

Jason's eyes flashed with a sudden show of anger, but he

quickly managed to control himself, and with an exaggerated show of politeness, he stepped over to the door and held it open for her. She averted her eyes so she would not have to look at the scornful mockery that curled up the corners of his mouth.

The instant she stepped outside, Kate realized Jason had been right, and only obstinacy and anger kept her from turning back. The saloons had obviously been filled for hours, and the patrons who spilled out of swinging doors onto the muddy street were already more than half-drunk. They were a free, unrestrained group—a kind of anything-goes society—and their rough frontier vulgarity was something Kate didn't know how to cope with. Bewildered, she glanced around hurriedly, trying to decide what to do. Only the scorn in Jason's eyes forced her to go on.

Stubbornly she turned to her left and began to walk slowly down the narrow boardwalk that separated the buildings from the wide dirt road. Without comment, Jason followed her lead, adjusting his pace to hers as he sauntered easily beside her. To Kate, each building they passed looked much like the one that had gone before, and she could barely distinguish one rough, unpainted facade from its neighbor, one narrow grimy window from the next.

As they passed by a dark alleyway filled with ominous shadows, Kate found her eyes searching its depths, waiting for something sinister or threatening to jump out and frighten her. When her eyes caught sight of nothing more terrifying than a row of barrels that obviously belonged to the general store next door, she had to smile at herself. Perhaps everything was like that, she thought hopefully. Perhaps when she got to know the West better, all the things that frightened or disgusted her would turn out to be as innocuous and harmless as a row of empty wooden barrels.

Just as they passed by the alleyway, Kate heard a sudden loud burst of raucous shouts that brought her feet to an abrupt halt. Not twenty feet ahead of them lay a busy saloon, and some disturbance inside had sent a mass of men onto the boardwalk, shouting and screaming in a confused babel of protest and accusation. Dismayed, she turned to glance at the street behind her, but she quickly saw that there, too, only a few doorways beyond the hotel, lay another saloon, nearly as boisterous as the one ahead. There was no point crossing the street, either—even if she had been willing to ruin her only pair of shoes in the mud—for other saloons and bawdy houses lined the boardwalk on that side.

"You see what I mean?" Jason's voice was not unkind, but it was cold and stern. "Are you ready to go back now?"

"I just . . ." Kate began, but she was unable to finish the sentence, for a loud commotion rang out at the end of the street, drowning out her words. To her amazement, she saw a group of men—there must have been a dozen at least—riding at breakneck speed down the center of the street, shouting at the top of their lungs, and sending the mud that spattered from their horses' hooves across the boardwalks and onto the sides of the buildings.

The loud crack of gunshots filled the air again and again as the men discharged bullets into the dirt at their feet or pointed their guns upward at the upper stories, occasionally shattering windows and sending glass down in a heavy barrage on the men in the streets below. Just before they reached the saloon, one of the riders swerved onto the boardwalk, followed by half a dozen of his companions. Most of them rode directly into the saloon, whooping and shooting and generally making as much noise as they could, but two of them continued down the boardwalk, the sound of their hoofbeats clattering sharply on the hard wood as men shouted and jumped out into the street to keep from being trampled. Jason grabbed Kate's arm and pulled her roughly into the protection of the alley.

Kate felt herself trembling as the hooves clattered past and the sounds died away. After a few moments, she and Jason were left alone in the darkness. An unnatural silence had settled over the street, a silence that was all the more eerie in its unexpectedness.

"*Now* you see," Jason said calmly. There was no hint of a question in his voice.

"I just wanted a quiet walk with you," she protested.

"I know what you wanted," he told her in a sudden burst of fury, as if the thin veneer of the evening's courtesy had abruptly shattered, leaving the full force of his anger and hostility to come rushing out all at once. "You wanted a nice romantic walk so you could flutter your eyelashes at me and remind me how demure and sweet you've become since this afternoon. Well, it won't work—not tonight, and not ever! I told you I didn't want you, and I meant it!"

"That's not true!" She didn't know if she was more surprised or hurt by his cold taunt, but she was determined not to let him get away with it.

"What do you mean?"

"I saw the way you looked at me tonight."

"And how did I look at you?"

Why did he have to sound so hard and bitter? she wondered. Why did his lips have to curl up in scorn? He frightened her when he looked at her that way. She wished she hadn't brought the whole thing up, but it was too late to turn back now.

"It was . . . well, you know what I mean. It wasn't the way a man looks at a woman he doesn't . . . love."

"Love?" he scoffed. "Are you by any chance laboring under the misconception that I am in love with you? Let me set you straight, my dear. That was not love you saw in my eyes. It was lust—plain, old-fashioned lust."

The ugliness of the word stung Kate, and to her embarrassment, tears began to slip out of her eyes and roll down her cheeks. "Jason . . ." she whispered.

"What do you want me to tell you?" he asked harshly. "That you're beautiful? You know that already. You have a mirror, and no doubt you spend hours in front of it. Or perhaps you want me to tell you you're desirable. You are, you know, very desirable. I saw that the instant you stepped off the train. Do you think any man could miss the way you swing your hips to emphasize their round firmness, or the way those ridiculous stays melt your waist away to where it looks as if a man could snap it in two in his fingers? Or perhaps you thought I hadn't noticed the soft fullness of those ripe young breasts that you contrive to jut out so enticingly?"

He reached out and caught hold of her shoulders in strong, rough hands, grasping them so tightly that she nearly had to cry out in pain. "Shall I tell you what I'd really like to do with you, my proud beauty? I'd like to drag you down in the mud at my feet and tear that falsely modest dress off your body. God only knows why I don't."

He pulled her even closer, until her face was directly beneath his. The sound of his breath came in short, heavy gasps, but Kate could not even hear her own breath, her body was so tense and still. She knew she had put herself in a dangerous position with him, but she was strangely unafraid.

"Perhaps I will," he taunted, looking hungrily into her eyes, but still she did not pull away. Suddenly, without warning, he lowered his lips harshly on hers, pressing his way ravenously into her mouth. There was no joy in his kiss, no tenderness, but Kate did not mind. She did not even mind the pain when his teeth cut into her lips, or the bruising agony of his rough fingers on her arms. That pain was nothing compared to the hot, thrilling sensation that racked her entire being in response to the strong touch of his body against hers, and her mouth was as greedy as his as she eagerly sought the ecstasy of his kiss.

"Oh, Jason," she cried breathlessly as his body finally parted from hers.

"Oooooh, Jason," he mimicked, raising his voice to a coy, unpleasant falsetto.

Roughly he thrust her back savagely against the wall. "Don't give me any of that 'Oh, Jason' crap. You can pull your coy, demure, lash-batting routine on any man you like, just don't try it on me. You and I both know, sweetheart, that underneath that pretty face and prim little dress, you're every bit as lusty and base-minded as I am. I daresay plenty of men besides your husband have enjoyed the pleasures of that sensual body of yours."

"That's not true," she gasped in astonishment. She could hardly believe he was saying such terrible things to her.

"If it isn't true now, it soon will be," he promised ominously. "You have the soul of a harlot, my dear. All you need is one of those red satin dresses with all the frills and feathers. You'd make some man a magnificent mistress, Kate—but not a wife. No, not a wife!"

Not a wife!

The words echoed in Kate's ears even after he had stopped speaking, and she felt herself grow crimson with shame and humiliation. After all, they were nothing more than she deserved. What a fool she'd been to chase after a man who didn't love her. Didn't *love* her? He didn't even *like* her. She made no protest as he clamped his fingers around her wrist and dragged her out into the street again.

"Here we are," he said with surprising cordiality. Looking up, Kate saw that Marc was waiting for them in the doorway of the hotel. "I told Mrs. Devlin the streets weren't suitable for a lady, but she had to come out anyway. I'm afraid it's ceased to amuse me. Show her around, will you?" He turned abruptly on his heel and hurried down the street, leaving Kate alone with Marc.

He must have seen by her face that something was amiss, but he was tactful enough not to mention it. "Come on, Kate," he said gently, laying a hand lightly on her waist to guide her inside. "You really shouldn't be out here. I'll see you safely to your door."

Kate spent a fitful night, tossing and turning restlessly, twisting herself up in the rough fabric of the sheets until she could barely move. Finally, she gave up even trying to sleep, and disentangling herself from the bedding, forced herself to lie quietly on her back, her open eyes staring unseeingly at the darkness of the ceiling.

Not as a wife. The words kept pounding away at her brain, as relentless as the harsh, monotonous clacking of the train wheels that had roared in her brain continually for days. *Not as a wife. Not as a wife. Not as a wife.*

That's unfair, she thought rebelliously. So unfair. And yet, even as she thought the words, she knew in her heart that she was wrong. It wasn't unfair. Not unfair at all. Who was she, a fallen woman masquerading as a widow, to claim the right to be any man's wife?

Morning brought relief from the darkness, but not from the doubt. Forcing herself to look at things objectively, Kate had to admit Jason was right. He had put it harshly—and cruelly—but he had spoken the truth. She could not expect to be his wife. And yet . . .

You'd make a magnificent mistress, Kate.

A mistress. One of those sinful but nonetheless glamorous women she had only dared to peek at from behind her fan. Even as the thought frightened her, it also tantalized, and Kate found herself thinking boldly: Why not?

Why not, indeed? What more could she expect? Besides, even for all his cruel indifference, Kate knew she wanted Jason. She had to admit that to herself. She wanted him at any cost.

He had told her to put on a bright red dress, one of those gaudy satin affairs with frills and sequins, but she owned no such garment. The white lawn would have to do, she decided, the pretty party dress all sprigged with green. It was far too tasteful for what she had in mind, but at least it was low-cut and showed her figure off to best advantage. Besides, the green brought out the deep highlights in her eyes.

Yes, the white lawn would have to do. She would tell Jason when he came to escort her to breakfast that she wanted to see him that evening alone, without Marc. Then, when she received him—in her bedroom—she would be wearing the white dress.

But when the knock came at her door, she flung it open to find Marc standing on the threshold alone. If he noticed the look of stunned surprise on her face, he was tactful enough not to mention it as he took her arm and escorted her down to the dingy, half-empty dining room. When they sat down at the same grimy table they had shared the evening before,

Marc spent the first few minutes in polite small talk, but it was clear to Kate that he had something on his mind. Finally, he came out with it.

"There's a train to St. Louis on Thursday," he told her. "Jason asked me to put you on it. You can make connections from there to Boston."

For a moment Kate was silent, stunned at his words. She had expected them, of course, but somehow she had hoped—unreasonably, she realized—that she would have more time.

"I won't go back to Boston," she replied slowly.

Marc leaned forward, attentive concern showing in his eyes. "Is there someplace else you'd rather go, Kate? I'm sure Jason would be willing . . ."

"No," she replied dully. "No place else." She caught her breath and tried to force her troubled mind to think. She had to see Jason once more—just one more time before Thursday. If only she could do that, her plans still need not fail.

"Tell Jason . . ." she began, holding her head proudly high, "tell him I won't stay if he doesn't want me, but he has to say it himself instead of sending a messenger to do it for him. Tell him I want to talk to him tonight—at eight o'clock. Then, if he still wants me to leave, I'll do it without any fuss."

It was a reasonable request, one that Marc would never deny, even if Jason could, and Kate knew he would have no choice but to agree to her terms. When eight o'clock came and there was no sign of him, and even eight-fifteen, she was not worried. She knew he would be there. She tugged anxiously at the neckline of the white-and-green dress, drawing it even lower, then pinched her cheeks to make them red. She wanted to look as pretty as possible. Jason would be angry with her for forcing him to come, and even more furious when he saw the way she was dressed. She might have only a few seconds before he stomped away in a rage. She had to look compelling enough to hold him there until she could explain.

As she heard the heavy, angry sound of fists banging against her door, she realized nervously that her fears had not been in vain. Jason was indeed furious, and he would be hard to deal with. A sudden, unexpected lump of fear caught at her throat, and she found herself wondering for the first time if she was doing the right thing. Pausing for a long, deep breath to calm her nerves, she forced herself to sweep gracefully across the room and fling open the door.

Jason stood in the open doorway, his hat held lightly in his hand, and Kate watched as the sullen expression on his face faded slowly into one of astonishment. He did not attempt to veil the emotion in his eyes, but let the heavy lust that permeated his gaze cut blatantly through the anger and the scorn. As she stared back at the deliberate insult of his leer, Kate suddenly felt all the pretty speeches she had carefully rehearsed vanish from her mind, and she could only stand and gape at him. When the silence was finally broken, it was Jason's voice that cut sharply through the still air of the hallway.

"Are you trying to prove something, madam?" Kate felt herself shiver at the ugly mockery in his voice, but she was determined not to back down. "I told you yesterday that I lusted after you. If you need further proof, your eyes will give it to you now." He glanced down pointedly, leaving no possible misinterpretation of his meaning.

Fascinated, her eyes followed his until they came to rest on the hard bulge of his crotch. She felt the trembling in her body grow to an almost feverish pitch, as much from the sensual magnetism as from the cold brutality of his words.

"You're trying to shock me," she told him, surprised at the calmness of her voice. The heavy beating of her heart was so loud, she was amazed he could not hear it. "But I want to talk to you. After that, you will decide what is to be done about me."

Surprisingly, her boldness seemed to have scored a point with him, and a half-smile crossed his lips as he stepped slowly into the room, his tall, lean body strangely out of proportion to the undersized furnishings. He looked pointedly at the bed, then seemed to change his mind, and sauntered over to the only chair in the room, lounging on it casually, with his long legs stretched out in front of him. Kate walked over to the bed and seated herself gingerly on the edge of it.

"I want . . ." she began, then paused awkwardly, swallowing the saliva that seemed to have accumulated all at once in her dry mouth. "I want . . . that is, I think it's time to tell you the truth."

"What a refreshing change." His tone was noncommittal rather than sarcastic. "I was getting tired of all the lies."

"I haven't lied since I got here," she snapped, beginning to lose her temper in spite of all her good resolutions. Why did the man have such a talent for making her angry? "I haven't!"

130

He only looked at her intently, the same careful, noncommittal expression on his face.

"Well, all right," she admitted. "Once. You were right. I am nineteen."

"I know," he said quietly. His voice was almost kind.

"But that's all . . ." She broke off abruptly, realizing suddenly that the lies she had told ran far deeper than that. "I suppose in a way it was a lie to let you call me Mrs. Devlin when I knew it wasn't true."

"So it's *Miss* Kate Devlin," he said calmly. He didn't seem too surprised.

"Yes," she admitted. "Well, no, that's not true either. It's Lady Catherine Devlin. Lady Catherine Anne Mary Bridget Devlin. My father was only an Irish potato farmer when he started out, but my mother is a second cousin of Queen Victoria. Twice removed," she added irrelevantly.

To her surprise, he began to laugh. She had expected him to be furious.

"You don't mind my being of the nobility?"

His eyes were twinkling as he looked back at her. "My dear Kate, I suspect there is far more of the potato farm in your veins than of the aristocracy."

She looked at him, puzzled, not sure whether to be angry or not. She was sure she had just been insulted, yet somehow his tone made it sound almost like a compliment.

"Tell me, what made you leave the fox hunts and the ballrooms? I would think you'd revel in that kind of world."

"That's what I wanted you to know," she responded simply.

It was hard at first to tell him, and the words came out falteringly, but he encouraged her gently with his eyes, using them to tell her mutely that he would offer only attentive sympathy, with none of the sarcasm she had grown to dread. As she talked, it became easier and easier, and soon she found the words tumbling out one after another. She spared herself nothing, not the tales of her willful rebelliousness against her father, nor the cruel way she had used her good friend Charles to get her way—not even that afternoon in a Boston stable when she had shamed herself forever by giving her body to a man who, no matter how much she adored him, was not her husband. Even at the end, when she had to speak of finding her lover's body beneath the still-smoking gun in her brother's hand, though her voice choked with tears, somehow she found the courage to continue. Finally, when she had finished, she sat silently on the edge of the bed, her head lowered and her lashes wet with tears.

"You should have told me this before, Kate," he said softly. His voice was as light and tender as a caress.

"I wanted to, but I was afraid."

The muscles in Jason's face contorted in a grimace. He remembered only too well the harsh, cold reception he had given her, and he understood why she was afraid of him. "Still, you should have told me," he repeated quietly. "I've been through enough myself to understand what you suffered. I don't condemn you for anything." He emphasized the word "anything," as though it was of special importance.

Kate felt a surge of hope rush through her body. He did not blame her, not for anything—perhaps not even for that spring afternoon when she had brazenly thrown herself into Philippe's arms.

He saw the hope shining in her eyes and was quick to discourage it. "Not *that*, Kate," he told her firmly but gently.

At first she was puzzled by his sudden rejection; then she felt her cheeks burn with a hot flush of embarrassment as she realized what he must have thought. "Oh, I don't expect to be your wife," she hastened to assure him. "I know that, but . . ."

To her surprise, the words stuck in her throat. Why couldn't she bring herself to utter them aloud? Why couldn't she just come right out and say: I know I can't be your wife, but I'm willing to be your mistress. I want you any way I can get you, and I'll take whatever crumbs you want to throw me.

Still, she could not make the words come out. She could only force herself to hint at them. "You told me to put on a red dress, but I don't have one," she said softly, her eyes cast steadfastly down at the hands folded tightly in her lap. Then, when he did not seem to understand, she knew she would have to be bolder. Her voice was hoarse, almost inaudible, as she whispered, "You said I'd make a magnificent mistress."

"What in God's name?" he bellowed furiously. Her eyes turned up quickly, to gape in astonishment at his face. "My God, Kate, are you offering yourself to me? As my mistress?"

"What else can I expect?"

"A hell of a lot!" To her surprise, he leaped up and began to pace angrily back and forth. The air was filled with tension, but she sensed that his anger was not directed at her. Finally he paused before her, leaning down to grip her tensely by the shoulder. "You've made one mistake, Kate, and you've paid for it. You don't have to go on paying for the rest of your life. You're a beautiful woman, and you'll make some man an exciting wife. . . . Only, not me. Not me."

"I know," she said dully. "That's why—"

"And not my mistress, either."

"But you said I'd make a magnificent—"

"Goddammit, are you going to keep throwing those words back in my face? I know I don't deserve it, but you have to believe me. I would never—*never*—degrade you like that!" He paused for a moment, visibly trying to control the emotion that vibrated tensely in his deep, resonant voice. When he continued, his tone was calm. "You're as beautiful as any woman I've ever seen, and as passionate, and once I'd have thrown myself at your feet. But not anymore. Now I'm tired, Kate, tired and weary. I want a soft, gentle woman, one who'll bring a little serenity into my life. You couldn't be that kind of woman if you tried for a thousand years."

She remained silent, her eyes cast down again, knowing there was no way she could argue with the truth of his words.

"But listen, Kate," he told her hurriedly, obviously trying to find a way to chase away the sorrow on her face. "You came here to find a husband—and a husband you shall have."

"What do you mean?"

"Pick out any man—any man in the whole town. They'd all be glad to have you. You're the loveliest woman they've seen in years. And nearly any one of them would make you a better husband than I would."

She stared at him, appalled. Didn't he understand? She didn't want any other man, no matter how good a husband he might be. She wanted Jason, only Jason, and her body ached for him with a passion beyond anything she had ever felt or dreamed. Longing for him as she did, how could she ever open her arms to another man?

"Look here," Jason told her, his voice filled with forced eagerness. "I'll support you until you choose someone. Take as long as you like. And if you decide on a man who's poor, I'll help him get a good start."

Kate knew it was fair, fairer than she deserved, but she knew at the same time that it wasn't what she wanted. She longed to cry out to him, to tell him that she wanted him and only him, that she would rather be his mistress than the wife of any other man on earth, but there was a cold, hard set to his face that held her back.

"All right," she whispered softly, after a moment's silence. "If that's the way you want it . . . all right."

13

THE WIND ALREADY HAD A WINTRY BITE TO IT, AND KATE shivered, pulling the black shawl tightly over her shoulders and tucking her knees up to keep her body warm. The stone ledge beneath her was cold, but she did not mind, for from its vantage point she could command views of both the sweeping, still-green plains, gently bisected by the meandering course of a lazy stream, and the tall, majestic mountains, now heavily capped with the snows of impending winter. It was a peaceful spot, Kate thought as she gazed across the fertile plains. It should have made her feel serene and contented inside, but it didn't.

She was angry at herself for the discontent that continually gnawed away at her heart, but she was powerless to stop it. She should have been happy, she reminded herself sternly. Weeks ago, she had been hoarding her last pennies in a dreary Boston boardinghouse, counting the days before she would have to drudge out a bare subsistence as a common streetwalker. Now she was in a new land, free and unafraid, soon to be the bride, not of an unknown stranger who had purchased her by mail, but of a man she could choose of her own free will. She ought to be down on her knees thanking God for her good fortune, instead of crying her eyes out into her pillow each night.

"You're lost in thought."

Marc's gentle voice startled her, and she turned to smile apologetically at him. Marc had been her almost constant companion in the last few weeks, and Kate had grown to rely on him more and more. From the knowing little smiles she caught on people's faces as they passed them in the street, she realized it had begun to be tacitly assumed that Marc would soon be her husband.

"I'm sorry," she told him. "I'm afraid I'm not very good company. I was just thinking how lovely it is here." Well, at least that was half-true.

"Don't apologize," he said kindly. As Kate looked into his warm, thoughtful eyes, she remembered again with a sudden pang of homesickness how much he reminded her of her dear friend Charles. If anyone had told her, only a few weeks ago, that she would marry someone as good and kind as Charles, she would have thought she was the luckiest girl in the world. If only she had never met Jason—if she had never laid eyes on him—how happy she would be!

"Could we take a look around?" Kate asked quickly, eager to shake off the sadness that threatened to cover her like a thick, heavy mantle. Without even waiting for his answer, she jumped to her feet, forcing a cheerful smile to her lips.

"Of course," he replied. She could see that her interest in the land pleased him greatly. "We can leave the wagon and walk—that is, if you can walk in those shoes." He hesitated, looking down doubtfully at her feet.

"Of course I can walk in them," she told him, laughing. "I'm used to hiking." Thank heaven her father had never thought girls should be raised as little ninnies who never ran through the fields or tramped the woods for fear of getting their clothes soiled.

"Come on, then." He held out his hand to help her over the rocks, and they quickly made their way down the hill to the flatlands below. "You see all this?" he asked, stretching his arm out in a sweeping gesture. "All this land—as far as the eye can see—it's all the Triple Crown, Jason's land."

"So much," she whispered softly. The vastness of his holdings seemed almost incredible to her.

Marc laughed lightly at her naiveté. "Things aren't the same here," he explained patiently. "Not the way they are in England. Land here is dry and rocky, and it takes more acres to support a herd of cattle. So you see, a man's holdings may look vast here, but actually, they're the equivalent of a tenth the acreage in England, or perhaps a twentieth."

"Even so, it's amazing." Kate looked out toward the mountains in the distance, trying to make her mind comprehend the fact that nearly all the land that stretched up to them belonged to Jason Hamilton.

"But look over here," Marc told her eagerly, turning her around to face the hill they had just walked down. "All the land around that hill and beyond—it may not be as vast as

Jason's land, but it's mine." There was a deep, quiet pride in his voice as he spoke of it.

"Your land?" She was surprised. "I thought you worked for Jason."

"I do," he said, smiling. "I'm his foreman. But I've been saving my money and investing it all in land. By now, I have enough to start my own ranch. And up there—that hillside we were sitting on—that's where I'm going to build my house." He did not go on to say it, but she knew by the softness in his voice that he was telling her: That's the house I want to share with you, if you'll marry me.

She turned away from him, confused and frightened, unwilling yet to confront the love he was prepared to offer her. "Where are the boundaries?" she asked, eager to change the subject. "Where does your land end?"

He sensed the fear that added an edge of tension to her voice, and he was gently patient with her. "You can't see the southern boundary from here," he told her quietly, making no further allusion to the home he would soon offer her, "but the northern boundary lies along the Jasper River." As he pointed, Kate followed the angle of his finger, looking across the gently babbling brook to scan the horizon. Marc watched her for a moment, a puzzled expression on his face, then began to laugh softly. "Not so far away. There." He directed her gaze toward the little brook.

"But that's just a stream," she protested. "That would hardly count for anything back home. How can you call it a river?"

"It will be a river," he promised her. "In the spring, when the snows melt and rush down from the mountains. Then we'll use it to water our herds and irrigate our fields, and soon it will become just a muddy little stream again."

Kate shook her head. Everything seemed very complex to her. Not at all like the fertile fields and deep, lazy rivers of England.

"Come over here," Marc urged, "and I'll show you the eastern boundary."

Kate walked slowly toward the fence she had not noticed before. It was an arrangement unlike anything she had ever seen, with rough wooden poles supporting browned and rusting wire. Every few inches, odd little barbs stuck out of the wire. Tentatively she reached out her hand to touch one of them with her fingers.

"Ouch!" she cried, pulling her hand back quickly in surprise at its sharpness. "What a nasty fence." She turned to look at Marc, surprised to see a dark expression on his face. She had never seen that kind of mood in him before, and she did not know how to react to it.

"Once, this land was all open," he said gloomily. "Free as far as the eye could see. Then the sheepmen came, and now everywhere you look, you see fences."

"Is that why you hate them so?" she asked. She had already sensed the violent hostility that lay like an open sore between the ranchers and the sheepmen in town—indeed, it would have been totally impossible not to notice it—but until that moment she had not been able to catch even a hint of its cause.

"Hate them?" Marc's voice had a strange, compelling quality that she could not comprehend. "Oh, Kate, you don't understand. The world is changing, even in this vast new land, and we couldn't stop it if we wanted to. Those ranchers that make citadels out of their homes—they sit there gloating over the land they think they possess, but in reality it possesses them. Those men are only sowing the seeds of their own destruction." He was silent for a long time, staring off into the distance with a sadness stamped on his features that tore at Kate's heart. When he turned to look back at her, his eyes were gentle again.

"The world is changing," he repeated, smiling softly. "If we want to survive, we have to learn to change with it."

We have to learn to change with it. The words followed Kate for the next few days, haunting her with an insistence that would not let her go. Adapt, she kept telling herself. Adapt! For in adaptation was the key to life.

She knew she had encountered the truth, and she knew, too, that unpleasant though it was, it was a truth that had to be faced. She was like the ranchers in their fortress-homes, she warned herself resolutely. They were longing for the freedom they could not retain, just as she was filled with a deep hunger for a man she could never possess.

She saw Jason frequently during those unhappy days, for he seemed always to find an errand in town that let him stop by the hotel, but she found little comfort in their meetings. The aloofness that had replaced his early mockery was equally impenetrable, and the invisible barrier he had erected between them was sufficiently strong to keep her at arm's length. He was always polite to her, and unfailingly kind, but he was careful to make sure that nothing personal could ever creep into their relationship. Slowly, Kate grew to accept the fact that he would never want her, at least not with the depth of passion she felt for him.

"You've been seeing a lot of Marc," he said unexpectedly one day. There was a strange smile on his lips. It was neither sarcastic, as his earlier smiles had been, nor friendly. Kate could not fathom what it meant.

"Yes," she admitted.

"He's a good man. Decent and kind. You'd be a fool to let him go."

Yes, she would be a fool, and she knew it. Never would she find another man like Marc. If only she'd never met Jason, she told herself again, as she had so many times during the past few weeks. If only she'd never met him!

But she had met him, she reminded herself bitterly. She'd met him and come to long for him deeply, and that was a fact she must learn to live with, just as the ranchers must learn to live with the sheepmen who fenced in their land and took away their freedom. She must accept life as it was. Pick up the pieces and start again. Firmly, in the darkness of her room late one evening, she made up her mind to accept Marc when he proposed to her.

She thought it was going to be simple—all she had to do was say one little word, "yes," and it would all be over. But in the end, of course, it was not that easy, and all the complex forces that had governed her emotions came into play to confuse her.

They were sitting on the same rocky ledge, the ledge on that beautiful, serene hilltop where Marc planned to build his home. Kate could hear the words coming, the words she thought she was prepared for, but suddenly her mouth was dry with nervousness and her heart beat at twice its normal rate.

"Please don't," she whispered, trying to postpone the dreaded moment at least a little longer. "Please give me a little more time."

"But surely you knew this was coming, Kate," he said gently, mild surprise showing in his soft, dark eyes. "I haven't exactly made a secret of how I feel about you."

"I know," she admitted. "But somehow, I thought . . . well, I thought when the time came . . ." She paused, unable to find the words to continue. To her embarrassment, a pair of huge tears rolled out of her eyes and began to slide down her cheeks. Why did she always have to cry at a time like that? she thought, furious with herself. It made her look like such a ninny.

Marc reached out tenderly with his hand to caress the soft skin of her cheek. Carefully he brushed the tears away, then took her chin lightly in his fingers, tilting her head upward so she had to look into his eyes.

"It's Jason, isn't it?" he asked softly.

She nodded mutely.

"You're in love with him?"

Love? She turned her head away abruptly so he could not see the startled expression in her eyes. Was it love, this deep and terrible passion she felt for Jason? She had known only that the blood ran hot through her veins whenever she thought of him . . . but love? Dared she call that violent emotion love?

"I don't know," she whispered hoarsely. But even as the words passed through her lips, she knew they were not true. Even as she expressed her doubt, she knew she could doubt no longer. Whatever cruel tricks fate had played on her, she had come to love with a deep and tormented passion this man who would not have her. Whatever chains he had used to bind her unwilling heart were subtle and invisible ones, but they were stronger than any chains she had ever seen. At last she understood what had happened to her. Somehow, without her even knowing it, she had grown to love him, and loving him as she did, she knew she could never bind herself to another man.

"No, that's not true," she contradicted herself quietly. "I *do* love him. Oh, I know I'm a fool. He doesn't love me at all. . . ."

"Doesn't he?" There was a sharp edge to Marc's voice that surprised her, and she found herself staring at him quizzically. There was a dark sorrow in the depths of his eyes that she didn't like to face. "Are you really so blind, Kate?" he asked gently. "Can't you see the man is head over heels in love with you?"

"But he said . . ." she stammered awkwardly. "He said he didn't want me." She turned crimson as she recalled that night in the dark alleyway when he had rejected her so cruelly. "That is, he said he didn't *love* me."

"If he doesn't love you, then why do you suppose he manages to be in town at least three or four times a day to catch a glimpse of you?"

"But when he does see me, he's so . . . Oh, I don't know. He's not rude exactly, but——"

"I know," Marc interrupted. Understanding mingled with

139

the sadness in his eyes. "He does everything he can to push you away. Don't you see, Kate? Jason is afraid of you."

"Afraid of me?" she gasped in amazement. "How could anyone be afraid of me? Why, I'm half his size, and—"

"I don't mean that," Marc broke in, laughing. "I mean afraid of your love. Jason is a strange man, Kate, strange and hard, with a dark rage inside him that even I can't understand. He wasn't always like that . . ."

His voice broke off, and he stared at her in silence for a moment. His face was troubled, as if he did not know how to find the words to express what he was trying to tell her. Before he continued, he leaned forward, taking her hand in his and pressing it gently in a gesture of friendship.

"We go back a long way, Jason and I. We grew up in Virginia, and we served in the war together. We were even together in a prison camp in Illinois—one of the most notorious prisons the Yankees had. Perhaps you've heard of it. It was called Rock Island."

Kate could only shake her head. The American war had always seemed wasteful and incredibly stupid to her, and she had paid little heed to tales of it.

"It was an ugly place, uglier than anything you could ever dream of. Not that we didn't have prison camps in the South, too. They were shameful places, particularly one in Americus, Georgia—Andersonville. Of the thousands of men imprisoned there, few survived. It wasn't that we were so inhumane, Kate. It's just that we were a defeated people, at the end of our resources. Many of our soldiers in the field got no better than our prisoners, but the Yankees didn't care about that. Once they heard what Andersonville was like, they were out for blood. They wanted to get an eye for an eye in their own prison camps—and they very nearly succeeded at Rock Island.

"I was wounded when I was taken there, and delirious. I couldn't have survived twenty-four hours alone. Jason begged and stole—and even killed—to get the medical supplies and food I needed. Without him, I would have died."

His voice broke, and Kate looked up at him quickly, surprised at the tension in his usually calm face. Catching her eyes fixed intently on his, Marc forced himself to throw off the burden of suffering that had enveloped him. As he continued, he smiled lightly.

"But I'm getting carried away with myself. You don't want to hear all that. Anyhow, it didn't last long. Soon the Yankees came along with an offer: help us fight the Indians out West, and we'll set you free. We didn't want to go, of course. We hated the Yankees with the fierce bitterness only a captive people can feel. Any sort of capitulation, even if it included our freedom, was abhorrent to us, but Jason quickly realized that I was too weak to endure the hardship much longer, so he signed us both up.

"I never fought again, of course. The minute I got out West, the army realized I was far too ill to be any use to them, and I spent the next year in an army hospital. By the time I finally managed to join up with Jason again, he was a different man, cold and hard, as if he'd built up a shell to protect him from the world. I don't know what happened to him during that time—he never talks of it—but somehow it took all the fight out of him."

"Took the fight out of him!" Kate gasped, fingering the still-sensitive bruises on her wrist and upper arms. She couldn't help picturing the angry, half-savage man who had nearly thrown her to the dirt in the alleyway outside the hotel.

Marc laughed at her reaction. "I didn't say it took the stubbornness out of him," he reminded her. "Or the anger. But he isn't a fighter anymore, not the way he used to be." He paused for an instant, to stare intently at her face. "You know, you remind me a lot of him. Perhaps that's why he's so drawn to you. He used to be ready to fight at the drop of a hat for anything he believed in, no matter how impractical or unrealistic it was. Now he's more calculating. Now he lets it all simmer inside him with a horrible intensity, and he never lets it out.

"That's why he's afraid of you, Kate, because of the excitement and challenge he feels in you. He's afraid you'll call to depths of emotion he's tried to keep buried safely inside himself until he can almost forget they're there. That's why he thinks he wants a gentle, passive wife. She would never be a threat to him."

"*Thinks* he wants?" she repeated, puzzled at his choice of words. "That's what he *does* want. He told me so himself."

"And I'm sure he believes it. But he is wrong. I know Jason, Kate, better than he knows himself. If he marries a woman like that, he'll be bored with her within a year, and even against his will, he'll find a thousand subtle, cruel ways to punish her for failing to fill his needs."

"But what can I do?" she cried out helplessly. How unfair it was for him to tell her of Jason's love when there was still no way for her to break through the hard shell he had built around himself. It only hurt double to realize he hungered for her as much as she did for him—but he would never dare to let himself reach out to touch her. "Even if he does want me, there's no way I can make him admit it."

"Of course you can," Marc assured her. "Jason may be stubborn, but he loves you desperately. He won't be able to hold out for long. You're a fighter, Kate. If you want him, fight for him."

Kate found herself searching Marc's face hopefully. Did he really mean what he said? Did she really have a chance with Jason? The gentle confidence she saw written across his features told her that she did, and her heart surged with excitement.

Jason would fight against her—that she knew. He would be rude and harsh and even cruel, but now that she knew he loved her, she was certain she would win in the end. She would have him for her lover.

"You know, I shouldn't be telling you this," Marc said, laughing lightly at himself. "If I'd let things go on as they were, sooner or later I'd have won you over. But I guess I couldn't do that."

He paused and looked at her quietly for a moment before continuing. "Jason is more than a friend to me. The things we've experienced have made us grow together until we're almost like brothers. No, more than brothers. More like one person. Two sides of the same coin, you might say. I share with Jason a depth of feeling I could never share with any other human being, not even you.

"Besides . . ." He pressed her hand tightly, then drew it toward him, holding it lightly for an instant against his lips. "You and Jason are the two people I care about most in the world. I want you both to be happy, even if it means losing you."

Happy? Yes, she would be happy, she knew, as she felt a thrill of excitement run through her body. Yet, still she felt an unexpected burden of sadness fall upon her. Why did it always have to be like that? she wondered, looking at the brave, lonely smile on Marc's face. Why did happiness with one man mean she had to hurt another?

"Thank you," she whispered lightly, leaning forward to kiss his cheek. "Thank you for being such a good friend."

14

KATE FLICKED THE REINS LIGHTLY WITH HER WRISTS, URGING the pair of spirited roans to even greater speed as they raced along the rough half-road that led to Jason Hamilton's ranch. With an expert hand she held them in just tightly enough to keep from losing control, but not so rigidly that she inhibited their high spirits or turned their friskiness into rebellion and stubbornness. Smiling, she remembered how appalled the man at the livery stable had been when she asked to rent them.

"Not without a driver, ma'am," he told her adamantly, surprise and scorn showing on his features. "They ain't used to a wagon none. 'Sides, they's too frisky for a little mite of a girl to handle."

But she had insisted, and in the end, knowing she was under Jason Hamilton's protection, he had to capitulate. He couldn't afford to antagonize the richest landowner in the area. As she rode off, the reins held tightly and surely in her hands, she was amused to glance back and see that the expression on his face was, if not approving, at least slightly mollified.

She was glad now he had given in to her, for it was exhilarating to drive alone down the road, guiding the horses skillfully through the potholes and muddy ruts that covered the trail and feeling the icy nip of the late-afternoon wind as it cut through the thin wool of her shawl. She threw back her head, feeling the full force of the wind rush against her neck and cheeks. How good it felt to ride across the wide plain, fast and free against the wind. How good it felt to be young and full of life—and eager to face the fight that lay ahead.

For fight it would be—of that she had no doubt. It would be bitter and filled with fury, but it was a fight she knew she would win in the end. What a little ninny she'd been to go to Jason all sweet and demure, with lashes lowered and wet with tears, to beg humbly for the right to become his mistress. No wonder she'd lost so quickly. It wasn't her style, and it didn't become her at all. No, Marc was right. She was a fighter, and the only way she was going to get what she wanted was to fight for it.

She felt a sudden urge to pull the heavy net out of her hair and free it to hang down to her waist, letting the wind blow exhilaratingly through the tresses that streamed out behind her, but remembering how long it took to coax all the little curls into place, she forced herself to curb the impulse. She wanted to look perfect that evening. She felt like she was playing a part, and she was determined to play it well.

Even the dress was perfect. She chuckled as she glanced down at the skirt, blowing briskly in the wind. He had told her to get red satin, and red satin it was, but not the bright crimson of the dance-hall girls and the prostitutes. Instead, it was a deep, rich burgundy that perfectly matched the darkest shades of her hair, accenting its vivid red and golden highlights. In lieu of feathers and sequins, she had trimmed it with the exquisitely fragile lace the town's dressmaker had brought with her all the way from Paris. The lace was a perfect touch, its snowy whiteness softening the edges of the low-cut bosom and bringing out the pink-and-ivory paleness of her skin. The only jewel she allowed herself was the heavy emerald brooch that had once belonged to her mother.

They told her Anne had picked it out for her soon after she was born, choosing the heirloom for her infant daughter because it was the color of her eyes. Instinctively, Kate slipped her hand up to touch its smooth, unfaceted surface, and for the first time, she began to feel a tiny tremor of doubt run through her body. What would her mother have thought, she wondered, her gentle, beautiful mother, if she could have known her daughter was riding wildly through the night to throw herself at the feet of a man who had already declared he would never marry her?

Kate pushed the doubt to the back of her mind and forced herself to hold the reins with both hands again. There was no point worrying about things she couldn't change, she reminded herself sternly. She had already committed herself to a course, and she would have to follow it through.

The terrain had grown progressively more rugged on the long ride from town, and Kate realized with a surge of excitement that she must be near the high hill Jason had chosen as the site of his home. The crest of the shallower hill she was driving up still blocked it from her view, but she was sure when she reached the top, she would finally see the house she had been picturing in her imagination for so long.

She tried to bridle the excitement that insisted on swelling through her body, for she knew she was bound to be disappointed. She had dreamed about this house too long. It could never fill her expectations. With a determined burst of realism, she tried to prepare herself for the ranch house she knew could be nothing more than a larger version of the weathered gray shacks that lined the streets of Jasper Springs and even Cheyenne.

Only when she rounded the crest and squinted her eyes into the glowing sunset did Kate realize her fears had been in vain. Far from the drab shack she had feared, or even the sturdy wood-frame house she hoped for, the mansion Jason had built for himself stood out in the stark, rugged wilderness with a grandeur and majesty that far surpassed even her wildest dreams. Jerking the reins abruptly toward her, she forced the startled horses to a stop as she sat and gaped at the sight on the hilltop before her.

Silhouetted in the fiery red of the dying sun, the house rose out of the face of a steep, rocky cliff, almost as if it had been carved from it, looming into the sky as boldly as an ancient medieval castle. Kate stared at its unexpected solidarity in the midst of a land of flimsy shacks and lean-tos, and it looked to her as tall and impregnable as any tower she had ever seen. Only after several minutes did she realize its height was an illusion. Built completely from heavy gray stones that blended perfectly with the color of the cliff, the house was nowhere taller than two shallow stories. Even the odd little turrets that graced the corners rose only a few feet higher, but the steep hillside beneath the house seemed to push it farther up into the sky, until it looked as if the four towers were reaching upward to the heavens like the spires of a majestic cathedral.

Like a citadel, she thought, wondering why the word gave her an eerie feeling. Then she remembered.

They sit in their citadels, Marc had told her. The ranchers in their citadels, gloating over the land they think they possess, the land that in reality possesses them. With an odd sense of foreboding, she wondered if he had been trying to tell her something about Jason.

One of the graceful roans shook his head impatiently, and taking her cue from him, Kate lifted up the reins again, eager to follow the road as it wound around the hill and snaked its way up the gentler slope that lay on the other side. When she got to the top, Kate found the house even more breathtaking than it had been from her earlier vantage point, and she caught her breath in amazement as she gazed at it.

The lawn was wild and unkempt, and the trail that led up

to it only a path of dirt worn down by countless horses' hooves, but Kate instantly saw the almost limitless possibilities it offered. How beautiful it would look with the green lawn neatly trimmed and tall, stately oaks edging a graceful, curving drive, paved with red bricks imported from the East. She could already hear in her mind the rough clatter of hooves and the groaning of carriage wheels as guests arrived from everywhere, even as far away as Cheyenne, to enjoy the splendid balls and barbecues. She would greet them at the door, dressed in velvet or satin, clinging daintily to Jason's strong arm. And they would all look down at her with smiles on their faces and say, "My, how lovely she is."

Now, stop that, Katie Devlin! she scolded herself sternly. You haven't come here as mistress of this house, that's for sure.

Or if she had indeed come as a mistress, it was not that kind. The task of the graceful lady greeting her guests at the front door was one that must be left to the woman who would one day become Jason Hamilton's wife. That was a role she could never aspire to play.

Kate stopped the horses beside the rough wooden fence that surrounded the house, and jumping down lightly, tied the reins securely to the top rail. Slipping the shawl from her bare shoulders, she began to make her way toward the massive front door, surprised at how calm and unfrightened she felt. Her heart was beating rapidly, that was true, but it was beating with excitement, not from nervousness. As she raised her hand to pound against the sturdy door, she tried to picture the look of surprise and indignation that would cross Jason's features when he threw it open and saw her standing there.

And yet, when he did open the door, she saw only surprise. There was no indignation, no anger, none of the righteous wrath she had expected. If anything, there was in his look— in that instant before he drew the veil back down over his eyes—a hint of pleasure, as if he were really glad to see her.

Why, this is going to be easier than I thought, she told herself exultantly. She knew better than to speak the words aloud, but the triumphant little smile she could not keep from her lips betrayed her, and his expression grew more guarded.

"Aren't you going to invite me in?" she teased gently. "After I've driven all this way to see you." She didn't wait for an answer, but glided past him, through the heavy doorway and into the narrow entry hall. He still offered no word of greeting, but he did not attempt to hold her back.

The hallway was surprisingly warm and homelike. Although the outside wall was the same cold, gray stone as the exterior, the inner walls were paneled with wood and draped with thick brown pelts that gave the small room a comfortable air. The wood floors were rough and unpolished, but they were covered almost completely with coarsely woven rugs of earth colors in strange geometric patterns that were unlike anything Kate had ever seen before.

She turned to tell Jason how much she liked his house, but the expression on his face stopped the words before they had a chance to leave her lips. Now that he had had a moment to get over his surprise, the look of anger she had expected to see was written boldly across his features. It seemed even colder and more forbidding than she remembered, and for an instant she was tempted to turn and run away.

"What did you come here for?" Jason's voice was rough and brash, but Kate detected a note of caution in it, too. He was just as wary of her as she was of him, she realized with surprise and amusement. She felt herself beginning to relax again.

He didn't fool her, not for a minute. He was doing just what Marc had said he would. He was trying to push her away, because he was afraid of her. Only, now that she knew about it, it wouldn't work anymore.

"I came to show you my new dress," she said, smiling slowly. "Red satin." She took a long, deep breath, holding on for just an instant before committing herself. "I figured if I came as a harlot, I should dress like one."

"My God, woman!" he exploded furiously. "Don't you ever learn? Surely you don't think I'm going to let you stay here?"

"What are you going to do about it?" she challenged. "Drag me out by the hair and carry me forcibly back to town?"

"And give you another hour or so to work your wiles on me? By heaven, no!" He grabbed a rawhide jacket from its peg on the wall and moved toward the door. "I'll get one of the men to take you back."

"I wouldn't do that," she cried out as he flung open the door. The sound of triumph was already ringing in her voice. She knew she had won. He would never be able to send her away. "If you do, I'll kick and scream and carry on something awful. And I'll cry," she threatened teasingly.

He turned slowly, to stare at her in amazement. "Do you seriously think your tears would have any effect on me?"

"Yes," she replied boldly. It wasn't true, of course. She didn't think the sight of feminine tears would have the least effect on his cool self-assurance, but it wouldn't do to let him see her doubts.

To her surprise, he did not scoff or even try to contradict her. If anything, the little lines she saw beginning to form around his eyes and mouth were expressions, not of anger, but of amusement. "You seem to have gained a lot of self-confidence," he said softly. "What happened to those sweet, demure, tearstained glances?"

"That was before I knew the truth," she told him boldly. "Before I knew you loved me."

His reaction was not angry, but guarded and cautious, as if she had somehow managed to put him on the defensive. "What gave you that idea, madam?" Icicles could have formed on his voice, but Kate refused to let herself be deceived by his coldness.

"Marc told me."

"He had no right to say that." Jason was still defensive, but to her amazement, he did not try to deny the charge. Kate watched his face closely, her eyes filled with wonder. She had hoped Marc was right—hoped she would be able to persuade Jason to accept her—but never in her wildest dreams had she thought it would be so simple.

"What a terrible host you are, Jason," she chided teasingly, sensing it was time to pull back for a moment. She didn't want to frighten him by pushing him into a corner too quickly. It was like going fishing with her father when she was a little girl, she thought. Don't pull the fish in too abruptly, he had warned her, or you might lose him. Give him a little line every now and then, play him along cagily until he grows tired and unwary. "Shouldn't you offer me a cup of tea? Or a glass of sherry?"

"I don't have any tea," he said briskly. His voice was still harsh, but it was a harshness that sounded habitual, as if the aloofness he had started with her weeks ago now continued under its own impetus, without any effort on his part. "I'll see if I can round up some sherry."

Yes, she decided, looking into his face for an instant before he turned and left the room. Those crinkly little lines around his eyes were definitely marks of amusement.

She was smiling to herself as she turned and made her way down a long hallway toward what she assumed was the parlor. Expecting another small, homey room, she was amazed to pass through a wide doorway and find herself suddenly in an area even larger than the grand hall of her own ancestral home. Her eyes glowed as she looked around, imagining the furniture removed and the floors polished until they gleamed brightly in the light of a thousand candles. Jason must have designed his house with a wife in mind, she thought, for it was the perfect spot for the grandest ball she could imagine.

It could use some changes, she told herself as she glanced around objectively, but it definitely had possibilities. The odd geometric rugs were all right in their place, she supposed, but there were far too many of them, and as for the massive pelts of thick brown fur that covered at least half the floor, they were far too heavy to walk on comfortably. And the decor . . . well, the decor was really dreadful. Too many pelts hanging on the walls, too many gray and tan paintings like the one she had seen in the hotel, and . . .

"My goodness," she gasped aloud, gaping in unconcealed astonishment at a large painting that hung just above the heavy stone fireplace at the end of the room. Unlike the paintings her chaperon had tried to keep her from seeing in Paris and in Florence, the unclothed body of the woman in the picture was neither ethereal nor graceful. She was, instead, crude and brash, painted in vivid colors and rough strokes, as she lounged seductively on a couch that was draped with a fabric Kate could only guess the unskillful artist had intended as satin.

So this was Jason's taste, this bold, gaudy painting of a harlot. No wonder she had failed to appeal to him. She had been too refined, too understated. Well, she would show him, she decided rebelliously. Firmly she forced herself to take a closer look at the crude picture, comparing the body of the painted harlot to her own with a cool, relentless objectivity.

Her hips curved more gracefully than those of the woman in the painting, she decided, and her waist was even slimmer. As for her breasts—she blushed as she looked up at the picture, seeing the ripe, firm breasts—well, her breasts were higher and firmer and even rounder, if that's what he wanted.

She was too engrossed to hear the sound of Jason's footsteps. Not until she felt his hand brush lightly against her arm did she realize he had joined her in the room, and she started guiltily, blushing at the immodesty of her own thoughts. He smiled knowingly—and not altogether kindly, she thought—as he handed her the sherry, properly served in a surprisingly delicate crystal glass. She noticed that his own glass, of a heavier, cruder variety, was filled with whiskey.

Kate took a seat on the large couch that faced the fireplace and daintily sipped at her drink, watching Jason step over to a box set against the wall and take out a heavy log. As he tossed it on the dying flames and reached in to stir the embers with an iron poker, the fire suddenly sprang to life again. Kate watched in fascination as bright yellow flames danced boldly upward and thousands of tiny sparks hissed and crackled, floating out into the room and up toward the ceiling for one single, brief second before their lights died out and they fell to earth again. The fire had an almost hypnotic effect on Kate, and for a few minutes she nearly forgot where she was and what she had come for.

"Well, how do you like my home?"

Startled, she turned toward the voice, then smiled as she realized how engrossed she had been in the fire. Jason had taken a seat in a high-backed chair that faced the couch, his drink clasped tightly in his hand. He was sprawled on the chair, with his long legs stretched casually in front of him, but Kate sensed neither relaxation nor ease in the coiled muscles of his body. There was a tension about him, as if he wanted to be ready to leap up at a moment's notice, and Kate was reminded again of the first time she had seen him at the railroad station. Even then he had looked to her like a panther poised to spring.

"It has possibilities," she told him, trying to match his cool, amused air. "But it needs some work."

His eyes moved pointedly toward the painting over the rough stone fireplace. "What would you change?"

She knew he was challenging her, and she was determined not to back down. "I'd change that for sure," she replied in what she hoped was a sophisticated, nonchalant tone. "It's coarse and cheap."

"It was a gift from a friend," he said calmly.

"Well, your friend has vulgar taste!"

To her surprise, he was not the least bit angry. Instead, he threw back his head and laughed. "Very vulgar," he agreed. "She likes red satin, too, but a brighter color, and with more appropriate decorations."

Kate felt her cheeks flame with embarrassment as she realized what he meant. That he consorted with prostitutes did not shock her, or even surprise her, for his was a rugged, masculine body with passions that would not go long unsatisfied. But that he could call such a woman his friend was an idea that was totally alien, and therefore frightening and unsettling, to her.

"Are you shocked?"

Damn the man! He was amused again. Furiously, Kate cast her eyes around the room, searching for something to change the subject. Catching sight of the heavy furs strewn across the floor, she quickly began to prattle on about them.

"And those silly furs have to go, too. Why, they're not even practical. How do you expect people to walk on them?"

"The furs are for warmth, Kate," he explained patiently. He was still smiling, but at least there was no more mockery in his voice. "So are the pelts that line the walls. The winters are bitter here, and they provide some insulation. Buffalo hide is thick and warm."

"Buffalo?" The minute he said the word, she remembered where she had seen that same thick, matted fur before. She cast her eyes down in confusion. She didn't like to think of Jason joining a greedy, ugly group like the one she had seen on the train.

"I didn't kill them, if that's what you're worried about." There was a sharp bite to his voice that startled her. Looking up, she saw that his face had grown hard with a deep, controlled anger. "As you saw yourself, it's hardly sport, and I could never use that much meat. I got all the skins I wanted—more than I could carry at one time—after one of the trains went by."

"I'm sorry," she said softly, fearing his anger was directed toward her. "I didn't mean—"

"I know that, Kate," he broke in quickly. He began to laugh again, but this time she sensed the laughter was directed at himself and not at her. "I don't know why I'm so defensive about it. Perhaps it's because the West is such a strange place. It will take you a long time to get used to it. I'm not sure I'm even used to it yet myself."

"I know," she agreed. "It's . . . well, it's downright bewildering. Every time I think I've got it figured out, something happens to surprise me. Like your house, for instance."

"My house?"

"It's not what I expected. I was looking for some gray wooden building, like the ones in town, only bigger. I never dreamed it would be . . . well, so imposing, like a medieval castle, you know."

"That's exactly what it is." There was a note of approval in his voice that surprised her. She wondered why he seemed so pleased with her observation. "It's like an old castle protected by high stone walls, and it was built for exactly the same reasons. The medieval world was not that different from the

West, you know. The need to find some security in the midst of violence was a dominant factor in both."

"Then it's a fortress," she said softly, remembering again with reluctance the words Marc had spoken about the ranchers hiding in their citadels. "Because of the sheepmen?"

"Oh, Kate, you're such a babe," he said impatiently. "Yes, of course, because of the sheepmen. There'll be a war over them soon, an ugly war, and anyone who hasn't taken care to protect himself will be destroyed, but that's only a part of it, a small part. There are Indians, too—"

"Indians?" She hadn't seen any Indians since she came to Jasper Springs. "I thought they were all wiped out, except for a handful of beggars, that is."

"You could say that," he replied with a bitter sarcasm. "But the few beggars that are left are sometimes willing to fight for their birthright."

"Birthright?" She could hardly believe her ears. "But they're only savages."

"For God's sake, Kate, look around you. Look at this rich, beautiful land. It all used to belong to them. The earth that we've taken, and the buffalo we've slaughtered. Once it was all theirs. What would you do if someone came along and took everything you owned? What would you do if they made treaties with you and broke them? If they gave you smaller and smaller parcels of land and then took even those away?"

She was silent. The picture he was painting for her was one that had never occurred to her. There didn't seem to be an answer to it, but he was insistent. He wasn't going to let her off so easily.

"What would you do, Kate?"

There was only one answer. "I'd fight!"

"With your green eyes flashing fire, you bet you would! And so do they. That's why I've made my house a fortress. That's why I have tall watchtowers and stone walls that can't be burned. Because of the range wars and the vengeful Indians and the marauding bandits. Because it's an ugly, violent world. Get out of it, Kate," he urged, his voice deep and compelling. "Go back home."

She shook her head slowly. "I haven't any home," she reminded him softly.

He gave her a long, compassionate look, and she felt her heart begin to beat in anticipation. She knew he desired her. She could see that in his eyes, and besides, he had already admitted as much to her. Now she had his sympathy, too. That was all she needed.

She took a slow sip of sherry, feeling its intoxicating warmth fill her mouth and slide down her throat. She was not used to drinking, and the warm glow that radiated through her body both surprised and relaxed her. Leaning back languidly against the cushions, she watched Jason through half-closed eyelids. He had turned to stare moodily into the fire, but she sensed his thoughts were still on her.

Very soon now it would happen, she thought with a flutter of expectation. Soon he would reach out and touch her bare arm gently, so gently she would not dream of protesting, and then the caresses would begin, the tender, romantic caresses that would drive her to such heights of ecstasy she could no longer resist his advances.

Why was he taking so long? she wondered impatiently, twisting the delicate crystal glass around and around in her fingers. She lifted it again to her lips, savoring the smooth amber liquid as it slid easily down her throat, warming her entire body. Why did it always have to be this way? Why did the woman have to sit and wait patiently for the man to make his move?

What if he doesn't come at all? she thought with a sudden surge of panic. What if she just sat and waited and waited and he never came? What if he was still too stubborn? Perhaps then she would have to go to him.

She looked across at Jason, still staring into the fire. If only he were sitting on the couch instead, it would have been so much easier. Then she could have slipped over slowly, inch by inch. Now it would be more difficult.

Still clutching the crystal glass in nervous fingers, she rose and began to move toward him. She was surprised at how light-headed and giddy she felt. Slowly she stepped over to him, but even when she stood directly before him, he continued to stare moodily into space, unaware of her nearness. Quietly, she sank to her knees beside him, raising her hand to lay it gently on his. As he turned to look down at her, she saw that his expression was neither angry nor surprised.

"Oh, Jason," she told him softly. "Don't shut me out."

"Kate, my beautiful Kate," he whispered, his voice hoarse with emotion. "If you only knew how much . . ." His voice trailed away as he clasped her hand tenderly in his for a moment. Then, leaning forward, he laid the other hand lightly on her hair, caressing it gently. "If you only knew."

The relief and exhilaration Kate felt at his words quickly

evaporated in a sudden wave of tenderness. She found herself longing to clasp this hard, strange man to her breast, offering him all the love and comfort she had to give. She felt his hand slip down from her hair, touching her shoulder lightly, and she yielded to the gentle pressure of his arm as he slowly eased her up until she stood beside him. Breathlessly she waited to feel him draw her toward the wide wooden stairway she knew must lead to the bedrooms upstairs.

"Finish your sherry like a good girl," he said softly. "Then I'll have Marc take you home."

"Home!" She took an instinctive step backward, gasping in surprise and frustration. She could hardly believe what she had heard. Her whole body reeled from the shock, and for an instant she was afraid she was going to faint. "But you can't do that," she whispered weakly. "Not after . . . well, you just can't."

"Can't I?"

"I won't let you," she cried out in desperation. "I won't go."

"I know." He smiled. "You'll kick and scream . . . and cry."

There it was again, that same infuriating mockery. Kate felt herself begin to boil with rage. "I will!"

"Go ahead. I'm sure your tears will move Marc to great depths of sympathy." Turning, he headed toward the doorway.

"No!" she cried out sharply, desperate to stop him before he could cross the threshold.

Startled by the violence of her outcry, he turned back for a second to face her. Kate knew she had to do something and do it quickly, or he would turn and leave her forever. Instinctively, she reached up and tore the net out of her hair, freeing thick red curls to cascade down to her waist.

"You can't let anyone come in and see me like this," she told him, tossing her head to make the mass of hair fall in disarray around her. "I'd be compromised. I'd never find a husband in this town then."

His expression was startled as he stared at her. She thought she caught a glimmer of amusement in his eyes, but there was a note of doubt in them, too. She knew she had him stopped for the moment, but that wasn't enough. She had to do something to hold him there. Awkwardly her fingers clutched at the back of her dress, trembling as they tried to undo the hooks that held it together.

She silently cursed the conventions that hemmed a woman

154

in with dozens of intricate fasteners, while a man could rip his clothes so easily from his body. Finally she felt the garment yield to her insistent fingers, and she slipped it slowly from her shoulders and down her arms, pausing at the last moment for an almost imperceptible second, frightened by the irrevocability of her act. Then, with one last shrug, she sent the dress floating to the floor. Jason stood silently on the other side of the room, his face a careful mask that voided all hint of emotion.

Now he would never be able to send for Marc, she thought triumphantly. Not while she stood there with nothing but a flimsy undergarment to cover her nakedness. Even Jason would be too much of a gentleman to do that to her.

But she had underestimated his determination.

"I suggest you put that back on, madam, and do what you can with your hair. You're right. It wouldn't do to be seen that way." Turning on his heel, he hurried from the room, his footsteps echoing on the hard wooden floor as he hurried down the hallway.

Kate was left alone in the center of the room, trembling with the anger of a thwarted child whose tantrums have accomplished nothing. He couldn't do that to her, she told herself furiously. She wouldn't let him! Let him go and get Marc if he wanted, but it wouldn't do any good. She was going to win in the end.

She lifted her fingers to touch the dainty bone buttons that fastened her chemise. It was a bold move, she knew, but it was the only one she could think of. Even if he brought Marc back into the rough, massive hall in which she stood, it wouldn't make any difference. Marc would only turn quickly and leave in embarrassment, unwilling to witness her shame. Then at last she would be alone with Jason, alone and eager to offer herself to him on the only terms he would accept.

She felt her eyes turning back toward the painting over the fireplace, the gift from a "friend," and for a moment she was tempted to pull on her dress again and cover her nakedness.

No, she told herself firmly. I can't do that. I can't let him get away from me.

She slipped the buttons easily through the buttonholes and let the light garment fall away from her body. The feel of the air against her naked flesh was icy cold.

As she heard the sound of footsteps approach, she felt her heartbeat quicken with excitement and fear. They were solitary footsteps. One man alone in the hallway. Only one man coming to join her. She closed her eyes, afraid to look up and see who that one man was. She heard the steps pause in the doorway, but still for one long moment she could not bring herself to open her eyes and face him.

When she could finally force her eyes to turn upward, the man she saw framed in the doorway was Jason. A rawhide jacket was stretched tightly over his broad shoulders, and he had a simple brown-and-tan blanket in his hands. His face was as guarded and expressionless as it had been before, but she knew she had won. The first traces of a welcoming smile began to form on her lips.

Jason stood perfectly still in the doorway, holding the muscles of his face in a tight, straight line as he stared at the pink-and-white softness of Kate's body. He was aware of a deep hunger that devoured him with an intensity he dared not show, even in his eyes. He dared not let her see the depths of his passion. There would be no controlling her then.

God, she was beautiful, he thought, so exquisitely perfect. Dark, fiery hair and smooth, milky skin. Suddenly he knew he wanted her more desperately than he had ever wanted any woman in his life. His arms ached with the urgent need to open themselves to her, clasping her warm, soft flesh ardently against his. His hands were greedy for the touch of a supple woman's body, his mouth burning to slake its seemingly unquenchable thirst in her sensuous red lips.

As he stood silently gazing at her, he struggled against the desperate craving that threatened to tear his body apart. It was all he could do to keep himself from taking the few long strides that would lead him to her, pulling her sensuous body down to the ground at his feet and devouring her ravenously with his love.

Only when he had managed to control the rebellious muscles that threatened to succumb to his passion did he allow himself to move toward her. With an abrupt movement, he shook out the blanket in his hands.

Kate felt the rough wool wrap itself around her naked skin almost before she was aware that he had even moved. "What are you doing?" she cried out in alarm.

"It's time someone taught you a lesson, you willful little bitch!" Bending down swiftly, he scooped her up and tossed her over his shoulder as easily as if she had been a twenty-pound sack of flour. She began to cry out in anger and indignation as she felt him carry her toward the door.

"Put me down!" she screamed. "Damn you, put me down. You can't do this to me!"

"Such language!" he scolded mockingly. "Why, my dear, if I didn't know better, I'd think you were no lady."

Kate stifled a cry of rage as she felt the hot, salt touch of tears stinging her eyes and pouring down her cheeks, until she could taste their bitterness in her mouth. How dare he say she was no lady? Why, he was nothing but an uncouth boor! She must have been insane to think she was in love with him. He was no better than an animal.

She felt the cold air bite into her cheeks as he carried her outside. With a furious burst of energy she struggled desperately to squirm out of his grasp. "Put me down," she cried again. "I can walk by myself."

He paid no more attention to her protests than he did to the icy wind that swirled around them as he hurried toward the wagon. She tried to pull her knee back to kick him savagely in the chest, but he was too strong for her, and she had to content herself with pounding futilely on his unyielding back.

As he dumped her unceremoniously in the back of the wagon, she twisted herself around quickly, rising to her knees so she would be on a level with him. Flailing out wildly with her arms, she aimed her clenched fists furiously at his head and chest, but she was so blinded by tears that she could not even see what she was doing. It only added to her humiliation when he laughed as he caught hold of her wrists to hold her steady.

"How dare you do this to me?" she sobbed. "Picking me up and carrying me out like . . . like a . . . like a sack of potatoes."

"Irish potatoes, my dear," he retorted, obviously more amused than angry at her outburst.

She felt herself reduced to impotent tears by the cruel scorn of his laughter, and she longed to fall to the floor of the wagon, sobbing in bitterness and frustration. Only the last traces of a fierce Irish pride she had inherited from her hot-tempered father saved her from that final pathetic humiliation. Pulling her hands back quickly, she forced herself to muster up whatever dignity was left her. Coldly she stared him directly in the eye.

"You son of a bitch!"

"Precisely, my dear," he agreed calmly. "Now that you realize that, I'm sure our little flirtation is over. Just be a good girl and stay put while I go back and get your clothes. I suggest you put them on during the ride back to town—unless, of course, you want to go back to the hotel dressed in a blanket."

Kate felt herself tremble with rage at the cool offhandedness of his mockery, but try as she would, she could think of no retort to call out after his retreating back. Nothing she could say would hurt him as he had hurt her—or even anger him.

What a fool she been to come there. What a fool to let him know how much she wanted him. Why did she let herself listen to Marc? "Jason loves you, Kate. He really does." What a crock of lies! Jason didn't love her. He didn't even want her all that much. She wasn't even worth the bother of being polite to for a single evening.

The bitter pain of humiliation flooded over her, and suddenly Kate knew it would be unbearable to have to face him again. She could not look into his mocking eyes one more time or listen to the sharp, cruel taunts of his tongue. It didn't matter how handsome he was, or how desperately she was attracted to him. All she wanted was to get away—to get away from him forever. She couldn't bear to see him again.

Impulsively she scrambled down from the wagon, clutching desperately at the blanket to keep it from falling away from her body as she hurried toward the rail where she had hitched the horses. Tugging at the reins, she pulled them free and jumped onto the high wooden bench. She was frantically eager to get away from there—to make her escape before he could come back—and she barely noticed, or even cared, when the blanket fell away from her, leaving her pale and naked flesh exposed to the bitter elements and the curious eyes of anyone who might have been attracted by her shouting.

The frisky horses, tired of being tied in place, responded to her urging with a speed she had not expected, and Kate had to grab onto the back of the seat to keep from sliding off. Not until she had regained her precarious balance and started the horses on their way down the road did she even notice the blanket that had fallen to the seat beneath her. Switching the reins to one hand, she began to pull it up, arranging it again around her shivering body.

The way down the hill was even more difficult than the way up, and Kate was nearly frantic at the slowness of their pace. No matter how desperately she urged the horses on, they could not seem to make good time. Stumbling on the steep incline, and weighted down by the unexpected pressure of the wagon as it relentlessly pushed them downward, the pair of dainty roans hesitated again and again. Kate found herself listening in an agony of fear for the sound of hoofbeats on the road behind her. How long would it take, she wondered, for Jason to saddle up a horse and follow after her? Or would he even try?

When she finally heard the sound she had been dreading, Kate was already at the bottom of the hill, and she began to cast her eyes around frantically, searching for someplace to hide. Even if she pressed the roans to a gallop, she knew there was no way she could outrun a single rider mounted on a swift horse. Her only hope was subterfuge. Why did the land have to be so flat and uncompromising? she asked herself as she looked around at the wide plains surrounding her. Why was there not so much as a nook or crevice to hide in? She would die if Jason caught her—if she had to see his icy, mocking eyes staring into her face again. She knew she would die.

There was only one chance. The moon was only a pale sliver of light in the intense blackness of the dark night sky. It offered barely enough light to see the road. Perhaps if she turned off now, cutting across the prairies, she would be far enough away before he passed. Perhaps then he would not see her. Even if she got lost, it would not matter. She could spend the night hiding on the dark plains, and in the morning, she would make her way back to town.

Impulsively she pulled the reins sharply to the left. The startled horses fought her for an instant as she tried to force them off the trail onto the dark, rough land that lay beyond it, but her will was too strong for them, and it took only a moment to turn them in the direction she had chosen.

The instant they were off the road, Kate felt the impact of deep ruts and sharp, heavy rocks that jolted the wagon and threatened to turn it on its side. Horrified, she realized she had made a mistake, yet she did not dare turn back. Mistake or not, it was her only chance. She had to take it.

Kate pressed the horses on faster and faster, pushing them against their instinctive caution, which urged them to move slowly. If only she could get far enough off the road, she told herself, then she would be all right. Then she could stop and wait for sunrise to guide her on her way.

Her terror began to communicate itself to the horses, and Kate found herself pulling harder and harder on the reins as the spirited pair began to race on in unrestrained abandon. Frightened, she knew she was beginning to lose control, but there was nothing she could do about it. All the pressure she could exert on the reins was not enough to stop their terrified flight, and she soon realized in a rush of horror that they had turned into a pair of runaways, each pulling the other along in a wild race of panic.

Kate felt the wagon jolt alarmingly back and forth as the horses swerved to avoid sharp rocks and treacherous prairie-dog holes, and it was all she could do to hang on to the back of the seat. She knew she had to try to hold her grip on the reins, had to somehow pull the horses back, but it was a task beyond her strength. All she could manage to do was cling desperately to the seat and pray they did not crash into anything.

Suddenly she felt the reins slip out from between her fingers. She made a mad grab at them, but even as she did, she knew it was no use. She knew she had lost her last chance to stop the wild flight that threatened to kill her—her and her horses both. In an agony of fear, she watched the reins slip away from her, until they fell useless into the pit of darkness that separated her from the horses.

All she could do then was hold on to the back of the bench, but she was bitterly aware that even that would accomplish little. It could be only a matter of minutes, or perhaps even seconds, before the horses stumbled, breaking the fragile bones of their legs in a prairie-dog hole, or the wagon crashed into a heavy rock and shattered into a thousand pieces.

When it finally happened, she did not even see what caused it, for whatever rock or crevice they crashed into was hidden by the heavy mantle of darkness that hung over the ground. She only heard the sickening crunch of wood as the invisible force crushed the side of the wagon, tearing away one of the wheels. She felt the wagon career dizzily, and in one last rush of desperation, she tried to sink her fingernails into the wood to maintain her hold, but it was no good, and she felt the dull ache of fear as she was flung with terrifying speed toward the ground.

For an instant, she was startled by the sound of a shrill scream that tore through the cold night air, but then she realized it was the sound of her own voice. She threw out her arms to try to break the impact of her fall, but it availed her little as she felt the rough, stony earth rise up to meet her.

A single flash of white, searing pain tore through her body. Then she felt nothing.

15

"KATE!"

She seemed to hear a voice calling out her name, calling from far away, but it was faint and unsure. She felt as if she were groping toward it, trying to press her way through a heavy fog that constantly swirled around her. The intense whiteness of its thick veil frightened her as it closed in tighter and tighter, until she thought for sure it must suffocate her. She didn't like the fog. She couldn't remember why, but she knew it made her afraid.

"Kate. Oh, my God, Kate!"

The voice grew more urgent, and suddenly Kate was aware of hands pressing her body, wrapping her tightly in a warm blanket, and pulling her up to clasp in strong, tender arms. She tried to speak, but the words would not come to her lips. It was as if she were far away in some dream world and had no control over the body that lay so still and lifeless on the ground.

The voice was still calling to her. She could hear it clearly now, but in her strange, white-misted dream, it was only a voice, disembodied and unreal as it floated on the cold night air. She wanted to see the face that went with it, but she couldn't seem to make her eyes focus. Everything was blurred and indistinct, almost as if she were blind to sight. Then, slowly, her mind began to clear, and she realized with surprise that her eyes were closed. Of course! That was why she couldn't see. Cautiously she let her lids flicker until they were open to the pale moonlight.

"Jason?" she whispered, surprised to see his face leaning over hers. At first, she could not figure out what he was doing there.

"Thank God, Kate," he cried, all pretense at mockery and coldness gone from his voice. "Thank God you're all right. Why did you run away from me like that?"

Run away? Had she run away? She looked at him, puzzled, trying to read in his eyes what he was trying to tell her, trying to remember what had happened. It came back slowly, one memory after another, and as the picture of herself standing before him in his house, naked and suppliant, flooded into her mind, she felt herself burn with shame.

"Take your hands off me!" she cried out hoarsely. Her sudden burst of anger startled him enough to release his hold on her. The instant she felt his hands leave her body, she struggled to her feet, clasping the blanket tightly around her. "How dare you touch me after what you've done to me?"

"What *I've* done to *you*?" he cried out, appalled. He felt all the fear and anguish that had been tormenting his body suddenly channel themselves into a wild burst of fury. As he stared at her in mounting rage, his piercing blue eyes flashed with anger.

"Just leave me alone," she shouted, the throbbing pain in her head adding fuel to the torment of her remembered humiliation. "I can get back by myself. I don't need you. I don't want you!"

"Be reasonable, Kate," he told her, making a visible effort to control his temper. "The horses have bolted God knows where with the wagon, and it's too dark to see five feet in front of you. I'd never have found you if I hadn't heard you scream."

"I don't care," she sobbed. "Just leave me alone." Turning, she began to run haphazardly across the dark plain, half-blinded by tears.

Jason was beside her in a few strides. Without further words he lifted her off her feet and carried her back the few yards to where his horse stood patiently waiting. She tried to fight him again, but quickly found she was too exhausted to offer more than a feeble protest as he lifted her up to the front of his saddle and mounted behind her.

The ride back up the hill was swift and sure. Kate felt the cold wind blowing in her hair, and she was acutely conscious of the warmth of Jason's body, hard and firm, beside her own. His arms were strong as they held her tightly against him, and she could feel the touch of his cheek against her hair. In spite of herself, even in spite of all the degradation she had suffered at his hands, she felt her body begin to swell with the same sweet yearning he always evoked in her.

I can't let that happen, she told herself furiously. I can't let it happen. I can't. But no matter how she forced the words to flow through her mind, she could not stop the yearning that filled her body, until she wanted to scream aloud in despair. All she could do was try to keep him from knowing it.

When they reached the top of the hill, he dismounted quickly, flipping the reins over the hitching rail before he lifted her down and began to stride purposefully up the walk.

"I'm not going to stay," she pouted angrily, but he paid no attention to her words. Still silent, he paused before the door only long enough to kick it open with his foot. At least he was carrying her in his arms, she thought gratefully, and not over his shoulders like an insignificant sack of potatoes.

With long strides he moved into the large hall, carrying her back to the same couch on which she had sat before, delicately sipping sherry from an elegant crystal glass.

"Let me go, Jason," she whispered hoarsely, suddenly frightened by the cold, hard lines that had formed in his face. "Please let me go."

As if in answer to her words, he leaned down and laid her on the couch. No sooner did she feel his arms leave her body than she jumped to her feet, dropping the blanket in her haste to scramble across the room toward the door. She didn't care. Nothing mattered anymore. She had to get out of that room and away from him. She had to get away before he found out he still had the power to enslave her body with the force of her own lust.

She was less than halfway across the room before she felt the strong grip of fingers on her wrist. "You little bitch!" he shouted furiously, pulling her arm until he had whirled her around. She tried to resist, but she was not strong enough, and soon she felt him hurl her back toward the same couch she had run from. The impetus of his force had propelled her nearly the full distance when she felt her feet twist under her as she stumbled on the thick buffalo rug. Crying out in frustration and anger, she fell in a tangled heap onto the matted fur. As she looked up, she saw Jason's face staring down at her, his eyes seething with a passion that terrified her.

"No, Jason," she whispered, more frightened than she had ever been in her life. "Please."

"Isn't this what you wanted?" he asked, his voice hoarse with emotion. "I was a fool to treat you like a lady when this is what you deserve."

She held her breath, terrified, as she saw his hands move down to undo his belt buckle.

"No, Jason," she begged again. "Not like this. Oh, not like this." This wasn't the way she had dreamed it would happen, the way she longed to see him come to her.

But his hands did not falter in their task, and the swelling

163

in his groin that stretched out the front of his trousers warned her he was not about to stop.

"You started this, sweetheart," he told her with a savage anger. "Time to finish what you've begun." He sank to his knees beside her, ripping open the front of his pants. She thrust her hands up desperately, trying to push him back, but she was not strong enough to stop the weight of his body as it crushed down on hers.

His mouth was hard and demanding on hers, devouring her without a thought or care for the tenderness she so desperately craved. He was like an animal, she thought, a beast that satisfies its own carnal appetite with a few moments of brutal, impersonal fornication. Where was the love she hungered for, the gentleness? She would not let him do this to her. With all her strength, she managed to push his shoulders away from her, and quickly she turned her head aside so she would not have to feel the rough, unwanted passion of his lips.

"Isn't this what you came here for?" he cried out hoarsely.

"No," she sobbed. "Not this, not this." Love, yes, and passion, but not this mindless, impersonal brutality.

"No?" he asked scornfully. "We'll see about that."

Pinning her arms down easily with one hand, he used the other to turn her face around so he could press his lips harshly on hers again. She tried to make herself pull away again, but even in the midst of her struggling, she felt her mouth begin to burn with passion, and her lips turned traitor, opening greedily beneath his to suck him ravenously into her mouth.

He felt the change in her body instantly, and knowing she would not try to run away again, he loosened the tight grip of his hand on her shoulders. Slipping his arms beneath her, he began to pull her body upward, pressing it strongly against his, making her feel as if her bones had sunk so deeply into his flesh that their bodies had suddenly been joined together.

Still she tried to resist him. Desperately she forced her legs to cling tightly together as she felt his knee cutting between them, trying to drive them apart to let his body invade the fortress she sought to protect. She was determined not to give in to the fire that had grown until it threatened to consume her whole body. She would not let herself be violated so brutally. She would not be taken like an animal in the dirt.

She fought him for as long as she could, but soon the sensual agony that reached every inch of her body became unendurable, and she felt her legs spreading apart eagerly, welcomingly. Her fingers clutched at the rough fabric of his shirt with frantic tension, seeking to cut through it, digging deeply into the flesh that lay beneath it, as she felt the source of all her pain and all her desire draw nearer and nearer to her body. When he finally entered her, she tried to cry out in protest, but she knew instinctively that any sound that left her lips would be one of joy.

She instantly forgot all attempts to stave off his lust as she felt the warmth of his body slide passionately into hers and move with a rhythm that matched the rhythm of her own fierce longing. All doubts, all fears were gone. Nothing mattered but the moment. Her body had mastery of her now, and it began to writhe in unison with his, raising the sweet torment that wracked her body to heights of pain and rapture she had never dreamed of.

"Oh, Jason, Jason," she cried out, mindless of the fact that only moments before she had pushed him roughly away from her. "Hold me closer."

The final moment of ecstasy tore at her body with a frenzy that seemed to pull it apart, and she clutched at him with the desperation of one who is about to fall from a high cliff. Slowly, the agonizing feeling of standing on the edge of a precipice began to leave her, and she felt the tension in her body gently ease away. A sudden flood of tenderness overwhelmed her, and she turned her face toward his, longing to kiss his lips with a sweet, lingering softness.

He did not respond to her gentleness, but pulled himself up quickly, fastening the front of his pants as he turned abruptly and walked over to the fireplace. He stood beside it for a moment in silence, his back turned toward her to shut her out.

Kate suddenly felt utterly lonely and bereft as she lay on the thick, matted fur that covered the floor. Tears began to well up in her eyes, but she fought them back, for she did not want him to see them. Once a fool, always a fool, she told herself bitterly. Why had she given herself to him so easily? He had told her he didn't love her, and he obviously meant it. Whether she was the seducer of his body or he the violator of hers made little difference. He still didn't care for her, and now that his lust was appeased, he no longer wanted to lie by her side. She began to rise slowly, determined to leave at once. Whatever little pride she had left would walk with her, back straight and head held high, out the door.

He sensed her movement and turned back toward her, hurrying to kneel beside her before she could rise. His eyes were clouded with pain, and there was a tenderness on his face Kate had never dreamed he could feel.

"I'm sorry, Kate," he whispered softly as he raised his hand and drew it lightly across her cheek. His fingertips were so gentle she could barely feel them.

"How could you?" She could no longer hold back the tears she had fought so valiantly. "How could you force yourself on me like that?"

"Isn't that what you were trying to do to me, my sweet?" he said, a light, amused laugh punctuating his words. "Didn't you come here to try to force your love on me?"

"But not unwillingly," she protested. "I knew you wanted me. That's why I came."

"And you didn't want me?" he prompted gently.

She was silent for a moment, her cheeks burning with embarrassment. It was true, in a way. She did want him. And yet . . . "Not like that," she whispered, so softly he could barely hear.

"I know, my darling," he said gently. "You wanted romance and tender promises . . . and you should have had them. Forgive me, Kate." He leaned forward to touch her lips lightly with his.

She laid her hand gently on his arm, feeling the rough texture of his heavy cotton shirt beneath her fingertips. For a long time they were silent, looking deeply into each other's eyes; then slowly she began to smile at him. How could she refuse to forgive him? How could she refuse him anything, when he was being so gentle and so good to her?

"And by God, you shall have it," he cried out impulsively. Rising abruptly, he scooped her up in strong arms and carried her swiftly toward the stairway—that same stairway she had dreamed he would lead her up, guiding her tenderly into one of the bedrooms that lay at its head. When he set her down again, it was on a wide bed covered with a gray fur throw that caressed her naked skin with sensuous luxury.

"You shall have all the tenderness you dreamed of, my love," he promised her. "And all the passion, too."

He sat in silence for a moment on the edge of the bed, not touching her with his hands, but giving her body long, lingering caresses with his eyes. After a while, his gaze lighted on the angry bruises that blemished the pale ivory of her skin, and his eyes grew troubled.

"I hurt you, Kate."

"It doesn't matter," she told him quickly. It didn't matter at all. Nothing mattered except the fact that he loved her . . . and that he was willing to accept her as his mistress.

"It does matter," he told her angrily. "God, what a brute I

can be sometimes." She saw in his eyes a haunted expression, a mingling of pain and grief that frightened her. She reached out her arms to pull him toward her, longing to offer him the comfort of her caresses. "No, Kate," he whispered gently. "Not now. Not yet." Taking her wrists gently in his fingers, he guided them down to the bed at her side. He let his hands lie lingeringly against her skin for a second, then pulled them away and rose slowly, walking toward the dresser at the side of the room.

When he turned back toward her, he saw that her eyes were bewildered and full of hurt. Too late, he realized she had taken his gesture as a rejection. He hurried over to the bed and sat at her side again.

"Now it's your turn, Kate," he whispered softly. "This will be for you. That . . . downstairs—that was for me."

"And for me," she told him, wanting him to know that she, too, had been driven to peaks of ecstasy by that tempestuous encounter, but he interrupted her with a soft laugh.

"I know that, my passionate little wench. Do you think I know so little about women that I couldn't tell that?" There was still laughter in his eyes as he continued, but his voice was serious. "I know I satisfied the hunger in your body, but not the hunger in your soul."

She lay still, looking up at him with eyes of love. How good he was, how sensitive, to understand the needs that still struggled, restless and unfulfilled, within her.

"Just lie there," he said quietly. For the first time, she noticed he had a small vial of dark-colored liquid in his fingers. He leaned forward, holding the bottle over the single candle that cast a flickering glow throughout the room.

"What are you doing?"

"Be patient, my sweet," he said softly, warming the liquid in the heat of the flame. "You'll find out soon enough." Finishing his task, he pulled the vial toward him and began to twist its stopper free. Then, impulsively, he glanced back at her, a look of mischief forming in his eyes. "It's a trick that was taught to me by a Spanish prostitute."

She caught the humor in his eyes and smiled. "Are you trying to shock me again, Jason?"

He smiled but did not answer as he poured out a measure of dark amber oil on his fingers. A heavy, earthy scent filled the room, the kind of smell Kate was sure a man would associate with lust and exotic Spanish prostitutes. Somehow, the thought made her nervous.

"Is that the same prostitute that gave you the painting?"

He looked at her with amusement. "Does that bother you?" he asked teasingly. "Her name is Carmelita, and she is a very lovely woman . . . and very understanding."

"Where is she now?"

"In Cheyenne."

Kate wished he would wipe away the look of amusement that lay on his face. It disconcerted her. She was careful to say nothing further about the exotic Carmelita, but she made a silent vow never to let Jason ride into Cheyenne without her.

He smiled down at her with an expression that showed, for the moment at least, more fondness than desire, and she realized instinctively that the time of teasing was over. She let herself relax into the deep pile of the fur that lay silky smooth against her skin. He reached toward her, the fragrant oil beginning to seep through his fingers, and laid his hands gently on her shoulders. Slowly, with infinite tenderness, he began to caress the warming oil into her skin.

"This isn't altogether authentic," he warned her. "I should put you in a hot tub and rub you all over first, until your body glows with the heat; then I should massage you, but I'm afraid I can't wait that long."

Wait for what? she wondered curiously. Surely, after what had happened downstairs, he had already quenched his lust. She tried to look down to see, but the heavy fur cover had bunched up, concealing the lower part of his body from her view.

His hands moved slowly over her naked skin, tenderly at first, then with compelling strength as he massaged her arms and shoulders, erasing every ounce of pain and tension. The rich aroma of the strange perfume floated up to the nostrils, its sensuous aura tantalizing her, while the warm oil made her body glow with pleasure.

"My God, how beautiful," he whispered, looking down at her with eyes filled with the agonizing thirst of a dying man staring at a desert mirage. "You don't know how long it's been . . . No, not 'how long.' Never. I've never seen skin like that, as smooth and pale as ivory. Or breasts so perfect."

His hands slipped down from her shoulders and began to caress her breasts, gently at first as he circled them carefully with his fingers, then with more and more insistence as his hands cupped the soft, warm flesh, pushing it upward until her nipples rose into the air, pressing up to meet his lips as they descended to hold her lightly, caressingly, in the soft, tantalizing suction of their passion.

She felt her body begin to cry out for him again, and she reached down with her hands, pressing her fingers into the thick golden curls of his hair as she drew his head tightly against her breast. Gently, almost before she was aware of it, his lips had left her breast and begun to move in a slow path down her belly, kissing her tenderly every inch of the way. Her body swelled with an aching hunger as she felt him coming closer and closer to the place she longed to feel him touch.

His hands moved slowly in front of his lips, guiding them on as a sort of vanguard of their tender invasion, and when finally she felt him touch her, she heard herself cry out in pleasure and in yearning. Gently he slipped to his knees beside the bed and pulled her slowly toward him, spreading her thighs apart until he could lay his head tenderly between them, his lips lovingly caressing the soft skin on the inside of her thighs. He moved so slowly that she was barely aware of the moment when his lips no longer touched her skin, but lay buried instead in the soft red curls between her legs. The gentleness vanished from his kisses, and they became more insistent, more passionate.

"What are you doing?" she cried out in alarm. It seemed to her that his mouth was in a place no man's mouth ought to be.

"Loving you," he replied, his voice choked with the harsh sound of desire.

"Is that what the Spanish prostitute taught you?" she asked, still horrified.

"With certain modifications," he agreed, laughing. "Now, hush, my love. Lie still. Trust me."

His hands continued to caress her thighs as he pressed his lips back against her body, pushing them with deliberate slowness ever lower and lower, until she felt the tender agony of his kiss on the center of all her desires. She wanted to protest again, to cry out for him to stop, but as she felt his tongue begin to touch the pulsating flesh of her body, lightly at first, cautiously, then with increasing boldness, she felt the passion of his act begin to pull her along in a flood of rapture she was powerless to control. Her body began to respond to him with a will of its own, and she was helpless to hold it back. There was no way she could keep from writhing with desire, even had she wanted to, and her legs, of their own accord, began to wrap themselves around his neck, pulling him tighter and tighter against her. She leaned back and closed her eyes, feeling the same sweet ecstasy flood over her body that had enveloped her before, until finally she lay exhausted and panting on the bed, the moisture of her sweat mingling with the sweet-smelling oil that poured off her skin.

When at last she opened her eyes, she saw that he had taken off his clothes and returned to sit naked beside her on the bed. Still feeling the glow of ecstasy, she reached up slowly to run her fingers lightly through the dark blond hair that lay in rough tangles on his chest.

He leaned forward slowly to touch his lips to hers again, first with an aching tenderness that took her breath away, then with a mounting passion that reminded her with haunting familiarity of the rapture just ended. When at last he released her lips, she looked down, seeing that he had grown hard and strong again with desire for her.

Tentatively she reached her hand toward him, knowing it was only fair to return the pleasure she had just received. She was angry with herself for the hesitancy she felt.

He laughed lightly, his eyes filled with good-natured teasing. "Surely, my love, you don't think I'm through with you yet."

"But . . ." What could he mean? After the heights of passion she had reached, what could be left for her?

"Beautiful Kate," he whispered. "Don't you know yet your body was made for rapture? Let me show you. Let me lead the way."

As he stretched his body next to hers and opened his arms to envelop her, she realized to her amazement that he was right. The same sweet pain began to renew itself within her, and she knew her body was preparing to receive him again.

"Oh, Jason," she breathed. "Is this what it's going to be like to be your mistress?"

"My mistress?" He pulled away from her sharply. She was dismayed to hear the harshness in his voice.

He did not intend her to be his mistress.

The cold brutality of it struck her like a hard blow in the pit of her stomach. It was all for nothing, then—this passion and this tenderness. All for a single night, and then he was going to abandon her again. She meant nothing to him after all, nothing at all.

He saw the pain that crossed her features, and he hastened to pull her tighter into his arms. "I told you I would never degrade you like that," he reminded her.

"But—" she protested.

"Not as my mistress, Kate," he told her with a firm tenderness. "Not as my mistress—as my wife."

His wife. She could hardly believe she had heard him right. His wife. The past and all its ugliness forgotten. Her heart swelled with gratitude and love.

He pulled her body against his again, his hands running with sweet strength down its length, and again she felt herself thrill to the excitement of his touch. Again she realized how right he had been. Her body *was* made for rapture, as was his. It was a rapture they would share together for the rest of their lives.

Part III

Storm Clouds Gather

16

WINTER ARRIVED EARLY, AND THE FIRST FLURRIES OF SNOW flakes were already swirling outside the small church where Kate and Jason exchanged their solemn vows. It was a quick, hurried affair, for the minister, who had ridden all the way from Cheyenne, still faced a long, hard race home against the ominous black clouds that hung low in the sky. As Kate turned to make her way back down the aisle with her new husband, she glanced at the small group of strangers huddled together in the front pews, surprised at the sudden pang of disappointment that jolted her serenity.

This wasn't how it should have been, she thought sadly. This wasn't the wedding she had always dreamed of.

There should have been a crowd of people, pressing the sides of the building nearly to bursting, and they should all have been friends, not these strangers whose features she barely recognized. And the church—Kate closed her eyes, visualizing the stately chapel in her family home, a grand room that epitomized all the dignity and majesty the New World would never contain. That's where she should have been, she and Jason, standing proud and tall before the rich-robed bishop as he intoned the long, elaborate ceremony that would bind them together for the rest of their lives. Not here in this shabby room, built with the crude, unskilled labor of local farmers and cowhands.

Until she felt the light touch of a hand on her waist, drawing her toward the warmth of her husband's body, Kate didn't even realize that she had nearly forgotten his presence in her preoccupation with childish daydreams. Glancing up guiltily, she saw that the deep blue eyes staring down at her were filled with solicitude. The instant she saw the love reflected in their depths, she felt all the doubt and disappointment slip away from her, vanishing like the first melting snowflakes that touched the earth. What a fool she had been to worry about elaborate ceremonies and ancient chapels.

What did they matter when she was married to the man she loved?

"I'm sorry, pretty wife," he whispered softly, and she knew he had seen the disappointment in her eyes. "It was too late in the season for a big wedding, and I didn't think you'd want to stay at the hotel until spring."

"Heavens, no!" She was horrified that he could even think of such a thing. She had been surprised enough to have to go back to the hotel at all. After the long, passionate night they spent together, she had expected to belong to Jason forever, but to her amazement, he had proved to have a deep conservative streak, so back to the hotel she had gone, to wait in chaste expectancy for the day of their wedding. "Two weeks was long enough, thank you!"

He laughed lightly at her response. "I'll make it up to you in the spring," he promised. "In the spring, we'll have the biggest, grandest party you ever saw. We'll invite everyone from miles around."

She wrinkled up her nose at the idea. She could just imagine all the rough frontier men and women trudging through her living room. Jason burst out laughing at the look on her face.

"We're not all as crude as you think, Kate. Some of us are remarkably refined and well-bred when we want to be."

"All the same, I'm not going to count on it," she told him coyly. "I'll let you make it up to me, all right. But not in the spring. Tonight."

Jason tightened the pressure of his arm around her waist. "A glass of sherry with friends first," he told her "And then . . ."

His smile was soft and light, but she could see that the look in his eyes was heavy with desire. She felt her body begin to tremble with anticipation.

The night that followed was even better than Kate had expected, and as the weeks passed, one quickly after the other, she basked in the rosy glow of perfect happiness. Even the thick blanket of snow that lay over the ground and drifted up until it nearly covered the windows, leaving her a virtual prisoner in the house, could not dampen her joy. This was the way life should be, she decided, and this was the way it was going to remain forever.

Kate was not even aware of the moment when at last she began to realize the days of perfect bliss were gone. At first she only smiled at it. The honeymoon was over, she told herself, imitating the words she had heard so often before. Now it was time to settle down to the hard job of making her marriage work, of building a solid relationship with this man whose body she had explored so eagerly, but whose heart and mind were still strangers to her.

At first, she was aware only of little things. A discontentment and restlessness within her own body that she vaguely attributed to the weather that isolated her inside the house. A moodiness and anger that seemed to be buried deep in Jason's heart—but couldn't that, too, be no more than a reflection of the dark, cold storms that cut them off from the world? Only as the weeks continued to pass and Jason's moods began to grow longer and blacker did Kate at last find herself wondering what manner of man this was she had married.

Nearly everything seemed to set him off—an ill-timed word or a chance happening, even a brief visit from a neighbor—and Kate was at a loss to know how to deal with him then. If only he would explode in anger, she knew how to handle that. Instead, he would seethe and simmer, somewhere deep inside himself, in some secret place she could not reach. How could she comfort him when she didn't even know what had angered or hurt him?

He lets it all simmer inside him with a horrible intensity, and he never lets it out.

Kate was to remember Marc's words often in those long, dark weeks as she watched whatever was inside Jason gnaw away at him until it almost seemed a miracle there was anything left of him. And still, it was all hidden away inside. Still she did not know what it was. In a frightening way, she realized, she did not even know who he was.

She was acutely aware of the position she had placed herself in, and she knew it was an odd and abnormal one. Back home, any man she married would have been a friend of long standing, perhaps even a childhood playmate. But here . . . here she had answered a stranger's advertisement in a newspaper, and after only the briefest acquaintance, she had become his wife. Now, long after the day of her wedding and the nights of shared physical love, she had to find a way to get to know this strange and moody man she had bound herself to for the rest of her life.

This strange and moody man. Wasn't that what Marc had said about him? *Jason is a strange man, Kate . . . with a dark rage inside him.* How strange? she found herself asking again and again. How dark? It was an answer she was to discover soon enough, and when she did, it made her tremble with fear.

It was a gray day, as cold and ugly as the days that had preceded it, and Kate had heard the sound of hoofbeats in the front yard with dread, for she knew it signaled the arrival of one of their neighbors. She admired these strong, stalwart men who cut their way through the snow, sometimes for days on end, to check on their herds and keep the lines of communication open with their neighbors, but Jason always greeted their coming with a grim set to his jaw that Kate quickly came to recognize and fear. When he opened the door and Kate saw Herman Rauss standing on the threshold, heavy clumps of snow matted on his hat and thick fur collar, she felt her heart sink. Jason always seemed to mind Rauss's visits most of all.

She found herself watching the closed study door nervously, dreading the moment it would open, dreading the dark look she knew she would see on Jason's face. When they finally came out, she forced herself to hurry over to them, anxious to acquit her hostess duties with good grace. She didn't want to give Jason an excuse to be angry with her when his temper was already so foul.

"Won't you stay to dinner?" she asked Rauss cordially. She didn't particularly like the tall, portly rancher, whose spread was, except for Jason's, the largest and most important in the area, but he was, after all, their neighbor. Besides, she knew that as long as he stayed, Jason would at least maintain a superficial veneer of courtesy.

"No, thank you, ma'am. I've a long ride before nightfall." Rauss buttoned the heavy fur-lined coat around him and headed for the door.

"Come again soon," Kate urged. She tossed her head coyly and smiled her gayest smile at him, trying to cover up the obvious insincerity in her voice. She didn't want their neighbor to know she didn't care if he never set foot in their home again.

Rauss smiled appreciatively and tipped his hat as he made his way outside. No sooner had he stepped across the threshold than Jason slammed the door behind him and whirled around to face her, the pupils of his deep blue eyes distended until they looked black with rage. Kate stumbled awkwardly backward, stunned by the naked rage she saw on his face. What on earth could she have done to make him so angry?

"Friendly, aren't you?" he snapped, his voice vibrating with controlled fury.

"Aren't I supposed to be?" she asked, puzzled and frightened.

"You don't have to toss your curls like a coquette. You're a married woman now, not a flirtatious hussy out looking for a husband . . . or a lover."

Kate could only gape at him in amazement. He was jealous! She could hardly believe it, but he was. The idea was so absurd that she began to giggle. Enraged by her laughter, he grabbed her by the wrist and pulled her toward him. "I won't have you whoring in my own house," he shouted furiously.

Eyes snapping, Kate pulled her hand out of his grasp and turned to walk away from him. What kind of a fool was he, anyway? Why, Herman Rauss was fifty years old at least, and fat, at that. How dare he treat her like that! Spinning around, she turned to face him again, her eyes as grim and hard as his.

"Well, you told me I had the soul of a harlot." She wasn't going to give him the satisfaction of arguing with him.

He looked surprised for an instant; then, to her amazement, he started to laugh. "What a talent you have for throwing my own words back at me," he told her. His voice sounded almost amused, but there was still a tenseness about it that warned her not to let down her guard. "The soul of a harlot, my love? Well, so you have . . . and I wouldn't have it any other way. I need a woman with passion. You convinced me of that. But I warn you, my love, that passion is only for one man."

He stepped over to her slowly and raised his hands, laying them lightly on her cheeks. There was no tenderness in the gesture. She could feel the tenseness that passed through his fingertips. "If you ever touch another man, Kate, I swear by all that's sacred, I'll kill you both."

Kate held her breath in terror as she looked into his eyes, frightened by the indescribably intense look she saw in their depths. Where had she seen that same look before, she wondered, that hard, frightening look? And then suddenly she remembered, and she felt her whole body go cold with horror.

It was the same look she had seen in her brother Eamon's eyes.

This is the face of a man who can kill. Why did those words keep pressing through her mind? Those were the words she had thought when she looked into her brother's eyes. They related to Eamon, only to Eamon. They had nothing to do with Jason.

Yet, even as she tried to convince herself, she knew it was not on Eamon that her thoughts dwelt.

But of course Jason was a man who could kill, she reminded herself with a surge of relief. Jason *had* killed. Jason was in the war. All men kill in the war. And after that, he was an Indian fighter. That was all there was to it. That was where the dark, brutal look in his eyes came from.

But he was not *really* a killer, not a man who could destroy another human life from greed or vengeance, or even from passion. The words he spoke now were an idle threat, an expression of a passing rage. He didn't really mean them. She knew he didn't.

And yet, as she continued to look into his eyes, she was not sure.

He saw the doubt in her eyes, and the fear, and it seemed to supply him with a grim satisfaction, as if it were a confirmation of the rage that was boiling up inside him. She trembled as she saw him looking down at her, the wild animal desire in his expression mingling with an anger that almost seemed to border on hatred. For an instant she thought he was going to push her away from him, but instead he slid his strong arms down around her back, crushing her against him with a violent force that threatened to crack her bones in pieces. With a gasp of horror she realized he intended to throw her on the ground again, all the fury and anguish of their first encounter intensified a hundredfold.

"No, Jason," she cried out, frantically trying to push him away.

"No, Jason?" he hissed furiously. "No, Jason? You're my wife. You can't say no to me now."

Angrily he pressed his fingers into the mass of red curls at the nape of her neck, grabbing a handful of hair and painfully pulling it downward, until he forced her face to turn up toward him. With a savage strength he thrust his mouth on hers, digging into her lips with a wild, hungry possessiveness. She tried to hold her mouth shut against the violence of his assault, but as she felt the pressure of his tongue and lips brutally attacking her tightly clenched teeth, she felt the same sweet pain rush through her body that always overwhelmed her whenever he touched her. Suddenly she was aware of a desperate craving to open her body to him, and her arms moved to enclose him, just as her mouth opened greedily under his.

She was conscious of a tremendous burst of anger that rose throughout her body, swelling with the very passion that seemed to have set every inch of her flesh on fire. How dare he treat her like that? Like a possession to be taken out and put away at will. How dare he press his savage advances on her in the hallway, threatening to drag her to the floor and pull up her skirt, entering her without ceremony, like the brutal beast he was. Yet, even as the anger rushed through her body, she felt it mingle with the lust his passion had aroused in her, strengthening and intensifying, until she realized, with a helpless despair, that her body was nothing more than a slave to his.

Ravenous for a culmination of the mad desire that surged through her body, she began to tug at him, trying frantically to pull him down to the ground. She felt her nails clawing into him with an agonizing frenzy. She wanted to hurt him, to punish him for the barbaric power that enslaved her, even as she wanted to heighten the passion that tensed every muscle in his body. To her surprise, she felt him resist her advances, tearing his body away from hers with a ruthless strength.

"Did you think I was going to throw you on the ground like a beast in the fields?" he shouted, doubly furious because he realized she had seen the brutality that was so inherent in his character.

She took a step backward, staring at him mutely in bewilderment. The scorching fires had not left her body, and she longed to throw her arms around him, but she was afraid. She did not know what he would do next to hurt her.

"Get upstairs," he told her sharply, the icy chill in his voice contrasting with the flames of lust that burned in his eyes. "Take off your clothes and get in bed—where you belong."

She felt the anger burn inside her again, and hot, furious retorts leaped to her tongue, but she knew she would not say them. She knew she would hold the humiliation inside her as she turned and walked up the steps, removing her clothes and slipping in between the cool sheets, to wait with rapidly beating heart and trembling thighs for him to come to her, quenching the burning thirst that consumed her body.

What gave him this power over her? she wondered. What manner of man was this who could still even her fiery temper with the promise of a few minutes or a few hours of savage lovemaking? What man could force on her humiliations she had never imagined, in exchange for a violently angry kiss, a bruising caress?

And yet, when he finally came to her, when at last he laid

his body beside hers to ease the pain that had grown nearly unbearable, he was as tender and gentle with her as he had ever been. Kate knew he had stayed downstairs on purpose, stilling the wild violence that racked his body, waiting to come to her until he could offer her the kind of love she needed. She knew it was his way of saying he was sorry, and she opened her arms to him eagerly, glad to accept a moment of truce with this strange, hot-blooded man who was now her husband.

Later, as she lay in his arms, her body still quivering with remembered pleasure, she tried to forget what had happened downstairs, but she couldn't keep his words from echoing in her mind.

If you ever touch another man . . . I'll kill you both.

But he didn't mean it, she kept telling herself. He was only angry. He didn't mean it.

She tried to keep the vision of his eyes from flooding into her memory, tried especially to forget the message she had read in their depths. But try as she would, she couldn't keep the image of their cold, cruel brightness from her thoughts. Who was this man, she wondered again, this man who was her husband? What was the darkness that lay buried in his heart?

In the days that followed, Kate was unusually quiet, and Jason, sensing her doubt and unhappiness, went out of his way to be good to her. She could see him making a special effort to control his moodiness and be cheerful in front of her, and she realized he was still trying to apologize for the wild burst of anger that had terrified her so cruelly, but no matter how hard she tried, she couldn't seem to respond to his geniality. She tried to tell herself she was just restless, that she was bored with the perpetually gray skies and the heavy snowdrifts that kept her confined to the house, but she couldn't quite convince herself. She felt as if she had been burdened with a continual mantle of depression that she would never be able to shrug from her shoulders.

Only when Jason came home early one surprisingly clear afternoon after a long, hard ride to town did Kate finally succeed in cutting through the veil of unhappiness that surrounded her. The curiosity she felt when she saw the huge box in his hand had no small part in the sudden metamorphosis.

"What on earth is it, Jason?" Kate cried, feeling excited for the first time in days as she opened the box and pulled out a heavy fur. "Good heavens, it looks like a whole buffalo."

"It very nearly is," he told her, laughing. "It isn't glamorous, I warn you, but it will keep you warm enough to go outside."

Outside! Kate's cheeks glowed with excitement as she heard the word. Perhaps she had been right, after all, she told herself joyfully. Perhaps it was only being cooped up in the house that caused her depression. Perhaps it was even making her imagine things in her husband's eyes that weren't there.

Kissing Jason excitedly in gratitude, Kate hastened to put on the long, heavy coat and foolish matching cap. He hadn't lied to her. They were far from fashionable, but even the fact that she could barely waddle like a duck as she hurried toward the door could not put a blight on her enthusiasm. She was going on an outing at last!

At first, the added weight of the coat made it hard to keep her balance on the frisky, prancing roan, but she quickly mastered the problem, and she and the spirited mare capered happily across the fields, kicking up the powdery snow until it flew in a fluffy white cloud around them. She leaned forward to pat the horse affectionately on the neck, calling out words of encouragement to her.

"That's it, Sunbeam," she cried gaily. "What a beauty you are."

Sunbeam had grown to be a great favorite since the day Jason had purchased her for Kate, nearly two weeks before their wedding. She was one of the pair Kate had driven madly across the fields the night of her wild escape from Jason's house, but she tried not to think of that now. She tried not to remember that there was another horse, too, as lovely and spirited as Sunbeam, a horse Jason had found the next morning when he searched the fields for them. He was lying on the ground, Jason said, his leg broken by a treacherous praire-dog hole. Sunbeam had stood by, quiet and sad, watching as he had to shoot her teammate.

It made Kate unhappy every time she thought of it, and she tried in little ways to make up to Sunbeam for the loneliness she was sure the pretty mare must feel. Never did she go out riding, or even just visit the stable, without a juicy carrot or sweet sugar lump in her pocket.

"What a pair you are," Jason called out, laughing lightly as he pulled up beside her. "That's why I bought her for you. Her hair's as red as yours."

"I thought it was because she's as spirited as I am," Kate shouted back, delighted to join in his laughter. She turned Sunbeam back on the trail, worn nearly clear of snow by the hooves of horses that had passed before them, and gave the little mare her head. As they flew lightly down the road, Kate felt the exhilaration of an icy wind that swept past her, nipping her nose and cheeks.

They continued down the trail, past the cutoff that led to town, and on into territory Kate had never seen before. Jason seemed to enjoy explaining things to her, pointing out landmarks and boundaries as they passed them. and for the first time Kate felt she was really becoming part of his life on the ranch. She started taking note of things, determined to prove later that she had been listening attentively. At first, it was hard to find intelligent questions to ask, and she had to force them out of her mouth, but soon she discovered to her delight that they were becoming easier and easier, growing naturally out of her interest. Jason was quick to sense the sincerity in her voice, and she was pleased to see him react to it with enthusiasm.

She was so engrossed with everything he was telling her that at first she didn't notice the small, fenced-in house that lay ahead of them down the road. When she did, she reined Sunbeam in abruptly, halting to stare at it in wonder.

"Why, Jason," she cried out in delight, "I didn't know we had neighbors so close."

When he didn't answer, she turned to look at his face, surprised at the troubled expression she saw there. Then slowly she turned back to look at the house again, and all of a sudden she realized what it was. She had never seen one before, but she had heard it described often enough. Instinct warned her now that was what it had to be. A sheepman's house.

She sat silently in the saddle for a moment, then nudged Sunbeam gently with her knee and began to trot after Jason, who had already continued slowly down the road. As she peered curiously into the little yard, she saw a couple standing in the doorway, the woman with a baby in her arms. It was a moment before she saw the other figure, a bulky man mounted on horseback, who had just come through the gate and was heading toward them.

It was Herman Rauss.

Kate felt her heart sink with despair. Why did they have to meet him then, of all days? Just when she and Jason were finally beginning to relax and enjoy each other's company. As the rancher drew closer, Kate saw that his face was nearly purple with rage.

"I offered the man a good price for his property," he

shouted hoarsely as he pulled up to them. "The damn fool wouldn't take it."

To Kate's surprise, Jason didn't try to quiet him. He usually refused to discuss anything serious in front of her, but today he seemed to have forgotten she was there.

"Where do you expect him to go?" he asked coolly.

"I don't give a damn," Rauss shouted furiously. He was so angry that he had completely forgotten his manners in front of Kate. "He can go to hell, for all I care."

Spurring his horse on, he began to tear wildly down the road. After he had gone about fifty yards, Kate was surprised to see him pull up abruptly, turning his horse around so swiftly that the startled beast reared up in protest.

"The time is coming, Jason," he warned, a blustering fury burning in his voice. "It's time to choose up sides."

Then, as swiftly as he had turned before, he whirled around again and began to gallop down the road, until all that was left of him was a little cloud of white in the distance. Bewildered, Kate turned back toward Jason, intending to ask him what Rauss meant, but the words died on her lips when she saw the expression on his face. He was staring fixedly at the small, dirty house, a hard, dead look in his eyes.

"I think the thing I mind most," he said slowly, "is the smell."

Kate sniffed the air and wrinkled up her nose in disgust. The cold wind had muted the odor, but it was there nevertheless.

"After a while, they get to smell like the animals."

"They must breed like them, too," she remarked caustically, looking with disgust at the woman in the doorway. "That woman's too old to have a baby."

Startled, he turned to face her. "Too old?" he asked. There was a faint catch in his voice that surprised her, though she couldn't understand what it meant. "She's the same age you are."

"Nineteen?" Kate was astonished for a minute; then she decided he must be teasing her.

"I didn't mean twenty-six," he replied with a wry smile. Before she could answer, he turned and spurred his horse down the road. Kate hurried after him in silence, her mind still dwelling on the terrible image of the sheepman's shanty throughout the long ride home. All she could think of was the woman she had seen, the tired, middle-aged woman who, incredibly, was no older than she herself. She could hardly force herself to believe it, and yet she knew it had to be true. She knew Jason wasn't lying to her. Could that be what poverty did to a person—poverty and drudgery? Make them into old hags before their time?

She was shivering with more than the cold when they passed over the last hill and headed gratefully for home. As Sunbeam sensed the nearness of the warm stable and fresh hay, she began to hurry her pace, and Kate, feeling the need of home as deeply as her mount, encouraged her on. They had already climbed to the top of the high hill when she saw Jason stop abruptly and stare out over the cliff, fixing his eyes on a point far in the distance. Kate pulled up beside him, turning to follow the direction of his gaze. Slowly, as her eyes scanned the distant hills, she began to pinpoint a long line snaking its way along the horizon. After a moment, she realized that the little black dots in the distance were people—a long line of people. Some of them were on horseback, but most were on foot, trudging their way wearily across the terrain.

"What on earth?" she asked, puzzled.

"Indians," Jason replied tersely.

"Indians?" She began to cry out in fright, but something in the hard, taut lines of Jason's face held her back. Slowly, almost hypnotically, she turned again to face the enemy, so far in the distance and yet so terrifyingly near. These were not like the straggling bands of captives she had seen in the railway stations. These were the real thing. These were the killers and marauders who had terrorized the West.

In her fear, her hand tightened on the reins, jerking them toward her in a movement that startled Sunbeam, making the frisky mare rear up in protest. Jason glanced over at the commotion, his face an angry mask of contempt.

"You don't have to worry," he said bitterly, his voice filled with a sarcasm Kate had not heard since the days before their marriage. "They won't hurt you. That's Gray Cloud and his people going south until spring, though God knows what they'll find there. There are no braves with them, just the old men, the women, and the children. The braves are . . ." He broke off abruptly, staring intently into her face for a long time. When he finally spoke again, his voice was softer. "The braves are somewhere else."

He did not speak again as they guided the horses around the house and toward the stable. Even Sunbeam seemed to have caught the somber mood, and did not try to prance or hurry as she headed for the warmth of her stall and blanket.

Jason was going to be in a vile mood again, Kate thought bitterly, biting her lip to hold back tears of disappointment. How unfair it seemed, how desperately unfair. Just when they seemed to be getting along so well.

Jason's silence hung in the air like a heavy pall, and it was a relief to get to the stable at last and find a group of friendly cowhands gathered to finish their chores. As Kate rode in on Sunbeam, they took a break from their work to call out cheerful words of greeting. They all admired their boss's spirited young wife, and today they took a special delight in seeing the bright pink roses that graced her cheeks after the weeks of gray depression that seemed to be hanging over her. One of the hands, younger and more enthusiastic than the rest, hurried over to help her from her horse.

"Thanks, Tommy," she said gratefully. She hadn't realized how hard it would be to climb down from the saddle with the heavy buffalo coat.

"How was it, ma'am?" He grinned.

"Lovely," she lied. How she wished she could have said that word sincerely. It *was* lovely for a little while—before the sheepmen and the long line of Indians spoiled it.

She noticed that Tommy held her hand a brief second longer than necessary as she dismounted, and the glowing appreciation in his eyes made her smile. She knew she should discourage the gesture, but it had been so long since she had enjoyed the admiring glances of young beaux that she let her hand linger in his a moment longer than she should have. Then, belatedly remembering Jason's jealousy, she hurriedly pulled it back. She was too late. Jason had already noticed the gesture.

"Pick up your pay and get out of here," he told the astounded young cowboy, his eyes laden with an almost murderous hate.

"Jason!" Kate cried out, astonished at his behavior. She had known he was jealous, but this was absurd.

"Pick up your pay and leave," he repeated. Such was the force of his anger that young Tommy did not even attempt to argue, but turned slowly and moved out through the doorway. The other cowhands shuffled their feet awkwardly for a moment, their eyes cast in embarrassment on the hay that coated the floor; then they too began to file out slowly. No one dared to speak or protest.

Kate watched them leave with a look of amazement on her features. "Jason, that's ridiculous," she protested furiously. "He's only a boy. He reminds me of my little brother."

"He wasn't looking at you like a boy." Jason's voice was icier than the chill air that poured through the open doorway as he turned away from her and began to hurry across the snow-covered path that led to the house.

"But where will he go?" Kate cried out, rushing to the door to shout after him. "It's winter. He'll never get another job now."

"Oh, I'll find another place for him," Jason called out over his shoulder. "I'm not as vindictive as all that. But he won't stay here. I won't have any man looking at you like that."

Kate's eyes followed him with dismay as he rounded the corner of the house, but she did not dare protest again. She stayed in the stable for a long time, talking softly to Sunbeam as the pretty mare nuzzled her affectionately on the shoulder, expecting more sugar cubes at any moment. As the late-afternoon shadows darkened in the doorway, Kate tried again to understand the dark, moody man she had married. Finally, when the sun began to go down and the air in the stable grew too cold, she made her way across the yard and toward the house.

"What am I to do with him?" she asked Marc that night as he lingered in the hallway for a moment after joining them for dinner. She tried to make her voice light, as if she were joking, but he saw the seriousness in her eyes.

"Be patient, Kate," he advised her. "Just be patient."

He held her hand comfortingly in his, and she held onto him tightly, needing to feel the understanding concern of another human being. Then, fearing Jason would come into the hallway and see them, growing jealous even of Marc, his oldest and most trusted friend, she pulled her hand slowly away from his.

In the coming days, she tried to heed Marc's advice, but patience was a quality she had practiced little, and Jason's indefinable moods were something that both frightened and angered her, almost beyond description. At first, he seemed to be sorry for his harshness on the day he had fired the hapless Tommy, and he went out of his way to be especially gentle with her, but soon, as the neighboring ranchers dropped in at odd hours and the Indians continued to wend their way through the hills, the black moods began again, worse than ever. Finally, it seemed to Kate that she could bear it no longer.

"The time has come to choose up sides."

Kate heard the words again and again from different lips in those troubled days, as, one after another, the other ranchers filed through their house and tramped out of the heavy doorway into the snow.

"The time has come to choose up sides."

Kate stood huddled in a shadowy corner where she knew the men could not see her as she listened to the dreaded words, this time on the lips of Herman Rauss.

"Gilkennen will be here in a few days, and Eidel soon after. The rest may not get here until spring, but they'll be here. The time is coming."

Standing alone in the shadows, Kate felt as if she could not listen to the words even one more time. What time was coming? What was it that she feared with a tightening of her throat every time she heard the words, even though she did not know what they meant? It was unbearable torture, she thought, this waiting for something—some indefinable thing—to happen. Better to know what it was, no matter how terrible it might be. Nothing was as frightening as the unknown.

"What does he mean, Jason?" she cried, as soon as the door had shut behind their visitor. "What time is coming?"

He seemed surprised to see her standing there. "Nothing, my sweet," he told her quickly, making an effort to fight off the anger that was etched on his brow. "Just man talk. It wouldn't interest you."

"Why wouldn't it?" she challenged. "Jason, I'm not a fool. I can see something is wrong. Please tell me what it is."

"You're imagining things, Kate." His voice was brittle for a moment; then he managed to fight off the harshness and put an arm gently around her waist, leading her back toward the living room. "It's being cooped up here that does it. Listen, love, I know it's hard for you, but I'll make it up to you soon. In the spring. Then we'll go into Cheyenne, and you can go shopping . . . and I'll give you that party I promised."

"Don't treat me like a child, Jason," she protested, pulling away from him angrily. "I'm your wife. Whatever the problem is, I want to share it with you. I want to help you."

"Oh, Kate," he began wearily, his voice heavy and tired, as though the strain of trying to deal with her at that moment was too much for him. Then, suddenly, without warning, he put his arms around her, drawing her toward him, until she could feel the hard strength of his body against hers. "There's only one way you can help me, pretty wife," he whispered huskily, leaning his head down until his lips nearly touched hers. "Shall I tell you what it is?"

She started to protest, but sensing it was a moment not for words but for unquestioning love, she pressed her lips up to meet his, enjoying the unexpected tenderness of his caress. Gently, almost as though she were a fragile china doll, he reached down to lift her in his arms, carrying her up the broad staircase with the same sweet passion that had marked their first night of love. Soon all thoughts of ranchers and Indians and black, brooding moods evaporated in sweet, furious rapture that transported them beyond the cares and fears of their lives.

But Kate did not sleep that night. Sweet as their lovemaking had been, it could not make her long forget.

The time has come.

What time? What time?

It was to be weeks before she found out, and then the knowledge seeped into her consciousness only piece by piece. Even when she saw the first man, she did not understand.

His name was Roy Hockam, and he had ridden in from Abilene. Jason had sent for him, he said, but Kate couldn't figure out why. Why would Jason take on a new hand in the middle of winter? She didn't like the look of this Hockam. He had an ugly, menacing air about him, but she didn't ask Jason who he was or why he had come. She had a terrible feeling she didn't want to know.

The next man came nearly a week later, from Dodge City, he said, and soon men began to arrive from all over, men from Ellsworth and Newton, men from places with strange-sounding names like Wichita and Ogallala. Soon there were over a dozen of them, and Jason set aside a separate part of the bunkhouse for their use. Kate noticed that the other men did not talk to them or associate with them, but left the newcomers to form their own tight little group. Still she did not ask who they were.

But then one day Earl Smead arrived. As Kate stood in the doorway looking out, she saw a tall, incredibly ugly man, slouched in the saddle, yet still bold and arrogant. An angry red scar ran down the side of his face, from his right eye to the corner of his mouth. He did not say a word other than to speak his name, but Kate knew even without being told that this man was the leader of the group. There was an air of power about him, and of strength—just as there was an air of evil.

"Howdy, ma'am," he said, tipping his hat as he spotted her standing in the doorway. He made even the polite greeting sound like an impertinent insult. "Mighty nice to see a purty woman hereabouts."

"Get inside, Kate," Jason said roughly. Kate hastened to close the door, but even as she did so, she heard Jason's next words to the stranger. "Your place is in the bunkhouse. I don't want to see you near the main house, and I don't want you near my wife."

Kate could have sworn she heard the sound of a bold chuckle, but the closing door obscured it, and she could not be sure. Leaning back against the door, she was surprised to find herself trembling at the memory of the man's words and the bold leer that crossed his ugly, scarred face as he gaped at her. Finally, all the questions she had been holding back so long surged into her mind, and she found to her surprise that the answer had been there all the time, staring her in the face, if only she had had the courage to look at it.

They were gunfighters, she thought, surprised at how dispassionately she could form the dreaded words in her mind. They were professional killers, and Earl Smead was to be their leader. That was what Rauss had meant.

Time to choose up sides, Jason.

Time to choose up sides in the range war that was coming. Time to prepare to slaughter the sheepmen and drive them from the land. Kate closed her eyes, but the picture of a tired, haggard nineteen-year-old girl rushed unbidden to her mind, and she opened them quickly to chase the unwelcome vision away.

She wouldn't think about it, she told herself. Jason was right. It was men's business, and no concern of hers. She wouldn't think about it. If she did, she couldn't bear it.

17

As THE BITTER WINDS INCREASED AND THE SNOWDRIFTS THAT assaulted the sides of the house heightened, Kate began to grow more and more on edge. It was the worst winter he had ever seen, Jason claimed, and the cruel snows and subzero temperatures contrived to keep them prisoners in their own house, making even an occasional trip to the stable or storehouse a major ordeal. Kate watched the ugly black clouds that perpetually gathered in the gray skies with a smoldering anger in her heart. It wasn't fair, she told herself bitterly. Everything seemed to conspire to drive a wedge between her and Jason, even the weather.

Yet, as the days passed, the stormy clouds and high drifts that had seemed so menacing to Kate slowly began to have just the opposite effect. It was as if the wild winds that raged outside somehow had the power to draw away the storms that existed inside, in their hearts, and suddenly Kate found a quiet lull in her life, a long stretch of days that extended into weeks, offering a new and welcome sense of security.

The deep snows that held them inside also offered protection against the violent world that existed around them. Now, the neighboring ranchers could no longer plow their way through impassable roads to come and darken Jason's mood, and even the gunfighters stayed close to the bunkhouse, sparing Kate the occasional glimpses that reminded her of their presence. Except for Marc and a few of the older cowhands who occasionally came to the house for a few minutes, they saw no one at all, and Kate sometimes had the illusion that she and Jason were all alone in the world. It was as if the snow that had wrapped itself around the house had sealed them in with the pleasant warmth of the fireplace and the rapture of long, idle afternoons to lie in each other's arms.

Kate enjoyed the unexpectedly gentle domesticity of those quiet days, enjoyed especially sitting before the fire, watching Jason sprawled out on the floor in front of her as he repaired a bridle or polished the leather of a saddle. It gave her a feeling of closeness to look down at the scowl of concentration that lay unawares across his features and to listen to the bright, snapping sounds of the crackling flames in the great stone fireplace.

"How fiercely you're glaring at that saddle," she told him one slow, lazy afternoon. Her voice was filled with light, happy laughter. He looked up at her quickly, pleased to see the contentment on her face. As he matched her smile with his own, she began to wonder if she could persuade him to lay down his work and take up a lighter, more frivolous task with his hands.

Suddenly, without warning, she heard the sound of hurried footsteps in the hall, and a voice called out Jason's name. He had barely answered when Marc appeared in the doorway, his face drawn and tense. Kate had never seen him enter the house so abruptly. He had not even taken time to scrape the snow from his boots, and already it was melting into little puddles at his feet.

Jason, too, noticed his unexpected haste. He had half-risen to his feet before Marc could even speak.

"Gray Cloud."

Though Marc spoke no other words, they were enough to spur Jason hastily into the hallway. Alarmed, Kate rose quickly to follow him, but he and Marc had both vanished before she could even reach the hall. She hesitated only an instant before she grabbed up a heavy woolen shawl from the peg by the doorway and hurried outside after them.

The icy wind stung Kate's nose and fingers, and her breath formed a white cloud of condensation in the air, but she paid little heed to the cold as she plowed through the heavy snow, picking her way through their footprints. What did it mean, she wondered, trying to hold down the fear that kept rising in her heart. What did Marc mean when he said "Gray Cloud"? Surely he couldn't mean Gray Cloud was there. It wasn't spring yet, nowhere near it, and Jason had told her the Indians wouldn't be back until spring.

Yet, as she reached Jason's side and followed his gaze down into the broad valley that lay at the foot of the cliff, she saw that her fears had indeed been well-founded. Gray Cloud was there, Gray Cloud and all his people, their tepees pitched at the foot of the cliff like the camp of some invading army stationed at the base of a beleaguered castle.

"Oh, my God," she cried, her heart throbbing violently with sudden terror. "Jason, what are we going to do?"

Jason turned to look at her in surprise, as if he had not expected to see her there. "For Christ's sake, Kate, that's Gray Cloud," he told her impatiently. "I told you he had no warriors with him."

"But it's winter," she protested. "You said they'd stay south till spring."

"I know," he replied slowly. His voice was cold and unemotional, but there was a faraway, troubled look on his face.

"Why do you suppose they've come back?" Marc asked, putting into words the question Kate was afraid to ask. "This is a cold, bitter winter. They'll die here."

"Things must have been bad down south," Jason said calmly. He was careful to keep all feeling out of his voice, but there was a wild, haunted look in his eyes. Kate watched his face with sinking heart, knowing the dark mood she had awaited with such dread during the past few weeks had finally returned. Even Marc seemed to sense the change in Jason, and was silent, as if he were reluctant to intrude on his thoughts.

Finally, it was Jason who broke the long, moody silence. "Saddle my horse," he shouted, spinning around to face the small group of cowhands who had gathered silently on the lawn. Two of the men hurried off to do his bidding.

"You aren't going down there?" Kate cried out, her voice quivering with sudden terror. "Not among those savages. They'll kill you."

Annoyed, Jason glared down at her, his lips half-opened to snap out an angry retort. Then, as if he thought better of it, he closed them again, staring down at her for a long time as he carefully assessed her features. Kate was terrified by the hard expression she saw in his eyes, but she did not dare look away. Finally, it was Jason who turned away from her.

"Get Mrs. Hamilton's coat," he shouted to one of the hands.

Kate felt her heart thump wildly in terror. Surely he didn't mean to force her to go down there with him. Surely he wouldn't put her in that kind of danger.

But of course he wouldn't, she thought suddenly, a flood of relief passing through her tense body. If he meant to do that, he'd have had them saddle Sunbeam. He was only worried about her standing in the cold. That was all. He was just worried about her.

But as she wrapped the coat around her cold, trembling body and watched them bring out Midnight, Jason's magnificent black stallion, she was not so sure. There was a harsh, stern look on Jason's face, one that she had seen before and that she knew from experience spelled trouble for her. She watched, barely daring to breathe, as he took the reins from the ranch hand and swung easily into the saddle. Turning slowly, he looked down at her.

"Get up behind me, Kate."

"Oh, no, Jason," she pleaded, terrified. It was as if all her worst nightmares were coming true.

"For God's sake, Jason," she heard Marc protest. "That's no place for a woman."

Jason's strong features were adamant. "This is something she has to see."

For a moment, Kate thought Marc was going to protest again, but he backed down from the force of Jason's determination, and it was only seconds before she felt his strong arms lift her firmly onto the tall black horse behind her husband. Still terrified, she buried her face in the thin fabric of the shirt that offered Jason his only protection against the bitter elements.

"Come down if you want to," she heard Jason's commanding voice call out to the men. "But leave your guns behind."

Leave their guns behind? Startled, she glanced down and saw that Jason, too, was without the gunbelt he always wore outside the house. How could he be so foolhardy? Whoever heard of riding into the midst of a pack of savages unarmed?

She pressed her face again into the back of his shirt, trying to shield herself from the horror that was gathering all around her. Tears of fright stung her eyes and turned to ice on her lashes as she felt the surefooted horse carefully pick his way down the slippery road. Even when they came to the bottom of the hill and hands reached out to help her dismount, Kate kept her eyes determinedly fixed on the ground. Whatever violence was coming her way, she did not want to have to see it.

Finally, after she had stood alone for several minutes in the deep snow that came halfway to her knees, waiting with tautly held breath for a blow that did not come, she felt her tense body begin to relax a little. Slowly, she started to grow angry with herself. What was the matter with her, anyway? She had never been timid before. Why on earth was she acting like a frightened little bunny rabbit? With quiet determination she forced herself to raise her eyes.

To her amazement, she saw, not the massive tribe of bold, strong Indians she had expected, but only a small flock of tired, dejected-looking people. Their faces were turned toward her, but there was no curiosity in the dark eyes that stared, blank and unseeing, in her direction. Kate had the eerie feeling that she was looking at people who were dead and had merely been frozen into position. To her surprise, there were no more than forty or fifty of them at most.

"Why, there are only a few," she gasped. "I thought there were more." She had been certain there were two or three hundred at least when she watched them winding their way slowly across the hills only a few weeks ago.

"There were more," Jason said quietly. His eyes were fixed on her face, as if he were trying to find something there. Kate couldn't figure out what it was.

"But where are the rest?"

"That's all that's left."

"What. . . ?" she began, then broke off quickly. What do you mean? she had started to say, but even before the question was out of her mouth, she realized she did not want to hear the answer.

Things must have been bad down south.

Jason's words echoed ominously in Kate's ears, and she realized with horror that she had discovered their meaning. Slowly she turned around, her eyes taking in the scene with uncompromising objectivity. Jason had been right, she admitted to herself. There were no warriors here. Except for the women, there were only the very old and the very young, the sick and the feeble. Some of them were wrapped in blankets, while others were clad in a motley assortment of jackets and coats, but all were inadequately clothed for the bitter, often subzero temperatures and icy winds that swept across the plains.

Suddenly Kate understood the cold, blank expression she saw in their eyes. It was the look of a people who had endured too much, who had passed beyond the breaking point, their bodies empty shells that plodded on from habit rather than motivation. It was the same look she had seen in the eyes of the nineteen-year-old sheepman's wife. It was the look of the living dead.

Shivering, she wrapped her coat tighter around her, as if the warmth of the fur could somehow protect them as well. No wonder there were only a few left, she thought bitterly. It was a miracle that even a handful had survived.

"Jason."

The sudden sharp note of warning in Marc's voice drew Kate's eyes toward him. Surprised at the hard tension she saw in his face, she turned nervously to follow his gaze. As her eyes moved toward the edge of the camp, she felt herself gasp in fear. There on the outskirts, mounted on scraggly, half-starved horses, was a small band of warriors.

There were no more than six or eight of them, but the cruel bitterness that had etched deep lines of pain into their faces gave them a look that was both terrifying and compelling, and Kate instantly sensed that they were a group to be reckoned with. Their rifles lay casually across the fronts of their saddles, but she noticed that their hands were poised on top of them with a lightness that belied the tenseness in the muscles of their arms. Instinct warned her that they were ready on a second's notice to sling their guns to their shoulders and fire.

Jason did not seem concerned. "John Little Wolf," he said quietly.

Slowly, with no abrupt or hasty movements, he began to

walk toward the little group. Terrified, Kate felt herself backing away from them, pressing the thick snow aside with her heavy boots.

"Injun-lover," a voice hissed in her ear.

Spinning around so abruptly that she made a cloud of snow swirl from her feet, Kate found herself staring at the unwelcome figure of Earl Smead. She saw that his eyes were fixed on Jason, and his thin, cruel lips twisted up in a scornful sneer.

"You keep a civil tongue in your head," she warned him furiously. The man was, after all, nothing better than a servant. How dare he criticize Jason? It *did* look like her husband was a friend to those savages, and while Kate didn't like it much better than Smead, she wasn't going to allow him to insult her husband.

"Reg'lar little spitfire, ain't ya?" he said, leering. To Kate's disgust, his eyes passed boldly up and down the length of her body. Angrily she pulled her coat tightly shut to protect herself from the obscenity of his gaze. She opened her mouth to reprimand him sharply for his impertinence, then stopped in amazement when she saw that his hand was resting lightly on his gun. How dare he disobey Jason and bring his gun down to the field? Livid with rage, she turned back toward the band of warriors, intending to call out to her husband and warn him of Smead's treachery.

The instant she whirled around, she saw that Jason needed no warning. He had already seen Smead's weapon, and he stood facing the gunfighter warily, a look of black anger on his features.

"Keep your hands off your gun, Smead."

"Who's gonna make me, big man?" the hired killer sneered. "You?"

Terrified, Kate watched as the two men faced each other boldly. Why on earth had Jason been foolish enough to leave his gun behind? Even if the Indians didn't provoke a fight, Smead would.

"Get away from him, Kate," Jason called out sternly. Alarmed, she searched his face hurriedly, but quickly saw that the anger painted darkly on his features was not directed at her. Instead, his eyes were fixed on Smead. Slowly she backed away from the gunfighter, until there was a wide stretch of snow between them.

"That goes for the rest of you," Jason warned. "Back off if you don't want to get in the middle of this."

Surprised, Kate glanced around and saw that, like Smead,

the other gunmen had come down the hill. Their guns rested comfortably on their hips. Kate saw them cast quick, almost surreptitious glimpses at each other, as if they were trying to decide what to do. Finally, after a long pause, the one called Hockam shrugged his shoulders and sauntered a few yards away. Slowly, almost as casually as if they were taking a short stroll, the others followed.

"What are you afraid of?" Smead ridiculed them.

"Ain't no point riskin' my life over a passel o' filthy Injuns," Hockam replied calmly, shrugging his shoulders again, as if to let Smead's insult slide off them.

"What's to risk?" Smead taunted, then turned back to Jason, squinting at him with eyes filled with amusement.

Jason didn't return his glance, but looked instead at the tall young warrior who had positioned himself slightly in front of his fellow braves.

"I had nothing to do with this, John," he said quietly.

The young Indian stared at him for a long time, his features stern and impassive; then slowly he nodded his head.

"What're ya gonna do about it, Hamilton?" Smead called out. "Shoot me with that big mouth o' yours?"

"I'm not going to do a thing, Smead," Jason replied coolly. He turned back to stare at the gunman. "I'm going to let Little Wolf do it for me."

For just an instant, a hint of alarm crossed Smead's face, but he quickly controlled it, standing warily with his hand resting on his gun.

"Try it, Smead," Jason urged. "You'll get one or two of them—you're good—but you can't get them all. Go ahead and fire . . . and you're a dead man."

Smead stood motionless for several seconds, his hand poised tautly above his gun, and Kate held her breath as she watched his dark, beady eyes flick over to the small group of braves, their rifles now held in readiness against their shoulders. Then slowly, with careful, drawn-out movements, he shrugged his shoulders, much as Hockam had done, and stretched his hands out in front of him. His elbows were slightly bent and his palms turned flat toward the ground in a gesture of submission. The slow, ugly grin that crossed his features accented the long red scar that cut deeply through his flesh.

"Anything you say, boss." His voice was laden with insolence and mockery.

"Unbuckle your belt and drop your gun to the ground."

A momentary spark of rebellion flashed through Smead's

eyes, but controlling it quickly, he reached down slowly and easily, unbuckling his belt and dropping the gun to the ground.

"The rest of you do the same thing."

Again, the other men glanced toward each other, but this time there was only a momentary pause before they complied.

"Now, get up to the bunkhouse."

Grumbling slightly, they began to head for their horses, but Jason's voice cut them off.

"On foot!"

Puzzled, they turned to gape at him, but the hard anger on his face warned them not to try to argue. Angry and sullen, they turned their backs slowly and began to trudge through the deep snow toward the road that led up the hill. Kate breathed a sigh of relief as she saw their retreating backs cut across the fields.

"I'm sorry, Gray Cloud," Jason said softly.

Surprised at the sound of his words, Kate whirled around. Now that she was no longer afraid of the Indians, she found herself consumed with curiosity. She knew from what Jason had said that Gray Cloud must be a chief, perhaps even one of the famous Dakota warriors whose names she had heard but never bothered to remember. She wondered how she could have forgotten his presence.

As she turned, she saw an old man slowly shaking his head, as if in great sorrow. "These are hard times," she heard him say quietly in English. His voice was hoarse and cracked with age.

She could hardly believe her eyes. Surely this couldn't be Gray Cloud. Not one of the great Dakota chiefs who struck terror into the hearts of the white settlers. Why, this was nothing but a tired, wizened old man, clad in rags as mean as those of the poorest of his people. Casting her eyes downward, she saw the tattered bundles of fabric that protruded from beneath the edge of his shabby, threadbare blanket. Horrified, she began to look around. No one had any better. Those whose feet were not swathed in rags went barefoot, leaving bright trails of blood behind them in the cold white snow.

"Jason, look at their feet," she cried out. As he turned to gaze at her, she saw that his eyes were filled with compassion, and she sensed that his pity was as much for her as for the Indians. "Can't we do something about it?" She looked down at her own feet, feeling guilty for the warm leather riding boots that covered them.

"Indians make boots and moccasins from animal skins," he told her. "Deer hide or even buffalo fur. But the winter's been too hard for the deer, and the white man has killed off most of the buffalo."

His eyes were sad and gentle as they looked down at her, and Kate found herself gazing back with rapt eagerness. Here at last was the Jason she longed to see, the kind, caring man whose heart bled for others' suffering.

"But we have so many furs, Jason," she urged him, thinking of the abundant pelts that decked the walls and floors of the house. "Couldn't we share them?"

He looked down at her with a puzzled expression. "Now, why couldn't I think of that?" he mused. It seemed to her she could detect a new note of respect in his voice. "George," he called out, beckoning to one of the older cowhands. "Take Mrs. Hamilton up on Smead's horse and get those furs. Bring them back in the wagon."

Kate was so excited at the prospect that she was already on the horse and halfway across the field before Jason could stop her. "And bring back some flour for bread," he shouted after her. "And vegetables and dried fruits. These people are starving to death." Eagerly, Kate waved her acknowledgment and turned to race away again, leaving the surprised George to catch up as best he could.

Once at the top of the hill, Kate wasted no time. Sending George into the house to collect the furs, she hurried to the storeroom, eager to sort out the things she would have him load onto the wagon. How good it felt to be doing something at last, she thought, after months of inactivity—and how good it felt to be sharing with those poor, suffering people who had so little, while she had such an abundance. They might be only savages, but they were, after all, living creatures. Why, she wouldn't even let an animal endure such a cruel existence.

She threw herself into the task with enthusiasm, carefully sorting out the best potatoes and tugging out bags of flour and bins of dried fruits and vegetables. She was so engrossed in the task that she didn't even notice she was no longer alone. When she finally became aware of the sounds of another human being standing behind her, she turned around eagerly.

"Done already, George? Here, come and help . . ."

She broke off abruptly, realizing she was staring, not into

the soft, kindly eyes of the old cowhand, but rather into Earl Smead's ugly, sneering eyes.

"What are you doing here?" she shouted furiously, trying to keep a nervous quiver out of her voice. "You're not supposed to be in here."

"You shouldn't oughta be up here alone, little lady," he drawled suggestively. His eyes played insolently over her body, leaving little doubt as to his meaning.

"I'm not alone," she told him firmly, trying to sound braver than she felt. "George is with me."

"Oh, old George." The idea seemed to amuse him. Kate wished she could take a rag and wipe the filthy smirk off his face.

"You get out of here," she told him furiously. "If you don't, I'll tell my husband about your insolence."

"Will ya listen to that fiery tongue?" He chuckled with mock surprise. "Fiery, like that wild red hair. Well, don't you pay that no never-mind, missy. Old Earl, he likes his women hot and wild."

Horrified, Kate watched as Smead began to cross the room, moving slowly toward her. Desperately she searched around for a weapon. Her eyes fell on a half-rotten barrel stave lying on top of the flour sacks, and she grabbed it quickly, holding it in front of her as she backed cautiously away from him, trying to get to the door.

"That's all right, missy," he told her, still chuckling. "You go ahead and fight. Old Earl, he likes a fighter."

Just when Kate thought he must reach her in another second, she heard the sound of the door creaking open. Shouting out in relief, she hurried toward it, nearly crying with joy as she saw George step into the room. There was a bewildered expression on his face as he looked from Kate to Smead, then back to Kate again.

"Thank God you're here," she told him.

Smead sauntered across the room, his eyes fixed coldly on George's face as he stationed himself between Kate and the door. "Old George were just leavin', weren't ya, George?"

To Kate's horror, George hesitated, then half-turned, as if to do Smead's bidding. "You get back here, George," she shouted, as much in anger as in fear. "If you leave me alone, I'll tell Mr. Hamilton."

George faltered awkwardly, pain and indecision written on his features. She knew he was trying to choose the lesser of two evils—Smead's wrath or Jason's—and it seemed to her absurd. After all, he was armed, and Smead had no gun.

What was he afraid of? What kind of power did this man exert over people?

"Dammit, George," she shouted, too angry and frightened to worry about being ladylike. "If you haven't got the guts to stand up to him, then give me your gun."

Frightened half out of his wits, George looked from one to the other in indecision.

"Give it to me," Kate repeated firmly, stretching out her hand toward him as she stared tensely into his eyes, desperately trying to subjugate his will to the strength of her own. Finally, to her relief, she saw his hand slide down and slip the gun out of its holster.

"That won't be necessary, George," Smead drawled calmly as he sauntered the few steps toward the door. He turned for a brief second as he reached the doorway, tipping his hat lightly to Kate. "We'll be seein' each other again, ma'am."

Trembling with anger and fright, Kate waited until she saw the door close, then turned to face the wretched George. She was amazed to see that he was shaking even harder than she was.

"You won't tell Mr. Hamilton, ma'am?" The words were half a question, half a plea.

Kate stared at him contemptuously. She certainly ought to tell Jason, that was for sure. George deserved to be reprimanded. But still she hesitated. Jason's wrath could be swift and violent—who knew that better than she?—and where could an old cowhand like George go?

"No, I don't suppose I will," she said wearily. "Now, help me get this stuff into the wagon."

Kate was still trembling as they started down the hill. The memory of Smead and the suddenness of his assault still lay heavy on her mind, and she paid only the scantest attention to the slippery, treacherous road. Finally, when the frightened George became too nervous to drive, she pulled the reins impatiently out of his hands and guided the horses safely to the base of the hill. Once there, she was surprised to see the camp bustling with activity.

She looked around hesitantly for a moment; then, seeing that Jason and Marc had busied themselves with a freshly butchered steer, she pulled the wagon over to the fire the women had made and began to help set up the heavy pots Cookie had brought down from the house. She was so busy, she completely forgot George, until she happened to glance toward the wagon and saw him standing awkwardly beside it.

"Well, don't just stand there," she shouted impatiently, hurrying across the few yards that separated her from the wagon. "Come on, I'll help you get this unloaded." She began to tug at a sack of potatoes, pulling it toward the edge of the wagon.

When George didn't move to help her, she turned toward him, annoyed. "What on earth is . . . ?"

Seeing the wary, frightened look that filled his eyes, Kate turned around cautiously. To her surprise, she saw that the small band of warriors had moved silently to that side of the camp. They were now surrounding the wagon, a look of harsh and vivid hatred emanating from their eyes.

Nervously Kate glanced around, looking for Jason and Marc, but she quickly saw that they were still at the far side of the camp, their backs turned toward her, unaware of her plight. Slowly she focused her gaze back on the Indians that surrounded her. What on earth could be wrong with them? she wondered, bewildered. Why did they look so angry, when all she was trying to do was help them?

"We don't want your charity," the one Jason had called John Little Wolf told her coldly. "Take it back."

"Take it back?" She gaped at him, aghast. That was absurd. These people were starving. Of course she wasn't going to take it back. "My husband told me to bring this down," she said icily, trying as best she could to match the firmness of his tone. "If you don't want it, talk to him about it." Furiously she turned back to the wagon, tugging at the heavy sack of potatoes, until it fell to the ground. Then she reached down, grabbing hold of the coarse fabric, and with all her strength began to tug it toward the fire.

"Stop!"

Little Wolf's voice was sharp and commanding. As Kate turned slowly, she saw his erect figure silhouetted against the gray sky, tall and strong in the saddle. His gun was raised halfway to his shoulder and rested tensely in the crook of his arm.

"Now, look here," Kate shouted furiously, dropping the sack of potatoes and standing as tall as she could to face him. "I've had just about enough of you!" All the humiliation she had suffered at Smead's hands, together with the horror she felt watching the starved, half-dead savages, had culminated in a sudden burst of rage. "Look at those people. They're suffering. Why, half the children will be dead in two days if they don't get help, and the women and old men are so weak they can hardly walk. If you don't want any of this food, you don't have to take it, but I'm not going to let a selfish son of a bitch like you keep it away from them."

To her surprise, she saw Little Wolf hesitate awkwardly, the gun lowering a few inches. Cautiously she glanced down at the heavy sack of potatoes. For an instant, both she and the Indian brave remained motionless, both wary, both cautious, both unwilling to give way.

You can't let him see you're afraid, Kate told herself firmly, trying to build up her courage. If he sees you're afraid, you've lost.

Slowly, with all the force of will she could muster, she bent down, reaching for the cold fabric of the bag. Her eyes were still fastened on his as she picked it up, half-lifting it from the ground. Finally, she knew the moment had come to test her courage.

It took all her strength to force herself to turn her back on the savage and inch her way, step by step, toward the circle of women who stood silently watching her. Every muscle in her body was tensed, waiting for the sharp crack of a rifle, the blinding flash of pain. When it didn't come, she knew she had won.

She walked back toward the wagon, now carefully avoiding the warrior's eyes, and was amazed to see George still standing in the same spot.

"Don't be such a ninny, George," she shouted out good-naturedly, the sudden exhilaration of victory sweeping over her. "You'd be scared to death of your own shadow if there were sun enough to see it."

She picked up a heavy bag of flour and staggered over to the fire with it. By the time she came back for her third load, she saw that George was at last ready to help her, and she left the rest of the heavy work to him.

Kate gladly helped the women prepare a rich, fragrant stew, studded with the fat white potatoes and dried mushrooms she had brought from the storehouse, but when it came time to eat dinner, she demurred graciously, not wanting to take even a single drop of food from their mouths. Only when Jason called across to her from the circle where the men were seated, telling her she would insult them if she refused their hospitality, did she agree to sit down with them, and even then, she was careful to eat sparingly.

Looking over to the men's circle, she noted with amusement that the protesting braves were eating as heartily as everyone else, but she was careful not to let them catch her staring. She wanted to give them a chance to partake of the healthful nourishment without having to forsake the last vestiges of their pride.

Later, when the sun sank behind the horizon and the Indians settled down into the cold night, Kate was finally able to relax in her husband's arms before the warm, blazing flames that danced invitingly in the stone fireplace. There was between the two of them a strong bond she had never felt before, and she was glad for the events of the day, tiring and frightening as they were, that had finally brought them close to each other.

She smiled to herself as she recalled the first night she had spent in Wyoming, the night she and Jason had misunderstood each other so cruelly. She remembered being frightened by shadows in a dark alleyway, then finding they were, in reality, nothing more sinister than a row of empty barrels. She had wondered then if everything in the West was like that—frightening only until you got near enough to see it clearly. Now she knew that was at least partly true. Even the Indians, the terrifying savages she had feared so dreadfully, were far from sinister close up. As for Jason . . .

She laid her head wearily on her husband's strong shoulder, rejoicing in the warmth and comfort of his body. How could she ever have imagined she saw dark, terrifying shadows in the depths of his eyes? What a fool she had been not to appreciate this good, kind husband of hers!

"I don't think I've ever been so tired in my life," she told him softly. "Every muscle in my body aches." She stretched her neck to look up at him. "I think I need some of that Spanish oil."

Her voice was low and husky, and her body trembled as it pressed against his. He knew it was not her aching muscles she was thinking of.

"What a brazen little hussy you are," he told her lightly, lowering his head until his lips played lingeringly on hers. "But you shall have it. You've earned it."

18

THE WORST STORM OF THE YEAR CAME LATE IN THE SEASON, and Kate spent many cold, bitter days standing beside the window watching the heavy snowflakes swirl thickly through the air, blocking out the dim rays of the sun. The drifts piled higher and higher against the side of the house, until finally, in their relentless assault, they reached to the top of the windows, completely shutting out the last traces of light. How harsh and bitter this land was, Kate thought as she stood in the living room gazing at the opaque square of white framed by the edges of the window. How cruel it was to the men who tried to conquer it.

"Jason?" she whispered softly, turning to look with pleading eyes at the man who stood beside her.

Marc reached out to touch her lightly on the arm. "He'll be all right," he assured her, but she could hear that his voice was troubled.

"Why did he have to go out there?"

Why did he have to leave her alone and go off to challenge the harsh elements? It had been a bold, foolish thing to do, and she had tried to tell him so. This stern, uncompromising land did not tolerate such challenges on the part of the mere men who tried to force a living from its soil. She had not even been surprised by the storm that began with such a cold, raging fury the day after he left.

"He had to, Kate," Marc explained gently. "I'd have gone for him if he'd let me, but he's too proud for that. It's too . . ." He broke off quickly, looking down into her troubled eyes. He had started to say: It's too dangerous. But he didn't want to frighten her. "It's his ranch," he told her, speaking quickly, to cover the brief break in his voice. "It's his responsibility. Someone had to go out there to check on the herds, and Jason would never let anyone do that for him."

No, Jason was far too proud for that, Kate knew. Jason would never let another man shoulder his responsibilities, or his hardships, for him, and so he had gone away—for a few days, he said, a week or two at most—leaving her alone, alone to stare at the blank sheet of white that rested where the window should have looked out on the world.

Well, at least there was one good thing about it, she told herself, trying to bring a small note of cheer into her troubled thoughts. At least that same snow, so cruel and dangerous for Jason, brought for her an oddly comfortable sense of security. That same snow that covered everything except the deep trenches connecting the ranch house with the outbuildings also protected her from the unwanted gaze of ugly, mocking eyes.

She realized to her surprise that she had not even thought of Smead for days, not since the heavy snows had begun. Before that, he always seemed to be lurking in the doorways of the bunkhouse or the woodshed, following her with a taunting, lustful leer as she scurried rapidly across the yard, averting her eyes so she would not have to look at him. Now, with the cover of the snow, she felt free to go anywhere she liked. Now she did not feel she had to have an escort every time she made her way to the storehouse for provisions or to the stables to tantalize Sunbeam with a handful of sugar lumps.

After Marc made his way outside to finish his chores and see that everything was all right in the bunkhouse, Kate found herself growing more and more restless. She tried to sit by the fire gazing at the snapping blue and yellow streaks that burst through the flames, but today even the hypnotic rhythm of its dancing movements failed to hold her gaze. She felt as if time were dragging by, each single second lasting a long, tedious hour. Finally, when she could stand the inactivity no longer, she made her way to the kitchen, grabbing up a handful of sugar lumps, and then hurried to the hallway to put on her coat. At least she could go and talk to Sunbeam for a while. Sunbeam would be glad to see her.

The sun was surprisingly bright as she threw open the outer door and caught sight of the shining rays that glinted against the brilliant white expanse of snow. As she hurried down the deep trench the men had dug, the subzero air nipping at her nose and cheeks, she felt as if the sheer, steep walls of white that rose well above her head were closing in on her. Looking up at the sky far above her, she was amazed to see that it was a clear, sparkling blue. Thank God there would be no more snow for a while, she thought gratefully. Jason had already suffered enough. Reaching the fork in the deep tunnel, she turned toward the left, heading for the stable.

"Hello, Sunbeam," she called out brightly as she pushed the heavy door open. The sweet, damp smell of hay rose to her nostrils, mingling with the earthy scent of the animals. The little mare whinnied an eager reply, and Kate rushed over to throw her arms around Sunbeam's neck, laughing as the pretty roan began to nuzzle the pocket of the heavy buffalo coat, knowing her mistress would not have forgotten to bring a treat for her.

"Now, ain't that tender?"

Horrified, Kate whirled around just in time to see Earl Smead's obscene leer rising slowly out of an empty stall near the door. She had the uncanny feeling he had been there a long time, lying in wait for her.

"Get out of here," she told him angrily. She was determined not to let him see the fear that was rapidly rising in her. The man was like an animal, she knew, and animals had a special sense that scented out fear. If he knew she was afraid of him, like any other wild beast, he would attack.

"Tsck, tsck, tsck," he clucked mockingly, his tongue working moistly against his sharp, pointed teeth. "Still as fiery as ever. Well, never ya mind. Earl Smead, he likes his women like he likes his horses, wild and untamed."

"Stay away from me," she shouted hoarsely, the note of fear she had fought against now rising plainly in her voice.

He ignored her cry, almost as if it hadn't occurred.

"Broke me a colt once," he told her. His voice was calm, but his eyes glowed with an insane light. "Wildest thing you ever saw. Couldn't nobody else touch that colt. Like to kill 'em all, he did. Broke 'em near in two if they went near him."

The idea seemed to delight him, and he began to laugh. At first, it was a slow, quiet chuckle, but it grew and grew, until Kate wanted to scream to drive the sound of it out of her ears. It was an ugly, coarse laugh, one that hung deep in his throat and gurgled with the moist, gushing sound of water pouring down a drain.

"Well, I broke me that colt. I broke him till thar warn't nothin' left of him." He kept on laughing and laughing, until Kate thought she couldn't stand it any longer. "You would o' thought he was just some dumb old draft horse, made for cartin' heavy wagons on the slow, bumpy roads."

Kate gaped at him in horror. He had not broken the colt because he wanted a spirited mount, as other men might do.

He had not even broken him for the sheer joy of the challenge, the excitement of pitting his strength against the wildness of an untamed beast. No, he had broken him because he enjoyed crushing a free spirit. He enjoyed destroying a thing of beauty.

"Always wanted to break me a woman like that colt," he drawled slowly. "A hot, spirited bitch with fire runnin' through her veins 'stead o' blood."

Cautiously, with slow, sure steps, he began to inch his way toward her. Kate watched him with terrified eyes. This must have been how the colt felt, she thought, standing his ground warily as he watched the harsh, uncompromising features and sure, deliberate steps of the evil brute who slithered slowly forward.

Kate stood absolutely still as he crept toward her, one cautious inch at a time. Only her eyes moved, darting around the room desperately as she searched for a way to escape. For her, time seemed to stand still, and the long moment dragged on interminably as she watched him moving ever closer and closer.

Then suddenly, just as he had almost reached her, she burst away from him, running in one mad dash toward the door. She almost made it, for he was taken off balance by her sudden movement, but the heavy weight of the buffalo coat held her back a second too long. She had just reached out to clutch at the rough handle of the door when she felt crude hands grasping at her arms, pulling her roughly backward.

"Well, ain't that a shame?" he gloated, laughing gleefully at her terror. "Jest cain't get nowheres with that heavy coat on, can ya? Now, why don't we jest take it off?"

"No," Kate screamed, horrified to think of coarse hands beginning to undress her body. She struggled desperately against him, but he was too strong for her. Pinning her tightly with one arm around the neck, he used his other hand to strip the coat easily from her body. She felt a cold rush of air assault her shoulders as he slid the coat down from them, dropping it in a heap at her feet.

"Well, now, that's better," he chortled coarsely. She was grateful that she could not see the obscene leer that must be painted on his evil features as he gazed boldly over her shoulder and down the front of her dress, but she was not to be spared the hot, moist feel of his panting against her cool skin.

Still holding his forearm tightly against her throat, he dug the fingers of his free hand deep into the thickness of her hair, tearing at it wildly, until the pins fell out, clattering on the floor. She shuddered as she realized her hair was now free to float seductively over his gross fingers.

"Ain't that jest the purtiest thing?" There was a hint of awe in his harsh voice. "Will ya look at all that red? Hell, I bet you're a redhead all over." The thought seemed to fill him with glee, and Kate could feel his body shaking with laughter.

Terrified, she felt him begin to pull her body toward the empty stall where he had lain in ambush for her. In despair, she realized there was no use screaming. The thick wooden door and heavy drifts of snow outside it would muffle any sounds.

"What's the matter?" he taunted, pressing her against the coarse wooden slats that edged the stall. "All the fight gone outta you? Shit, this is jest too easy."

For a hideous moment, his ugly features were contorted in a look of bitter disappointment, and Kate felt her terror increase. He actually wanted to hurt her, she realized. He was looking forward to it. He didn't lust after her flesh; he lusted after the pain he could cause her. He enjoyed hurting.

Then, to her surprise, a soft light began to glow in his eyes. "Or mebbe ya don't wanna fight," he said, amused by the idea. Kate could already see his repulsive body puff up with pride. "Mebbe ya don't hate old Earl after all. Mebbe you enjoy this." He laid his hand coarsely on the soft, pale skin of her breast, sliding a disgusting finger down the cleavage that pressed out of the front of her low-cut dress.

That was too much for Kate. "God damn you," she spit out furiously. "You filthy pig! Do you think I'd ever let you touch me?" With a new strength born of fury, she managed to push him away. Astonished at her sudden burst of rage after the silent terror that had preceded it, Smead stumbled awkwardly backward, giving Kate a chance to dart across the floor to the other side of the stable.

A slow, grotesque grin began to spread across his features as he caught his balance and gazed across the room at her. Kate realized again with sickening horror that he enjoyed her fear. It was all a game for him. The hungry, sadistic leer on his face was the look of the bloodthirsty hunter as he gazes down at the terrified eyes of the cornered fox.

Kate glanced around quickly, trying to assess her situation. With sinking heart, she realized she was no better off than before. She was still too far from the door to reach safety, and there was no way she could defend herself against his superior strength. Catching sight of a bridle hanging on a peg beside her, she grabbed at it abruptly. It wasn't much good, but it was better than nothing. Even if he was going to have his way with her, she wasn't going to make it easy for him. She wasn't going to sell her body cheaply.

Smead did not speak as he saw her take down the bridle and let the long leather strap swing slowly from her fingers, but the same low, gurgling chuckle lay deep in his throat, and it was more terrifying than words.

Slowly, with infinite caution, he began to circle around her, forming broad arcs as he moved back and forth, each time sliding an inch or two closer to her. Kate watched him warily, every muscle in her body tense as she waited for him to make his move.

Then, suddenly he lunged forward, but she had read the gathering tension in his muscles correctly, and she was ready for him. The sharp leather thong lashed through the air with an eerie whistling sound that broke only with the loud crack of its impact against the side of his neck. Astonished, Smead let out a sudden yelp of pain and leaped instinctively backward.

His eyes grew warier, and in them Kate could see a sudden new respect for her as an opponent, but the ugly grin that brought such terror to her heart still lay across his scarred and brutal face.

It was the same game all over again, the same circling and the same waiting; only, this time he was slyer. This time he was not underestimating her. As he leaped forward again, he found she was ready for him once more, and her improvised whip whistled through the air, finding its mark on the side of his face. Kate watched in fascination as the deep, ugly cut slowly began to fill with red, until his face seemed to have two hideous scars running across it.

Blood poured freely from the wound, clogging his eye and dripping soggily onto his clothes as he turned to face Kate again. This time—at last—the grin was gone. This time, his eyes were cold and deadly serious.

He did not wait to circle again, or play coy games with her, but started walking toward her with firm, bold steps. Terrified, Kate lashed at him again, but this time he had steeled himself for the blow, and his body barely quivered as the sharp leather tore into his flesh. Again and again she struck out at him, but the iron strength of his body would allow nothing to halt his sure advance. It was only a matter of seconds before Kate saw his rough hand lunge out at her wrist, wrenching it painfully, until she dropped the bridle into the straw at her feet.

She was sobbing bitterly in anger and frustration as she felt him thrust his crude arms around her, pressing the foulness of his body against hers and forcing her down toward the floor. With an agonizing surge of effort, she struggled to push him away from her, but it was no use, and she felt her hands slide helplessly across the strong muscles that traversed his chest and belly. She was already on her knees, struggling with the last ounce of strength in her body to keep him from pressing her down rudely on her back, when her fingers, desperately clutching for anything that might help her, suddenly came in contact with the unexpected feel of cold metal.

It was his gun! The gun in the holster at his side. Instinctively she curled her fingers around it, pulling it toward her.

He realized instantly what she had done and reached out with strong fingers to tear it from her grasp. Knowing she had only a second to keep it in her hands, Kate pointed it toward him and pressed her finger tightly against the trigger.

The sound of the shot was deafening. Kate could hear it ringing in her ears for a long time, even as her nostrils picked up the harsh, bitter smell of burning powder. Smead staggered backward, a stunned, angry look on his face. Blood was pouring from a wound in his side.

Horrified, Kate jumped up, backing away from him, with the gun still in her hand. She could not take her eyes off him. The hate she saw in his eyes was the most intense and terrifying thing she had ever seen in her life.

He pulled himself slowly, painfully erect. To her horror, Kate saw that he was still standing between her and the door. She had no choice but to back away from him farther and farther into the gloomy depths of the stable. For a long time they stood silently facing each other; then, slowly, almost before she was aware of what was happening, he began to walk toward her again.

"Get back," she warned, raising the gun with both hands to hold it steady. "If you come closer, I'll shoot."

"Will ya, now?" he said calmly, as if they were discussing a fact of little consequence to either of them. He did not falter for an instant as he kept advancing toward her.

Kate continued to back away from the ugly violence she saw in his eyes. She was strangely afraid to pull the trigger, strangely reluctant to end a human life, even one as disgusting and useless as Smead's. Suddenly, without warning, she felt her foot catch on a saddle that had been left carelessly on the floor, and before she knew it, she had tumbled awkwardly to the ground, the gun flying from her fingers.

That was all Smead needed. He flew across the floor, kicking the gun away from her before she could even think to clutch at it. Kate screamed in terror, though she knew it would do no good. Looking up, she saw Smead's body leaning over her, his face a mask of gloating hatred. The blood that dripped profusely from his body began to coat her with its sticky moisture.

Kate closed her eyes in terror, unable to bear the ugly vision of his mad lust a moment longer, and waited in an agony of suspense to feel the hateful touch of his fingers against her flesh. When it didn't happen, she opened her eyes cautiously, wondering what other cruel tortures he had in mind for her before he worked out his gross lewdity on her body. To her surprise, she found he wasn't even looking at her.

She gaped at him in astonishment for a moment. His eyes were raised above her head, staring warily at the door. As he rose cautiously, pulling his body away from hers, his hands stretched out in the same mute gesture of surrender she had seen him use in the Indian camp. Turning slowly, she saw Marc silhouetted in the open doorway, a gun level in his hands.

Smead's eyes flickered for a moment toward his own gun, lying only a few feet away, where he himself had kicked it. Marc did not miss the glance.

"Go ahead and try it," he urged, his voice grim and determined. There was a light in his eyes that frightened Kate.

This was not her Marc, she told herself incredulously, not the kind, gentle friend she had come to know so well. This was a hard, savage stranger, as brutal in his own way as the man he faced. What manner of person was this who could urge another man to reach for his gun so he could shoot him down in cold blood?

Kate felt herself shudder as she watched the hard, cruel light that shone out of his eyes. Was this what the West did to men? Was the savagery and violence that surrounded them so strong and compelling that it eventually permeated even the lives and souls of decent men, turning them into brutal, cold-blooded killers? Had that happened to Jason, and was it happening now, before her very eyes, to Marc?

To her relief, Smead was not fool enough to accept Marc's challenge, but pressed his hand painfully against his side as he shambled slowly toward the doorway. Marc did not even give him a second glance, but moved swiftly across the floor, stopping only long enough to pick up Smead's gun as he hurried to Kate's side. Gratefully she threw herself into his arms, forgetting the coldness she had seen in his eyes as she laid her tearstained cheek against the strength of his shoulder.

"It's all right, Kate," he told her softly, holding his arms tightly around her trembling body. "Everything's all right now." Gently he leaned down and laid his head comfortingly against the hair that flowed wildly over her shoulders. In a mute expression of comfort, he pressed his lips lightly against its fragrant profusion.

"So that's how it is."

Smead's harsh voice rang through the stable with all the force of thunder on a quiet night, and Kate and Marc looked up suddenly, startled to find him still standing in the open doorway.

"Seems as how the boss's lady don't have no time for the hired help," he drawled. "But I reckon she ain't so particular when it comes to the boss's best friend."

"Smead, you are the foulest thing that ever walked the face of the earth," Marc called out, his face livid with rage. "You get your ass out of here or I'll have it carried out." He reached pointedly for his gun.

"Oh, I'll go." Smead sneered. "But I ain't gonna forget what I seen here. Someone'll be interested to hear about it. Someone'll be mighty interested indeed."

"Oh, my God," Kate whispered in horror as she watched the man slink through the doorway and disappear from view. "He's going to tell Jason." Smead was just mean enough to do it, she knew. He wasn't likely to forget the recent humiliation he had suffered at her hands, nor was he the kind of man to be cheated out of his revenge.

"Tell Jason what?" Marc asked puzzled. "We weren't doing anything wrong. I was only comforting you."

"That won't be the way it'll sound when Smead gets through with it," she said ominously. The man was clever enough to twist the story around to suit his own ends.

"So what?" Marc said patiently, obviously more than a little surprised at her distress. "Jason wouldn't believe anything that swine said, and anyhow, you're his wife. Why would he doubt you?"

Why indeed, Kate thought bitterly, but she didn't dare voice the words aloud. Marc hadn't been there to see the look of rage on Jason's face when she had smiled at a neighbor in parting or let a young boy hold onto her hand as he helped her from her horse. He hadn't heard the cold fury in Jason's voice when he threatened to kill her if she ever touched another man. Marc didn't know the extent of Jason's jealousy. How could he understand?

She closed her eyes, picturing for a moment another stable, picturing another man's hands that had caressed her warm and eager body, a man who was not her husband. Oh, why had she ever been such a fool to tell Jason about it? Why hadn't she kept on masquerading as a widow?

You have the soul of a harlot, my dear.

Tears stung her eyes as she recalled his words. Oh, yes, she told herself bitterly, Jason would indeed doubt her. He would always doubt her.

"Promise me you won't tell Jason anything about this," she implored, looking pleadingly into Marc's kind, sympathetic eyes. "Not anything at all."

"Kate—"

"Promise me," she begged.

His eyes looked troubled for a minute; then, glancing at the tears that threatened to roll down her cheeks, he sighed wearily. "All right, I promise. I guess it's better that way anyhow. Smead has to stay here, and if Jason knew about this . . . well, it would only cause trouble."

"Thank you, Marc," she whispered gratefully.

"Don't worry, Kate," he promised her. "Jason will be home soon. Then everything will be all right again. I promise you."

19

JASON BARELY FELT THE ICY STING OF THE BITING WIND AS he sat atop the motionless horse, gazing with outward calm at what was left of the empire he had carved for himself in the wilderness. "Damn," he muttered under his breath, feeling bitterly the inadequacy of words to express the helpless frustration that welled up inside him. How infuriating it was, and how cruelly unfair.

He felt a sick feeling turn over in the pit of his stomach as he looked around him. Everywhere, as far as the eye could

215

see in the wildly swirling snow that half-blinded him, vast heaps of dark brown carcasses, the last remnants of his own great herds, lay in long stretches in the snow now nearly covered with a soft, cold blanket of white. Dammit, what a fool he had been. Whatever made him think he could hold together scattered groups of cattle in this hostile terrain? Unlike the massive herds of buffalo who had wandered the plains before the coming of the white man, the cattle could not claw with sharp hooves through the layers of ice to find the browned grasses beneath them. Only inches from the food that could have saved them, they had starved to death, their bodies frozen in rigid postures by the subzero temperatures.

The vast, open ranges, unfenced and free, had seemed ideal in the good years, Jason reminded himself bitterly, in the years when the weather was mild and the grass plentiful and easy to get at. Now it was a different story. Now, in the harsh, cruel winters, with freezing winds cutting across the plains and ice burying the meadows beneath a thick, impenetrable mantle, the vast open stretches of land could no longer be serviced. The herds could not be drawn together for the food and protection they needed to survive.

It was all over, Jason thought, silent as he felt the bitterness well up inside him. It was all ended now, the life he had loved. No more for him the vast, unfenced lands, stretching as far as the eye could see, and beyond. No more the wild, unfettered freedom that matched the recklessness of his own spirit. The others might not see it yet. It would take more hard years and even harsher blizzards to show them the truth, but Jason knew in his heart he had seen it already. It was a truth that grieved him even as he accepted it.

Jason felt the horse move impatiently under him, shaking his black mane into the biting wind, and he reached down quickly to stroke the stallion's neck reassuringly. Midnight was a good horse, strong and sensitive, and Jason understood instantly what he was trying to tell him. It was as if the horse had a voice to speak, saying to him: What the hell are you doing, you damn fool, dawdling around here mourning over losses that can't be helped? Don't you know you're risking both our necks? We have to get to shelter before the storm gets even worse.

And he was right, Jason had to admit. He *was* a fool to sit there worrying over the future, when the present was so precarious. Hell, if the weather held, he wouldn't have to worry about anything—ever again. A few more hours of this blasted storm, and his troubles would be over permanently.

Throwing a hurried glance up at the darkened sky, Jason realized grimly that he had been a fool to push on so far. He was miles away from the crude hut he had left behind, but still too far from home to make it before twilight shut off the little light that remained. Well, there was nothing for it, he told himself with a cold determination. He would have to stay where he was until morning. Thank heaven for the wall of dead cattle, he thought, half-smiling at the bitter irony of it all. The gruesome heap of corpses marked the end of the world he loved, yet it was that same heap that provided a break from the cruel wind that threatened his very life.

Tugging at the blankets in his saddle roll, Jason tossed one of them hastily over Midnight's back, wrapping it carefully around the horse to help hold in his body heat as he backed the animal slowly against the mound of snow that covered the pile of carcasses. He eyed the heavy flurries of snow that coated the blanket, turning it almost immediately to a bright, clean white, with a cool appraisal. If only the snow didn't fall too thick and fast, he thought, burying the horse until he suffocated beneath its weight, perhaps it would offer just enough protection to keep the animal from freezing.

When he finished tending to his horse, Jason began to search the length of the long, seemingly uncompromising wall, until he finally found a deep crevice, half-hidden in the snow, between the stiff, frozen bodies of two of his cattle. Wrapping himself in the blanket, he settled his body tightly inside the crevice, letting the snow cover him, too, with its protective mantle. There was no point trying to start a fire, he reminded himself grimly. With the icy, howling wind and the heavy snow, it would be nothing more than an exercise in frustration.

The hours passed slowly as Jason huddled in his small, snowy sanctuary, staring out at the deceptively fragile snow-flakes swirling through the air around him until at last darkness settled over the land, cutting them off from his view. Even then, he could still feel the moist, oddly warm sense of their touch as they landed like thousands of tiny kisses on his cheeks and nose.

After the darkness settled, Jason no longer had any concept of the time, nor did he know how many hours had passed since he buried himself in the snow to wait out the long, bitter night. He only knew that he felt cold, incredibly cold, as the icy touch of the cold night air beleaguered his body, until he was sure he could bear it no longer. Then, suddenly, just as it had grown intolerable, he felt the cold begin to subside, and a warming flush seemed to spread over his body, as if at last the blood from his veins had begun to heat his icy flesh. Alarmed, he reached out, pinching his arms and cheeks with gloved fingers to make sure the sensation was not the first false glow of frostbite. To his relief, he could feel the tight pinch of his fingers. The warmth was real, he thought gratefully. Enough snow had fallen at last over his shelter to insulate him from the outside, letting his own body heat keep him warm.

At last he could afford to relax a little, letting himself ease back into the shelter, grateful that the heavy shivering of his limbs and body had finally ceased. What a relief it was to feel even a momentary release from vigilance and tension.

But he dared not let his eyes close, he warned himself as he felt his lids grow almost unbearably heavy. He dared not fall asleep. If the snows grew heavier or the winds changed, forcing the heavy drifts to move in his direction, the beautiful, brutally uncompromising blanket of white that now protected him could easily become both his burial shroud and his tomb. Somehow he had to stay awake until morning, until he could make his way back to the shelter and warmth of home. Home . . . and Kate.

Kate. He felt a new strength of will burst through his body with all the power and fire of a rocket flare as he visualized his wife, her dark red hair floating softly against the snowy whiteness of the pillow. Kate. God, how beautiful she was, and how exciting. Even in the tension and bitter cold of his dubious haven, Jason felt his body grow hot again at the very thought of her. How perfect she was for him, and how unexpected. He who had thought he would never love again, at least not with the same wild, untamed passion of his youth—what a miracle it had seemed to him when suddenly there was Kate.

He could see her as if she were before him at that very instant, her deep green eyes wide with interest and intrigue, her lips parted in eager expectation, just as she had looked as she stood on the station platform, staring at him with undisguised interest . . . and yes, though she would never have admitted it, desire, even though she did not yet know he was the man she had come to meet and marry. He could see her standing in the hallway of his own home, dressed in one of the pretty gowns he had bought for her, her curls bobbing with disconcerting charm as she tossed her head vivaciously, offering a flirtatious smile to greet one of their guests or bid him a hospitable adieu.

He was surprised at the sudden rush of anger that flooded over his body as he thought of Kate, laughing and flirting coyly with every man who came into their home. Goddammit, how could she do that to him? Didn't she know how much it hurt him? Did she think all she had to do was smile coquettishly and toss her long golden curls . . .

Golden? But Kate's hair was dark—a deep, pure shade of red. Jason felt his body begin to relax again, and a wry, bitter smile turned up the corners of his lips as he realized, perhaps for the first time since he had met his wife, what he was doing. It was not Kate he was angry at, not Kate he cursed and threatened, not even Kate whose body he sometimes forced with a wild and burning rage. Not Kate, but Celeste. It was Celeste who flirted outrageously with every man she saw, laughing charmingly at their jokes, and sharing their beds, too, he'd warrant, if they were wealthy enough or powerful enough to have anything to offer her.

"God damn her," he shouted out bitterly. Why had thoughts of her come back to his mind tonight? Why now, when he hadn't thought of her for months, not since the first instant he'd laid eyes on Kate? What a fool he was to think of her, what a fool to harbor bitterness in his heart after all this time. He had been wrong to punish Kate for Celeste's sins, wrong to be suspicious of her, only because Celeste had once been guilty. Dammit, how unfair he'd been. Kate was only sweetly gracious to their guests, not boldly calculating, the way the other one had always been. Kate wasn't like that. She couldn't be. God help him, he couldn't stand it if she was. He'd rather see her dead.

Jason felt a cold sweat break out over his body as he recalled the violent words that had poured out of his own lips, harsh, angry words uttered only in the rage of the moment, but bearing more truth than he cared to admit. *If you ever touch another man, Kate, I swear by all that's sacred, I'll kill you both*. God help him, he knew he meant it. He couldn't stand that kind of betrayal again, especially not from Kate. He'd see her dead before he'd let her do that to him.

Jason clutched at the blanket, pulling it tighter around his body to block out the cold moisture of snowflakes that had begun to melt against the heat of his body. "Dammit," he cursed again, but this time he muttered the words softly, under his breath. This time he knew that no matter how hard he tried, he was not going to be able to drive bitter memories of Celeste from his thoughts.

And why the hell should they go away? he asked himself

coldly. What made him think he could erase all those years from his mind? Celeste was there, firmly entrenched in his memories, as she always would be, along with the gracious plantations, long since burned, and the carefree life that was no more. How could he expect to drive them away, those enduring visions of a world he had reveled in with an uncritical passion, and the girl he had worshiped since early childhood? They had all loved her, he remembered with a wry half-smile, he and Aaron, the orphaned cousin who had been raised in his home, and Marc, the son of a neighboring planter. They had been inseparable, the "three little musketeers," as his father laughingly called them, more like brothers than cousins and friends. They had grown up together and fallen in love together—with the same girl.

And how could they help loving her? Even as a child, Celeste had been perfectly, incredibly beautiful, like a little Dresden doll no one dared touch for fear of breaking her. Then maturity had come, years earlier for Celeste than for the other girls, and suddenly every young man in the area— and a few of the older ones, too, if the truth were known— found a thousand excuses to reach out and touch her, their hands resting lightly for an instant against the silken smoothness of her bare arm, their trembling fingers longing to reach forward just a few inches farther, coming to rest at last against the soft swell of her breasts, rising from the low, tight bodice of her dress. And yet, it was all a dream, an intense, unattainable dream, for as long as they could remember, they had always known Celeste was not for any of them, not for Jason or Aaron or Marc. Celeste belonged to the son of the richest planter in the area, young Beau DeLys, and it was always understood that one day she would grow up to be his bride.

And yet, one afternoon, one amazing, incredible afternoon in the summerhouse by the river, Celeste had become his. She was barely fifteen that warm summer afternoon, but she gave herself to him freely, with a freedom far beyond her years. It had not occurred to him to wonder at the practiced skill with which she manipulated his body, for it was an introduction to love for him, and he was content to revel in the ecstasy that was beyond his wildest dreams. If he noticed that the advances had been made by her and not by him, his male vanity did not bristle at the challenge, but accepted instead without question the miracle of the gift she had offered him. He did notice she was not a virgin—how could he help it, after all those countless adolescent sessions, exchanging crude biological facts, that had made all the boys feel like men?— but surprisingly, it had not bothered him. He cared naught about the past. There was no jealousy in him then. It didn't matter what she had done before, or what mistakes she had made. It was enough that she loved him, enough that he could feel the silken smoothness of her flesh against his lips and fingertips, enough that he could bury himself in the moist, yielding warmth of her body. The past was dead, he had told himself with a conviction only the very young could feel. The future was golden . . . and the future was Celeste.

Yet, that was the last time he possessed her. She had let him dip his fingers deeply into the bodice of her dress often enough after that, and even slip his hand up beneath her skirt, resting it for a second on the quivering moisture of her thighs, but always at the last moment she had stopped him. Always there was an excuse. "Someone might come, my love." "I fear you will get me with child." "We must be married, my darling. If you want this again as much as I do, then we must be married right away."

It was all right with him. He had hungered for her with a deep passion that drove all thoughts of reason from his mind. He would have married her that very afternoon if his father had not put his foot down—and put it down hard. Jason felt a hard, bitter smile cross his face as he thought of his gentle parents, now dead and lost to all but memory. How hard it must have been for them, how agonizing, to watch their only son reach out so determinedly for the one thing that was certain to ruin his life. No doubt they had already seen what it would take Jason years to realize—that Celeste's sudden interest in him had coincided remarkably with the fact that young Beau DeLys's father had lost the family plantation, and indeed, their entire fortune, in a poker game.

But even despite his parents' objections, Celeste had nearly won. He remembered with a vague sense of bitterness the last ball he had ever gone to in his native state, remembered Celeste's coyness, the last desperate ploys she had used to try to trap him into a hurried marriage. He remembered searching for Celeste that night, coming out to the terrace unexpectedly and catching her in Marc's arms. He saw enough of the scene to realize that this young friend was trying desperately to fight off his own temptations, trying with only a moderate degree of success to extricate himself from her wiles, but it didn't matter. He was furious, furious with both of them, even though he knew in his heart he was being unfair to

221

Marc. His friend had been embarrassed, red-faced, and stammering awkwardly, but Celeste had only laughed gaily and tossed a knowing glance over her shoulder as she flitted back into the ballroom, as if to warn him she was ready to find someone else if he did not marry her—and marry her soon.

All evening she had tormented him. With Aaron she found far more success than she had with Marc, for his cousin had no compunctions about accepting her advances, even when he knew she had been virtually promised to Jason. For the first time, as he stood on the sidelines and watched her tempt scandal by dancing dance after dance with Aaron, he felt the cold fingers of jealousy wrap themselves around his heart. For the first time, he began to wonder who it was, which of the young men floating lightly through the room with pretty ladies in their arms, that had possessed her before he had. Was it Aaron? he wondered, with a sick sense of disgust. And yet, even besotted with love though he was, he knew that could not be true. Poor and landless, Aaron would never have been able to tempt Celeste. Let him bask in his glory now. Let him glance over at Jason as often as he wanted, a gloating smile marring his handsome features. When the night was over and she no longer needed him to make her lover jealous, Celeste would drop him without so much as a sweet good-bye or a coy backward glance.

Still, if it wasn't Aaron . . . Jason found himself scanning the room with a new, unfamiliar kind of suspicion, eyeing his friends and neighbors with a hostility that unnerved him. The sensation of jealousy was a strange and unpleasant one. Jason did not yet know it was a sensation that would never again leave him completely free of its ugliness.

Celeste had played her cards well, and she very nearly won the game. After that evening, after the torments she threatened him with, Jason would have moved heaven and earth to marry her. Nothing could have stopped him. Nothing except the fact that it was April—and April was the month Virginia seceded from the Union and the war began in earnest.

Well, it was all over now, he told himself grimly, surprised that he could still feel such bitterness for the past. It was all over, and Celeste belonged to Aaron now, God help him. Despite all the letters of passion that had passed between them, all the promises of love and fidelity from the prison camp and beyond, Celeste had not waited for him. She had not even bothered to write him of her marriage, leaving it for him to find out instead from the casual, gossipy letter of an old friend. He could still feel the surge of rage that had swept over him when he learned the truth, the bitter humiliation of her betrayal. God, how he had longed to have her before him then, longed to punish her for the pain she had created inside him—longed to feel the pallor of her slender white throat beneath the bruising vengeance of his own strong hands.

Damn the anger and the bitterness that never quite left his heart, he thought with a sudden burst of rage. What difference did it make anyhow? Aaron had her now, the cold, calculating little bitch, and from all he could tell, he deserved her. Aaron had done well in the war, Jason thought with rising disgust. He had figured out early on that there was more to be gained from profiteering than from soldiering. Jason supposed he must be a rich man by now.

Bitterly he tried to force the memories from his heart. They were all part of the past now, the black, ugly past that was no more. They had nothing to do with the present . . . or the future. The future was Kate, not cold and calculating, but soft and beautiful and loving. He'd been unfair to her, he reminded himself, unfair to burden her with the darkness of his own past. He'd make it all up to her when he got home, he promised himself. Things would be better then. He'd force himself to stop this insane, stupid jealousy that must be a torture to her. From now on, he'd be a good husband to her, loyal and generous . . . and trusting. Just as soon as he got home.

If he got home, he reminded himself. *If* he got home. He reached out blindly into the darkness, feeling the thickness of the mantle of snow that covered him. Dammit, it had to be all right. He had to get home to her. He couldn't have come so far, learned so much about himself and his love for her, only to have it end now.

"He's all right, isn't he, Marc?" Kate heard the soft, pleading sound in her own voice, as over and over she mouthed the same words.

"Of course he's all right," Marc told her again and again with quiet patience. "It just takes more time to get back in all this snow." His voice was earnest, but he couldn't hide the growing anxiety in his voice.

As the days passed, Kate felt her worry turn slowly to despair, and soon she could think of nothing but Jason, alone and suffering, perhaps even dead, in the snowdrifted fields far away. Every other thought dwarfed in significance beside that fear. Even her fears of Smead, even the ugly memories of the brutal attack she had endured in the stable faded from her consciousness. She barely even remembered the cruel threats he had made when he saw Marc's arms comfortingly around her. All she could think of now was Jason. All she wanted was to have her husband home again, alive and safe.

Then, one day, just as she had begun to give up hope, she heard Marc shout out from the front door of the house. Hurrying out to him, she was just in time to see Jason walking toward her from the stable. She felt her heart leap with joy as she raced down the path to throw her arms around him in welcome.

His hat and coat were matted with snow, and little icicles had formed in his hair and the scraggly beard that had grown on his face, but Kate barely noticed them as she threw her arms around him, sobbing with excitement and relief. His face was lined and his eyes weary, but he was her own Jason, the same Jason who had gone away from her three long weeks ago, and she was beside herself with joy.

He leaned down to cover her eager, tearstained face with kisses, reveling in the warmth of her caresses after the long, cold nights of dreaming of her beauty. Clutching her up in his arms in a great bear hug, he half-led, half-carried her back into the house.

"Why were you gone so long, Jason?" she cried out. "I was terrified. What happened to you? What took—?"

"Easy, pretty girl." He laughed, still reluctant to take his arms from around her body as he tried to shrug off his heavy coat, now drenched from the melting snow. "Easy. There'll be time enough for talk when I get these wet clothes off and settle in front of the fire with a good strong whiskey."

But when they had finally brushed the snow from Jason's scratchy new beard and planted themselves comfortably in front of the fire, Kate found she had forgotten all her questions. All she wanted was to sit beside her husband, resting her head lightly on his shoulder and feeling the protective strength of his arm around her. It was enough to nestle quietly beside him, leaving the questions to Marc.

"Was it bad?" Marc asked tersely.

Jason nodded. "Worse than you can imagine. Everywhere I went, I saw piles of dead cattle."

Kate sat absolutely still, trying not to make any movement that would remind Jason of her presence. If she did, she was afraid he would send her away. Always before, when he talked business, he would not let her hear, but this time, surprisingly, he didn't seem to mind. This time, he seemed to want to cling to the warmth of her presence.

"How many do you think we have left?" Marc asked, his voice sober and heavy.

"We'll be lucky if we can save a tenth of the herd," Jason replied wearily. Kate looked up suddenly, glancing from one face to another. A tenth of the herd! Why, that meant almost everything would be lost.

"Too much land," Marc said quietly. Kate couldn't tell if there was a question mark at the end of the phrase or not.

"Too much land," Jason repeated slowly. There was a heavy reluctance in his tone. "It's too spread out, too hard to reach. There's no way to maintain it. Oh, it's all right in mild weather, but every time we get a winter like this, we'll be wiped out."

They were both silent for a long time; then Marc's voice cut through the stillness. "The world is changing."

It was the same thing he had told Kate a long time ago, in the days when he and not Jason was courting her. There was the same sadness in his voice then, too. She wondered if he remembered telling it to her. It had meant little to her then, but now she was beginning to understand.

"Yes," Jason agreed. It tore at Kate's heart to hear the pain in his voice. "The world is changing. But I hate it. I hate it like hell."

The silence that followed was so heavy that Kate could almost feel the weight of it pressing down on her shoulders. The only sound that broke its oppressive emptiness was the loud snapping of the flames, jumping out in the still air like loud bursts of gunfire.

Later, when at last she could lie in her husband's arms, weary and spent from the ecstasy of their lovemaking, she remembered the words and began pondering them again.

"Jason," she whispered softly.

"Ummm?" he replied dreamily, shifting the weight of her body to press her closer in his arms.

"Please tell me what's happened. About the cattle, I mean. Are we ruined?"

She was surprised to hear the soft sound of his laughter. "Of course not, Kate," he told her gently. "It's a setback, but I've had setbacks before. We'll manage, I promise you."

He pulled away from her gently and stared into the green depths of her eyes, watching the tiny golden highlights that reflected flickering candle flames. His gaze grew tender and compassionate.

"It's been hard for you, hasn't it?" he asked softly. "I'm sorry, Kate. I never dreamed the winter would be this cruel. I never even knew there were winters like this. But it will be better in the spring, I promise. Spring will be full of parties and gaiety."

"Sometimes I wonder if spring will ever come."

"It always does, my love. It always does."

Kate lay awake for a long time, even after Jason had drifted off to a deep, healing sleep, his arms still tightly entwined around her body.

Spring always comes.

Dear heaven, how she longed for spring. How she longed for the lush green grasses and the brilliant, perfumed flowers. Her soul was sick and weary, tired beyond endurance of the endless cold from which there seemed no relief, tired of the long dark nights and lonely days. Would it ever really come? she wondered.

20

ON THE LAST DAY OF WINTER, WHEN THE SKY SEEMED darkest and the menacing gray clouds had grown almost unbearable, Kate noticed the snow at last begin to melt, letting dark patches of muddy earth show through its cloak of whiteness. Soon she watched in wonder as it disappeared altogether, and the first sprigs of green valiantly pushed their way through the cold earth in the perpetual miracle of reawakening. Kate felt as if a burden had been lifted from her shoulders now that the long gray days were over, the cold days of confinement in the house with nothing to see but vast sheets of whiteness outside, long fearful days of waiting for Smead to make good on his idle threats. At last she felt happy and alive again. She felt as if she wanted to run through the fields with her hair loose, floating in the wind behind her. She had forgotten what it was like, forgotten how sweet it felt to hear the first soft trill of a bird, to see a bright unexpected shaft of light burst suddenly upon the pale yellow-green of new leaves beginning to sprout on barren branches.

Suddenly the party Jason had been promising her, that same party she had ridiculed so offhandedly the first time he spoke of it, no longer seemed a foolish idea. Suddenly Kate found she was hungry for human companionship, for the sound of voices and soft music, and the light touch of a man's hands as she floated gracefully through the sensuous rhythm of the dance. When Jason again suggested the idea, urging her to choose a date, she found herself responding with an enthusiasm she had not expected to feel.

Kate felt as if she were floating in the center of a dream, an amazing, only half-believable dream, as she stood beside Jason in the entry hall, listening to the awkward sounds of the musicians tuning up, and waiting with quickened pulse for the first trace of hoofbeats clattering up the road. This was her own daydream, the very image she had set in her mind the first day she drove up the long, twisting road and into the wide front yard. The dirt was still unpaved, and the tall oaks had not been planted, but it didn't matter. It was still the same dream—and it was a dream come true.

You really are mistress of the house now, she told herself silently, smiling at the silly fears she had felt on that day that now seemed so long ago.

She glanced up almost shyly at the tall man who stood beside her. This was her husband, she reminded herself, the man she loved. And yet it almost seemed as if he were a stranger.

She had never seen him look so elegant, or quite so exciting. The supple grace of his tall, lean body was accentuated by his stylishly cut clothes, and thick, wavy hair, now turned dark blond without the summer streaks of gold, provided a dramatic frame for the bold, strong lines of his face.

Kate smiled as she remembered the slicked-back hair and dark, ill-fitting suit in that first photograph she had seen of Jason. Where on earth had he gotten such a clumsy, unbecoming outfit? she wondered idly. And he had accused her of dissembling! Why, that first picture was every bit as deliberate a misrepresentation of him as her own letter and photo had been. How lucky they were to have somehow managed to cut through all that falseness to find each other!

Sensing her gaze on his face, Jason looked down at Kate, the intense blue of his eyes brightened by the pride that shone in their depths.

"How beautiful you look." His voice was soft and low, as if the words were for her ears alone, a delicious secret of love and joy to be relished in private.

She smiled happily at him. Her mirror had already told her she looked particularly pretty that night, but it was good to see the confirmation in his eyes. She was desperately eager to make a good impression on his friends. Her rich green velvet dress, scandalously low-cut by Western standards, hugged her body in the latest fashion, which she had coaxed the local dressmaker to cut from the sketches she drew. Its lush, deep splendor provided the perfect backdrop for the scintillating glitter of diamonds at her throat, studded delicately with tiny emeralds that just matched the emerald earrings Jason purchased for her from a gambler passing through Cheyenne.

The corners of Jason's lips curled into a smile as he looked down, watching his wife's delicate fingers reach up unconsciously to touch the jewels at her throat. He remembered the look of surprise in her clear green eyes when he had pulled them out of the bottom of a drawer and handed them to her.

"I bought them for my wife," he told her simply.

For a moment she didn't understand, knowing he must have had the gems long before he married her, but then suddenly she realized what he meant. The jewels were like the castle he had built on top of the hill, or the crystal and china he had crammed into the cupboard shelves. Everything had been prepared in readiness for the wife he would one day bring from the East. How carefully he had planned for her, and how thoughtfully.

"But how did you know you'd get a wife with green eyes?" she teased, touching the emeralds lightly with her hands.

"Perhaps I've always known," he said, smiling gently. "Perhaps I knew I would never settle for anything less."

The first sound of an approaching carriage clattered on the dry dirt, drawing their eyes away from each other. Kate felt her heart begin to thump wildly, following the rhythm of the hoofbeats. The party was beginning at last.

Kate was surprised at the apprehension that passed through her body, spreading even to her trembling fingertips, and she realized she was frightened of the strangers she would soon meet, inhabitants of a world she did not yet understand. For the first few minutes, she greeted them shyly, barely daring to look up into their faces, but soon she felt her fears beginning to melt away like the last of the spring snows.

Just as Jason had promised, their neighbors were neither as crude nor as gauche as she had feared. None of the women had dyed and frizzled hair or grotesquely painted faces, and not one of the men spit out dark brown tobacco juice on her newly polished floors. As they stepped up, one after another, to greet and welcome her to their community, she saw that they were every bit as elegant and perhaps even more gracious than the people at home. There was a roughness about America that still frightened her, but there was an essential fairness, too, that was appealing. Where else in the world would plain Kate Hamilton, a former governess, have been welcomed with all the courtesy that London society would have accorded only to Lady Catherine Devlin, a second cousin of the queen (three times removed)?

"Whoever expected such a jewel in the middle of the wilderness?" a new voice chimed out. Kate was aware of beaming lips that framed a perfect set of pearly white teeth. "What a rare and delightful pleasure."

Kate stared in astonishment at the young man who bowed with supple grace over her fingers, kissing them lightly with dry, firm lips. His voice was hauntingly familiar, and yet there was nothing about the vaguely pretty face or immaculately modish clothes that called to her memory. Then, with a sudden rush of homesickness, she realized what it was. The man had spoken with a perfect English accent.

"A countrywoman is always a pleasure," he told her with the easy charm of one who is accustomed to courts and ballrooms. "But such a beautiful one . . . ah, we hadn't expected that."

Kate looked up at him with a warm smile, enjoying both the lighthearted compliment and the sweet sounds of a voice from home. It was an instant before it occurred to her to ponder his words.

We hadn't expected . . .

That meant there were other Englishmen here. Here in the Wyoming territory. Here where she thought at last she was free of the influence of her father and brothers. She felt herself stiffen with fear.

Jason noticed the sudden tension of her body next to his, and he slipped his arm quickly around her waist, drawing her closer. Although he did not try to speak of it, even to whisper words of assurance in her ear, he told her with his eyes that he understood and with his tender smile that she was not to be afraid. As she looked up at him, meeting his eyes with her own, she found the fear easing away from her body, and her lips began to answer his smile.

After all, there was no sense being a ninny about it. Even if there was someone who had known her in the past, would he recognize in the stately, sensuous beauty who stood so proudly beside her husband the same awkward, gangly teen-ager he had known in years gone by?

As the hours passed, Kate began to laugh more and more at her fears, seeing how foolish they really were. Although a surprising number of Englishmen passed over their threshold, she did not recognize any of them, nor did they seem to see her as anything but Kate Hamilton, the English-born wife of their host. When the music started and her toes began tapping involuntarily against the floor, Kate was delighted to see that the Englishmen flocked quickly around her, vying with the young Americans for her dances. As she floated happily in their arms, it took no great perception to see that their warm smiles were turned, not toward a lady with a suspicious past, but only toward a graceful, pretty dancing partner.

What fun it was to live in the West, she thought for the first time since she had arrived in the rough frontier town. What fun it was to live in a land with so few young women, a land where even a matron could dance as many dances as a beautiful young belle with dozens of beaux. Otherwise, with Jason off in a corner comparing the effects of the long winter with one neighbor or another, she would have had to sit against the wall with a long line of matrons, pretending to enjoy watching the young unmarried girls dancing every dance.

"As light of foot as you are beautiful. What a wonder!"

The voice startled Kate as she stood for a moment between dances, trying to catch her breath. Looking up, she was delighted to see the vapid but charming features of the young Englishman she had spoken to earlier.

"Reggie Sheffield-Jones," he reminded her tactfully. "Deuced hard to remember so many new names all at once, isn't it?" As she smiled gratefully, he held out his arms invitingly. "May I have this dance, or do I have to fight off all your other young gallants with a branding iron?"

Kate laughed, delighted with the empty-headed frivolity of his compliments, and stepped easily into his arms, moving in rhythm to the music. Reggie was, she decided quickly, as foolish and silly a human being as she had ever met, but he was good-natured and fun to be with, and even the inanities that passed out of his mouth, one after the other, were refreshing to ears accustomed to the long, slow sound of silence. Besides, the foppishness of his dress and manners reminded her of all the young dandies in London, and she suddenly realized that she missed her homeland with a yearning she would never have believed she could feel for a clod of earth and a few old buildings.

For all his foolish airs, Reggie was a superb dancer, and Kate quickly relaxed into the lightness of his arms, enjoying the faultless rhythm of the steps almost as much as the easy humor of his chatter. Even when the imperfect orchestra strayed from the music, picking up a wrong note here and there, Reggie could not be lured into a misstep, and Kate followed him confidently as they whirled gracefully around the floor.

All too soon she heard the sound of the music stop, and with a sudden touch of sadness she watched Reggie bow lightly to her. She had forgotten how much she loved dancing . . . and how much she loved smiling at young men and flirting harmlessly with them.

Reggie stayed by her side for a moment as she heard the musicians strike up another piece of music. The tune was unfamiliar to her ears.

Reggie saw the puzzled look on her face. "The reel," he explained. "Do you know it?"

"No." She shook her head. Jason had warned her about the reel. He said no Virginian could hold a dance without it.

"Let me show you," Reggie urged, enthusiasm lighting up his face as he stretched out a hand to draw her toward the long lines of dancers forming in the center of the floor.

Kate hesitated for a moment. It would be scandalously improper, she knew, to dance two dances in a row with the same man. And yet, this was a new country with new rules. The old customs and taboos no longer held here. Would anyone really notice—or care—if she decided to have a little fun?

Who cares anyway? she thought with a sudden burst of frivolity. Who cares if a lot of old fuddy-duddies disapprove? This was her night, and she was going to enjoy it. Smiling her assent, she reached out her hand to place it in his.

She felt a little foolish as she took her place in the long line, not knowing what to do, but it was only seconds before she felt her toes tapping to the lively music and her hands clapping in rhythm as she bobbed happily back and forth, swinging on her partner's arm with a wild abandon that sent her skirts flying out from her sides. By the time it was finally her turn to romp briskly down the long aisle with Reggie between the twin rows of dancers, she was ready to join in the boisterous fun with the pent-up laughter of months bubbling out of her lips.

The reel ended with Kate faint and out of breath from girlish laughter. The giddiness made her suddenly light-headed, and she held on to Reggie, leaning against him breathlessly for support. Giggling almost as hard as she, he reached out an arm to place it around her waist, and the two smiled at each other like a pair of children who had just invented a wonderful new game that no one else can understand.

The music started up again, a melodic, graceful waltz, and without warning, Reggie swung her into his arms, whirling her giddily onto the floor. At first Kate was horrified. Three dances with the same man! And yet, what difference did it make? Who cared about propriety? Now when she was having fun. Not in this brave new land where people were free and unfettered.

Only when Kate glanced over at the side of the room and saw Jason standing there, watching her with a terrifying intensity, did she realize with the horrible clarity of hindsight that propriety did, after all, matter. It mattered a great deal. How could she have forgotten, even for a few brief hours, Jason's wild, angry fits of temper? The look she saw on his face at that moment was the same black rage she had not seen for months, and her heart sank with despair. How could he do this to her? How could he ruin this, of all nights? This night he had planned especially for her amusement and happiness?

Reggie caught the expression on her face and turned quickly to look at Jason. "Oh, I say," he stammered awkwardly, his face turning red with embarrassment. "I'm sorry if I've caused you trouble."

"Don't be silly," she told him, her voice sharper than she had intended. How could Jason be jealous of Reggie? she asked herself, amazed. Why, Reggie was just like all the London dandies she had ever known, one of those foppish, inane young men all the girls loved to flirt with but no one ever wanted to marry. Glancing up at him, she saw the troubled look that had replaced the vapid humor in his eyes. "It's all right, Reggie," she assured him, forcing as much lightness in her voice as she could manage. "Don't worry about it."

The dance seemed to go on interminably, but at last Kate heard the music stop, and she excused herself with relief. Brushing off the other young men who tried to flock around her, she hurried toward the kitchen, though she knew she was needed there just about as much as she had been in her father's house. Jason, like Patrick, had been careful to see that she had proper kitchen help so she would never have to lift a finger.

Sick at heart, she lingered in the kitchen for a few minutes, her brain reeling with shock. How could she have been so foolish, she berated herself angrily, and so improper? And yet, why should it have made such a difference? Philippe wouldn't have minded her dancing with other men, or Charles. Would she never be free of this hideous jealousy Jason tormented her with?

Kate spent the next half-hour busying herself in the dining room, helping the servants arrange things for the formal dinner that would follow the dancing. How exquisitely beautiful it looked, she thought in sadness as she looked down the length of the massive banquet table. How many times she and Jason had laughed at that same long table as they enjoyed their dinner there, huddled together in one corner. Once they had even sat at opposite ends, pretending they were a grand lord and his lady, shouting bits of formal conversation at each other. What fun it had been, what wonderful silliness.

She fought back the tears that stung her eyes as she thought of that night, remembering how much she had loved the silly game they played. She should have loved being here tonight, too. She should have loved looking down the long table, seeing the elegant crystal and highly polished silver that glittered with the sheen of a thousand diamonds in the rich golden candlelight. How unfair it was of Jason to spoil it all for her.

Finally, when she could make no more excuses, she knew she had to force herself back into the ballroom to watch the festive dancing that no longer intrigued or delighted her. Although she dragged her feet as slowly as she could down the long hallway, she knew she must come finally to the end. All too soon, she saw the bright lights of the party directly in front of her.

As she looked out into the gaily lit ballroom, she saw Marc standing just on the other side of the threshold. Turning, he caught sight of her and stepped quickly through the doorway.

"It's a lovely . . ." he began, then broke off abruptly as his shrewd brown eyes caught the troubled look on her face. Gazing down at her, his voice filled with concern, he asked, "What's the matter, Kate?"

"Nothing," she told him hurriedly, forcing as much cheer into her face as she could.

He reached down and took her chin lightly in his fingers, tilting her face up so she had to look into his eyes. "You're not a very good liar, you know."

She felt the tears begin to well up in her eyes again, and angrily she tried to force them back. She wasn't going to make a fool of herself in front of him. She wasn't!

"It's Jason," she whispered, dropping her eyes in embarrassment. "He thinks . . . Well, I was dancing with Reggie. He's just a silly goose, but he's fun, and Jason . . . Jason . . ."

Her voice faded away, unable even to whisper the hideous words of his suspicion.

"I know, Kate," Marc said quietly. She had the feeling he really did understand. "Didn't I warn you you'd have to be patient?"

"Oh, I've tried," she cried out. At last the tears she had been fighting refused to be contained any longer and began to pour freely down her cheeks. "I've tried so hard."

"Now, look here," he said, a mock sternness in his voice. "We can't have you crying over this, do you hear?" Pulling her gently toward him, he wrapped his arms comfortingly around her, letting her sob softly on his shoulder.

When at last she stepped back from him, her tears spent, she was conscious of a feeling of foolishness.

"I'm sorry."

"Don't be," he whispered softly, reaching out his hand to brush the tears lightly from her cheeks. Seeing the kind patience on his face, she strained to reward him with a smile, but even as the corners of her lips began to turn up, they stopped abruptly, frozen with horror and fear.

There in the doorway, not six feet away from them, stood her husband, his eyes filled with hate.

As Marc caught sight of the stunned expression on her face, he turned quickly. Seeing Jason in the doorway, he pulled away from Kate and swung around to face his friend. "Jason—"

But Jason would not even let him begin. Turning on his heel, he hurried away from them, heading back into the crowded ballroom.

"Don't worry, Kate," Marc called out hurriedly over his shoulder as he started after Jason. "I'll find him and explain everything."

Kate followed the two men for a few steps, then halted on the fringes of the brightly lit room, watching helplessly as Jason hurried toward a group of men standing on the other side. Marc followed as best he could, but there was no way he could talk to Jason in front of the other men, and he was forced to stop a few feet away, hesitating awkwardly with a troubled look on his face.

Sick with dread, Kate watched for a minute longer, then turned toward the hallway again. She was no dissembler, and there was no point spoiling the party for her guests. Just as she was about to move back down the hall, seeking the quiet refuge of one of the dark, empty rooms, she became aware of a figure standing stiffly on the side of the room. Half in curiosity, half in dread, she raised her eyes to look at him.

It was Earl Smead.

What was he doing there? she thought furiously. Like the cowhands, who had all been invited to the dance, Smead was dressed in a suit and wore no gun at his side. Still, Kate found the intrusion of his presence in her house intolerable, no matter how much superficial courtesy he might have cultivated for the occasion.

He had not chosen to join in the gaiety of the party, but stood instead on the sidelines with a look on his face Kate could not identify. Then, as he noticed her standing across the room, staring at him, Smead turned his gaze directly toward her. With a sudden rush of horror, Kate finally identified the brutal expression she saw in his eyes. It was a look, not of hatred, as she would have expected, or even a look of lust. Instead, it was the cold, cruel expression of gloating vengeance.

Too late, Kate realized what had happened. Too late, she saw what had made Jason suspicious of her. Now she realized what voice had been whispering evil words into his ears. Now she knew why he happened to come to the doorway just at the moment Marc was comforting her.

What a fool she had been. By flirting with Reggie, she had played right into Smead's hands. That was all he had been waiting for these long, silent weeks when she had begun to think his angry words were only an idle threat. By seeking sympathy and advice from Marc, she had only put the finishing touches on her own ruin.

Was it too late now, she wondered, too late to undo the cruel rift he had caused between her and Jason? If only she knew what kind of evil he had poisoned Jason with, then she might know how to fight it.

Oh, please, dear God, she thought, too frightened now even to cry. Please don't let it be too late.

21

For Kate, the rest of the party seemed a long, bleak nightmare, as if a series of hazy, distorted images was passing one after another before her eyes and yet somehow she couldn't make herself bring them into focus. It was one of those long, seemingly endless nightmares in which she felt as if she were trappped in some nameless, indefinable place with no hope of escape.

She sat obediently at the end of the long damask-covered table, feeling like a mechanical, jointed puppet being pulled on strings over which she had no control. Even as she forced her lips into a studied smile, affecting the gracious geniality of a hostess, she knew it was no use. No matter how hard she tried, she would never succeed in looking natural or carefree. She could only be grateful that her guests didn't know her well enough to realize that the wooden gestures and stilted conversation were not really her.

As she turned mechanically to this side and that, following the demands of convention, she found her eyes holding firmly to the other end of the long room, where Jason sat like a king at the head of a heavily laden banquet table.

Jason was far better at pretending than she. Kate noticed he moved with a casual ease, playing the perfect host as he smiled a solicitous query at one guest or laughed with approving mirth at the sallies of another. Yet, all the time, even with the superficial grace he exhibited, Kate sensed that his body was as tense as a tightly coiled spring or a gun with the trigger pulled halfway back, ready to explode at any second.

Kate jabbed her fork into the raw oyster that lay in its bed of chipped ice in the delicate monogrammed crystal bowl before her, and lifted it to her lips. Its subtle flavor was lost in the bitter taste of fear that filled her mouth. Even her jaws found it too hard to concentrate on the task of tearing it apart, and finally she let it slide in a single lump down her throat.

She had been so proud of those oysters, she remembered.

They were only tinned, but they were enough of a delicacy to impress Jason's friends, and that had been important to her. She had planned that course as carefully as she planned the rest of the meal.

As the oysters were cleared away by servants who were, if not as meticulous as Kate would have wished, at least enthusiastic and eager to please, hot consommé was quickly ladled from heavy tureens into the bowls set at each place. It was only canned soup, but Cookie had exercised his wonderful imagination, flavoring it with sherry and dried herbs that hung from the rafters in the storeroom, and floating long grains of rice through its translucent brown succulence.

The remaining courses flowed swiftly, one after another, with the perfect harmony of a well-orchestrated symphony. First came delicate salmon croquettes, topped with a rich egg sauce and surrounded by Saratoga potatoes, then sweetbreads formed into patties and colored with a garnish of canned green peas. The roast beef that followed was Kate's pièce de résistance. Unlike the Western style of beef—freshly slaughtered meat tossed into a pan and seared hastily over high heat—it was perfectly aged and slowly roasted to perfection. The pudding that accompanied it had puffed up to a heavenly lightness as it cooked in the juices of the meat, and cauliflower and cabbage were a perfect complement to the rich blend of flavors. After the beef came succulent prairie chickens and currant tarts, then at last the palate could be cleansed with the cooling taste of salad, prepared from canned asparagus Kate had been hoarding for just such an occasion. Even the heartiest eaters began to slow down when it was time to nibble at the cheese and crackers and savor the lightness of sherbet, but Kate noticed that somehow they still found room for the homemade cakes and cookies that ended the meal.

Kate felt heartsick as she watched her guests relishing the meal she had worked so hard to plan. How little that triumph meant to her now. Now all that mattered were the stern cold eyes that avoided hers from the other end of the long table. Watching her husband's face closely, Kate saw to her dismay that the hard set of his jaw had not abated during the long meal. It was with relief that she finally pushed back her chair and suggested to the other wives that they retire, leaving the gentlemen to their brandy and their cigars.

During dinner, the grand hall had been filled again with furniture, and as Kate led her guests into the room, she was surprised to see not the slightest trace of the ball that had taken place such a short time ago. In an odd way, it was a relief. She felt almost as if the ball had never taken place, as if it had been only a hideous, terrifying nightmare. Wearily she sank into the soft cushions of an overstuffed chair, grateful for the heavy meal that made any further question of dancing impossible. Fortunately, the lethargy that settled over the plump matrons as they eased their overfed bodies into chairs and couches around the room made any attempt at small talk slow and languid, and Kate's sudden weariness went unnoticed.

When at last she heard the sound of rough male voices laughing in raucous mirth at their own humor, Kate realized the men had come out into the hall and were preparing to rejoin the ladies. With a sudden flash of panic she realized she couldn't face Jason again, at least not for a while. She couldn't bear to sit across the room from him, watching the coldness on his face while she tried to pretend nothing was wrong. Abruptly she rose and excused herself, pretending that she had to see to arrangements for the guests who were staying with them instead of risking the hospitality of the local hotel.

She slipped quickly through the doorway before the men could draw near, and hurried around the corner, heading for the wide stairway that led to the second floor. Hearing the muffled sound of voices, now well in the distance, she breathed a sigh of relief. No one would venture this far down the hallway. She would be alone here.

As she tiptoed lightly toward the stairs, careful not to make even the slightest noise that might attract attention to herself, she was startled to hear the sound of voices coming from the entry hall. Hastily she pressed back into the shadows beneath the stairway, listening tensely to the words that floated across the still air.

"Didn't I tell you?"

Kate would have recognized that gloating sound of triumph anywhere. It was the voice of Earl Smead.

What was he doing in the house? He should have left at the end of the dance, when all the cowhands had gone. If he was here now, it could only be at Jason's invitation. The thought made her blood run cold.

"Get out," Jason hissed furiously, his voice low but filled with venom. Kate felt her heart beat faster in a sudden burst of hope. Perhaps, after all, Jason hadn't believed Smead's lies. Perhaps she had overestimated his anger.

Smead only laughed at Jason's fury. It was a low, nasty

laugh, buried deep in the cavern of his throat. "Are you calling me a liar?"

There was a long pause, too long, and suddenly Kate knew she had been foolish to hope. When Jason finally spoke, the words came out slowly, reluctantly, as if they caused him physical pain.

"You know goddamn well I can't."

"I told you," Smead gloated, wasting no time picking up on Jason's anguish. "She ain't nothin' but a whore. Anyone can have her, even old Earl, if'n he wanted her."

"You filthy son of a bitch," Jason cried out hoarsely. To Kate's surprise, she heard a sudden scuffling sound, as if Jason had thrown himself on the man. "Damn you to hell."

"Come on, boss," Smead sniveled obsequiously. The placating sound of his groveling seemed to Kate even slimier than his evil, gloating laughter. "Cain't kill a man for tellin' the truth."

"If you've lied to me, Smead—"

"Ain't no lies," he whined. "Didn't I steer you right before? Didn't you catch her with him in the hallway, jest like I said? Bet she didn't tell you what happened in the stable, neither, did she?"

The silence that followed was as eloquent as an answer.

Suddenly Kate realized what a fool she had been not to tell Jason what had happened in the stable. She had played right into Smead's hands, letting him frighten her into keeping the incident a secret. Now her silence could only look like guilt.

"I didn't reckon she'd say nothin' about it," Smead added snidely after a long, meaningful pause.

"By heaven, I trusted that woman," Jason called out, the sound of anguish ringing with a deep resonance in his voice. "I loved her."

Frightened as she was by the horrible finality of his words, Kate felt herself torn apart by the desperate suffering she heard in his voice. She longed to run out to him, to hold him in her arms and comfort him. Only fear held her back.

"As God is my witness, I'll . . ." He broke off abruptly, unable for a moment to go on. When he finally continued, his voice was calmer, but there was a quiet despair in it that was more terrifying than all the shouting and raging in the world.

"May God show her mercy, for I won't."

The long silence that followed was broken only by the sound of the front door opening and slamming shut again, and the sharp clatter of Jason's leather heels against the wooden floor as he moved down the hall. Kate pressed herself farther into the shadows, not even daring to breathe until he had passed.

She could still hear the sound of his voice echoing in her ears.

May God show her mercy, for I won't.

She closed her eyes, trying to visualize his features as he said the words, but instead, the face of her brother Eamon kept intruding in her mind. The face of Eamon as he stood over the body of her lover, the cold, hard look of death and killing in his eyes.

If you ever touch another man . . . I'll kill you both.

They were so alike in many ways, she thought, her husband and the brother she had feared since early childhood. Both so aloof and self-contained in the things they felt deeply about. Both so strong and sure of themselves. Both so determined never to leave a course, once they had set their feet on it.

Would it do any good to protest her innocence? she wondered fleetingly. Or would it be only a futile effort? He was already predisposed to believe her guilty, of that she was sure. Everything had been building toward that from the first moment they saw each other on a station platform and he caught her looking at him, a stranger, with lust in her eyes.

You have the soul of a harlot, my dear.

Why would he believe her, a woman who had had a lover before him? A woman who had ridden through the night to thrust her naked body at him like a common whore? In his eyes, she was a fallen woman, a woman who had sinned before and would surely sin again.

If you touch another man . . . I'll kill you both.

And he had found her in another man's arms!

That he was capable of keeping his threat, Kate did not doubt for a moment. Jason was a man who could import gunmen to slaughter the innocent sheep ranchers for claiming open land he did not even own. What lengths would he go to in order to hold on to the possessions that were really his? And Kate knew, beyond the shadow of a doubt, that to Jason she *was* a possession, perhaps his prize possession. He would never let any other man have her, even if it was only in his own imagination. He would see her dead first.

With a sudden rush of horror, she realized there was nothing she could do. To stay in Jason Hamilton's house, no matter how desperately she loved and needed him, meant certain death. Perhaps not for the next day or two, not with guests in the house, but sooner or later it would be inevitable. Sooner or later, they would have to be alone again, and then she would be at his mercy. There was no way she could defend herself against him.

Even as she tried to push the thought from her mind, she knew she had no choice. There was only one thing she could do. She had to get away from him. She had to leave this man with whom she had known such ecstasy, and she had to do it quickly, that very night, before he had a chance to formulate his plans against her. To hesitate, to let her passion sway her in her resolve, might cost her her very life.

Perhaps if she left quickly, she told herself, he might be satisfied to vent his rage on her instead of taking it out on Marc or poor, foolish Reggie. She wished she could warn them, but she knew there was no time.

She leaned back for a minute against the banister, closing her eyes in weariness. She was sick of violence and death, sick of the terror of running away. For a moment she was tempted to stay, tempted to let Jason do with her what he would, but then the fighting spirit returned and she began to race stealthily up the stairs.

22

KATE STARED DOWN AT HER HANDS IN FASCINATION, watching them with an odd detachment, as if they belonged, not to her, but to someone else, some stranger she had never met. She had never seen hands quite like that before. They were trembling so violently they looked like the pale new leaves that shuddered on the branches of trees in strong spring breezes.

She ran her quivering fingers lightly over the rough fabric of the dark brown riding habit she had stretched out on the bed. It was not her most becoming garment, but it was the most practical. Jason had insisted on having it made for her, promising she would find good use for it. What irony it seemed that the very use he had promised should turn out to be nothing less than running away from him.

Kate stood for several minutes beside the bed, hesitating

reluctantly. Once she had put the garment on, she knew, the action would be irrevocable. There was no way she would be able to explain the drab riding habit while guests in elegant finery awaited her downstairs. There would be nothing left for her, once she had draped its severe folds over her body, but flight.

She knew she could not afford even the moment of indecision she had already allowed herself, but still she wavered. How long would it be, she wondered, before Jason became suspicious of her absence and came to search for her? Fifteen minutes? Twenty? Half an hour perhaps? No, she could not afford to linger any longer beside the bed trying to make up her mind. Soon it would be too late, and the moment of choice would be gone.

Suddenly, with a violent impulse that tore against the resistance lying deep in her heart, she pulled off the expensive party dress and thrust it on the bed, heaping a pile of frothy petticoats beside it. Reaching up toward the back of her neck, she was surprised to find her fingers stumbling on the clasp of the necklace at her throat, as if she was reluctant to give up the solace of its beauty. It was the same sparkling necklace she had rejoiced over only hours before—that very bauble that seemed to offer promises of a lovely, shining life—and for a moment she clutched tightly at the clasp, holding on to it as if it were a life raft in the middle of a turbulent sea. Finally she forced her fingers to pull the dainty pieces of metal apart, and removed it slowly, staring at it with the hunger of lost love as she laid it gently on the dresser.

Mechanically she pulled the drab brown dress over her body and fastened it quickly, then sat on the side of the bed to tug at the soft leather boots that covered her legs nearly to the knee. When she had finished with that, she grabbed up a plain black woolen shawl, drawing it lightly across her shoulders. She would have preferred the heavy buffalo coat, for its warmth could have protected her against the chill night air, but it was downstairs, and she knew better than to try to fetch it. The shawl, light as it was, would have to do. Besides, it was oddly appropriate. It was the same shawl she had arrived in that eventful night months ago. It seemed fitting that she should also leave in it.

Her eyes lingered for a moment on the superb emerald brooch that lay carelessly beside the necklace on her dresser. With a pang of regret, she realized it was her last link with the past, and with the lovely, gentle mother who had now passed almost beyond memory. For a moment she was tempted to bring it with her; then, slowly, reluctantly, she forced herself to abandon the idea. The brooch would pay for the horse she was taking and the small amount of cash she had tucked into her pocket. She did not want to leave any debts behind her.

Kate slipped quietly across the room and leaned against the heavy wooden door, pressing her ear to its sturdy surface. She listened carefully, her ears straining for the faintest hint of a footstep outside the door. One misstep, one false move, might prove fatal.

Finally, hearing nothing but silence, she pulled the door slowly open, cringing at the harsh sound of creaking hinges that echoed in the still hallway.

Silent as a ghost, she slipped out into the hall and stood for a moment, motionless as a statue in the dim, flickering light of the candles set in heavy iron sconces on the walls. After a short time, hearing no sound, she began to glide stealthily toward the narrow back stairway.

As the gay sounds of laughter drifted up from the party below, Kate felt a heavy lump beginning to form in her throat. Only a few hours ago, she, too, had been laughing and happy. How unfair it all seemed. She should have been downstairs with the others, chattering and giggling like a young bride, instead of standing joylessly and alone in a darkened hallway awaiting the destruction of all her hopes and happiness, perhaps even her life.

She paused as she reached the stairs, and leaned against the wall, letting her lids close heavily over eyes that stung, not with tears, but the remembrance of tears, hot and bitterly shed. Suddenly she was tired, more tired than she had ever been in her life. Suddenly she did not want to run anymore.

She was tempted to give up, tempted to throw herself on Jason's mercy. Perhaps she could explain. Perhaps she could make him understand.

But even as the thought crossed her mind, she knew it was impossible. She knew she could never make him believe her. All she could think of was the ugly memory of hard, cold eyes, eyes that would never understand or forgive.

If you ever touch another man . . . I'll kill you both.

Icy, bitter eyes. Cold and cruel. Eyes she had seen before, but not in Jason's face. Eyes she had seen staring out of the impassive features of her brother Eamon before he had killed her lover. There had been a warning in Eamon's eyes, a warning she had not heeded, and now Philippe was dead. There was a warning in Jason's eyes, too, one she knew she dared not ignore. If she did, this time the corpse that lay cooling on the floor would be her own.

What kind of land was this she had come to? Kate wondered. What kind of land could breed the senseless violence that lay all around them, warping even decent men, until they too became a part of its ugliness? The cruelty she had seen in Jason's eyes was born here; Marc had told her that. And Marc, would the cold light she had seen shining out of his eyes when he urged Smead to go for his gun continue to grow, until he too was capable of the same mindless brutality?

What a fool she had been to come here, she realized with terrifying clarity. It had been a ridiculous mistake to think she could find a husband through a mail-order ad—and an even greater mistake to marry a handsome stranger even after she had seen the cold anger that lay behind the back of his eyes. It was a mistake she might have to pay for with her life.

With a sudden burst of will, Kate forced herself to stand up straight again. No matter what happened, she was not going to give up her life easily. She listened attentively for a second, then began to walk slowly down the stairs, dreading the heavy creaks that marked each cautious footfall. She knew the lively party noises would cover the sounds that seemed so loud in her own ears, but still it was hard to force herself forward, moving step by creaking step down to the bottom of the stairs.

The dark, narrow hallway that lay at the foot of the stairs would be dangerous, she knew. It was only a small area, no more than a few feet long, but from there she would be visible from the doorway of the large living room.

She held her breath as she stood on the bottom step, knowing that for her the moment of truth had come at last. This was the time she would escape . . . or be captured.

Still holding her breath, she counted slowly to ten, then forced herself to push out abruptly from the safety of the stairway. Darting across the hall, her heart beating rapidly in a frenzy of panic, she threw open the outside door and ran out into the cold night air. When she heard no sound behind her, she dared to hope she had made it, but she knew she could not be confident yet. Only the next few minutes would tell if anyone had seen her and decided to come out looking for her.

Kate hurried across the light new grass sprouting on the wide lawn and swung open the heavy door to the stable, leaving it agape behind her. There was no time to find a lantern and light it. The moonlight that streamed in through the open doorway would have to suffice.

Sunbeam whinnied an affectionate greeting, and Kate hurried over to the mare, throwing her arms around her neck and talking to her softly, trying to coax her into silence. She felt the spoiled little roan nuzzling eagerly at her pocket.

"No, Sunbeam," she whispered softly. "No sugar lumps today. No more sugar for a while, my pretty."

The mare seemed puzzled, but did not protest as Kate led her hastily from the stall and threw a bridle over her head, fitting the cold bit gently into her mouth. She didn't dare take time to saddle the horse. She had already used up far too many of her precious minutes dressing and coming downstairs. She would have to take her chances riding Sunbeam bareback.

She led the horse outside, walking stealthily ahead of her, then pushed the door carefully shut behind them. The frisky roan was happy to be outside again, after being pent up all day, and it was all Kate could do to control her eager prancing. She did not want to get caught now. Not when she was so close to safety. She could not afford to let Sunbeam whinny her eager approval of a wild ride through the cold midnight air.

When at last Kate had led the horse around the first turn in the road and was out of view of the house, she finally allowed herself to climb on the mare's back and press her heels lightly into her side. That was all Sunbeam needed. Tossing her mane in the breeze, she began to gallop easily down the road.

Kate dug her knees tightly into the roan's sides, grateful for the split riding skirt Jason had forced on her. It was ugly, but it was sensible, and she found to her relief that she could ride in it as easily as she had in her brothers' outgrown trousers when she was a child.

She let Sunbeam have her head, and soon they were racing swiftly down the hill in the bright light of a nearly full moon. The wind bit into Kate's face and tore through the thin weave of her shawl, but she barely noticed it. Every corner of her awareness was concentrated on her fear.

Kate had expected to feel safer once she was out of the house, but now that the swift flight had suddenly become reality, she found her fear growing instead of abating. It was as if every thump of Sunbeam's hooves pounded the icy terror deeper and deeper into her heart. Her ears strained with an almost unbearable tension, listening for any sound that might give even the slightest hint of pursuit.

When at last she had reached the bottom of the hill and begun to cut across the fields, she allowed herself the luxury of stopping for a moment, reining in the frisky horse as she looked back, her eyes scanning the hill for any sign of a rider. When she saw nothing, she realized that she had gotten away safely, and she allowed herself a small sigh of relief.

Urging Sunbeam forward again, this time at a slower, steadier pace, Kate waited for the wave of relaxation that should have flooded over her body, but it did not come. In its place was a new fear, a quieter, subtler fear, but one that kept growing until it became almost unbearable.

It was a fear of tomorrow, that unknown tomorrow, and all the days to come. It was a fear that she thought she had left behind forever on a wintry day in a small frontier chapel when she and the man she adored exchanged the vows that should have endured till the end of their lives.

At least I'm alive, she told herself firmly.

It was true. She was alive, and that was what counted. She was young and strong and full of life. Whatever tomorrow might bring, she would face it somehow. She had endured hardships before. She could endure them again. She was a fighter, and nothing was ever going to make her curl up in terror and give up.

Throwing her head back, she tossed off the warm shawl she had wrapped around it, letting the cold wind play through her hair until it tore out the pins, sending it tumbling out behind her. She was a fighter, she reminded herself. She would make out all right.

Turning Sunbeam back on the road, she began to gallop toward Jasper Springs, eager to get through the outskirts of town long before the sun could rise.

Part IV

The Storm Breaks

23

THE BRIGHT GOLDEN MOON WAS NEARLY A FULL CIRCLE AS IT hung high in the deep blue sky. Sometimes, as Kate glanced up at it, it almost seemed to wink at her, as if it were trying to offer the cheer her heart was too heavy to accept. Every rock and crevice along the side of the road, every tiny blade of grass, was illuminated in the clarity of its light, but Kate could barely see them. Instead of the soft, undulating hills in the distance, she saw only the image of dark golden hair falling in gentle waves around the strong, potent lines of an inscrutable but passionate face. Instead of the deep, pure light of the sky, she was aware only of the memory of clear, midnight-blue eyes.

Why did she have to think of him now? she asked herself bitterly, gazing down the road that seemed to be a pale satin ribbon twisting its way through the deep blue landscape. Why did his eyes come back to haunt her, filled with the sudden flashes of tenderness that could flare out from depths of dark passion? Why did even the mockery and cruelty she had too often seen in those same eyes call out to her with a deep yearning to return to the man she loved? For love him she did; even now she had to admit that to herself. Even if he caught her, even if he raised his hand to strike her down in death, she knew she would still love him with the same violent passion that was no more reasoning than the instincts of a wild beast.

She felt a deep sense of loss as she forced herself to continue down the road. There was in her a terrible hunger for the joy she was leaving behind, as if she sensed that, no matter what life had in store for her in the future, the best of it already belonged to the past. As she slipped quietly through the outskirts of Jasper Springs, leaving none but a few inquisitive eyes to stare after her in the moonlight, and left the main road to cut across the fields, she felt a deep weariness settle over her body that shut out even the grief and fear that had weighed so heavily on her heart.

Kate turned Sunbeam west, following the bright stars that decorated the clear spring sky. She didn't know what lay ahead across the prairie or beyond the next hill, but it didn't matter. All that mattered was escape, and one way seemed much like another to her. Besides, to the west lay the new land—California and the seacoast. Surely life would be better there, newer and purer, without the ugly violence that had settled so brutally over the Wyoming territory.

She pressed the pretty roan on relentlessly, even as the sun rose and pushed its way higher and higher into the sky. Only when she realized her exhausted horse could continue on no longer without rest did she allow herself to stop, and then for no more than thirty or forty minutes at a time. Even then, she did not dare shut her own eyes, for fear they would grow too heavy to open when the time was up and they had to press on again. Each time she climbed back on Sunbeam's back, she felt a little wearier than when she had left it, and soon she realized she could not go on much longer.

The land she had been riding through was flat and nearly empty, dotted only here and there with a sparse collection of isolated ranch houses and small farms. As afternoon began to deepen into dusk, bringing her flight nearly full circle from night to dark night again, Kate found herself scanning the horizon anxiously. She didn't want to stay on the prairies much longer. She felt like an easy target on the long stretches of land that showed a hill or a house or even a human form miles in the distance. Hopefully, she began to study a series of shallow hills to her left, and on a sudden impulse she tugged at the rein, veering Sunbeam off course and turning toward the safety of their refuge.

Sunset had already brightened the tips of the hills to a rich blaze of vivid crimson as Kate and Sunbeam rode wearily up to the first crest. Pausing for an instant at the top, Kate found herself gazing down at a surprisingly fertile valley nestled in the gentle slopes below. Just at the edge of the valley lay a lone farmhouse, poised hesitantly in the midst of the rich green grasses and deep brown earth, as if it were not sure of its right to be there. The house was small and unpainted, surrounded by a low, crude fence, and the barn that was perched behind it was equally unpretentious. To Kate's eyes, both buildings seemed gray and uninviting.

Cautiously she began to urge Sunbeam down the hill, heading for the simple house that lay below. She knew it was dangerous to encounter people, even so far from the Triple Crown, for Jason's influence spread for many miles, but she knew, too, that she and her horse were both desperately tired. She would have to go to these people, whoever they were, and beg for help. She had no choice.

The farmyard was empty and curiously devoid of any sound as Kate rode in. She hesitated for a moment, her uncertainty heightened by the uncanny silence around her, then slipped resolutely from Sunbeam's back onto the muddy ground below. She thought she caught the glimmer of a faint, flickering light in the twilight dimness of the windows, but she could not be sure. She felt the eerie sensation of eyes staring at her unseen from behind crisply curtained windows. Finally, the door slid open, barely more than a crack, and a man stepped out, shutting it tightly behind him. He had a heavy rifle gripped tensely in his hands.

He was a young man, no more than twenty-five or -six, Kate judged, but his face was already lined with care and tension, and the dark brown hair around his temples was streaked with gray. He was short, barely more than an inch or two taller than Kate, but his body was strong and stocky, as if he was accustomed to heavy labor.

Kate took a step toward him, then stopped uncertainly, confused by the hard, unfriendly look on his face. "I'm Kate ..." she began, then broke off awkwardly. "Kate Devlin."

It sounded strange to use the name that was no longer hers—the name she had vowed would never cross her lips again—but she dared not say Kate Hamilton here. It was too close to the Triple Crown.

"What d'ye want?"

Kate felt her heart sink. There was even less welcome in his voice than in his face.

"My horse and I are tired. We've come a long way, and we need food and shelter." When there was still no sign of response in his face, she continued awkwardly. "I can pay you well."

Cold gray eyes looked carefully into hers, and for a long moment Kate was sure he was going to turn her away. Then, just as she had begun to despair, he moved his arm slowly, sliding the butt of his gun to rest against the dark earth.

"I'll take no money for helpin' a stranger," he said quietly. Then, turning his head, he called out in a loud voice, "Caroline."

The door swung open almost immediately, giving Kate an opportunity to stare into the interior of the house. The room was simple and sparsely furnished, but even in that brief first glance, Kate could see that it was well cared for and immac-

251

ulately clean. The woman that hurried through the doorway to greet Kate would have been gently pretty if it weren't for the weariness that lay like a gray veil on her face. Her dress was faded and patched, but it was as clean as the rough wooden floor beneath her feet.

The baby she carried on her hip was plump and rosy-cheeked, gurgling with amusement at the stranger who stood in front of him. His was the carefree laughter of the infant who has not yet learned in that first sheltered year of life what it is to fear. It was a lesson the little girl who stood beside them with solemn, cautious eyes had obviously learned. She could have been no more than seven years old, yet already she judged things with the alert, searching eyes of an adult. She was a miniature copy of her mother, dressed in a long gray skirt with curling wisps of pale brown hair escaping from the bun at the back of her head, to float lightly around her pretty face.

"Why, you poor thing," the woman cried out in sympathy as she caught sight of Kate's disheveled appearance. Throwing her husband a scolding glance for greeting a stranger so inhospitably, she hurried back into the house, calling out over her shoulder, "Come over here to the stove—here's a chair for you—and warm yourself. I'll have you a cup of tea in no time."

"Thank you," Kate called after her. "But I have to take care of my horse first."

The man threw her a quick, approving glance. "My brother'll see to that. Ben!"

A young man suddenly materialized from the shadows in the corner of the small room. Short and stocky, with a thick shock of brown hair, he looked like a younger version of his brother.

"I'd be right glad to, miss," he told her eagerly, a warm grin lighting up his homely features.

His smile was a bit too welcoming for his stern older brother. "See that ye take good care o' *Mrs.* Devlin's horse," he said sharply. Kate was surprised at the emphasis on the word; then she remembered the heavy gold band that she still wore on her left hand. Ben saw it, too.

"Yes, ma'am, I'll take right good care o' her," he stammered awkwardly, his eyes cast down in apologetic embarrassment. Kate smiled at the crestfallen look on his youthful features as he hurried toward the barn.

Only seconds later, she found herself resting comfortably on a heavy wooden chair beside the warm stove that was

Pardon this interruption, but...
if you smoke
and
you're interested
in tar levels
you may find the
information on the back
of this page worthwhile.

A comparison of 57 popular cigarette brands with Kent Golden Lights.

FILTER BRANDS (KING SIZE)

REGULAR	MG TAR	MG NIC	MENTHOL	MG TAR	MG NIC
Kent Golden Lights	8	0.6	Kent Golden Lights Menthol	8	0.7
Parliament	10	0.6	Kool Super Lights	9	0.8
Vantage	11	0.7	Multifilter Menthol	11	0.7
Marlboro Lights	12	0.7	Vantage Menthol	11	0.8
Doral	12	0.8	Salem Lights	11	0.8
Multifilter	12	0.8	Doral Menthol	11	0.8
Winston Lights	12	0.9	Belair	13	1.0
Raleigh Lights	14	1.0	Marlboro Menthol	14	0.8
Viceroy Extra Milds	14	1.0	Alpine	14	0.8
Viceroy	16	1.0	Kool Milds	14	0.9
Raleigh	16	1.1	Kool	17	1.3
Marlboro	17	1.0	Salem	18	1.2
Tareyton	17	1.2			
Lark	18	1.2			
Pall Mall Filters	18	1.2			
Camel Filters	18	1.2			
L & M.	18	1.1			
Winston	19	1.2			

FTC Method

FILTER BRANDS (100's)

REGULAR	MG TAR	MG NIC	MENTHOL	MG TAR	MG NIC
Kent Golden Lights 100's	10	0.9	Kent Golden Lights 100's Menthol	10	0.9
Benson & Hedges 100's Lights	11	0.8	Benson & Hedges 100's Lights Menthol	11	0.8
Vantage 100's	11	0.9	Merit 100's Menthol	12	0.9
Merit 100's	12	0.9	Virginia Slims 100's Menthol	16	0.9
Parliament 100's	12	0.7	Pall Mall 100's		
Eve 100's	16	1.0	Eve 100's Menthol	16	1.0
Virginia Slims 100's	16	0.9	Silva Thins Menthol	16	1.1
Tareyton 100's	16	1.2	Benson & Hedges 100's Menthol	17	1.0
Marlboro 100's	17	1.0	L & M 100's Menthol	18	1.2
Silva Thins	16	1.3	Kool 100's	18	1.3
Benson & Hedges 100's	17	1.0	Belair 100's	18	1.3
L & M 100's	17	1.1	Winston 100's Menthol	18	1.2
Raleigh 100's	17	1.2	Salem 100's	18	1.3
Viceroy 100's	18	1.3			
Lark 100's	18	1.1			
Pall Mall 100's	19	1.4			
Winston 100's	19	1.3			

FTC Method

Kings only 8 mg tar

100's only 10 mg tar

Simply put, they're as low as you can go and still get good taste.

Of All Brands Sold: Lowest tar: 0.5 mg. "tar," 0.05 mg. nicotine.
Kent Golden Lights: Kings Regular 8 mg. "tar," 0.6 mg. nicotine.
Kings Menthol 8 mg. "tar," 0.7 mg. nicotine av. per cigarette ,
FTC Report August 1977. **100's Regular and Menthol**—10 mg. "tar,"
0.9 mg. nicotine av. per cigarette by FTC Method.

Warning: The Surgeon General Has Determined
That Cigarette Smoking Is Dangerous to Your Health.

© Lorillard, U.S.A. 1977

perched nearly in the center of the room. As she sipped gratefully at the hot tea Caroline had given her and watched the woman bustle efficiently around the stove, she offered tentatively to help. She couldn't help feeling a sense of relief when the offer was politely refused.

"No need for that," Caroline assured her. "Sarah will give me all the help I need."

As Kate watched the little girl hurrying back and forth between the stove and the table, she quickly realized Caroline was right. Though she was only a small child, she was already far more useful than Kate could ever be. Feeling a little embarrassed, Kate contented herself with sitting comfortably by the fire, playing with the baby, whose name, she learned, was Emmet.

Caroline talked quietly as she prepared dinner, and from her Kate learned much of the family who had so unexpectedly become her hosts. She listened with fascination to tales of the young couple, Jeb and Caroline Allen, who had left the harsh, rocky slopes of New England to carve a new life for themselves in the fertile fields of the West, bringing with them only their infant daughter, Sarah, and Jeb's teenage brother, Ben. She learned of the bitter hardships of the journey and the sore trials of the new life, of crops that failed and babies that lay in the bleak stillness of the gray, unyielding earth. As she listened, she began to sense a quiet courage about this young family that was beyond anything she had ever seen or dreamed of. Looking around at the sparse and barren hut they called home, Kate found herself forgetting her own problems for a moment as she voiced in her heart a secret, silent prayer for the brave and generous people who had taken her in. She could only hope that soon they would find the good life they had worked so hard to create for themselves.

By the time they all sat down at the clean wooden table, Kate felt as if the Allens were old friends, friends she had long loved and respected. As they bowed their heads in grace, she was aware of a strong sense of inner peace she had never felt before.

Dinner was simple, but to Kate in her hunger, it tasted like a banquet prepared for kings. She heaped her plate eagerly with thick slabs of potatoes fried with succulent, salty chunks of pork. The biscuits were strange to her taste—Caroline told her they were raised with baking powder because they had no soda—but they were not unpleasant, and she used them to soak up the thick gravy on her plate. Even the heavy brown sugar, although it was alien to Kate, had a rich, delicious taste as she stirred it into her coffee.

Kate felt her strength beginning to return, surging through her body with a warmth that reminded her of the warmth of a fire on a cold evening. She had just leaned back, her coffee in her hands, thanking God for her good fortune—not just for the wholesome food, but for good friends to share it with—when, to her surprise, she saw Jeb bang his coffeecup abruptly on the table with a loud clatter. All conversation ceased at once, and Kate gaped at him in amazement, watching as he cocked his head, like a dog who has heard a strange noise before anyone else's ears can pick it up. An instant later, Ben followed his example, and soon even Caroline and Little Sarah had placed their utensils quietly beside their plates and sat listening to a sound Kate could not hear.

It was minutes before she finally heard it, and then it was only a dull, rumbling sound, like thunder off in the distance. It was a long time before she recognized what it was. When she did, it made her blood run cold with fear.

It was the sound of hooves.

It was the sound she had dreaded all through the long day and the dark night that preceded it. Could it be that Jason had found her already? Judging from the heavy sound of hoofbeats, he must have brought many men with him.

Kate sat paralyzed with fear as she watched Jeb rise and hurry toward the door, picking up the gun he had left carelessly leaning against the wall. Ben hurried to the side of the room, and reaching up toward a rack Kate had not even noticed on the wall, took down one of the heavy guns that rested on it. In contrast to their haste, Caroline was a study in slow, elegant grace as she rose and leaned forward, blowing gently against the lamp until the flame flickered away into darkness. Crossing over to a small table beside the stove, she did the same thing to the only other lamp in the room. Even Sarah seemed to know what to do, for she jumped up hastily and pulled Baby Emmet from his chair. Struggling with his weight, she carried him to the corner and sat quietly beside him, her arm around him, as she gazed out with solemn eyes. Only Kate remained at the table, unable to think or act.

Even as the sound of hooves grew nearer and nearer, Kate could not bring herself to move. Only when they approached the house and Kate heard them stop outside did she finally realize she had to force herself to get up and go to the window. If the thing she feared had come to pass, then she had to walk outside quietly, surrendering herself without a struggle to whatever evil faced her. She could not let these good people endure any further suffering on her behalf.

As she cautiously eased aside a corner of the curtain and peered out at the shadowy figures beyond the fence, she felt herself breathe a quick, unexpected sigh of relief. It wasn't Jason. Thank God she was safe.

Only when she heard a sharp intake of breath and turned around to see the ashen features of Caroline beside her did she realize the significance of what she had seen. She felt the blood drain from her face until she knew she was as pale as the woman at her side.

"Dear God, what are we to do?" Caroline whispered in terror.

As Kate turned back to the window, she saw the shadowy figures dismount in the distance, then begin to slither stealthily forward. The rays of the full moon landed on their faces, picking up with eerie clarity the vivid primary colors of the feathers in their long, dark braids and the streaks of paint laid out in almost geometric patterns on their faces.

The figures moved slowly toward the barn, sometimes under cover, sometimes with bold, arrogant daring. As they brazenly pulled the heavy door open and slunk inside, Kate heard the loud sound of startled whinnies, then watched furiously as she saw them leading both horses and livestock out of the building and away from the yard. Whirling around quickly, anger flashing in her dark green eyes, she cried out in astonishment to Jeb, "Are you going to let them get away with that?" She couldn't believe he was just standing there, his gun hanging limply at his side.

"D'ye think I be such a fool as to shoot?" Anger and impatience cut through the calm control Jeb tried to maintain in his voice. "We're two men, and there be a dozen out there at least."

Kate caught the bitter edge in his voice and realized how galling it must be for a man to have to stand aside and watch someone steal his property without being able to lift a hand to defend it. She wished she hadn't said anything. Her words only served as a cruel reminder of his failure.

Turning back to the window, she was just in time to see one of the braves lead a prancing red roan from the barn. For a moment, she had forgotten that her own horse was in there. In a sudden burst of fury, she headed toward the door. She wasn't going to let them get away with that! If Jeb wouldn't stop them, she would. She had faced Indians before. She could do it again.

Jeb reached out and grabbed her by the wrist, dragging her back before she could make it even halfway to the door. He pulled her down under the window, where she couldn't be seen from outside.

"The horse is gone," he said sharply. "Pray ye that's all they want today."

Ben turned toward her, sympathy shining in his eyes. "They've come before," he explained. "Just to steal food and livestock. Maybe that's all . . ." His voice trailed off, as if he did not want to jinx himself by speaking the hopeful words aloud.

"Aye," Jeb agreed, his voice dark and heavy. "But that was before. Now, with new treaties broken, they're out for blood. They're a dying people now, and the dying fight with a rage beyond their strength."

Kate saw Caroline slip into the corner with the children, sinking to her knees beside them. At first, she thought Caroline had gone to comfort them, but then she realized the woman was praying. Little Sarah slipped her arms away from her baby brother for the moment and knelt beside her mother.

Kate did not kneel, but she forced her fear-numbed lips to mouth silent, half-remembered words of childhood prayers. "Dear God," she whispered finally, "please help us. Please make them go away."

But even as her lips formed the plea, she knew it was useless, for the shadowy figures had already finished their raid, but they did not go away. Instead, they tied the livestock securely to trees beside their own horses, then turned to creep back toward the farmhouse and position themselves in a circle around it, taking care to remain under cover every second of the time. Now she wished Jeb had shot at them a few minutes before, when they had made such inviting targets of themselves in the yard; but now it was too late.

"Caroline. The guns." Jeb's voice was crisp and quiet, and his wife obeyed quickly, rising and hurrying toward the wall rack, which still held two heavy rifles. She placed one beside Jeb, then hurried to his brother, who had stationed himself at the far wall, and laid the other by his side. Then she opened the drawer of a large wooden bureau and pulled out a brace of pistols, bringing them to a spot nearly in the center of the room.

As soon as she had finished that, she began to pull out powder and rags and long sticks to load the guns, which she laid out methodically on the floor beside the handguns. As soon as Kate realized what she was doing, she rushed eagerly to help her. Here at last was something she could do. She could handle a gun as well as any man she knew.

When the two women finished their preparations, they sat in the center of the floor, every muscle strained for the task they would soon be called on to perform. The unearthly silence that filled the room dragged on for half an hour, or perhaps even an hour. The only sound Kate could hear was the rough rasping of their own breath. It was as eerie and heavy as the silence before a violent storm.

Kate wondered if they did it on purpose, the Indians. Were they using the time for their own preparations, or were they waiting on purpose, toying with the people inside the house, knowing what a devastating effect the unnatural silence would have on them?

When at last the first shot was fired, it was almost a relief. The glass in the window shattered with a sharp, crashing sound that at least broke the eerie silence as it sent tiny fragments flying into the room. Kate was surprised to feel a sharp sting of pain bite into her hand, and she looked down in disbelief as the tiny cuts that began slowly to fill with the deep crimson of fresh blood. She did not mind the pain. In a way, she almost welcomed it. At least it took her mind off the terror.

She was too busy for the next few minutes even to think of fear. Only the task at hand occupied her mind. As the men answered the opening shot with fire of their own, they began to throw back their rifles, reaching out with tense hands for a freshly loaded weapon. Both women pushed themselves to work quickly, but as Kate glanced over at Caroline, marveling at the way her deft fingers raced through their task, she was put to shame. The other woman was far more skillful than she.

After the first barrage of gunfire, the fighting slowed down, as if both sides had suddenly become aware of the scarcity of their own ammunition. Random firing would gain them little. It was becoming painfully obvious that the outcome of the battle might well depend on who was thrifty enough to make their ammunition hold out longer.

As caution grew and the men were slower in handing over their guns, Kate found herself alternating with Caroline, one reaching out for the gun at hand, while the other sat patiently to wait for the next. In one of the moments she was at rest, Kate's eyes drifted toward the unused pistols on the floor beside her.

There was really no point sitting there loading guns. Caroline was far better than she. Even when the firing had been heaviest, Caroline would have been able to keep up with it by herself. Picking up the pistols, Kate crept carefully across the floor toward one of the windows on the side wall.

She had already noticed that the men were trying desperately to cover all sides, moving from window to window to follow the heaviest fire. Another gun would help, and she was a crack shot, better than all her brothers—except Eamon.

Ben glanced up sharply when he saw her crawl across the room with the pistols in her hand, but a quick burst of gunfire occupied his attention before he could object. Kate stationed herself at the window, pulling the curtain aside cautiously so she could look out and assess the situation. The moonlight was bright, far brighter than she had remembered, and she was sure she could make her first shot count. Laying the barrel of the gun carefully on the windowsill, she waited until she saw a figure leap out of the shadows, obviously confident he could make it to the next cover safely, since the men inside the house were plainly occupied in other areas. He hadn't counted on Kate. Taking a split second to sight him carefully, she tensed the muscles of her finger tightly against the trigger. The sound of the explosion burst with an unexpected loudness in her ear. Kate was relieved to see the man jump up with a wild, convulsive jerk, then fall back to the ground.

"Good shot."

Kate was surprised to see Jeb at the window next to her, drawn to that side by the sudden escalation of gunfire. She knew from the terse approval in his voice that he accepted her as a fighter. He would have no fears that her use of the gun would be a waste of precious bullets.

She emptied the rest of her gun with less success and tossed it aside hastily, picking up its mate. That, too, she emptied to no avail, and as she fired the last shot, she turned away from the window to reload. She begrudged the time it would take, but she knew Caroline had enough to handle trying to load for both the men. As she threw the empty gun down and reached for the box of bullets, she was surprised to see tiny fingers holding the first gun out to her. Startled, she stared down into solemn brown eyes.

My God, only seven years old, and she already knows how to load a gun, Kate thought bitterly as she stared for a moment at the grave little face. Her heart ached as she thought of other seven-year-olds, carefree and at play. What should a child like that know of death and killing? How unfair it all seemed.

But there was no time to dwell on sadness, for even as Kate looked down into Sarah's eyes, she was aware of a sudden change, as if someone had dimmed the lights, and she hurried to look out the window again. Glancing up toward the sky, she saw a dark, heavy cloud just beginning to slide over the bright face of the moon. For one last, brief second, a tantalizing hint of light still quivered in the sky; then, like a dying ember, it disappeared, leaving everything covered with a thick mantle of darkness.

The sudden strain of watching, of turning eyes into shadows that did not yield, became almost unbearable. Kate found herself peering out of the windows with a tenseness that almost seemed to be pulling her eyes out of her head. She could barely see two feet in front of her. At any moment, she knew, a bold, painted face might leap out of the darkness to leer at her with its obscene mockery. Her eyes burned with the effort of staring ceaselessly, but she did not even dare to blink. Even that single fraction of a second might cost her her life.

The sound of a shrill scream broke through the eerie silence, and Kate spun around in horror to gape at Sarah, who was pointing at the far wall, a look of terror fixed on her face. There in the window, barely visible in the dim light, were traces of lurid red and white stripes, leaping out boldly from a face that was completely covered by the darkness.

The sound startled Ben, and he jumped as he whirled around. The sharp crack of a gun rang out at the same time, but Ben's back, such an inviting target only an instant before, had pulled away in time, and the bullet grazed his side instead. Kate raised her pistol automatically, pulling the trigger before the savage outside could get off a second shot.

She watched in horrified fascination as the vivid red streaks of pigment that marked his vengeful wrath seemed to melt over his face, obscuring even the last bold traces of white. Only after a moment did she realize that what she had mistaken for paint was in reality the crimson of his own blood as it poured from his body, drawing away the vitality of his body. After what seemed forever to Kate, he slowly slipped beneath the edge of the window, vanishing at last from view.

"Good girl," Ben told her, clutching at his side with his hand to stanch the heavy flow of blood that trickled out between his fingers. As Caroline rushed over to him, ripping at the hem of her petticoat to make a bandage, Jeb and Kate turned hurriedly back toward the window, just in time to see the last traces of the cloud blow away, leaving the world again bathed in a soft blue light.

Kate saw half a dozen figures snaking rapidly through the unexpected brightness as they tried to get to cover, and she aimed carefully, felling one and wounding at least one other. To her surprise, the Indians didn't stop at the edge of the yard, as they had before, but seemed to be pulling back even farther. She followed them carefully with her gun, trying to pick off at least one more of them, but their undulating movements were too clever for her, and soon they were out of range of her pistol.

"They're retreating," she cried out, the sound of surprise ringing in her voice. They had done it! Only three brave guns against a marauding band of savages, but they had done it anyhow. They had put the savages to rout!

"Aye," Jeb replied gloomily. "For the moment."

"Maybe not," Ben said quietly, forcing an enthusiasm into his voice that Kate sensed he did not feel. She wondered if he was doing it to keep their morale up, hers and Caroline's. "They had pretty heavy losses."

Kate glanced quickly around the yard. Ben was right. The Indian losses had been heavy. She could see at least five, or possibly six, bodies, and there must have been others, out of sight, who were also dead or badly wounded. That meant that out of twelve or at most sixteen men, no more than eight or ten could be left. If they were also low on ammunition . . .

"Their losses are *too* heavy," Jeb's gloomy voice cut in. "Their pride won't stand for that. They'll be back."

In the end, Jeb proved wiser than either Ben or Kate, and the Indians did return, coming back to attack with all the savage intensity they had shown before. Again and again they closed in, teasing their quarry with light fire as they waited for the thick clouds to obscure the moon again, providing them with the darkness they needed to press closer. Each time it did, they would charge forward with the same bold foray, pulling back only when the pale blue light burst forth again. Yet, each time, no matter how violent their attack, they still managed to inflict no serious damage on the small group of fighters inside the house.

Kate knew her body must be tired, but she could no longer feel even the weariness. All she was aware of was the tenseness that tightened every muscle. She did not know how long she had been stationed at the window, the pistol clutched tautly in her fingers. It could have been an hour or a century.

For her, time had lost all meaning, and she existed only in the brief second that comprised the present.

Suddenly she was surprised to see a faint, almost imperceptible change in the quality of the darkness. At first she thought the moon had grown brighter, but then, slowly, she became aware of a faint gray line at the edge of the horizon.

"Why, it's nearly morning." She could hardly believe her eyes.

"Aye," Jeb agreed cautiously.

"But that's good," she cried out. "They can't attack in the daylight, can they? They'd be easy targets then."

"No. They can't attack in the light."

Kate couldn't understand the hesitation in Jeb's voice. When daylight came, the Indians would have to go away. They wouldn't dare stay near the farm, risking sight by a chance traveler who might ride for help. Excitedly, she turned toward Ben, expecting to see confirmation in his eyes.

He met her gaze slowly, reluctantly, as if he were still trying to decide what he should tell her. When he finally spoke, the words were soft and hesitant. "The light's near an hour away yet. There'll be one more attack, and it'll be a thing of despair. It'll be the worst yet."

Kate knew in her heart he was right, and she shivered with fear as she turned back toward the window. The Indians wouldn't leave now, not after suffering such bitter losses. They would have to give it one last try.

There would be another attack, but only one. It would be savage and brutal, she knew, but so had all the onslaughts that had come before it during the long, cruel night. Yet, each time, somehow they had managed to keep the Indians back. Each time, the savages had lost. Surely they had worked all their worst, most terrifying tricks already. What more could be left?

The answer came suddenly and without warning, reaching Kate's consciousness before anyone else in the room could even notice it. At first, all she saw was a lone arrow whistling through the dark night air, but soon she found herself staring at it in fascination, watching the ghostly arc of light it cast into the pale gray air. Only after it sailed through the broken window and landed in the center of the floor did she realize what it was. The mystery of its light was nothing more than a plain rag tied to the shaft and ignited until it burned with a pure yellow flame.

Ben hurried over it to, stooping cautiously to keep his silhouette from showing through the windows, and began to stomp on the flames with his heavy boots. Caroline, her face pale, hurried over to the bed and tugged off the blankets, tossing them in the center of the floor. Picking up a heavy bucket of water, she began to pour it on the blankets. Although she doused them thoroughly, Kate noticed she was careful not to spill even a single drop of the precious liquid on the floor beneath.

Fire! Of course. Why hadn't she thought of it before? What was it Jason had said to her? I built my house of stones and metal, nothing that would burn. If only the Allens had planned as carefully.

The first arrow was followed fast by a second and then a third, until soon the air was filled with a mass of fiery missiles, flying in thickly toward the house. Most of them fell short of their target or extinguished themselves in the flight, but those that found their mark wreaked havoc in the little house.

Kate watched in horror as the curtains in front of her went up in a sudden blaze of golden red, ignited by sparks flying off an arrow that passed through them only seconds before. Reaching out instinctively, she tore them down from the rod that held them against the window and threw them wildly on the floor. Almost before she realized it, Sarah was at her side, a dripping blanket heavy in her small hands as she beat the bright flames into submission.

Soon the fire was all around them, forming into tiny clusters that threatened to get out of hand at any moment. When it became apparent that it was more than Caroline or Sarah could handle, Jeb turned around to size up the situation.

"Leave the guns to Kate, Ben," he barked out quickly. "She's a better marksman than you are."

Without even a second's hesitation for false male pride, Ben slid the heavy gun across the floor to Kate and hurried to snatch up a blanket, barely showing the effects of his wound as he helped beat at the flames that were already beginning to mount in their fury. Only Kate and Jeb remained at the windows, firing at shadowy forms in the distance and pausing intermittently to load their own rifles.

The firefighters raced back and forth across the room, hurrying from one danger point to another with a desperation that tolerated no concern for their own safety. As they stood beside the brightly glowing flames, they knew they were silhouetted in their sharp, clear light, but they could not afford to waste even a second to take the precautions that might spare their lives.

Kate heard Caroline cry out in pain, and she turned quickly to look at her, but as soon as she saw that it was only a shoulder wound, she fixed her gaze back on the yard, having no time for pity or compassion. Caroline grimaced in pain, but she did not falter for an instant as she continued to pull up the blankets with her wounded arm, heaving their weight forcefully against the floor and walls.

To Kate, it felt as if the room was growing unbearably hot, too hot even for the many fires that blossomed up in every corner, but she didn't have time to think about it. She only had time to stare down the barrel of a gun, waiting for one of the Indians to dash out carelessly into her sight. Only when she turned to pull the gun back inside and reload it did she notice the rosy glow that hung like a pink halo around the top of the window.

"Look!" she cried out in horror. Hungry red and yellow tongues of flame lapped at the upper edges of the window.

"The roof!" There was a sound of terror even in Jeb's stern voice.

An instant later, the flames burst through the ceiling and began to run down the walls in colorful little rivulets. Kate and Jeb threw down their guns and grabbed at the blankets, soaking them in the buckets to make sure they were dripping wet.

Encouraged by the lack of gunfire, the Indians began to creep closer and closer to the house. Kate could see them through the windows, but there was nothing she could do about it. She didn't dare drop her blanket even for a second, not even to send off a single shot that would drive them scrambling back again.

Thick black smoke now lay heavy in the room, and Kate could barely breathe as she felt the incredibly hot air pour into her lungs, searing them with a sharp, burning pain. She grabbed at the woolen shawl she had thrown down on the floor when the fighting began. Dipping it in the residue of hot water that still remained in one of the buckets, she wrapped it around her head, covering her mouth and nose from the deadly fumes. As she picked up the blanket again, she was aware of the shrill sound of Emmet's screams carrying across the crackling static of the flames.

To her horror, Kate felt the fire catch at the hem of her skirt, and she struck at it desperately with the heavy blanket in her hand. When that wasn't fast enough, she bent down and beat at the flames with her hands, smothering them quickly beneath her palms. The fire was already out before she even noticed the searing pain that marked the spots where the flames had eaten into her flesh.

She was aware of an acute stab of pain in her left hand, and glancing down, she saw that the hot metal of her wedding ring was still burning into her skin. Wrenching at it with her other hand, she tore it brusquely from her finger. Although she tried desperately to hold onto it, her pain-racked fingers betrayed her, and with a poignant stab of regret she saw it slip to the ground and roll away from her.

"We've got to get out of here," Caroline screamed, her voice filled with terror and despair. The cruel, sizzling flames were fast flooding the room with their blazing heat.

"It's no use," Jeb called back. "We're better off here than outside with those savages."

"But the children," she argued. "They might spare the children."

Although Kate could barely see Jeb's face in the dim light that pierced the heavy smoke, she was aware of the agonizing decision echoed in his eyes. The torture his wife might endure if they killed her slowly had to be balanced against the chance that his children might live. Finally, after what seemed like forever, he nodded briskly.

More by instinct than by sight, Caroline rushed to the corner where little Em sat sobbing, and sweeping him into her arms, she protected him with her own body as she darted through the flames, trying to make her way toward the door. Kate, seeing Sarah standing helplessly beside her, her face streaked with smoke and sweat, bent down and picked the child up in her arms, barely feeling the pain that shot through her body as her blistering hands came into contact with the rough fabric of Sarah's dress.

The two men walked before them, blankets in hand, beating off the flames as best they could to clear a path to the door. It took an agonizingly long time to reach it, but finally they were there, and Kate cried out in relief as she saw Jeb's foot rise up to kick it open with a single hard blow.

The blast of fresh air that swept in to touch Kate's burning cheeks offered an instant of relief, and she shook her head to loosen the shawl that covered her mouth so she could gulp in a cooling breath to ease the searing pain in her lungs. The instinct for survival was stronger than either reason or fear, and for just a moment her body rejoiced in the cold purity of the morning air.

Only after that first second did she begin to remember her peril, and then she forced herself to peer slowly through the swirls of smoke that still poured from the burning cabin into the pale gray light of dawn. What she saw reflected in the soft pink rays of the rising sun was enough to bring all the terror back again with an intensity she could hardly endure.

There in the cool dawn, mounted again on their horses, stood a solemn row of savage warriors, stationed in a curved arc, half-surrounding their captives. The gaudily painted decorations on their faces were oddly out of keeping with the harsh implacability of their expressions. Their guns were raised and held to their shoulders as they aimed at the small band that had fled from the cruel flames.

24

KATE PULLED DEEP GULPS OF COLD AIR INTO HER LUNGS, coughing and choking as she felt the sharp sting of its impact. She stood absolutely still for a moment, watching dark billows of smoke pour from the flames that now engulfed the house, then slowly she lowered little Sarah to the ground. Never for an instant did her eyes leave the small band of warriors in front of them.

She expected at any second to hear a thundering volley of shots and feel the sharp stab of pain that would accompany them, but to her amazement, the Indians sat immobile, their guns raised but silent in front of them. At first, she could not understand. Then slowly she became aware of the dark hatred that blazed out of eyes set in impassive faces. Shuddering, she realized with terrifying clarity that their bitterness left no room for mercy. They would be in no hurry to ease their captives out of life.

Kate found herself staring, with a curiosity that seemed oddly out of place, at the men who were to be her murderers. But perhaps it was not all that strange, she told herself. Hard and cruel as they might be, they were, after all, the last faces she would see on this earth.

There were only seven of them, but they sat tall and proud in the saddle, looking as if they were a small army instead of just a ragged little band, garbed in a motley assortment of Indian garments and white man's clothes. One of the warriors, obviously their leader, had positioned himself well in front of his comrades, and Kate could not keep herself from gaping in fascination at the heavy fur vest he wore over his shabby jacket. It looked to her almost as if it had been fashioned of the same buffalo hide she herself had brought down to the wretched, starving remnants of a once proud tribe camped at the base of the hill beneath her husband's home. How strange it would be, she thought with a curious sense of detachment, almost as if the whole subject did not really relate to her, if this young brave was in reality one of that same small band. Perhaps it was her own fur that now rested so comfortably on his body, providing him with the warmth and protection he needed to stay alive. Perhaps if it were not for her small act of charity, her own life would not be in danger that very day.

Suddenly, as the flickering light from the flames fell on the warrior's face, Kate realized with a vague sense of awe that her instinct had indeed been true. She had seen those same proud, cruel eyes before. With a sharp chill of fear, she realized that this was the same young brave whose will she had once defied with such foolhardy boldness. That time, she had won. This time she knew she had little chance.

How ironic it all was, she thought with a sudden weariness that almost took away the fear. She had fled from death at the hands of the man she loved, only to find it waiting for her here on a windswept plain in the guise of a familiar enemy. She was silent for a moment as she looked deep into the young warrior's eyes, waiting for him to recognize her. Then slowly, quietly, she stepped out of the circle of her friends and began moving slowly toward him.

"Hello, John," she said softly.

The sound of her greeting seemed to unnerve him, and he lowered his gun to stare at her. The others, obviously confused by his gesture, began to stir nervously in their saddles. Kate noticed that the barrels of their guns tipped down an inch or two until they were pointing toward the ground.

"I do not use the white man's name." There was a cold anger in his voice that frightened Kate, but she was determined not to back down from him.

"Little Wolf, then." Her eyes were filled with tears from the thick, black smoke that lay heavy in the air, but she managed to hold her head proud and high.

"Hamilton's wife is far from home." There was a measure

266

of doubt in the Indian's voice, or perhaps it was disapproval. Kate could not tell which. It was a subject she did not wish to pursue.

"Why don't you take the livestock and go? We've done you no harm. Why do you want to hurt us?"

"No harm?" His voice was both cynical and incredulous. "I leave behind me eight men when I ride away, eight young, brave men whose souls have gone already to dwell with the Great Spirit. You have killed them."

"In self-defense," she cried out passionately. "Surely you would not expect us to die without defending ourselves. You fired the first shot."

When he did not answer, she began to hope her argument had reached him, and she hastened to press her advantage. "These are good people," she cried out, gesturing with her arm toward the small family that stood huddled together a few feet behind her. "They've never done you any harm, nor have I. Why, I fed you when you were starving, and put those very furs on your body to warm you. If it weren't for me, you wouldn't be alive today to threaten us."

She could see that her words were not lost on him, for he stared down at her with dark and searching eyes, but as she gazed back at him, she realized there was no trace of mercy or compassion in them. Finally, after what seemed an eternity to her, she began to give up even the last shreds of hope. Then, to her surprise, she saw him open his lips to speak.

"Hamilton's wife speaks wisdom," he said slowly. "You may go."

Kate fought to control the relief that threatened to flood over her face. She did not want to let him know how frightened she had been, or how unsure. A strong show of self-confidence was important in dealing with John Little Wolf. If she gave that up now, it might well provide him with the excuse he needed to change his mind. Slowly, as calmly as she could, she turned to rejoin the others.

"No!" Little Wolf's voice rang through the air with harsh clarity. Puzzled, Kate turned back to face him again. "Not them. You."

"Dear God, why?" Impulsively she began to run toward him, anguish and undisguised fear written boldly across her features. Surely he could not really mean to kill them! Not after he had just raised their hopes so cruelly.

The young savage leaned forward as she approached, softening his voice until it reached her ears alone. "I have not that power, Hamilton's wife. I could not save them if I

267

wanted to . . . and I don't." He leaned down still farther, until his head was so low his eyes were almost on a level with hers.

"We are dying, Hamilton's wife, dying of wounds inflicted by the white man. Surely you do not expect us to die without defending ourselves." His voice was still soft, but it was filled with a bitter mockery as he deliberately threw her own words back in her face. "The Indian is like a wounded beast crawling into a corner to die. He will attack anything that comes near him, kill anything he finds alive, just as the wounded beast will kill."

Kate felt the blood run cold in her veins as she remembered the same words on Jeb's lips only a few hours before. The dying fight with a rage beyond their strength, he had told her. Now she understood what he meant.

John Little Wolf pulled himself straight in the saddle again, looking down at Kate with an arrogance that befitted, not the last tattered remnant of a dying savagery, but rather a resplendent and mighty prince. As Kate watched in horror, he drew his arm up slowly and extended it full length in front of him. Pointing with his long forefinger at the wagon tracks leading away from the house, he spoke only a single word: "Go!"

Knowing there was nothing she could say or do, Kate turned slowly to obey, tears of frustration mingling with the moisture the stinging smoke had brought to her eyes. She tried to force her feet down the narrow path, but she found them strangely reluctant to move. She knew the gift of life she was being offered was a precious one, but it was a gift she found surprisingly difficult to accept if it meant she must leave her friends behind.

Kate knew she was being foolish. There was nothing she could do to help her friends now. It would be stupid to stay behind. It would accomplish nothing but the vain sacrifice of her own life. Still, she could not help feeling guilty.

Was it always like this, she wondered, for the survivor? Did it always hurt so much to walk away in safety when others must stay behind to face a cruel and ugly death?

Anguished, she turned to face the family she was leaving, her eyes pleading mutely for help. Tell me what to do, her eyes begged them. Tell me to go . . . or tell me to stay and face my fate by your side. Don't leave this horrible decision to me.

It was Jeb alone who seemed to see the silent appeal in her eyes. His voice was rough and hoarse from the smoke that had burned raw spots in his throat.

"Go."

Kate felt an involuntary sigh quiver through her body like a heavy shudder of physical pain. At last, she prepared to go.

Only at the last second did her eyes meet Caroline's. The despair she saw in their depths was echoed in the words her burned lips mouthed in mute appeal.

The children.

Kate looked down at little Sarah, standing bravely by her mother's side. The child's eyes were wide with fear, but she did not allow herself to move, not even enough to let her tiny lower lip give way to trembling. Only the baby whimpered softly, his pudgy body clasped tightly in his mother's arms. As Kate stared at them in silent anguish, she could not bring herself to believe the Indians meant to slaughter any so young and innocent as these.

Slowly she turned back to face John Little Wolf again, her eyes filled for a brief moment with hope, but the instant she saw him, she knew it was no use. His arm was still stretched out, rigid and unyielding, as if he were a statue, frozen into the space of a single moment.

With a desperate feeling of helplessness, Kate realized that further words would be futile. If she wanted to save the children, it would take a bold move. With a sudden impulse of daring, she hurried over to Caroline and held out her arms. The other woman understood immediately what she was trying to do and quickly shifted the weight of the infant to her arms. Kate adjusted him on her left hip, then reached down with her right hand to Sarah. The little girl glanced hesitantly toward her mother, then, seeing her quick nod of approval, gave her hand willingly to Kate. Together they turned and began to walk slowly down the road. To Kate's relief, no one tried to stop them.

Out of the corner of her eye, Kate saw one of the braves beginning to herd the animals into a field beside the road. With a pang of regret she caught sight of Sunbeam's bright red coat. For an instant she was tempted to try to rescue her horse, but common sense warned her not to press her luck too far. It was enough that her life was being spared, and the lives of the children. It would be foolish to linger a moment longer, no matter how tempting the errand. Every minute they were still in sight gave the revenge-driven Indians that much more time to change their minds.

"Sorry, Sunbeam," she whispered as they passed by the field and continued down the road. Her eyes began to well up with tears as she watched the young brave rudely herding the horses together. She hoped the Indians would be good to her pampered little mare. Poor Sunbeam. There would be no more sugar lumps for her now.

Kate was surprised at the catch that came to her throat when she thought of Sunbeam, surprised and ashamed. How could she cry over an animal when she was also leaving cherished friends to suffer an agonizing fate? And yet, perhaps it was really not so unnatural, she consoled herself. Perhaps she could think of the one parting, and weep for it, because it was bearable. The other parting was one she could not even face.

Kate did not try to turn back, not even for one last, fleeting glance of farewell. She knew she could not bear to see the three brave, silent figures standing in the charred ruins of their home, waiting patiently for the death they knew must come.

Go straight ahead, she kept telling herself, mouthing the words she did not even dare to whisper aloud. Go straight ahead. She picked up her feet with mechanical precision, forcing them to move one after the other down the road. Her body was so numb to feeling that she was scarcely aware of the weight of Emmet's plump body against her hip. With her right hand, she continued to hold fast to Sarah.

The little girl clutched her hand tightly, hanging on to it as if it were a lifeline to be held at all costs. Agonizing currents of pain shot up Kate's arm from the raw and blistered skin on her palms and fingers, but she paid them little heed, nor did she attempt to loosen the child's grip. She and Sarah both needed something to hold on to.

They were already halfway up the hill before the loud, staccato sound of gunshots tore through the morning air. The noise shuddered through Kate's body with a hot burst of pain, almost as if the bullets had been aimed instead at her. She could feel Sarah's hand trembling in hers.

The silence that followed was a relief, but it lasted only for a moment. In its place the air was suddenly filled with the shrill, agonizing sound of a prolonged scream. To Kate, it sounded hideously like the wail of an animal in pain. At first, she could not understand what it was. Then, slowly, with an awareness that seemed to increase with the intensity of the scream, she realized what it was.

It was the sound of a woman's voice.

The baby began to cry in terror, and squirming in Kate's arms, he turned to stare back over her shoulder. Hurriedly Kate tore her hand out of Sarah's grasp and slipped it over his eyes. She didn't know how old a child had to be before he would remember things, but she didn't want to take any chances. She didn't want him to go through life with the vision of his mother's agony stamped indelibly on his memory.

She glanced down quickly at the little girl at her side, intending to shout out: Don't look back, *don't look back!* But one look at Sarah's face told her the warning was unnecessary. The child was staring straight ahead down the road, her tiny features set in a grim, unflinching mask. In her eyes was a look of anguish and hatred Kate had never seen even on the face of an adult.

They continued to trudge down the road, their steps now hurried and unfaltering as they sought to put more distance between themselves and the grief and suffering that lay behind them. Kate had no idea how long they had been walking when she suddenly realized it was not safe to stay on the road. At any moment, the Indians might return that way, and seeing their former captives, regret their one spontaneous act of mercy.

With Sarah at her side, Kate turned onto the gently blowing grasses of the hillside. As they stumbled hurriedly up one side of the hill and down another, Kate was aware that she didn't even know where they were going, nor did she care. All she wanted was to get away. She was no longer capable of making a rational judgment, or putting together a viable plan. Finally, when a decision was made, it was left to Sarah to make it.

"I know a cave," the little girl said quietly. To Kate, her voice sounded numb and dead, like the voice of an old person who has lived too long.

The cave Sarah led her to was dark and humid. At first, it was a relief after the brutal heat of the flames, but soon the moisture that dripped relentlessly down its walls began to exert a subtle torture of its own, emphasizing the bitter chill that dug into their bodies until their bones began to creak. Still they did not leave.

They stayed within the dark protection of the earth until sunset painted the sky a vivid red, making the front of the cave seem to drip with blood in the graying light. They stayed there through the long, sightless night, waiting for sunrise to illuminate the world with a soft, rosy glow that faded slowly into the cheerful, clear blue of the morning sky. Still Kate could not bring herself to leave.

Only after the sun had ventured nearly to the center of the heavens did she finally creep out of its gloomy haven, leaving Sarah behind to care for her baby brother. Even when she stood in the brisk winds of the hilltop, her eyes carefully scanning the horizon, she found herself longing to cling to its shelter. She knew the Indians must have left long ago, and it was time to go and search for food, but still she could hardly force herself to move. At first, she could not understand why.

It was not until she recognized the course her feet had automatically taken through the ankle-deep grasses of the hillside that she finally began to understand the reason for her hesitancy. Without being aware of it, she had allowed instinct to turn her feet back to the same path she had climbed the morning before. She was already halfway there before she even realized she had begun the long walk to the small farmhouse that now lay in charred ruins at the bottom of the hill.

Even as her feet pulled her inexorably along the path they had set for her, Kate knew she had to follow them. She had to search for whatever scraps of food the Indians might have left behind. And yet, she was not sure she was strong enough to go on. Horror filled her mind at the thought of what she had to face.

Perhaps she was only making it worse in her mind, she told herself hopefully. Perhaps when she got there, she would find no traces. The Indians might have buried the dead, or at the very least, cleansed the whole site with the searing purity of fire. Just as long as there was no trace of her friends, no trace of the valiant comrades she had fought beside, then she would be all right.

Please heaven, she prayed, remembering the gentle God of her childhood who had always granted her desires, please don't let there be any traces. But even then, she knew in her heart it was a vain hope.

The blackened remains of the house and barn stood out against the bright green and blue landscape, and Kate could see them a long time before she reached them. The dark heaps of ashes that covered the ground had already been scattered by the winds, until they rested on the nearby fields, touching them with hints of deep charcoal gray. Rising from their midst, a handful of poles and rafters, charred but otherwise strangely untouched by the flames, lifted their blackened fingers toward the heavens like an obscene joke.

As Kate approached, her eyes began to pick out more and more details of the appalling devastation. Although she tried desperately to keep from staring at the spot in the yard where she had last seen her friends, she found her eyes drawn toward that same place with a dreadful fascination. At first, she could see nothing there, and she began to hope her prayers had been answered. Then, as she drew nearer, her eyes began to distinguish the outline of mangled bodies in the heap of rubble. The clotted brown blood, heavy on their skin and clothing, mingled with the earth and ashes that half-buried them, leaving them barely exposed to Kate's view.

Kate's eyes took in the picture for only a single, vivid second before they closed tightly in shock. Taking a long, deep breath, she tried to hold her body steady, but she found that her knees were trembling too much to support her weight. It was only an instant before she felt her legs crumble slowly beneath her, and the soft gray ashes flew up to coat the skirt of her riding habit as she sank awkwardly to the ground.

The trembling from her legs spread throughout her entire body, until even in the bright sunlight she found herself shivering uncontrollably. For a moment she was tempted to turn and run away, leaving behind her all the grief and ugliness, as if it had never happened.

Even as she fought to control the violent trembling that engulfed her body, she knew she could not give in to that temptation. Horrifying as it was, she had to stay. Even if she hadn't needed the food she might find there, she still could not let herself run away, leaving the bodies of her friends to decay in the yard. There was little enough she could do for them now. At least she could see them decently buried.

The trembling in her body now stilled, she rose wearily, carefully averting her eyes so she would not have to look at the pathetic heaps of human flesh that lay beside her on the ground as she moved toward the remains of the barn. After kicking around in the rubble for a short time, Kate was lucky enough to find a shovel that had somehow escaped the holocaust. She picked it up gratefully and began to search the nearby slopes, looking for a green and restful spot.

Her eyes lit on a small, well-kept knoll, not far from where the house had stood. As she approached it, she noticed two tiny wooden crosses protruding from small mounds of loose rock that had been carefully arranged, one beside the other. Perhaps this was where the little girls lay, she thought, the two infant daughters Caroline had told her about. It seemed fitting that their parents should rest beside them.

The blisters on her hands sent sharp stabs of pain through her body as Kate labored with the shovel, but she willed her mind to ignore them, striking again and again with the spade into the surprisingly hard earth. Even when blood began to ooze through the tender flesh on her hands and run in bright red streaks down her arms, she still continued to toil, scooping up spades of earth and tossing them to the side until she had formed a wide opening nearly two feet deep.

The grave was shallower than she would have liked, but at least it was better than leaving them to rot in the sun, prey to vultures and scavengers. Kate rested for a moment before she went back to get the bodies, trying to prepare herself for the ordeal that lay ahead. Finally, when she thought she was strong enough to face it, she laid the shovel under a nearby tree and forced herself to walk slowly toward the spot where the bodies lay. The minute she got there, she knew all her preparation had been in vain. She could steel herself to look down on the bodies of her friends in death, but there was no way she could prepare herself for the horror of witnessing the tortures they had faced. As she forced herself to gaze down at the mangled remains of Jeb Allen and his brother, now close enough to see every detail of their suffering, she felt her body begin to shake with acute convulsions, and only the fact that she had had nothing to eat in the last twenty-four hours saved her from retching violently, vomiting in the blood and ashes at her feet. She dug her fingernails into her already pain-racked hands to keep from screaming aloud in anguish and disgust.

The two men lay close together, one beside the other, the dark brown stains on their clothing intensified near the wounds in their chests and sides. Kate shuddered as her eyes moved toward their heads. She had heard that Indians sliced the scalps from the bodies of people they slaughtered, but she had never believed it before. Now she had no choice.

How could such horror exist? she wondered bitterly. It was too savage for anything that bore the name of human. Looking down at the mutilated bodies of her friends, she tried to force the tears that would not come. For the first time in her life, she learned that things can lie too deep for tears.

The ugly wounds that coated the heads of the two men were strangely clean and bloodless, and Kate remembered, as if from somewhere in a dream, that she had once heard the body did not bleed any more after it was dead. At least, she thought with gratitude, that pain had been spared them. At least the Indians had waited until their victims were dead to collect their grisly trophies.

Caroline's body lay several yards away from the men, as if in her last agony she had tried to crawl away, prompted by some deep instinct to hold off the terrifying finality of death, even if it was only for a moment.

Kate heard herself gasp aloud with a sharp cry of horror as she stared down at the dark mass of dried blood that coated her friend's face and fell down onto her shoulders. If that much blood had flowed freely from her scalp, that meant . . .

Those savages!

Kate shut her eyes tight in horror, remembering against her will the long, agonized wail that had followed her up the sloping hillside the day before.

It was a long time before Kate opened her eyes again, and an even longer time before she could force herself to touch the bodies of her friends, dragging them unceremoniously through the dirt, with none of the dignity that befitted the last human rite.

When she had finished her sad chore, she found two strips of charred wood, and tying them together with a piece of her petticoat into a rude semblance of a cross, she impaled it in the rocky earth at the head of their shallow common grave. It was all she could do for them.

As she looked down at the mound of brown earth that pushed its way out of the fertile green grasses around it, taking leave of her friends at last, she tried to erase the ugly memory of their bodies from her mind. She tried to remember instead the last look of desperate hope she had seen in Caroline's eyes, echoing the mute appeal of the words that played silently on her lips.

"At least, I've done that," she said aloud, raising her voice as if she thought the woman beneath the earth could hear her. "If I've done nothing else, at least I've saved the children."

Sarah asked no questions when she returned. Kate had not expected her to. But she knew that, even without words, the child was aware of everything that had happened that afternoon. She could see the unspoken thought in Sarah's soft brown eyes as she looked up at her, but still they did not speak of it.

Instead, they spoke of the meager supplies Kate had dug up from the charred ruins of the house, and began eagerly to rummage through them. Kate had carried them in an old bucket she had found near the house, wrapping the excess in her shawl and tying it to her arm. Now it was Sarah who took the supplies from their containers, sorting them out carefully and neatly on her own petticoat, which she had spread out on the ground. Kate felt as if her hands were too painful ever to touch anything again.

There were a few potatoes—only a few, but they would be enough to last for a while. Like everything else at the farm, they had been burned in the fire, and their skins were black and charred, while the insides were as soft and mushy as if they had been baked in an oven. There was a slab of salt pork, too—like the potatoes, already cooked—and a small chunk of smoked venison. It wasn't much, but it was all they had. With the fresh berries they could gather from the hillside, it would suffice for a while.

They stayed in the cave for two days. Kate let Sarah bandage her swollen hands with the last shreds of her petticoat. When they began to heal, she decided it was time to leave.

Kate carried little Em, bearing the bulk of his weight on her hip, while Sarah took up the small bucket with all that was left of their provisions. With a slow, quiet determination, they set their feet on the road that led away from the farm. Once again, Kate was headed west.

25

JASON COULD FEEL THE SMOOTH, HARD MUSCLES OF HIS HORSE rippling in an easy rhythm beneath his body, giving the long climb up the hill a deceptively lazy quality. The tension in his own lean body seemed to flow into Midnight's sinewy grace, almost as if he and the black stallion formed a single entity. It had always been thus with Jason and his horse. Sometimes he thought they shared a single soul. It seemed to him fitting that Midnight should be there with him then, at the time of his trial and anguish.

That was as it should be, he told himself bitterly. A man and his horse together. The only comfort a man could accept, the only companionship he could trust.

"God damn the woman, anyhow," he shouted out with a force that startled the horse beneath him, causing a momentary break in his stride. He had loved that woman. More than that, he had trusted her. For the first time in years, for the first time since Celeste, he had let himself trust again—and again he had been betrayed.

There were only two people he had trusted in these last, lonely years, his wife and his best friend, and they had both betrayed him.

God damn her, anyhow! Why had he made such a fool of himself over her? There were other women with smooth, pale skin and firm, rounded breasts. There were other bodies made to satisfy lust. Why did he have to pick hers? Above all, why did he have to let himself love her? Trust her?

He spurred the horse angrily forward, urging him to greater speed. He wanted to feel the wind rush by his ears, whistling with such a violent intensity that he would concentrate on nothing else. He wanted to shut out all memories of long, languid nights with soft arms clinging to his sweating body, and sweet, flowery perfume lingering in his nostrils. He wanted to still the echoes in his ears of sharp cries that marked the sweet anguish of love.

God damn her, he thought again. God damn her to hell for what the thought of her was doing to his unwilling body. He knew if he had her before him that very instant, he would think, not of the revenge he had craved day and night since she left him, but only of slaking the burning hunger that tormented his body, in the rich voluptuousness of her flesh.

Jason rounded the top of the hill and began his hurried descent, eager to turn his thoughts from his wife and the angry confusion she caused in his mind. He would hurry toward the farmhouse below, he told himself forcefully. He would ask the friendly couple who lived there if they had seen a stranger in the past few days. Then he would spend a few minutes in pleasant conversation, taking his mind off the cares that oppressed him until his shoulders seemed to bend down with the weight of them.

It wasn't until he was well down the trail that he let his thoughts drift away from his troubles for long enough to gaze at the farmhouse in the valley below. When he did, he reined his horse in abruptly.

"My God."

The words rushed out of his lips in a startled gasp. There below him, on the edge of the fertile valley where the house used to stand, was nothing but a mass of charred ruins.

He knew instantly what had happened, but he would not let himself believe it until he had spurred Midnight down the hill and stopped at the edge of the heap of ashes. There, his worst suspicions were confirmed by the shafts and heads of arrows that lay scattered in the yard.

"The savages," he cried out furiously. God damn the violent animals! Why did they have to keep on perpetuating this senseless brutality? He had seen too many ugly things Indians had done to white men, too many equally ugly things the whites had done to Indians. Where would it all end?

Jason knew Jeb and Caroline Allen. They were decent, hardworking people. He knew of the hardships they had suffered, knew too of the tiny graves on the hillside where two infant daughters rested. They had just begun to wring a living from the wretched soil, and now . . .

He broke off his thoughts abruptly. He didn't want to go on thinking. He didn't want to visualize the agony the brave young pioneers had suffered. He took a long, deep breath, then squared his shoulders with determination. There was nothing he could do for them now, he reminded himself. Nothing but give them a decent burial.

Jason began the slow, sad search through the ashes and charred ruins, expecting at any moment to find the bodies of the Allen family. At first, when he did not see them, he was not too surprised. There was so much rubble to sift through. But after a while he was puzzled.

He couldn't have been wrong, he told himself, glancing around in confusion. There must have been a battle. Nothing else would account for the arrows on the ground. But if there was a battle, where were the bodies?

He was about to give up when his eyes lit on a piece of gold that glittered temptingly in the dark ashes. Leaning down, he picked it up and held it in the palm of his hand. It was the thick yellow gold of a heavy wedding band.

He felt the first tight contractions of fear stab at his heart as he looked down at the dainty circle in his hand. It was far too heavy, far too expensive, to belong to Caroline Allen. Holding his breath with an ominous sense of foreboding, he tilted it in his hand until he could read the initials engraved inside.

JH/CD.

Jason Hamilton and Catherine Devlin.

Kate. Dear God, Kate. Kate was in that house. He forgot all his anger, all his hatred as he stood alone in the bright sunlight that glinted off the gray-black ashes of the charred and ruined house. Kate, his beautiful Kate, tortured and killed, her wedding ring torn or cut from her hand.

Why did it bother him so much? he wondered. Why did he

feel such an intense sense of suffering for a frivolous and unfaithful wife? Hadn't he vowed to kill her himself if he caught her? Why, then, did he grieve so much at her death?

He clutched the ring tightly in his hand, surprised at the sudden sting of hot salt tears inside his eyelids. Angrily he forced them back. He hadn't cried since he was a boy. He wouldn't cry now, especially not for a faithless wife.

Forcing a determination he did not feel, he turned and began to look for another spot where the bodies might lie. As his eyes moved toward the two little graves on the hillside, he saw to his surprise that a fresh mound of brown earth now lay beside them. Hurrying over, he realized with a rush of horror that there was indeed a new grave on the grassy knoll. The earth that capped it was still moist and reddish. It could not have been more than two or three days old.

As he stared down at the crude wooden cross, already askew from the heavy winds that traversed the hills, he could not control the bitter pain he felt rising in his body. He realized then that he had been hoping in his heart that somehow the occupants of that house had escaped, that somehow—by some miracle—Kate was still alive. Now that hope was dead, and he knew he had to face reality. With a heaviness in his heart almost too great to bear, he forced himself to admit he was looking down at the common grave of the valiant defenders of that little house, his wife among them.

He knew he was not the first man in that wild, only half-tamed country that had buried his heart in the deep, cold earth, but that didn't make it any easier. Somehow he had always assumed that the commonality of bereavement and of death would make it easier when the time came for him to face them. He was surprised to find that it did not.

He was so engrossed with his own thoughts and his own pain that he did not even hear the sound of approaching hoofbeats. Even when the rider stopped beside him, he did not notice. Only when he heard the soft sound of a voice did he look up.

"Indians?"

At first, he was not even surprised to see Marc beside him. Slowly he nodded in answer to his question.

"Poor devils. Life was hard enough for them as it was," Marc said quietly, forcing down the bitterness in his voice. He knew that Jason had always been a friend to the Indians. He didn't think this was the time to let him see the ambiguity of his own feelings toward that race of people who could be at once so brutalized and so brutal.

Suddenly Jason's mind began to clear, and he stared at Marc, who had dismounted to stand beside him. "What the devil are you doing here?" he bellowed furiously.

Marc was calm in the face of Jason's anger. "You didn't think I'd let you rush off alone, did you?" he replied simply. "Not in the state you were in. I've followed you since you left, and I'll keep on following you until you find Kate."

Jason's eyes flashed with a momentary burst of fury; then, suddenly, as quickly as it had flared up, the light faded away, leaving them as cold and lifeless as the eyes of a dead man.

"I've found her," he said. He spoke so softly that Marc could barely hear the words. Carefully he opened his hand, letting the sunlight shimmer on the tiny circle of gold that lay on his palm.

Marc could only stare at it speechlessly. He recognized it instantly. The two men faced each other silently for a long time. Then slowly Jason closed his hand around the ring.

Marc turned to look again at the wide mound of earth, a puzzled expression growing on his face. "But why the grave?" he asked slowly.

Jason could only gape at him like a crazy man. Why the hell did he think there was a grave? Because there were dead people in it, that was why.

Marc saw Jason's look of amazement and understood instantly. "I mean, how did it get there? You haven't been here long enough to dig it. I've been following you closely."

"Of course not. I just . . ." Jason broke off, staring at Marc in astonishment.

Indians didn't bury their victims, much less erect rough wooden crosses over them.

"Someone must have come along later," he suggested cautiously. He didn't want to let himself start hoping again.

"Or they drove the Indians off," Marc prompted. "Or someone escaped and came back later to bury the others."

Jason turned away from him quickly, rushing to search the ruins for something that would tear open that mysterious grave, but Marc beat him to it. He had already seen the shovel where it lay under a nearby pine. Grabbing it up hurriedly, he sank it into the soft, fresh earth. When Jason saw him, he rushed over immediately.

"Goddammit, Marc. Give me that shovel. She's my wife."

"That's why you'd better let me do it," his friend replied with a calm strength.

As Jason listened to his words, he felt a shudder pass through his body. He knew Marc was right, and yet there was still a moment when he could not give in. His eyes flashed with a quick anger; then, abruptly, he forced himself to spin on his heels and stride forcefully away, keeping his back to the grave where Marc was toiling.

The sharp sound of metal striking against rocky earth filled the air as Jason stared with unseeing eyes at the blue-gray mountains in the distance. There was a cold finality to the sound of a gravedigger's shovel, he thought, feeling himself shiver in the bright sunlight. It was hard to make himself believe that the grave Marc's shovel was violating was that of his own wife.

Was he so soon to touch, for one last time, the same soft flesh that made the blood run hot in his veins, only to find it now cold and lifeless? And long red hair, would it spill its vibrant beauty only on limbs that were rigid in the pose of death?

Long red hair spilling vibrantly . . .

He felt a bitter salt taste rising from his stomach and fought desperately to choke it back. Long red hair spilling no more from the ugly scar of an empty scalp. Long red hair that served only as an obscene trophy for some brave young warrior, skilled in the murder of helpless women and children.

Oh, God, long tresses he would never see again. Warm, beating flesh he would touch no more. Haunting green eyes closed forever in the last long sleep of death.

At least, he hoped they were closed, he thought with a shudder, imagining the pain and suffering he would see in their gaping expression if they were open. Yes, Marc was right. Better that he should open the grave first.

After no more than a few minutes, Jason was surprised to hear Marc cry out with a hoarse shout. Turning toward him, he saw that he had not yet dug more than a foot or two. He couldn't possibly have come upon the bodies yet.

But Marc was already on his knees as Jason hurried over, gently brushing the dirt from the figures in the newly opened grave. Jason could see three forms, two men and a woman. The men were obviously Jeb Allen and his brother, but the woman . . .

Dear God, he wasn't sure. In all the terrible fantasies that had poured through his brain as he listened to the harsh sound of the shovel grating against the earth, it had never occurred to him that, in the end, he might not even recognize her.

It was Marc who saw more clearly. "It's too thin to be

281

Kate, Jason," he said quickly, bending over the horribly mutilated body. "It must be Caroline Allen."

Even when Jason heard the words, he was dubious. Quick to reassure him, Marc lifted the lifeless hand as far as the rigidity of the arm would allow. "Besides, look at this." There, on a hand callused with toil, was a thin gold wedding ring.

Jason closed his eyes, a surge of relief flooding over his body. In a moment, when he opened them again, he was in control of himself.

"Help me get them out of there," he barked. "We can at least give them a decent grave."

As they lifted the bodies gently out onto the grassy knoll, Marc's brows were pulled together in a puzzled expression. "Didn't the Allens have children?" he asked.

"Two," Jason said quietly. Seeing Marc's eyes move quickly toward the little graves beside them, he added, "Besides those."

"Perhaps the Indians took them," Marc suggested hesitantly.

"No," Jason disagreed. "God knows, the Indians love children, and they used to steal them all the time. Whenever one of their own children died, they thought it was their God-given right to take another in its place, but not anymore. Now they're starving in droves. They wouldn't take on any more mouths to feed."

"Then Kate must have escaped somehow and taken the children with her."

The two men did not speak of it again as they toiled side by side in the ever-deepening grave, but they were both keenly aware of it. Both saw the shallow grave, and both were thinking it could have been dug by a woman. Both saw the tattered edges of lace on the rag that held the cross together, lace that could have been torn from an expensive petticoat. Both were thinking: Kate is still alive.

Only as they stood beside the deep new grave, looking down at a sturdy cross carved from the rails of the fence, did Marc broach the subject again.

"With the two children, it should be easy to track her. We won't have any trouble finding her."

Jason's face grew hard and cold. Now that he knew Kate was alive, now that he was no longer afraid of holding her mutilated remains in arms that ached with love for her, all he could think of was anger and hurt again. All he could remember was that she had betrayed him.

"I'm going on alone."

Marc's face reflected stunned amazement. "My God, Jason, you can't believe the stories that stupid, vindictive man told you."

"I don't know what to believe, and until I do, I'm not going to trust anyone."

"Even if you don't trust me after all these years, surely you can trust your own wife."

"I want to trust her," Jason cried out, forgetting for a moment the cool facade he was trying to maintain. Marc could hear the pain that rang clearly in his voice. "I want to . . . but how can I? Not after the way she behaved. I saw her with my own eyes—in your arms!"

"Goddammit, Jason," Marc shouted impatiently. "She came to me for comfort—because of your damn-fool jealousy!"

Jason's mouth was set in a grim, hard line. "I could almost believe that," he said quietly. "But if she's innocent, why did she run?"

Marc was silent. He, too, had wondered why Kate had fled. Jason saw his hesitancy and knew he had no answer.

"By God, if I find she's guilty, I'll . . ." He left the words unfinished, but their meaning hung heavy in the air. It was several minutes before he spoke again.

"Don't try to follow me, Marc. If you do, I swear I'll kill you."

Marc faced Jason's anger with eyes that were cool and fearless. "If that's what you want," he said quietly. "You saved my life years ago. In a way, I figure it belongs to you now. If you want to take it, you will."

Jason glared at him bitterly, rage turning the piercing blue of his eyes to a dark, midnight black, but still Marc did not back down. Finally Jason whirled on his heels and strode angrily over to where he had tied his horse.

Marc watched as he faded into the distance, waiting until both horse and rider had disappeared on the horizon. Then, slowly, he walked over to his own horse and swung gracefully into the saddle.

26

Kate stared at the small, drab farmhouse with dismay, for there was an ugly, unwelcoming air about it. The unpainted boards that comprised its exterior were no grayer than the Allen house had been, but unlike Jeb and Caroline's carefully kept home, it was in shabby disrepair, as if its inhabitants cared for nothing but the strictest utilitarian needs. As Kate caught sight of a broken pane of glass in one of the windows, carelessly covered with an old board, she noticed that the curtains behind it were dingy and yellowed with age and neglect.

For an instant she felt an almost irresistible urge to turn and run away, so unpleasant was the feeling the house created in her, but she forced herself to stand her ground. She knew she could not afford the luxury of self-indulgence now. She and the children had been walking for three days, and in all that time, they had seen no other trace of a house or even a reasonably well-traveled road. Their provisions were gone, and even the wild berries that had seemed so abundant at first were now in scant supply in this barren area. Besides, they were weary almost beyond endurance. Even with the sling Kate had made of her shawl so she could carry baby Em like the Indian women toted their papooses, she knew she could not bear his weight much farther.

"We'll stop here," she said quietly. "We can't go on without food and rest."

Sarah's eyes turned quizzically toward her face, and Kate could see the doubt written in their depths. Even the child seemed to sense the ugliness that hung like a heavy pall over the house, but Kate noticed she did not try to voice her objections aloud. Perhaps, little as she was, she, too, realized they had no choice.

Kate was surprised that no one had come to greet them in the yard. Surely the inhabitants of the house must have seen them by that time. It seemed unlikely that anyone in such a dangerous land would let strangers enter their yard unawares.

Still, no one came out of the house, and at last Kate reluctantly trudged forward, beating with her fists against the sturdy wooden door.

The sound that greeted her ears was eerily hollow, as if the house was vacant and still, with no one inside to answer her summons or come to her aid. Then, just as she began to fear her instincts were right and the house was indeed uninhabited, she heard the heavy, thumping sound of approaching footsteps, and at last the door creaked warily open.

Kate felt her heart sink as she gazed at the man who stood on the threshold. He was every bit as uninviting as the house in which he dwelt.

He was a tall man, well over six feet, with a lean, powerfully built body and thinning blond hair that had half turned to gray. With his strong bone structure and intense, dark eyes, he might have been strikingly handsome in a rugged sort of way, had not the hostile, uncompromising set of his eyes and jaw given him a cold, unpleasant air. As Kate gazed into angry eyes that obviously considered her an intruder, she was once again tempted to turn and run away. Only the knowledge that she and the children needed food and protection from the cold night kept her feet firmly rooted to the spot.

"Good afternoon," she said politely, hoping to melt his coldness with the cordiality of her own greeting. She was surprised to receive no response to her words, not even a subtle, almost involuntary nod of the head to acknowledge her presence.

Kate's concentration had been centered so completely on the man in the doorway that she had not even noticed there was someone else inside the small house. Only when a slight movement caught her eye did she finally stare past the man toward the thin gray-haired woman who fluttered through the room with the vague insubstantiality of a ghost. She seemed about forty-five or fifty, though she was so weary and broken in spirit it was hard to tell. She might easily have been younger.

Kate turned her gaze back to the man. "We've been traveling a long time, and we're tired and hungry. We desperately need food and shelter."

The man's expression grew even more hostile as he passed his eyes up and down her body in a slow, frank appraisal that turned Kate's stomach. It was getting harder and harder to force herself to hold her ground when every instinct within her urged flight. When the man finally deigned to speak, Kate noticed that his voice, though harsh and sharp, had a natural resonance to it.

"We be hardworkin', God-fearin' folk here. Think ye we have extra to squander on the likes o' ye?"

"It would only be for one night," Kate hastened to assure him. "Tomorrow you can direct us to the nearest town."

"There be no town here," he told her angrily, as if he resented the fact that she had even dared to mention the word. "We hold no truck with the sinners who live in town, not with the evil men who drink intoxicating liquors nor the women with their painted faces. We live here, where we choose to be, close to the clean, good earth of God's country."

Kate gaped at him in amazement. How could he talk of God and still refuse charity to the needy and helpless? Was it possible that he didn't even realize the incongruity of what he was saying?

"We won't be a burden," she promised. "If you'll just let us stay for a few days, I'll be glad to help with the work."

"Ye?" he snorted contemptuously. "What use would ye be? Town women who paint their faces and dress like harlots have no place on a farm."

Kate was stunned by his words. Surely he couldn't have meant them for her. Even if she had been willing to touch her fresh, youthful skin with paint, it would long since have worn off, and the brown riding habit she was wearing was one of the most modest garments she had ever owned.

"I have money," she told him slowly. She was reluctant to give even a cent into the hands of this loathsome man, but she was desperate and knew they had to have help. "I can pay you."

The man was still wary, but his dark eyes began to glow with ill-disguised greed.

"How much?"

Kate slipped her hand into her pocket, curling her fingers around the money that lay inside. She had already started to pull it out when instinct warned her not to let him see how much she had. Quickly she let most of it slip back through her fingers and pulled out only a small handful of coins. Holding out her hand, her open palm turned upward, she showed them to him.

"That?" he scoffed. "That'll not pay for your keep even for a single night."

Kate knew it was more than sufficient to cover food and lodging for several nights, but she dared not antagonize the man by calling him a liar. Instead, she said simply, "It's all I have."

His eyes caressed the coins greedily, and Kate knew he would not let them go.

"It's just for a few days," she assured him again. "Only until I can figure out what to do."

"All right," he agreed reluctantly. "I'll feed ye at the table, but ye'll sleep in the barn."

"No, Amos!"

Surprised at the sudden outburst, Kate turned to face the thin, pale woman who had moved across the room toward them. She could have sworn the woman would never have had the courage to defy her strong-willed husband. Amos, too, seemed surprised, for he whirled around to gape at her, his eyes filled with anger and reproach.

"Keep out of this, Elisheba," he warned sternly.

"But it's too cold for the children," she protested. Although she eyed her husband cautiously, she seemed determined to stand her ground. "Why, the little one's no more'n a baby. Let 'em sleep in the kitchen, Amos—by the stove. They won't take up hardly no room at all." There was a hunger in her eyes as she looked at Em, and Kate sensed she had no children of her own.

Amos opened his mouth to answer her with a sharp retort, then suddenly snapped it shut again. Kate was surprised, for she was sure he was still angry. He did not seem the kind of man to tolerate insubordination.

"All right,' he agreed sullenly. "They can stay in the kitchen, but *she*"—he jerked his thumb toward Kate— "goes to the barn." There was an ugly light in his eyes, and Kate felt a cold chill pass over her. Elisheba noticed it, too, for her face grew even paler, but she said nothing as she turned back into the room, her eyes fixed firmly on the floor.

Kate followed the woman silently into the house. As soon as she had laid the baby in a basket beside the warm stove, she began to help, as best she could, with preparations for the meager meal they were about to share. Her assistance was of little value, she knew, for her hands had still not healed, making her clumsy and awkward. Besides, she was embarrassed to realize she didn't have the vaguest notion what to do in a kitchen. What little she accomplished was thanks to Sarah, who despite her age proved a patient and apt teacher.

Dinner in the drab farmhouse was a far cry from the meal she had shared with the Allen family. Although Caroline had no more to work with, she had prepared her meal with great care, making it both nourishing and tasty. Obviously, Elisheba no longer felt the same concern, and the soggy, indifferent meal she served showed it.

Dinner centered around the inevitable fried potatoes, but these were overcooked and laden with greasy salt pork. The biscuits raised with baking powder had no rich, succulent jelly to accompany them, though Kate was sure berries must grow somewhere on the nearby slopes. She noticed that the plate was passed first to Amos, who carefully picked out all the pieces of salt pork, heaping them on his own plate. By the time the dish was passed to the others, there was nothing left on it but potatoes. Kate couldn't help glancing at Elisheba, amazed that she should tolerate such rudeness without protest.

"Amos needs more to eat," the woman said apologetically. "A man works hard."

Far from being grateful, Amos only glared at his wife, as if he were furious with her for daring to suggest he needed defense. Kate felt sorry for the woman, but she knew there was no point trying to say anything to her. Even the slightest comment could obviously set off Amos' ugly temper. Heaping a modest pile of potatoes on her own plate, she picked up her fork and began to eat.

Before she could even raise the food to her lips, she heard a loud bellow from the end of the table. Dropping the fork back on her plate with a loud clatter, she looked up to see Amos glowering at her furiously.

"Where be your manners?" he demanded angrily. Kate could only gape at him in amazement. *He* was the one who had no manners. "Do ye not wait for grace before ye shovel the food into your mouth?"

Embarrassed, Kate hastened to bow her head. The man was right. She *had* been rude. She should have waited, but somehow she hadn't expected him to say grace. Despite all his talk of God, she had no sense of His presence in that house.

"Almighty God," Amos' voice rang out clearly. "Protect us from the evil, sinful ways of the world."

To Kate, it seemed a strange way to start grace, with no mention of thanks for the food they were about to receive. She listened to the surprisingly resonant sound of Amos' voice as he raised it to an almost fanatical pitch.

"Almighty God, protect good, God-fearin' men from the lust of painted women who liken themselves to harlots and arouse the evil desires of the flesh. Let no such woman in this house, Lord." He paused to stare pointedly at Kate, until, unreasonably, she felt herself begin to blush, as if the intensity of his hostile gaze was enough to make her guilty of sins that were not hers. "God punish all women who tempt the weak and sinful flesh of man. Amen."

"Amen," Elisheba added softly, and Kate, reluctant to incur again the wrath of this strange, hard man, quickly echoed the word.

She was concious of Amos' dark eyes fixed on her throughout the meal, staring at her with the same fanatical intensity she had sensed during his angry, fiery prayer. Suddenly she was conscious of the long red hair that flowed freely to her waist, the pins that held it in place long since lost in the wilderness, conscious, too, of the brown riding habit, which, although modest even by Western standards, could not begin to conceal the voluptuous curves of her body.

Even after dinner, she was not to be spared the intense embarrassment of his eyes following her face and form silently around the room as she helped Elisheba clear away the dishes. Though she barely glanced at him out of the corner of her eye, she knew he was constantly watching her, waiting for the moments when the soft fabric of her skirt would mold itself suggestively around the contours of her hip. It was agony for her to feel him staring at her, but she dared not protest, for she knew they were at his mercy. He could throw them all out in the cold at any moment, and she feared the children could not stand another night of bitter exposure to the elements.

It was a relief when everything was finally cleared away and Amos ordered them to retire so they could be up before sunrise to begin their chores. Even when he forced Kate out into the darkness, grudging to spend even a cent of the money she had given him on candlewax, she did not mind. She was glad to be out of there—glad to be away from him.

Even in the bright moonlight, her footing was treacherous as she moved slowly toward the barn, for the path was ill-kept and rough. The more she tried to hurry, the more awkwardly she stumbled along. All of a sudden, she was startled to hear the sound of a sharp hiss behind her. She spun around quickly, not knowing what to expect.

To her amazement, she saw Elisheba hurrying toward her, a dim light flickering from the small stub of a candle she held in her hand. She pressed it quickly into Kate's grateful fingers, then turned to hurry back into the house before her husband could discover what she had done.

Astonished, Kate stared after her for a moment, surprised at the sudden, bold courage that had prompted her brief moment of defiance. What a cruel, hard life the woman must lead, married to a monster like that. Suddenly it occurred to Kate to wonder what kept her there. If it had been she, she would have run away for sure. She would never have endured such cruelty, not for a minute.

Or would she?

Kate closed her eyes for a moment, surprised at the tears that leaped to their surface as the image of Jason came into her mind. Jason. Strong, handsome features outlined boldly against the dark golden frame of his hair. Deep blue eyes staring out at her with a tender, savage passion.

Yes, she would endure cruelty, she told herself bitterly. She *had* endured it. Jason's cruelty was different from Amos', subtler and more insidious, but it was every bit as hard to bear. Yet, she had borne it, and willingly—and all for the passion with which he had enslaved her body. If it weren't that her life was in danger, she would never have left him. Even now, after all she had endured because of him, she was tempted . . .

Angrily she erased the image from her thoughts. She didn't dare think about him. His hold on her heart was still too strong. She couldn't trust herself to fight the urge that threatened to send her racing back to him. She had to keep on running. She had to preserve her life, even if that very life turned out to be nothing but drudgery and sadness, nothing more than the lonely memory of lost delights.

As she pushed open the door to the barn, the candle still flickering faintly in her hand, Kate was disgusted by the rank, stale smell that rose to greet her nostrils. Reluctantly she forced herself to step inside and pull the door closed behind her, shutting out the last traces of cool, fresh air. The sound of scurrying footsteps echoed across the floor at her entrance, and Kate was careful not to look too closely into the straw. She did not want to see whatever it was that rustled through it.

Kate glanced around briefly at the barn that was so unlike the tidy, well-kept stable at her husband's ranch. She could look at the unfamiliar tools with a minimum of curiosity, but she could not help being puzzled by the lengths of cheap muslin that hung like canopies over the stalls. What on earth could they be? she wondered.

It was only seconds before she found out. The sound of scurrying in the rafters had increased after she brought the light inside, and suddenly she heard a loud, unnerving squawk as one of the rodents fell from the ceiling onto the floor below. That was what the fabric was stretched across the stalls for, Kate realized with a shudder. It would catch the falling rats and mice before they could land unceremoniously on the backs of the livestock below. No doubt Amos had learned from bitter experience that the startled animals could set up a loud enough commotion to disturb his precious sleep.

Kate took another moment to glance around, more carefully this time, and she was relieved to spot an empty stall in the far corner. She, too, would sleep under a canopy that night. She was at least as sensitive as the livestock.

Reluctantly she began to heap masses of damp, stale-smelling hay on the floor of the stall. She was determined to be as far off the ground as possible. She knew it would provide little protection against the vermin that crawled the floor, but it made her feel better to try.

Even when she had accumulated a sizable pile and laid her shawl on top of it to protect her from the sharp spears of hay, it was hard to force herself to lie down. She knew she had to sleep. She didn't want to have to stay in that hideous place for more than a few days at most. It was important to build up her strength so she could face the arduous trip that lay ahead.

Only at the last minute did she remember the money, and she reached down in her pocket to pull it out. She hesitated for a moment, then tugged at a loose board in the rough floor and hid the money beneath it, tucking it firmly against the damp earth. She didn't trust the mercenary farmer who talked so freely of God but had no charity in his heart.

Although she was sure she would never be able to fall asleep in that awful place, Kate quickly found she was more exhausted than she had realized, and it took only a few seconds after she blew out the candle for her eyelids to grow heavy. Despite the rustling sounds in the straw, she felt herself begin to drift off. She had just begun to slide from the twilight world of half-sleep into blissful unawareness when she was jolted back into consciousness by a loud, creaking noise. For an instant, it almost sounded as if someone were pushing open the door to the barn.

At first, she tried to tell herself it was only her imagination, but when the sound was repeated, she realized with a rush of horror that she had been right. Someone *had* come through the door. Slowly, cautiously, she opened her eyes, turning them toward the source of the sound.

There in the open doorway, silhouetted in the dim light of the lantern in his hand, was Amos, his tall, strong body standing out menacingly against the dark sky.

Kate gasped in terror at the sight of him. Then, with a tremendous effort of will, she forced herself to breathe more evenly, trying to calm the rapid beating of her heart. Surely there was nothing menacing about his being there, she reminded herself sternly. After all, it was his barn. Perhaps he had just come back to take care of some chore he had forgotten.

But that hope was quickly dispelled as she saw the man look around slowly, as if he was searching for something. Only when he spotted her in the stall at the far end of the barn did he begin to move again. Slowly, with no effort or haste, he walked toward her, the lantern raised high in his hands to illuminate her features. He didn't stop until he had reached the front of the stall.

"What do you want?" She was surprised at how strong her voice sounded.

"God's will be done."

Kate trembled at the sound of his voice. She couldn't tell if it was lust or wrath she saw in his eyes.

She wanted to cry out: What do you mean? But she was too frightened to speak. She could not force the words to rise out of her terror-constricted throat.

"Ye come here with painted hair and swaying hips to tempt a good man of God," he told her ominously. "Think ye not that God be angry with ye? Aye, sore angry, and for that ye must be punished cruelly."

Kate stared at him in horror. The fear she felt as she gazed at the fanatical light that gleamed out of his dark eyes was beyond anything she had ever known before. Even when she had looked into the eyes of Indians aiming their guns at her breast, she had not felt the same deep terror. Horrible as their rage had been, she could at least understand the lust for vengeance she saw in their eyes. The expression on this man's face was beyond comprehension, beyond even sanity.

"My hair is as God made it," she told him angrily. Her voice was still bold, but her heart and mouth were dry with fear. "And so are my hips. As for why I came here, I came only to beg for the charity God bids you grant to all his creatures."

"Liar!" he shrieked. "Hussy. Satan sent ye to tempt me,

but now ye'll know the wrath God hurls down on the evil temptress." Kate was suddenly aware of the brutal size of his rough hand as he thrust it toward her. She backed away from him quickly, but the stall was shallow, and she soon found herself pressed against the hard wood of the wall.

"No, please . . ." she whispered, but even as she spoke the words, she knew they would not help her. There was no mercy in his eyes as he lowered the lantern to the floor and began to step slowly toward her.

Again he thrust out his massive paw, and Kate shivered with fear as she realized there was nothing she could do to stop him. Then suddenly, to her surprise, he reached down toward her skirt, ripping at the fabric until he had torn the pocket right out of it.

The money! So that's what he was after. The money. Kate felt her body go limp with relief. She had expected him to hurt her—or even kill her—and all he was after was her money.

"I told you that was all I had!" How glad she was that she had taken the time to hide the rest of it beneath the floor.

"Then ye be a fool," he told her coldly. "Ye should never have given all to me."

I didn't, she thought exultantly, but she knew better than even to hint at it to him. She stood facing him defiantly, trying to will him with her eyes to back away from her. When he didn't move, she began to grow frightened again.

"We'll leave in the morning," she stammered awkwardly. "I promise we'll leave then."

"It be God's will that ye be punished," he insisted. "God's will be done."

Kate wondered if he meant what he said, or if he was just angry because he couldn't get any money from her. She thought for a brief instant of digging up the money and offering it to him in exchange for her safety, but she quickly rejected the idea. He would just rob her and then go ahead and do whatever he had planned anyway. Trembling, she wondered what that was. Did he intend to punish her by beating her? Or killing her? Silently she faced him, her body shaking with fear.

When she saw his hand slip down to his belt and unbuckle it, she was sure she had been right. He did intend to beat her. She could already feel the painful sting of the welts the sharp leather would raise in her tender flesh. Only when he failed to pull it out of the loops of his trousers did she realize that he had a far uglier punishment in mind for her. In horror, she saw his fingers paw at the fasteners of his pants, then rip them impatiently open.

"Oh, dear God, no!" she cried out. Remembering the beating she had feared only seconds before, she realized how welcome it would be now. Even death would be welcome if it would spare her from this cruel lust masquerading as righteousness. "Do anything you want," she begged him. "But not that. Please, not that!" Sobbing, she threw herself to her knees at his feet, imploring the mercy she knew he did not have in his heart to give.

"It be God's will," he repeated sternly. "And this be the instrument of his will."

Reaching a crude hand inside his pants, he pulled out the rough red instrument of divine will he had threatened her with. Kate's heart sank as she stared at its massive hardness. Instinct warned her there was no way he would let her go now that he had let his lust grow to such proportions.

Kate knew she had only to open her mouth and scream. The sound would carry across the yard and into the still house, where Elisheba would hear it, her eyes overflowing with sadness. It tormented Kate to think of adding yet another load to that poor woman's burden of unhappiness, but as she cast her eyes frantically around the small stall, searching for something to defend herself with, she realized she had no choice. The instant she felt him sink to his knees beside her, pressing his coarse body lewdly against hers, she opened her mouth to cry for help. The long, shrill scream that issued from her lips sounded hideously harsh, even to her own ears.

Kate expected to feel a rough hand pushing across her mouth at any moment, stifling her screams and choking her until she could barely breathe. She was prepared to fight with all her strength against that hand, prepared to fight to the death to maintain the screams that were her only defense against his brutality.

To her surprise, he did not even attempt to stop her, as if her screams were of no consequence to him. Instead, he reached down with the same rough male hand she had expected to feel across her mouth, and clutched at the fabric of her skirt until it gave in his grasp, the seams ripping apart with a sickening sound. Thrusting her roughly down into the dank, foul-smelling hay, he flung what was left of her skirt above her waist and tore the flimsy undergarments from her body until she lay naked before him, exposed to the gross lewdity of his eyes. He wasted not a second admiring the smooth perfection of her pale skin and soft, voluptuous flesh, but threw the repugnant weight of his body immediately on top of hers.

Kate fought against him desperately, realizing with rising panic that there was no way she could defend herself against his superior strength for more than a few minutes. It would be all she could to keep her knees clamped tightly together until Elisheba rushed irately into the barn to pull him off her.

Why doesn't she come? Kate thought with a mounting sense of urgency. Surely she must have heard the screams by then. Surely she had had plenty of time to respond to them.

Then suddenly Kate realized the truth. Elisheba was not coming!

Of course not! What a fool she had been to count on her. Elisheba was too thoroughly browbeaten, too afraid of her husband to defy him. Even now, she must be lying in her bed, her hands clapped tightly over her ears to shut out the sound of screams, her cheeks crimson with shame. But still she would not come. No, she would not come.

Nothing could save her now, Kate realized helplessly. Nothing could keep this vile animal from violating the sanctity of her body. She held her legs pressed tightly together as long as she could, but as she felt his knee pushing relentlessly between them, she knew it could be only a matter of seconds before his strength won out.

When it finally happened, Kate felt herself sob with despair and frustration, knowing that she was now open to the final moment of his cruel assault. The agonizing physical pain that shot through her body as he intruded into her resisting flesh was violent and brutal, but in a strange way, it was almost a relief. At least it took her mind off the shame.

She heard the harsh, rasping sound of loud grunts, reminding her of a beast in the field, as he pumped his vulgar body up and down in a fierce, awkward rhythm, rubbing savagely against the wounded flesh of her body, until she thought she must scream from the pain. Then, just when she was sure she could bear it no longer, she felt merciful faintness overtake her, and she slipped gratefully into unconsciousness.

When she awoke, she was lying alone in the straw. Even in unconsciousness, she had been weeping, and her lashes and cheeks were wet with tears. As she became aware of the pain that still racked her violated flesh, she felt a flood of hatred surge through her body, a hatred more intense and terrifying than anything she had ever known.

For the first time in her life, she knew what it was to desire to kill. If she had the man before her then—the man who had so brutally and viciously violated her body—and if she had a gun in her hand, she would not hesitate to pull the trigger. She would even enjoy watching his lifeless body drop to the earth, a threat no longer to her or any other woman.

At last she began to understand the dark glow she had seen in Jason's eyes, and in Marc's. Violence begets violence, she thought, until you become violent yourself. Was this what had happened to Jason, this same cruel thing that was happening to her?

Jason.

The tears stung more bitterly as she thought of him. Jason. The man with whom she had shared her body so ecstatically and so lovingly. Now that same body had been touched by coarse, brutal hands that violated and shamed it. Now she was little better than the whore Jason had accused her of being. Now, even if she could somehow manage to see him again, she could never hope to effect a reconciliation. Even had he been willing, she knew her flesh had now been defiled too grossly to offer again to a man in tenderness and love. Her shame was too great to live with.

Her bitter reverie was cut short by the creaking sound of the door swinging open, and Kate leaped to her feet abruptly, searching desperately for some kind of weapon to grab up. If the beast had returned to work his vile, filthy ways with her again, he would not get away this time unscathed.

But before she had time to find a weapon, she was startled to catch sight of a small, hesitant shadow in the doorway. Squinting into the moonlight, she saw the slight figure of little Sarah, a huge, long-handled pot grasped tightly in her hands.

"Oh, darling," she cried, rushing to the child and dropping to her knees to embrace her. Sarah must have heard her screams, and small as she was, she had come loyally to her defense. "It's all right, darling," she assured her, comforting her in her arms. "It's all right."

Sarah looked doubtfully at Kate, her eyes taking in the disarray of her clothing, but she relaxed enough to loosen her grip on the pan.

"It was only a prowler," Kate lied. "I scared him away with my screams." She could see that Sarah was still not convinced, and her heart went out to the frightened child who had suffered so much in the past few days. She was determined to ease her mind. "Go on back to bed now, sweetheart. I'll be all right . . . but leave the pan here with me."

If Amos came back, she was determined to be ready for him.

But Amos did not return until sunrise, and then only to attend to his chores. Kate shuddered when she saw him enter the barn, and she tightened her hold on the heavy pot in her hand, but it quickly became apparent that he was no longer interested in her. Indeed, he walked calmly around the barn, tending to his tasks with a total unconcern, as if she were not even there. Even when she took advantage of his being on the far side of the barn to slip hurriedly outside, he barely seemed to notice her. It was as if nothing were amiss. As if nothing at all had happened. Kate could almost believe it had been only a bad dream if it weren't for the burning pain between her legs that continually reminded her of her shame.

Breakfast was a nightmare. Kate didn't know which she hated most, Amos' cool, appraising stare or Elisheba's pale face and troubled, averted eyes. She was grateful when it was finally over and Amos rose to go to the fields. At least, it would give her a few hours to prepare, a few hours to figure out how to defend herself against him.

At the last moment, as he stood in the doorway, Amos turned to face her.

"Ye can stay here again today," he told her, as if to imply that the money she had given him was all used up and she was staying only at his bounty. "But ye'll sleep in the barn again tonight."

Tonight!

Dear God, he intended to visit her again tonight, to work out his lewd lust once again on her defenseless body. What a fool she had been to think she could protect herself from him. Nothing could save her, not as long as she stayed there.

She spent the early part of the morning carefully mending her torn skirt. The inner panels were ruined, and she knew she could not make it into a split riding skirt again, but that didn't matter. She expected to do no more riding. A plain narrow skirt would do. She tried to do something with the damaged undergarments, too, but she quickly realized it was hopeless. They were beyond repair.

After the skirt was mended, Kate waited until Elisheba was outside doing chores, then called Sarah to her. The words she had to say to the child were the hardest she had ever spoken, but she knew she had no choice. The journey that lay ahead would be long and arduous. There was no way the children, especially Em, could endure it. They would have to be left behind.

Sarah greeted her announcement with fear-filled eyes, but she did not question it. Even the child seemed to sense that Kate would be in danger if she stayed in that house.

"But I'll send for you," Kate promised. "I'll send for you."

And she would, too, she vowed to herself. She didn't know how, but somehow, when she reached safety, she would find a way to bring the children to her.

When she slipped out into the barn to dig up her money, she was careful to leave most of it lying in plain sight on top of a bale of hay. Elisheba would be kind to the children, she knew. Perhaps the money would serve to soften Amos' heart as well.

She took only enough to provide train fare to San Francisco.

27

Jason rode mechanically through the outskirts of Cheyenne, barely noticing the drab gray buildings that seemed even shabbier under the glowing red rays of the dying sun. Only after he had neared the center of town did he realize he was following the railroad tracks, clinging to them with a certain grim persistence that was as pointless as it was stubborn. He knew very well there would be no more trains before morning. He could not hope to find Kate until then.

Resolutely he tugged at the reins, turning Midnight away from the tracks. There was no point being doubly the fool. He was not going to let himself camp at the station until morning, waiting there on the slim chance that his wife might come that way.

As he guided his horse sharply into a side street, he suddenly realized to his surprise that he had turned automatically into a narrow lane that was heavily laden with memories. How many times had he passed that way before? he asked himself. How many times had he ridden down that same street toward the warm, unquestioning welcome he knew he would find at the end?

Carmelita. He pictured coarse black hair rippling fluidly to her waist, and gay, dancing eyes sparkling with dark lights of merriment. Yes, Carmelita would be glad to see him. She always was. And he would be glad to see her.

She was only a *puta*, the lowest of the low, even in this rough society, but she had a heart filled with compassion and understanding. Besides, who was he to scoff at a *puta*? Didn't he have a wife who was no better? At least Carmelita was honest enough to take the name of prostitute. He couldn't say as much for Kate.

"Damn her," he cursed hoarsely, hurling out the same angry words that had crossed his lips countless times each day since he discovered her treachery. It did him no good, but he shouted them out anyway, as if somehow the force of his curses could drive out the anger that threatened to tear him apart and purge his system of it once and for all. Damn her for betraying him . . . and damn her for proving his suspicions were right.

If he had ever doubted his harsh judgment of her, he could doubt it no longer. God, he could still see the ugly, sneering features of that coarse farmer before his eyes as if it had not already been two long days since he spoke to him.

"Ain't been no female here," the man had sniveled. "We don't hold none with them painted city hussies." What kind of fool had the man taken him for? Didn't he realize the presence of the Allen children branded him as a liar instantly? He only had to talk to the man for a few minutes, watching the sly, half-boastful leer that pulled up the corners of his mouth, before he realized with a sick feeling in the pit of his stomach what had happened.

The man was handsome in a cold, cruel way. Jason had to admit that to himself. He had the kind of spare, rugged body that would appeal to the passions of a woman like Kate, and his features were well chiseled and attractive, except for the fanatical gleam in his eye and the bitter set of his jaw. My God, was that all it took—a handsome face and a strong masculine body—to get his wife to jump into bed like a bitch in heat?

"I couldn't help myself," the man whined self-pityingly. "She threw herself at me like one o' them harlots on the street. How's a good, God-fearin' man to protect himself?"

There was a plea in the man's voice, but Jason ignored it. You didn't resist her, you son of a bitch, he thought furiously. You were only too glad to bury yourself in that soft, pliant flesh. For an instant he felt an intense, almost overpowering urge to kill the man. It gave him a certain grim satisfaction to watch as both he and his pale, gray wife cowered backward into the shadows. Only after a few seconds did he realize he was actually gripping the handle of his gun. Slowly, with the greatest reluctance, he forced his fingers to release it.

After all, how could he kill the man for sins that were Kate's—and Kate's alone? No doubt she had thrown herself at the poor farmer, just as she had done to him months ago. How could he blame the man for giving in to the same temptation that had conquered him? Kate was lovely, incredibly lovely . . . and obviously she was any man's for the asking. It would take a strong man to say no to her beauty.

Catching sight of the bright lights of the saloon ahead, Jason tried to force his thoughts back to the present, thinking only of the dark Spanish *puta* inside and the welcome hours of sweet forgetfulness he would find in her arms.

Maybe Kate didn't really lust after the man, he told himself hopefully, unable to tear his thoughts away from his pain and disillusionment. Maybe it was just a bribe. Maybe she only slept with him to pay for the children's keep. Yet, if she truly cared for their welfare, could she have entrusted them to such a cruel, self-obsessed man? Thank God he had found them and gotten them out of there. At least they were safe now.

No, Kate obviously didn't care a whit about the children. What she did, she did for self-gratification. She had opened her legs to that bastard, with the instincts of a whore who could never get enough of a man's body.

Angrily he pushed all thoughts of his wife to the back of his mind. No, not his wife, he reminded himself bitterly, his *whore*—his and everyone else's. With a cold fury he flipped the reins over the hitching post and hurried inside, eyes searching for a flash of scarlet capped by a shining mass of black hair. He was not disappointed.

"Jason!"

Carmelita's dark eyes were sparkling with undisguised delight as she hurried toward him, crudely pushing away the other men who had flocked around her. There were loud murmurs of protest, for the men were as anxious to enjoy the brightness of her laughter and zest for life as they were to relish the soft resilience of her complying body in the rooms upstairs. But she paid them no heed.

"It is good to see you again, *caballero*." Her voice had a teasing tone as she hooked her arm in his and pulled him casually toward the bar, treating him with the same affectionate warmth he remembered so well. For an instant, he almost had the illusion that nothing had changed since the last time he saw her. Though she must have known of his marriage, she said not a word about it, tactfully leaving it for him to mention if he chose. She must have known, too, that his wife had run away from him, he thought bitterly—no doubt the whole town was buzzing about it—but again, she was discreet enough to say nothing about it.

"What are you drinking, *amigo?* It's on the house. *Everything* is on the house tonight." Her voice was heavy with a meaning he could not possibly mistake.

"I don't want a drink." He pulled his arm out of hers and threw it roughly across her back, drawing her body toward his until she could not miss the hard bulge of desire that pressed demandingly into her belly.

She was quick to sense the torment and anguish in his eyes, understanding that he was seeking the only solace he knew to ease the deep pain burning inside him.

"I'll have the whiskey sent upstairs."

There was a fury in Jason's hands as he gouged his fingers into the soft flesh of her body, bruising her skin painfully, but Carmelita did not cry out in protest, not even when she felt him thrust himself into her with a brutal savagery that took her breath away. She was used to the rough, violent ways of men, and she saw the anguish that was tearing his soul apart, even as her own flesh was being torn. Even without understanding its cause, she sensed the deep thirst for forgetfulness Jason sought to quench in her warm body.

Even later, when she had coaxed Jason's weary, aching body into the sensuous luxury of a hot bath, Carmelita sensed that the anger and tension had not left him. She knelt beside him, her generous body now wrapped in a translucent, flowing robe, its whiteness broken by gaily embroidered flowers and birds, and ran her fingers soothingly over his skin, letting them slide across his tired muscles with the slippery ease of soap-laden water. For the first time that evening, he looked up at her and smiled wearily.

Jason had been aware of her eyes on his lean, hard body, and as he gazed back at her, he was suddenly surprised to realize he was seeing her for the first time that evening. He had joined his body to hers with a lust born as much of rage as of hunger, but he had not really been aware of her presence at all. He had reached out to grasp coarse black hair in clutching fingers, but all he had been able to think of was the silken luxury of fine red tresses. He had sensed the aroma of rich perfume assailing his nostrils, but his soul was filled only with a yearning for the light, flowery fragrance that evoked memories of so many flights of ecstasy.

No, Carmelita had not been there at all. Not for him. Even as he had worked out his anger on her body, it was another body he had longed to tear apart with the fury of his passion.

"Gently, *hombre*." Carmelita's voice cut into his bitter reverie. "What angry thoughts you must be thinking. See how your muscles are straining."

Looking down, he saw to his surprise that she was right. The muscles of his chest and arms strained tautly against his skin, stretching it to its limits.

"I'm sorry," he said contritely, using the words that rarely crossed his lips. How unfair it was to take his anger out on her. Even if he paid her handsomely, it would never be enough. What a jewel she was!

"Don't worry, eh, *caballero*," she teased gently, careful to keep a light, sparkling note in her voice. "I don't mind. I'm used to it. But I think it is hard for you. You should relax . . . and Carmelita knows how to make you do that, *sí*?"

She winked knowingly at him, then rose and moved with sensuous grace toward a cabinet in the corner. Suddenly he realized what she intended to do.

"No oil!"

His voice sounded harsh and angry. As she turned to stare at him in amazement, he was annoyed to see that he had frightened her.

"Come here," he ordered gruffly. She obeyed instantly, and he leaned forward, dripping water on the tiled floor as he put his arms around her. "I just don't want the oil," he told her, trying to make his voice sound gentler.

"But you always loved it."

He knew she was puzzled, but he could not explain. How could he bring himself to talk of long, idle afternoons of love, long afternoons spent gazing down at warm oil glistening on perfect white skin, long afternoons of listening to the soft, sensuous sounds of ecstasy?

"No oil today."

He slid his hands up to her shoulders and slipped the loose neck of her robe over them, letting it slide silently to the floor.

"Today, I need something different."

He wrapped his strong arms around her willing body and pulled her into the warm, fragrant water beside him. At long last, he lost himself in the forgetfulness he had craved so desperately.

At first, Kate had no idea where she was. She knew only that she had wandered into the fringes of a large city, and as she looked around at the shabby buildings, she felt herself breathe a heavy sigh of relief. Here, at last, she could feel safe. Here she could blend in the anonymity of the crowds.

Only after she had moved closer to the center of town did she begin to have an uneasy sense of familiarity. Then, suddenly, as she passed a building that was unmistakably recognizable, she realized what had happened.

She was in Cheyenne!

She had come full circle, back to the place she had started from. She was so discouraged, she could have sat down at the side of the road and wept.

Blinking back tears of frustration, she forced herself to examine the situation realistically. Perhaps it was not as bad as she had feared. After all, she had been gone nearly two weeks. Surely by now, unless he had somehow been able to follow her tracks, Jason would assume she was far away. He wouldn't be looking for her in Cheyenne. Besides, her dilemma had a bright side, too. Cheyenne was a major center. Trains passed through every day, even those headed for the new railway line that led to the coast. If she was lucky, she might be able to get a train to San Francisco that very day.

For once, luck was with her, and it was only a few short hours later that she stood on the platform, her ticket clutched tightly in her fingers. As she glanced around with incurious eyes, she found it hard to make herself believe that she was really going to get away at last. She was surprised at the odd little twinge of grief that tugged at her heart, now that she was leaving forever, but she refused to let herself think about it. She was doing what she had to do, and it was too late for regrets.

For the first time in two weeks, Kate felt completely safe. She knew she blended in perfectly with the other anonymous travelers waiting beside the tracks. Before she had reached the town, she had stopped beside a small stream to freshen up and tie her hair back with a few threads pulled from her hem. She knew she didn't look elegant, but she looked presentable, and that was even better. Elegance would have been out of place on that rough platform.

She was so sure of herself that she was totally unprepared for the hard grip of a hand reaching out from behind to clutch the flesh of her upper arm. She felt a surge of pain shoot through her body as the fingers gouged into her skin, but she barely noticed it, for the terror that racked her senses in response to that sudden rough touch was all-encompassing. Even before she turned around, she knew what she would see.

"Jason!" Her voice was so soft he could not hear it. He could tell what she said only by the form her lips made as she mouthed the word.

With a sudden roar, the train rushed into the station, wheels churning loudly against the prolonged, whistling noise of the steam engine, drowning out the harsh, angry sound of Jason's breathing as he gazed down at her with the treacherous feeling of a man who was drowning in his own hatred. Kate stared back at him, feeling a sudden rush of longing flood through her body that both amazed and terrified her.

How could she feel that way about the man who stood before her with murder in his eyes? This was the man who had threatened to kill her! Why, then, did her body react so strangely? Why did she feel a sudden surge of breathless anticipation pouring through her until it penetrated even her fingertips?

For a long time Kate and Jason stood alone on the platform, staring tensely into each other's eyes, until finally they heard the shrill sound of the train pulling out of the station, leaving them at last alone with each other. Suddenly, without warning, Jason tightened his grip on her arm, and turning abruptly, he began to drag her along the platform.

Where was he taking her? she wondered with a sudden rush of hope. And why? Perhaps he was not planning to kill her after all. Perhaps she had been foolish to be so afraid of him.

But as quickly as her hopes had been raised, they were dashed to earth again, and belatedly she began to feel the cold fear that should have seized her the instant she turned around and saw his enraged eyes boring into her face. Of course he was not going to kill her there, she reminded herself. It was far too public a place. Someone might see them. He would have to take her out to a dark, wooded place. There he could do with her what he would. There he could leave a hasty, shallow grave that no one would ever find.

Her worst suspicions seemed to be confirmed when he dragged her angrily toward the horse he had hitched outside. Still clutching her wrist so she could not even attempt to run away, he swung easily into the saddle, then turned to look down at her. His sharp eye caught sight of her narrow skirt, and realizing she could not ride astride, he pulled her up in front of him, where he could hold on to her as she rode with both legs dangling awkwardly on one side.

He knew it was a mistake the minute he urged Midnight into an easy trot down the street, but he was too stubborn to admit it and change her position. He could already feel his flesh beginning to respond to the temptation of her warm body pressing close to his, and the light, seductive touch of silken strands of hair brushing against his cheek. No matter how furiously he fought it, he was powerless to control the lust that began to swell in his body. Even after long, hard days on the road, her hair was still sweet and fragrant, and the scent reached his nostrils with the urgency of remembered passion. He felt his body calling out to him, stabbing him with aching thrusts, begging him to press his hardness one last time into the soft, yielding warmth of her flesh.

By the time they finally reached the open road, his need for her had grown until it was a thing of desperate urgency, and reason no longer had any control over his body. Spying a thick clump of trees, well away from the road, he turned Midnight quickly off the trail and raced toward it. There was nothing in his thoughts save the all-consuming fire that burned through his body until it was an agonizing torture.

As he dropped her rudely from the saddle onto the hard earth beneath, Kate looked up at him in terror, cringing from the dark rage she saw in his eyes. This was where he was going to kill her, she thought with a rush of panic. This was the perfect place for it, isolated and secretive.

As she watched him dismount, she began to back away slowly, painfully aware that there was no place she could go to escape from him. She opened her mouth to plead with him, to beg for her life, but she could not force the words to come out. They would do no good, she knew. They would only turn her at the last moment—the moment of her death—into the kind of sniveling coward she had always despised. If she was going to die now, at least she could do it with dignity.

She stopped and waited as he moved across the short space that separated them, his eyes blazing with hatred.

"Whore!" His hand lashed out swiftly, landing forcefully on the side of her face. Her head reeled with the impact, and she stumbled awkwardly, falling backward against the cold earth.

When she had recovered her senses, she looked up at him in amazement. She had expected him to kill her, but she hadn't expected to be beaten first—though heaven knows why not. He was angry enough to do it, she knew.

"Pull up your skirt, whore!" he cried out hoarsely. Kate could only gape at him, stunned. This was not what she had expected at all.

"Pull it up!" he shouted furiously, leaning menacingly over her body. With trembling fingers she managed somehow to obey him. The air felt cold against her naked flesh as she rolled the rough fabric awkwardly to her waist.

She could see his hand reaching out, ready to rip the thin undergarments from her body. He paused, surprise filling his eyes for an instant when he saw she was no longer wearing any.

"Well, at least you come prepared," he told her sarcastically. She bit her lip to keep from crying out in shame.

"Now spread your legs apart."

"What?" At last, she was indignant. He could kill her if he wanted, but she wasn't going to let him treat her like a common prostitute. She kept her legs clamped tightly together.

"I said, spread your legs apart, whore! What's the matter? You spread them fast enough for everyone else. Isn't there anything left for your own husband?"

Kate pressed her teeth deeper into her lip until she could taste the bitterness of her own blood. She was determined not to answer his cruel taunts. She knew she would gladly give her body to him anytime he asked, but she was not going to let him force her like that, without even a semblance of tenderness or love.

"You can make love to me anytime—" she began, but he would not let her finish.

"Love?" he cried hoarsely. "Do you think it's love I want from you? I want to satisfy the urges of my body with a whore, just like everyone else has done. Now, spread your legs apart, or I swear before God I'll kill you now!"

Kate knew from the black rage in his eyes that he meant what he said. Slowly, her whole body taut with anguish, she pulled her legs apart for him. She tried to tell herself she obeyed only out of fear, but she couldn't keep herself from recognizing the sweet pain that began to burn between her thighs, torturing her again with its own special delight now that she knew she was going to feel Jason's strong, hard body against hers once again.

Jason looked down at her for a moment, contempt and anger playing in his eyes. "If I were any kind of man, I wouldn't let you do this to me. I'd kill you now."

But Kate was not frightened by his words. She saw that his hand was reaching, not for his gun, but for the front of his trousers.

No sooner had he ripped his pants open than he flung his body on hers, his breathing coming in a series of short, heaving grunts. They were not so different from the horrible sounds the gross farmer had made when he violated her body, but unlike those disgusting sounds, these hoarse gasps increased her excitement until it reached a fever pitch. As she felt his hands explore her body roughly and his mouth press hungrily down on hers, her hips began to writhe in the joy of anticipated rapture.

She knew she should not let herself succumb to the savage violence of his assault. He should not be able to command her to spread her legs, then leap on top of her, expecting her to twist beneath his body, moaning with ecstasy. She was not a possession he owned. She was a human being with feelings and needs of her own. Still, her angry brain could not force her eager body to reject him, and she felt her legs begin to entwine themselves around him, trying to press him deeper and deeper into her body.

She sensed that he, too, was angry at the lust his mind could not control, for his movements were brusque and harsh, and when he sank his teeth deep into the flesh of her shoulder, she knew he was trying to punish her with pain for the sensuality that had enslaved his body. She did not attempt to resist, for his anger told her that he needed her as desperately as she needed him. When at last she felt her body rush toward the final moment of ecstasy, she knew instinctively that her cry of joy would be mingled with the moan that escaped his lips.

For only the briefest of moments, their bodies clung together, and Kate could feel the love and tenderness that emanated from Jason's flesh. Then, abruptly, as if he were ashamed of that moment of softness, Jason pulled away from her and rose to his feet.

"Get up!" His voice was filled with anger. Kate knew the anger was directed inward against the passion he could not control, but she knew, too, that he would not hesitate to take it out on her. Slowly, reluctantly, she drew her skirt down around her naked thighs and pulled herself to her feet.

"What are you going to do with me?"

The eyes that looked back at her were cold with hatred.

"I'm going to take you back to face your accuser. And then, if I decide you're guilty, I'm going to kill you."

Kill her! Dear God, he still meant to kill her! Even after what had just happened. Even after he had proved that he still desired and needed her.

She wanted to protest. She wanted to tell him she was innocent, but one look at his hard, cruel eyes warned her it would be no use. Jason was a harsh judge, and a merciless one, and he had already condemned her in his heart. Suddenly she felt a wild surge of anger flood through her body.

How dare he treat her like that? How dare he throw her on the ground and arouse passions she thought she had buried, then tell her as calmly as you please that he had the right to kill her if he wanted to?

She didn't have to put up with that! He was strong enough to kill her if he chose, but he was not strong enough to arouse her passions or her love again. No! Let him do what he would, he would never receive another word or gesture of love from her again. Not even enough to plead her innocence or beg for her life.

"It seems you're a slave to all your passions," she said tartly.

A momentary flash of hot rage seared through his eyes, then died quickly as he regained his control and turned away from her.

A bitter smile crossed her lips. She had meant the taunt to hurt. Obviously, it had.

He was careful to put her behind him on the horse this time, even though it meant they would have to walk slowly down the road so she wouldn't slide off. He wasn't going to take any chances on making a fool of himself again.

28

JASON WAS CAREFUL TO WALK HIS HORSE SLOWLY DOWN THE road, guiding him gingerly around the multitude of ruts and potholes that impeded their progress, but to Kate, even that cautious journey seemed as frightening and treacherous as her wild gallop across darkened plains the first night she had tried to escape from Jason—the night she had finally become his wife in all but name. It was hard to tell what terrified her most—the ultimate fear of what would happen to her when they reached their destination, or simply the desperate agony of the moment as she tried frantically to cling to Midnight's strong, smooth back, which suddenly seemed to her as slippery as if it had been slicked down with oil.

It was all she could do to keep her tenuous seat on the horse. Despite her pride and her anger, she was forced to clutch at Jason's back from time to time, catching a handful of rawhide jacket to keep from sliding off. She would not allow herself to throw her arms around him, even to secure her position. She would rather fall painfully to the ground, rather even be trampled beneath the black stallion's sharp hooves, than give him the satisfaction of knowing she needed him.

Jason was conscious of Kate's hands as she clutched awkwardly at him, fighting for space with the bulky blanket roll tied behind his saddle, but he tried to block it from his mind. Damn the bitch, it served her right anyhow! He was not going to put her in the front again, no matter what happened. He was not going to fall prey to her sensuous beauty even one more time.

Without warning, she suddenly threw her arms around him, clinging to him with a desperate urgency that caught him completely by surprise. He had been sure she was too angry—and too stubborn—to press her body close to his, no matter what the reason. As he felt the violent trembling of her limbs, he suddenly realized she was frightened, badly frightened. Automatically, he began to scan the surrounding countryside, curious to see what had caused such a violent, abrupt reaction.

At first he saw nothing that could possibly account for her strange behavior. There were people ahead of them, a mile or so down the road, but they were only Indians—a small, peaceful group of thirty or forty Dakotas, headed no doubt for the sun dance that was to be held a few days' march north of Cheyenne. That couldn't be what had terrified her. Kate had seen Indians before, at closer hand than this. She couldn't be afraid of them any longer.

And then suddenly he remembered. Kate *had* seen Indians at closer hand, seen them in a terrifying and evil light. She must have been in that small house when it was attacked and overrun. Perhaps she had even seen her friends slaughtered before her very eyes. Impulsively he turned in the saddle, swinging around to look at her. As he caught sight of the ashen pallor of her cheeks, he felt an overpowering urge to sweep her into his arms, whispering soft words of comfort to her. It took all his strength of will to resist.

"There's nothing to be afraid of," he told her gruffly. "They're peaceful." He meant the words to be comforting, but his voice was laden with anger and self-disgust at the tenderness that surged through his breast whenever he looked at her. He felt her trembling begin to increase, and he cursed himself silently, knowing he had frightened her even more.

"Goddammit," he shouted out, as impatient with himself as he was with her. "This is something you have to face."

Angrily, he touched his spurs to Midnight's side. The startled horse bolted forward, rapidly closing the space between them and the Indians ahead. Jason could hear Kate's gasp of surprise and terror.

What the hell was he doing, anyhow? he asked himself, startled at his own impetuosity. This woman was his unfaithful wife, and he had planned for her the same fate doled out by strong men to faithless women since the beginning of time. Why, then, should he try to make her face her fears? Why teach her about life, only to prepare her for death?

But it was too late for questions, or for qualms, for the small group ahead had already spotted them and turned to watch their approach with eyes glistening with curiosity. Jason recognized their leader immediately, Plenty Horses, one of the minor Dakota chiefs, who was riding proudly at the head of his people. There was nothing warlike, or even cautious, in their manner as they watched the strangers gallop toward them, and Kate felt her trembling ease, although she was still afraid.

She held her breath as she peeked out from behind Jason's broad shoulder, trying to convince herself that these friendly savages intended no harm to her. She thought she had just managed to still the anxiety that quickened the beating of her heart when one of the squaws, bolder and livelier than the rest, approached and extended a curious hand to touch the fabric of her skirt. Kate could not keep from recoiling in horror. She was sorry the instant she did it, for the woman pulled back abruptly, her face a mask of embarrassment and shame.

One of the older women hurried over to the young squaw, grasping her by the shoulder and shaking her with a force that matched the torrent of scolding words that poured from her lips. For a moment the entire group of laughing, chattering women fell silent; then, with a timid awe, their faces turned slowly toward Kate. Although she could not understand the words they whispered to each other, Kate sensed that their eyes were filled with sadness. They nodded gravely, as if they understood her fear, as if they even knew what torments she had been through. She wondered if they had heard the story of what happened to Hamilton's woman, or was it just that her experience was so common in these troubled times that the women could guess with accuracy the cause of her fear?

At that moment, an elderly man inched his way on horseback through the crowd, and Kate guessed from the way the others deferred to him that he must be their chief. These Indians, she quickly realized, were more prosperous than Gray Cloud's tribe had been, for many of the men were mounted on horses, and their burdens were borne, not on their women's backs, but on travois that trailed behind the horses.

The old man raised his hand in solemn greeting. *"How kola."* His voice was grave, but a warm smile deepened the creases in his dark skin, and Kate sensed he was greeting Jason as a friend.

"How kola," Jason responded in the same serious tone. Dismounting quickly, he lifted Kate to the ground with surprising gentleness before turning to address the old man in a long discourse in his own tongue. Kate watched as the man nodded solemnly from time to time, breaking out in an occasional broad grin. He waited patiently until Jason had finished, then responded with an even longer speech, punctuated every few seconds with a lively gesture.

When the man had finished speaking, Kate was surprised to see Jason turn back toward her. "He says they are going to the sun dance. Do you know what that is?"

Kate could only shake her head. She had heard the words mentioned from time to time, but she had so little curiosity about the ways of the savages that she never stopped to wonder what they meant.

"I guess you could call it a sort of coming-of-age ceremony for the young braves," Jason explained. "But it's really much more than that. It epitomizes Indian feelings and beliefs—their religion, if you will." He fell silent for a moment, studying her face with care. "It's something everyone should see."

Kate caught her breath sharply, listening to the harsh sound of air passing through her own lips as she heard his words. Surely he couldn't mean what she was thinking. He couldn't be suggesting that they travel with these savages—savages of the same tribe that had attacked her and murdered her friends.

"This will be one of the last sun dances," Jason went on. "The government will outlaw them soon."

Kate gaped at him in surprise, wondering if he even realized what he had said. What difference could it possibly make to her whether this was the last dance or not? Hadn't he already warned her she wouldn't live long enough to see another ceremony anyhow? She held her breath as she waited tensely for his decision, not even knowing what she wanted to hear him say. She was terrified of the Indians, and God only knew she didn't want to travel with them, but she was even more terrified of going home with Jason.

"We're going," he said suddenly, swinging back into the saddle. Kate noticed that he let her ride in front again, but she didn't dare say anything about it, not even to thank him. She sensed he would consider even that small act of consideration a weakness.

She and Jason rode in front of the long procession, next to the chief. It was a long time before she felt comfortable enough to turn around and stare at the others with curiosity. When she did, she noticed to her surprise that, while many of the men were on horseback, the women were all expected to walk obediently behind them. She felt her cheeks redden with embarrassment, sensing that the laughing taunts hurled at Jason by the other men were because he had chosen to share his horse with his woman. She was relieved to see that Jason bandied back their teasing with equally good-natured jests. Thank heaven for the Southern chivalry that would not allow him to force her to walk, even angry as he was with her.

The sun had already begun to set behind the distant purple hills when they finally broke their march for the evening rest. Kate was amazed to see that the Indian women, even though they had trekked for miles down the long, tiring road, were the ones to begin pitching the tents, while the men sat around on the ground chatting and joking with each other.

When Jason caught sight of her bewildered look, he began to laugh aloud at her.

"Let's see how good an Indian wife you'd make," he challenged sharply. Pulling a small hatchet out of his saddle roll, he began to stride purposefully toward a nearby grove of trees.

Kate stared after him in bewilderment for a moment, then turned back to the women, intrigued by the bustling activity she saw before her. Each of the squaws had taken three long poles from one side of the travois and laid them carefully on the ground, lashing them together with stout leather thongs.

When she had finished, the squaw would take several smaller poles, tying them onto the others, then set the entire creation upright to form the crude skeleton of a cone. One by one, each of these rough frameworks the women had erected so quickly and efficiently was covered with buffalo hides, gaily painted with bright and primitive designs.

Kate was so deeply engrossed in the women's handiwork that she didn't even notice Jason's approach. She became aware of his presence only when she heard a loud sound beside her. Whirling around, she saw that he had dropped a pile of rough wooden poles at her feet.

"What on earth do you expect me to do with those?" she asked, startled.

"I expect you to be a good wife—for a change!"

There was a hardness in his voice, a barely controlled anger, that warned her not to disobey. Glancing down helplessly at the pile of wood on the ground, she bit her lips to keep from asking him for help. Whatever else he might do to her, she was never going to let him make her beg. Mutely she stared at the poles, wishing she had the vaguest notion what to do with them.

Her dilemma was solved far more easily than she had feared, for the other women, finished now with their own tasks, quickly began to flock around her. With laughter and patience, they showed her how to lash the poles together and set them erect. It seemed no time at all before she had her own framework standing stoutly on the hard prairie earth.

As she worked alongside the Indian squaws, Kate slowly became aware of one young woman who always seemed particularly helpful. Glancing over at her, Kate was aware of a shy smile shining on the woman's warm brown face. She looked especially familiar, but for a long time Kate could not figure out why. Then suddenly she remembered. This was the same young woman who had tried to touch the fabric of her dress and been rebuffed with such rudeness! What a wonderful capacity for warmth and generosity she must have to be able to forgive so easily, and even help to build Kate's tepee. With a quick burst of affection, Kate turned to flash her a warm answering smile.

Jason was standing some distance away, talking and joking freely with the men, but his eyes had never left Kate for a moment, and he was aware instantly of the bright smile that lit up her face. He was stunned to see how beautiful she looked. He had almost forgotten how much her smile delighted him.

He was filled with self-disgust as he felt a familiar, unwelcome yearning flood through his body, working its same inexorable magic on him again. What kind of witch was she, to enchant him so thoroughly, even at the moment he despised her the most?

Angrily he turned and strode toward his horse, trying to ignore the burning ache that was beginning to grow in his loin. Pulling the blankets from his saddle roll, he hurried over to her, throwing them at her feet. His face was a mirror of scorn and contempt.

Kate could not understand what he wanted, but the other women were quick to catch his meaning. Grabbing up the blankets, they showed her how to attach them to the frame she had already made, and within minutes her tepee was complete. All that was needed was the loan of a few buffalo robes to spread across the floor. The interior had no cot for Jason to sleep on, but that was hardly necessary. The buffalo robes would be soft and warm.

Kate stood back for a second, gazing at her handiwork with a kind of awe. It was not perfect, she knew. It was not as sturdy as the other tents, nor as decorative, but it was serviceable, and it was the first thing she had ever built with her own hands. Pushing aside the limp flap the blanket had created in the doorway, she stepped inside, surprised at the sense of satisfaction that engulfed her. It was not until she saw a dark shadow fall across the floor that she realized Jason had followed her inside and was standing on the threshold.

Timidly she turned, not knowing what to expect from him. When she saw his face, a thrill of cold despair ran through her body.

"Very good," he told her. There was a grudging approval in his voice, but it was so muffled by his sarcasm that she did not even recognize it. "Now, let's see if you're *really* a good Indian wife." Unbuckling his gun belt, he tossed it carelessly on the floor and began to unfasten his pants.

"My God, Jason, no!" She could hardly believe he was doing this to her. How could she bear the shame again?

"An Indian wife's only pleasure is serving her husband," he told her crudely. "It's your duty to bear my burdens on the trail, erect my tepee, and prepare my meals . . . and open your legs to receive me whenever I want to satisfy my lust."

Kate felt a sick sense of disgust flood through her body at his words, but she fought it back desperately. She was determined not to give him the satisfaction of knowing how deeply he had hurt her. "As you wish," she replied coolly. "I assure you I know how to do my *duty*." She was amazed at how steady and calm her fingers were as she unfastened her dress and slipped it from her body. "You're strong enough to force me anyhow if you want. You can force me to do anything . . . except want you."

"Why, you little fool!" he cried out, reaching toward her and pulling her naked flesh against his. "Don't you know yet you have no control over what you want? Your body was made for lust, and all your other senses are a slave to that."

She wanted to cry out that he was wrong, that no man but he had the power to set her blood on fire with a mad frenzy that sometimes seemed as if it would tear her apart, but she bit her lip to keep from speaking the thoughts aloud. She knew he would not believe her. As she felt his hands pressing into the softness of her flesh, she knew her body would soon betray her again, responding to him with an abandon that seemed to lend truth to his cruel words. Even as she felt her body begin to move hungrily in unison with his, she knew there was no way she could ever keep him from enslaving her again with the force of his passion and her own.

Soon the ecstasy that enveloped her, flowing even to the tips of her toes, erased all thoughts of anger and even shame. All she could feel was the joy that surged through her body as it mingled in perfect harmony with his. Even the cries of pleasure she had tried so desperately to hold back issued freely from lips that pressed blissfully against his, until at last all thoughts of resistance were forgotten. Finally, when the moment of climax came, all she wanted was to press her body tighter against his to make the moment last just a little longer. All she could remember was that this was her beloved husband, returned at last to her.

It was Jason who broke the moment of tenderness. Pulling himself abruptly away from her, he rose and began to dress hastily, fastening the gun belt once again around his waist. Only when he had stepped over to the doorway, raising the flap to move outside, did he turn to look at her. When at last he spoke, his voice was harsh and icy.

"Just because I want you, don't make the mistake of thinking I love you."

Kate felt her body shiver in the draft of cold air that swept through the doorway as she watched Jason step outside and disappear into the deepening dusk.

Twilight had darkened into early evening before Kate could finally force herself to brush away the bitter tears that had begun to dry on her cheeks and pull the coarse fabric of her dress back over a body that was bruised and aching from the angry brutality of Jason's passion. She knew she had to go outside again, had to force herself to join in the activities of the camp, but it was all she could do to make her reluctant hands lift up the flap of the makeshift tent so she could step across the threshold. Everything inside her called out to remain in the darkness of the tent, hidden inside its shelter as if it were a warm cocoon, but she knew she had to step over to the campfire and help the other women with the cooking. Jason would be furious with her if she didn't. He had already made it clear that she was only one of the squaws. God help her if she didn't keep up her end of that sorry bargain.

Kate had expected even the cheerful, friendly squaws to be more than a little irritated with her when they found out how hopelessly awkward she was around the campfire, but to her amazement, they were the soul of merry patience as they taught her how to help them prepare the dinner, explaining what they were doing in sign language and even helping her to learn a few simple words of Dakota. No matter how clumsy she was, or how much extra work her lack of skill made for them, they never seemed to grow cross, and not once did they think to scold her for her ineptitude. Instead, each new mistake she made would send them into rollicking fits of laughter, a bright, happy laughter that was so contagious they soon had Kate forgetting her problems and joining in the hilarity.

By the time she sat down in the women's circle to partake of the fruits of her own labor, Kate was amazed to find that she was almost in a cheerful mood. It was just as well she was, she quickly discovered, for dinner itself was a sorry affair. Even later, when she had grown accustomed to Indian food, it as was hard enough to stomach, but that first time, when she was not yet used to it, she was afraid she would retch at the smell and taste of it. The watery soup had only a few tiny chunks of dubious meat floating in it—Kate did not dare ask what it was—and the soggy wheat cakes were vile with rancid bacon grease. Still, she forced herself to choke it down. Portions were meager enough as they were, and she sensed she could not count on getting as much—or even as good—the next day. She wondered how the Indians managed to survive on such a scanty and unwholesome diet.

After dinner, the men began to gather in a large circle, the women in a smaller one, and Kate realized to her surprise that some sort of festivities were about to begin. She soon learned it was their custom. No matter how far they had walked or how tired they were, the Indians never allowed themselves to be deprived of the dancing and entertainment that were so vital a part of their spirit. Glancing toward the men's circle Kate quickly saw that Jason, too, had mellowed, obviously enjoying the Indians' merry company as much as she did, and she dared to creep away from the women's circle so she could join him in the darkness, asking him in soft whispers what was going on.

Far from being annoyed by her boldness, Jason seemed to welcome her presence. "When the Indians are at home," he explained patiently "the *wachkeepe tonka* is held in a rough wooden hut, with mud chinking the holes between the logs. Here, where there are no huts, they have to hold the dances outside."

It hardly seemed to Kate that the rude huts were any loss. What a shame it would have been to hold the dance inside a dim, smoky room instead of here in the crisp, cool air, with stars twinkling in the dark sky overhead. What better place than this to be in perfect communion with nature?

Kate felt a strange thrill of anticipation run up her spine when she heard the men begin to beat their tom-toms softly, commencing the eerily unmelodic rhythm of their music, as they chanted odd songs that seemed to have no tune at all. At first, their music sounded alien and unpleasant to Kate's ears, but as the time passed, it grew to have a familiarity that was both haunting and compelling, until soon it almost seemed a part of her, its rhythm vibrating into her bones with every beat of the drums.

The drums began slowly at first, softly and gently, but soon their beat began to grow with an ever-increasing frenzy. Dancers threw off their robes and blankets, prancing into the center of the circle of watchers, their eerie shadows, cast against the firelight, giving them the semblance of ghosts as they hopped with strange, only half-graceful steps around the ring.

They really were a magnificent sight, she thought, clad only in breechclouts their bodies coated with gaudy streaks of paint as they pranced around the ring, moving with a dynamic arrogance that was thrilling to watch. Their bodies were thin and angular now, with every rib outlined sharply against their dark skin, but as Kate watched them she imagined how the dancers must have looked in the old days—in the days when there was enough food and each young brave's body would have been a mass of rippling muscles standing out boldly against the strong flesh and gleaming skin. How exciting it must have been then for the young Indian maidens who peered in from the edge of the circle with no pretense at modesty.

As each dance ended, the men resumed their seats around the edges of the circle, only to be replaced by others when the music started up again. Occasionally, one man would leap out alone, pacing back and forth between the flickering firelight and the shadows, chanting strange words Kate could not understand. Sometimes the listening men leaned forward, their faces rapt and attentive; at other times, they burst out suddenly in loud and raucous laughter.

"What on earth is he doing?" Kate asked, intrigued and puzzled at the same time.

"Counting the *coups*," Jason explained. Then, seeing the bewildered look on her face, he continued. "His *coups*. His brave deeds in battle. They must be awarded to him by the council before he can recount them all at the *wachkeepee tonka*."

Fascinated, Kate watched the man's impassioned face as he called out Indian phrases, some of them over and over again. One of them he seemed to relish, for the words were long and drawn out, like a haunting wail.

"What's he saying?"

" 'Great deeds are the children of my heart,' " Jason translated softly. Kate noticed a gentle smile on his lips. "You see that stick he's carrying in his hands? That's his *coup* stick. Each notch in the stick signifies a brave deed—a *coup*. These deeds are important to the Indians. They never tire of talking about them. Sometimes, if you get a real braggart, he'll go on for hours." Jason laughed softly, but there was no trace of mockery in his voice.

"I'm surprised you don't recount your own brave deeds," Kate said boldly, encouraged by his laughter to dare tease him a little. "You're almost as much of an Indian as they are. At least, they seem to accept you as one."

As he turned to look at her, his eyes filled with icy scorn, she realized too late she had made a mistake.

"What, would you have me count my *coups*?" he asked coldly. His voice was filled with self-scorn, although she was too frightened by his sudden anger to recognize it as such. "I assure you I have done no great deeds in battle that make my heart swell with pride."

"But you have been in battle," she responded contritely. "I just thought you must have some deeds to tell."

It seemed to her that the dark fury of his eyes was boring through her body. "I have done no deeds in battle I am proud of."

Abruptly he turned away from her, staring with fixed attention at the circle of dancers Kate stole a glance at his angry profile silhouetted against the flickering golden firelight, then turned to slink away, her eyes filled with tears she was too proud to shed. Quietly she crept back through the shadowy camp, until she found her own tent again and hurried inside, eager to wrap herself in the warm buffalo pelts and give way to her tears.

She was certain Jason had not even noticed her when she crept away from him, but she could not have been alone more than three or four minutes when he appeared in the doorway. She could not see his features in the faint moonlight, but it seemed to her his shadow loomed up dark and raging against the silent midnight sky. He did not speak for a long moment When he did, his voice was harsh and angry.

"Why is it, the more of a bitch you are, the more I want you?"

"Oh, my God, no!" Her voice was hoarse and tense as she realized what he intended Surely, angry as he was, he did not intend to force himself on her again. "I can't bear it."

"You'll bear what I tell you to," Jason shouted angrily. Kate knew she could expect no mercy from him—no more than she could from her own traitorous body. Even as she felt his weight crushing down on her, she knew her arms would reach out automatically to enfold him, paying no heed to the troubled brain that sought desperately to reject him.

"You're an animal!" she hissed in a last hopeless attempt to stave off the humiliation she knew must come soon.

"So are you, my beauty! I may be as randy as a dog, but remember, a dog always knows how to find a bitch in heat." He paused grabbing a handful of hair and pulling her head back so tensely that hot, sharp tears burned the inside of her eyelids "And you are a bitch!"

With one last indignant cry of protest, Kate tried to pull away from him, but as she felt his lips close hungrily on hers, she knew it was too late. She knew, even before it happened, that her body was going to rise eagerly to meet his.

Afterward, as she felt his body fall away from hers, the sweat that dripped from his skin mingling with her own, she gave one last desperate gasp of anguish.

"I hate you!"

He pulled himself up on his elbow, looking at her coolly in

the dim light that filtered through the blankets covering the tent.

"At last I seem to have made an honest woman of you." Pulling himself away from her, he pushed his body to the far side of the tent, as if he could not bear to be near enough to touch her, even accidentally, in his sleep.

Kate lay awake, deep into the late hours of the night, her eyes dry but stinging with regret and humiliation. This was what it would be like, she knew, every night that she spent with Jason. Each time he reached out for her, with no tenderness or softness in his touch, her body would turn traitor once again, offering itself willingly, even eagerly, to his caresses, and then she would turn into the animal he had accused her of being, hungry for the demanding thrusts of a man who would not even pretend to love her.

29

As the days passed, Jason and Kate continued to wend their way through the wide plains and gently sloping hills, following the Indians toward their mysterious sun dance. With the passage of time, Kate had hoped to learn enough endurance to make the agony of her relationship with Jason less intense, but instead she found that each day it was growing more and more unbearable. As evening approached and it was time to set up camp, her cheeks would begin to glow with the hot pink of anticipated humiliation, and she would wait with dread for the moment her tasks were finished and Jason would draw her into the newly erected tepee to claim his rights as her husband.

Each long night, she would lie awake, muscles taut and thighs moist with anticipation, waiting for the moment he would wake and reach out for her, demanding the response her body was only too ready to give. Some nights, she tried to lie beneath his weight passively, hoping he would spend himself before her passion was aroused; other nights she kicked and struggled frantically, praying to hold him off until he grew bored with her games and left her alone. But in the end, it mattered little, for each night her body betrayed her, accepting his unloving embraces with all the passion buried deep within her. Each night, her degradation was complete, for it was a degradation she created herself with the power of the desire she could not control.

And yet, even with all the humiliation she suffered at the hands of her own husband life among the Indians was far from an unmitigated misery. There were far too many new and interesting things for her to see and do to spend her time wallowing in self-pity. The nearer they came to the area where the sun dance was to be held, the more the excitement seemed to grow, and despite her basic unhappiness, Kate was surprised to realize that she was actually looking forward to seeing the festivities she had heard so much about during the long trek.

At last they reached the site of the long-anticipated dance, a vast windswept plain ringed on two sides by majestic snow-capped mountain peaks. As they pitched their tepees for the last time in many days, Kate gazed around in excitement and wonder. Everywhere, as far as the eye could see, there was nothing but an enormous sea of gaily painted buffalo skins rising to sharp peaks against the clear blueness of the sky. Each morning, as she rose and stepped outside, she saw that even more tents had been added, as if the entire Dakota nation, ignoring all the hardship and poverty they endured, had decided to come together, one last time at least, in brotherhood and festive jubilation.

The first days of the ceremony were busy ones, for in addition to cooking and other daily chores, the women had to construct the huge enclosure that would house the dance.

It took days to erect the three high walls that partially surrounded a large area measuring perhaps one hundred and fifty feet across. First, large branches with the leaves still intact, were woven together to form rough skeletons of the walls; then when they were complete the gaps in the framework were filled in with whatever materials they could find—smaller branches and brush even tall grasses and hay—until finally a rustic wall rose nearly ten feet in the air. At last, the tall structure was ready to be completed.

As Kate watched, the Indians began to crowd into the enclosure, and she felt the sense of anticipation and excitement suddenly mount to an even higher pitch. In amazement, she stared at the ceremony, both puzzled and delighted by all the elegance and power the Indians seemed to have been able to put into their rite. Surely even the knights of medieval England, with all their pomp and solemn pageantry, could have offered nothing grander.

The ceremony began with the sound of many tom-toms, loud and hauntingly rhythmic as they beat out their atonal melody. Slowly the Indian warriors began to ride out into the open field. Mounted on horses, their nearly naked bodies decked out in war paint, they formed a perfect straight line a few hundred yards from the open side of the enclosure. There were so many of them, Kate was sure every young Dakota brave must have been there that day. The warriors held to their line, seated silent and erect on their mounts for a long time. Then suddenly, without warning, the beating of the drums stopped. For an instant there was nothing but a long line of men silhouetted in absolute silence against the bright sky. To Kate, watching quietly from the sidelines, it seemed the eeriest and most impressive sight she had ever seen.

Then, as if in response to a signal Kate could neither see nor sense, the drums began again, and the warriors all started in unison to gallop toward the enclosure. Each man paused only briefly as he swooped down to catch up a branch from the massive pile that lay on the ground, then continued his wild ride forward, waving the branch exultantly in the air and whooping with wild abandon. Kate could feel the earth vibrating under the heavy beat of hundreds of hooves.

The instant the warriors reached the unfinished enclosure, they pulled their horses to an abrupt stop, holding their seats gracefully as their mounts reared high into the air. No sooner had the front hooves of the first brave's horse touched the earth again than he trotted forward, moving toward the space where the final wall of the enclosure was yet to be constructed. Dashing his bough to the ground, he moved aside quickly, making room for the next brave in line. One by one, each of the young men added his branch to the pile, until soon the rough skeleton of the fourth wall stood in place.

No sooner had the warriors finished setting the branches in place than the squaws rushed forward, filling in the spaces with grasses and brush, just as they had done with the other walls. When they were finished, only a small opening remained in the center of the last wall.

The first days of the ceremony were, if sometimes primitive, at least colorful and exciting, and Kate found herself enjoying the novel experience. Only as the strange rites neared their end did she begin to sense a subtle difference, and for the first time, although she couldn't put her finger on the reason, she began to feel the first hints of trepidation. At first, it as only an intangible thing, just an odd indefinable awareness of a mounting excitement of a very different kind. Only on the morning of the fourth day did her fears begin to take form.

On that morning, Kate watched as the young boys of the Dakota tribes were led into the enclosure. There was something about them that was far different from the festive jubilation of the preceding days. To Kate, it seemed they emitted an air of solemnity and nervousness that existed side by side with a kind of cocky bravado. For the first time, she remembered that the sun dance was actually a coming-of-age ceremony for the young men.

"They won't be hurt. will they?" she asked nervously. It seemed cruelly unfair that these young boys should have to face a sudden test of manhood with such forced boldness.

Jason scowled at her impatiently. "No one is forcing any of them to do this," he said coldly "They do it by choice. This is how they prove their courage. After the ceremony, they will be entitled to call themselves braves and take part in the councils Any young man who fails to prove his courage here will be known forever as a *jontay sutah wanitch*—weak-hearted one—and he will be scorned by men and women both for the rest of his life."

And no one forces them to do it! Kate thought indignantly, but she did not dare risk Jason's wrath by uttering the words aloud. Angrily she turned back to look at the young men again.

And yet, she had to admit it didn't really look that strenuous, after all. The boys had fasted for over twenty-four hours, taking no nourishment save tea, but they were all young and healthy, and they did not seem to suffer too much. As they entered the enclosure, Kate saw the medicine men hand them whitened bone whistles Almost in unison, they turned their heads upward to face the sun and began a slow, strange dance composed of nothing more than a series of small hops, to the shrill accompaniment of their own whistles.

Throughout the dance, the young braves-to-be barely moved from their places, as if each was rooted to the spot where he stood Careful to keep their toes on the ground, they lifted only their heels, and those no more than three or four inches Kate was puzzled by the lethargy of their movements, until she realized that the dance was to go on continuously without rest from morning until sundown. They had obviously learned how to conserve their strength.

After a while, the monotony of the dance grew tiring, and

Kate began to glance around, curious to see the reaction of the other Indians. To her surprise, they were barely watching the youths in the center of the ring. Instead, their attention was focused on the activities that were taking place in the audience.

A number of grubby-looking men—Jason had told her they were called "medicine men," but they looked more like the sideshow attractions at a cheap carnival to her—were making their way through the crowd, shaking long, filthy sticks with chicken claws attached to the end of them. Kate wasn't surprised to see that they were every bit as busy as hucksters at the carnivals, but she was amazed to see what they were doing. They seemed to have built up a booming business in ear-piercing.

Babies were carried to them by eager mothers to have their tiny earlobes pierced, either with a long, thin knife or a red-hot needle. Kate could not help noticing that these sleazy-looking men were paid handsomely for their services. No beads or calico for them. Instead, they took their pay in the form of blankets and heavy furs the poverty-stricken Indians needed so desperately themselves, or in some instances, even horses or ponies.

The squaws, too, seemed to have their own strange ceremony with the medicine men, but Kate could not tell what it was until she drew closer to one of them. When she realized what was happening, she heard herself gasp in shock.

The medicine men were cutting chunks of flesh from the upper arms of the Indian women!

Kate noticed that not one of the women so much as flinched when the stinging blade dug deeply into her flesh, although the sharp cut must have been terribly painful. She watched in amazement as the tiny pieces of severed flesh were wrapped in strips of filthy muslin, then buried with elaborate ceremony in the ground.

"That's barbaric!" she protested to Jason.

He glanced at her with an angry scowl, and it seemed to her there was a thinly veiled warning in his eyes. Realizing he was afraid she would do something to embarrass or disgrace him, Kate felt herself begin to bristle with indignation.

"I assure you I am perfectly capable of conducting myself properly," she told him coolly. And she would, too, she promised herself. She might have made a fool of herself, throwing her love—and her body—at a man who cared nothing for her, but she was determined to prove to him that she still knew how to conduct herself with strength and dignity.

And yet, as she quickly learned, that promise she had made to herself was going to prove far more difficult to keep than she had ever guessed. Even as sunrise brought the opening of the final day of the rites, Kate sensed from the heightened sense of anticipation that surrounded her that strange things would soon come to pass, things she had never even dreamed of, or dared herself to face.

At first, despite her trepidations, she found it little more unpleasant than the preceding day. In frightened fascination she watched as the medicine men brought in long poles with lines attached to their ends, like overgrown fishing poles. Walking slowly around the ring, they dangled the long lines temptingly in front of the young men's eyes. Whirling around dizzily, their eyes blinded by the sun, the dancers were forced to make wild attempts to snatch at the elusive ropes, which the medicine men skillfully kept just inches beyond their reach. For the first few minutes, it all seemed deceptively simple and innocent, and even mildly amusing. Only after she had watched the youths stagger and fall to the ground time after time did Kate realize the dance was in reality a cruel torture.

"This is only preparation," Jason warned her. She caught a surprising hint of compassion in his voice, as if he was sorry he had brought her there.

"What do you mean?"

"See how dizzy they get," he told her. "So dizzy they fall to the earth again and again. The exhaustion makes them less sensitive to pain."

Kate held her tongue. She didn't want to ask any more questions. Suddenly, she didn't want to know any more about the mysterious rite she was about to witness. Filled with a vague sense of impending horror, she watched the medicine men help the youths to their feet, then lead them into pens set up at the opposite sides of the enclosure. The pens were formed around four sturdy poles at the corners, each about six feet high. As Kate watched, wide-eyed with horror and disgust, the boys were divided into two groups. The first group was shunted to the sidelines, as if to be held in reserve for later. Thongs were threaded through the backs and pectoral muscles of the boys in the second group, cutting painfully through their flesh. As if that were not torture enough, the thongs were then attached firmly to the posts, and the youths had to writhe and strain against the inflexible force, trying desperately to tear their own muscles apart to work themselves free.

Kate realized instantly what an agonizing choice the young men had to make. The harder they pulled, struggling to tear the thongs from the backs, the more excruciating their pain would be. Yet, if they were gentler, sparing themselves the most agonizing torture, the ordeal would only last longer.

"How can they do it?" she cried out, forgetting all her promises to behave properly. "How can people be so cruel?"

"Try to understand Kate," Jason said softly. There was a warm sympathy in his voice as he placed his arm reassuringly around her shoulders "This is what they believe in."

"They believe in torture? In suffering?"

"Of course not," he hastened to assure her. "This ceremony is a tribute to the sun It's a kind of religious rite. You see, to the Indians, everything in nature is *wakan*, holy—the sun and the moon. the stars and the earth. everything. But the sun, the giver of life, is the holiest of all. The sun is *wakan tanka*, the creator. Each year, this ceremony is held to worship the creator."

"Worship?" She was disgusted. "Is this what they call worship? This agony?"

"This is the only way they can worship, Kate. An Indian believes the only thing he truly owns is his own body. Therefore, it is the only thing he has to offer. It's the only way he can express his deepest feelings—worship or love or even grief. That's why many Indians cut their flesh at the death of a loved one, to show their bereavement."

Kate had to admit that Jason's words made sense—intellectually—but she still found it hard to accept the primitive ceremony. All she could feel was the disgust and anger that welled up in her when she listened to the cries of encouragement from the old women on the sidelines. *"Ohetekha, ohetekha, cosha metowah."* Be brave, my son, be brave. How easy it was to call out for bravery from the sidelines How easy—when they were not the ones who felt the cruel thongs cutting through their flesh.

The time passed slowly, each hour seeming as if it would never end as, one after another. the newly proven braves worked themselves free and fell into the dirt, lying passively on the ground to wait for the women to rush up to them, coating their bleeding bodies with a soothing white powder.

The sun was already high in the sky when Kate noticed a young warrior standing not far from her, staring at her with a passive solemnity The intensity of his gaze was so strong that it drew her eyes toward him. The instant she faced him, she felt a cold flood of fear rush through her body.

"You!" she whispered, feeling her legs go weak with trembling.

The brave moved toward her with a slow, easy gait. Not until he stood directly in front of her did he speak.

"So Hamilton's woman has come to the sacred place of the Indians."

Kate saw that Little Wolf's eyes, filled though they were with deliberate mockery, still held traces of surprise and even admiration, as if he recognized how much courage it had ⸺en for her to come there.

"I had not thought to see you again," she said with a coolness she did not know she possessed. After the initial shock of coming face to face with him, she found it amazingly easy to stare into the eyes of the man who had nearly taken her life.

"No doubt," he replied wryly, allowing his lips to curl up slightly at her words. "Tell me, Hamilton's woman, are you curious? Don't you wonder about me?" She could have sworn she saw little dancing lights of amusement in the back of his dark eyes. "Don't you wonder how I know your customs so well? How I speak your language without flaw?"

"I have wondered," she admitted. "But it is not for me to ask those things. They are for you to tell, but only if you want."

"Well said, Hamilton's woman," he told her with quiet approval. "But I do wish to tell you. Perhaps then you will be able to understand a little. You see, I am a product of your schools. I was one of the Indian children who was dressed in *wasichu* clothing and taught *wasichu* ways, so I could take my place in your world."

"Then why . . . ?" She broke off uncertainly, suddenly aware of the impertinence of her question.

"Why did I come back to my people?" he prompted gently.

She nodded silently.

"For just that reason—because they are *my* people. You can dress me up in the white man's clothes and teach me his language, but you cannot make me white, nor can you make the other *wasichus* accept me as their equal. No, my place is here, to live—or die—with my own kind."

"Then you will die," Kate said softly.

"So you see that?" His voice was soft and low. "But then, you have only to look around you. We still have the last remnants of our finery, but they are just that—sad, pathetic remnants. We still have our feasts, too, but now, instead of buffalo meat, rich in its own gravy, we have only thin, watery soup made from bony dogs."

Kate swallowed uncomfortably, remembering squeamishly the dubious meat she had eaten, but she said nothing.

"And so you see, we die." His voice was flat and unemotional.

Kate turned away quickly, unable to face the mute accusation she was sure she would see in his eyes. As she faced the ring once again, she was surprised to see that ropes or leather thongs had been hung from the tall pole in the center. As she watched, a group of boys—those that had not yet tried their courage—walked slowly out into the arena, forming a wide circle around the pole.

Kate turned toward Little Wolf, eager to ask him what they were doing, then caught herself abruptly. Snapping her mouth shut again, she turned back grimly toward the spectacle. There was no point asking a question when she already knew the answer.

Even before it happened, she knew what she would see. She knew that these young men were to be tested with the same primitive savagery as the others. Only, this time it was going to be even uglier, even more brutal.

As Kate stared at them in disgust, the medicine men threaded the cords through the chest muscles of each youth. Kate clenched her fists, digging her fingernails into her skin to keep from screaming aloud as she watched their bodies being slowly suspended in the air. There they were left to dangle and swing at the end of the thongs that pierced their flesh. Kicking and flailing their bodies grotesquely through the air, they attempted to free themselves from the cruel bonds while their blood flowed freely down their bodies, dripping onto the ground below.

"Does it disgust you?"

Kate was surprised to hear Little Wolf's voice in her ear. She had completely forgotten he was there.

"It's brutal," she told him angrily.

"Life is brutal."

"But you don't have to make it harder than it is."

"We make it no harder," he insisted "But neither can we make it easier. All we can do is prepare ourselves for the suffering that lies ahead."

"And this is how you prepare? By inflicting more pain?"

"These youths are still eager and young, still at the peak of their strength This is the time to give them the chance every young man needs—to test his courage and his endurance. In the old days, we used to say that a young man met at the sun dance the hardest pain he would ever have to endure. After that, nothing else would ever seem as difficult. Now, of course, that is no longer true."

"What do you mean?"

"Now the *wasichu* has devised for us agonies beyond any we could inflict on ourselves. Not only suffering of the body, but of the spirit as well. There is no way to prepare for pain like that."

Kate and the young Indian warrior stood for a moment in silence, each feeling the sudden sadness in a different way as they stared at each other. Then, without another word, Little Wolf whirled around and walked away, leaving her alone again. She could only stare after him in stunned surprise.

Could he really have meant what he said? That pain was the only way to prepare for even greater pain that lay ahead? And yet, how was that possible? How could any pain be great enough to justify the cruel torture the Indians had devised for themselves?

Looking around, Kate was surprised to see that the Indian women were still offering their arms to the filthy medicine men. Did they, too, think they were preparing themselves for future pain? The idea was so repulsive it seemed like an obscenity to her.

Suddenly she heard a loud cry rise from the crowd, and turning toward the arena, she saw that one of the dangling young braves had finally crashed to the earth. As the women rushed forward to rub their powder in his wounds, Kate was astonished to see him wave them back. Instantly the whole flock of medicine men hurried over to him.

For one horrified second Kate could not believe her eyes. Then she realized that it was true. With loud words and broad gestures, the youth was ordering the medicine men to tie the cords again through his back and raise him once more into the air. The crowd roared its approval as the same bleeding body was elevated a second time, to begin again the same brutal round of torture.

"*Ohetekha, ohetekha, cosha metowah.*" God, how bloodthirsty they sounded.

Kate felt her stomach churn as she watched the ugly ritual, and she knew she could stand it no longer. Making her way hurriedly outside, she took deep, eager gulps of the fresh air. Grateful for the cool afternoon shadows that lined the sides of the enclosure, she stood alone for a few minutes beside the high wall of greenery, listening to the sounds of drums and chanting that now seemed mercifully far away.

Suddenly, as she lingered by the wall, she was startled to hear the sound of a familiar voice breaking through the chaotic sounds issuing from the building behind her. Surprised and curious she hurried over to the corner of the enclosure and peered hastily around it.

There, not twenty feet away from her, deep in conversation with her husband, stood Marc. The attention of both men was fixed on the other, and neither saw Kate where she stood in the shadows.

Her first instinct was to rush toward her friend, her arms outstretched to welcome him but something about the tense set of Jason's back warned her not to try it. Instead, she moved deeper into the shadows holding her breath as she tried to pick up the words of their conversation through the noise of the tom-toms and the raucous sounds of the Indian festivities.

". . . always were a goddamn hotheaded fool," she heard. The voice was Marc's.

"I told you before, and I'll tell you again, keep out of this!" Kate thought she had never heard Jason's voice sound quite as menacing.

"Not after I followed you all this way . . . and it wasn't easy. You cover your tracks as well as an Indian."

"Goddammit Marc I'll deal with my wife in my own way, and when I finish with her . . ."

He left the sentence unfinished. For a moment, the only sound in the air was the heavy beating of the drums.

"When I finish with her," Jason finally continued, "I might very well come after you. You'd better get as far away from here as you can. I've already warned you I won't hesitate to kill you."

At the sound of his words, Kate felt herself begin to shiver violently It was all she could do to force her trembling legs to move back around the corner and hurry toward the entrance of the enclosure Suddenly she remembered that this was the last day of the sun dance, and she remembered what the last day of the dance meant for her.

This was the day they would all pack up and leave, the day Jason would take her back to the Triple Crown and force her to stand trial at a kangaroo court of his own making. Perhaps this was even the day he planned to hand down his judgment and enforce its execution.

She knew she had to get away from there, and quickly, but

she did not dare attempt it as long as Jason was standing just outside the walls. No matter what direction she headed, he would be sure to see her in that huge open field. Scurrying around the corner, she spotted the narrow entryway that led back inside the enclosure and slipped quietly through it. She would wait there until it was time for her to escape.

No sooner was she inside than she saw that she had positioned herself only a few feet away from one of the medicine men. She cringed as she saw his ugly face leering mockingly at her. Slowly he raised the long, dirty blade in his hand high into the air, shaking it menacingly at her. At first she stepped back in alarm; then, to her surprise, she saw that he was not threatening her, but rather daring her to take the same test of courage that the Indian women had borne so bravely. She saw by the mockery in his eyes that he was sure she would be too afraid.

Kate felt a slow wave of anger begin to rise in her. How dare he assume, just because she was a *wasichu*, that she had no courage? Did he think a white woman never had to bear torments as cruel as those that faced an Indian?

Suddenly she realized the truth. Little Wolf had been right, after all. There were far greater tortures than those the Indians practiced on each other. Who should know better than she? Wasn't she facing a nearly unbearable ordeal that very instant?

Soon she would have to slip outside again, searching for an escape that would offer her, not hope, but despair. Soon she would be caught in a cruel web of torment, torn between two agonies—fear of death at the hands of her own husband or despair at the aching loneliness that would flood through her body as long as she was separated from that same man.

Suddenly she found herself wondering if the Indian way was not the right way, after all. Perhaps when the Indian women offered their arms to the medicine men, they were proving they had found a universal truth that Kate had only begun to glimpse. Perhaps there was, in some small measure at least, a way to prepare for the pain and suffering that lay ahead. Impulsively she thrust out her arm.

She could see that the medicine man was startled, but after taunting her so openly, he could hardly refuse to perform his harsh arts on her. With reluctant fingers he reached out and pulled her arm toward him, his face mirroring repugnance, as if mere contact with white flesh was distasteful to him. The Indian women gathered around eagerly, anxious to see how well the *wasichu* would stand up under the pain.

Kate set her jaws in a grim, tight line as she saw the blade of the knife advancing slowly toward her, but the actual moment of contact was far less painful than she had imagined She knew her eyes blinked when she felt the first sharp edge of pain but she did not flinch or cry out When she heard the murmuring sounds of approval around her, she knew she had acquitted herself with credit After that. she was content to sit with the same stoical expression she had seen on the faces of the Indian women as she watched the squaws coat her wound with the same white powder they used on the young braves who had endured far greater pain than she.

Kate let them wrap her severed flesh in fabric and bury it in the earth With that burial of a small part of herself, she knew—like the Indian women—that she had proved she could bear pain with pride and strength.

There would be other suffering, she knew—greater suffering, soon to come—but now that she had passed through pain once, she knew she could face it again without fear of faltering. From this point on. she knew that like the Indians, she could be confident of meeting the trials and tortures of life with the same courage and dignity she had shown that day.

Part V

Flight into Darkness

30

"A WOMAN ON A TRAIL DRIVE?" SANDY MACTAVISH'S PALE gray eyes narrowed in amazement as he stared at Kate. "Never!"

"Why not?" Kate knew her boldness was far from justified, but she was desperate With her money gone, and having only a train ticket she dared not use because Jason would be watching the depot, she had no choice Sandy and his trail drive to Stockton was the only way to get out of the area quickly and inconspicuously. "I can handle a horse like a man if I have to . . . and I'm a good cook, too."

At least the first statement was true, she reassured herself. As for the latter . . . well, after weeks on the trail with the Indians, she at least knew how to set up a campfire and prepare an adequate stew.

Sandy squinted his eyes even further, until they were nothing more than narrow slits in his deeply tanned, leathery face. He needed a cook, there was no two ways about that. He'd already been laid over three days since he had the misfortune to lose the last one. Damn that fool cook, he thought irritably. How the hell had he managed to find a cook stupid enough to think he could tangle with a rattlesnake?

A pox on these stupid cattle anyhow, he told himself peevishly. Sandy had always loved the Black Angus, with their long, lean faces, but that didn't make him blind to their weaknesses Not that the rancher in Stockton who had ordered them wouldn't get his money's worth The Angus were ideally suited to the rugged climate of northern California, and they could stand the cold and snow as well as any. If only they traveled better, they'd be pretty near perfect.

But they didn't travel well. Sandy reminded himself with a sigh, and that was the whole problem. As skittish as babies they were, apt to start up at any little thing They had to be watched every second of the time. He couldn't afford to give up one of his cowhands to tend to the cooking chores; but he couldn't afford to hang around any longer looking for a new cook, either. He was already late enough. The rancher in Stockton would be waiting for his new herd with something less than patience.

Sandy eyed Kate dubiously for a minute, trying to find a way to convince himself that somehow he could make the preposterous idea work. Then, realizing how ridiculous it was, he pushed the thought out of his mind.

"Nope," he said decisively. "We canna have a woman on the trail. Why, lass, a woman has nae got the stamina for a long drive, nor the courage."

Kate fought back the surge of anger that began to flood through her body. Did not have the stamina or the courage, indeed! Why, she had already been uprooted from her home, and cradled the barely cold body of her murdered lover in her arms. She had fled for her life from her own husband and endured brutal rape and savage Indian attack. How much more did she have to suffer to prove she had stamina and courage?

She could think of no adequate words to prove to this tough trail boss that she had already proven herself. Finally, deciding against words, she mutely rolled up the sleeve of her dress. If he knew anything at all about Indians, the open wound would be testimony enough that she had already proved her courage to a race that did not accept such proof easily.

Sandy realized instantly what she was trying to tell him. In his years on the prairie, he had learned a grudging respect for the savages who all too often wrought havoc with his trail drives.

"All right," he admitted reluctantly. "You're a tough one, I can see that, but that is nae enough. I canna have a woman in the middle o' a passel o' men. Why, lass, how would ye protect yourself?"

Kate could hear a subtle difference in Sandy's tone, a kind of momentary weakening, and she was quick to capitalize on it. "Give me a gun," she demanded brusquely.

"What?" Sandy was too startled to do more than stare at her.

Kate did not repeat the words, but merely stretched out her open hand. Doubtfully Sandy removed his gun from his holster and held it out to her. Grasping the cold metal firmly in her fingers, she tested the weight of it against her palm.

"Now, pick that up," she told him, pointing to an empty can in the heap of rubbish beside the cook wagon. She would prove her skill by playing the same game she had often played with her brothers. She had always been the best, she remembered—except for Eamon. If only she hadn't lost her skill. "Throw it in the air."

Sandy's face registered disbelief. He recognized the common gunfighter's trick, and he knew from experience that the showy game was far harder than it looked. Still, he said nothing as he obediently tossed the can high into the air.

Kate waited expectantly, her gun aimed carefully at the shiny missile, until she saw it reach its peak, hovering for a brief second in the air. Then, carefully, she squeezed the trigger. A sudden thrill of triumph shot through her body as she heard the sharp ping of metal against metal followed almost instantly by the little Scot's hoarse gasp of surprise. The bullet ricocheted off the can, spinning it dizzily through the air, even higher than before. Kate waited only a split second before aiming again and again she hit her mark. By the time the can crashed noisily to the earth she had hit it a total of five times. As she raised her gaze to look at Sandy again, she knew she would see capitulation in his eyes.

"Have ye a gun?" he asked cautiously.

Kate shook her head.

"Well, I'll give ye one." His voice was still reluctant, but he knew he had no choice. He had to have a cook. Besides, if the woman could defend herself, perhaps it wouldn't be so bad. "But ye canna wear those clothes, lass. Why, every time a man looks on ye in that dress, he'll be thinkin' ye're a bonnie woman. Ye'll wear loose-fittin' men's clothes, and that's that. And ye'll carry a knife as well as a gun."

Kate smiled in triumph at his words. She did not in the least object to wearing men's clothing. She had often worn her brothers' cast-off clothes as a child and found them far more practical for riding and romping than her own frilly skirts and petticoats. Besides she had been wearing the same dress for weeks now, and though she had washed it often in the cold streams that flowed down from the mountains, it had grown so bedraggled and grubby that she would be glad to trade it for something more sensible.

But when she saw the clothes Sandy had in mind for her, she was half-tempted to call the whole thing off. They were the shabbiest, filthiest things she had ever seen in her life. She could only gape at them in dismay.

"Put them on," Sandy ordered firmly. Something in his voice warned her not to disobey.

Kate stepped behind a cluster of low-lying shrubs and reluctantly removed her dress. Even though the cold breeze that swept over her body raised goose bumps on her bare skin, she found it hard to force herself to don the well-used garments. The shirt was foul and stiff with sweat as she slipped it on and tugged at the buttons, trying to pull the resisting fabric over the fullness of her breasts. The pants, if possible, were even more disgusting, and Kate clenched her teeth to keep from retching as she tugged the filthy, mud-coated denim over her naked flesh. At last she was ready, except for the dusty red handkerchief Sandy had given her to tie around her neck.

Still holding the bandanna in her hand, Kate stepped out from behind the shrubbery. To her dismay, Sandy ordered her to put it on immediately.

"But it's filthy. It stinks!"

"Ye can wash it out later if ye feel the need. A cowhand canna do without a bandanna. Ye'll learn why soon enough."

Even after he made her tuck her abundant auburn curls beneath a dusty, felt-brimmed hat, Sandy only stared at her glumly, shaking his head back and forth slowly in dissatisfaction. "S'pose ye'll have to do," he grumbled. "But even wi' all that, there's no makin' you look any less o' a woman. Well, I hope ye're as good wi' this as you are wi' the gun."

To Kate's dismay, he held out a long, savage-looking knife.

"Tuck that in your belt," he told her. "And dinna go any-place without it—*ever!* Nae even to get up in the middle o' the night to relieve yourself under a tree."

Kate reached out tentatively, taking hold of the sharp, cold blade with reluctant fingers. Even if she was threatened, she was sure she would never be strong enough to use it successfully against a man.

"I feel safer with a gun," she admitted.

Sandy's sharp eyes took in the situation instantly. "Then ye better learn to use it," he told her quietly. "There be times a gun'll do ye no good."

Slowly he leaned down, pulling up his trouser leg. From the inside of his high leather boot he took out a wicked-looking blade. To Kate, it looked like the twin of the one she held in her own hand.

"First ye must learn how to hold yourself," he explained patiently. "Not all timid and frightened, like ye're standin' now. That ain't no good at all."

Kate suddenly realized to her horror that he was planning to give her a lesson in the use of a knife. She found herself shuddering at the idea, but she did not dare refuse. Besides, she knew he was right. Someday, this very lesson she was so reluctant to learn might even save her life.

She stiffened her back and legs quickly, trying to hold herself the way she thought a fighter should stand. Gripping the knife firmly in her fingers she faced Sandy staunchly, trying to put on a bold show The stance felt good to her, and for a moment she imagined she looked as invincible and ferocious as the terrible warriors of old. To her annoyance, her efforts only drew laughter from Sandy.

"Not tense like that, lass Ye're only makin' it harder for yourself See, relax your muscles like this." Kate watched in fascination as he tossed the knife lightly back and forth between his hands. his shoulders flexing carefully in unison with the movement. "Bend your knees like this, and roll your weight up on the balls o' your feet. Ye have to be flexible enough to move in a split second " Sandy was a small man, perhaps an inch or so shorter than Kate, but his tough, wiry body and lithe, catlike movements warned her he was a force to be reckoned with.

Kate mimicked his movements as best she could. To her surprise she was rewarded with a quick glance of approval. It took only a few seconds for her to realize that Sandy was right. This stance was not as dramatic as the one she had chosen but it left her feeling free and supple. She knew she would be able to move much more rapidly.

"Before ye even begin lass there's one thing ye have to learn," he warned her solemnly. "There ain't no way a little mite like you is ever gonna win in a fair fight against a man. Ye have to learn to fight dirty . . . and fightin' dirty means to hit a man *here*." He lowered his hand to his groin to dispel any possibility of misunderstanding. "Hit him with your knee or your foot, but hit him hard and fast. And don't let him see it coming."

Kate looked at him in amazement, trying to decide whether he really meant what he said He did.

"Go ahead Try to kick me there," he urged.

Cautiously Kate obeyed raising her foot up and swinging it out tentatively toward him She didn't know which alarmed her the most—annoying him by missing her target or making him even angrier by hitting it.

She needn't have worried for Sandy sidestepped the blow easily. "Nae like a timid little bunny rabbit," he shouted. "Try it again, harder this time."

Kate felt her hot Irish temper rising as she heard his shouts grow louder and louder, his taunts more and more impatient.

Furiously she aimed her foot at his crotch, kicking with all the force she could muster.

To her amazement, he did not even try to duck her blow, but reached down quickly, catching her ankle in his hand and jerking it sharply upward until he sent her sprawling painfully in the mud.

Stunned and furious, she fought back the tears that rose to her eyes as she struggled slowly to her feet.

"Faster!" Sandy shouted harshly. "If ye take that long to get up, ye're in trouble, sure as anything. Anyone fool enough to get knocked down had better learn how to get up fast as lightnin'." Outrageously he bent down and clutched Kate's ankle again, flipping her once more to the ground.

"Damn you!" she shrieked. She couldn't keep the curse from bursting out, even though she knew it would do her no good. Sandy would never relent for her anger, nor even, she supposed, for her pleas. Desperately she tried to pull herself up quickly, but she knew even without being told that she had not been fast enough. If it were a real fight, she would have felt the cold touch of his blade against her flesh for sure.

Again he threw her to the ground, and again she tried to rise quickly, but just as before, Sandy was unsatisfied. With cruel relentlessness, he forced her to practice the same fall over and over again, teaching her the light, rolling movement that would enable her to pull herself up swiftly. Even when she had finally accomplished it well enough to earn a terse "Good girl!" from him, he would not let up.

Damn him, she thought furiously. Would he never relent? How much of this did he think her bruised and aching body could bear? Finally, when she knew she could stand it no longer, she began to rebel. Who the hell did he think he was, anyway? She'd show him!

All right, she reminded herself, he'd warned her she could never beat him in a fair fight, and he was right. But if he thought the only way to fight dirty was a good, swift kick in the groin, he didn't know much about devious feminine wiles. Glancing down quickly, she noted with satisfaction the slippery earth at his feet, still muddy from the early-spring rains.

Dropping her knife hand abruptly, as if she were too weary to hold it up any longer, Kate let the first choking sob press out of her throat. Her tears followed immediately on the sound. She did not have to force them. Her pain-racked body and humiliated spirit were only too ready to weep.

Through half-closed eyes, Kate saw Sandy lower his arm

slowly, a look of bewilderment spreading across his features. He had realized she was tired, but after all, she had begun to do so well. How could he have known she was so close to breaking? He began to feel guilty about working her so hard.

Kate saw his confusion, but said nothing. It was all she could do to keep from smiling.

Letting her shoulders droop in discouragement, she slumped forward, as if she felt a great weight pressing down on her. She let the sobs that had begun softly in her throat grow until it sounded as if she was on the edge of hysteria. That was too much, even for Sandy.

"I warned you it was rough, lass," he said awkwardly, his voice choked with embarrassed sympathy. Lowering his knife hand, he began to step toward her.

That was all Kate had been waiting for. Glancing down surreptitiously from beneath tear-coated lashes, she saw him place his foot on a particularly slippery patch of muddy ground. Quickly, before he could even notice the movement, she had lashed out with her foot, twisting it treacherously around his ankle. Almost instantly he was thrown off balance, landing in a clumsy heap at her feet.

Sandy was too surprised to recover as quickly as he should. When he finally curled his legs under himself and pushed his body upward as he had taught her to do, he found she was ready for him, her knife stretched out to meet his chest.

Kate had only meant to touch the blade against his body in proof of her advantage, just to show him what she could have done had she wanted to, but she was not skillful enough to master the subtle movement. Instead, to her horror, she saw that she had torn through the fabric of his shirt with the sharp point of her knife. Even as she stared back at him in shock, she saw a thin stream of blood begin to ooze out of the dark brown of his shirt.

Kate stepped back hesitantly, gaping at him in shock. The wound was only a scratch, but it was deep enough to be painful. Now, surely, he would be furious with her. If he had been harsh and unrelenting before, when he had merely been dispassionately teaching her, what would he be like now?

Instead, as she stared at him in fright, she saw a slow, broad grin begin to spread across his features. Slowly he raised his hand, wiping it across his wound, then glanced down in wonder and astonishment at his blood-drenched fingers.

"By God, ye drew blood!" There was the sound of awe in

his voice. " 'Tis years since any's drawn blood from Sandy MacTavish, and you only a wee lass at that!"

Without even glancing again at his wound, Sandy slipped the knife back into his boot. Wiping his bloody hand hastily on his pants, he held it out to her. Kate, too, tucked her knife away, noting the strange sensation of hard steel against her body, then placed her hand in his.

"Aye lass," he told her, taking her hand heartily. "Ye'll find Sandy MacTavish is a hard master, but ye'll never have cause to say he dinna admit his mistakes. I was wrong about ye, lass. Ye'll do fine here. Just fine."

Kate felt a warm glow at the approval she heard in Sandy's voice, and for a while it made her feel comfortable and secure. Only when it came time to meet the men did she begin to remember the doubts she had felt when she first approached the stern little trail boss. Only then did she finally stop to think that they might be far more troublesome—and dangerous—than she had even begun to guess.

She had been lucky in the fight with Sandy, she knew—lucky that it was only a mock battle. Otherwise, she would have been beaten a thousand times over. Next time, fortune might not be so kind to her. Next time, the fight might be in earnest. The thought was a chilling one.

The instant she met the men, she realized her fears were far from groundless. They were as rough and crude a lot as she had ever seen. No doubt they would prove to be quick-tempered and quarrelsome, too.

As Kate eyed the men warily, only half-listening as Sandy introduced them to her, she felt the tip of her nose curl up in disdain. Never, not even in Jasper Springs, had she seen men as ugly and filthy as these. Gaping at them in disgust, she half-expected to see lice begin to crawl out of their shaggy hair and beards. Instinct warned her that these were wild, coarse men, used to months on the road without a woman. They would not be gentle or polite if they decided to press their attentions on her.

Shuddering, Kate remembered the crude farmer who had forced his foul body on her in the darkness of his barn. Her hand reached down automatically to touch the comforting steel at her belt. For the first time, she was glad Sandy had given the knife to her. The time might come when she would need it. Never again would she let herself be so viciously brutalized.

Kate spent her first few hours in the trail camp trying to get her bearings. Cautiously she observed each of the men out of the corner of her eye, trying to peg their characters before they could catch her staring at them. To her surprise, she quickly realized that they were studying her just as intently and just as warily.

They were as rough and crude as she had thought at first sight, she decided—and not a one of them was self-conscious about leering at her openly—but there was an awkwardness about them, and even a shyness, that puzzled her until she had a chance to think about it. It was the shyness of men who had spent all their time on the road, with little chance to make the acquaintance of women. To her amusement, Kate suddenly realized that they were in awe of her. Perhaps it would not be so hard to keep them in line, after all. Perhaps a sharp tongue and a swift display of sharpshooting would be all she would need. Only one of them—a rough, ugly cowpoke with the unlikely name of Big Hogan—looked like he was going to be a problem.

Oddly enough, Big Hogan wasn't really big at all. He was about average height, and only a little overweight, but he had a big man's swagger and carried himself as though he were six-feet-five and weighed three hundred pounds. Kate quickly realized that the men not only called him Big, they reacted to him as though he actually were a giant of sorts. In some odd, indefinable way, they were all afraid of him, just as the other imported gunslingers had feared Earl Smead. With cold objectivity Kate warned herself that she could expect no help from them if she was ever unfortunate enough to tangle with Big Hogan. She decided to keep her distance from him.

As it turned out, it was not difficult, for their duties kept them well apart throughout the long, tiring days. Big Hogan, as one of the more skillful cowhands, rode in the point position at the front of the herd, while Kate drove the cook wagon, well to the rear. In most trail drives, the wagon moved in first place, well ahead of everyone else, even the men who rode point, but Sandy, perhaps because of Kate's inexperience as a driver, or perhaps because he sensed the need to keep her well separated from Big Hogan, had ordered her to drive behind the herd, staying far enough back to keep out of their dust. On the first hard day's drive, Kate soon found herself forgetting about Big Hogan and all her fears of him, not only because he was out of sight, but because her own duties were far more rigorous and exhausting than she had ever imagined.

Kate was used to driving wagons, but they were small wagons, pulled by well-trained, light-footed horses. Nothing had prepared her for the wearying effort of guiding clumsy, plodding oxen dragging a heavy burden behind them. She quickly learned how hard it was to lean forward for hours on end, arms outstretched, tugging with all her strength on the reins. Even before the end of the first hour, she had already been exhausted enough to weep. and she knew she still had most of the long day's trek ahead of her.

It was all she could do to force herself to hold on to the reins through the hours that followed, but she knew Sandy could not spare one of the riders to spell her, even for an hour or so. Somehow, she had to keep on going. Even if she had wanted to spend the time thinking about Big Hogan and the threatening menace he seemed to pose for her, she would not have had the strength to do it.

When they finally stopped to set up camp for the evening, Kate's only reaction was one of sheer relief It was several minutes before she even remembered Big Hogan, and when it finally occurred to her to glance around the campsite, trying cautiously to see where he was, she felt her fears begin to ease. He was at the far end of the camp with the other cowhands tending to his chores. He seemed completely oblivious of her presence.

How foolish she had been to worry, she told herself with relief. As long as she had her knife and gun. no one would come near her. Stretching her arms and shoulders out to ease the pain of cramped, aching muscles she took a long deep breath, gulping in the cool air. It felt good just to lay down the reins at last. Even when she began to gather up heavy armloads of wood, heaping them up to build a fire, she felt a respite from the weariness that had tormented her all day. Just moving limbs that had been imprisoned for hours in the same position was pure heaven It was only when the time finally came to begin preparing dinner that the feeling of well-being suddenly deserted her.

With a rush of anxiety, she realized she didn't have the vaguest notion how to go about it!

Oh, she could make a stew, all right. It would be none too tasty, since she didn't know the first thing about seasoning it, but it was probably as good as the men were used to. But that was all she knew. She couldn't even prepare a batch of biscuits raised with baking powder, since she didn't have an oven to cook them in. She had a feeling the men wouldn't tolerate the soggy, grease-soaked Indian cakes she could make.

As she stared helplessly at the utensils she had pulled out

of the wagon, near tears from weariness and discouragement, she was surprised to hear a soft, gentle voice in her ear.

"I know how to cook, ma'am. I'd be right proud if you'd let me help you."

Kate stared with relief at the young cowboy who stood beside her. His name was Lonnie, she remembered, but she knew nothing else about him. Right then, he looked like an angel from heaven. Whatever he knew about cooking, it couldn't be less than she did.

As it turned out, Lonnie knew a great deal. It was Lonnie who taught her how to bake in a heavy iron kettle over the open flames, preparing moist, fluffy biscuits, and Lonnie who taught her how to gather wild herbs from the fields to make the meals tastier. It was even Lonnie who taught her to recognize the wild vegetables and edible grasses that added needed vitamins to their foods, staving off the scurvy that was so lamentably common in the West.

"Where did you learn to cook, Lonnie?" Kate asked him one day, unable to suppress her curiosity any longer.

"From my ma," he told her. "She was too sick to do much for herself as long as I kin remember. The older kids had to work in the fields, so she taught me to take care of the house."

"Where's your mother now?"

"Died six months ago, God rest her soul. Now, don't you be takin' on, Miss Kate," he added hastily, noting the look of pity that had swept across her features. " 'Tis best this way. There ain't no more sufferin' for her now. But seein' as she's gone, there weren't no more reason for me to stick around. I'm goin' to my older brother out to Stockton. He wouldn't send for me—figgered I got too soft, all those years workin' around the house—but he says if I kin make it there myself 'fore the snows hit, he'll take me on."

Kate smiled at the young man. Lonnie was a good and willing worker. She had a feeling his older brother was in for a pleasant surprise.

It took only a few days for Kate's body to adjust to the drudgery, and soon she found, to her surprise, that she was approaching each morning with enthusiasm. Each new day that lay ahead, she knew, would be a delight, leading her through different and always fascinating territory. Now that she had grown accustomed to the work, she began to feel more at home. Even her fears about getting along with the men—particularly Big Hogan—began to abate as time passed and no unpleasant incidents occurred. Perhaps she would be able to make it to Stockton without problems, after all. She could see that even Sandy had begun to relax and was spending less and less of his precious time checking to make sure she was all right.

But comfortable as she had become, Kate never relaxed enough to forget Sandy's advice. The gun remained strapped to her waist at all times and the sharp knife was tucked into her belt, even while she slept. She was soon to be glad that she had the foresight and good sense to keep up her guard.

It happened on a dark, silent night, when only a few faint rays of light flickered in from the dying campfire and the air was still, save for the faraway, eerie howling of a coyote. Only a moment before Kate had been sleeping soundly beneath the shelter of the cook tent; then, suddenly, she was wide-awake. She didn't know what it was that alerted her, a sound perhaps, or even a sensation of movement, but she was sure she could feel something—or someone—inching stealthily through the darkness toward her.

Slowly she opened her eyes careful to make no movement or even to vary the quality of her breathing. Whoever—or whatever—it was, she didn't want to give warning that she was awake and ready to protect herself. As she moved her eyes cautiously to scan the space around her, barely illuminated in the faint firelight that filtered through the shadows, she was just in time to see a huge, hairy hand slithering its way cautiously toward her. Before she could react, it reached forward abruptly, snatching the gun from her holster and tossing it on the ground yards away.

As the figure moved, Kate caught sight of a man's face, accented against the darkness by the golden rays of light. It was Big Hogan, and he had gotten her gun! Instinctively she rolled out from under the wagon and leaped to her feet with the swift, catlike motion Sandy had taught her.

"What the hell are you doing?" she shrieked at the top of her lungs.

As she heard the heavy rustling sounds coming from all directions, she knew she had awakened the entire camp. Sleeping cowhands instantly tumbled out of bedrolls and reached for their guns. As Kate saw them, their eyes illuminated in the flickering glow of the fire, she could have wept for relief. Now, surely, Big Hogan would slink away embarrassed.

But she had underestimated his determination. Crawling out from under the wagon, he rose to face her, seemingly oblivious of the eyes that glowed out of the darkness at the edge of the circle of firelight.

"I aim to git me a woman," he said confidently.

With a rush of fear, Kate remembered her first assessment of Big Hogan. He was the kind of man other men feared, the kind of man they would never stand up against, not even to protect a helpless woman.

"Like hell you will," she shouted coarsely. The only way to deal with a man like that was to meet him on his own terms—to try to bluff him down.

But Big Hogan was not about to let himself be bluffed. "I aim to git me a woman," he repeated calmly, a broad grin spreading slowly across his moon-shaped face. "And a right purty one, too!"

Kate was suddenly aware that, without a hat, her dark, silken hair was free to stream abundantly down her back. The golden light of the campfire that picked up its sensuous red highlights must have made her a tempting sight to men who had not had a woman for months, even years. Slowly, warily, she turned to cast her eyes around the circle of light, assessing the silent watchers in the shadows. She was not encouraged by what she saw.

Not a face in that circle was turned toward Big Hogan. All eyes were on her, and the expression she read in their depths was not one of pity or regret, but rather of deep hunger and even heightened anticipation. With a sudden rush of horror, Kate realized that if she could not keep Big Hogan from having his way with her, he was not the only man who would violate her unwilling body that night. Instinctively she drew her hand down to feel the comforting hardness of the knife handle. The blade glinted menacingly in the firelight as she pulled it out.

Big Hogan only threw back his head to roar with laughter when he saw her resistance. "You're a right fiery little one, ain't ya?" She could hear the admiration in his voice.

Shifting her weight to the balls of her feet as Sandy had taught her, Kate waited for him to draw his own knife and ease his bulky body toward her. Instead, she saw to her surprise that he had reached down to unbuckle his belt and slip it through the loops in his pants. It was only a moment before the long strip of leather dangled from his fingers, swinging back and forth through the air with a slow, menacing power.

Horrified, Kate could only stare at him. This was something she hadn't anticipated. With the belt, he could lash away at her without ever once coming into the range of the sharp blade in her hand.

Big Hogan wasted no time. Flipping the belt backward, he sent it whistling through the air with brutal strength. Kate cried out in pain as she felt the sharp leather cut into her wrist. It took all her strength to manage to keep her fingers clutched around the hilt of her knife. She knew she would not be able to do it again.

Kate felt fear and despair begin to rise in her throat, choking her with sudden urgency. She had always known she would not be able to hold out long in a fight with a man, but she had never realized it could end this quickly. She would have to fight dirty, as Sandy had warned her—but she would have to fight fast too. She would have only one chance to attack, and it had better come quickly or it would not come at all.

Reacting swiftly, Kate lowered her hand that held her knife and with the other hand reached out to massage her battered wrist. Just as she had done in the practice bout with Sandy she let her shoulders heave up and down in racking sobs. It required no effort to force tears of pain and fear to roll down her cheeks.

The ruse worked even better than Kate had anticipated. The instant he saw her tears, Big Hogan dropped his belt to the ground and began to chuckle in unrestrained mirth at the feminine weakness that forced her to give in so easily. As Kate watched him step eagerly toward her, she steeled her body to wait until the last second. She dared not move too soon.

Then, just as he had begun to reach out his repulsive hands to drag her resisting body toward him, Kate shifted her weight to her left leg, drawing her right knee up swiftly and digging in sharply into his groin. It was even easier than she had expected, for he was caught completely off guard.

Big Hogan let out a harsh cry as he felt the brutal impact of her knee, and almost instantly he doubled over in pain. Kate wasted no time lashing out her foot and twisting it around his ankle, knocking him swiftly to the ground. With a wry smile of satisfaction she noted that she hadn't even needed a patch of muddy ground to throw him off balance.

No sooner had the man crashed to the earth than Kate was on top of him. Twisting her fingers through the filthy tangles of his hair, she pulled his head back roughly, leaving the surprising whiteness of his throat exposed to the sharp point of her knife. She was amazed at the strong surge of pleasure that filled her body when she drew the tip of the blade in a shallow cut along his skin. The few drops of blood that welled up in its wake were intensely satisfying.

Big Hogan ceased struggling the instant he felt the blade scratching lightly into his throat. He knew he was at her mercy.

"Enough?"

Kate heard the loud sound of laughter that greeted her challenge. and she realized that the men had drawn closer around her. Glancing up for a quick second, she caught sight of a fierce look of pride on Sandy's face.

Pausing only long enough to remove Hogan's gun from his holster, Kate jumped up quickly, replacing the knife in her belt. Her fallen adversary rose much more slowly, his body still doubled over from the painful kick in the groin.

"You leave me alone from now on." she warned him.

"Ma'am, I ain't never gonna mess with you agin."

There was a sound of resignation in Big Hogan's voice. but it was mingled with an awed astonishment and even admiration. In that second Kate suddenly realized that she had won more than just one battle that night. She had won her safety for the rest of the journey. for neither Big Hogan nor any of the other men would ever tangle with her again. Now, at last, she had earned the right to ride beside them as an equal.

From that day on, though she still slept with her knife in her belt. Kate knew she had nothing to fear. The men respected and even looked up to her.

31

SANDY MACTAVISH'S FACE WAS GRIM AND UNHAPPY, BUT there was a hard set to the little Scot's jaw that warned Kate he meant business. It was an unpleasant task he had to perform, but he knew there was no point putting it off.

"Sorry lad." he said gruffly. "Ye canna go any farther. We'll have to leave you behind at the next town and take on a replacement."

Lonnie looked up at him miserably, but he didn't try to

coax him to change his mind. One glance down at the foot that was already swollen to double its normal size was enough to persuade him that all his entreaties would be in vain.

Kate's heart bled for the crestfallen boy. Being left behind, she knew, was heartbreaking for Lonnie. With his injured foot, there would be no way he could cross the mountains before the first winter snows made the passes too dangerous to attempt. Kate knew only too well how much it had meant to him to reach his brother's ranch that season, not just because of the job that was waiting, but because it was so important for him to be able to prove himself to his stern older brother.

"Dinna take it so hard, lad," Sandy urged awkwardly. " 'Tis nae your fault. 'Tis a bit of bad luck, is all."

It had been bad luck all around, Kate thought. Bad luck that Lonnie was in the lead as half a dozen of the men had raced down the steep embankment in search of game to supplement their monotonous meals. Bad luck, too, that he'd been too poor to replace the thin soles of his boots, even though they were worn nearly clean through. When his foot had landed on the sharp, thick stub of a dead branch that rose invisibly from the scrub covering the rocky soil, there had been nothing to keep it from ramming right through the ball of his foot.

Lonnie had tried gallantly to overcome his injury, but the task would have defeated a far stronger man than he. After two days, the foot was badly infected and so agonizingly painful that he could no longer even step on it. Sandy had taken a sharp knife to the wound, draining it and cutting out as much of the woody spike as he could, but it was all too clear that some of it was still embedded deeply in Lonnie's flesh. It would be days, or even weeks, before it worked its way out through the top of his foot, and a long time after that before the wound would heal completely.

"Couldn't you keep him on anyhow?" Kate urged, forcing a brightness into her voice that she did not feel. "He could help me drive the cook wagon."

"Ye know I canna do that," Sandy shouted out impatiently. Kate could tell by the gruffness of his voice that he was as sorry as she to have to leave the boy behind. "I canna afford to carry food and water for a man that canna pull his weight."

Kate was silent for a moment. She knew Sandy was speaking the truth. There were hard mountain crossings ahead, and stretches of dry, arid land. The cattle would be skittish and hard to handle. Sandy would need every hand he could get.

"But someone has to drive the wagon," Kate protested, determined not to give up before she had to. "Let Lonnie do that, and I'll ride drag for him."

"What in hell, lass?" Sandy burst out in exasperation. Kate was a good worker, he had to admit that, and having her on the drive had worked out far better than he'd expected. But a woman riding herd! Impossible!

"I can do it, Sandy," she pleaded. "You know I can ride as well as any of the men. Besides I'm no more inexperienced than Lonnie was, and you took him on."

"I'm sorry Kate," he told her firmly. She could tell by his face that his mind was made up. "Maybe on an easier drive, but I can't afford to take any chances on this one."

Neither Kate nor Sandy had noticed the shadow that fell over them as they spoke. Only when Big Hogan strode out to a spot directly in front of them did they finally see him. They both glanced up at him in surprise.

"If Miz Kate says she kin handle drag, then she kin handle it," he said emphatically.

Troubled as she was, Kate had to smile at his words. Ever since the one brief battle they had fought with each other, he had gone out of his way to be not only her protector, but her friend as well and when Big Hogan set out to be someone's friend, he obviously did it in style.

"Now, Big— " Sandy protested, but the round-faced cowpoke refused to listen.

"You wanna leave that kid in the next town, you kin leave me, too."

Sandy shook his head in silence, too surprised to be able to find the words to object. He and Big both knew there wasn't a chance the man was going to be left behind. He was far too valuable a cowhand to lose at that stage.

"If'n she wants to ride," Big repeated emphatically, "she rides."

And so it was that Kate found herself mounted on horseback, sharing with the men the responsibility for holding the herd in place. She quickly found out what it meant to be the least experienced rider on a trail drive.

The more experienced— and hence the more valuable— men rode point, stationing themselves at the front of the herd to guide the cattle and hold them to an appropriate pace. Next came the men who flanked the herd, riding out on one side or the other to hold the strays in check and keep the animals on the well-worn path, which by now, after the many drives that had passed over it, was almost as clearly defined as a paved road. Last came the two least experienced riders, Kate and a youth named Cal Bennett, riding in what was called the drag position. Only Charley Cassidy and the extra horses rode behind them, and they were careful to stay far enough back to avoid the heavy dust kicked up by the herd. Even the cook wagon, now that Lonnie was driving it, had taken its accustomed place well in front of the others.

At last Kate understood why Sandy had forced her to wear the bandanna. If she hadn't been able to wrap it around her mouth and nose, she would never have been able to breathe in the thick cloud of dust that swirled around her. Even with its protection, she found herself choking and coughing painfully through the long, dry days.

Sometimes her eyes stung so badly from the dust and the hot rays of bright sunlight that she could barely see. It was at moments like that, when she thought she could bear it no longer, that she reminded herself of Lonnie and how important it was for him to reach Stockton. She could get back the relatively easy job of driving the cook wagon any time she wanted it, but that would mean Lonnie would be left behind in the next town they passed. She had to succeed, for his sake.

Kate would sometimes find herself looking down at the coarse, reddened hands that gripped her reins and wonder with a kind of detached awe if they could really belong to her. Could those really be the hands of that same girl who only months before had cherished the milky smoothness of her skin? Sometimes, it almost seemed, as she looked back on her past life, that her memories were nothing more substantial than a dream, or perhaps a story she had read once in a book and now half-forgotten. Surely this woman dressed in rough, filthy clothes, with a knife and gun at her waist, could not be the same pampered aristocrat who had embarked for the New World barely more than a year ago.

Kate dug her spurs irritably into her mount's side, trying for at least the thousandth time that day to urge the unresponsive beast forward into the thick brown dust. The horse was a far cry from the spirited, light-footed steeds she was used to, but she did not dare complain. She knew the lowest-ranking rider had no choice but to accept what was offered, no matter how inferior it might be.

Each man on the drive had brought his own horse. As Lonnie's substitute, it fell to Kate to ride Lightning, his sadly misnamed mount. She knew only too well that the boy couldn't afford a really good horse, but she still found herself cursing his bad taste in horseflesh every time she had to climb onto the beast's back.

In addition to Lightning, she—like the other riders—had half a dozen working horses from the remuda, the herd Charley Cassidy tended At the beginning of the drive, Sandy had let each of the men choose his own horses from the remuda Starting with the highest-ranking rider they had each chosen one horse before beginning a second round of selections and then a third. As low man on the totem pole. Lonnie had no doubt been at a disadvantage but Kate couldn't help thinking poor judgment had played a part in it, too, for he seemed to have drawn the six worst horses in the lot. Several changes of mount were made each day to keep the horses from getting too tired, but with the heavy-hoofed beasts Kate had drawn, it never seemed to be enough.

Kate squinted her eyes into the hot sunlight, tilting the brim of her hat down to block out the bright rays as best she could. For several days now, they had been riding through a long, dry stretch, and gazing ahead she could see no relief in sight. The herd had been without water for two days, and while Sandy spoke confidently of the water they would reach the next afternoon Kate could see no hint of it as she looked around at the arid landscape.

Several times during the day, Sandy stopped the herd for an hour or so, but by midafternoon, heat and thirst had made the cattle so restless that it was impossible to force them to graze, much less lie down It was all the point men could do to hold the herd to a walk For the first time, Kate did not envy the men who rode in front Perhaps, despite the dust and the discomfort, it was easier to ride drag.

Late in the afternoon Sandy sent Charley Cassidy ahead to overtake the cook wagon. Once they reached a suitable campsite, Charley was to tie up the night horses. The thirsty cattle would be skittish and nervous that night It would be nine or ten o'clock at least before they could be grazed and bedded down Until then, they would continue to use the working horses, saving the more valuable night horses for the important task that lay ahead.

Even with twice the usual amount of space for bedding down the cattle, it was well after ten before they could coax them to lie down Even then the cowhands did not dare relax. They knew that thirsty cattle were always more likely to stampede, especially if the strong night winds carried the scent of water to their nostrils—and the Angus were even more nervous than most breed on a drive.

As an extra precaution, Sandy doubled the guard that night. Six riders would be on duty for the first half, six for the second. Kate was not scheduled until the second watch, but she was far too nervous to catch more than an hour or so of fitful sleep. She got up long before she was needed, and headed for the cook wagon to grab a cup of hot, bracing coffee before it was time to mount up.

To her surprise, Kate found that the other riders from the second shift were already there before her. Lonnie had heated up the stew and made fresh biscuits, and Kate noticed that despite the strain and weariness, morale was high as the men enjoyed their nourishing late supper. She marveled as she sat beside the campfire, listening to their jokes and joining in their songs, at the lighthearted spirit they all showed. They might just as well have been a bunch of little boys on a picnic instead of a group of men facing the grim, dangerous task of holding together a group of thirsty cattle through the long, dark hours of the night.

The moon was only a narrow sliver in the cloudless sky as Kate drained the last bitter dregs from her cup and headed toward the night horse that had been assigned to her. She cringed as she neared it, realizing only too well that it was no better than the clumsy mounts that carried her during the day.

Many times, around the campfire, Kate had heard the men bragging about their night horses, talking of them with deep pride and affection. She had always known how important they were to the cowhands, but somehow it had never seemed to matter too much to her that she had nothing better than a tired old nag to carry her through the long, slow night. Always before, that had seemed like the easiest part of the drive anyhow. But now, with stampede an imminent possibility, she realized with a cold rush of foreboding that a good horse on a night like this could well mean the difference between life and death.

A good night horse, she had heard the men say often enough, had eyes for darkness where none else could see. A good night horse could make his way safely through treacherous gullies and prairie-dog towns, where a lesser steed would stumble, thrusting himself and his rider both beneath the sharp hooves of the stampeding herd.

"Put your faith in God if ye will," she had heard Sandy say more than once. "But make sure ye have a good night horse. Now, me, if I had to choose between God and a night horse . . . well, lads, I'd take the horse."

Well, it wouldn't do any good to fuss about it now, Kate told herself firmly. This was the only horse she had, and that was all there was to it. Besides, she was probably making a mountain out of a molehill Surely there wasn't going to be a stampede that night, not when half the night was already gone and everything was still quiet.

Kate was about to swing into the saddle when she saw Big Hogan coming toward her walking his horse beside him. Puzzled, she stopped and waited for him to draw near.

"That ain't no horse for a lady," he told her indignantly, casting a suspicious eye on the hapless steed beside her. " 'Specially on a night like this." His practiced eye took in the skittish herd with a wary glance. "A little mite like you needs a horse what kin protect you." To Kate's amazement, he thrust the reins of his own horse hurriedly into her hands.

"Why, Big," she exclaimed, startled. "I can't take your horse."

"Aw, hell, Miz Kate," he protested, blushing at his own sudden and unexpected generosity. "I kin ride that old nag o' yourn Why. I been herdin' fer years. I know how to handle myself. But you . . . well, you *need* Lulu."

Kate had to agree that she felt more secure the instant she felt Lulu's strong, broad back beneath her. The horse looked as preposterous as her name, drab and stodgy and unprepossessing. but she was as bold and surefooted a mount as Kate had ever ridden The minute she felt Kate on her back—a far lighter burden than she was used to—her step grew jaunty and almost carefree Kate sensed she appreciated the light, deft hand that guided her with perfect but gentle skill.

As Kate watched Big ride off on her own horse. she felt a momentary tremor of doubt and even guilt sweep across her body. but she quickly reassured herself. remembering his own words. Big *had* been herding for years. He would know what to do if . . .

But she was being silly, she told herself impatiently. Nothing was going to happen The herd was resting peacefully, as they had on many other nights. She was letting herself get spooked by the cowboys' talk around the fireside Taking a deep breath she felt herself beginning to relax as she guided Lulu skillfully in a wide. slow circle around the herd. Out here, under the silent, open sky, with a responsive horse beneath her. she felt too much at peace with the world to let her nervousness take over.

> I ride an old paint and I lead an old Dan,
> I'm goin' to Montana to throw the Hoolian . . .

Kate let her voice ring out in a deep, pure alto as she sang the familiar words of the lonely cowboy refrain. The men had taught her to sing as she rode at night on her solitary rounds, telling her that the sound reassured the animals. Now Kate found that it comforted not only the animals, but herself as well.

> Ride around little doggies,
> Ride around them slow,
> For the fiery and snuffy
> Are rarin' to go . . .

Kate heard the words echo faintly through the night air, hopelessly out of rhythm with her own, as the next rider emerged slowly through the darkness, circling his way in the opposite direction around the herd. He touched his fingers to the brim of his hat in a mute salute as they passed by each other in the dark night.

> I ride an old paint and I . . .

And then suddenly, in the midst of all the quiet and calm, something—some indefinable, invisible thing—happened. Before Kate's eyes, the whole herd rose in unison, lowing pitifully as they began to run in what seemed a mindless, directionless panic.

Kate could hardly believe her eyes. One moment, the cattle had been lying quietly on the ground in apparent peace and contentment. The next moment, they were an ugly, milling mass, fleeing blindly through the dark night, running from nothing, headed nowhere.

In that instant, Kate suddenly realized the sacrifice Big Hogan had made for her. Even before her startled brain could begin to comprehend what had happened, Lulu had changed from an ordinary, stodgy mare into a supercharged bundle of dynamic energy. Ignoring Kate, who in her panic and bewilderment had pulled at the reins with a force that would have stopped a lesser horse, Lulu began to move swiftly and surely through the darkness.

Kate could not help remembering the panic she had felt on another wild, frantic dash across rugged plains in the pitch black of night. Only, that time it had been two frightened runaways who pulled an awkward rented wagon. This time, it was different. This time, Kate was clinging tightly to the back of a surefooted beast, holding on tightly until it almost seemed as if she and the horse were one single being. This time, Kate realized quickly, she did not need to look in terror for ruts or ravines crisscrossing the ground, or even shadowy prairie-dog holes, for Lulu knew her business, and knew it well.

Kate had been told often enough what to do in a stampede, but even had she been a complete novice with no instructions at all, it would not have mattered, for Lulu was not waiting for her to give the orders. With perfect instinct, the stocky mare raced to the front of the herd, seeking out the lead cattle in the midst of a darkness and chaos that Kate could not yet begin to decipher.

Kate knew that in any stampede the fastest and strongest animals would work their way quickly to the front of the herd, setting a killing pace that the others must follow. The only way to stop them was to head off the leaders, veering them sharply to the right in an arcing pattern, then slowly closing the circle, until finally the animals used up all their energy running around and around in a tight little ring. It was that task that Lulu had set herself to accomplish.

Kate forced her mind into a total blank, giving Lulu her head as she raced toward the front of the herd. If she dared let herself think about the danger, she would panic for sure. She could already feel the rough, powerful side of one of the lead cattle against her leg as Lulu pushed steadily into the beast, trying to force him even an inch or two off his course.

Only after her eyes had become accustomed to the milling mass of bodies did Kate realize she was not alone. Another rider, too, had made it to the head of the herd. Kate felt a surge of excitement as she made out the bulky form of Big Hogan atop her own horse. She longed to call out to him, shouting her joy at finding a better, more skillful cowhand beside her, but she didn't dare distract him, even for a second. It could be too dangerous.

Then, suddenly, even as her eyes were on him, she was horrified to see the horse stumble beneath his body, falling abruptly to the earth. Desperately she tugged at Lulu's reins, trying to force the horse to turn back. She had to go to Big, had to find some way to pull him out from beneath the butchering hooves that must even now be tearing his body apart.

But Lulu knew her job too well. Kate could not budge her an inch from her self-appointed task. She had been trained to break the stampede, and break it she would. She would not veer aside for anything not even for the fallen rider who only minutes before had been her master.

Numb with shock Kate clung to Lulu's back, too tired and too horrified to know or even care what was happening around her Soon her movements became as mechanical and instinctive as those of her horse, and she felt neither surprise nor exhilaration when at last the lead cattle began to swing in a graceful arc, moving slowly but inexorably back toward the end of the herd.

It wasn't until Kate had turned the swifter animals completely around, closing ranks at last with the slower beasts in the rear that she realized she was completely alone. The other riders had moved in closer, but seeing that she already had the herd under control they tactfully kept their distance, leaving her to savor the moment of victory alone.

But it didn't seem like victory, she told herself bitterly. Not without Big The men thought she had done it alone, but that wasn't true It was Big's horse—and Big's help at the beginning—that had enabled her to do it. He should have been there to share the triumph with her.

The rest of the work was simply mechanical. With the other cowhands Kate helped to squeeze the circle ever tighter and tighter, taking care to keep the wilder animals from escaping and beginning the stampede anew. After a while, Kate noticed that the herd had begun to slow down perceptibly.

She was not sorry to see Sandy riding toward her. "Go warm yourself by the fire, lass, and get a cup o' coffee. The men'll take care o' the rest. Ye've done more than your share."

Weary and despondent, Kate was only too glad to hand Lulu's reins to a hobbling Lonnie and shuffle slowly toward the fire She was nearly there before she noticed the broad, moon-faced figure seated beside it, a bright stream of blood trickling from his mouth.

"Big!" she shouted excitedly. "I thought you were dead for sure."

"Aw, shit!" His broad face broke into a bloody grin as he saw the joy in her eyes "Didn't I tell you I know all about herdin'? Why it'd take more'n a few tired ol' cows to git Big Hogan " To Kate's horror, the blood continued to spurt out of his mouth and in the midst of all the red she caught sight of loose chips of white that looked suspiciously like teeth.

"But your teeth!" she cried out in horror.

"Why, hell, that ain't nothin'," he boasted, glad to be able to show his bravery in front of this spunky young woman. "Ain't no good for a cowpoke to have all his teeth nohow. Looks like he's layin' down on the job."

Soon, as the cattle were bedded down at last and the night air was still once more, the other cowhands began to drift toward the fire. Pouring out the steaming mugs of coffee, they delighted in relating over and over again the events of that exciting night.

Always, in the stories they told, Kate was the heroine. They seemed to relish reminding themselves over and over in tones of unmuted awe how the stampede had been stopped by a lone *woman*. But as she listened, Kate did not feel like a heroine. She felt something even better. Looking around at the circle of admiring faces in the flickering firelight, she felt—for the first time in a long, long time—that she had found a place where she belonged.

As she leaned back and closed her eyes, Kate could hear once again in her imagination the melodic waltzes that had flowed so richly through the rooms of her father's house. She could see again in her mind's eye the glittering lights of chandeliers reflected on highly polished floors.

She knew she would always miss the romantic charm of the graceful world she had left behind. Even more, she would miss the passion and excitement Jason had brought into her life for a few brief months. But the life she had found to replace it, if nowhere near as splendid or stimulating, at least brought with it an unexpected peace and contentment.

It felt good to lie on the earth beneath a clear and starry sky. It felt good to pit her strength against the forces of nature and know she had not been found wanting. There was a camaraderie in this life that was warm and fulfilling, a camaraderie with the men she worked with, the horses she rode, and even the elements of nature that continally challenged her. It was a camaraderie Kate would not have minded sharing for the rest of her days.

The firelight was warm on her face as she felt herself drift into forgetfulness.

32

THE DAYS THAT FOLLOWED WERE PLEASANT ONES FOR KATE. Although life on the trail was far from easy, it offered a satisfaction that ran deeper than anything she had known in earlier, more pampered days At long last, she told herself proudly, she had managed, through her own diligence and even pain, to carve herself a niche in the harsh, insulated masculine world that made up the West. For a while, it was enough to bask in her good fortune without questioning it. Only toward the end of the drive was she forced to come to the sudden bitter realization that all her contentment and new-found sense of security was nothing more than a flimsy illusion, like the conjurer's myriad gaudy silken handkerchiefs that vanished into the air as quickly as they had appeared.

They were less than a week out of Stockton when Sandy called her aside late one afternoon. At first she thought nothing of it, but as she caught sight of the hard, determined look on his face, she began to feel nervous. His first words quickly confirmed her fears.

"Here's your pay, lass." Sandy was careful to let neither sentiment nor affection show through the gruffness of his voice. "There's a bonus, too—ye've earned it. Take one of the horses from the remuda for your own, and keep the knife and gun, too."

"But, Sandy, we've nearly a week to go yet," she protested.

"Aye, but I'll get another man to fill in easy enough now."

"But I *want* to go to the end."

"I dinna think it wise," he said solemnly. "When the men draw their pay, lass, the first thing they'll do is go out and get all liquored up. The men like ye, Kate, and respect ye, but the minute they're filled with liquor, they'll be thinkin' o' only one thing, and that's that ye be a bonnie woman. 'Tis none can protect ye then."

Kate heard his words with sinking heart, for she knew there was no way she could contradict them. What Sandy had told her was nothing but the truth—and it was a bitter truth to face. The West was still a man's world, and there was no way she would ever be able to meet it on her own terms. Any woman who tried to live in that world alone, free and independent of masculine aid, would live always in the shadow of brutality and degradation.

"What can I do?" she whispered, suddenly overwhelmed by the enormity of the problem that faced her.

Sandy squirmed sympathetically. He was painfully aware that there was little he could say or do to help her. "Why dinna ye try one of the smaller cattle towns where ye can find a nice young man? Ye'll make some man a hell of a wife, lass," he told her earnestly. "But whatever ye do, dinna go near the goldfields. There's nae gold left now, and 'tis none ye'll find there but opportunists and cutthroats."

Go to one of the cattle towns and find yourself a husband. It was good advice, Kate had to admit bitterly—perhaps the only good advice for a woman alone in this strange, barbaric land. She wondered what Sandy would think if he knew she already had a husband, a man she was bound to for the rest of her life—for better or much, much worse.

The trail suddenly began to look very lonely to Kate as she made her solitary way through the cool green foothills of the Sierra Nevada mountain range. It seemed strange to be so far from the milling cattle and horses and the dusty cowhands who had grown to be her friends in the long weeks that now belonged to the past. Slowing the stocky horse to a comfortable walk along the rocky trail, she stiffened her back and forced her chin up boldly into the air. No matter what happened, she was not going to let herself be frightened by thoughts of the bleak future that lay ahead.

It was not so much the emptiness of the future—or even the loneliness—that frightened her, for those were things she had already learned to accept. The aching sadness that filled her body through the long, dark nights was as intimately familiar as an old friend, and she knew only too well she would never be able to stop herself from yearning for the man she was doomed to love for the rest of her life, no matter how cruel or heartless he had been to her. But she knew, too, that there was a cure for the sweet agony that spread through her body whenever the memory of passion invaded her heart, and that cure was good hard work. Muscles that cried out in weariness left no room for soft, weak flesh to mourn the lascivious touch that seemed to turn her blood into molten lava.

No, it was not the loneliness that flooded her heart with

fear, but rather the sudden cold realization that even the barest survival was going to be a desperate struggle She had a pocket full of money now, and a good horse, but without a means of earning a living. how long would they last? She had neither the impeccable references to be a schoolmarm nor the skill to be a dressmaker, nor was she free to accept the protection of a man What on earth was she going to do?

But whatever ye do. dinna go near the goldfields.

Kate felt an odd twinge of guilt as she heard Sandy's voice again in her memory It was the same feeling she had always had when she was a small child and knew she was about to disobey her father's orders Don't go near the goldfields, Sandy had told her. But if she didn't go there, where was she to go?

Even though most of the gold was gone, Kate knew that rich strikes were still being made from time to time. Besides, she reminded herself she didn't need a really big strike. If only she could make enough to increase her modest stake, even a little bit she would be able to buy a small store or a rooming house some little enterprise that would make her independent and self-supporting And if she happened to be lucky enough to hit a really good strike . . . Well, that would solve her problems forever.

And so it was that, almost before she realized it, the decision had been made and she had turned her horse around, heading toward a town whose name she had never even heard.

Murphys, by the early 1870's, had become a wide-open town, as filled with saloons and gambling tents as it was with dysentery, diarrhea, and scurvy. As Kate rode down the main street that ran through the center of town, she had to smile wryly at herself, for she knew she must look exactly like those same rough cowhands who had seemed so intimidating to her when she first arrived in Jasper Springs. Glancing at the dirty boardwalks and gray ramshackle buildings that lined the street, she was conscious of a certain sense of satisfaction. She had to admit the town was every bit as crude and raucous as Sandy had threatened, but it was a crudeness Kate could deal with after weeks with rough cowhands on the trail. Besides. in Murphys she would not look out of place.

Even though she saw no other women dressed in male clothing on the crowded main street, Kate was relieved to realize that she had attracted no disapproving or curious stares. Here, she sensed, was a place where everyone was so

362

outrageous and individualistic that one more eccentric in the midst of it all didn't even cause a raised eyebrow.

The town of Murphys, she soon learned, had been founded barely more than twenty years before, in 1848, by the Murphy brothers, John and Daniel, who had come to the valley to set up a trading post. In no time at all, John Murphy had persuaded the Indians to mine for him, and by the time he left the camp in December 1849, he had already managed to accumulate nearly two million dollars in gold, making him one of the wealthiest men on the West Coast.

The claims in Murphys were among the richest in the Calaveras area. During the boom years of the fifties and early sixties, the town was, if a bit rough, at least vital and exciting, but the years that followed brought with them only diminishing prosperity as even the richest of the claims began to dry up. By the time Kate arrived, all that was left of the raucous opulence that had once flooded through the town was an army of opportunists and hangers-on.

It was not a very promising place to seek a fortune, but Kate refused to let herself be discouraged. After all, she had not come for wealth, she reminded herself sternly, but only for a modest strike to help her get started in some kind of business. Besides, while she was trying to make her small stake, Murphys might not be such a bad place to stay after all. The town itself was coarse and filthy, but the surrounding countryside was beautiful and serene, with tall green mountains rising in bold silhouette against the clear blue and white of the sky. And even in the town itself, there was a surprising number of pleasant oases, not the least of which was the delightful Sperry and Perry Hotel.

The instant she saw the building, Kate felt as if she should rub her eyes to make sure she wasn't dreaming. Surrounded by dozens of ramshackle wooden structures running up and down the length of the main street, the thick stone walls of the Sperry and Perry rose like an unexpected symbol of solidarity and strength. It had never occurred to Kate that any of these buildings in such a rough-and-tumble area would actually have been built to last. It gave her a comfortable feeling of continuity to realize she had been wrong.

The instant she checked into the hotel, she knew the comfortable feeling the building had given her was not just an illusion. Although it was nowhere near as elegant as the European hotels she was accustomed to, or even the hotels of the East, her room was clean and the bed wonderfully inviting. The meals, after months of nothing but plain stews and biscuits, tasted like gourmet treats prepared for a king's banquet.

The windowless dining room at the rear of the hotel was dark and gloomy, with acoustics that emphasized the clatter of utensil and the raucous sound of voices, but it didn't matter, for the food was fresh and superbly prepared. The fresh vegetable that were brought in daily from nearby ranches were a delight to Kate, and the soft water that was hauled to the hotel from a spring a mile away seemed like an unbelievable luxury.

Perhaps the most remarkable feature of the Sperry and Perry, at least to Kate, was the small, elegantly furnished salon that had been reserved for the exclusive use of the ladies, most of them visiting gentlewomen who had come to see the magnificent sequoia forest at nearby Big Tree. Kate could hardly believe her eyes as she peered into the small room, marveling at the quiet taste and gentility of the furnishings. To her surprise, she found she could not force herself to step inside. She was no longer comfortable with those perfumed silk-clad ladies, their hands smooth and white, their hair tidily coiffured until each dainty curl rested obediently in place. These same women, only months ago, would have seemed so far below her station that she would have greeted them with no more than a cool, polite nod of her head. Now they seemed to belong to an elegant world beyond her reach.

It took Kate no time at all to realize she would be more comfortable if she remained as she was. By far the wisest thing she could do was hide her beauty beneath the rough masculine garb she had already been wearing for weeks. Her only concession to dainty femininity was to wash out the filthy jeans she had traveled in for so long. As for the rest, she willingly adopted miner's garb. She quickly learned to roll her jeans up to the top of her high boots to keep them dry and clean on the muddy streets, and she bought herself a red flannel shirt just like all the miners seemed to have. All she lacked was a floppy, broad-brimmed hat, but with an eye on her diminishing resources she decided against it. The felt hat she had worn on the trail would have to do.

Kate was careful to hold her expenditures to a minimum, but even so, she was alarmed to see her modest store of money dwindling rapidly in the expensive mining town. It was good to have a soft bed to sleep in, and a warm quilt to wrap around her body in the middle of a cold night, but she knew it was a luxury she could not afford much longer. Soon she would have to find a way to make money—not an easy prospect, since all the nearby claims had been taken, and there was nothing left for the drove of immigrants who flooded in each day—or she would have to leave Murphys before all her money was gone.

The solution to her problem came far more easily than she had expected As she walked into the Sperry and Perry dining room to enjoy a tasty, nourishing meal—the last one she would be able to afford for a long time. she told herself sternly—she was surprised to hear a loud angry commotion at the end of one of the long communal tables Boisterousness was hardly out of place in Murphys even in a restaurant frequented by ladies but this quarrel seemed exceptionally vicious and surly. Kate saw instantly that her eyes were not the only ones fastened on the scene with interest.

"What in hell d'ya think yer gonna do, Foster," a loud voice boomed out Kate looked across the room with distaste at the huge bearded man on the other side. She recognized Mike Pritchett right away. for she had often seen his unpleasant face around town Pritchett's massive size enabled him to be a domineering bully but Kate had noticed more than once that heavy layers of fat were mingled with the muscles on his tall body forming ripples of blubber beneath his shirt Obviously the lean years that had hit the mining camps had not affected him overmuch.

"I'll manage." a quiet voice replied.

Kate stared with interest at the young man who rose from the table to face Pritchett Though barely more than a boy— Kate judged he could be no more than seventeen or eighteen—he seemed undaunted by the bully's threats. With pink cheeks still puffed with baby fat, he faced the other man with the bold fearlessness of youth.

"You'll manage all right " Pritchett snarled. "*If* you throw in with us!" Like all true bullies, Prichett never traveled alone, and now, as if on cue two slimy little men known locally only as Mac and Sammy, stepped up behind him. They were, Kate thought just the kind of leeches that were always attracted to braggarts and swaggerers. "You ain't got but one man on your claim Foster since your partner died. Ain't gonna find no one else 'less'n you throw in with us."

Instantly Kate realized what had happened. She had already discovered that claims in Murphys were limited to eight by eight feet but with a partner they could be extended to eight by twelve. Young Foster obviously had one of the larger claims and no partner to share it with. Ordinarily, it would have been an easy matter in a crowded area like Murphys to find someone to take over an established claim, even an insignificant one, but with those ruffians trying to cut themselves in, everyone else had been scared away.

"Get out of here, Pritchett," another voice broke in emphatically. "We'll get someone else. Don't worry."

Kate glanced at the speaker in surprise. She hadn't even noticed the two fair-haired boys sitting beside Foster. No doubt they had the next claim to his and had decided to cast their lots together.

"We'll see about that," Pritchett snarled menacingly as he stomped out, followed by his two unappealing henchmen. It seemed to Kate that the whole room heaved a sigh of relief when they were gone.

Kate continued to watch the three young men. She could tell by their expressions that they were far more troubled than they had admitted. Suddenly it occurred to her that this might be just the break she had been hoping for. They needed someone who wasn't afraid of Pritchett and his cronies to share a claim, and after everything she had been through, she wasn't afraid of anyone anymore. Slowly she sauntered over to their table and pulled up a chair.

"Kate Hamilton," she said tersely as she sat beside them.

The young men looked at her warily. "Johnny Johnston," one of them said slowly. He was the blond youth that had talked back to Pritchett. "My cousin, Bill Elsey. And this is Rafe Foster."

"I hear you're looking for someone to share your claim," she said immediately. There was no point beating around the bush. No matter what she said, they were bound to be suspicious of her anyway, just because she was a woman. Might as well get it right out in the open. "I might be interested."

Kate was surprised to see Rafe Foster's face light up. "You would," he asked eagerly, but young Johnston was quick to squelch the idea.

"No chance!"

"Who else do you have in mind?"

The silence that followed her question was as eloquent as an answer.

Finally, Bill Elsey, quieter and more thoughtful than his cousin, spoke up. "She's right, Johnny."

"No!" Johnny retorted angrily. "It's hard enough as it is. We don't need some little prima donna to wait on. Hell, how much work do you think she'd do?"

"I'm used to hard work," Kate said quietly. Without another word, she stretched her hands out on the table in front of her. The calluses that coated her palms and fingers were mute testimony to her sincerity.

Johnny shrugged his shoulders. "I don't think you even know what hard work is."

"I could do extra," Rafe broke in, his pink cheeks glowing with excitement.

Johnny whirled around angrily to face him. "Goddammit, Rafe, don't you know a woman in a mining camp is poison?"

Kate almost smiled as she heard the words They sounded just like Sandy's objections when she had asked for a job on the trail drive.

"I can protect myself." She patted the gun at her waist.

"And I'll protect her, too," Rafe promised.

Johnny's black scowl was still doubtful, but he turned slowly toward his cousin, a questioning look on his face. Bill was silent for a few minutes as he pondered the problem. Kate could catch no hint of what he was thinking from his expression. She was as surprised as the others when he finally spoke up.

"Seems to me we're barely making it now with two claims. If we have to cut down our base of operations, we're through."

"All right." Johnny said reluctantly, then turned to glare with open hostility at Kate. "But if it gets too rough for you, you have only yourself to blame."

The claims that Rafe and the two cousins had staked for themselves were not in Murphys, but in Angel's Camp, some ten or twelve miles to the west The four new partners decided to remain overnight in town before beginning the hard, hilly trek back to camp in the morning Kate rose early the next day, and after a hearty breakfast she made her way to the general store, where she had agreed to meet the others. She felt a moment's anxiety as she laid the rest of her money on the rough wooden counter to pay her share of the grub-stake, but she forced herself to shrug off her nervousness with a smile. After all, she had to commit herself sooner or later. Now was as good a time as any.

The road that led to Angel's Camp was steep and rocky, but Kate enjoyed the rugged climb. The crisp mountain air felt brisk and refreshing on her cheeks, and the majestic beauty of the adjacent Sierras gave the countryside an aura of serene purity. Surely, she told herself hopefully, Angel's

Camp was going to be a pleasant place to live. With a name like that, it almost had to be.

Kate knew, of course, that the name of the mining camp was hardly the result of some heavenly instinct, but referred rather to Henry Angel, one of Colonel Stevenson's New York regiment. It was Angel who had first established a trading post at the junction of Angel's Creek and Dry Creek to serve the miners who arrived to pan for gold. Still, no matter where it had come from, the name seemed to Kate a good omen, and she was filled with high hopes as they approached the camp.

But the instant they drew close enough to see the area clearly, Kate felt her hopes dashed to the ground. What a fool she had been to commit herself so deeply, spending all of her money, without taking time to see what she was letting herself in for. Angel's Camp, indeed! It should have been Devil's Pit, for surely it was the worst hellhole she had ever seen.

The claims were small and close together, and the adjacent free space was limited and rocky, forcing hundreds of men to crowd into a cramped, compact area, fighting with their neighbors for decent space to pitch a tent. Rats and lice ran rampant throughout the camp, and the stench of garbage and urine filled the air.

Fortunately, the spot the three young men had found to erect their tent was relatively decent. Although it was a fair hike from their claim, it was yards away from their nearest neighbor, and rested on relatively flat earth. Best of all, it was upwind of most of the other tents.

After glancing at the small, flimsy canvas structure, Kate quickly decided it would be impractical, if not downright immoral, to try to crowd into the cramped space with three members of the opposite sex. Fortunately, there was enough space beside it to erect a structure of her own.

Thank heaven for her Indian training, she thought gratefully, as she set out with Rafe's hatchet for the woods. It took her less than an hour to hew half a dozen ralatively smooth poles for herself and drag them back to camp. The boys watched curiously as she skillfully began to erect the framework of a tepee. They said nothing as they watched her lash the poles together, then cover them with blankets from her saddle roll, but when she had finished, she saw that even Johnny was beginning to look at her with newfound respect. She knew he was reevaluating her worth as a partner. By early evening, she had managed to win at least a grudging acceptance from him.

While Johnny was impressed with her willingness to work—and with the fact that she wasted no time whining or complaining about the ugly, primitive conditions—she knew it was her skill at the campfire that finally won him over. As she watched the three young men struggling to light the perpetually soggy twigs that made up their fire she decided it was time to take them in hand. Remembering the old Indian tricks she had learned, she taught them how to find the driest wood, choosing the best twigs and branches with great care. It was no time at all before she had a warm, pleasant fire burning before the tent.

"Well it's not as bad as I thought it would be," Johnny admitted reluctantly. as she heaped their plates high with rashers and an ample portion of hardtack fried in grease "Maybe it will work out." He turned to look at her thoughtfully, his eyes taking in the glow of her cheeks and the stray curls that crept becomingly from beneath her hat. The intensity of his gaze unnerved her. "Maybe you and me should join up together—just for a while, you understand."

Aghast Kate stared at him "Do you mean . . . ?" She couldn't bring herself to say the words aloud. What kind of woman did he think she was, anyhow? Some kind of cheap harlot?

"Sure " He grinned broadly, stuffing a big bite of hardtack into his mouth. "You need a man to protect you. Why not me?"

"I can protect myself." Kate's hand slipped down automatically to her gun She had done her own fighting before. She could do it again, if need be. She was not going to ask for any man's protection again—especially not at such a cost.

"Have it your own way." A dark frown crossed his features. "But you'll be sorry. Comes the time you need a man, don't look to me for help."

"Don't worry, I won't! I don't need you."

"Oh, you'll need me, all right," he predicted darkly. "That is, if you last that long. Most likely, though, you'll pack up and leave in a day or two. I don't think you're going to like it here."

Not like it here, Kate thought later in the dark solitude of her miniature tepee. Why, that was the understatement of all time. She didn't dislike it here, she *hated* it. She hated listening to the sound of guttural snores coming from dozens of tents around them, hated the soggy feel of the rain-drenched earth that never seemed to dry completely. But it was a hatred she would have to endure, for she had no choice. Now that she had spent her last cent on supplies, she would have to see it through.

In the bright light of morning, she saw the owners of many of the snores that had kept her awake the night before, but except for a few of their closest neighbors, the men passed back and forth in her range of vision with the anonymity of large-city dwellers. They were too tired, Kate realized, and too suspicious of each other, to form even the most cursory of friendships. To her surprise, even though Mike Pritchett and his cohorts were frequent visitors to Angel's Camp, they, too, maintained the same aloofness as the others, as if to prove their bullying was nothing more than an insubstantial wave of hot air.

Only one man—Mr. Herrick—seemed to stand out from the others. Kate never learned his other name. It was only "Mr. Herrick," but it suited him so well that it was a long time before she even thought to wonder at this strange bit of polite formality in such a savage, brutal camp. Mr. Herrick was their nearest neighbor, and except for Rafe, who had all the eagerness of a puppy dog, and perhaps Johnny and Bill, he was Kate's only friend.

She took to him instantly. Perhaps because he, too, was English, and his clipped, precise accent reminded her of the clean purity of the countryside of home; or perhaps because he had been ill for a long time and was by now almost completely helpless. In the morning, when all the men shouldered their tools and moved off to work their claims, Mr. Herrick had to remain alone in camp, sitting in front of his tent. He would be in the same place each evening when they returned.

At first, Kate wondered how he managed to live, but soon she saw rough, seemingly unapproachable miners from nearby tents slipping him an occasional handful of biscuits or a plate of rabbit stew. It was not long before she found herself doing the same thing. It was a constant source of amazement for her to see these simple gestures of humanity in an otherwise inhumane world. It was as if, in Mr. Herrick's illness, the other miners had all caught a sense of their own vulnerability. Perhaps the food they brought him was like the primitive sacrifices savages made to the gods—a kind of bribe that they at least might be spared the cruel vagaries of fate.

"What's wrong with him?" Kate asked Rafe one day. To her surprise, the young man turned bright pink and began to choke and stammer, as if the explanation was unsuitable for her feminine ears. Only when she insisted could he force himself to stammer out the single word: dysentery.

Dysentery. Poor Mr Herrick Kate had watched many of the men suffer from it, and it seemed both painful and horribly debilitating. Still most of them seemed to recover after a few days or at worst a few weeks, but with Mr. Herrick, all the medications urged on him by concerned neighbors seemed to accomplish little.

"Shouldn't you go back to Sacramento?" Kate asked him many times. "You could get proper medical treatment there."

"Nonsense, my dear," he would tell her with a falsely cheerful smile. "It will go away in time."

And so Mr. Herrick stayed, sitting patiently in front of his tent every morning as the others left. It nearly broke Kate's heart to look at the hope in his eyes, as though he really thought that somehow by evening he would finally be better. Sometimes his eagerness was contagious, and she almost began to believe he was right, but then she would catch a glimpse of the other men's faces, their eyes purposefully averted so they wouldn't have to look at him, and she knew he was not going to get better.

After her first day on the diggings Kate understood why Mr. Herrick did not even make the feeblest effort to work his claim. In his debilitated condition, he could not possibly manage any but the lightest work—and nothing on the diggings was light! Kate quickly realized Johnny had been right when he told her she didn't even know what hard work was.

The site of their claim was well up on the hillside, at least thirty or forty yards from the river. Earth from the claim had to be carried in sacks down a steep, dangerous path to the river, where it was emptied into a cradle for washing. Kate was not expected to help carry the earth, for it was too laborious a task, but she had to take her turn at the pick and shovel so that each man could have a chance to "rest" at the relatively easy job of rocking the cradle.

Struggling to break up the rock with the pick was hard work, and at first Kate looked forward with eagerness to the light layers of dirt and sand that often covered it. Soon, however, she learned to dread them, for they had to be discarded as worthless. Only the heavy rock bore fruitful returns, and she found herself watching for it hopefully, prying it out of the resisting earth and breaking it into fine pieces that could be shoveled into a bag and carried down to the river.

Once at the riverside the bags were emptied into heavy cradles for the deceptively simple job of floating away the useless gravel and dirt. At first, Kate thought she would enjoy the job, for it looked as if it would be both simple and pleasant, but she soon learned that, like anything else in mining, it was short on amusement and long on hard work.

Her arms ached from rocking the cradle nearly as much as they had from working with the pick. To her surprise, she found it incredibly difficult to master the smooth, rhythmic movements required to swing the heavy cradle with one hand while scooping water into it with the other. Too violent a motion, she quickly discovered, would push the fine gold over the cleats in the bottom of the cradle, and it would be lost forever; but too gentle a motion would hold the dirt behind the cleats, packing it in and clogging up the entire machine. Kate learned to curse every bit as well as any man in camp as she stood in the water, her clothes cold and soggy, trying to master the perfect rhythm that would enable her to finish the work efficiently.

Only after the earth had been washed thoroughly in the cradles did the work become relatively easy, but Kate was not allowed to assist in that, for it required more skill than she had yet learned. When she had finished her long, wet stint with the cradles, all that was left for her was to scoop out the heavy black sand that remained behind the cleats and set it carefully aside. It was in this sand that the gold was to be found.

It was usually Bill, or sometimes Johnny, who would sit by the river's edge with a tin pan in his hands. After he put a handful of dark sand into the pan, he would tilt it into the river to admit water, then tilt it back again to let the water float out, carrying the lightweight sand with it. The heavier gold would sink to the bottom. This operation would be repeated with extreme care several times, until the gold that remained in the pan was nearly clean. Then he would set the gold on a plate in the sun to dry. The remaining sand could be cleaned off easily by blowing on it lightly, leaving only pure gold to be poured into a buckskin.

A full bushel of earth and stones was the usual load that was carried down the steep hill. Even though they dug and washed as many as seventy to seventy-five bushels a day, they seldom found gold enough between them to make up more than five or six dollars' worth. It was discouraging work, and Kate often found herself wondering why she hadn't listened to Sandy's advice.

The days passed slowly into weeks. Kate was not even sure when she began to be aware that the shortened days were growing colder and colder, and the leaves on the trees were beginning to be tipped in yellow. Soon it would be winter, she thought with a cold dread. She didn't want to be caught in a makeshift tepee in the foothills when the mountain snows began to fall, but she knew there was nothing she could do about it. She had spent everything she had for her grubstake; yet, they had barely made enough to keep going. She had no money to move on, even had she known where to go.

The cold autumn days and nights were hard on everyone, but they were especially cruel for Mr. Herrick. Every night, all night long, Kate could hear the moans that escaped from his lips, and her heart ached for him, even though she knew there was nothing she could do to help him. Each morning as she shouldered her tools and headed for the rocky riverbank, she tried to give him a cheerful smile of farewell, but the tense muscles in her face betrayed her, and the look came out more of a grimace. Each time, she was sure it was the last time she would see Mr. Herrick; yet, each evening when she came back, she would find him seated in the darkening shadows, eager to greet her and ask how her day had gone.

Until, finally, one day he was not there.

Kate did not think too much about it at first. When she did not see him seated on a blanket in front of his small tent, she assumed he had just gone inside to sleep. She would not disturb him, she decided. The rest would do him good.

She had come up early to put the rabbit in the pot and begin the stew. And about time, too, she told herself, wrinkling her nose in disgust. It was beginning to smell perfectly dreadful. When the men first showed her how they prepared the wild rabbits they were sometimes lucky enough to shoot, she had been downright shocked. It was the French style, they told her, but she could hardly bring herself to believe it.

The rabbit was kept hanging in the open air for several days, until it was tender and blown by the bees and wasps that swarmed over it. After only a few hours, it began to stink, and as time went on, the stench grew truly vile. Still, Kate had to admit, when it was finally cooked, the result was tasty and succulent.

When the boys came back and the stew was beginning to smell a bit more tempting, Kate began to worry about Mr. Herrick. Even the hearty fragrance of rabbit and herbs had failed to draw him from his tent. Anxiously she sent young Rafe to check on him. The minute the boy returned, she knew by the stunned, sick look on his face what had happened.

She shouldn't have sent the boy, Kate scolded herself angrily. She should have gone herself. He was not yet hardened toward the cruel ways of this savage land. He had not yet steeled himself to face untimely death.

The next day was gray and cold. The site the men had chosen for Mr Herrick's grave was a far, lonely spot, way up on the side of a hill. It embittered Kate to think that his body would be so far removed from the hub of busy activity he had given his life to stay in Still she knew it could be no other way. Land nearer the camp was far too valuable to waste on a mere corpse Maybe it was better this way anyhow, she reminded herself. She would hate to think that someday Mr Herrick's grave might be violated because a rich strike had been found nearby.

The preacher the men found for the burial was a far cry from what Kate thought a man of the cloth should be. In fact, she had her doubts about his validity, but he was known in the camp as the Preacher, and that was enough for the men. He had once been an important minister back East, Rafe told her, but then the gold fever struck, and he succumbed to the evil temptations of the flesh.

Taking one look at the man Kate decided his problem was not so much gold fever as drink but she was careful to say nothing to the others gathered at the graveside. She did not want to tarnish Mr Herrick's last rites, such as they were, with quarreling or bitterness.

Only when she looked around at the miners, many of them strangers to her, and saw that their hands were engaged, not with hymnals but with bottles did she begin to grow angry.

"I suggest we get on with the service," she told the Preacher tartly.

The man turned to look at her with a puzzled expression on his face Disgustedly Kate realized from the glazed look in his eyes that the nearly full bottle he had clutched in his fingers was not his first that day Obviously the man was too far gone to be of any use. If Mr. Herrick was going to have any kind of service at all, it would be up to her.

"Give me your prayer book " she whispered quickly.

"Prayer book?" Pathetically the Preacher began to search his pockets. patting them hopefully, one after the other, until it was obvious to everyone that he was not going to succeed in his task.

Dear heaven, Kate thought desperately, what was she to do now? She had attended only a few funeral services in her life, and she could barely remember any of the words she had heard. Still, she had to say something.

"Let us pray." She was surprised at how loud and clear her voice sounded, as if she really felt the confidence she projected.

To her surprise, every rough and shaggy head bowed obediently at the sound of her voice. Perhaps the nearness to even the barest semblance of a religious service had shocked them back, for the moment at least, to the remembrance of gentility.

She felt herself begin to panic in the heavy silence that followed her words. Dear God, why couldn't she remember at least something from the services for the dead?

"Almighty God, we are gathered together here in thy holy sight . . ." Oh, no, that was all wrong. Surely that was from the marriage ceremony. "We are gathered together here to bid our last farewell to a good and faithful friend, Mr. Herrick, whom thou in thy infinite wisdom has seen fit to take from us."

That wasn't right either. Why couldn't she remember the words of the Anglican service she knew Mr. Herrick would have liked? "In the midst of life, we are in death." There, that was better. Those were the right words. She was sure they were. "In the midst of life, we are in death. The Lord giveth, and the Lord taketh away. Blessed be the name of the Lord.

"Man that is born of woman hath but a short time to live, and is full of misery. He cometh up and is cut down like a flower. He fleeth as it were a shadow and never continueth in one stay."

Goodness, how had she ever managed to remember all that? She tried desperately to force more words from her memory, but fight as she would to drag them forth, they would not come. Sensing the men's restlessness in the growing silence, she concluded lamely, "May God bless you and grant you his eternal peace."

Leaning down, she picked up a handful of loose earth and tossed it lightly on the blanket-clad corpse in his cold grave. "Earth to earth, ashes to ashes, dust to dust, in the sure and certain hope of resurrection through Christ Jesus our Lord."

There. That was the best she could do. She knew it was not very good, but she had a feeling Mr. Herrick would have understood.

"Amen."

"Amen," the voices echoed, a rich baritone chorus in the

midst of dark, fragrant pine trees. For a brief instant Kate had an illusion of beauty and peace, but it was quickly shattered as the men, breaking out of their solemn mood, clapped each other on the back and passed their bottles back and forth in a rare show of generosity. Kate watched in bitter anger as they laughed and made coarse jokes while they stumbled drunkenly down the hill.

The hillside suddenly seemed incredibly lonely as she stood by herself and looked down at the solitary grave. Was this all it came to in the end? Only a rocky grave on an alien hillside, far from the fertile green fields and peaceful streams of home?

Was this what would become of her, too? Was this all she would find in the end? A lonely, poorly marked grave on some cold and rocky slope with none to mourn or even note her passing? Suddenly the loneliness seemed to tear her body apart, and her heart ached so much she thought she could not bear it. Suddenly she felt an intense longing to return home. Home to Jason, to wrap herself once again in the warmth of his arms, even if she should die for it. Home, even to her father, despite the ugliness and hatred that had separated them so cruelly. The loneliness curled itself up in her body like a giant parasite, eating away at her soul, and all at once she knew it was too much for her. She knew she did not have the strength to go through life as Mr Herrick had, a lonely and solitary figure, with neither friends nor family to belong to.

The desperate loneliness followed her into the dark, still night, until she felt as if she could not bear the solitude of her tent a minute longer. The light raindrops that trickled through the thin blankets set up a constant pattering sound that seemed to intensify the lonely beating of her heart. Finally, as the agony closed in on her, shutting her into the ugly darkness of the tent, it began to stifle her until she was afraid she wouldn't be able to breathe anymore. She knew she had to get out of there.

Pulling off her sodden clothes, dripping with the moisture that had penetrated her flimsy shelter, she hurriedly tugged on dry jeans and pulled another shirt from beneath the rubber sheet where she kept her supplies. Covering her shivering body as swiftly as she could, she rushed outside into the cold night air.

Even the light raindrops and the cold, crisp air felt good after the stifling confinement of her tent. She glanced up at the full moon as it struggled to peek out from behind the heavy clouds that half-covered it, delighting in the clean purity of the golden-white orb as it hung suspended in the dark sky. Making her way through the shadowy forms of tents and rough huts toward the edge of the camp, Kate sought a place where she would not feel choked by the filth and ugliness around her.

Tomorrow she would leave this place, she promised herself. She wouldn't worry about money, or even about where she was going. She would just get on her horse and ride away. Anyplace had to be better than this.

She had nearly reached the edge of the camp when she heard a strange sound behind her. For an instant it sounded like an ugly, guttural chuckle, but she wasn't sure. In the midst of all the snores and pattering rain, it was hard to tell.

Whirling around with instinctive caution, she was appalled to see the ugly features of Mike Pritchett leering at her. Quickly she reached down to clutch the gun at her side.

And then she remembered. It wasn't there!

Dear God, what a fool she had been. When she had thrown off her wet clothes, hurriedly pulling on dry ones, she had forgotten to pick up her weapons from the ground where she had tossed them. It was the first time she had gone out without either her knife or her gun. It was the first time she had ever been so careless, but once was enough!

Sick with horror, she watched a foul grin of amusement spread across the man's coarse features. His gross red lips gleamed expectantly from behind the dark hair of his beard. Slowly he began to move toward her.

33

The grin on Pritchett's ugly, leering face broadened as he watched the look of fear in Kate's eyes. "Now, ain't that jest like a woman?" he drawled, punctuating his words with a guttural laugh. "I jest knew you'd fergit your gun one o' these times. Jest took a little waitin', that's all."

"You mean you've been lying in wait for me? Every night?" Kate was horrified. It had never occurred to her that Pritchett was capable of such cool, subtle calculation.

"Every night," he admitted. "Now I got me what I want."

Whirling around swiftly, Kate began to race down the path away from him, certain that her agile grace would let her outrun him To her amazement, he didn't even try to pursue her. She hadn't gone more than twenty yards when she realized why. At the sides of the path. hidden deep in the shadows of tents and hovels, stood Pritchett's two henchmen, Mac and Sammy, effectively cutting off her escape. Glancing around desperately, Kate searched for some other way through the crowded maze of dwellings, but she quickly realized it was hopeless. She was trapped.

"God damn you," she cried. spinning around to face Pritchett again. "What are you going to do to me?"

"Shit, if you was a man, I'd kill you sure for messin' with a claim I wanted. Hell, I still might . . . but I aim to have me a little fun first."

He signaled to his two henchmen, and Kate turned quickly to face them as they closed in on her. She waited, her body tense, until they had almost reached her, then thrust her knee violently upward, aiming with all her force at Mac's groin. Catching the movement out of the corner of his eye, Mac pulled himself aside quickly, taking the blow on his thigh. Sammy wasted no time hurling his arm roughly around her shoulders, pinioning her body back tautly against his With a loud cry of rage and frustration, Kate bent her head forward, sinking her teeth into his forearm.

Though her teeth ripped through the fabric of his shirt and cut into his flesh, Sammy did not release his hold for an instant. Even when a bright stream of red began to pour through Kate's lips, trickling down on her breast and belly, he managed to hold the viselike lock of his strong arm. It was only a second before she could feel Mac's powerful fingers grasping a handful of her hair, pulling her head back painfully, until she could no longer hold the grip of her sharp teeth.

"Well, hell, will ya look at that?" There was laughter in Pritchett's voice that matched the ugly grin half-hidden by his beard. "Get her shirt off, Mac. I want to see what I got."

Kate struggled frantically as she felt rough hands jerking crudely at the collar of her shirt, ripping it forcefully away from her body. The buttons gave almost instantly, and Kate heard herself cry aloud in anger and shame as the fabric pulled away from her breasts, leaving them exposed to the evil leer of the gross man who stood in front of her, his breath now coming in short, heavy pants.

As the shirt fell away from her body, Kate was appalled to hear an audible sound rise from the hordes of men who had gathered around, creeping out of the shadows to stare at her torment. To Kate, the sound they made as they watched the pale moonlight caress her soft ivory skin and firm full breasts seemed halfway between a collective grunt and a moan of expectation. She shuddered in horror as she realized that Pritchett had accomplished just what he had intended. If he had simply dragged her into his tent, determined to keep her for himself, there was always the ghost of a chance that one of the men might decide to help her. This way, they were all on Pritchett's side. They were ready, even eager, to help him satisfy his lust, hoping he would throw the leavings to them.

"Ain't near so skinny as she looks, is she?" a loud voice called out. Kate realized with mounting despair that it belonged to one of the onlookers. When she heard an answering laugh rise up from the crowd, she knew they were all waiting, tense and expectant, for a chance to abuse her soft body with their own.

"Swine!" she screamed furiously, praying that her anger could somehow shame them into helping her. Instead, she heard only muffled sounds of excitement, as avid and intense as the blood lust that rose from fox hunters at the moment of the kill.

Pritchett leered at her obscenely. "Pull her pants down," he cried. There was a roar of approval from the crowd. "I can't fuck her with her pants on."

"No!" Kate shrieked. Dear God, this couldn't be happening to her. It had to be a nightmare, a terrible, hideous nightmare, and she would wake up soon, tears on her cheeks, her body wet with sweat. She could not endure this—not the pain or the shame. It was more than anyone could bear.

She struggled desperately as she felt rough hands tearing at the heavy denim fabric of her jeans, but they were too strong for her, and soon they had managed to drag her naked body, kicking every inch of the way, down into the mud and slime of the path. They pinned her shoulders to the ground easily, pressing her down tightly, but they could not control the wildly kicking feet, still incongruously clad in boots, that flailed viciously at anyone who came near.

"Get her legs," Pritchett shouted shrilly to the onlookers, too cowardly to risk his own manhood at the sharp leather points of her boots. "Anyone what holds her down can fuck her when I'm through."

A handful of men stepped forward eagerly at his words,

each protecting the swelling mass that protruded from the crotch of his pants with one hand while he tried to grab at her feet with the other. They stepped back quickly enough when they heard the thick heel of her boot connect with a sickening crunch against one man's jaw.

"Hell she's a reg'lar wildcat, ain't she?" one of them said in awe. For an instant it looked as if there would be no more volunteers.

But that hope was quickly shattered. "You get one leg. I'll get the other," a familiar voice cried out. With horror, Kate looked up to see the hard, determined eyes of Johnny Johnston. *But if it gets too rough for you, you have only yourself to blame*, he had warned her once. It looked like he meant what he said.

"You should have let me have you before," he told her. "When I first wanted you. None of this would have happened if you were my woman." She could hear the anger and vindictiveness that mingled with the lust in his voice. He reached down and grabbed her ankle fearlessly in his strong hands, ripping her boot off before he pulled her leg down into the mud.

She struggled so desperately to tear her leg free from Johnny's brutal grasp that she did not even notice the man who approached from the other side until it was too late. Feeling stout fingers around her ankle, she tried to lash out at her anonymous attacker, but he was too strong for her, and it was only seconds before she felt herself being pinned helplessly to the ground. Filled with anger, she turned toward her new tormentor. The instant she saw him, her blood ran cold with shock and disgust.

"Dear God, Rafe . . . not you!"

Kate closed her eyes in sick horror. This was the worst thing yet. It was foul enough to have her body violated by strangers—but by a friend? That was ugly beyond endurance.

"I never had a woman before," he told her. "I can't help it. I just got to."

There was a pleading sound in his voice that Kate could hardly believe. How could he be pleading with her when she was the one whose body was about to be torn apart by foul rapists? Summoning a last, frantic burst of energy, she pulled her leg back violently, trying desperately to wrench it free so she could smash her bare heel into Rafe Foster's baby-pink face.

"Don't fight so hard," Rafe begged, as he dug his fingers

into her leg, struggling to maintain his hold. "You'll only get hurt."

She'd only get hurt? Dear heaven, what did he think they were doing to her now? Did he think the pain of a few more bruises on her leg would matter after she felt the searing agony of rent flesh as man after man entered her unwilling body? Did he think even that pain could compare to the agony of the spirit she would suffer as she was forced to endure their cruel degradation?

And yet, in the end, there was no pain, either of the body or of the spirit, for the sick disgust that rose in her soul finally overwhelmed her, and she felt with relief the deepening blackness that drifted over her, easing her tortured mind mercifully away from consciousness. Only the haunting, tormented dreams that racked her unnatural sleep and were to stay with her for the rest of her life bore witness to the degradation she endured as friend and foe alike compensated for their weaknesses and the embittered failures of their lives in the battered, bleeding flesh of her body.

It was hours before she woke, and when she did, she found herself alone. She could see by the dim morning light that filtered through rents and tears in the shabby canvas that she was in an unfamiliar tent, but at first she could not remember where she was or what had happened to her. Her mind was a blank, a gray, fuzzy blank, and for some reason she could not yet comprehend, she could not will herself to bring her thoughts into focus. Only as she became aware of the pain, the sharp, thrusting pain that jabbed between her legs, did she remember what had happened the night before.

Choking back her sobs, she felt once again the full terror and humiliation of the vile acts she had been subjected to, not only by Pritchett and his henchmen, but by her own friends as well. It was not the pains of her body that tormented her, for she knew that time would apply its soothing balm to all wounds of her flesh. But how could she ever find relief for the wounds of her spirit and heart? What could ease the pain of her soul?

Kate forced herself to move her arms tentatively, and was surprised to find that they hardly hurt at all, despite the bruises that had turned them into a nearly solid sheet of black and blue. With her legs, however, it was a different matter, for even when she tried to move them only an inch or two, she felt sharp pains shoot through her inner thighs. Looking down at them, she gaped in horror at the mass of congealed blood, thickened with semen, that had caked on her skin and drenched the earth beneath her naked body. She could not even wash the vile stuff from her body, for there was no clothing in the tent, and she dared not walk outside nude, not in the midst of those sex-starved maniacs.

She did not know how long she waited in the tent alone, but the sun must have been reaching its peak before she heard a noise that warned her her privacy was about to be invaded. Anxiously she looked up as the flap of the tent opened and Mike Pritchett stepped in, his head bowed to keep his floppy black hat from scraping against the low roof.

"Well, now, ain't that a purty sight?" he said, a broad grin spreading across his homely features as he leered down at the bruised and battered body lying drenched in its own blood in the dirt at his feet. He had a mass of shiny red satin clutched in his hand. As he tossed it casually to the ground, Kate saw that it was a cheap, poorly cut dress, the kind that only a whore would wear. "That's the kind of dress you'll have from now on." He chuckled. "The only kind. But don't put it on jest yet." His hands slipped down to his waist, beginning to unfasten his belt buckle.

"Oh, no," Kate whispered, horrified. Not again. She couldn't bear it if he touched her again. "Please don't." To her embarrassment, she began to whimper like a beaten puppy.

"Now, lookee here, Miss High-and-Mighty," he roared furiously as he sank to his knees beside her. "You belong to Mike Pritchett now, get it? You do what you're told, and no whining." He punctuated his words with a sharp blow on the side of her head.

Kate screamed in pain, but instead of arousing his pity, the sound only angered him more. Ripping his belt furiously from his trousers, he brought it whistling across the naked flesh of her belly. Kate felt her body jump convulsively in pain, but she bit her lip to keep from screaming. She knew it would only make him hit her again.

She held her breath in an agony of terror, watching him with the belt in his hand, sure that he had not yet finished the painful tortures he intended to inflict on her before once again humiliating her flesh with his own. She saw him raise his hand again, swiftly, surely, when to her amazement he stopped, the sharp strip of leather still poised in the air. His eyes were glittering with greed. Even when she realized he was staring at her earlobes, it still took her a moment to remember the pair of dainty emeralds that glistened against the ivory pallor of her skin.

"Hell, those must be worth a fortune," he cried, triumphant gloating ringing in his voice. Kate cringed as she saw his hand reach toward her, steeling herself against the agonizing pain she knew she would feel when the delicate trinkets were ripped brutally from her ears.

Kate did not dare cry out in the searing pain that wrenched her body, but she felt a flood of fury course through her veins as she saw him toss the earrings to the floor beside her, smugly confident that he would be able to retrieve them when he had worked his brutal way with her once more. As she felt his bulky weight on top of hers, pressing his way through the clotted blood that matted her hair, half-sealing the entrance of her body against him, she knew she could endure it no longer. He could beat her again if he wanted—or even kill her—but she was not going to suffer this shame any longer. Desperately she pulled her hands up to his chest, and with all her strength tried to heave him away from her.

"What the hell?" he muttered furiously, pulling away from her for an instant as he drew his hand back to send another crushing blow against the side of her face. At just that instant, she caught sight of the knife that had always been stuck casually in his belt. It had fallen to the side, just inches away from her hand. Pritchett was so engrossed in his own lust and his own anger that he did not even notice what she was doing.

Her hand moved automatically, without an instant's hesitation. She reacted not from an instinct for escape or even the stronger instinct of self-preservation. Instead, she felt only an overwhelming instinct of pure hatred. There was no compassion in her, no thought of the life she was about to take. She did not try to aim at his chest, where a rib might deflect the sharp blade, but buried it instead in the deep flesh at the side of his neck.

A strange gurgling sound poured from his throat as she buried the blade up to the hilt. For a second he did not move; then his eyes glazed over and his weight began to sink down heavily on top of her. Blood gushed from his wound, spilling over Kate's body as she pushed him away from her and began to rise slowly to her feet.

For an instant she stood solemnly over the body of the man she had just killed, staring down at him with a calmness that would have amazed her had she not been too shocked to be able to think clearly. Only after a minute or two did she turn and move slowly toward the corner of the tent where

Pritchett had tossed the red satin dress he had brought for her. The sleekness of the cheap fabric felt almost slimy against her body as she pulled it up over her naked skin.

The dress fit well enough, but it was so sleazy and vulgar that Kate cringed to feel the cool touch of it. Even in that brutal mining camp, even after what had happened to her the night before, she could not bear to walk out in the sunlight looking so completely like a harlot. With a cool detachedness she never dreamed she possessed, she stepped over to the corpse of the man she had just killed, kneeling calmly beside him as she unfastened the buttons of his red flannel shirt and tugged it from his body. Oblivious of the warm, sticky blood that saturated the collar and upper part of the garment, she slipped it on over the hated dress and stepped quickly to the door of the tent.

When she peered outside, there was no one in sight, neither the other miners, though that was hardly unusual in the middle of a working day, nor, more surprisingly, Pritchett's two henchmen. No doubt the foul beast had sent them off on some trumped-up errand so he could have her all to himself. Well, so much the better, she thought with grim determination. With Mac and Sammy out of the way, she would have a better chance to escape.

Kate glanced quickly around the silent camp, noting to her relief that someone had tied a tired old nag to a tree just a few yards away. The poor animal looked as if it could barely move, much less give her a good swift race should she need it, but it was the best she had. Perhaps if she was fast enough about it, she would be able to leap on his back and make her way out of the camp before anyone realized she was gone.

Without even looking back to see if anyone had spotted her, Kate ripped the reins from the brittle branch of the tree and tossed them over the startled horse's head. With an almost superhuman effort she managed to pull herself up onto the animal's bare back without even a rock or stump to stand on. Letting her dress ride up nearly to her waist, she managed to get a firm seat on the horse. As she kicked it sharply in the ribs with her bare heels, she was relieved to feel it give an abrupt start, then begin to gallop clumsily toward the woods.

She did not attempt to make her way to the road, for she knew she would be an easy target there. Instead, she kept to the woods, listening with almost unbearable tension for the sound of pursuit. To her surprise, although she could hear everyday noises drifting up from the camp, now well beneath her on the wooded hillside, there were no sounds of hoofbeats or even the heavy clumping of pursuing footsteps. Perhaps she had been lucky after all. Perhaps no one had seen her hasty flight, or learned its grisly cause. Even if they had, she reasoned, they still might not pursue her. Pritchett had been an unpopular bully, and no one besides his two henchmen would be likely to mourn his death. Besides, most of the men in camp were at heart decent and even sensitive. She was sure that the cold light of morning brought with it for most of them nothing but sharp stings of conscience for their vicious cruelty of the night before. Perhaps if anyone had spotted her escape, it was someone who was actually glad to see she had gotten away.

Still, she dared not take the chance. As soon as the woods grew thicker and the underbrush began to catch at the horse's hooves, she pulled it to a stop and slid down onto the ground. Slipping the bit out of its mouth, she slapped it sharply on the rump.

Kate watched the horse lumber off with mixed emotions. It would be hard walking on bare feet, but a horse was too much of a hindrance in the woods. Besides, the poor old nag was so tired and scrawny, it would be nearly useless to her. It would never be able to keep up the pace she had to set.

The sun was already beginning to tinge the late-afternoon sky with pale hints of pink before she dared at last to stop beside a cooling mountain stream to cleanse the foul residue of men's lust that still clung to her legs and thighs. The touch of the clear water was sharp and icy, but Kate barely noticed the cold. It was enough to luxuriate in the purifying coolness that seemed to sweep away the filth from her soul as much as from her body.

Only when she caught sight of her own reflection in the still, clear water did she feel herself begin to shiver. She barely recognized the gaunt face that stared back at her with a haggard pallor. Surely that must be another woman, she thought, a much older one, whose image was reflected on the silvery water. The woman's eyes had a strange, lifeless look about them. It was a look Kate recognized but could not place at first. Then, suddenly, she remembered what it was.

It was the same look she had seen in the eyes of the dying Indians. The look of the sheep rancher's wife. It was the look of the living dead.

In the morning, the first snows of winter began to fall, lightly at first, then heavily enough to coat the ground with a thick blanket of white. Kate tied the flannel shirt tightly around her body and slipped the long sleeves down over her hands, but there was nothing she could do about her feet. Gritting her teeth against the pain, she forced herself to trudge on through the biting snow.

Looking behind her, she was surprised to see that, like the Indians she had once pitied so long ago, she was leaving a trail of red in the clean white mantle that covered the earth.

34

JASON WATCHED THE FROTHY SNOWFLAKES SETTLE LIGHTLY on Midnight's black mane. They looked to him like tiny pieces of fragile gossamer that had fallen from a spider's delicate web. How could anything so soft and dainty be so treacherous? he wondered, then winced at the irony of his own thought. Just like a woman, he reminded himself bitterly. Just like his own enticing, exquisite wife, soft as a feather floating on the breeze, delicate as a fragile Dresden angel . . . and as treacherous as the beautiful snow-covered crests of the mountains that lay ahead.

Jason touched Midnight's side lightly with his spurs, urging the horse to a trot, even on the slippery uphill path. He did not want to chance getting caught on the ridge after nightfall. If the snow continued, the road would soon become impassable, and he would be trapped there. Jason could not help remembering the fate of one group of pioneers who had attempted to cross the Sierra Nevadas only twenty-five years before. Even now, the pass he was approaching had already begun to be known by their name—the Donner Pass.

It was well into the afternoon before Jason reached the crest and could look ahead at the long road that twisted like a white snake down the hill and into the valleys below. On a sudden impulse he turned and looked over his shoulder at the uphill route he had just left behind him. There, just as he had feared, plodding steadily but much too slowly up the winding path, was a dark form silhouetted against the brightness of the snow.

"Damn the fool," he hissed under his breath. "Why

doesn't he turn back?" Jason had known for weeks that Marc was following him, for the other man had taken no precautions to conceal his presence, but Jason had hoped he would turn back when he saw the snow begin to fall. Didn't he know he was much too far down the mountainside to attempt the crossing now? He was going to get himself killed for sure.

And why should it matter to him whether Marc lived or died? Jason asked himself bitterly. Even after all these months, he could still close his eyes and picture his wife's soft body in the arms of his friend. Why the hell should he care what happened to Marc? If he died now, it would only save Jason the trouble of having to kill him later.

Yet, even as the words crossed his mind, Jason knew there was no conviction behind them. Much as he hated his friend for touching his wife, he knew he could not blame him. Kate was a witch and a devil! When she set out to enchant a man, no power on earth could stop her. Who should know that better than he?

God, how could he ever forget? The soft, warm glow of firelight shining on pink-and-ivory skin. The fiery look of welcome in green eyes half-shut with desire. Red lips parted to join his mouth to hers. What man would have the strength to deny himself such ecstasy? God only knows, he hadn't.

If only Marc had been honest about . . . But how could he be? What chance did he have, with Jason stomping around, waving his gun, and shouting for revenge?

Jason squirmed uncomfortably in the saddle. If he was going to be fair about the whole thing, he knew he had to admit the rift with Marc was his own fault. He couldn't blame the man for responding to the lust of a cheap harlot, and he couldn't blame him for not daring to admit it, either.

He continued to watch the horse and rider far below him on the hillside, as they pushed their way with plodding determination up the long, slow trail. They seemed no closer than before, yet still they insisted on pushing forward. Jason felt an urge to cup his hands to his mouth and shout out, "There's still time to turn back," but he knew that, even if he could make himself heard, Marc would pay no attention.

Damn! It was hard to turn around and leave him. It was crazy, but he couldn't force himself to ride away. Even though he hated Marc, he couldn't leave him to face danger, and perhaps death, alone.

As Jason watched the snowflakes settling lightly in a pile of fluff on the ground, he couldn't help remembering another winter, far away and long ago. It had been cold then too, the same bitter cold, and the same relentless snows had covered the ground. Unbidden, the picture came back to his mind of a prison camp in Illinois. Men without boots or coats shivering in the subzero weather. Men racked with hunger and dysentery and exposure lying on the ground until their bodies froze in the rigid posture of death. Marc, too, lay near death, his body sweating even in the snow from the heat of the fever that left him half-unconscious in his delirium.

As long as he lived, Jason was sure he would never forget the face of that son of a bitch turncoat who kissed all the enemy asses—and betrayed not a few of his compatriots in the bargain—to weasel the food and medication he sold to his fellow prisoners.

"Well, sonny boy, you ain't got nothin' to give me. Ain't nothin' I kin do fer you," the man had drawled, his soft Southern tones sounding harsher to Jason's ears than any Yankee accent. "Why don't you write yer folks fer some cash or somethin' to trade?"

"Goddammit, you bastard. You know very well, even if I had someone to turn to, it would be too late before the money got here. Can't you see he'll die if he doesn't get that medication?"

"Ever'one's dyin' here, sonny," the man said calmly, as if there were no room left in his black heart for compassion or concern. "Might as well save the supplies for them what kin pay for 'em."

Jason had watched the look on the man's face as he strangled him. It was the first time he had ever faced anyone he had killed, but even the look of pain and fear in the man's bulging eyes did not arouse his pity. For the first time, he realized it was possible to enjoy killing a man. The medication he stole without qualms had been enough to save Marc's life.

It was hard to let go of a man, once you had saved his life, Jason thought. He was keenly aware of the irony of the situation as he watched Marc continue to climb slowly up the hill. He knew now there was no way he could ever leave him to face the dangers of that snow-covered mountain peak alone. He would have to sit silently on Midnight's back, waiting with patience for the darkness, so they could go on together. Whatever bond had grown between them in that miserable prison camp was beyond the strength of human will to break.

At last he began to understand what had driven Marc to follow him all these long weeks, what was driving him even now up the mountainside, though he risked his life to do it. The same bond was as strong for him—no stronger, for he had the debt of gratitude to add to it. Marc was no more capable than he of letting his friend ride into danger alone. And that was exactly what he was doing, Jason had to admit to himself. He was hell-bent on destroying himself, and if he had his own way, he was going to succeed.

And for what? A devious auburn-haired beauty who wasn't worth a minute of the anguish he had suffered for her! For that he had left his ranch alone, hoping a leaderless flock of loyal cowhands would keep it from falling apart. For that he had journeyed over dangerous winter roads on a mission of vengeance that would no doubt bring him nothing but justice at the end of a hangman's rope.

He should have stayed at the Triple Crown and forgotten the few months of ecstasy he had found in her treacherous arms. God knows he had tried hard enough, but even when he brought Carmelita out from Cheyenne, setting her up in splendor as the pseudo-mistress of the house in Kate's stead, he had known no peace from the thirst for vengeance that sucked all the vitality from his soul. It was inevitable that he should stay for only a few weeks—and equally inevitable, he supposed, that when he left, Marc would feel he had to follow him.

As he watched his friend drawing nearer with the maddeningly slow pace of a snail, Jason felt his body leaning forward, urging him on with the same futile effort of spectators at a horse race. Dammit, why didn't he move faster? They had to get over the ridge before dark. Wasn't that what had happened to the Donner party?

Jason tried to remember what he had heard about the Donners. George Donner had set out in 1845—no, it must have been 1846—for Sutter's Fort with a party of just under a hundred people. Fewer than half of them ever made it. From the beginning, the journey seemed to have been jinxed, Jason recalled. Every mishap that could possibly occur on a wagon train seemed to plague them. Accidents were to be expected, of course, and untimely deaths, for the trails were rough and hard, but the Donners had more than their share of them. That, added to quarrels and thieving—and bad guidance—brought them to the Sierra Nevadas too late in the season to count on a safe crossing.

Poor devils. They almost made it. They had nearly reached the crest of the mountain pass, that same pass Jason was waiting at now, but the snow had already begun to fall, and the weary and weakened pioneers were too cold to go on. Instead of pushing over the pass and heading into the valley below, they set a pine tree ablaze and made a camp to warm themselves. That was their fatal mistake. By morning, when they awoke, they found snow deep on the ground. Their mules and cattle had strayed, and they were hopelessly stranded.

Hardened as he was to suffering, Jason shuddered to think of the ordeal the pioneers endured that bitter winter. Rescue parties were sent out to bring back help, but few survived the snows and wind to reach their destinations. Fate was even crueler to those who had remained behind. Jason could not even imagine the horror the survivors must have felt, watching their friends die one by one, then knowing, with no food remaining, their only choice lay between starvation and eating human flesh.

Midnight pawed at the earth impatiently, jolting Jason back from his unpleasant reverie. "Easy, boy," he said soothingly, running his hand firmly along the dark, sleek neck. He couldn't blame him for being nervous. Even the horse must have sensed the dangers they faced, waiting immobile on a snowy mountain pass for darkness to fall.

Dusk was already heavy in the air when Marc finally approached the crest. He showed no sign of surprise when he saw Jason waiting for him.

"You should have gone on," he said quietly as he pulled up beside him. "It was dangerous to wait this long."

"You know goddamn well I couldn't go off and leave you to face this alone," Jason retorted gruffly.

"I know," his friend replied softly. Traces of a smile played with the corners of his lips, but he was careful not to let his friend see them.

"There's still bad blood between us," Jason warned.

"There shouldn't be."

"Not even when I . . . ?" Jason broke off abruptly. There was no point saying again: Not even when I found you in my wife's arms? Marc would only repeat that he was comforting her—and perhaps, for him at least, that was the truth. For Kate, no doubt, it was a different matter. "Not even when you're in love with my wife?" he continued coldly. There! Let Marc try to deny that one.

Marc looked uncomfortable for a moment, then set his jaw in a hard, firm line that matched the sternness of Jason's face. "I never said I didn't love her, Jason," he told the other man quietly. "I've loved her since the first time I saw her, and I love her still. But I've never tried to do anything about it—not since the day you decided to make her your wife—and as

390

long as she's still your wife, I never will. But I swear before God, Jason, if you're ever fool enough to let her go, I'm going to do everything in my power to win her."

"After I find her, there won't be anything left to win," Jason threatened menacingly. His brows tightened in a dark fury as he remembered Kate's beauty and how fiendishly she had betrayed him.

"Because you're going to kill her? Don't be a fool, Jason. You know you'll never go through with it."

"What the hell makes you think——?"

"Did you kill her when you found her before? When you took her with you to the sun dance?"

Jason glared at him in fury. "I didn't kill her, because I still thought she might be innocent." No, I didn't, he told himself silently. I knew what she was all the time—just like I knew about the other one—only I shut my eyes to the truth. Like a fool, I prayed she was innocent, even though I knew damned well she wasn't.

Marc caught the grim look that spread across his face as bitter memories of Celeste flooded over him, but he refused to acknowledge it. "Kate *is* innocent," he insisted. "You'll learn that when you find her."

Jason squinted at him suspiciously, realizing suddenly how much—more and more each day—his friend's features reminded him of his cousin Aaron. "When I do find her, I warn you, keep out of the way. She's my wife, and I'll decide what to do with her."

"No, Jason," Marc said quietly. "I told you I love her. I'll never let anyone hurt her—not even you."

Jason reached his hand instinctively toward his gun. "There's nothing you can do about that."

Marc kept both hands lightly on the reins. "All I ask is that you let me be there when you confront her. I want to make sure your temper doesn't run away with you. It has been known to, you know."

Jason smiled wryly at the accusation he knew he could not deny. "All right," he agreed, "but only on one condition. When the time comes, you leave your gun behind. The decision—whatever it is—has to be mine."

Marc returned the smile. "I'll unbuckle my gun belt and drop it at your feet," he promised easily.

"Hell, the snow's getting worse," Jason said abruptly. "What are we sitting here for?"

Together the men turned their impatient horses down the road and gave them their heads, letting them pick their way cautiously through the slippery snow. The sun no longer attempted to peek out from behind the heavy clouds, and soon the world was bathed in deepening gray. The nearly cloudless night was half-over before the surefooted beasts found their way to the bottom of the steep trail.

Part VI

The Long Winter

35

As Kate stared at her reflection in the gold-framed mirror, she was delighted to see her own glowing red lips curl up in a gentle smile of satisfaction. It was true she had added a touch of rouge to bring out the bright color, but it was only the faintest touch. Besides, it was so becoming, she could hardly look on the artifice as a sin. Never before, she told herself contentedly, had she looked so good.

Her long auburn hair was piled elegantly on top of her head, the curls twisted into the latest fashion, and her skin had already begun to lose the rough coarseness of months in the outdoors, regaining as if by a miracle the perfect ivory silkiness she had been so proud of. With her ravishing form draped once again in the shimmering perfection of emerald satin, she felt almost as if all the cruel memories that had bruised her heart were nothing more than a bad dream.

Only traces of freckles on her nose—freckles she knew would stay with her for the rest of her life—reminded her of long days of exposure to the blazing sun. Still, they hardly mattered now. A discreet touch of pale face powder nearly hid them from view.

Kate could hardly believe her good luck. It was as if fate had suddenly decided to make up for all the cruel tricks it had played on her, rolling up her allotment of good fortune and prosperity in one final, gigantic bonus. Glancing again at the elegant creature in the mirror, Kate had to pinch herself to believe it was really true. To think that only two weeks ago she had been shivering on a cold, rainy street corner, miserable and half-starved to death.

She had thought then that San Francisco was one of the ugliest places she had ever seen, surpassing even the squalor of the hideously misnamed Angel's Camp. Everything about the city was new, but it was a newness of buildings hastily and cheaply thrown together, of muddy, unpaved roads and arrogant horsemen who pushed their way swiftly through them, rudely spattering mud on the scurrying pedestrians.

There was a roughness about the vulgar, gaudy town that almost made Cheyenne, and even Jasper Springs, seem refined by contrast.

Kate could still remember how cold it had been. Huddling deep into a filthy doorway, she had tried futilely to keep dry in the heavy drizzle that perpetually seemed to hang over the bayside city. She remembered looking out in angry envy at the loud, brassy women who made their way confidently through the raucous crowds that lingered on the boardwalks and the edges of the muddy streets. They must have been the wives and mistresses of the newly rich, she surmised, for all the wealth in the world could not buy them even a single ounce of good taste. Every last one of them looked as if she would have been perfectly at home with her old friend Stella walking the darkened night streets of Boston.

If only she had some decent clothes, Kate thought desperately. She could easily hold her own against any of those women. In this rough society, she would not have to worry about an impeccable background or good references. If she had just one presentable dress, surely she would have no trouble finding work as a governess or shopgirl, or even as a maid. And yet, without a cent in the world, how could she ever hope to . . . ?

"Hey, girlie, wanna earn a dollar?" a coarse voice burst into her melancholy reverie.

Looking up, Kate was appalled to see a drunken face leering down at her as she sat huddled in the dingy doorway. The lewd obscenity in his eyes left no doubt as to his meaning.

"A dollar?" she said, disgusted. How dare he suggest she would be willing to sell herself for a dollar? No matter how cruelly her body had been abused, she had not sunk that low.

"Sure, baby. You look like you could use it."

To her horror, Kate found herself dwelling on his words. What could a dollar buy? she wondered. A good meal? A decent dress? Angry at herself, she brushed the thought out of her mind. Her body was no longer the chaste vessel of purity it had once been, God only knew, but she was not ready to sell it for cash.

"Get away from me, you foul, filthy beast!"

The man was so drunk, he hardly understood her words. Digging awkwardly into his pocket, he pulled out a dollar, dropping it with fumbling fingers into the mud at her feet.

"Go ahead, whore," he challenged. "Pick it up."

"Get away from me," she shrieked, suddenly frightened as she felt his drunken body lurch toward her. It couldn't be starting again, she told herself desperately, not the violence and the degradation. She couldn't stand it anymore. "Just get away and leave me alone."

He ignored her protests as his staggering body leaned down to press against hers. She fought desperately to push him away, but drunk as he was, he was still too strong for her. She had almost given up hope, when she heard a voice call out.

"Take your hands off that poor girl, you varlet!"

The voice was soft and feminine, but it held a confident, imperious note, too, as if the speaker was used to giving commands. Kate instantly recognized heavy traces of a French accent.

Kate and her attacker both looked up at once. When the man saw a fragile, daintily dressed lady, her white hair tinged with a faint touch of lavender, he began to laugh.

"Who's gonna make me, lady?" he said, slobbering, brave enough in the face of two women, one weakened and half-starved, the other too old to be a threat even to a drunk.

As if in answer to his question, a huge shadow fell over the doorway. Looking up, Kate saw the largest human being she had ever seen in her life. The man could not possibly have stood less than six-feet-six or -seven, with a mammoth girth that matched his height. He was coal black in color, and Kate nearly forgot her fear as she stared at him in fascination. She had never seen one of these strange, dark men the impetuous Americans had fought their cruel war over.

Kate's drunken assailant seemed far less curious about the black man than she. Slinking back against the wall, he began to inch his way along it until at last he was out of the giant's reach. Turning with an awkward stumble, he began to race down the street as fast as his feet would carry him.

"Thank you, John," the elderly woman said calmly. The black man turned and mounted easily to the coachman's seat of a surprisingly fashionable carriage. The woman remained where she was, staring at Kate.

As Kate stared back at her, she was aware of piercing blue eyes, as bright a color as she had ever seen, set in the midst of a face so filled with good humor it actually seemed to twinkle. The woman was considerably shorter than Kate, and of a very delicate build, but the feeling of fragility that emanated from her was heightened by the frothy white lace that seemed to float around her neck and wrists, accented as it was by the modest gray taffeta of her dress.

"Why, you poor little thing," the woman murmured sympathetically. Her eyes were clear and warm, her smile remarkably ingenuous. "*Et si belle, aussi* . . . so pretty. *Mais certainement, ma chère,* we cannot leave you here, not with all those foul villains along. *Viens, viens* . . . come with me, *ma pauvre petite.*"

Kate stared at the woman in amazement, but she did not protest as she felt herself being pulled to her feet and led toward the carriage. She couldn't understand why this kind stranger was going out of her way to help her, but she wasn't about to question her good luck. Leaning back against the soft, luxurious cushions of the carriage, she felt herself begin to relax. The sound of the heavy wooden wheels turning through the muddy streets blended pleasantly with the woman's prattle.

"*Mais, ma petite,* I have a boardinghouse. *Comme c'est grande, c'est belle* . . . so lovely, so big." Although the woman's English seemed nearly perfect, she obviously enjoyed throwing in little French phrases every now and then, which she carefully translated for Kate's benefit. Kate was too tired even to think of telling her she needn't bother, for she had had a good education and her French was nearly as fluent as a native's. Looking out of the window, she watched the ugly, dirty streets go by, one after the other, twisting and turning their way through the vulgar town. She was grateful that she could look at them from the security of the closed carriage.

"It is full of refined girls, *ma maison,*" the woman went on. "*Si elegante.* You will love them, I know. They pay me from their wages, *vous comprenez.* I think somewhere in the big house, we must find a little room for you, *eh, ma petite?*"

"But I couldn't pay you," Kate explained haltingly. "I don't have a job."

"*Non, non, ma chère,* that is not a problem," the woman told her kindly. "I will advance you a little money for some pretty clothes, then we'll find you something, *eh bien?* Don't worry, *jolie fille,* you will repay me later."

And so it was that Kate found herself in the house of Madame du Plessine, for that was her benefactress's name. True to her word, the gracious woman found a warm, pleasant room for Kate. It was not very large, but it had a pretty charm about it, and for the first time in months she began to feel comfortable and secure again.

That same small chamber, with only one tiny window looking out on the filthy, raucous street below, was all Kate was to know of the house for the first two weeks she was there. Madame de Plessine had insisted that she remain in the room, resting until she had regained her strength. Even her meals were sent up to her.

"It wouldn't do to let the other girls see you," the old woman teased her, her voice filled with warmth and humor. "Not until you have some decent clothes and your cheeks are filled again with the roses. *Sacre bleu, ma petite*, you are so pale now, *si blanche*. You would terrify the other girls if they passed you in the hall."

Kate smiled ruefully at her words. Surely she must look like a filthy little ragamuffin. No wonder Madame du Plessine did not want to suffer the embarrassment of having her seen in the hallways. But how thoughtful she was, how kind, to express it so tactfully. So warm and sincere was the woman's manner, so sweet and ingenuous her smile, that it never occurred to Kate to think that she might have some other reason for keeping her confined to her room. Never for a moment did she wonder if there was something in that house the woman did not want her to see—not yet, at least.

Kate felt no sense of menace about the house; neither had she any apprehensions about her future there, but she was intensely curious about it. She was eager to see the other rooms, and especially to meet the girls she could hear chattering and giggling on the other side of the heavy wooden door. She had been so long without companions of her own sex that she found herself hungry even for a few minutes of idle, foolish chatter.

At last, just when she had begun to feel as if she were a prisoner, even in that pretty room, the message came that she had been waiting for. Her fingers trembled with eager anticipation as she patted her fashionable curls tidily into place, preparing eagerly to go downstairs to meet the prospective employer Madame du Plessine had found for her.

Her feet fairly flew down the steps, and she found herself humming a cheerful tune as she hurried toward the little parlor at the back of the house, where she knew the tea things would already have been laid out. The eager hopefulness that rose in her breast seemed vaguely familiar in an unpleasant way, but she could not place it for a moment. When she did, she found her feet halting suddenly in place.

It was the same hopeful enthusiasm she had felt more than a year ago when she danced down the long hallway toward her father's library, certain she would be able to persuade him to let her marry Philippe. And yet, when she got there, she found instead only an ugly, unwelcome suitor.

The sudden thought brought a touch of cold foreboding to

her heart. Pushing the unpleasant comparison to the back of her mind, she continued to move, with slower steps this time, toward the small back parlor. Even before she reached the room, she was aware of the heavy, stifling aroma of over-sweet perfume.

Kate hesitated just inside the threshold, appalled by the sight of the elderly man whose bulky form spilled over the edges of the dainty parlor chair. With sinking heart she realized that the sudden cold sense of intuition that had flooded over her only seconds before had not been wrong. Her prospective employer, whoever he was, was no more than half the size of the repugnant Burton-Styles, but he was every bit as unpleasant-looking. Surely she could not be forced to work for such a disgusting creature.

And yet, what choice did she have? She was suddenly angry with herself for the dainty fussiness that made her turn up her nose at the man. How out of place it seemed in a woman who only weeks before had been nothing more than a drudge in a dirty mining camp. Besides, she could not afford to be particular, even if she could claim any right to it. She had to have a job, any job she could get. She could not go on living off Madame du Plessine's bounty forever.

If Madame saw the look of anguish on Kate's face, she said nothing about it. Rising gracefully, her bright eyes twinkling merrily, she swept over to the girl, her arms outstretched. Kate saw that the blue of her eyes had been accented by the rich blue-gray color of the expensive silk in her modest dress.

"*Bonjour, Madame,*" Kate greeted her as warmly as she could manage. She had long since learned that it pleased the woman to be addressed in French.

"But we must speak English now, Catherine," Madame reprimanded gently as she led her across the room. Kate relaxed enough to smile at the sound of her full name on Madame's lips. It had a feeling of gracious formality about it, a kind of old-world charm she had nearly forgotten. "Here is Mr. Hartwell, Catherine. He's looking for a lovely girl, just like you." Kate noticed that the little French phrases she usually affected had disappeared. Despite her fragile appearance and continued charm, she had suddenly developed a very businesslike mien.

Kate noticed that Mr. Hartwell did not attempt to rise in courtesy, or even to speak. Instead, he gaped at her as blatantly as if she were a piece of merchandise that had been offered for sale. Kate could have sworn she saw the look of lust cross his stupid face.

"Now, isn't she exactly what I promised, Mr. Hartwell?" Madame du Plessine wheedled, her voice filled with an ingratiating enthusiasm that was somehow unpleasant to hear. "Come, come, Catherine, turn around so Mr. Hartwell can see how elegant and graceful you are."

Feeling awkward and uncomfortable, Kate began to swivel around slowly, listening to Madame de Plessine extol the virtues of her tiny waist and long slender limbs, the full voluptuous curves of her hips and bust, the fiery red highlights of her shining, silken hair, and the cool, dark green of her eyes.

"I ask you, Mr. Hartwell, have you ever seen eyes so green? They are like cool, limpid pools in the deep forest."

Kate listened to Madame du Plessine with a growing sense of uneasiness. She suddenly felt as if she had been put up on the auction block like some kind of cheap harlot being offered for sale to the highest bidder. As she listened to Madame's voice drone on and on with a strangely oily quality, like a barker at a circus, she felt her previous sense of suspicion begin to turn to certainty in her breast.

Forcing herself to turn around slowly one last time, she reminded herself that no doubt there was a very good explanation for Madame's behavior. Perhaps Mr. Hartwell was looking to engage a girl for some position that would place her in view of the public.

"Why, Catherine, you mustn't blush like that," Madame teased lightly, mistaking the cause for her embarrassment. "Isn't she charming and modest, Mr. Hartwell? Now, Catherine, do come and sit on the sofa beside me and let Mr. Hartwell find out all about you."

She had just guided Kate skillfully to a position beside her on the small velvet love seat when her attention was suddenly drawn toward the doorway. Following her eyes, Kate caught sight of the little French maid, Yvonne, hovering nervously just inside the threshold, an uncertain expression on her face.

"Yes, Yvonne, what is it?"

"Oh, Madame, there's trouble in the kitchen. You'll have to come."

"Oh, dear, not now," the woman protested. Still, the expression on poor Yvonne's face was so distraught, she knew she could not possibly avoid the tiresome task. Rising quickly, she patted Kate's hand reassuringly, then hurried from the room. So deftly was the entire operation accomplished that it did not even occur to Kate to wonder if the girl had been lingering outside the door, waiting for a subtle signal from her mistress before she burst into the room.

Kate thought only of her own dismay as she found herself alone with the silent and uncongenial employer Madame du Plessine had found for her. Turning back toward the man, Kate was surprised to see that he looked almost as nervous as she. Glistening beads of sweat had formed on his forehead and begun to run in comical little streams down the broad expanse of his nose and cheeks.

Why, he's uncomfortable, too, Kate told herself, amazed at the discovery. No doubt he didn't know anything more about conducting interviews than she did. She noticed he hadn't spoken a single word since she came into the room. Perhaps it would help to get off on a good footing with him if she tried to put him at ease.

"What kind of position did you have to fill?" she asked courteously.

To her surprise, he did not attempt to answer, but only continued to stare unblinkingly at her. When he finally deigned to open his lips, all he uttered was a single word.

"Lovely!"

Kate noticed with disgust that his breath was coming in heavy pants. But aloud she only repeated her question. "I said, what kind of position do you have for me?"

He still did not answer, but pulled his bulky form from the chair and plopped it heavily beside her on the love seat. The sickeningly sweet smell of perfume that had almost overpowered her when she came into the room grew stronger, and she realized with revulsion that it emanated from his body.

"Why don't we get better acquainted?" he wheezed noisily, leaning forward until his face was only a few inches away from hers. Suddenly Kate realized why he wore the perfume. The strong stench of his foul breath mingled almost unbearably with the sweaty odor of his body. Sick from the nauseating smell, Kate closed her eyes and leaned backward as she felt a wave of faintness sweep over her.

Taking her gesture for encouragement, he pushed his gross body even farther toward hers, raising his fat fingers to thrust them abruptly down the low-cut bosom of her dress. Gasping in surprise, Kate snapped her eyes open and pulled away from him, trying to dislodge his fingers from the softness of her skin.

"Now, now, dearie," he protested as he felt her draw away from him. "You should be nice to me. I can do a lot for you."

"Sir, how dare you?" Kate cried out, clutching his arm and tugging at it frantically, until she finally managed to pull his hand out of the intimacy of her bosom. If he thought she needed a job that badly, he had another think coming! How horrified Madame du Plessine would be if she knew he had misused the hospitality of her home so vulgarly.

"Don't you know when a man is throbbing with desire for your beautiful body?" he grunted huskily. Filled with disgust, Kate suddenly realized that the man had no intention of stopping with a mere ego-raising flirtation. For an instant she was alarmed, but then she realized he was not strong enough to be any real threat to her. Besides, repulsive as he was, he was still a guest in Madame du Plessine's home, and that would be a shabby way to repay her generosity. Instead, she pressed her hands against his ample chest, pushing him back as hard as she could.

He turned out to be far stronger than she had thought. Struggle as she would, she could not manage to keep him from wedging his body tightly against hers, and she began to feel an ugly knot of fear rising in her breast. In horror, she saw his hand go down to unbutton his satin breeches. She renewed her effort to push his fat body away from hers, but he continued to hold her tightly, his obese hips writhing rhythmically as his pudgy fingers groped beneath her skirt, trying frantically to pull it up above her waist and leave her open to his attack.

Suddenly, just as she had begun to panic, realizing how grossly she had misjudged his strength, she felt his body jerk convulsively, making the love seat tremble as if it had been hit by an earthquake. Then, as abruptly as it had begun, the quivering stilled.

"Now, look what you've done," he scolded peevishly as he pulled the weight of his body off hers.

"What *I've* done?" She was aghast as she gaped at the pasty white that marred the shiny surface of her skirt. "Look at my dress. It's ruined!"

"Now, dearie, don't be angry," he coaxed, his own anger suddenly mollified. "I'll buy you another."

"I wouldn't take anything from you," she cried out, horrified. "I don't ever want to lay eyes on you again. Just get out of here."

"You're beautiful when you're angry, dearie. Your green eyes flash with fire." He sighed as his eyes settled once again on the plump contours of her breast. With no more pretense at subtlety than he had shown before, he reached out and

403

grabbed hold of her skirt, tugging at it insolently. "Be a good girl and come here."

"Really, you're too much!" she snapped angrily. Pulling her skirt out of his coarse fingers, she turned and hurried from the room. She hadn't meant to tell Madame du Plessine about his crude behavior, knowing how mortified that refined, kindhearted woman would be to learn of the cruel humiliation one of her boarders had suffered at the hands of her own guest, but she knew now she had no choice. The man's presumption was too insupportable to bear.

To her surprise, as she hurried down the hall she heard the soft sound of padding footsteps behind her. She realized with amazement that Mr. Hartwell was actually following her. Really, the man was impossible! He should have been fleeing in shame at that very moment.

Kate found Madame du Plessine, not in the kitchen, as she had expected, but in the front parlor, calmly working on a piece of needlepoint. She rose quickly, the expensive gray silk of her skirt rustling around her ankles, the instant she caught sight of Kate standing in the doorway. Her expression remained calm and placid even when she saw the rage and indignation flashing in the girl's green eyes.

"Madame du Plessine, this vile man—" Kate began, but she got no further, for Mr. Hartwell, who had followed her into the room without even pausing to button up his pants, quickly interrupted her.

"What kind of girls do you keep here, anyhow?" he whined.

What kind of girls do you keep here? Kate felt a sick chill rush into her heart at the sound of the words. There was no mistaking their meaning. *What kind of girls do you keep?* Dear heaven, Madame du Plessine could be none other than the keeper of the kind of house Kate had never even been allowed to speak of in the sheltered days of her childhood. Glancing at the woman in horror, Kate still found it hard to believe that such a sweet, demure exterior could conceal such cunning and evil.

"I warned you she'd be hard to get, Hartwell." Madame's eyes were still alight, but this time Kate could see they were glittering with malicious amusement.

"But she didn't give me a chance," he complained. "Not even a little teensy chance." His voice sounded petulant, like a spoiled child about to throw a tantrum.

"If she was a sure thing, I would have charged you the full price," the woman replied coolly. "As it is, because she isn't

404

broken in yet, you had to pay only ten dollars to have a try at her. It's not my fault you didn't succeed."

Not broken in yet? What was she that they should talk about her that way? An untamed horse from the fields?

"But I want her." He pouted and looked even more like a thwarted child as he began to stamp his feet up and down on the polished wooden floor.

"Well, go back to the parlor," the woman replied calmly. "I'll see what I can do. But if she agrees, I warn you, you'll have to pay full price."

"I'll pay anything you say. I want her."

Kate and Madame du Plessine faced each other in silence. Finally the older woman spoke.

"Well, my dear, I suggest you go back to the parlor."

Kate ignored the comment. "You sold me," she whispered, her voice barely audible in her horror.

"Hardly," the woman replied tartly. "I told you it was a job, and it was. You were free to accept or reject the man as you chose. No one held your legs apart while he raped you—a situation I daresay you are not totally unfamiliar with."

"And just because I've had some hard luck, you thought I'd let that obscene man force himself on me for a lousy ten dollars!"

"*Non, non, petite.*" Madame du Plessine chuckled, reverting again to the affectionate French endearments of their earlier camaraderie. "You're worth much more than that. Do you think I would ever have let him try if I thought you'd agree?"

"Then why—?"

"This way, I get an extra ten dollars. Besides, the new girls, they are always unpopular. They cause so much trouble, *vous comprenez?* I wanted to—how do you say it?—whet his appetite."

"I'm afraid you've whetted it for nothing," Kate replied sarcastically. "I'm not going anywhere near him."

"But of course you are, *ma chère*," the woman replied with a calmness that only added to Kate's anger and indignation.

"I'm sure I don't know what makes you think that."

"Come, come, *chérie*. You are a sensible young lady. I'm only making you a business proposition—and a very good one, at that. If you leave, you'll only have to go to one of the other houses, and most of them are not nearly so congenial."

Kate gaped at the woman in amazement. She could hardly

believe that she, Lady Catherine Devlin, the pampered daughter of British aristocracy, was actually standing there comparing merits of various brothels with a woman who, no matter how fragile and ingenuous she might look, was actually one of the notoriously evil madams of San Francisco. Of all that had happened to her since she had left home, surely this was the most ludicrous.

"It's a good business, *ma petite*," the woman told her. "I pay you ten percent of everything you earn, and you can keep anything extra you wheedle out of the men. Out of that, of course, you have to pay your room and board, as well as clothes and personal needs. If you don't make enough at first, I'll advance you the money, but soon you'll be able to save enough to set out on your own."

Kate was appalled. "And for that—a chance to save money sometime in the future—you expect me to go back down the hall and face that fat, obscene old man?"

"Naturally, if you want to wait for someone younger and more presentable, that's up to you. But I warn you, Hartwell pays more because he wants the popular girls. Besides, some of the handsome ones have . . . well, let's just call them idiosyncracies that aren't particularly appetizing. Hartwell at least is easy to please, as I can see you've already found out." Her eyes traveled down with mirth to the dried semen that stained the front of Kate's dress.

Kate found herself shivering. The old woman's eyes turned toward her in a combination of anger and impatience.

"Of course, I can always give you back those filthy rags you were wearing when I found you, and turn you loose on the streets again."

Kate turned away slowly, realizing at last the painfully subtle horror of the choice she had to make. Death on the street, or degradation in Madame du Plessine's house. It was like the Indians at the sun dance, she thought, choosing between the harsh, agonizing movements that would free them of their pain and the gentler motions that would not hurt as much, but would last much, much longer. Staying with Madame du Plessine would certainly preserve her life, at least for a while, but would it be worth living then? Kate had an unpleasant feeling that the Indians would consider staying the cowardly choice.

For an instant Kate had almost steeled herself to leave, facing her fate boldly and quickly, but suddenly she caught sight of her reflection in one of the many mirrors that graced the large room. It was the same elegant, pretty reflection that had pleased her so much earlier in the day.

At last she understood how clever Madame du Plessine had been. If she had brought Kate to the house and told her right away what was expected of her, the girl would simply have turned and fled back into the dark night. By giving her a taste of comfort, and even luxury, for two weeks, she had made it nearly impossible for Kate to leave. Never again would she be able to force herself to face the squalor and loneliness, the utter degradation, that lay in wait for her in the cold streets. Oh, there would be degradation here, too, of a subtler and perhaps even a crueller kind, but at least here she would have clean surroundings and pretty clothes. At least there would be other girls, all in the same position, to laugh and chat and while away the hours with.

She winced. Really, it made little difference. Her fate if she went outside would be exactly the same. There in the streets, the same kind of violation awaited her body. Here at least she would be paid for it. Here at least she would have a chance to save enough money to buy her independence.

She turned slowly back to face the madam of the house. "All right," she whispered softly.

"Then go to the parlor . . . or are you waiting for someone more agreeable to the eye?"

Kate hesitated for a moment, then squared her shoulders stiffly. "No," she said quietly. "I'll go to the parlor." It would be better to get it over with quickly, she told herself. Besides, she had a hideous feeling Madame du Plessine was right. No doubt there were far more unpleasant things than satisfying fat old Mr. Hartwell's uncomplicated lust.

All right, she would go, she told herself as she moved reluctantly down the hall. She would go, but she could never bring herself to like it—or even pretend to. She had an uncanny feeling that Mr. Hartwell wouldn't even notice the omission. Somehow, that only increased her disgust.

36

To Kate's eyes, Madame du Plessine's front salon seemed to be a completely different room at night. The plush red furnishings and glittering gold-framed mirrors had merely seemed garish in the bright sunlight that poured through the open draperies. Now, bathed in the dim, flickering rays of artificial light, they took on a tawdry, vulgar tone that made her feel cheap even to be standing in their midst. Still, she had to admit, with a vague sense of surprise, that it didn't look like a brothel at all—at least, not the way she had imagined a brothel should look. Surely there ought to be a motley assortment of plump women, heavily rouged and caked with mascara, seated in various stages of dishabille on the couches and lounges to wait for the men to wander around and peer obscenely at the merchandise for sale. Instead, Kate was amazed to see only girls dressed as fashionably as herself, their hair piled elegantly on top of their heads and their slender bodies sheathed in luxurious though scandalously low-cut satin and velvet gowns.

Kate blinked in surprise for a moment at the unexpected glamour and sophistication of Madame du Plessine's salon. It was a while before she even began to realize that the surface veneer of elegance was nothing more than a cleverly wrought illusion. No wonder the lights were always kept dim, she thought as she took a closer look at some of the other girls. Not a one was as young as she appeared at first glance. The faces beneath heavy, caked layers of powder were creased, not only with age but also with care.

To Kate's secret delight, she quickly saw that none of the other girls was particularly pretty. She was ashamed of the surge of pleasure that swept through her breast at the thought, but she was unable to control it. With competition like that, she told herself happily, she would surely become a favorite of the customers in no time at all. With a little luck, she would soon be able to make enough money to buy her way out of that hideous place.

For her first hour in the salon, Kate found her body trembling, not only with nervousness, but also with an odd kind of excitement. No matter how ugly life in the brothel might be, she was sure she would do well there. It was only after a while that her newfound confidence began to fade. Only then did she realize she had been overly optimistic, for she had assumed that beauty and youth would be the key to success in Madame du Plessine's salon. Yet, time after time she watched in amazement as the more attractive girls were left to sit alone in corners of the room, while drab, plain women laughingly escorted clients up the stairs that led to the small chambers. One in particular, a thin, emaciated woman named Elise, seemed to be chosen far more often than the others.

"What do they see in her?" Kate asked one of the girls seated next to her on the couch.

The girl turned to cast a suspicious eye on Kate. Plainly, she was not disposed to be overfriendly with the new girl. "You'll see," she replied cryptically.

Kate had no further time to muse on the oddities of the salon, for she soon learned that another role had been set aside for her to play. The heavy double doors that lay on both sides of the long hallway had been thrown open, and to her surprise, Kate saw that a number of bars and gaming tables had been set up in the rooms that lay behind them. This, she quickly learned, was an important part of Madame's operation, and she saw to it that the rooms were always staffed with the youngest and most attractive of her girls.

Here, at last, was a place Kate could feel comfortable—and even happy. She felt her heart give a little jump of hope the instant she saw the gaiety and liveliness of the smoky rooms. Perhaps life here was not going to be so bad after all, she told herself excitedly. It was almost like the gay parties and balls she had always loved. If she could make money working in rooms like these, she would not mind at all. It would even be fun.

She was cautious enough to take a few minutes to observe the other girls, and she was glad she did, for she quickly caught on to the way things worked. The liveliest and cleverest of the young women, she noticed, were wise enough to attach themselves to the heaviest drinkers or to the gamblers who were high on a winning streak. From time to time, these men seemed willing to pay Madame the full price for one of the girls just for the privilege of keeping a favorite drinking companion, or holding a pretty girl by their sides at the gambling table. "To bring me luck, Madame, to bring me luck!"

Kate quickly learned all the games she needed to know, and she even found herself enjoying them. It was a challenge to flirt with the men, coaxing them to buy just one more bottle of expensive champagne or daring them to bet "just a little more"—and a little more again. She could tell by the laughter in their eyes that the men all understood exactly what she was doing, but they never seemed to mind, not as long as they had a laughing, pretty companion at their sides.

As long as the men were drinking heavily and throwing their money recklessly on the gaming tables, Kate found Madame more than willing to let her stay in the midst of the cheerful gaiety. On nights like that—when she could nearly forget where she was—Kate was almost happy. But there were other nights, too, nights when business was slow, and Kate would watch with dread for the inevitable moment when Madame would suddenly materialize by her side, her lips cold and set, her thin brows slightly arched. "Really, Catherine," she would say coolly, "I don't think you're doing your share, *ma petite*." And then it would be time to go back to the salon and face the one thing she had tried desperately to block from her mind.

When that time came, Kate always felt a sick feeling in the pit of her stomach. No matter how many times her body had been abused, it was something she could never manage to get used to. It was one thing to remind herself in the cool light of morning that she was a whore, but it was quite another thing to face that same fact in the dim candlelight of the front salon. To be a whore at moments like that seemed the lowest form of life on earth. All she could do then was remind herself over and over again that it was only temporary. If she thought she would have to endure it for the rest of her life, she would rather have died.

Whenever the moment came to summon up her courage, stepping over the threshold into that hated room to offer up the use of her body to one stranger or another, Kate was always careful to remember the advice Madame had once given her. Always her eyes sought out the older men, the less attractive ones, the ones who had to pay more. It was not difficult for her to look to the less appealing men. Indeed, she cared nothing about the physical qualities of those who violated her body. They were all repugnant to her. If she had to suffer, why not choose the man whose money would enable her to buy her freedom a little sooner?

Kate soon noticed that many of the other girls, especially

the more popular ones, seemed to have made the same decision. Although a few of the handsome young gallants seemed to have found a following among the girls, many of the most charming men were forced to go upstairs with women no one else wanted. If that fact puzzled Kate, it didn't seem to bother the young men themselves. While many of them had teasingly asked Kate to share the pleasures of her bed with them, none seemed offended, or even surprised, when she put them off. They would simply shrug their shoulders, and with a casual "Another time, perhaps, my beauty," turn their attention back to the bar or the gaming table—or one of the other women.

Only after a few days did Kate begin to understand why these men were so unpopular, and when she did, she felt cold shivers run up and down her spine. Why, with a little less luck, one of those unfortunate girls returning slowly down the stairs, her face and arms marred with the marks of bruises, and tears still wet on her cheeks, might have been her. Thank heaven instinct warned her to avoid those men! It was torture enough to endure the abuse of the more normal men.

Normal? Kate thought with a shudder of the indignities she had suffered in the brothel, and she wondered if she would ever be able to think of any man as normal again. Once she had thought that the cruel abuses her body suffered in the mining camp would be enough to inure her to future horror and shock, but now she knew that, even hardened as she was, there were still new, subtle humiliations, not only to her body, but to her woman's spirit as well, that were almost beyond her power to endure. In the camp, at least, she had had some slight protection, for until she lost consciousness, the miners had to fear the vengeful wrath of her sharp nails and strong teeth. Here, being paid, she had to give the men whatever they asked, of her own "free will." As she felt her head pressed down for the first time to that part of a man's body her lips had never yet touched, she wanted to cry out in shame and humiliation. How dare these strangers force from her the most private intimacies of her body, intimacies she had never even offered to the man she loved so passionately, even at the same moment that she hated him for the cruel agony he had made of her life.

The days in the brothel passed slowly, almost as slowly as the long nights of tears and degradation. At first Kate thought the humiliation of her body was the worst thing she would have to endure, but she soon learned that humiliation of the spirit, though subtler, was far more agonizing. It was not only the knowledge of how low she had sunk that tore her soul apart, but also the less obvious yet all the more insidious torture of the slowly dragging time that never seemed to pass. Kate had never realized boredom and loneliness could be such terrifying enemies.

The companionship she expected to share with the other girls somehow never seemed to materialize. Although they were a surprisingly cheerful lot, considering what they had to endure each night, there was little amusement in their conversation, perhaps because of the inherent grimness of their profession, or perhaps because, except for the never-ending procession of strangers that passed through their lives, they had nothing to talk about. Nor did they seem inclined to form the kind of fast friendships that would have offered at least a modicum of comfort amid the ugliness and boredom of life in the brothel. Each girl was far too cautious to trust the next, Kate quickly learned, knowing that very girl would be her competition in the dark night hours soon to come. What few friendships were offered were given to the plain, unpopular girls, never to lively beauties like Kate, who only made life more difficult for the others.

Kate could look forward to only one thing; the day she would be able to buy her way out of there. So far, she had not even been able to earn enough to pay back what she already owed Madame du Plessine, much less set aside any savings, but she was determined to work harder and accomplish her goal. She had to get out of there. She wasn't going to let herself end up like that poor, sad creature at the end of the hall.

They talked about that poor woman often. All the girls seemed to forget, for a time at least, their own petty rivalries and jealousies as they stared with frightened eyes at the closed wooden door. It was as if in the fate of that one aging prostitute they all caught a glimpse of what was going to happen to them in the years not too far distant, and it made them a little more charitable to each other.

"They're going to send her away soon," Elise whispered to Kate one day in hushed tones. Elise was one of the few girls who had ever been at all friendly to Kate, perhaps because she was popular enough herself not to feel threatened by Kate's beauty.

"But why?" Kate could not believe anyone could be so cruel.

"She's been sick for weeks now. She won't ever be able to work again. I'm surprised Madame has kept her as long as this." There was a sharp edge of bitterness in Elise's tone that surprised Kate. She had never heard her voice sound anything but soft and gentle.

Kate looked back at the closed door with a mixture of pity and apprehension. Yes, she could well imagine Madame throwing an aging prostitute out to die on the streets. God help that poor woman. She closed her eyes with a tremor of dread. And God help her, too, if she didn't find a way to provide for herself before she got that old or that sick.

The closed door seemed to haunt Kate. She found her eyes returning to it again and again. Finally she could bear it no longer, and she knew she had to see what was on the other side. Besides, she told herself, trying to justify her curiosity, that poor woman must be dreadfully lonely and frightened. It wouldn't hurt to go in and try to offer her a word of comfort or cheer.

The door stuck in Kate's fingers as she tried to push it open, and the only way she could force it to budge was by pressing her shoulder firmly against the resisting wood. It held fast for a moment, then gave with a startling jolt that threw Kate off balance and set her stumbling awkwardly over the threshold. She was too startled for a moment to pay more than the scantest attention to the gaunt woman who lay inside the room, her face as white as the sheets beneath her frail body. When Kate finally looked up, staring into the other woman's face, she felt her heart begin to ache with pity.

The woman was obviously a prostitute, for even though the coppery hair that frizzed garishly around the ashen pallor of her face was tinged with gray at the roots, it still blazed out from the white bedsheets like an emblem of her profession. She seemed shocked at Kate's noisy, unexpected entrance, and gaped out at the girl with a horrifed expression that made Kate regret bursting in so abruptly and so rudely unannounced.

"Oh, my God," the woman whispered from between dry, cracked lips. "Kate!"

Kate was astounded to hear her name on the woman's lips. Peering closer through the dim light of the room, she searched the ashen features for some clue that would jog her memory. When it finally came, she could hardly believe her eyes.

"Stella!" she cried in stunned disbelief. Surely this travesty of human life that lay half-dead before her could not be the lively, vivacious, fun-loving friend she had once laughed and chatted with so gaily.

Kate was surprised to see that Stella's face was filled with the same horror she herself felt. It took a moment for her to realize that Stella's shock and grief were as great as her own. No doubt she was as sad to see a friend reduced to working in a brothel as Kate was to see her pale, emaciated condition.

"It's all right, Stella," she hastened to assure her, sitting beside her on the bed and clasping her hand comfortingly in her own. "It's not so bad here—not after what I've been through. Besides, I'll soon save enough money to get out of here, and I'm taking you with me!"

To her surprise, Stella gave a hoarse, dry laugh. "You poor little lamb. You're new here, aren't you?"

Kate could only nod her head in surprise. What could she have said that made Stella aware of her relative innocence? The older woman wasted no time enlightening her.

"Buy your way out indeed!" She snorted. "Tell me, lamb, how much have you saved so far?"

"Well, nothing," Kate admitted. "But after all, I *am* new here, you know. I still have to pay back the money Madame advanced me when I started."

"And in the meantime, your current expenses are adding up. Ah, lovey, don't you know you'll never catch up? No matter how hard you try, you'll always be farther and farther behind. Listen to Stella, pet. There's only one way you can get out of here—except for the grave, that is."

Stella gripped Kate's arm tightly, drawing herself up painfully from the thin, hard pillow until her face was only a few inches from the girl's. "Find yourself a rich man, lamb," she urged. "A very rich one. He can afford to pay Madame back and buy your way out of this hellhole. He'll set you up as his mistress and take care of you as long as you please him. If you're smart, you'll sell the baubles he gives you and save something for when he tires of you. Don't turn out like Stella, precious. Don't let this happen to you."

"Don't be silly, Stella," Kate reassured her friend hastily, speaking with a confidence she could not force herself to feel. "I'm sure I can make enough to buy my own way out, but if I can't, I promise you I'll find a rich man. One way or the other, I'll get us both out."

"It's too late for me," Stella replied wearily. "She'll throw me out on the streets where it's cold and wet. I'll never make it there, but don't you mind too much about that, lovey. My time is pretty well up. Just don't let the same thing happen to you."

"It won't happen to either of us," Kate promised vehemently as she bid her friend good-bye and hurried down the stairs in search of Madame du Plessine. She tried to keep up a bold front, but as soon as she was out of Stella's sight, she found she could not maintain her veil of artificial confidence any longer. What on earth could she hope to do? she asked herself bitterly. What kind of position was she in to help the friend who had once saved her from an equally unthinkable fate?

"I will not have you throwing Stella out on the street," Kate declared stoutly the instant she found Madame du Plessine. Her bold impertinence surprised them both. "I'll share my food with her. She just needs time to get her strength back. She's not as young and pretty as she might be, but she's warmhearted and cheerful, and I know she'd be a great favorite with the men."

Madame du Plessine was too astonished to interrupt the sudden outburst. Never in all her years as a brothel keeper had one of her girls dared to speak to her so boldly. "All right," she agreed with a noncommittal air. "I'll give her a couple of weeks, but that's all."

A couple of weeks, Kate thought bitterly. What good would a couple of weeks do? She and Madame both knew Stella could not possibly get well by then, and there was no way on earth Kate could ever earn enough to pay her own debts to Madame, and Stella's too, in so short a time.

Still, she had to try. Even though she was sure it was hopeless, she had to coax more and more of the high-paying clients upstairs with her, begging and wheedling them for the extra change that might add to her store. It made her furious to see the way Madame's eyes narrowed in devious greed as she watched her hurry one man after another up the wide stairway.

That old cat! she thought angrily. She's making plenty of money off me. She could afford to keep Stella, too.

But she knew there was nothing she could do about it. Unfair as it was, she had to keep on trying. She had to get the money somehow.

Only as the two-week deadline began to draw to a close did Kate finally realize the futility of her mission. She had worked as hard as she could, and she still had not even managed to keep up the expenses of her own meals and elaborate wardrobe, much less get ahead. As she stood in the crowded salon looking around impatiently at the unpleasant assortment of customers vying for her attention, she felt her eyes begin to sting with bitter tears of defeat. Fighting them off desperately, she forced the corners of her lips into a semblance of a smile.

To her surprise, she suddenly noticed a young man—a newcomer, she was sure—staring at her hungrily. Automatically, she brightened her smile. Although one glance at his shabby clothes had already warned her that it would be a foolish waste of time to take him upstairs with her, she knew how rigidly Madame enforced one of her favorite rules: the girls must be friendly to everyone. To her amusement, the boy turned purple with embarrassment when he felt the warmth of her smile light on him.

He could not have been more than seventeen, Kate guessed, or eighteen at most. She was sure he had just come to San Francisco from one of the nearby small towns. He looked as if he had never even talked to a girl—except for his sisters—much less tried anything as daring as holding hands or kissing them. Impulsively she stretched out her hand toward him.

"Come here."

The boy looked startled, but he obeyed, stepping over awkwardly to stand before her. Kate could not help laughing at his nervousness, although she saw instantly that her mirth was causing him even greater embarrassment.

"I'm not laughing at you," she said kindly, grasping his hand. "I'm enjoying your company. There's a difference, you know."

The boy was too tongue-tied to answer or even to smile back at her as she pressed his hand invitingly. He had an awkward innocence about him that was strangely appealing to Kate, and she suddenly found herself longing to be the one who initiated him into the mysterious rites of love. And after all, why shouldn't she? No matter what she did, she wasn't going to be able to earn enough money anyhow. There was no point sticking to the fat old men any longer.

"What's your name, lad?"

"R-Richard," the boy stammered.

"Well, Richard, would you like to come upstairs with me?"

The boy's eyes fairly popped out of his head at her question. He opened his mouth to speak, but could not seem to make the words come out.

"This is your first time, isn't it?" she asked gently.

The boy blushed and lowered his eyes as he nodded slowly.

"That's all right, love," she said gently, trying not to laugh at his embarrassment. "I'll be good to you, I promise." She would, too—better than any of the other girls, except perhaps Elise. The others would be amused by him, not realizing how cruel their jokes and taunts would seem to a sensitive youth. "If you don't take me," she advised, "take Elise." Suddenly, to her surprise, she realized she had stumbled on the secret of Elise's popularity. There was an inherent look of kindness and understanding that never left her eyes.

Richard looked doubtfully at Elise for a moment, then turned back to Kate. "I'd rather have you," he said, finding his tongue at last.

"Good." Slipping her arm gently around the boy's waist, she began to guide him expertly toward the stairs.

"But I haven't much money," the boy protested, obviously astonished that a beautiful woman would want to seek him out from all the other men. "You must be very expensive."

"Not for you." Kate was surprised at the sexy huskiness she affected in her voice. It was a game she did not usually play. Still, what harm could it do? The boy would never learn she didn't mean it, and it would make his first encounter with love a joyous and pleasant thing if he thought the woman who lay beneath his body was not there simply for the money.

Young Richard turned out to be no less awkward in the bedroom than he had been in the salon, and Kate was careful to tease him only lightly as she taught him how to undress her, taking each layer of clothing off with seductive slowness to heighten his sense of anticipation. She made her voice even heavier with the semblance of lust, and was delighted to see how quickly it excited him. At the moment he finally gazed on her body, his eyes were filled with a look of eagerness and pleasure that offered her a kind of flattery she had nearly forgotten. The look of astonished awe in a boy's eyes was a far greater tribute to her beauty than all the fluent compliments and leers of practiced lechery she had grown accustomed to in her long weeks in the brothel.

"Why, Richard, how big you are," she teased boldly as she unbuttoned his pants and thrust her hand inside. "What a devil you are going to be with the ladies."

The boy blushed, but it was a blush of pleasure. Her teasing had accomplished the goal she intended, for he was no longer shy with her as she drew him down beside her on the bed. For the first time since she had left Wyoming, Kate felt she was offering her body freely.

He was clumsy and inept at lovemaking at first, but Kate was patient with him and soon taught his eager hands and lips how to please a woman before assaulting her body. She knew Madame would be furious with her for lingering, for he had paid for only one brief use of her flesh, but she could not help enjoying the awakened sensitivity she felt in his body. By the third time he possessed her, he had already developed a reasonable amount of skill and confidence. She was only half-teasing when she said, "What a good lover you are going to be, Richard."

She was pleased to see that the shyness in his eyes had been replaced with quiet confidence. "Do you really think so?"

"Truly," she answered earnestly. The boy had earned the compliment. As Kate felt his hands still lingering on her body, caressing her skin tenderly, she knew that the moans and sighs of ecstasy that escaped her lips would no doubt have been sincere if she had not buried her heart long ago, on the day she left the man who had earned her passionate love and hatred both. "It's a lucky girl who'll catch you for a husband."

Kate remembered the words again as she remained alone in her room for a few minutes, having sent Richard downstairs by himself. Somehow, she could not force herself to face the lechery of the brothel again, at least not right away. It was pleasanter to stay upstairs, thinking of the boy. Someday he would marry, Kate told herself, feeling a warm glow of pleasure, and his wife really would be lucky. Now that he had learned a woman's body was made for pleasure, too, he would be eager to find ways to please her. In her own small way, perhaps Kate had helped pave the way for a good marriage for a kind, gentle boy and the bride he had not even met. It made her feel good inside to have accomplished something. For the first time since she had come to the brothel, she felt clean again. For the first time, she did not feel as if her body had been used and violated.

Kate could hardly wait until the next day to tell Stella what had happened. Stella was even more generous than she, and had a far warmer heart. Surely she must have had many experiences like Kate's in the past, and they must have made her feel good inside, too. It would be pleasant to have happy memories to share with her friend for a change.

But when she reached Stella's room, the woman was not there. Instead, Kate saw only Yvonne, who was cleaning out the room with a furious burst of energy.

"Where is Stella?" Kate cried out, her throat already beginning to constrict in fear.

"Why, ma'am, she's gone," Yvonne told her nervously. The poor girl was obviously frightened by the glowing rage that flashed out of Kate's dark green eyes. "She couldn't pay her keep anymore."

Kate fairly flew down the steps, not even giving herself a second to think as she hurried toward the outside door. It didn't even occur to her to wonder why Madame du Plessine had chosen that particular day to evict the hapless Stella. If she had, she might have realized that her friend had been safe as long as she was working frantically, bringing in the extra money that whetted Madame's greed. But the instant she realized it was hopeless—the instant she let herself relax enough to spend extra time with a lad with little money to spend—the incentive of Stella's presence in the house lost all of its effectiveness.

"Oh, Stella, thank God you're here," Kate cried out in relief as she caught sight of her friend huddled on a doorstep across the way. "I never thought I'd find you." Hurrying across the muddy street without even taking time to hoist up her skirts, Kate threw her arms impulsively around her friend.

"I couldn't leave without saying good-bye to you," Stella told her, the tears brimming up in her eyes. "You're the only real friend I ever had."

"And you're not leaving now!" Taking hold of Stella's hand, Kate pulled her forcefully to her feet, and without giving her time for more than a weak protest, she led her hastily back to the house and up the front steps. She wasn't going to let Madame du Plessine get away with such selfish inhumanity.

"Really, Madame, this is intolerable," she announced furiously as she burst into the parlor. She barely even noticed Madame's guests, although they stared at her in frank curiosity and amusement. Not even the darkly handsome man who seemed vaguely familiar in a charming, carefree way caught her eye. All her concentration was centered on Madame.

"Now, see here, Catherine . . ." the woman began angrily, quickly surmising the cause of Kate's outburst when she saw Stella hovering behind her in the doorway. "I warned you she'd have to go if—"

"She's not going!" Kate said emphatically. "I bring in enough money to keep both of us, and you know it. No one makes more than I do, except maybe Elise. If you want to throw Stella out, you can just give me back the rags you keep threatening me with, because I'm going with her. She can't stay alone on the streets. She'd die without help."

Madame du Plessine's eyes narrowed, but she did not say anything for a moment. She knew Kate was angry enough to keep her threat, and she had no intention of losing the girl. She was far too valuable. Besides, it was ridiculous to quarrel over an aging woman who who could not live much longer anyhow, especially if she stinted on her rations and forced her to sleep in the cold, damp attic.

"You're a fool," she snapped angrily. "If you want her, she can stay, but you'll have to pay for her keep out of your earnings. And I warn you, my girl, it'll be a long, cold day in hell before you find any man who'll be willing to buy the two of you out of here."

As Kate prepared to go downstairs that evening and face the ugly menagerie of men who had gathered to look her over, she couldn't help remembering Madame's words. With sinking heart she realized they were all too true. No doubt, once the mistress of the brothel got over her initial anger, the situation would suit her just fine. Obviously she didn't want Kate to leave, and this virtually ensured her staying. Besides, now she had a hold over Kate, and the girl would have to be docile and obedient.

Kate lingered for an instant in the doorway of the front salon, finding it almost impossible to step inside and greet the early arrivals with the warmth and friendliness that was expected of her. It seemed to her they were a particularly unappealing assortment that night, and she felt herself shivering as she glanced around the room. Always before, she had been able to take the ugliness in stride, confident that she would soon escape from it. Now she was not so sure. Even if she could somehow earn enough to buy her own way out, she would never be able to buy Stella's too, and where would she find a man generous enough to pay for both of them? Her eyes flitted around the room, taking in one fat, wrinkled face after another, and she knew that not one of them—though they could well afford it—would have the generosity or the kindness to help Stella too.

For the first time since she first set foot in that front parlor, Kate wondered with a cold chill of apprehension whether she would ever get out of there. It suddenly became appallingly personal to realize how old most of the other "girls" were. Before she knew it, she thought with a tremor of apprehension, the years would have passed by, and she, like Stella, would one day be that poor wretch at the end of the hall.

37

THE SAME DARK STRANGER WHO HAD SAT WITH AMUSED EYES and upturned lips in Madame du Plessine's salon, listening to Kate deliver her angry ultimatum, returned again that evening for another look at the fiery beauty who had piqued his curiosity; but as before, she wasn't even aware of his presence. Her mind was on her own troubles that night. Her smile was mechanical, her eyes unseeing.

Undaunted, the dark man stationed himself calmly in the center of the room, confident that she would notice him sooner or later. Ordinarily he would have preferred to spend his time at the gaming table with a drink at his elbow. Women were something he took for granted, knowing that with no effort on his part they would soon flock around him like moths dancing around the flickering candle flame. But this woman, he sensed, was something special. This was a woman worth pursuing.

It took half the evening, but he was patient, watching with an oddly amused smile as she dutifully escorted one unpleasant man after another up the wide stairway. Finally, just as he had known she would, she became aware of the dark eyes that had been fastened on her face for hours. When she did, her reaction was beyond his wildest expectations. Dropping her mouth open in amazement, she stared at him as if he were a visitor from another world.

"I am not unused to adulation from the opposite sex, madam," the stranger said lightly as he sauntered over to her. "But I assure you this is even more than I deserve. Dare I hope the expression I see on your face reflects your amazement at my overwhelming grace and charm?"

Kate did not answer him at first. When she did, her mouth formed only a single, soundless word.

Philippe.

The stranger could not make out the word on her lips, even though he leaned forward to try to pick up the sound with his ears.

"I beg your pardon?" he asked, genuinely puzzled by this unlooked-for response from a pretty prostitute.

"Oh, no, sir," the girl replied with a sudden grace. "It's I who must beg your pardon. I'm afraid I was thousands of miles away. I can only hope you'll be kind enough to forgive me. My name is Catherine."

The bright radiance of her smile was mechanical, but in it the stranger sensed a warmth and sensuality that made the long wait worthwhile. "Cathy," he said lightly, running the word slowly across his lips to savor the sound. "What a pretty name. I like it." He did not notice the slight tremor that ran through her body at the sound of a nickname she had not heard since a warm spring afternoon in a stable far away. "It is my pleasure to meet such a beautiful woman, Cathy. I am Anton Levesque."

There was a trace of French in the man's voice, tinged with something else Kate could not recognize. With a pang, it called back the rough French tones of Philippe's Canadian accent.

"You are French, Monsieur Levesque?" The question was half polite conversation, half curiosity.

"Partly." His smile crinkled the corners of his eyes attractively. "My mother was a gypsy. Does that shock you?"

Does that shock you?

Why did the words come back and hit her like a slap in the face? Who had always said that to her?

Jason. Dear heaven, Jason. Why did she have to think of him now? She had managed to push him out of her mind for weeks. Why were the memories flooding back? Jason, with that absurd painting hanging over his fireplace, the one given him by the Spanish prostitute in Cheyenne. She could only suppose he was seeing enough of the woman now. *Does that shock you?* Eyes filled with laughter. Jason, with the dark, warm oil that same prostitute taught him to use so effectively. Always, deep blue eyes bubbling with laughter. Always, *are you shocked?* Oh, God, why did she have to remember? Why did all the pain have to come back?

"Of course I'm not shocked," she retorted quickly, trying to push away the thoughts that had drifted unbidden into her mind. "It would take a lot to shock me now—certainly more than the details of someone's parentage."

Anton Levesque laughed lightly. How hard she sounded,

this pretty girl, and yet how soft her expression had been only a moment before. She had been far away, he was sure, dreaming of someone else. It occurred to him that he would like to see the same look on her face when she was thinking of him. "What were you thinking of, *chérie?*" he asked casually. "You looked at me so strangely, as if you had just seen a ghost."

"In a way, I have," she admitted. "You look very much like someone I used to know. My first love."

So that was it. She had been thinking of her first love. And yet, it was strange, now that she was speaking of him, the light had died again from her eyes.

"Your first love?" he teased. "Or your first lover?"

"Both." She smiled.

"How fortunate." He was still teasing, but there was no sarcasm in his voice. "Most of us are not so lucky. Perhaps, pretty *chérie,* for memory's sake, you will let me share your love tonight."

Kate shook her head gently. "I never go upstairs with the handsome young men. The old ones pay more."

"Why, you mercenary little bitch!" Anton burst out laughing, delighted at such unexpected candor. "If sentiment won't persuade you, I suppose I'll have to lay out a king's ransom for you."

"But the answer would still be no, sir." Damn the girl, he thought irritably. How could she smile at him so coquettishly even while she was refusing him? "If you spend all your time in brothels instead of romancing the obviously acquiescent young ladies of San Francisco, I suspect you have a few—how shall I put it?—idiosyncrasies that make you somewhat less than appealing. I don't like to come downstairs with cuts and bruises showing. It's bad for business."

Instead of being offended by her directness, as she had expected, Anton burst out in a loud roar of laughter that caused the others to turn and stare at them.

"I do not romance the young ladies because the games they play bore me," he told her, smiling. "Although I do admit to more than my share of 'idiosyncrasies,' as you so charmingly put it. I have no doubt you will find me intolerable in time, but perhaps not right away. Besides, *ma belle amie,* I never leave marks on beautiful women—though I think perhaps you will not find that an advantage. Haven't you learned yet that wounds of the flesh heal? It is the other kind, beatings of the spirit, you must fear."

Kate felt herself grow cold at his words. It sounded almost

as if he were warning her. But against what? Himself? "I'd better go now," she said, turning away from him abruptly.

"Wait." He reached out with a strong hand to grasp her arm, pulling her back toward him. As she turned to face him again, she was surprised to see that his eyes were no longer laughing. "I will have you tonight, pretty Cathy, and you will find me gentle and considerate. Later, perhaps, there are other things, less pleasant things, I will want from you, but I will never force them on you against your will."

"What on earth makes you think I'd ever agree?" she snapped, annoyed with the man's presumption. "Do you seriously think you could make me like your peculiar perversions, whatever they are?"

"Of course not," he replied calmly. "If you enjoyed them, too, they wouldn't be perverted, would they?"

"I think you're unspeakable," she hissed, careful to keep her voice low enough so Madame could not hear her rudeness. "I will never go upstairs with you—not tonight or ever!"

He only laughed at her, a soft, gentle laugh that warned her he knew she could not quite force herself to mean the angry words she barked at him. He released his hold on her arm, and she flitted immediately across the room, eager to put him out of her mind. There was something about the man, a kind of magnetism radiating from his dark eyes and flashing white smile that unnerved her, and she was determined to have nothing more to do with him.

But despite all her firm resolutions, she was constantly aware of the force of his eyes on her body, and even against her will she found herself turning again and again to meet his gaze. To her amazement, she realized that she was actually hoping he would come over to her again. The man was arrogant, and he was insufferable, but there was laughter in his eyes, and understanding, and she suddenly realized she hungered for these things with a yearning that bordered on despair.

"You see," he whispered, slipping at last to her side and laying a hand lightly on her waist. "You can't keep your eyes off me, any more than I can keep mine off you."

"I don't know what you mean," she retorted coldly, but they both knew she was lying. He let his hand slip down to her hip and then her thigh, slowly caressing the flesh that lay beneath the heavy satin of her dress. She was surprised to feel her body responding with a warmth she thought she would never feel again.

"You will lie with me tonight because you want to," he whispered hoarsely in her ear. "Later, you will come to me because you have no choice."

"What do you mean?" She didn't like the confidence in his voice. For all his attractiveness, there was something frightening, almost sinister, about him.

"Who else would be willing to buy you and your tired old friend both?" Hearing his words, she pulled out of his grasp and spun around to face him. "Oh, yes, I heard you throw your beautiful tantrum, my fiery little vixen. How wild you were, how magnificent! I decided then I had to have you."

"And *you* are going to buy me out of here?" She looked at the man with disdain. "It's obvious, sir, that you are a gambler. I wonder you have enough to keep yourself in silk shirts. You could never afford to pay all my debts to Madame du Plessine."

"Don't be so disdainful, my beauty." He laughed. "Even gamblers win fortunes every now and then."

"Well, I'm certainly not going to hold my breath."

"Aren't you, *chérie?*" Kissing her lightly on the cheek, he left her to ponder his words.

Just as Anton had predicted, Kate let him take her upstairs that night, and for exactly the reason he had said—because she wanted to. For the first time in months, she felt her flesh quivering eagerly for the tender caresses of strong, masculine hands. She was sure Anton could never make her love him, or even arouse in her the passions that lay buried in her soft flesh, but there was a gentleness in his fingers that could warm her whole body, making it tingle with the same heat that flowed through her thigh when he caressed it in the crowded salon. Besides, he brought with him the gift of laughter, and as Kate had come to learn through the long, cold months, that was no small gift indeed.

Knowing what was expected of her as one of the higher-priced girls, Kate went through the charade of letting him undress her, peeling off one expensive layer after another as if they were soft veils concealing an innocent, virginal body he was eager to seduce. When at last he removed his own clothing and lay beside her on the bed, his hands and mouth caressing her naked flesh, she opened her lips easily to let the practiced moans escape from between them. To her surprise, at the first cry he pulled away from her abruptly.

"What kind of a fool do you think I am?" he whispered, his voice hoarse with anger. "Don't pretend with me."

"What makes you think I'm pretending?" Kate challenged

425

irritably. She was not used to having her lovemaking criticized. "Perhaps the magnificent ardor of your skillful caresses has lifted me to peaks of ecstasy."

Reaching up swiftly, Anton clutched a handful of the thick auburn hair that sprawled across the pillow, pulling her head back until she cried out in pain. "You'll moan in ecstasy, all right, but it won't be fake. Until then, just keep your mouth shut."

"You'll never make me want you," she told him, angry green flames snapping in the depths of her eyes. "My heart is dead to love."

"I don't want your love, you little fool." He laughed hoarsely. "Nor do I want to touch your heart. I only want to touch the passionate flesh of your body and feel it quiver beneath my weight."

Kate bit her lip to hold back the angry retort that threatened to slip out. If he wanted to make a fool of himself by trying to arouse her passion, then let him. There was no point arguing with him. Time alone would prove him wrong.

And yet, somewhere in the long, dark hours between midnight and dawn, time played a trick on her, proving her, and not Anton, wrong. Somewhere in those sweet, slow hours, Anton's skillful fingers began to evoke from her unwilling body the passion that had too long been sealed up in the warm, soft coffin of her own flesh. She did not feel the wild surges of tumultuous passion she had known with Jason, nor even the innocent expectations of her first encounter with Philippe, but the tender warmth that swept over her body as she lay in Anton's arms was enough to drown her troubled heart for a few moments of blissful forgetfulness, until at last, no longer mindful of the challenge she had intended to defy, she opened her lips to let a soft moan of pleasure pass between them.

"You see, *chérie*," Anton told her, laughing lightly as he covered her face and body with the gentlest kisses she had ever known. "I knew you could not deny the passions of your flesh."

"But I don't love you," she protested, confused by the strange, unfamiliar reactions of her own body.

"Of course not, my treasure," he told her gently. "Passion comes often without love. That's nothing to be frightened of. Haven't you learned that yet?"

It was all well and good for him to tell her there was no reason to be frightened, but as the days turned into weeks and the craving to feel his strong, hard body against hers increased, the fear that would not leave her began to turn into despair. Jason had been right, after all, she told herself as she lay beside Anton's sleeping form in the darkness. She did have the soul of a harlot.

Dear God, was she really as fickle as all that? Could she so easily forget the one deep love of her life in the passionate caresses of another man? She must be far steeped in sin indeed if the touch of any skillful lover could arouse the lust of her body. Instead of recognizing the strong passion that love had awakened in her body, and seeing it for the normal, healthy emotion it was, Kate felt only a deep guilt that grew stronger and stronger every day.

Often she would wake up in the middle of the night to find she had been sobbing in her sleep. Then she would lie quietly in the darkness, trying to make no sound or movement that would disturb Anton, but almost as if he could hear the near-silent drop of her tears onto the pillow, he would awaken and take her lightly into his arms, kissing away the moisture from her cheeks. But instead of making her feel better, the gesture only made her feel guiltier.

For a while she tried to force herself to break off the foolish flirtation, for even in moments of passion she realized that was all it was. How absurd it was for a prostitute to get emotionally involved with a client. But then she would see him again, standing across the room from her, smiling with a wry kind of amusement as she flirted with the other clients. Her heart would give a funny little skip, like an innocent young girl seeing the boy she has set her heart on, and she knew she would never be able to say no to him, not as long as he wanted her.

And then, one night, suddenly and without warning, Anton did not appear in the salon, nor was he there the next night, nor the night after that. Each night for nearly two weeks, Kate came down the long flight of stairs with a little less hope and a little more apprehension, until finally she had to admit to herself that it was over. She wondered why she felt such a lonely ache in her heart: the end of that unwise affair was, after all, nothing more than she herself had wanted but been too weak to initiate. Still, she could not bring herself to accept the sudden abandonment she was so ill-prepared to face.

"Really, *petite*, you must learn how to end an affair gracefully," Madame complained, making no attempt to disguise the impatience in her voice. Kate knew she must really be annoyed with her, for it was not Madame's custom to call the girls down for a morning chat unless it was serious. "After all, these things happen. Surely you didn't think the man wa in love with you?"

Kate shook her head. "Nor am I in love with him."

"*Sacre bleu*," the woman burst out, annoyance getting the better of her. "Then why is it you moon around all the time like a lovesick calf? The men are beginning to complain They don't like seeing long, sad faces."

"Well, that's too bad for them. My God, what do they ex pect? They're willing to rob a woman of her last shred of dig nity by paying for her body, then they're annoyed when she' unhappy."

"That's enough, Catherine." There was a cold finality in Madame's voice. "Have you forgotten that I was willing to keep your friend in my house out of the kindness of my heart? If you wish that arrangement to continue, you will pull yourself together, and you will do it *now!*"

A dozen angry retorts occurred to Kate, but she forced herself to swallow them back. It was hard having Stella so dependent on her. If it weren't for her friend, she would gladly have told Madame exactly where to go, and in words tha were far from ladylike.

"You old cat!" she cried out angrily, but caution held her back, and she said nothing more.

"Here, now, what's all this?" a new voice chimed in. Kate and Madame both turned eagerly toward the door.

"Anton!" Kate was so delighted to see him that she didn' even think to ask where he had been.

"Come, Madame, have you been hard on my pretty little favorite here?" Laughing lightly, he flung his arms around Kate, kissing her full on the lips. "She's right, you know, you are an old cat." But his voice was filled with warmth and af fection, and his scolding fooled no one.

"And where have you been, *mon cher?*" the woman asked gruffly, trying with little success to fill her voice with cool in difference. "Once you returned to San Francisco, I though for sure you weren't going to desert us again so quickly."

"You know I'd desert anyone for a good poker game." An ton laughed easily.

"But, Anton," Kate interrupted. "Two weeks? Surely a game doesn't last that long."

Anton looked down at her in amusement, his arms still comfortingly around her body. "It can last much longer than that, *mon ange*, if it's a good game—as you'll soon find out. How else could I get enough to buy you for my own?" Disengaging her from his arms, he reached down in his pocket and pulled out a sum of money that looked absolutely enormous to Kate. He threw it casually on the couch beside Madame du Plessine. "Count it, Madame. I'm sure there's more than enough there to ransom *ma petite jolie*."

Kate was surprised to see Madame's eyes turn into angry, gleaming slits, with the blue barely showing through.

"Come, Madame," Anton teased. "Surely you don't begrudge happiness and bliss for one of your little pigeons—especially when you know you'll have her back again soon enough."

The reluctance on Madame's face began to melt away before Kate's eyes. "But of course not, *mes enfants*. You know I wish you all the joy in the world."

"Besides, when you finish counting out the money, you'll know you've made a pretty profit, eh?"

Madame threw an amused, understanding smile at him, then turned to Kate. "Run upstairs, *petit chou*, and pack your things. You don't want to keep Monsieur Levesque waiting."

"And pack your friend's things, too," Anton added with a smile. "She'll follow us in Madame's carriage. Only, I warn you, Cathy, you'll have to keep her hidden away somewhere. I can't bear the sight of sick people. But never you mind. The house I've bought is big enough for all of us."

Even later, when her baggage had been carried downstairs and she found herself safely settled in the carriage with her lover's arm around her, Kate could hardly believe her good fortune. "But, Anton, it's all so sudden. I didn't know . . . I didn't expect—"

"Hush, pretty girl," he told her, silencing her with a kiss. "It is always that way with me. You must get used to that."

Kate was so happy to have escaped at last from the terrible house where she had spent so many painful months that she did not even object when Anton began to take outrageous advantages in the open carriage. She knew now, with her changed status, she should not permit such liberties. After all, she was no longer a whore in the local brothel, but instead the mistress of a newly wealthy man. A subtly different code of manners applied to her now. Still, she was so pleased, she could hardly find the will to protest, even when he pressed his lips boldly against hers, fondling her body with caresses that were meant for the bedroom.

"Really, Anton," she jested, when at last he gave her a moment to catch her breath. "I should not let you do such shameful things."

"Why on earth not?" He laughed. "Don't tell me you're trying to become a respectable lady at this late date."

"Certainly not," she replied. "I don't think I'd even know how anymore." She cuddled into the warmth of his arms, content with the newfound sense of belonging to someone at last. She did not love Anton, but that did not matter, for she would never love again. But she did like him, and that was enough.

Only when they had nearly reached the new house did a sudden thought make her pull away from him abruptly. Surprised by her gesture, Anton looked down at her, a puzzled expression on his face.

"What did you mean when you told Madame she'd have me back soon?"

"My poor innocent," he teased. "Did you think it would last forever? How long do you think I'll be able to afford you? I'm a gambler, my love. When the good luck is gone, the money will go, too."

"But all the money you won—the house, the carriage—what about that?"

Anton's eyes clouded over with sadness as he continued to look down at her. She sensed his sorrow was not for himself, but rather for the last traces of innocence she had yet to lose.

"I'll lose it all, my sweet, just as I've lost everything before. Don't you know gamblers never reform . . . or want to? Besides"—teasingly he bent down and kissed the tip of her nose—"I may get tired of you before then."

Tired of her? How could he grow tired of her, when she was so eager to please him? "Do you think so, *mon cher?*" She forced herself to smile brightly back at him. She was not going to let anything spoil the pleasure of that beautiful, perfect day. "Maybe I won't let you grow tired of me."

"Won't you?" He laughed easily. "Well, perhaps not. I like a girl who's fun. Are you fun, my dear?"

The sudden coldness in his voice unnerved her for an instant. Then, brushing off the uneasy feeling, she replied, "Anything you like."

"But see," he said suddenly, his face lighting up with enthusiasm. "There is our house."

Kate gasped in amazement when she saw it. It was not as big as her father's house or the fortress Jason had built for himself in the wilderness, but it was larger and more elegant than anything she had expected. Leaping out of the carriage, she tugged up her skirts to keep them from being ruined in the mud and hurried toward the walk that led to the house.

Unlike most of the homes in San Francisco, the house Anton had chosen was fashioned, not of wood, but of sturdy red brick. Its lines were as hopelessly vulgar and ugly as those of its neighbors, but there was an earthiness about it that seemed appropriate for the brash newness of the city. Inside, it seemed even larger than she had guessed, and without waiting for Anton, Kate raced from room to room, rejoicing in the spaciousness that seemed like a balm to her spirit after months of cramped brothel rooms and small, flimsy tents.

When she had finished exploring the upstairs rooms, she raced back down the broad curving stairway that led to the ground floor. Anton stood at the foot of it, just inside the doorway, looking up at her with amusement.

"You look like a little girl," he told her, laughing with pleasure at her delight.

"Oh, Anton, it's lovely . . . so lovely. I know I'm going to be happy here."

"For a little while, my dear," he said softly, the knowing smile on his lips tinged with sadness she could not understand. "For a little while."

Outside, the rain began to fall, dropping in heavy pellets through the darkening gray atmosphere, but Kate barely noticed it. Nothing, she promised herself—*nothing*—was going to cast a pall over the sunshine in her heart.

The same cold rains that fell in San Francisco turned to snow when they reached the foothills of the Sierra Nevada mountain range. Thick, moist snowflakes clotted in Rafe Foster's hair and melted, to run in icy streams down the back of his neck. There was a broad grin on his features as he faced the stranger.

"What'll ya give me for 'em?" His eyes were alight with eagerness as he glanced down at the dainty emerald earrings in his hand. "Ain't no one here's got enough to buy 'em off me."

"Where did you get them?" Jason's voice was controlled, but there was a black anger flashing in the depths of his eyes.

Rafe was too concerned with his own embarrassment to notice the tension in the other man's face and body. Shuffling his feet nervously in the snow, he mumbled, "Took 'em off the body of a guy what got hisself knifed. But hell, they warn't really his, neither. He ripped 'em out of the ears of a hot-tempered little redhead we had · here." Rafe always thought of her as "the redhead" now, never as Kate. Somehow, it gave him a funny feeling in the pit of his stomach—though it couldn't be guilt, he knew, for what was there to feel guilty about?—when he remembered she was once his friend. "She weren't nothin' but a whore anyhow."

"Whore?" Rafe didn't notice the sharpness in Jason's voice.

"Sure. She weren't no better'n a harlot. We all of us had her."

"And you?" Jason's voice was deceptively casual. "Did you have her, too?"

"Well, I sure as hell did—and she was great too. She was the best I ever had." He didn't add that she was the only woman he had ever had, but that was hardly necessary, for Jason wasn't interested in his feelings. If Rafe had not been so wrapped up in his own erotic memories, he might have noticed that Jason's fingers had slipped down to curl around the handle of his gun.

"And she came here to be a whore?" Jason asked, his voice choked with a sick disgust he could no longer conceal. "She did it willingly?"

"Hell, yes," Rafe retorted, looking at the man with a puzzled expression. Why on earth did he sound so disgusted? Wasn't it in the nature of women to whore for men? Didn't they all love it, if only they would admit it? "Oh, sure, we had some trouble with her to begin with."

"Trouble?"

"Shit, we had to hold her legs apart at first." The idea seemed to fill him with mirth, and he could not control the obscene chuckling sound that rose from his throat. "We all took her that way. But after a while . . . well, hell, she didn't kick up no more'n a whimper every now and then."

Jason's face contorted with rage. They held her legs apart and forced themselves on her! Much as he hated Kate for what she had done to him, and much as he knew what a vixen she could be, luring men on, he couldn't make himself believe any woman deserved that kind of treatment. No human being should ever be used so cruelly. No human being? Hell, he wouldn't even let a dog be treated like that.

Rafe was stunned when he saw the gun being raised slowly toward his face. "Here, take 'em," he screamed, tossing the jewels brusquely toward Jason. "Just don't hurt me. Please don't hurt me." Jason did not even glance down at the emeralds where they landed in the snow. Stammering nervously, Rafe took a step backward.

The sound of the gunshot echoed across the mountain valleys, but none of the half-frozen miners in that violence-ridden camp even stepped outside to see what had happened. Jason watched Rafe's face disintegrate, turning to a mass of bloody plup before his body slipped to the ground.

A sound in the shadows prompted Jason to turn his head. He watched apprehensively as a dark figure approached, silhouetted against the bright snow.

"He had to die," Jason defended himself, his voice choked with fury. "The filthy swine!"

Marc nodded quietly. "If you hadn't killed him, I'd have done it myself."

Jason reached down to pick up the two emeralds, sparkling in the crisp, new snow. He stood silent for a moment, looking down at them where they lay in his open palm.

38

"MY DEAR, YOU SHOULD HAVE SEEN HER. EVEN IF SHE IS A duchess, she does make a terrible fool of herself, don't you think?" Lady Caroline Croftleigh's shrill, high-pitched voice rose unpleasantly above the murmur of the idle chatter in Kate's salon. "The man is . . . well, darling, he's at least twenty years younger than she, and an obvious gold digger besides. How I wish you had been there to see them. She really was behaving in a most *unladylike* manner."

Kate listened only halfheartedly as Lady Caroline's sharp tongue skillfully dissected her social rival. What did she care about the Duchess of Eastbourne, anyway? Why, she wasn't even a real duchess. Anyone could see that. She barely had the manners to be a scullery maid. The closest she had ever come to the title, as far as Kate could make out, was a brief kitchen-table affair with the doddering old duke, but that, coupled with her English accent and the wealth her gold-miner husband had left her, provided credentials enough to make her claim believable in the brash, nouveau-riche society of San Francisco.

Not that it could possibly make any difference to Caroline, anyway, Kate told herself with a vicious, catty satisfaction that surprised her. Lady Caroline's real name—so the local gossip had it—was Carol Crowley. She had been born in St. Louis (a few years earlier than she would have it known), and had no better right to her title than she did to the atrocious English accent she affected. Kate wondered what Caroline would have thought if she knew she was sitting opposite a genuine aristocrat—and a cousin of the queen, at that. For an instant she had a mischievous impulse to tell her, but common sense quickly warned her to keep her secret hidden.

"Really, Caroline," she protested peevishly. "I can't get at all excited about the duchess. Frankly, I find her love affairs decidedly tiresome."

And they were tiresome, too, Kate thought bitterly—the duchess's love affairs, and Caroline's love affairs, and all the other petty, trivial gossip that had flooded through her world in the past few weeks. She stared idly at the heavy rain that coated the glass windowpanes behind the thick, expensive mulberry velvet draperies. If only it weren't so gray, she thought miserably. If only it didn't rain all the time. Perhaps if she could just go outside for a while, then maybe everything wouldn't seem so incredibly boring.

"Why, how blasé you are, darling," Caroline teased, a hint of chiding in her voice. "I know it's fashionable to look bored nowadays, but don't you think you're overdoing it a bit?"

Kate glanced over at Caroline with distaste. She wondered why she disliked the woman so intensely. Surely she was no sillier—and no more vicious—than any of the others. Perhaps it was because of the name she had affected. Kate couldn't help thinking of her own Aunt Caroline, a woman for whom the word "lady" was more than an inherited title. It was also an appropriate description.

No, it wasn't Aunt Caroline she had been thinking of, Kate suddenly realized with a jolt of conscience. It was another Caroline—Caroline Allen! She felt her cheeks burn with shame as she remembered the mute appeal in the dying woman's eyes as she held out her children toward Kate. Dear heaven, how could she have forgotten them so easily? She had been so worried about how she was going to get enough money to support herself and Stella, she had pushed all thoughts of the children out of her mind. And yet, dammit, what was she supposed to do? How unfair it all seemed. Her responsibilities just kept mounting and mounting, but the chances of fulfilling them grew slimmer every day.

"No doubt you're right," she told Caroline quickly, eager to drive unwanted worries from her mind. There was no point dwelling on them now, not when there was nothing she could do about them. "Still, you must admit it's all too wearying. One lover after another, and all just about the same. Surely it's the most boring thing in the world to talk about."

"Boring, darling?" No doubt Caroline thought her laughter was light and tinkling, but to Kate it sounded shrill and bitter, like the dry cackling of a tired old hen. "What could be more fascinating than lovers? Why, even the duchess's lovers aren't always dull. Did you know, darling—though, of course, I don't believe it for a minute, do you?—she even claims to have had an affair with Damien Dru?" Her eyes turned hungrily toward a tall, impeccably groomed man on the far side of the salon. "Now, you must admit, he is a most intriguing topic of conversation."

Kate's eyes followed Caroline's gaze without even a hint of reluctance. Yes, she had to admit Damien Dru was fascinating in every sense of the word. The superbly tailored suit that molded his broad shoulders and narrow hips could not begin to conceal the taut muscles or catlike grace of his body, and his thick, wavy black hair formed a perfect frame for swarthy skin and dark, flashing eyes. Even the slender scar that cut across his cheek, gently tugging at the corner of his lips, only added to his romantic appeal, giving him the tantalizing aura of a bandit or a revolutionary. He was older than any of the other men Kate had ever flirted with—forty at least, she was sure, or even forty-five—but somehow, that only added to the mystique.

"He *is* attractive," she admitted reluctantly, trying to stem the warm flush she knew must be turning her cheeks a vivid crimson. Like many of the women in her crowd, she had shared with Damien Dru the stolen treasure of moist, clinging kisses, her body quivering passionately beneath the touch of bold, inquisitive hands. Kate felt her blush deepen as she watched the sly, knowing smile on Caroline's crafty features.

"How lucky you are, darling," Caroline told her pointedly. "Anton isn't jealous at all. Why, most men won't allow their mistresses the least little bit of fun. Not even a harmless flirtation, much less . . . well, *you* know what I mean."

Kate certainly *did* know, though not the way Caroline meant. She felt herself bristle with indignation at the implication in the other woman's words. She may have allowed herself a few harmless flirtations, but she had certainly never tried to extend any of them into full-fledged love affairs.

Not that Anton would have minded, she told herself realistically—or had any right to! Anton's constant infatuation with anything that crossed his path in skirts had come as a shock to her. Somehow, when he asked her to live with him, she had assumed a deeper commitment on his part, or at least a deeper sense of possessiveness. She quickly learned it did not. They had not been living together a full week when Anton took to philandering again, taking no pains to hide the heavy scent of cheap perfume that permeated his clothes, sometimes not even bothering to come home until the first bold streaks of dawn had already begun to color the winter sky.

At least he was fair about it, she had to admit. While he was out dallying with other women, he had no objections to her carrying on a flirtation with the men who flocked to her salon on the days she was "at home." If anything, he seemed to take a certain pride in the popularity of her salon, delighting in the number of powerful politicians and railroad kings who sought out her beauty and her charm.

Kate's eyes flitted toward the figure of Damien Dru again, watching the casual ease of his body as he chatted with one of the wealthiest cattle barons on the West Coast. She wished Caroline hadn't mentioned him. She didn't like the way her eyes kept seeking him out, but there was nothing she could do to stop herself.

Caroline's sharp eyes caught the glance Kate would have preferred to keep a secret. "What you need is a new diversion, darling," she purred impishly, her fake English accent nearly lost in the overpowering amusement of the moment. "No wonder you're so bored. You need to take a new lover."

"Oh, I couldn't!" Kate was scandalized. A flirtation was one thing, but a love affair . . . She didn't even want to talk about it.

"Not a serious thing, darling—just a casual little diversion. You know, Anton wouldn't object. Really, I think you owe it to yourself."

Kate was surprised to catch her eyes returning again to Damien Dru's tall figure. Surely she wasn't seriously considering Caroline's advice, she thought, horrified at the sudden fluttering of her heart that half took her breath away. To her annoyance, Dru seemed totally unaware of her presence, as though he had forgotten she was his hostess.

In the dull, rainy days that followed, Kate found herself thinking more and more of Caroline's words, and the more often they crossed her mind, the less outlandish they seemed. After all, why shouldn't she take a lover? Caroline was right,

Anton wouldn't mind—as if he had any right to object, anyhow! Besides, she *did* owe it to herself. Life was drab enough as it was, with the endless succession of days and nights that all seemed the same. Why should she deny herself the "little diversions" that might add a bit of spice to it?

Once she had made up her mind, she was amazed, and even a little frightened, at the cool calculation of it all. How could she possibly bring herself to glance calmly around her salon, choosing a lover with the same cold deliberation as a cut of meat in the butcher shop? And yet, she told herself with a tingling thrill of anticipation, if she was going to be honest about the whole thing, she would have to admit the choice had already been made.

To Kate, Damien Dru had always had an unattainable air about him. For all the kisses he handed out so freely, he emanated an almost untouchable quality that made him all the more tantalizing. Many of the women who had shared fleeting hints of passion with him in an empty drawing room or chilly, windswept garden had tried with all the wiles at their disposal to lure him to their beds, but none of them, so far as Kate knew, had ever succeeded. Perhaps that was what made him so tempting to her—not just because he was a challenge, but because she felt safe with him. No matter how far she carried the flirtation, no matter how avidly she offered her body to him, she was sure in the end she would fail, just as the others had, meeting with nothing more than a cool, amused rejection.

And yet, when the time came, it was not like that at all. To her amazement, Dru offered no resistance, not even the cat-and-mouse game she had somehow expected from him, although he must have seen through the transparent ruse she used to lure him into the parlor late one afternoon after the house had emptied of guests. Even when she coyly closed the door behind them, he did no more than lift a slightly mocking eyebrow.

"So you've made up your mind at last," he said coolly. His voice had a hoarse, earthy tone that made it sound as if it were perpetually tinged with lust.

"What do you mean?" Kate was puzzled and wary both. This was not the reaction she had expected.

"I've waited a long time for you." His voice seemed to have grown even huskier, and Kate felt the rapid beating of her heart begin to accelerate. Could it really be true? Could this experienced man of the world truly have been waiting for her? Was that why he had turned down all the others?

"I've been patient with you because you're new to this game. Otherwise, I'd never had let you hold me off so long."

"I don't know what you mean, sir," she told him archly, flitting away from the reach of his strong hands like an elusive butterfly. She was determined not to let him know how inexperienced she was in the ways of the world. "Just because I didn't throw myself at you right away doesn't mean—"

"Don't be a stupid little bitch," he snapped angrily, his eyes filled with fire and ice at the same time. "I loathe coyness. You haven't played those games before. It's part of your charm. Don't start now."

Without another word, he stepped forward swiftly, clasping her boldly in his arms with a raw strength that took her breath away. Leaning down deftly, he swooped her into his arms and carried her with sure swiftness to a couch at the far side of the room. As he drew his own body down beside her, he began with skillful, knowing hands to caress her flesh, while his tongue searched her mouth, setting it on fire with the flame of his desire.

Even when Kate saw the door open abruptly, she barely had the presence of mind to call herself back from the rapture that had already begun to transport her body to peaks of ecstasy. It was only with the greatest effort of will that she forced her eyes to focus enough to distinguish the outline of Anton's body standing just inside the threshold. Even when she finally realized what had happened, she was not frightened, only annoyed. What a time he had picked to come home unexpectedly!

"You damn filthy little bitch!" he roared furiously. "What the hell do you think you're doing?" Stunned, Kate struggled to pull herself up, tugging at her skirts in a vain effort to smooth them out. Damien rose easily from her side, a look of wry amusement on his face.

"B-but, Anton," she stammered. "I didn't think you'd be angry."

"You didn't think I'd be angry?" he shouted, his dark eyes flashing ominously. "Have you any idea how much it costs to keep you in the grand style you love so much? What the hell do you think I'm paying for, anyway?"

"I'll tell you what you're paying for!" Kate retorted furiously, forgetting in her anger that she was risking her security. "You want a beautiful woman at your beck and call anytime of the day or night. Well, you have that, so what are you complaining about? While you're out dallying with your whores—your *other* whores, I mean—I don't see what difference it makes if I have a little fun, too."

"Do what you want," he replied coldly. "But do it somewhere else. Not in my house, on my couch!"

Kate opened her mouth to shout out another angry retort, then snapped it shut abruptly. Anton was right! She did have a right to do whatever she wanted—he had set the terms of the relationship himself—but it was the height of bad taste to take a new lover in such a conspicuous place. No wonder he was so furious.

The look of dismay on Kate's face was so sincere and so anguished that Anton could not resist the smile that insisted on turning up the corners of his lips. Finally he burst out laughing. "All right, *chérie,* don't look so downcast. I'm not as angry as all that. Tell me, did you really want him so much?"

Kate was frightened at the new light that suddenly gleamed out of Anton's eyes. She didn't know what it meant, but she knew she didn't like it. Shrugging her shoulders with studied casualness, she replied coolly, "It's just that I was bored, Anton. You're away so often, and there's really nothing else to do."

She thought she had accomplished the scene with a certain jaded quality that was bound to be effective, but to her annoyance, she heard the sound of laughter behind her. Whirling around angrily, she saw Damien staring at her, his eyes filled with bold amusement.

"I hate to contradict a *lady,* madam, but that was no kiss of boredom."

"You . . . you swine!" How dare he call her a liar? She was a fool even to have considered him as a lover. Obviously, he was no gentleman.

"Come, Cathy, don't be angry," Anton coaxed gently, barely able to control the laughter that bubbled just beneath the surface of his voice. Why was he being so placating? Kate wondered nervously. She didn't like the sudden conciliatory tone. "You want Damien, you shall have him. But not here. Come upstairs to the bedroom, my pretty. You agree, it's much more suitable there." There was an oily confidence in his voice as he slipped his arm around her waist and began to guide her adroitly toward the wide, curving staircase.

Kate held back, confused, but the pressure of his arm was too strong for her, and slowly he forced her to move with him up the stairs. She felt her panic begin to mount. Why was he leading her to the bedroom? Was he really going to give her so easily to another man? But she didn't want him anymore, she longed to shout out. It had all been a flirtation, just a silly flirtation that got out of hand. Now she wanted to stop the game. Dear heaven, why was Damien following so boldly, the corners of his mouth turned up in a lewd half-smile? And why was Anton still with them, if he truly meant to give her to the other man?

"Oh, God!" Kate stopped, horrified, as she suddenly realized what he intended to do. Even to her far-from-innocent mind, it seemed disgusting and depraved. Desperately she tried to pull herself out of Anton's strong grasp.

Anton tightened his hold on her. "Come, my love. You'll like it, I promise you."

"I could never like anything so . . . so perverted!"

Anton only laughed. "I've shared women with Damien before, my precious. He is very ardent . . . and very skillful. With a passionate body like yours, you'll never be able to resist for long."

"No!"

This was too much! She had already learned, much to her sorrow, that Anton wasn't lying when he told her he had a few small "idiosyncracies," but she had never dared say no before, knowing how dependent she was on him, not only for her own support, but Stella's too. Even when he had forced her to dance nude before him, or touch her own body in ways that seemed to her obscene, she had not refused, but this she could not endure! She closed her eyes, feeling as if she must faint from shock and disgust.

As he felt her weight begin to sink slowly toward the ground, Anton leaned down and lifted her lightly into his arms. He was surprisingly gentle as he carried her up the steps.

Later, when they were alone again, she and Anton, she felt his fingers caress her face, lightly brushing away the tears. Turning her head away, she buried her burning cheeks shamefully into the pillow. *You have the soul of a harlot, my dear.* Oh, God, he was right. Jason was right. Why didn't he kill her when she was his captive? She would have been better off dead.

"Don't be so hurt, *chérie,*" Anton's voice whispered gently. "You still haven't accepted your own sensuality, have you? And yet, there's nothing to be ashamed of. Your body is like a perfect, finely tuned musical instrument. Any skillful musician can play a beautiful melody on it."

Kate supposed it was better being called a musical instru-

ment than a harlot, but somehow the contrast in words offered small comfort. No matter what Anton told her, she
knew the intimacies of her body should be shared only with
love. It was bad enough to have to do those things to stay
alive. But to enjoy them, too—that was the crowning humiliation!

Perhaps, after all, Anton was right, she tried to tell herself.
Perhaps she was a fool to complain. No matter what happened, she would never love again. It was unreasonable to expect her body to go through life without the sustenance
nature intended it to have. And yet, the physical act alone,
without love, was like a wholesome meal prepared without
seasonings. It satisfied the body, but not the soul.

"My dear, you don't know how lucky you are," the other
women would prattle on. "He treats you so well—and he's so
handsome."

"And such a good lover. Such a good lover."

Kate could never keep from turning pink when she was
forced to listen to the silly giggles that inevitably accompanied the word "lover" when the other women talked of Anton. How many of them, she wondered—how many of these
silly, frivolous women—had lain at one time or another at
her lover's side? Most of them, she'd warrant. Anton was far
too much the gallant cavalier to spurn the affections of any
reasonably pretty woman. How absurd it was to feel jealous
over an unloved lover; yet, still Kate couldn't keep the blush
from her cheeks. She wondered if the other women noticed it.
No doubt they did. Perhaps that was why they insisted on
talking about it so often.

After a while Kate began to feel as if she couldn't bear it
another minute—not the drabness of her life or the pettiness
of the gossip. Or the boredom. Especially the boredom.
Sometimes she thought for sure she would have to scream out
loud to drive away the boredom. Dear God, how unbearably
stifling life had become, as if the fresh air from the gray,
foggy streets outside was not strong enough to penetrate into
the vulgarly glittering salons and bedrooms of San Francisco.

I wonder if this is what life would have been like if I had
married Philippe? she thought, and the suddenness of the idea
made her catch her breath in amazement.

Of course that's what it would have been like! It would
have been exactly the same. Endless days of idle chatter,
endless nights of gambling and infidelity. And yet, with Philippe the degradation would have been even greater, for he

would have been her husband. She would have been bound to him forever.

With a sudden rush of insight, she was forced to admit her father had been right. Dear foolish Papa. He had only her best interests at heart. If only she had known more about life then! Marriage to Lord Burton-Styles, no matter how odious it might have been, could have been no more degrading than the long nights in the brothel or the mining camp, and at the end of that ugliness, at least there would have been a fortune waiting for her. If it hadn't been for Eamon and his murderous arrogance . . .

But such thoughts were foolish, she scolded herself. After what Eamon had done, she could never go back. That part of her life was finished forever. Besides, things weren't all that bad. She was already beginning to save some money. Soon she would have enough to start out on her own.

With each new trinket Anton bought her, Kate played the same game. She would wear it for a while, then set it aside until she thought he had forgotten it. Then she would take it out and sell it. Anton knew what she was doing, she was sure of that, but he did not seem to mind.

"Here's a pretty little bauble for you, love," he would say, tossing a diamond ring or ruby bracelet at her as casually as if it were a cheap trinket. "I suppose you'll wear it a dozen times, then it will disappear like all the others." But there was a twinkle in his eyes as he said it, and Kate knew he was amused at her.

"Here, beautiful green-eyed vixen," he told her one day. "See what I have for you this time." His eyes glistened with pleasure, and Kate knew the gift was something special.

"What's it for?" she asked warily, barely glancing at the tiny jeweler's box he had placed in her hand. She had long since learned that unexpected gifts usually meant something unpleasant—a long, tedious poker game that would clutter up her salon for days, or worse yet, an unwelcome visit from Damien Dru or one of Anton's other friends.

"Don't worry." Anton laughed, guessing her thoughts easily. "I don't want anything. I just couldn't bear to wait for an appropriate occasion." His eyes sparkled mischievously as he glanced at her expectant face. "Still, if you're grateful enough, perhaps we might ask Odette to call on us one idle afternoon."

Odette? Kate was surprised at the tension that clutched her throat when she heard the name. Odette was one of the girls from Madame du Plessine's house, but Kate hardly knew her at all. Still, as far as she could recall, there was nothing particularly frightening or intimidating about her. How strange it was that her mouth had suddenly gone dry and her body grown tense. Was there something in the soft, amused sound of Anton's voice that had unnerved her, or was it something else, some little fact in Kate's memory that she had pushed to the back of her mind?

Kate tried to remember everything she knew about Odette. She had never been close to her, nor, for that matter, had any of the other girls. They all seemed to hold themselves aloof from her. Even the men didn't care too much for her, Kate recalled. Rarely had she ever been invited upstairs alone, but went instead as a third when one of the men had more diverse pleasures in mind. Looking back, Kate suddenly realized what it was that sank in the pit of her stomach, turning her hands cold and clammy with sweat, as she thought of Odette. It was the odd, self-satisfied smirk she had seen all too often on Odette's face when she returned downstairs from one of the cozy little threesomes she specialized in. How pointedly—and how lewdly—she had stared at the other girl. And how ashamed the other girl had always looked, her eyes cast down toward the ground as if she could not bring herself to face the others, even through moist lashes.

"Good God, you are a beast," Kate burst out when she finally realized what he had in mind for her. "You don't expect me to enjoy that little perversion, do you?"

"Enjoy it, my pet? Hardly. Oh, you'll respond, all right, like the passionate little beauty you are, but you'll hate yourself for it. I warned you once, I wouldn't be amused by my little perversions if you enjoyed them."

"Amused? Really, Anton, do you know how disgusting you can be sometimes?"

Her revulsion only made him laugh, as she had known it would. It gave Kate a sick feeling, but she did not dare show it. That would only make him torment her more.

"Come on, Cathy, don't pout so," he teased lightly. "Don't you want to see your present?"

Still furious—and frightened at the new torment he had in store for her—Kate would have liked to throw the gift disdainfully back in his face, but curiosity got the better of her, and slowly, with a growing sense of expectation, like a small child at Christmas, she opened the tiny box. When she saw the dainty emerald earrings lying on clean satin, all thoughts of Anton's cruel teasing, and even of the odious Odette, vanished from her mind.

Unconsciously, her hand went up to touch the scarred ear lobes where those same earrings had been painfully ripped from her flesh. "But they're mine," she whispered in a voice that was barely audible.

"Of course," Anton replied, puzzled at the strangeness of her tone.

"No, I mean . . ." She paused, unwilling to revive old memories. "What an odd way they've come to me."

"Not at all, my dear," Anton contradicted quickly. "They're just a gift from your lover. Nothing odd about that." He made his tone brighter than he felt. He did not want her to know how much her reaction had unnerved him.

It *was* odd the way the earrings had shown up—like a pair of ghosts returned to haunt him. How long had it been—a year at least—since he had sold them to that rancher in Cheyenne when he was down on his luck? He had been amazed to run into him again, especially at Madame du Plessine's, of all places. He hadn't thought the man would even remember him—or, for that matter, the earrings. He had been astounded when the man had reached into his pocket and pulled them out.

It was just a coincidence, of course, but it was strange the way fate stepped in sometimes and took a hand in people's lives. He had often remembered the earrings in the past few months, thinking how magnificently they would match his Cathy's eyes, but he never expected to see them again.

"You wouldn't want to sell them back, would you?" he had asked the rancher casually, with little hope of success. After all, if the man had carried them halfway across the continent . . . Still, it didn't hurt to ask. "I have a mistress with green eyes."

The man had looked at him oddly for a moment, his strange, magnetic eyes as cold as ice; then, shrugging his shoulders, he had tossed the earrings over to him. "Why not? I don't need them anymore." Letting his eyes drift around the room, he had picked out Elise carefully from the crowd and walked over to her.

"How pretty they'll look with your eyes," Anton told Kate lightly, anxious to dispel the strange memory. "Still, I suppose I'll see them a few times, then they'll be gone too."

"No, I . . ." Kate stumbled on the words. How could she tell him they reminded her of the love and passion she could never feel again? "I like them too much to lose them."

Wasn't it strange, she thought, the way she still clung to the past? The sad, hopeless past. Jason. Cruel, gentle Jason.

She closed her eyes, seeing for a fleeting moment the smile on his face when he'd brought the same earrings to her in another tiny velvet box. She remembered his look of pride when he saw how pretty she looked in them.

Dammit, why was she thinking of him? Why was she longing for a man who hated her? A man she hated, too—even more than she loved him. It was stupid to idealize a past that was far from ideal, to romanticize a man who had threatened to kill her for false accusations of infidelity.

Well, at least they weren't false anymore.

If she ever had any hopes that Jason could forgive her for the past, he would never be able to forgive her for the present.

Besides, what did it matter, anyway? Jason was gone—gone forever. No doubt he had long since given up his vengeful quest for her. She would have to put him out of her mind. The tall, snowcapped mountain peaks that rose high to the east were like a wall, locking her in on one side, Jason on the other. She would never see him again.

39

THE STENCH OF FOUL TOBACCO SMOKE FILLED EVERY CORNER of the house. Even in her small dressing room, just off the bedroom she shared with Anton, Kate could not get away from its oppressive odor. She wrinkled her nose in disgust as she stared at her image in the dainty silver-framed mirror that hung over the vanity table. Dear heaven, how vile it was! She could even taste the stale, filthy flavor in her own mouth, although her lips had been nowhere near the fat, brown cigars.

Throwing down the elaborately engraved silver hairbrush in her hand, Kate rose impatiently, her long auburn hair still flowing in a silky stream to her waist. This stupid card game had gone on far too long—well over a week, in fact—and she was beginning to fret with restlessness. To her surprise, she found she missed the gay comings and goings of the brightly garbed men and women who frequented her salon, missed even the idle prattle that had seemed so boring until it was gone.

Kate reached the top of the wide, curving stairway and paused for a minute to stare down with distaste at the thin wisps of white smoke that filled the hallway, floating with slow, undulating movements toward the ceiling. They looked, she thought, like so many miniature ballerinas dancing on the bright rays of morning sunlight. At least Anton didn't insist on holding his game in the front salon this time, Kate reminded herself gratefully. Last time, the smoke had been so thick that the heavy mulberry draperies had to be carried out into the yard and beaten with a carpet whisk to drive out the stale tobacco smell.

Kate drifted down the stairway as lightly and aimlessly as the smoke curls, hesitating only an instant at the bottom when she saw that the door to the small library was open. She was surprised at the sight of the door, for it had been tightly closed every day since the game began. No doubt the heavy smoke had grown so stifling to the men that they were even willing to give up their privacy to find some relief from it.

Kate approached the open doorway tentatively. She was curious to see this game, for she sensed it was far different from the others. Yet, at the same time, she was conscious of a sharp edge of uneasiness. This was a grim, serious thing, with none of the laughter and easy mobility of the other games she had seen in the house. She did not know what to make of it. She only knew it frightened her.

As she peered cautiously through the doorway, Kate counted six men around the table. They were all slouched in their chairs, with an affected, studied casualness that barely missed being convincing. Each of them was eyeing the others carefully, but it was done so subtly, so surreptitiously, that Kate would not even have noticed, had it not been for the unbearable tension that made even the slightest movement stand out. There were no onlookers in the room, no jovial, laughing men joining in for a while, then dropping out again. This was just six grim-faced men seated around a table, six men who had been sitting in the same spot, save for an occasional two- or three-hour break to catch a bit of sleep, for well over a week. The constant tension that permeated the room was beginning to show on their faces.

Kate stared nervously at the taut, strained expressions around the table. She could see in the faces of these men the look of hungry animals on the prowl, desperate for the kill.

She wished Anton had made them leave their guns at the door, as some of the other men did when the games were in their homes, although of course that was a token of respect for their wives. She was in a different category. She did not qualify for that kind of consideration.

Kate lingered for a few moments in the doorway, her eyes stinging from the heavy smoke. She did not dare move, not even enough to brush away the tears, or cough to drive the vile, burning fumes from her throat and lungs, for she was afraid Anton would send her away if he saw her. Instinct warned her that the tension in the room could accompany only a high-stakes game, one in which her own fate as well as Anton's would be decided. She could not bear to be sent into the other room to wait and wonder alone.

"That's too rich for me," one of the men said quietly, breaking the oppressive silence at last. He was a thin, wiry little man called Macklin. Slowly, as if he had all the time in the world, he dropped his cards facedown on the table.

"Me too," another voice chimed in, and then another, until, one by one, four of the men had folded their cards neatly in their hands and dropped them onto the bright green felt. Only Anton and one other man, a man Kate had never met before, remained in the game. Kate looked into Anton's face, appalled by the deep, tense lines she had never seen before, then turned her gaze toward the stranger, wondering what kind of man he was. He had been introduced to her as Robert Landry, but she knew nothing else about him. He was a tall man with a thick waist and a huge handlebar mustache that made up for the lack of hair on his shiny scalp.

Kate must have made some slight noise, even without being aware of it, for Anton glanced up suddenly. "What the hell are you doing here?" he snapped furiously, rage glittering in his black eyes. "This is no place for a woman."

Kate felt herself begin to shiver. She knew his anger was a sign that the game was not going well for him. Always before, at other games—when he was winning—he had enjoyed seeing her in the doorway. Often he would call out to her, urging her to come in for a moment and stand by his side for luck.

"Don't be so hard on her, Levesque," Landry said in an easy drawl that spoke of the South. "It's always good to have a pretty woman in the room. Maybe you'll bring me luck, ma'am." His face glowed with a quiet confidence. Kate knew even without looking at the pile of money in front of him that he was winning.

Anton flashed an angry look at her, and for a second Kate was afraid he was going to tell her to go away again. Finally, bringing his temper under control with an obvious effort, he shrugged his shoulders. "As you wish. It is of little import." He glanced down at the cards in his hand for a second, then looked up with a quiet, studied smile. "They say you're a bluffer, Landry."

Kate's eyes were drawn toward the center of the table. She could barely control the gasp of surprise that slipped through her lips when she saw how much money was there. No wonder the others had folded. She found herself hoping Anton would not try to stay in the game, not at those stakes.

"Try me, Levesque," Landry challenged, an edge of mockery in his voice. "If you can, that is. It doesn't seem to me you have enough money to call."

Anton bristled visibly at the taunt. He shouldn't do that, Kate thought desperately. Even with the little she knew about poker, she realized he had made a bad mistake. He should never have let Landry see how quickly he reacted to a challenge.

"I have this house."

"No, Anton!" The words slipped out of Kate's lips before she had time to think. To her annoyance, Landry turned slowly to face her, his eyes sparkling with amusement. Kate glared back at him, wishing desperately there were some way she could recall her foolish outburst. Now, even if Anton wanted to drop out, he wouldn't be able to. He was much too proud to give in to her, especially in front of his friends.

"You goddamn bitch!" Anton's voice was hoarse with anger. "Do you think I don't dare? Do you think I have a weak-spirited woman's heart?" Reaching into his pocket, he pulled out a paper and pen. After scribbling a few words. he tossed the paper in the center of the table. "That's my note, but you don't have to trust me. The deed is in a cabinet in the front salon. Catherine will get it for you if I lose."

Kate bit her lip to keep from crying out again as she watched Landry pick up the paper, carefully scanning its contents before he tossed it back again. An amused smile played on his lips as he turned his cards over slowly.

"A pair of treys?" Anton gaped at the cards that lay faceup on the table, as if he could not believe his eyes. "You risked all that on . . ." He broke off, a relieved laugh ringing in his voice as he threw down a full house.

Don't do that, Kate thought anxiously. Don't let him see

how scared you were. But this time she was cautious enough to keep her fears to herself.

"What a fool you are, Landry," Anton gloated, relief and exhilaration robbing him of every last shred of gambler's caution he had learned over the years. "That was a stupid way to play that hand."

"Do you think so?" Landry drawled calmly. Kate caught herself scanning the man's face carefully. She didn't like what she saw. This was a man capable of losing a big hand with no trepidations if he thought it would make his opponent overconfident. Then, next time, when Anton thought he was bluffing again . . .

Kate broke off the thought abruptly, shivering at its implications. She didn't like to think about what could happen next.

"Get some whiskey, Cathy," Anton called out genially, his good humor restored. Kate breathed a sigh of relief as she stepped over to the sideboard and pulled out a heavy bottle. No doubt she was just being foolish to worry. After all, Anton knew more about gambling than she did, and he sounded secure and happy again. Besides, with all the money he had won on that last hand, he would certainly be all right, for a while at least.

As she brought the bottle to the table, Kate was unnerved to catch sight of a bright glint of eagerness shining for a brief instant through Landry's usually expressionless eyes. No, she had not been wrong to worry, she warned herself nervously. Landry was dangerous—there was no question about that. As for all the money Anton won . . . well, money that had been won in a single hand could be lost just as quickly.

Kate began to pour the whiskey into the men's glasses, taking care not to stint, for she knew Anton was always generous with his liquor when he played. Men with a full glass were more likely to take a sip now and then, Anton had once told her, and a man who was full of whiskey was not an opponent to be feared. Anton himself was always careful never to drain his own glass. As Kate poured out the clear amber liquid, she couldn't help noticing that Landry's glass, too, lay full at his elbow.

"That's my girl," Anton told her warmly, as he watched her fill the glasses to the brim. "Now, get us another bottle, so we don't run out . . . and toss me a couple of fresh decks from the top drawer while you're at it."

Although the comment was casually tossed out, Kate felt her back stiffen at the sound of the words. Mechanically she reached into the sideboard for more whiskey, then drew the drawer open and stared down for a moment at the cards that lay inside. They were mingled innocently beside a dozen other odds and ends, their seals carefully drawn across their surfaces, but Kate didn't like the look of them—though she couldn't for the life of her figure out why. Anton usually played with cards he kept in a locked cabinet in the front salon. She would have felt more comfortable if he had asked for those.

As she turned and tossed two decks of cards on the table beside Anton, she was startled to catch sight of Landry's eyes, fixed with carefully concealed interest on her face. Had he picked up her nervousness? she wondered. And if he had, what did he make of it?

"I'll leave you alone now, gentlemen," she said quietly, setting the whiskey bottle beside the cards. Although she tried desperately to inject a note of coolness into her voice, she had the uncanny feeling that Landry was not fooled for a minute.

"Close the door behind you," Anton called after her. There was a smile on his lips, but the grim, hard look had not left his eyes.

Kate spent the rest of the morning and a good part of the afternoon in the salon, staring out at the raindrops that pelted bleakly against the windowpanes. Dear heaven, why did it always have to rain? If only the sun were shining, perhaps then she would not mind the dark despair in her heart so much.

As Kate gazed out at the gray, empty street, she was conscious of a deep sense of foreboding—a sense so strong that it went even beyond fear. The game was going badly for Anton, she knew—if nothing else, the closed door was proof of that—and intuition warned her it was going to get even worse. Anton's lucky streak was over at last, just as he had once warned her it would be, and soon there would be an end to the big house and the expensive carriage . . . and the pretty mistress.

"Dear God, help me," she whispered aloud, then laughed quietly at herself. Who was she to ask God's protection? She was nothing but a common whore. And yet, she had no one else to turn to. She had no friends—no real friends—and she had not yet saved enough money. Oh, there was some cash buried in a small metal box in a corner of the backyard, and a handful of jewelry she could sell, but it was not enough. Not nearly enough.

The afternoon shadows had already turned the rain-darkened streets nearly to black when Kate suddenly became aware of a commotion at the back of the house. Hopefully, she rose and hurried out into the hallway. Perhaps the game was breaking up at last. Perhaps Anton had not lost everything, after all.

But the instant she reached the hall, she realized that she was not hearing the jovial sounds of camaraderie that should accompany the end of a game, but rather harsh, angry, brutal noises. Heedless of Anton's orders, she rushed to the library doors and thrust them open.

The scene that met her eyes was even more grim and terrifying than she had feared. Four of the men had backed away from the table, and stood, silent and expectant, against the wall. Only Anton and Landry still stood at their places, facing each other warily, their fingertips resting lightly on the soft felt surface of the table in front of them. Kate could not help noticing that their hands were only inches from their guns.

Although she was sure she made no sound, Landry seemed aware of her presence. Without turning around, he spoke to her, his voice filled with a quiet force that was all the more frightening for its lack of bluster. "I'd suggest you leave the room, Mrs. Levesque. This is something a lady shouldn't witness."

His concern, together with the courtesy use of a name they both knew she didn't deserve, was more terrifying than any angry raging could ever have been. How ludicrous it seemed for a man to be thinking of courtesy at a moment like that—a moment when he must also be thinking of death. Kate could not force herself to speak. She could only shake her head mutely.

To her surprise, one of the men—she thought it was the one called Macklin, though she was so frightened she could not remember clearly afterward—moved over to her, positioning himself in front of her, as if to shield her body with his own. She remembered wishing he was taller so she would not be able to see over his shoulder. She hated watching the scene that was being enacted before her, but she did not have the power to turn away.

Landry paid her no further heed. "I called you a cheat," he said calmly, "and I'll repeat it. Those cards were marked. Every man in this room knows it."

Anton's face turned gray, but he did not back down. "There's only one way I can reply to that." Taking his time, he slipped off the black wool jacket he had worn even in the warm room. Landry did not attempt to remove his own coat, but unbuttoned it casually, shrugging it loose from his sides so it would not impede his access to his gun.

Oh, God, they're going to shoot it out, Kate thought, gaping at the pair with wide-open eyes. Why was she watching them? She didn't want to see this. Why couldn't she force her eyes to shut?

Anton was a good shot, she knew. They had often played shooting games together, for far from feeling threatened by her prowess, he had actually thrived on the competition. He was nearly as good a shot as she, she had quickly discovered, only much, much faster. She began to feel hopeful—until she glanced at Landry and saw the supple, tense set of his muscles beneath the light wool of his jacket. He would be fast, too, she sensed. Very fast.

Kate held her breath for what seemed like forever, watching the two men as they faced each other, their hands poised lightly in the air, inches from their guns. Then suddenly she saw Anton's hand fly downward, almost too fast for her eyes to follow. She did not even see Landry draw his gun, for her eyes were fixed on her lover.

The sound of the shot was deafening, but Kate barely noticed it. All she was aware of was the expression on Anton's face. The look that swept across it was one of surprise. She could not detect even the faintest note of pain in it.

Only after what seemed like minutes did Kate finally notice the open wound that spurted blood from the center of his chest. Lurching forward, Anton clutched at the table, perhaps in a last desperate attempt to steady himself, but somehow it looked to Kate as if he were reaching for the pile of money in the center. He almost made it. Only at the last moment, when the tips of his fingers rested against the shiny coins and wrinkled bills, did his hand fall back, sliding across the bright green felt. Kate watched dispassionately, almost as if it were not her lover, but some actor in a play, whose body sank to the ground, limbs twitching convulsively one last time before falling still forever.

"Oh, God," Kate whispered. "Philippe."

Dear God, was this how it was meant to be? Was this second cruel death only a reminder of the inexorability of fate, hers and Philippe's both? He had died by her brother's hand, and yet, perhaps death had been his intended legacy all the time. It was as if she had been given a second chance to see that this was the gambler's logical end, this bloody, ignominious death on the gaming-room floor. Even if things had been different in the beginning, even if she had somehow managed to escape with Philippe, would she have come in the end to this same dark room of death?

She stared down at her lover's blood seeping into the deep red pile of the carpet. Dear heaven, why did it have to be red? It was red before—that other carpet where another lover had died. Why did she have to keep on reliving the same torture again and again?

The men were startled by her words at first, staring at her curiously as she called out the wrong name, but they quickly managed to rationalize her behavior. After all, they reminded themselves, the poor woman had just suffered a terrible shock. No wonder she was disoriented.

Landry slipped his gun casually back into his holster. "Sorry, ma'am," he told her. Oddly enough, he sounded sincere. "But he *was* cheating."

Kate did not try to reply. She knew the man was right. In a way, she did not blame him. Philippe had lived—no, not Philippe, she reminded herself, Anton—Anton had lived by the gambler's code. When the time came, he had to die by the same code.

"I'm afraid I've won the house, too, ma'am," Landry told her hesitantly, as if he were embarrassed at having to intrude on her grief. "While you're a very beautiful woman, I'm afraid I'll want to bring my own adornments."

"Of course," Kate replied quickly, surprised at how easily the sad, gentle smile came to her lips. "I'll be out by nightfall."

"Oh, now, that won't be necessary, ma'am. Take a few days—a week or two if you need it."

"No." Kate shook her head slowly. "I'll be out by nightfall." She turned her eyes back to the body on the floor, barely noticing when the men took up their hats and shuffled slowly, awkwardly through the door, their eyes downcast to avoid her gaze if she should happen to turn their way.

Was this all there was to it, then, she asked herself with a wearying sense of futility—this empty shell of a human life? Strange that he should look so cold and unreal. Strange, too, that she should feel nothing for this man whose bed she had shared for months. Had she grown so callous that she had no feeling left, no pity? Or was it just that she had endured so much she had grown numb to pain?

The lights glittered brightly in the wall sconces and chandeliers as Kate paused hesitantly for a moment at the top of the stairs. She had thought it would be easier to walk down that broad carpeted stairway—after all, she had descended those same steps hundreds of times before—but now she felt the saliva choking her throat as she listened to the sounds of forced gaiety that drifted up from the floor below.

She had chosen a red dress, a vivid red satin that clashed boldly with her hair, and soft red feathers that could be fastened with gawdy rhinestone clips in her abundant curls. This was a night for tawdry cheapness, she told herself bitterly. She wanted to look as vulgar as she felt.

How strange it was that she had never noted that Madame du Plessine's carpet was red, she thought as she placed her foot tentatively on the first step. Funny, the whole world seemed full of red carpets. Suddenly the thought made her want to giggle.

In the midst of life, we are in death. Where had she heard that before? Oh, yes, she had said the same words herself once, long ago, over the grave of that miner—what was his name? It all seemed so far away now. In the midst of life, we are in death. In the midst of prosperity, we are in poverty. In the midst of hope, despair.

There was no sense procrastinating, Kate told herself sternly, forcing her feet to the next step and then the next. This was her life now. She had to face it. That pathetic little pile of money still buried in a box in Landry's backyard was not even enough to make a start for herself, much less take care of long-standing debts, like helping Stella or the the two children she had left behind but never quite forgotten. No, back to the brothel she had come, and in the brothel she would have to stay. She might as well make the best of it.

When she finally forced herself downstairs, Kate stood for a moment in the doorway of the front salon, unable to bring herself to take that last inexorable step over the threshold. The warm, perfumed air floating out of the room was so stifling she thought she would choke on its heavy sweetness. Finally, closing her eyes for a second against the faintness that threatened to flood over her, she walked with a semblance of calmness through the door.

At first, in the flickering light, she did not notice the tall man who stood across the room, his back toward her as he bent over to converse with Elise. It was an instant before her eyes lit on him, but when they did, she saw in his easy grace and carriage a haunting familiarity that took her breath away. Her heart seemed to jump into her throat, pounding so rapidly that she felt as if it must burst.

Dear God, it wasn't fair. Not fair at all. Why tonight of all nights should she see a man that called forth memories of days when life was young and beautiful—days when she thought love and joy were hers for the taking, just like shiny red apples hanging on low branches of autumn trees.

As if he sensed the intensity of her gaze, the man turned around slowly. The instant Kate saw his face, she realized that the memories he evoked were not merely an illusion. She felt herself turn hot and cold all at once.

It couldn't be him! He couldn't be here. Surely the mountains had cut him off from her, the mountains with all their snow.

"Jason," she whispered. Her voice was too soft to carry across the room.

Though he did not speak a word, Kate could see that his eyes flashed with a cold fire, and the tension of every muscle in his body was visible through his clothes. The rage that emanated from his presence was so violent that everyone in the room fell silent, their eyes turned toward him. For a long time he stared at Kate mutely; then finally he opened his lips slowly.

"It seems I was right, madam," he drawled with cold contempt. "You are a whore, after all. But why do you look so surprised, my dear? I told you I would kill you. Did you doubt my resolve?"

As she stared back at the cold, hard eyes fastened on her face, Kate realized in despair that he meant what he said. His hatred and lust for vengeance were as strong as they had ever been. Once again she felt the bitter edge of fear, as she had all too often in the months since she had married this strange, cruel man. It took her only a second to decide what to do.

Clutching her skirt in her hands to keep from tripping, she spun around and raced out into the hall. She knew she would have only a second or two before Jason pushed his way through the crowded room and hurried after her. By that time, if she was lucky, she could already have made her way through the front door. If the night was still dark and moonless, perhaps she could find a way to hide from him.

Luck was with her, for the heavy darkness that greeted her eyes as she flung open the door was broken only by the pale light filtering out of the windows of Madame du Plessine's house. Slamming the door behind her, Kate fairly flew down the steps, slipping awkwardly in the treacherous pools of water that lay on the ground, a residue from the heavy rain that had let up only a moment before. The air was freezing cold, but she did not notice. All she could think about was trying to reach the dark alleyway at the side of the house. If only she could get there before Jason came through the door—before he could see where she had gone—then she might be able to escape.

40

THE ONLY TRACE OF LIGHT THAT PENETRATED THE DEEP blackness of the alleyway was a single shaft of gold spilling out of a window at the side of the house. Kate crouched, shivering, in a damp corner behind a high pile of old boxes and refuse, staring out at the nearly hypnotic pattern the flickering light formed against the muddy brown earth that covered the alley's surface. So far, so good, she told herself hopefully. She was sure she had made it to her hiding place unseen.

She could already feel icy moisture coating her legs and thighs as the trailing satin of her skirt dipped into deep puddles on the ground, soaking up the muddy water like a sponge. She longed to reach down and pull the skirt up from the dampness, wrapping it closely around her, but she didn't dare move, or even let her teeth chatter from the cold. It was too still in the alleyway, too intensely silent. She was afraid even the slightest sound might betray her. All she could do was huddle in her dark corner, her eyes still fixed on the single patch of light, her ears picking up nothing but the muted sound of her own breathing. Finally, after what seemed forever, she heard the one thing she had been dreading.

To Kate's ears, the footsteps sounded loud and insistent, beating against the damp earth with an angry determination. She held her breath in terror, her rigid body tensed against even the slightest movement, until at last she heard them draw so near that she was sure they must be right beside her. Still she could see nothing.

Only when her invisible intruder drew at last into the dim shaft of golden light did Kate suddenly become aware of a pair of heavy brown boots capped by tight brown pants tucked into the top. Kate could see nothing else of the man, for the light extended no higher, but she did not need to see him to know who it was. Surely no one but Jason would have followed her out into the dark alleyway. Still holding her breath against the unbearable tension, she waited to see if he would stop and search for her or hurry on down the alley in his angry pursuit of vengeance.

To her relief, the boots paused only a second in the pool of light, then disappeared again into the darkness. Kate could still hear Jason's footsteps for a long time, rushing and stumbling, stopping only briefly as he crashed into the heaps of trash Madame had piled up in the alley. Thank God she had fooled him, she thought with a sob of relief. He was so sure she had already raced through the narrow passageway, hurrying to the dark street at the other end, that he hadn't even wasted a minute or two searching it.

Kate remained in her cramped corner even after the footsteps died away, her skirt now completely drenched from the mud that lay in thick puddles beneath her trembling body. It was a long time before she dared move, and even then she took great care to push the boxes aside cautiously, shoving them forward only an inch or two at a time. She didn't want to take any chances. One false move could send them crashing down around her, and she didn't know if Jason was far enough away not to hear.

She had barely begun to push the boxes carefully away from her, when a sudden change in the quality of light caught her attention, startling her enough to draw back into the safety of her little corner again. At first, she tried to tell herself that the light only looked different because she had begun to inch the boxes away from her protected corner, but she quickly realized she was wrong. The new light that had begun to flood the alleyway was far too bright for that. As Kate stared out in horror, too frightened even to remember to pull the boxes back around her, she saw the glow of light become stronger and stronger.

It was a lantern! There was a man with a lantern silhouetted at the edge of the alleyway! Kate felt her heart stand still as she squinted her eyes into the dim light. With a rush of horror, she recognized the strong, angry features of Jason's face.

But if that was Jason, who was the other man who had just stumbled hurriedly through the darkness?

Kate had no time to dwell on the mystery, for Jason had

already begun to move slowly forward, swinging the lantern back and forth in his hand to erase the dark shadows that lay in the corners of the alleyway. Kate pushed herself farther back in the darkness, wishing she had had the presence of mind to pull the boxes in tighter instead of leaving a gaping hole he could peer into all too easily. Now it was too late. Now even the slightest movement or sound might attract his attention.

She held her breath, sick with dread, as she watched the light creep slowly forward, illuminating the dark corners formed by the pile of boxes, until it lay only inches from the bright red satin skirt that would be so visible in its pure yellow rays. Finally, when she thought she must scream with the tension and the suspense, she saw the light begin to recede slowly, drawing back, until her body was safely encased again in darkness.

Kate felt tears of relief begin to stream down her cheeks, but she was careful not to let her sobs become audible. Still shivering in her cold, damp corner, she watched with fascination as the light grew fainter and fainter. Obviously, Jason was making only a cursory search of the alley. No doubt, he too—like her earlier intruder—was sure she had already fled in aimless terror down the street.

It was several minutes before she could work up the courage to inch her way slowly out of her hiding place again, but this time she met with no obstacles, and it took her only a minute more to make her way stealthily back to the front of Madame du Plessine's house. She stood hesitantly for a second, just outside the front door. Then, realizing how boldly the red of her dress must stand out in the light that filtered through the windows, she began to run swiftly, impulsively down the long street. She didn't know where she was going, or even care. It didn't matter. All she knew was that she was going the opposite direction from Jason—Jason and the other mysterious intruder who had preceded him into the dark alleyway.

She hadn't gone more than a block or two when the rain began to drive down again, this time with renewed force. Cutting sharply into her body, it seemed to massage her cold flesh with a thousand icy fingers. In seconds, her hair and dress were completely drenched, clinging to her body and limbs with a cold persistence that only added to the terror and exhaustion she already felt.

Suddenly Kate knew she could go on no longer. It was as if the cold rain somehow had the power to intensify her fear

458

and anguish until it drove her to the brink of despair. Feeling her legs begin to buckle beneath her, she sank down on the cold, wet steps that led to a darkened house, letting her head drop heavily into her hands. She did nothing to try to control the compulsive sobs that began to wrack her body, but let them run their course, waiting until they began to subside of their own accord. Only when, at last, she felt them begin to taper off did she let her mind take over again.

She had to make some sort of plan, she reminded herself over and over again with a mounting urgency. She had to! But it was hard to force her shivering body to rise again, harder still to force her mind to concentrate. It would have been so much easier to give up, so much easier to curl up in a dark, wet corner, sobbing her heart out, until finally she succumbed to exhaustion and exposure.

Only through the greatest effort did she finally manage to force her fear-numbed mind to focus again on the problem she had to face. At first, it seemed too great, too insurmountable, ever to solve, but then, slowly, as it always had before, Kate's fighting spirit began to take over. As she recalled all the terror and humiliation she had been subjected to over the past few months, she began to grow more angry than frightened, and with the anger came a fierce determination. She was not going to let herself be cornered like some pathetic little fox, shivering in fear at the sportsman's game! She was going to fight for her life!

There was no sense sitting around crying like a little ninny, she reminded herself firmly. She had to make up her mind what to do, and she had to make it up quickly. At least one thing was certain. She couldn't go far, even if she could find the means to do it. Stella was still here, and Stella needed her help. She had to find a way to be reunited with her again.

Well, that shouldn't be too hard, she reminded herself bitterly. No doubt, Stella, too, would be on the streets the next morning. As soon as Madame found out why Kate had run away so suddenly—and realized she wasn't likely to return—she wouldn't bother with Stella for another instant. All Kate had to do was hide herself somewhere nearby. Then, when Stella came out in the morning, she could follow her, staying carefully out of sight until she was sure it was safe to make her presence known.

That would take care of one of her responsibilities, at least. As for the other, Kate didn't even like to think about it. She had already left the Allen children far too long with that brutal farmer and his wife. There was nothing she could do about it, she told herself over and over again, trying to find some balm for her conscience. Perhaps one day soon she and Stella would be able to make their way to Wyoming. Then they could pick up the children and take them back East. If only she could get them to her aunt's house, she knew they would be all right.

"But that's in the future," she said aloud, trying to bolster her courage with a show of determination. Right now, she had to figure out a way to get hold of some money, even if she had to steal it.

Money! But of course she had money! Not much, but a little. At least it would keep them from starving for a while.

Jumping up suddenly, with a new sense of purpose, Kate began to hurry down the dark street. She barely even noticed the heavy rain that molded her dress to her body, drencing it with an icy liquid that grew even colder in the biting wind. Now, at last, she had hope and purpose to keep her warm.

The house was dark and still when she got there—how strange it was to think of it as *the* house instead of *her* house—and the windows were closed and shuttered. Obviously, Landry had made good on his offer, forbearing to take possession until she had had a decent amount of time to adjust to her grief. It hadn't seemed to matter before, but now she was grateful for his courtesy. With no one in the house, she could run lightly across the yard, wasting no time hiding from prying eyes that might be peering out of shadowy windows.

She had buried the small metal box beneath a heavy clump of shubbery in a corner of the fenced-in backyard, and now she hurried toward it, her feet moving with unerring familiarity through the thick darkness that half-blinded her. The instant she reached the spot, she fell to her knees in the mud, scratching her way frantically through the soft earth with her bare hands. She was so engrossed in her task that she did not even notice the light sound of footsteps until they were almost upon her. Hearing them suddenly, she gasped in terror, struggling desperately to her feet, but she was too late. Even before she could bring herself erect, she felt powerful arms reaching around her, pinioning her tightly against the hard strength of a rough male body.

"Let me go!" she screamed in terror.

"It's all right, Kate. It's all right," a gentle, familiar voice called out from the darkness behind her. "Why are you trying to run away from me?"

"Marc!" she cried out eagerly. Hearing the relief in her

voice, he released his hold tentatively, freeing her to whirl around and face him. "What are you doing here?"

"I was there tonight, at Madame du Plessine's, although you didn't have eyes for me." Distraught as she was, Kate still couldn't miss the note of sadness in his voice. "I had the feeling you might come back here—to your old house. I was waiting for you."

"Oh, Marc, I'm so glad you're here," she sobbed. Suddenly too weary to hold up the weight of her body any longer, she sank gratefully into his strong arms. "I was so frightened."

"Poor, darling Kate," he whispered. His arms enfolded her tenderly, pressing her reassuringly against the warmth of his body. For an instant, his lips rested lightly against the tantalizing fragrance of her hair. "I always seem to be comforting you." He ran his fingers gently through her hair until they brushed against a soggy bit of feather that was still stubbornly attached to the cheap rhinestone clip. His face reflected his distaste as he ripped it from her hair and threw it down in the mud.

"My God, Kate, where did you get such a vulgar outfit? And what were you doing in that place?"

"What do you think I was doing there?" She pulled away from him, her voice filled with bitter sarcasm and self-disgust. He could not help noticing the wet tears that still lingered on her cheeks and lashes.

"Oh, my dear, I didn't meant that," he told her hastily, realizing instantly how deeply his thoughtless words had hurt her. "I know you'd never have been in a place like that if you had any choice. But how did you get there? What happened to you?"

"Oh, Marc, it was terrible, so terrible," she sobbed, grateful at last to have a sympathetic shoulder to cry on. "I went to a farm for shelter, and there was this man there—this horrible, disgusting man. He . . . he raped me. I thought that was the worst thing that could happen to me, but it wasn't."

"Hush, Kate," he soothed. "It's all right. You don't have to go on." He didn't want to stir up memories of that ugly experience, nor did he want her to have to relive the horror of the mining camp.

"It's so hard to be a woman, Marc. It's not fair. I'm not strong enough to protect myself. Don't you see?" There was an urgent plea in her voice that tore his heart apart with its sadness and despair. "Anything was better than trying to survive on the streets of San Francisco. Anything. Even *that*."

"It's all over now, Kate," he promised her, comforting her

with the light, tender caresses of his hands. "You're safe now. You'll never have to be afraid again."

"No!" she cried out in terror, remembering the look of insane anger in Jason's eyes. "I have to get away from here."

To Marc's amazement, she pulled away from him abruptly and fell to her knees again, clawing in the dirt like a wild animal. "What are you searching for, Kate?"

"My money! I buried it here. It's only a little, but it's all I have. Somehow, I have to take care of Stella, too, and the Allen children—I can't leave them with that dreadful man any longer." She was vaguely aware that she was babbling incoherently, but she couldn't stop herself. She was too frightened to try to be reasonable. Her fingernails were half torn off and her hands bleeding, but still she scratched desperately in the dirt.

"Stop it, Kate," he told her firmly, grasping her hands and pulling them back. "I'll do it for you, if it's that important." Picking up a sharp rock that lay nearby, he gouged at the earth until he had managed to uncover the box. Handing it to her, he watched as she ripped it open. His heart ached when he saw how pitifully small her cache was.

"It's not much," she said defensively as she caught the look of pity in his eyes. "But it's all I have. Somehow I have to make a new start with this."

"I'll give you more money if you need it," he told her gently, his voice choked with emotion. "But come with me now, darling. Come with me." Tenderly he raised her to her feet, holding his arms tightly around her, as if he thought somehow they might be able to protect her from the pelting rain. "Come with me."

Kate had little recollection of the long carriage ride that followed, or even the facade of the stylish, elegant house they pulled up in front of. Even when they went inside, she was shivering too much from cold and fright to notice the superb taste of the architecture and furnishings. Only for an instant did it cross her mind to wonder where she was. She was sure Marc couldn't afford to buy or even rent such a place, but she pushed the thought quickly to the back of her mind. It wasn't important. She had far more pressing things to think about.

Marc led her upstairs to a small, tastefully furnished bedroom. "Take off that hideous dress, Kate," he ordered brusquely. Then, fearing he had hurt her feelings again, he added more kindly, "It's soaked through anyhow. I'm afraid I haven't anything to offer you but this dressing gown. It's far too big, but at least it's warm and dry."

Kate tried to reach out her hand for the robe, but she suddenly found she was too tired even to move. Letting herself crumple down on the bed, she dropped her head in her hands and began to weep unashamedly.

"Come on, Kate," Marc urged gently. "You have to get those wet clothes off." When she still did not respond, he slipped his hands lightly behind her and began deftly to unfasten the back of her dress. As he slid it off her shoulders, he felt her body begin to tremble violently beneath his fingers, but sensing she was shivering, not from fear of him, but from the cold, he continued to undress her.

The flimsy undergarment that barely covered her voluptuous body had turned translucent in the heavy moisture that drenched it. Marc caught his breath as he saw the deep pink of her nipples straining against the clinging fabric. With trembling fingers he unbuttoned the chemise and pulled it off, laying bare the smooth pink and ivory of her flesh.

My God, she was beautiful. He was conscious of a throbbing ache in his body, stronger than anything he had felt since the days he had first known her, the days before she had become Jason's bride.

"Here, put this on," he said gruffly, thrusting the robe toward her. Hurrying across the room, he tossed the dripping chemise and dress angrily over the back of a chair. Goddammit! The woman was still Jason's wife. He had to keep his hands off her.

Kate sensed the difference in his attitude, and even though she didn't understand it, it frightened her. Slipping on the robe obediently, she sat in silence on the edge of the bed. Only when she saw him step over toward the door did she finally speak.

"Where are you going?" she asked tensely.

He spun around to face her. "To find Jason."

"No!" she cried out, terrified. "You heard him. He threatened to kill me."

"That was because he thought you were unfaithful to him."

"*Thought* I was unfaithful?" She was surprised at the harsh, bitter laugh that escaped from her lips. She could hardly believe how calloused she had become. "My God, Marc, he found me in a brothel. Of course I've been unfaithful to him. How could I deny that now?"

"Don't, Kate," he begged her. "Don't torture yourself like this. Jason has the blackest rages of any man I've ever seen, but even he wouldn't blame you for seeking refuge in a brothel when you had no place else to go."

"Wouldn't he?" Kate asked bitterly. "He might understand, but he'd never be able to forgive."

"Maybe you're right," Marc agreed, surprised at the surge of hope that raced through his body at the thought that Jason might not be willing to take his wife back again. Dammit, he told himself furiously, Jason was his friend—and Kate, too. If they still loved each other, he had to try to get them back together again. He had to forget the unceasing pain that was becoming a burning agony in his groin. "At any rate, we have to stop this craze for vengeance. Jason went half-mad when he thought you were unfaithful to him. We have to prove he was wrong—at least while you lived under his roof. What happened afterward was as much his fault as yours for accusing you falsely."

"He'll never believe that. I doubt if he'd have believed it before, but now . . . well, now he has proof that I'm the whore he always thought I was."

"Don't be ridiculous, Kate." Marc's dark eyes were filled with pain, as if he had been physically hurt by her words. "No one who knows you could ever believe that of you. Why, beneath that stubborn Irish temper, you're as warm and sweet, as generous and loyal . . ." He broke off abruptly, suddenly aware that he had said far more than he had meant to. "Why do you think Jason fell in love with you in the first place? For your beauty, yes, and your fiery vitality, but most of all because he believed in you and knew he could trust you."

"No!" she burst out. "He always knew about me." She saw the confusion on Marc's face and tried to stammer out an awkward explanation. "You see, I had a . . . well, I had a lover before Jason." She felt her cheeks grow crimson under his gaze as she blurted out the truth. Averting her eyes, she turned them toward the floor so she would not have to see the disillusionment in his eyes.

"You don't have to tell me this, Kate," Marc said gently. Looking up, she was surprised to see, not revulsion, but only kindness and even pity in his eyes.

"But I want to," she cried out. Suddenly the words began to spill out of her mouth, one tumbling quickly over the next, in her eagerness to tell him the truth at last. She told him first that she had lied when she claimed to be a widow, and then she told him everything else—how she had fallen in love with Philippe despite her father's wishes, how she had defied everyone to run away with him, even how she had given herself joyfully, unrepentantly to him on the filthy straw of a common stable floor.

"So you see," she said quietly when she had finished, "that's why Jason doesn't trust me."

"Yes," Marc replied thoughtfully. "That explains a lot of things. Jason is very possessive. It would be hard for him to accept the fact that his woman had given herself illicitly to someone else. I wish I had known about this before. I wouldn't have treated his jealousy so offhandedly."

"Then you aren't going to look for him now?" she asked hopefully.

"I have to, my sweet," he replied lightly. "We have to settle this once and forever. You can't spend the rest of your life being afraid he'll track you down and kill you."

Goddammit, why did she have to look up at him with those sad, trusting eyes, framed by dark lashes glistening with tears? Didn't she know how precious she looked at that moment, how vulnerable? Didn't she know how much he wanted to fold her into his arms and make love to her?

"Listen, Kate," he said, trying to make his voice sound light and casual. "I'll be gone just a little while. Lock the door behind me, and don't open it for anyone—not *anyone*, do you hear?—until I come back."

She nodded mutely, still looking up at him with the same soft, pretty, frightened look. It was all he could do to force himself to step across the threshold and pull the door shut behind him. He waited until he heard the soft scraping of the key in the lock before he turned slowly and started down the stairs.

41

KATE WRAPPED THE BLANKETS TIGHTLY AROUND HERSELF, forming a kind of cocoon that soon picked up the heat of her body and created a cozy haven for her. After a few minutes, the comforting warmth began to soothe her exhausted, fear-wracked body, and as her eyelids grew heavier and heavier, she felt herself drifting off into a deep and dreamless sleep.

She had no idea how long she slept, but when she awoke, she saw that the single candle on a table across the room had burned until it was only a tiny stub. Yet, still she was alone. Suddenly the sound of the rain beating heavily on the roof took on an ominous, oppressive tenor, like thousands of tiny nails being pounded into a box sealed around her.

As her nervousness increased, she sat up anxiously and began to look around the room, searching for some clue to tell her what time it was. Surely Marc had been gone too long, she thought, growing more and more frightened. Could something have happened to him? Jason's temper was black and vile, she knew, and he was nearly as angry at Marc as he was at her.

By the time she heard the sound of the downstairs door opening, then closing again, she had already worked herself into such a state that she was sure she would never see him again. It was all she could do to keep from sobbing with relief as she listened to the heavy sound of his solitary footsteps slowly ascending the stairs. Tying the dressing gown tightly around her body, she set her bare feet on the cold floor and hurried over to the door. Her fingers fumbled with the lock for a moment before she finally managed to undo it and swing the door eagerly open.

"Marc," she began to cry out joyously, but even before she could finish the word, it died on her lips. Her mouth still half-open, she watched in horror as a tall blond figure strode purposefully up the stairs. He stopped the instant he saw her, his eyes as wide with surprise as her own.

"Jason!"

Backing away slowly, she watched with terror-filled eyes as he advanced steadily toward her. She was too frightened to try to run away again, or even to slam the door swiftly shut in his face. Almost before she knew it, he was standing on the threshold of the bedroom, his eyes passing boldly up and down her body.

"I see you've made yourself at home." His voice was hoarse with an angry sarcasm she didn't understand at first. "Marc didn't waste any time, did he?" His cold, brittle eyes flitted suggestively toward the rumpled bed linen.

"Why, you son of a bitch!" she retorted furiously, her fear half-forgotten as she suddenly grasped the foul implication of his words. "Say what you want about me—I'm used to it!—but don't you dare accuse Marc." Stomping furiously over to the chair, she picked up her discarded garments, still dripping from the heavy rain, and flung them angrily on the floor at his feet. *"That's* why Marc had me put on his dressing gown. As for luring me into his bed, every man isn't as foul-minded as you are. I expect he thought I'd be safest there. Besides, you know perfectly well, Marc isn't the least bit interested in me."

"Are you really that naive, my sweet, obedient wife?" The sharp sarcasm in his voice stung her bitterly. For an instant, she felt an almost irresistible urge to reach out and slap his sneering face. "Marc always wanted you, but I'm sure you know that."

"Don't be ridic . . ." Kate stopped abruptly, suddenly recalling the strange look on Marc's face when he had thrust the robe irritably toward her. Jason was right, she thought in amazement. A belated crimson flush began to burn her cheeks. How could she have been such a fool? Heaven knows she had seen that same look often enough on other men's faces. This time, she had been too wrapped up in her own troubles to notice or understand. "I didn't realize," she said softly. Then, seeing the scornful, doubting look in Jason's eyes, she felt a dark anger begin to rise in her again. "All right. Maybe he did want me, but he didn't touch me. He's too much of a gentleman to do that. That's something *you* wouldn't understand."

Jason raised an eyebrow irritably as he continued to stare at her. He didn't like the turn the conversation had taken. Damn the woman! How had she managed to gain control of herself so quickly? She should have been sobbing and groveling at his feet, begging for her life.

"You're a cool little bitch, aren't you?"

"Oh, for God's sake, Jason," she cried out. Every muscle in her body was so taut she felt as if she was going to snap from the tension, like a dry and brittle twig underfoot. "If you're going to kill me, get it over with. Why do you have to torture me first? Does it give you some sort of sadistic satisfaction? Is that why you didn't kill me before, when we traveled with the Indians? Because you wanted to find new ways to hurt and degrade me first?"

What the hell was she trying to do? Jason thought furiously. What did she think it would accomplish, staring at him with those wide green eyes, so helpless and forlorn? She must have taken him for twice the fool he was if she thought he would fall for that. He knew it was just a trick she was playing, a stupid, coquettish trick.

"Do you really want to know why I didn't kill you, my love?" His voice lingered over the last word, managing somehow to turn even that tender endearment into a scornful insult. "Because I couldn't force myself to believe you were really the faithless, vicious little cat you are. Oh, I knew the truth, all right, but I tried to hide from it, tried to cling to that last little shred of hope that maybe I was wrong. Well, we settled that tonight, didn't we, my pet? Do you have any idea how I felt when I saw you parading your gaudily festooned body in front of a pack of prospective buyers, that same soft body I've run my hands over a thousand times, waiting to feel it writhe with pleasure beneath my touch?"

Dammit, Jason thought furiously, feeling his body begin to swell with familiar yearning as he thought of the lascivious delights of her ripe, warm body. What a fool he had been to speak of it, to let his mind dwell on it now. Desperately he tried to turn his thoughts away from remembered passion, but it was too late.

"Do you think I wanted to sell myself?" she asked, filled with a sudden intense loathing. She wondered vaguely who it was she despised the most—Jason or herself? "Do you think I enjoyed it?"

"Of course you enjoyed it, my dear. You enjoyed every minute of it. You love tantalizing men, don't you, luring them on with your beauty and your sensuality?" With rising anger he watched the tears that began to well up in her eyes at his cruel taunts. Damn her anyhow, he thought angrily, pounding his fist sharply against the door frame in a bitter rage. It was all he could do to keep from smashing it into the smooth whiteness of her face. Why the hell did she have to look so sad and put upon, as if everything were somehow his fault and she was not to blame at all? "A different man to pleasure you each night—how you must have loved that!" He spit the words out in rage and pain.

"Several men each night," she retorted with a savage fury. How dare he taunt her so cruelly? She wouldn't give him the satisfaction of knowing how much he had hurt her. "And of course I absolutely adored it. Every woman loves to feel a man shoving his way into her body before she's even dry from the man who used her before. And every woman loves to have her flesh torn apart by some brutal, selfish beast who pushes himself into her with no regard for her discomfort or pain, much less her pleasure."

"Don't try to make me feel sorry for you, bitch! You love being forced, don't you? You love to tempt a man until he loses control, then cry rape when he does what you were asking for all along. Come, my savage beauty, tell the truth. With every one of those men, no matter how you pretended, didn't you always end up writhing in pleasure beneath the weight of his body? I know you always did with me."

"And despised myself for it," she replied with a quiet sadness and dignity he had not expected. "As I suspect you despised yourself for responding to my body. Let's face it, Jason. There's something between us, some kind of animal passion that neither of us is strong enough to resist. But that's where the resemblance ends. I assure you, *I* take no pleasure in brothel encounters."

His eyes narrowed until they were dark, angry slits of midnight blue. What the hell was she doing? Trying to put him on the defensive? "Are you blaming me, madam, for seeking solace in whorehouses when I have an unfaithful wife?"

"You didn't have an unfaithful wife, sir, until you drove me away with your violence and black rages. If I, too, have sought 'solace,' as you put it, it has not been in whorehouses." Angrily she tossed back her head until the still-damp curls that lingered around her face flew backward, exposing the brilliant flash of green in her ears.

I have a mistress with green eyes. Dammit, why did those words have to come back to taunt him? Why did he have to see again in his mind's eye the vision of laughing black eyes and a gay, disarming smile? So that was where the earrings had gone.

"You have a penchant for gamblers, I see," he said coldly. He took a certain grim satisfaction in watching the color drain from her face as she guessed where her lover had gotten the earrings. "I suppose you're going to tell me you didn't enjoy sharing his bed, either."

"No, I'm not," she cried out defiantly. "Anton was good to me—and kind, in his own way. I didn't love him, nor did I ever pretend to, but in his arms I managed to forget my cares for a few minutes at least. That's something you'd never understand . . . but I can't believe it's so terrible."

Jason felt himself squirm uncomfortably. It was almost as if the little minx could read his mind. Hadn't he thought often enough of the sweet forgetfulness he found in the arms of the passionate Carmelita, or even the gentle, understanding Elise?

"He used to say—Anton—that my body was like a finely tuned instrument, and any musician could make a beautiful tune on it." She had intended to shock him with her bluntness. She could see by the angry expression on his face that she had succeeded.

"Fine musical instrument? Isn't that a bit high-class for a harlot, my dear? But then, I'm sure you were a very high-class whore." He tossed the words out in a harsh, biting tone, trying with the force of his anger to fight the agonizing desire that continued to mount in his body. He was no better than she, he thought bitterly. His body, like hers, clamored for the basest kind of satisfaction.

"All right, whore," he shouted out, giving in at last to the urges of his body. "Let's see how well you earn your money."

Reaching into his pocket, he pulled out a filthy, crumpled dollar bill and flung it carelessly on the small nightstand by the bed. For a moment, Kate felt herself cringe at the crudeness of the gesture. Then, reminding herself it was no worse than she had suffered at other hands, she stiffened her back with determination.

"A dollar, sir?" she said with carefully affected lightness, as if it were only an amusing jest they were playing with each other. "How dare you insult me? I assure you I am worth much more."

"How much?"

In spite of her resolve, Kate could not help feeling the cruel sting of his savage barbarity. "For you . . . fifty dollars!"

He did not flinch at the amount, but reached calmly into his pocket. Pulling out a roll of bills, he carefully counted out the sum and laid it on the table. "I doubt if you're worth it," he sneered, "but if you earn it, you can keep it."

The arrogance in his voice and mocking smile taunted her until she longed to kick and claw at him, scratching his face until she pulled his eyes out of their sockets. It took all her strength to hold her hands at her sides. An angry show of spirit would accomplish nothing, she reminded herself over and over again. It would only succeed in giving him pleasure in some perverse way. No, if she wanted to hurt him, there was only one way she could do it—with cold indifference and half-smiling scorn. She could defeat him only by lying limp and motionless beneath his weight. Taking off her robe, with no show of either haste or reluctance, she reclined lazily on the bed.

"Do whatever you want with me," she told him, contriving to make her voice sound tired and bored.

Jason looked down at her furiously. Damn the little bitch! She was escaping him, running away into the shelter of her indifference. He couldn't let her get away with that. Ripping off his shirt and pants with trembling fingers, he thrust his naked body angrily on top of her flesh, and without preliminaries, forced himself savagely into her.

"Whore!" he cried out violently. Almost uncontrollably, his body began to pump up and down against her flesh with frantic urgency, partly to satisfy his own burning craving, but more in a vain attempt to stir her up to the same wild frenzy. "Now, tell me you don't love this," he shouted out. "Tell me your body isn't aching to twist and turn under mine."

"No!" she cried out triumphantly. "No!" At last she had won, defeating his lust and her own. All she could feel was the pain he had caused in her body with the abruptness of his entry after so many months of none but willing lovemaking. Thank God for the pain, she thought gratefully. If only she could keep concentrating on it, perhaps it would be enough to prevent the swell of desire she feared so desperately.

Her victory stirred in him an irrational rage. Bitch! How could she escape from the anguish that was flooding his own body, tearing his spirit and heart in pieces? His mouth sought hers with an urgent hunger, clamping down on her tender skin until he forced her to cry out in pain. He pushed his tongue greedily inside, exploring with a violent possessiveness the territory that had once been so familiar to him. Even when her body remained passive beneath his, he did not relent, pushing his frantic assault, until at last he could feel the stiff tension in her limbs begin to melt away. At that moment he knew that the familiarity of their intimacy had finally evoked in her flesh a remembered passion she was powerless to control.

"I knew you loved it, bitch!" he hissed in triumph, rotating his hips with the swift, undulating movements he knew she could not resist. All the anger and pain he had felt at her betrayal swelled in his body, forcing out a torrent of raging words—words that were a cry of pain and grief, although Kate was too hurt by them to understand. "Is this how it was when you lured that poor, stupid farmer into the barn, then pretended you weren't aching for the feel of his hard shaft in your body? Is this how you felt when you pitched your tent in the goldfields and waited for them to hold your legs apart, playing the proper little lady until the passions of your body took over and you couldn't control yourself anymore?"

"God, you are a swine!" she cried out, but her words lacked force, for her body had already betrayed her. She and Jason both knew she had lost her battle against him. He was a beast, a brutal, savage beast, but now he owned her flesh, and there was nothing she could do but surrender to the swelling passion that carried them together to the same high peaks of rapture.

When at last their sated, sweating bodies fell still, they lay for a brief moment in each other's arms, unwilling captives to the heavy exhaustion that left them too weak to do anything but gasp for breath. Finally, with a harsh, abrupt movement, Jason jerked his body roughly away from hers, rolling hastily to the other side of the bed. To Kate's surprise, she suddenly felt lonely and bereft.

Damn him! How easy it was for a man. He could turn away, his lust satisfied, while her woman's heart still cried out for tenderness and caresses, even from the man who had savagely abused her.

Furiously she pulled herself up to her knees beside him. "Well, I hope you got your money's worth," she snapped bitterly. There was an icy coldness in her voice as she looked down at him.

"God, you are a cold-blooded little bitch!" he said with a short, harsh laugh. "But you're one hell of a lay. I have to admit that. You can keep the fifty dollars."

The white-hot flash of anger that raged through her body in response to his insulting taunt was tempered by a sudden, surprising impulse to laugh. "Keep the money?" She didn't know if the sound that accompanied her words was the beginning of a long, hysterical laugh or merely a tortured choking sob. "Keep it as long as I live, you mean—which, according to you, won't be long at all. I suppose you can retrieve the money from my body later."

He was startled by her words. To his amazement, he realized that he had completely forgotten the sole reason he had spent nearly a year of his life tracking her down. His eyes grew cold and hard as he continued to lie on his back staring up at her.

"How strange you are," she taunted, trying desperately to find some way to hurt him as much as he had hurt and humiliated her. "You hate me so much you want to kill me, but you still make love to me."

"Make love to you, whore?" Jason drawled with a slow, cold anger. "I didn't make love to you. There's a difference between making love and fucking, you know. You can consider yourself fucked."

"Why, you . . . you bastard," she hissed furiously, tears of humiliation stinging her eyes. How dare he force his body on her, then dismiss her so cruelly? How unfair it all was! Why was it that only women could be raped and humiliated?

Goddammit, she wasn't going to let him get away with that! Maybe he *was* going to kill her, but not before she had a chance at her own kind of vengeance. She wasn't going to die without making sure he had a taste of degradation, too— the same kind of degradation he had forced on her.

"But why are we quarreling, pet?" she asked with deceptive lightness, making her voice honey sweet and soft as velvet. "It's foolish to quarrel." Slowly she slipped her hand down his body until it rested lightly between his thighs.

He looked wary. "Why all this sudden sweetness?"

"Why not, my love?" she teased, letting her voice sink deep in her throat until it was earthy and sensual. Quickly, before he had a chance to realize what she was doing, she dropped her head down, letting her mouth rest against the flesh her hand had touched only a moment before. With a show of eagerness, she sucked it between her lips.

Jason's body jerked with a convulsive movement when he felt the warm moisture of her mouth on his body. "What the hell do you think you're doing? Don't you know I'm through with you now?"

But I'm not through with you! she thought gloatingly, though she dared not open her lips to speak the words aloud. Instead, she moved her jaw ever so slightly until the edges of her teeth rested menacingly against his flesh. She felt his body stiffen as he recognized her threat. He did not try to move for an instant; then his hand slipped down to clutch at the long auburn curls that flowed freely down her back, and she knew he was ready to tear her head backward, jerking her mouth away from his flesh. Slowly, carefully, she tightened the pressure of her teeth, until, with a surge of triumph, she felt him draw his hand away.

Jason held his body rigid and tense beneath the touch of her lips and tongue, but he dared not resist. Fighting desperately to keep from responding, he let her explore his flesh with the deft, skillful movements she had learned in long, hard months in the brothel. In spite of his resolve, it was only moments before he began to feel the same sweet, agonizing pain begin to swell his body again, and he cursed himself bitterly for it. He knew she would recognize his surrender the instant she began to feel his hardness fill her mouth, and she would gloat. God, how she would gloat! But even that humiliation was not enough to quench the burning desire that raged through his body. The more he tried to fight it, the more aware he was of the provocative movements of her tongue, driving him to the edge of a despair he could no longer resist. He was surprised at the harsh, tormented groan that escaped his lips when he finally gave in to her, forgetting every last shred of his masculine pride as he let his hips gyrate urgently beneath the moist touch of her mouth.

The instant she heard the sound, Kate knew she had won. Pulling her lips abruptly from his flesh, she cast her body on top of his, thrusting it down sharply until she felt that sweet moment when they had finally joined together, becoming for a brief instant in time one single being.

When it was over, Kate pulled herself abruptly away from him, rose, and slipped on her robe. As she stood beside the bed for a moment, looking down at him, she saw the same conflicting emotions blazing out of his eyes that he must have seen many times on her own face—the conflicting emotions of hatred and satiated passion, both fighting for dominance in his body. At last he understood, she thought bitterly. At last he knew what it was to feel the same degradation he had so often forced on her.

She stepped over to the doorway quietly, pausing only briefly to look back at him.

"Consider yourself fucked!"

By the time she reached the fragile velvet chair in the hallway and sank down on it, her body had already begun to tremble with uncontrollable convulsions.

42

Kate didn't know how long she sat in the dim hallway, shivering as she huddled on the fragile chair, the voluminous folds of the dressing gown tucked tightly around her body. She only knew that it seemed like an interminably long time. She closed her eyes for a moment, trying to make her mind a total blank so she wouldn't have to remember or feel anything, but it didn't work. The pain and the longing kept closing in on her, no matter what she did. It didn't for a moment occur to her to run down the long flight of stairs or even to try to lock herself in one of the other bedrooms. She knew it would do her no good. Jason was far stronger and swifter than she. There was no way she could escape him now.

Through the open door of the darkened bedroom, Kate was acutely aware of Jason's shadowy figure, his long, lean form barely visible in the faint light as he reclined on the bed. He had put on his trousers, but made no other concessions to propriety, and she was painfully conscious of the dark blond hair that curled on his chest, and the muscles that ran through his shoulders and arms. He did not move, but rested motionless, his shoulders propped up against the headboard, his deep blue eyes staring moodily into space.

Kate did not notice the moment when he first moved, for she had turned her head away to stare aimlessly down the broad, brightly lit stairway. It was only after a moment that she slowly became aware of a tall figure leaning against the door frame, staring at her with an intensity that drew her gaze toward him like a magnet. Turning her head slowly, she was startled by the raw, naked pain she saw cutting through his eyes. There was a weary resignation in his expression she had never seen before. It was as if he had dropped his mask for a moment, letting her catch a glimpse of the sadness and vulnerability that lingered behind his strong, invincible facade.

"I loved you," he said slowly, the words rasping through his lips as if they had been torn from his throat. "As God is my witness, I loved you."

Kate saw the pain in his eyes, and it cut through her body with a tender compassion she would never have believed she could feel for him again. For the first time, she realized that Jason, in his own way, had suffered as deeply as she. She longed to say something to him, to offer him some word of comfort, but she knew he would not be able to accept it from her. All she could do was stare at him mutely, her pensive eyes glittering with unshed tears.

Jason was silent as he gazed back at her, but he, too, longed to reach out and offer words of comfort. He felt as if his heart was being torn in two by the pallor of her listless face and the quiet sorrow in her deep green eyes. It took all his strength of will to keep from running to her side, throwing his arms tenderly around her soft, fragile body. "You killed something inside of me when you were unfaithful," he cried out in anguish. "You deserve to die for that."

"I was never unfaithful to you—until you drove me away,"

she replied with a quiet conviction that unnerved him. "But you can kill me if you want to. I'm tired of living anyhow."

She laid her head wearily against the back of the chair, her eyes still open, but as unseeing as the eyes of the dead. Yes, let him kill her now, she thought with cold resignation. She didn't mind dying anymore. It would be so much easier. She wouldn't try to run away again.

Jason leaned silently against the doorpost, his taut expression giving no hint of the aching desire that had once again begun to surge through his breast as he watched her sitting so helplessly, so invitingly, not six feet away from where he stood. God, what a fool he'd been to think he could ever revenge himself on her. He could never do it, not as long as that same tender yearning clung to every fiber of his body—yes, and his heart, too. What kind of witch was this woman, that she could cast such a spell on him? Even now, after all she had done to hurt him, he longed to crush her in his arms, taking her breath away with the passion of his lovemaking, then lie beside her the whole night long, covering her body with tender kisses, smelling the sweet fragrance of her skin and hair.

At that moment, Jason felt himself surrender, completely and finally, to the violent emotions that had racked his body and tormented his mind for all these long months. At last he understood that the commitment he had made with his marriage vows—those same words he had uttered so glibly and easily—ran far deeper and truer than he had ever known. She was his love—his only love—for better or for worse, to the end of his days. There was no way he could ever fight it.

And yet, what the hell was he supposed to do with her? he asked himself bitterly. He couldn't kill her—he knew that now—or even cast her away, but neither could he share her caresses with any other man. What other choice did he have? Lock her up in a tower room and never let her out except when he wanted her to share his bed?

He was painfully aware of the heavy silence as he stared down at his wife's pale, ashen cheeks, and wondered how the hell he had managed to make such a mess of his life. Dammit, he had always been the practical one, the sensible one—the man who never let emotion get in the way of reason. How could he have let this happen to him?

Jason was so engrossed in his own thoughts and the vision of Kate's soft body in front of him that he barely heard the sound of the door opening downstairs. He was only vaguely aware of Marc's tall body as he hurried up the steps to stand protectively at Kate's side.

"I see you've managed a reconciliation," Marc snapped sarcastically, his eyes taking in Jason's half-naked body.

"Why shouldn't I bed my own wife?" Jason retorted sharply. "What business is it of yours what I do with her?"

"By God, Jason, you're the stubbornest human being I've ever met—except maybe for her." He looked down at the taut, strained expression on Kate's face. "Haven't you two ever tried *talking* to each other?"

"He doesn't want to talk to me," Kate retorted defensively. "All he wants is—"

"Goddammit, I've had enough of this," Jason broke in furiously. "You keep out of this, Marc. This is between my wife and me."

"I have a stake in this, too, Jason, and you know it."

Kate was surprised to see Marc's hands move slowly toward his gun belt. Unbuckling it easily, he slung the weapon toward Jason, waiting tensely until it clattered to the ground at his feet. For several minutes the two men faced each other silently, angry determination written on their faces. It seemed to Kate that they were carrying on a mute dialogue with their eyes, although she could not even begin to understand what they were saying to each other. Finally, after what seemed like hours to her, Jason nodded slowly. With no change in expression, Marc turned, and with a deliberate casualness sauntered over to the stairway and flipped himself down on the top step, his long legs stretched comfortably in front of him.

"Well, let the trial begin," he said with a light mockery that belied the serious undertones in his voice.

Jason glared at him furiously. "I'm glad it amuses you."

"I don't find it amusing at all. I'd just like to get it over with."

Kate sat stiffly in her chair, gazing at them in amazement. How arrogant they were, these two men, calmly deciding her fate without so much as a glance in her direction. As far as they were concerned, she might as well not even have been there. "Aren't you gentlemen going to ask me how I feel?" she asked sarcastically. "Or is this mockery of a 'trial' going to go on without even a word from the defense?"

Jason spun around suddenly to face her. "*Can* you defend yourself, Kate?" he cried out. She was astonished at the tension in his voice. For an instant, it almost sounded as if he really wanted her to convince him. If she hadn't known better, she might almost have been fooled into thinking he was still in love with her. "Do it, Kate. I want you to prove your innocence. I'd sell my own soul—if I still have one—to believe in you again."

"Would you, Jason?" she replied coolly. "Forgive me if I find it hard to believe you. You certainly haven't tried very hard so far. You weren't even willing to give me the benefit of the doubt. You always believed I was guilty—just because you weren't the first man to stake a claim on my body."

"That's not true." Damn the little witch. How had she managed to turn the tables so neatly, putting him on the defensive?

"Isn't it? Then why did you carry on like a maniac, threatening to kill me every time I so much as flirted with someone else? Oh, yes, I admit it, I flirted. I'm really a shameless little flirt, but it was never anything but harmless fun."

"If it was only harmless fun, if you never did anything wrong, then why did you run away?"

"Why did I run away?" She stared at him aghast, unable to believe the words that spilled out of his mouth. Was he really as blind as all that? Surely it must have been obvious from the very beginning why she had fled. "I ran away because I was afraid of you."

If she wanted to hurt him, she had succeeded at last. For a moment, the careful mask slipped again from his features, and he looked as if she had slapped him sharply across the face. "I suppose I deserve that," he admitted. "But, my God, Kate, I've lost my temper with you many times—yes, and threatened you, too—but you never ran away before. Oh, I'll admit I'm moody—"

"Moody? I'd hardly say that's the word for it."

"What would you call it, then? Black rages? All right, I'll even admit to that. But you know damn well I always pulled out of them, and I always tried to show you how sorry I was."

"Did you, Jason?" she asked bitterly. "Oh, yes, you made love to me afterward, gently and tenderly, but you could never bring yourself to *say* you were sorry, could you? Come to think of it, you never really said anything to me. Oh, sure, words of passion sometimes, and a little casual chitchat, but when it came to anything important, it's as if I wasn't even there. You always made me feel shut out." She could see by the pained expression on his face that somehow, without really knowing what she had done, she had scored a point. She hastened to press her advantage. "You're very unforgiving, you know. I was afraid you'd never forgive me, and that I'd have to die for it."

"Unforgiving? Kate, that's not fair. Harsh, I suppose, and even cruel sometimes—but only to those who deserve it. Never to someone who's innocent."

"Like that poor cowhand you fired because I smiled at him?"

"Cowhand?" He sounded genuinely puzzled, as if he couldn't understand what she was talking about. Was he really so callous, she wondered, that the incident had completely slipped his mind?

To her surprise, she heard Marc give a light chuckle. "Tommy," he reminded Jason.

Jason looked uncomfortable—almost embarrassed, Kate thought, if indeed he was capable of such an emotion. "Oh, hell, I'd forgotten that. Do you have to remind me what a bastard I can be sometimes?" To Kate, it sounded almost as though he were laughing at himself, but it was a dark, bitter laughter.

"He hired him back, Kate," Marc said gently. "That same day. You didn't see him again, because the boy had enough sense to keep away from you. He didn't want another run-in with Jason."

Was that really true? Kate looked up hopefully, seeing the confirmation she longed for in Jason's eyes. Could she have been wrong all the time, she asked herself in amazement— wrong about the murderous blackness she thought she saw in his eyes? Dear heaven, had it all been a mistake? Had she fled from him, bringing untold suffering on herself—yes, and on him, too—all because of a stupid misunderstanding? A silly lovers' quarrel?

And yet . . .

Some little thought kept tugging at the back of her mind, some memory demanding recall. It was not just Jason's temper that had frightened her, she reminded herself. There was something else, too, something worse—some terrible, ugly thing that even now she could not bring herself to face.

Smead!

Earl Smead, his face dark and malignant, staring at her with savage malice, Earl Smead, the angry red scar running down to the corner of his sneering lips. Smead the liar, Smead the troublemaker, Smead the hired gunman!

"But of course you're only cruel to those who deserve it,"

she said coldly. Her voice was an empty, hollow echo of his own words. "You would never harm an *innocent* person."

Why did the image of that sheep rancher's wife have to keep racing through her imagination? That poor, tired girl, old before her time, her eyes as dead as Kate's own eyes had once looked in the reflection of a mountain stream. It gave her a sick feeling in the pit of her stomach.

Kate looked up to face the darkness in Jason's eyes. Suddenly she knew she couldn't stand it any longer. She was tired of running away, tired to death of the ugly fears that had too long hung over her like a dark pall. It was a relief to face things at last.

"You're a killer, Jason," she said bluntly. "A cold-blooded killer—as ruthless in your own way as Smead is in his. That's why I ran away from you."

"Goddammit, now you've gone too far!" he roared, thrusting himself furiously forward. Marc raced quickly up from the stairs, as if to pull Jason back from her body, but by the time he reached them, Jason had already stopped of his own accord. He stood only inches from her, his powerful body hovering threateningly over hers. "By God, madam, explain yourself, or I swear by all that's holy, I'll teach you a well-deserved lesson."

"I've seen what this country does to men," she told him defiantly. She was not going to let him frighten her anymore. He could strike her if he wished—or even kill her—but she was not going to live in fear any longer. "I've seen the look in a man's eyes as he prepares to gun down another human being, and it's not anger I see, or even hatred—but a passion for death. This land is so violent that it breeds nothing but violence, until it turns men into something lower than animals. Life is so cheap here that a man can be killed as casually as you'd shoot a wildcat or kick a tin can out of the way on the street."

Kate stopped abruptly, surprised by the naked anguish she saw reflected in the deep blue pools of Jason's eyes. She suddenly realized that the accusation she had hurled at him disclosed nothing more than a truth he had already learned about himself.

"There is a violence in me," he admitted slowly, "a kind of cruelty I would never have believed possible. I'm sorry you had to see it, but I suspect it was unavoidable. But I swear before God, Kate, whatever else I've done, I've never killed an innocent man."

"I suppose the sheep ranchers aren't innocent men—just because they smell bad! Oh, Jason, I know you hired gunmen to drive them off the land . . . and kill them if necessary. And that land doesn't even belong to you! How can you tell me you aren't every bit as evil as the gunmen you hired to do your dirty work for you?"

A long, stunned silence followed her outburst. The two men stared at her with surprise, astonishment, written on their faces. Finally, after a moment, Marc opened his mouth to speak, but Jason silenced him abruptly with a wave of his hand. For a long time he stood over Kate, staring down at her mutely. Then, to her amazement, he threw back his head and roared with laughter.

The sound stunned Kate, hurting her—and infuriating her—far more than his rage of a moment before. It seemed to her the final humiliation. How dare he make fun of her for caring what happened to the innocent sheep ranchers?

"God, Kate, I may have been a fool," he bellowed out, the sound of laughter still catching at his voice, "but you've been twice the fool! If I judged you on short evidence, you've been even quicker to leap to conclusions. Do you seriously think I'd slaughter innocent families just to steal their land?"

"I'm not a fool, Jason," she retorted sharply. "You may not have been willing to talk about it, but I overheard enough to put the pieces together. Besides, why would you import gunmen if you weren't planning to kill someone?"

"Oh, I'm planning to kill someone, all right, but I give you my word, no one I'm gunning for is either helpless or innocent."

Kate could only gape at him in disbelief and horror. Surely he didn't really believe that—or did he? Was he so far steeped in the violent madness of this land that he actually believed those poor, pathetic sheepmen were dangerous? Or had he convinced himself that, by settling on the open range, they had in essence stolen something that belonged—morally, if not legally—to him?

"I'll grant you one thing," Jason said, a wry half-smile twisting up the corner of his mouth. "If I were really that kind of monster, you would have been right to run away from me."

"*If* you were . . . ? But I saw with my own eyes—"

"You didn't see enough," he replied calmly. Then, turning to Marc, he added, "Go get her clothes—if you can find any that aren't all covered with plumes and sequins. And pay the good Madame whatever you think will appease her for losing such a pretty employee." When he saw Marc hesitate, the dark, angry look returned to his face. "Good God, man, do you think I'm going to hurt her? Get moving, now."

"What are you going to do with me?" Kate asked tensely as she watched Marc's back disappear down the stairs.

"I'm going to take you back to Wyoming territory so you can see for yourself whether the people I'm planning to 'slaughter,' as you so charmingly put it, are really as innocent as you believe."

"Oh, no!" Kate felt an icy hand of fear clutch at her heart as she looked into the cold, hard eyes that stared back at her. There was no pity or kindness in their depths.

Surely he couldn't mean it, she told herself desperately, trying somehow to convince herself that the fear that had begun to form in her mind was a foolish, insubstantial thing. Surely he wasn't going to make her witness the carnage he was planning. Even Jason couldn't be cruel enough to force her to stand and watch as he murdered them one by one, even the women and the children. That would be the supreme degradation, worse than anything else she had ever endured.

"Now, madam, no tears," he said coldly, reaching down to clamp her wrist tightly in a strong, painful grip. "You are coming back with me to judge for yourself."

Kate closed her eyes so she would not have to look into his face, but that was even worse. Dear God, why did the tired, washed-out features of that sheepman's wife keep intruding on the merciful darkness? How dreadful they were, those eyes—how tormenting. Heaven help her, she did not want to have to watch that woman die. She would rather be back in the mining camp, crying out as crude, filthy hands pawed her flesh, and cringing as she felt the lice from men's hair and beards crawling across her skin. Anything—*anything*—would be better than this final degradation Jason had planned for her.

She was beyond feeling pain as Jason jerked her roughly upward, thrusting her angrily back into the bedroom. She was surprised—and relieved—when he did not try to follow her into the room, but remained instead in the hallway, slamming the door tightly shut between them. She barely noticed the sound of the key as it slid softly in the outside lock.

Part VII

Spring

43

As Kate sat on the high wooden fence, feeling the rough, hand-split rails beneath the smooth fabric of her skirt, she gazed out in contentment at the broad, fertile valley that stretched as far as the hazy, majestic mountains in the distance. At moments like that, she thought with a smile at her own naiveté, she could almost believe she had never left the ranch. All she had to do was close her eyes and smell the sweet, tantalizing scent of new grass, and she could imagine that she was once again an innocent young bride, about to spend her first spring in the West. Even when she opened them again, catching sight of the delicate buds of profuse spring wildflowers that were already beginning to coat the meadow, the illusion remained intact. It was almost as if time had turned back full circle, giving her another chance to relive that bitter year in which she had made so many mistakes.

"You're lost in thought."

Kate spun around quickly, nearly losing her balance on the rail. She was startled to see Jason's tall figure standing beside her, his cool, aloof eyes staring down into her face. She had seen so little of him in these past weeks that he almost seemed a stranger to her.

"I didn't mean to startle you. I'm sorry."

He smiled easily, but Kate sensed no warmth in the gesture. She felt herself begin to shiver lightly as she stared back into the cold, hard depths of his eyes. As long as she had been alone, it was easy to turn the clock back—to pretend that everything was just the way it used to be—but the instant she felt the icy chill of Jason's eyes on her face, the illusion was shattered and she was forced to remember once again the ugly, terrifying thing he had brought her back to the ranch to face. He had been careful not to mention the sheep ranchers again, not since that night in his house in San Francisco, but the threat of them hung constantly over Kate's head, and she could not look into his eyes without remembering the brutal torture he had in store for her.

"I'm going back to the stables," Jason told her casually. "Why don't you come with me?"

Surprised, Kate slipped off the fence and began to follow him obediently. Ever since that night in San Francisco when they had made such brutal use of each other's bodies, Jason had been distant and aloof with her, much as he was during her first few weeks in Jasper Springs, when he had been trying to marry her off to someone else. This was the first time since their return that he had shown any interest at all in her company. To her annoyance, she found that she was almost pathetically grateful for the attention, willing and even eager to follow at his heels like a devoted spaniel puppy.

She was so engrossed in her thoughts of Jason—and of her reaction to him—that she barely heard the familiar sound that greeted her ears as they entered the stable. Even when it finally intruded on her consciousness, it took a moment for her to realize why the joyous, high-pitched whinny evoked such strong, sweet memories. For a moment she felt her heart skip a hopeful beat, then quickly she forced herself to take a long, deep breath. Surely it couldn't be . . .

Yet, as she squinted into the darkness of the stable, she was amazed to catch sight of a glint of reddish gold, caught up in a shaft of light that burst through the open doorway.

"Sunbeam!"

She ran toward the horse, then stopped abruptly and whirled around to face Jason, her eyes wide with amazement and delight. She thought she caught the trace of a smile on his lips, but in the darkness, she couldn't be sure.

"I bought her back from John Little Wolf. He drove a hard bargain. I paid a hell of a lot more for her this time." He strode over to the mare and ran his hands affectionately down the length of her neck. Kate was surprised to see Sunbeam nuzzle expectantly against the pocket of his rawhide jacket.

Why, she expects a sugar lump Kate thought in astonishment. Had Jason taken to bringing treats to her horse, just as he had often seen her do? Kate was surprised, for she knew it was a thing he rarely did, even for Midnight. Could it be that he had missed her, after all? Was that why he had gone out of his way to be kind to the horse he knew she loved?

Hopefully she glanced up at his face, but the same hard cold look that had shrouded his deep blue eyes for weeks warned her she was being foolish. Whatever love he had once felt for her now belonged to the past. His behavior on the long, hard journey back to the ranch and his aloofness in the days that followed, proved beyond the shadow of a doubt that he no longer cared for her. In all that time, she had never once caught him looking at her with warmth or tenderness—or even desire.

Once, she had thought that all she wanted from Jason was that he leave her alone—stop abusing her with the humiliating passion she could not control. All she had feared on the long train trip was the moment his eyes would begin to fill with desire again and he would turn toward her demandingly, ready to unleash the force of his animal passions on her unwilling body. And yet, as the journey progressed and it became more and more apparent that the thing she dreaded was not going to happen, Kate found to her amazement and self-disgust that she was filled, not with relief, but disappointment. Even when they returned home and she felt her body begin to tremble, half with fear, half with anticipation, Jason did not try to come near her. Instead, he seemed content to move into a remote corner of the house, leaving her to sleep alone in the bedroom she had once shared with him, as if the lust that had consumed them both was nothing more than an ugly memory for him. Kate didn't know if the changes in his feelings stemmed from the moment she had turned the tables on him, forcing him to taste the same degradation she herself had so often endured, or if the time had simply come when he had finally grown tired of her. She only knew that freedom from the terrifying cruelty of his lust brought with it, not the feelings of joy and relief she had expected, but only a deep passionate longing for a renewal of those same bittersweet chains that had enslaved her.

Too late, she realized that the instincts of her body were also the instincts of her heart. No matter how hard she tried to fight it, no matter how afraid she was of Jason and the brutal torture he had yet in store for her, she still longed to feel the touch of his fingers against her flesh, even if she had to accept his caresses only on his own harsh terms.

It was a bitter realization for Kate, and one that she could barely bring herself to face. As the days at the ranch turned into weeks and she saw nothing but a cool, indifferent courtesy on Jason's handsome face, she found it harder and harder to hold back the hot, stinging tears that threatened her eyelids. She wasn't sure what it was that hurt her most—the sudden coldness from his man who had once loved her, or her own immature, foolish inability to accept it. If it hadn't been for Stella and the fact that the woman still needed her so much, Kate didn't know how she would have endured those long, miserable weeks.

Jason had been surprisingly generous about Stella. "Good God, Kate, you can't expect me to support the whole prostitute population of San Francisco," he had grumbled noisily, but she knew it was only a token protest, for he had immediately dispatched Marc to fetch Stella before "Madame, with her renowned generosity, tosses her out with the rest of the trash." Unlike Anton, he had not insisted that Stella be shunted off to an out-of-the-way corner, but had treated her quite unexpectedly like a member of the family. He and Marc had actually seemed to enjoy vying with each other over her care, and even after Marc left, beginning the long ride that would bring Jason's horse and his own back home, he had continued to dance attention on her, pampering her with a spontaneous thoughtfulness that almost made Kate envious.

Stella was not the only unexpected gift Jason had planned for her. There was another, and it was, if possible, even better—and certainly more of a surprise. The last thing in the world she had expected to see when they rode into the ranch yard after the long, slow trip from the train depot was a bright blur of blue calico streaking across the yard. At first, she couldn't believe her eyes.

"Sarah!"

Unashamed tears flowed down her cheeks as she dropped to her knees in the muddy yard and threw her arms around the child. Only an instant later, Emmet followed his sister, toddling toward them eagerly on pudgy legs.

"Thank God you're safe," Kate cried out in delight. Jason had already promised that he had taken care of the children, but with characteristic reticence, he hadn't mentioned that he had brought them to the ranch. How very like him, Kate thought, to be so secretive, and yet, at the same time, so generous.

With the children to care for and play with, and with Stella growing healthier ever day, Kate's life in many ways was nearly content. Only when she caught sight of the relentless coldness in Jason's eyes—such a vivid contrast to the heat that burned through her own body whenever she saw him—did the sadness and the fear begin to grow in her heart again. Only then did she remember that she and Jason still had unfinished business between them, and it was a brutal, ugly business. The business of murder.

Sometimes Kate tried to drive the thought to the back of her mind, hoping against hope that the bitter thing she dreaded would never come to pass. At other times, she tried to force her thoughts to dwell on it, reminding herself that it would only be harder to bear if she hadn't prepared herself to face it. In the end, she realized it made no difference, for try as she would to steel herself against it, when the moment finally came, it was even uglier and more terrifying than she had imagined.

She knew the instant she saw the hard, brutally determined look on Jason's face that the time had come. She thought she had already seen the worst of the dark violence in his soul, but she quickly realized she was mistaken. Never had she seen a look like that.

"Get one of the men to put on a sidesaddle for you," he told her harshly. "We haven't time to wait for you to change into a riding skirt."

"I'll do it," she whispered, the words catching on the cold lump of fear in her throat. "I don't like anyone else to handle Sunbeam."

"Not Sunbeam," he told her sharply. "Tell them to give you an older horse, one who's"—he hesitated briefly, setting his jaw in a taut line—"one who's expendable."

"Oh, no!" She closed her eyes against the faintness that threatened her. How could she bear this? "Please, Jason . . ."

He gripped her arm firmly. "No fainting, and no hysterics," he warned. "It's time you saw the truth for yourself."

Time you saw. Time you saw. The words rang through her head in rhythm with the horses' hooves as they rode out, a small army, turning into the warm, bright rays of the late-afternoon sun. *Time you saw.* Yet, there were things she couldn't bear to see. Brutal, unspeakable things.

It was a nearly perfect afternoon, the kind of day when it's almost impossible to tell whether spring had already slipped into early summer, and the fresh, clean scent of new leaves and grass still hung on the light breezes. It was the kind of day when she should have been thinking only of life, Kate told herself bitterly; yet, there was nothing in her heart but ugly visions of death.

"I won't be a part of this," she whispered over and over again as they rode down the muddy trail. "I won't be a part of this senseless, brutal slaughter." But even as she whispered the words to herself, she knew they were meaningless. By her very presence, by her lack of resistance—even if resistance meant almost certain death—she, too, was contributing to the brutality. She, too, was guilty—as guilty as if she had held a gun to the heads of the innocent sheep ranchers and pulled the trigger herself.

God help her, she told herself desperately, this had to be the ultimate degradation. To be forced to participate in the torture of others—surely that was far worse than being tortured herself. As they neared the sheep ranch, she felt a sick disgust begin to flood over her soul, a disgust that was all the more horrifying because it was directed against herself. She knew she should die rather than let herself become a part of such a heinous act, yet somehow she could not find the courage to express her defiance.

For the first few minutes of that fateful ride, Kate had let herself pray desperately that the house they were going to attack was not the same one she had ridden past with Jason more than a year before. She didn't think she could bear to see that same woman's eyes, already so lifeless in life, staring up at her in death. Yet, as they drew nearer and nearer, she realized with sinking heart that even that torture was not to be spared her. At last, when they were near enough to see the place distinctly, Kate recognized the shabby, pathetic hovel she had seen but once before. Its drabness was unrelieved even by the bright rays of the dying sun.

Agonized by the sight of the home she had come to destroy, Kate turned her eyes away for an instant, staring intently into the vivid red of the sunset sky. She felt herself shivering as she looked up at it. Suddenly it seemed as if it was streaked with blood—the blood of the countless pioneers who had given their toil and their souls to mold a brash new land out of the wilderness.

To Kate's surprise, they rode to the gate unchallenged, though she was sure that terrified eyes must be watching them from behind the grimy windowpanes, just as she and the Allens had once stared out at an approaching band of savages. Without haste, almost as casually as if they had simply come to call, the men dismounted, pulling down heavy rifles from their saddles. With a dozen hired killers and twice as many ranch hands, they must have looked like an invincible army to the occupants of the tiny hovel; yet, still there was no sign of threat or even protest from within. And after all, Kate asked herself bitterly, why should there be? No doubt they were afraid, just as the Allens had been, of provoking the fight they still hoped desperately to avoid.

At Jason's signal, Smead gathered a small group of men and began to lead the horses toward the flimsy shelter of the barn. Another small group formed around Jason. The rest, led by Marc, headed for cover in the rocks and gullies of the surrounding terrain.

When the other men had scattered, Jason gripped Kate

ightly by the arm, then began to lead his own small group oward the door of the house. Though all the men carried ifles, Kate was surprised to see that they slung them easily over their shoulders instead of clutching them in tense readness. It was as if they were all so arrogant they expected no esistance.

To Kate's amazement, the door opened silently as they approached it. The man who stood inside, just on the other side of the threshold, held no gun in his hands. What kind of fool was he, Kate wondered, to open his door so readily to his own murderers? Or was he just too much of a coward to fight or his own life?

Still clenching Kate's arm tightly in his own strong fingers, ason moved to the side, gesturing to his men to precede him nto the house. Then, forcing Kate ahead of him, he too tepped into the small room. An eerie, unnatural silence hung neavily in the air.

Inside, the small shanty was even more of a hovel than it nad appeared from the outside. Kate was appalled as she glanced around at the soft dirt floor, still damp with the moisture of spring, and the crude, filthy furnishings. Bewildered, she watched as the men silently began to stack the few shabby chairs and tables on top of beds in the corners of the room. What on earth were they doing? she wondered, her dread half-forgotten in her curiosity. What was going on? She onged to ask, but neither Jason and his men nor the sheep rancher had spoken a single word, and she was afraid to break the heavy silence. Even when she saw the men begin to station themselves in the cleared-out spaces in front of the windows, she still could not understand what was happening. Only when she saw Jason kneel in front of one of the windows, resting his gun carefully on the ledge beside the sheepman's, did the truth finally dawn on her.

"Oh, my God," she whispered, horrifed and ashamed of the ugly suspicions that had filled her mind for months. "Why didn't you tell me, Jason?"

He turned only briefly to glance at her. "You had to find out for yourself. Besides, stubborn as you are, you probably wouldn't have believed me." There was a trace of humor in he lines around his eyes.

"But why are . . . ?" she started, then broke off as she realized Jason had already turned away from her, centering all his concentration on the darkening space outside the window. Why *was* he doing this? Jason hated the sheep ranchers, hated the way they were cutting up the open range and destroying the life he loved. How could he bring himself to help them now? That he should want to keep his hands clear of their blood was something she had prayed for, but never in her wildest dreams had she imagined he would actually *help* them. What kind of strange, unfathomable man was this she had married?

Kate had no time to ponder on it further, for the sound of hoofbeats began to ring in her ears, and it was only minutes before the first shot was fired. For all the men Jason had brought with him—and all the cleverness he had used in stationing them around the area—it soon became clear that victory would not be an easy thing to achieve. Instinctively Kate picked up one of the guns and moved toward a window. She was no stranger to battles, and she was not going to remain in the corner, huddled behind a table with the sheep rancher's wife and children. Jason caught her movement out of the corner of his eye and whirled around angrily to face her. Before he could open his mouth to speak, Kate silenced him effectively.

"You brought me here, Jason. Now you have to let me do what I feel I must."

Jason did not reply. He had already begun to have second thoughts about exposing her to danger, but no one knew better than he how important it was for people to follow the dictates of their own conscience. Turning resolutely away from her, he forced his attention back to the window, firing another round into the darkness.

It was a long night and a cruel one, but the first light of dawn brought with it at last the bitter taste of victory. Kate held her breath as she stood in front of the small house scanning the yard and the nearby slopes with her eyes, appalled at the evidence of butchery she saw on every side. Kate had seen dead men before—hadn't she even looked down in shock at the corpse of the man she herself had killed?—but never before had death and carnage left her so sick with disgust. How appalling it was, she told herself with a quiet hopeless fury, how stupid and wasteful to destroy so many lives in a vain attempt to stave off the destiny that was certain to overwhelm the West anyway.

The greatest toll had been taken among the ranks of the enemy. Kate shuddered as she looked around, seeing far too many faces that she recognized. Herman Rauss was dead, that hot-tempered, portly neighbor whose visits had caused Kate so much grief. One of their other neighbors, too, a good friend, lay battered on the ground, and Kate saw half a dozen ranch hands whose faces were nearly as familiar. No doubt the rest were hired killers, or perhaps cowhands Kate had never had a chance to meet.

Kate felt herself shiver as she counted the number of the dead. Why, there were nearly two dozen of the enemy alone. What an army Rauss and his friends must have brought to attack them! Only surprise had been on Jason's side, she realized, feeling her trembling increase at the thought. If Rauss had expected such strong resistance, the outcome might have been far different. Kate was glad she had not known during the long dark night how close she had come to being slaughtered alongside the people she had helped to defend.

Their own losses were nowhere near as great, but they were far harder to bear. The defenders of the little house had been lucky, and though there were several slight wounds, no one had been killed. Smead's men, defending the barn, had gotten off even lighter. Only in the field did their forces suffer casualties, but those were crushing. Marc himself had been wounded in the shoulder, and he had lost seven of his men—seven of the three dozen that had ridden up with them the night before.

Several of the gunfighters were injured, but only one did not survive. Kate found herself wishing it had been Earl Smead, but fate, with her usual disdain for a man's virtues or evils, had let him off without a scratch, and he lived to accept his pay with a mocking smile before riding off jauntily across the prairie to find another battle to fight—or another man to kill. Instead, the gunslinger who died was Roy Hockam, the man who had once sneeringly refused to risk his life fighting over a passel of Indians at the bottom of a snow-covered hill. Yet, now he had given that same life for a handful of gold coins he would never spend. It really didn't make any difference in the end, Kate thought—not any difference at all.

The ranch hands, perhaps because they were less experienced fighters, had fared far worse than the hired killers, and six of them now lay dead in the fields—six good men who had sacrificed their lives for a cause they could not possibly believe in. Kate saw the bitterness on Jason's face, and she knew what he was thinking. He was reminding himself that these men had died because they loved him enough—and respected him enough—to follow him blindly into any battle, even one they would not have chosen for themselves.

Kate felt her eyes well up with tears as she looked down at the strangely peaceful features of young Tommy, still a teenager. She remembered the day Jason had fired him because he dared hold her hand an instant too long as he helped her from her horse. How much better it would have been for him if Jason had not relented only a few hours later! Not twenty feet away lay George, poor old George, who finally had atoned for his cowardice with one last blazing act of courage, trying to save Tommy after he had been hit. Perhaps she should not feel so sad about him, Kate told herself. The West could be cruel to old cowhands. At least in death George had a chance to taste what he had never found in life—courage and gallantry.

What an appalling waste, she thought as she looked around, her shoulders bowed down with the weight of her sadness. And yet, for all the horror of it, at least it had accomplished its end. With two of the ringleaders dead, the ranchers would put a halt to their violent resistance of the sheepmen, and the savage range wars that had already lasted for years in other places would end in Jasper Springs with only one brief battle. More fences would go up now, and the vast open land Jason loved would be no more, but with its passing, peace would begin at last to spread its healing balm over the wounded, bleeding land that was the West.

Sadly Kate turned back toward the house, rolling up her sleeves above her elbows as she prepared to help with the wounded, who were already being carried into the small hovel. At first she expected Jason to object when he saw her tending enemies as well as their own men, but she quickly realized she had been mistaken. If anything, Jason was watching her with a new and deepened respect in his eyes.

Why, he's as sick of this as I am, she thought in amazement. It seemed almost incredible to realize that Jason, like herself, was appalled and disgusted by all the death and devastation that surrounded them, yet she knew it was the truth. Theirs was a common cause now, healing the wounds they had helped to inflict.

Kate became so engrossed in her work that the time passed quickly, and she was surprised when at last she felt the touch of a hand on her arm. Looking up quickly, she saw Jason bending down over her as she knelt beside a wounded gun-slinger on the ground.

"Come on, pretty girl," he said with a gentleness she had never expected to hear from his lips again. "It's time to go home." His voice was so soft and filled with love that she longed to throw herself into his arms. Only the same guarded look that had filled his eyes for weeks prevented her.

"But there's still so much to do," she protested wearily. "So many men were hurt."

"The others will take care of them," he said, gently pulling her to her feet. "You've done enough. Besides, there are still too many things left unsaid between us."

There was a strange, dark look in Jason's eyes as he led her toward her horse. It was a look of sadness, she knew, but there was something else in it, too, something she couldn't quite recognize. What was it—fear? And yet, it couldn't be. Jason wasn't afraid of anything.

They rode back to the ranch in silence, listening only to the heavy clumping of their horses' hooves beating through the still morning air. When they arrived at last at home, they found the downstairs rooms empty and quiet, although someone had been thoughtful enough to build a warm, blazing fire in the grate. Jason stirred up the logs for a moment, then replaced the poker in the rack at the side of the fireplace and came over to her, sitting down on the rug at her feet. The same dark, unfathomable look lay in the depths of his eyes.

"There's been a darkness hanging over my soul, Kate," he said simply. "But I suspect you know that already. Perhaps that's what frightened you so much about me. Only, I think that darkness has begun to lift a little today. Maybe, at last, it's time to talk about it."

"I don't understand," she replied, surprised and annoyed at the little tremor of fear that ran through her body. Why was she shivering? She had longed for him to talk to her, *really* talk to her—she had begged him to—yet now that it was finally happening, she was afraid.

He seemed to be shivering too. "I suppose I should have told you long ago, my love. I had no right to marry you without letting you know what kind of man you were getting, but you see, I was afraid of losing you." He broke off with a harsh, self-mocking laugh. "That's a good one, isn't it? Me, the strong, independent one—the one with no holds, no emotional ties—me afraid of losing a woman! Oh, my darling, that's why I could never bring myself to tell you, and that's why I have to tell you now. Because I love you too much to hide the truth from you anymore, even if I lose you because of it."

Silently she nodded her agreement. She was still afraid, but she knew it was something she had to hear. Perhaps now, at last, she could finally begin to understand this bewildering, complex man she loved so deeply.

"All I ask is one thing," he said softly, lifting her hand for an instant to touch it lightly with his lips before releasing it again. "Let me finish without interrupting. No matter how you feel, let me go on. Then, when I'm through, you can say anything you want."

44

"YOU HAVE TO UNDERSTAND, MY LOVE, I CAME TO THE WEST as a man dedicated to anger and hatred, a man filled with a desperate longing for the searing flames of clean and honest battle to purify a soul sickened by brutality. War had become, for me, a stinking, malignant thing. I was sick to death of fighting in the ruins of farmers' fields and setting fire to the homes that men had devoted their lives to building, even if those same men were the enemy, sicker still of the inhumanities of prison camp—inhumanities on both sides. All I wanted to do was wipe away the ugly vision of men lying on frozen ground with gangrenous, rotting limbs, or worse still, the memories of men whose souls died before their bodies as they traded away their dignity, and sometimes even the lives of their friends, to buy one more day of miserable existence. I tell you all this, not to justify what I did, but so that you will understand what it was like.

"You can't begin to realize how important it was for me to come West. The West was something different, something better. The West was a world apart from the weariness and death I had known. Here at last was a clean, decent place, a place as yet untouched by the corrupting fingers of civilization. All we had to do was root out a group of primitive, bloodthirsty savages, and then mankind would be free to build a new world—honorable and decent and just.

"That the Indians were savages, I had no doubt, for besides the stories I had heard about them ever since I was a boy, I had seen traces of their ugly handiwork throughout the long trek west. They made sure of that, the Yankee colonels and majors who brought us out. We were nothing but a group of rebels who had half-sold our own souls when we escaped our captivity, trading it in for a blue uniform and the right to ride alongside men we would have fought—and killed, if we could—only months before. The only thing that kept us going was the knowledge that we were going to a cleaner war than

496

any of us—blue or gray—had known before. Our officers wanted to make sure we had the proper incentive to maintain discipline and fight together.

"And incentive they gave us! Although the burned-out cabins and covered wagons meant little to us—for hadn't we seen far worse devastation in our own lands?—the grisly trophies of human hair that had been retrieved from dead savages were enough to send our blood boiling for revenge. The long tresses, we knew, could not have come from the scalps of men in battle, and tiny, soft clusters of curls could only have graced the heads of small children. Here at last was something that could unite us, Yankee and rebel both. Here was a common cause that could join us together in a quest for justice and human rights.

"I can't put my finger on the exact moment when things began to change, and the fervor the Yankee officers had instilled in me slowly started to slip away, but I know it was not long after I arrived at my post in Fort Lyon. Looking back, I suspect the first thing that began to shake my smug, complacent judgment of the savages was my growing sense of respect for the commanding officer, a man as renowned for his stern, unyielding discipline as he was for his honesty and scrupulous fairness. At first it shocked and even angered me when I noticed the blatant sympathy he displayed in his dealings with the Indians, but then it began to make me uneasy. If this man—a man I was growing to trust and respect more each day—was actually a friend to the Indians, could they really be the savages I had imagined?

"The actions of some of my fellow officers were even more unnerving. One of them in particular, an idealistic captain named Silas Soule, was extremely vocal in his defense of the Indians. 'What a lot of damn fools we are!' he would shout time and again, his face growing red beneath his dark beard. 'We break every treaty we make, we attack unarmed Indians and slaughter them, and then we wonder why the "savages" fight back!'

"I found myself growing to like Silas Soule, partly because of the strength of his character, but more, I suppose, because he went out of his way to be kind to me. Rebel officers were hardly popular in the Yankee army, at least not until they had proved themselves in battle, but Soule never treated me like an outcast. Perhaps because we were both captains, or perhaps because he recognized in me a compatibility of ideals I had not yet sensed myself, he went out of his way to befriend me.

"Grateful as I was for Soule's companionship, I was careful to hold my tongue whenever he started in on one of his wild tirades about our treatment of the Indians. At first, I told myself I was doing it because I did not want to jeopardize our friendship, but soon I had to admit that there was more to it than that. Soule's words were finally beginning to strike an answering chord in my own thoughts. In the few weeks I had been in the fort, I had had ample opportunity to see many Indians at close hand, primarily Cheyenne and Arapaho, and some of their Dakota friends from the north, and it disconcerted me to realize that there was nothing savage or warlike about them. They had an aura of warmth and friendliness—and a gift for laughter—that puzzled me, for it was unexpected. Still, I found it hard to believe that they could be anything but the vicious savages I had been taught to believe in.

"I might have gone on like that indefinitely, wavering back and forth in my indecision, if it had not been for Major Anthony, the new commandant brought in to replace our former commanding officer, who had become—so it was rumored, at least—'too soft on the Indians.' Anthony was a squinty, red-eyed, deceitful man, and as I watched his shady dealings with the Indians, I was finally forced to admit that Soule was right, in part at least. It was a chilling thought.

"Everything came to a head in the late fall, at the end of November. I still remember the ugly foreboding that cast its cold chill over me as I stood in front of Major Anthony's office and watched Colonel Chivington's Colorado volunteers march down the dusty road into the fort.

"There were six hundred of them, six hundred rough, crude, unprofessional 'soldiers,' and every last one of them was a ruffian who had come for excitement and loot—or to escape a prison sentence. At their head rode a huge, barrel-chested, thick-necked Methodist minister named John M. Chivington. Chivington had spent much of his time in the rough mining camps, organizing Sunday schools, and he still had the ways of a 'preacher' about him. He sat tall and arrogant in his saddle as he gathered his men around him—and anyone else who would listen—while he made a fiery, blustery speech that made my skin crawl.

" 'Well, men, you all know what we're here for,' he roared, or words to that effect. 'You've been raised to kill Indians, and that's what we're going to do. I want you to remember one thing, and one thing only—kill those damn Cheyenne whenever and wherever you find them.' The cheer that greeted his words was bloodcurdling.

"Chivington's welcome among the officers was, to my surprise, far less enthusiastic. Several of the men were openly disapproving, although most of us took care to remain cautiously neutral as we eyed the colonel and his undisciplined followers. Only Major Anthony greeted him with unmixed warmth.

" 'Just in time,' the major enthused, his eyes glittering with pleasure and excitement. 'Black Kettle's camped on the banks of Sand Creek with some of the other chiefs and a passel of those tricky Arapaho. But, hell, they won't be any trouble at all. I told 'em to send all the warriors off to find food. Go on a buffalo hunt, I told 'em.' I don't know why I didn't understand the uncharacteristic chuckle that accompanied his words. At the time, I only knew it made an uncomfortable chill run up and down my spine.

" 'Well, Major, looks like we'll all be collecting scalps tomorrow,' Chivington responded with fanatical fervor.

" 'I hope so, Colonel.' Anthony's enthusiasm was ghoulish. 'We've all been waitin' for a chance to pitch into them.'

"I was careful not to say anything, although I could hardly believe the words I was hearing. Surely this was an unprofessional way to conduct a campaign; yet, Anthony was regular army. Didn't he know we were supposed to be there to protect innocent settlers, not to satisfy our own private needs for vengeance or, God forbid, amusement? Yet, that was how our leaders were talking.

"Some of the men were not as cautious as I. Predictably, Silas Soule, together with a pair of young lieutenants, led the opposition. 'But, Colonel,' Soule protested, 'we've given the Indians a pledge of safety. They're here in peace. If we attack Black Kettle now, it would be murder in every sense of the word.'

"The young lieutenants agreed, but Chivington would have none of it. 'It's time we taught those savages a lesson.'

" 'Such an action would dishonor the uniform of the army,' Soule said with a courage and dignity that I envied. 'I for one refuse to participate in it.'

" 'Damn anyone who sympathizes with the Indians,' Chivington screamed with a rage that turned his face into a bright reddish purple. 'Need I remind you, Captain, you will obey orders or you will face a court-martial. I have come here to kill Indians, and I believe it is right and honorable to use any means under God's heaven to do so.'

"Soule's face turned nearly as red as the colonel's, but he knew he did not dare say anything. One look at the colonel's dark, raging eyes was enough to warn him he was not bluffing. It was only later, as we sat up through the long, dark night, contemplating the fight that lay ahead, that he could finally speak his mind.

" 'Christ, the warriors are all off hunting buffalo," he complained bitterly. 'There's no one there to defend the camp. What kind of a fight will that be?' There was despair in his voice, and I could feel it with him. Much as we all loathed the task that lay ahead of us, we knew we had no choice.

"It was a grim and silent group of officers that set out under cover of darkness the next evening, leading a small army, several hundred strong, toward the banks of Sand Creek. I cast a glance at the taut, angry faces of Soule and the two young lieutenants who had defied Chivington, and in an odd way, I almost envied them. I knew that sometime in the long, dark hours of the previous night, they had come to an agreement not to order their men to fire in the forthcoming battle. I only wished I could make up my mind as easily. I deplored the colonel's unprofessional behavior, just as I deplored attacking men who had been given a pledge of safety, but I couldn't forget that the Indians were, after all, wily, tricky devils. Perhaps they only pretended to go along with the hunting idea, I told myself hopefully, using it as a ruse to set up an ambush. If that was true, then the battle that followed might yet be an honorable one.

"We reached the camp just as the first gray light of dawn was creeping over the horizon. The cluster of tepees pitched in the bend of the creek looked remarkably quiet and peaceful. The tents of Black Kettle's people and the other Cheyenne were in the center, with Left Hand's Arapaho slightly to the east. Even at our approach, only a few curious heads peeked out of flaps of the tepees. It was as if they had not been alerted to our approach—yet, surely they must have had sentries. I think it was at that moment I finally realized all my hopes were futile. If the Indians felt safe enough not to post sentries, Soule must have been right. They really *had* come in peace.

"I was ordered to circle around to the west, so I missed the first horror of the battle, thank God. I don't think I could bear the memory of sleepy, frightened people pouring out of tents and rubbing their eyes in bewilderment. The men who did see it could only talk about it later with pale and ashen faces. There were old men, they said, and frightened women with babies in their arms, and little children crying with confusion and terror. That was all, they said—there were no warriors.

"By the time we reached our post and turned to face the 'battle,' it was already appallingly clear that it would not be a fight, but rather a massacre. I could see by the sick look on my men's faces that they felt no differently than I did. The lust for blood and slaughter seemed to come primarily from Chivington's six hundred volunteers.

" 'My God, Captain,' a young sergeant cried out in anguish, 'I can't kill women and children. It isn't decent.'

"It wasn't decent. I have never seen anything farther removed from the concept of decency than the atrocities committed at Sand Creek that day. I saw women shot down and impaled on sabers, children torn from their mothers' arms and clubbed to death, screaming with pain and agony. For a long time, I could not bring myself to issue any kind of command to my men, or even to speak a word. Finally I was jolted out of my horror by a frightened voice.

" 'What are we going to do, Captain?' It was the same young sergeant.

" 'Hold your fire!' I shouted out, suddenly spurred to action. The words were hardly necessary, for without an order to fire, all my men had stood rigid and immobile, staring with unbelieving eyes at the bloody massacre. 'Don't shoot—except in self-defense.'

" 'But the colonel—'

" 'Damn the colonel!' How I wished I'd had the courage—or the wisdom—to stand up with Soule before when he had defied his superiors' orders. Now all I could do was follow his example and refuse to take part in the disgusting slaughter.

"I stood beside my men, silent after my one angry outburst, and watched with horror as Chivington's volunteers tore through the camp. At first, everything was too confused and chaotic for me to discern what was happening, but all too soon, incidents and actions began to stand out with hideous clarity, and I was forced to witness things so appalling I would never have believed they could be committed by human hands. I can't even being to describe some of the things that occurred before my eyes, nor would I even try. They are too brutal and ugly to share.

"After a few minutes of watching that disgusting spectacle, I was surprised to see some sort of order beginning to arise from the Indians' confused, aimless attempts at flight, especially in the distance, far to the east of where I stood. As I stared harder at the spot, I became aware of an old man who stepped out of an imposing lodge and gathered a group of frightened women and old men around him. To my amazement, he carried a pole in his hand, topped by an American flag—the same red-white-and-blue Yankee colors that had flown over my own enemies in battle. He raised it high, waving it over his head until it was caught up by the cold dawn winds and streamed out behind him. Over and over, he kept shouting out words I could barely hear, but could not understand at all.

" 'That's Black Kettle,' a voice said in my ear. Spinning around, I was surprised to see the half-breed that Chivington had routed out of his bed and forced to become our guide. His face was void of expression, but I knew there must be bitterness in his heart, for I had been told the Cheyenne were his mother's people.

" 'What is he saying?' I asked, almost against my will. Already I sensed I didn't want to know.

" 'He's telling them it's a mistake,' the half-breed said. 'He's telling the people not to be afraid—the bluecoats are their friends. They won't shoot when they see the flag.' He turned and spat on the ground.

"The smoke and confusion of battle quickly clouded the area, until, to my relief, I could no longer see the innocently trusting Black Kettle and his people. But as I turned to survey the scene nearer at hand, I saw a sight that was even more hideous to my eyes. Another old man—another chief, I assumed—had gathered his people around him, only this time he was so near I could see the deep creases on his dark brown face. To my horror, I realized he was also carrying a flag, and many of the people with him had hoisted conspicuous white banners on poles above their heads or were waving white rags in their hands. With the old men at their head, they began to march slowly toward the main detachment of troops. They had an air of confidence and trust about them that was frightening.

" 'What are they doing?' I shouted out in horror. 'Don't they know they'll be shot down?'

" 'But they're under white flags, Captain,' the half-breed replied sarcastically. He looked as if he wanted to spit again but couldn't quite force the bitterness out of his mouth. 'Besides, didn't the Great White Father Lincoln himself promise the chiefs no soldier would fire on them if the flag of the United States flew over their heads?'

"Even as I watched the old man—I later learned he was Chief White Antelope, but I knew him then only as the old man—he held out his arms and called out in English, so clearly that I could understand every word from where I stood. 'Stop firing,' he begged the soldiers. 'It is all a mistake. We are your friends.' They shot him down where he stood, the Stars and Stripes still clutched in his hands.

"I could only stare at him mutely, sick with horror at what I saw. Even when I heard the emphatic sound of approaching hoofbeats, so dramatic and forceful that they seemed to have an anger of their own, making them echo above the din of the massacre, I barely noticed them. Only when I saw the look of bitter contempt that slipped through the half-breed's careful mask for an instant before he hurried away did I turn around.

"Colonel Chivington in his wrath was as terrifying a sight as any man must ever have seen in battle. As he sat boldly on his horse, furiously facing me, his dark hair floated around his bearded face and his eyes flashed with a black fire of rage. What a terror he must have been in the pulpit, spewing out threats of fire and brimstone.

" 'Get your men moving, Captain,' he barked furiously. 'You're here to fight Indians. Do you want to be court-martialed for cowardice?'

" 'Good God, Colonel, what do you expect me to do? Fire on a bunch of children?'

" 'Nits turn into lice,' he snapped viciously; then, spurring his horse savagely, he whirled and rode away.

" 'He means it, Captain,' the anxious sergeant said. 'We'll all be court-martialed sure.'

"How I wish I'd had the courage to stand my ground. If only I had said to my men: Stay here and hold your fire, and the devil take the consequences. But I didn't. Instead, I found the easy way out.

" 'The horses!' I shouted to the men. 'Capture the Indians' horses.' At last—a way to join in the melee without having to slaughter innocent women and children.

"When we got to the horses, we quickly found we were not alone. More than a dozen other men had already set themselves to that self-appointed task, trying—as we were—to flee from the carnage and brutality that surrounded us all. And it worked—at least, for a while. We still heard the screams of terror, but we no longer had to look on the atrocities, at least not then.

"Later, it was unavoidable. Later, when the slaughter was over and most of the men were gone—even those who searched for grisly souvenirs among the bodies of the slaughtered—I stood alone at the edge of the eerily silent battlefield. There were no sounds, not even the whimpers of the wounded.

"I later learned that the wounded had been too terrified to

cry out—even while their scalps were being cut from their heads. They knew they would be killed if they did.

"How can I describe the scene that met my eyes? There were bodies everywhere, but they were not the bodies I was used to seeing after a battle. The men were old, and there were women and children—all savagely mutilated. I saw women with their breasts sliced off and their private parts gouged out to decorate the pommels of their murderers' saddles. I saw a pregnant woman whose belly had been sliced open, with the dead and bloody fetus lying beside her. Men had fingers cut off to remove their rings, and testicles chopped off as a souvenir . . . or to make a tobacco pouch.

"Dear God, I never thought I'd have to see anything so terrible or so inhumane in my life, and I'd rather die than have to see it again.

"Altogether, there were over a hundred and thirty dead, more than one hundred of them women and children. Several of the chiefs had been killed. Black Kettle escaped, but not White Antelope or One-Eye or War Bonnet. Left Hand, too, the Arapaho chief, had been shot down, but miraculously escaped death. I was grateful I had not been there to see that.

"It had been an eerie sight, one of the young lieutenants told me on the long ride back to the fort. He was obviously still stunned by the experience. Left Hand had just stood there, the boy said, stood quietly with his arms folded on his chest, refusing to fight, because the white men were his friends.

" 'He just stood there singing,' the boy told me in awe. 'And do you know what he was singing? His *death song.* Nothing lives long, only the earth and the mountains.'

"Nothing lives long. Only the earth and the mountains.

"I was to hear those words often enough in the weeks and months that followed, but even though they seemed to offer comfort to the dying men who chanted them, they did nothing to ease the chill that settled over my own heart.

"To this day, I can still distinctly remember the expression on the faces of my fellow officers as we rode home during the dark night that followed the massacre. I knew by the grim set of their jaws, barely visible in the pale moonlight, that they were asking themselves the same question that tormented me. How could we have let it happen?

"Oh, sure, some of them spoke out against the slaughter even before it began, and many more of us refused to shoot, but we let it happen, all the same. It's tempting to try to justify it, to say we were outnumbered by those hundreds of volunteers out for blood, but brave men have been outnumbered and still fought before. Many times during the 'battle'—how can I call it a battle, when no one fought back?—I was tempted to order my men to turn their guns on the volunteers, but I lacked the courage. How often in the long, dark nights that followed have I wished I had done just that. I might well have given my life for it, but at least it would have been death with honor . . . and dignity.

"There are things a man can't live with, my love, and still call himself a man. Standing by and watching innocent people slaughtered—no matter how hopeless resistance would have been—is one of them. It is something that will haunt my nightmares every last hour of my life."

45

THE FAINT FLICKERING RAYS OF THE DYING FIRELIGHT touched Jason's face with a soft caress as he finished his tale and fell silent. With a loud snapping sound, the last heavy log rolled from the top of the embers and fell with a bright barrage of red and yellow sparks to the bottom of the hearth. Jason turned his head at the sound and reached out his hand toward the poker, intending to stir up the flames again and dispel the twilight darkness of the room. Before he could reach it, Kate leaned forward, covering his hand with her own and pulling it back toward her.

He raised her hand to his face, laying her fingers gently against his cheek. "Now you understand why I had to fight for the sheepmen, even if I hated them and all they stand for. Once before, I had to stand by when innocent people were slaughtered. I could not do it again. This is my way of atoning for that . . . of making peace with myself again."

Silently she nodded, running her fingers lightly across the dark stubble that lay on his cheek.

"Now maybe I can make you understand why I seemed so aloof from you, and so unreasonably jealous. I'd like to say it was because of someone I knew before—a lady who lives in the deep, dark past—but that's only half-true." He closed his eyes for an instant, letting a half-forgotten memory of light golden hair and pale eyes drift surprisingly across his thoughts. He could no longer even remember the sick feeling that had lain like a giant tumor in the pit of his stomach when he had learned of her treacherous betrayal. "No, that's not even half-true," he contradicted himself, smiling lightly as he opened his eyes to gaze at his wife again.

"You see, my love," he told her softly, "deep in my heart, I always knew—always—though I could never admit it to myself, what a cruel, hardhearted little minx she was. But with you, it was different. With you, I sensed I had found someone decent and faithful and true—only, I knew it wouldn't make any difference. I knew my fear of the past was making me shut you out of my life, forcing you to be a stranger to my heart. I knew that sooner or later that would drive you away from me. The hell of it was, I couldn't blame you . . . but I hated you for it all the same.

"It wasn't reasonable, my love, but then, I rarely am. Every time I saw you laughing and joking with some man, I would ask myself: Is this the man who is going to take her away from me? And then I would grow afraid."

"Oh, Jason," she cried out, her arms longing to press his body against hers in comfort. "You're being too hard on yourself."

"I know what you're going to say," he broke in quickly. "You're going to tell me I couldn't help what happened, that it wasn't my fault because I didn't participate in it, but don't you see, that isn't true. Everyone who didn't do something to prevent that massacre has to accept a share of the guilt."

Kate shook her head slowly. She would offer him no words of false comfort. Hadn't she felt exactly the same way herself when she thought she was riding to the massacre of the innocent sheepmen? The fact that she wasn't a willing participant hadn't made her feel any less guilty.

"No," she said softly, "I wasn't going to say that at all."

Perhaps it had all been for the best, she told herself with a wry smile, all those hideous, degrading things she had been forced to endure. If she hadn't suffered them, it might have been harder for her to understand Jason now, when he needed her compassion and her love.

He pulled himself up to his knees beside her, his eyes still fixed firmly on her face. A new hope began to shine in them as he saw his mute appeal answered by the tender understanding that lay in the soft green depths of her eyes.

She did not try to speak, for she knew there were no words

hat could ease his heart. Silently she slipp..
eside him, giving in at last to the urge to offer her knees
n the only way she knew he could understand and accomfort

In the long, sweet hours that followed, Kate felt her
reawaken to the nearly forgotten delights of tenderness, an..
he knew at last that she had truly come home again. As she
nestled in her husband's arms, in the same bed where they
had shared their first joyous night of love, she finally understood what it was that had carried her through the cruel, bitter
months now forever behind her. She knew at last why she had
fought so desperately to preserve her life, even when she had
thought it was worthless and empty. Love was the answer, she
told herself happily, the ultimate reason for her existence.

"You look like a cat curled up before the hearth, my love,"
Jason told her, laughing softly as he pressed her even closer
into his arms. "So contented and so smug. Tell me, precious
wife, do you by any chance think everything will go smoothly
now? Do you think I will be gentle and even-tempered, and
you will see no more of my black moods?"

"Be as moody as you like, sweet husband," she replied
pertly, deliberately mimicking the teasing tone of his voice.
"But it shan't do you any good. From now on, I'll know how
to handle you."

"Good God, it sounds as if you mean that," he said, raising himself on one elbow to look down at her with an expression of mock horror and surprise. "What kind of demon
is this you've become? Where is the gentle, sweet-tempered
woman I married?"

"Go ahead, Jason, joke all you want to. From now on, I
intend to wrap you around my little finger."

"Oh? . . . And how do you propose to do that, pray tell?"
His tone was still light and teasing, but Kate could sense a
half-serious challenge in his eyes.

"I'll show you." Rising quickly, before he could reach out
and hold her back, she slipped over to the bureau and pulled
open the heavy drawer.

"What are you doing?"

"You'll see," she replied lightly as she returned to hold the
vial of amber liquid over the single candle that cast its golden
rays across the bed. "It's an old Spanish prostitute's trick,"
she told him, the teasing sounds of her voice now echoing
with the mellow tone of passion as she poured the fragrant
oil on her fingers and began to caress it lightly, lingeringly
into his skin, "but it was taught me by the man I love."

About the Author

Susannah Leigh was born in Minneapolis and raised in St. Paul, Minnesota. After graduating from the University of Minnesota she moved on to New York City, where she worked at a variety of jobs and appeared in many off-Broadway productions. She stayed in New York for twelve years and then left for a year of traveling to such spots as Morocco, Nepal, and Afghanistan.

Ms. Leigh is currently living in West Los Angeles, where she spends her nonwriting time indulging her interests in reading, travel, history, and lying in the sun.

Hoglund

A Locked Stable In Victorian Boston

where young Kate Devlin was initiated into physical love by a man determined to leave his brand on her forever.

A Splendid English Country Estate

where sexual assault was but the prelude to nightmare bondage for the aristocratic red-haired beauty.

An Isolated Ranch On The American Frontier

where Kate gave herself to a stranger body and soul, for better or for worse.

A Raw Mining Camp

where Kate risked being a woman alone in a world of brutal, hungering men— and paid the unspeakably savage price.

An Elegant San Francisco Bordello

where Kate perfected the sensuous skills that made the act of love her gateway to freedom and instrument of vengeance.

These are but some of the blazing scenes that highlight this sweeping saga of a beautiful woman's passionate odyssey— in a novel that goes further than any before in fiery candor and irresistible romantic adventure. . . .

WINTER FIRE

Big Bestsellers from SIGNET